Gloria

Gloria

KEITH MAILLARD

SOHO

Published by Soho Press, Inc.
853 Broadway
New York, NY 10003

Published by arrangement with HarperCollins Ltd. Canada

Library of Congress Cataloging-in-Publication Data

Maillard, Keith, 1942–
Gloria / Keith Maillard
        p.   cm.
ISBN 1-56947-206-8 (alk. paper)
1. Young women — Fiction.   I. Title.

PR9199.3.M345 G57 2000
813'.54 — dc21   00-026548

10   9   8   7   6   5   4   3   2   1

For Mary, Jane, and Elizabeth

Who list her hcount, I put him owte of dowbte,
As well as I may spend his tyme in vain:
And, graven with Diamonds, in letters plain
There is written her faier neck rounde abowte:
Noli me tangere, for Cesars I ame;
And wylde for to hold though I seme tame.

— Sir Thomas Wyatt

Gloria

PART ONE

1

It was well past the time when anyone should feel the least bit embarrassed by asking for another drink. The worst of the day, in fact, was nearly over—that tedious span of muggy afternoon when one deeply regrets the second helping of Crab Louis and the second (or was it the third?) Scotch, while the sun—fat and yellow and simple as a kid's drawing—blazes away in an impossibly blue sky complete with the corniest of cotton batting clouds, and one must, somehow, maintain the pretense that one is having a hell of a good time on one's day off.

A faint breeze had sprung up; now it stirred the drapes in the open window of the guest room upstairs; through that window one could see the pool and the patio and much of the gently sloping land beyond as it led to the row of apple trees marking the distant edge of the property line. The untended woods behind the apple trees were already being absorbed by night; the childish disk of the sun was settling into the highest of the branches where it created the illusion that the treetops were burning up—furiously but silently. And, across the vast expanse of exquisitely clipped lawn (in the hard, oblique light, it appeared to have a perfect nap, like quality velvet) were creeping the long, inky shadows that signaled the steady advance of evening. Soon—but, thank God, not too soon—it would be time to dress for dinner.

The only sound was the steady splash of someone swimming. Ted Cotter and his wife Laney—the nickname still persisted from her Vassar days—were stretched out side by side on reclining chairs by the pool, his eyes covered with green sunglasses, hers with a yellow plastic gadget shaped like two picnic spoons, their handles joining over the bridge of her nose. Neither had moved for some time.

Both Ted and Laney enjoyed hearing it said that they made a handsome couple; they'd heard it often and had come to expect it. No one meeting Laney for the first time ever believed she was in her forties; she had the sleek, fine-boned figure that is usually called "thoroughbred." Ted had the look of a successful middle-aged man who keeps himself fit; the gray sprinkled liberally through his thick hair was the perfect touch for a man who liked to think of himself as mature and resourceful and steady under fire—a man who would naturally take command in any disaster. Ted and Laney did, indeed, make a handsome couple, and if, during their twenty-two years of marriage, neither had been seriously unfaithful to the other, it had not been for lack of opportunity.

Reclining in a third chair, set off some ten feet to the side of the others, was

Billy Dougherty, Ted's old executive officer from his last command in the war, now Ted's employee. Billy appeared to be built entirely out of slabs of thickly bunched muscle, and he looked more like a roughneck steel worker than what he was, the general superintendent of the "Old Reliable" Indian Works in Millwood. Though only a year younger than Ted, Billy had never lost something of the perpetual boy—maybe it was his winsome, lopsided grin or his habit of rubbing the back of his neck and looking off to one side as though he were about to say, "Aw, shucks, ma'am," in a Jimmy Stewart voice—and he had always been successful with the sort of woman who mistakenly thinks she can make something of him.

Billy sat up and yawned and lit a cigarette; he leaned forward to get a better view of Gloria Cotter swimming laps in the pool. She had passed on the Crab Louis, had eaten instead half a grapefruit, two rye crackers, and a cube of Swiss cheese; she had not been offered a gin and tonic, and, if she had, would have refused; she thought that adults (or, as she caught herself still referring to them despite the fact that she had recently turned twenty-one, "grown-ups") drank too much.

This was the first day since Gloria had come home when she hadn't awakened feeling utterly miserable. Her boyfriend—she presumed she no longer had the right to call him her fiancé although things had been left in such an inconclusive state she wasn't sure even of that—but at any rate, Rolland Spicer, the boy she'd been planning to marry, had, the week before, driven her home from Briarville, Pennsylvania, to Raysburg, West Virginia, in what must have been record time. He'd said hardly a word to her and hadn't stopped once, not even for a cheeseburger. After he'd dumped Gloria and her five pieces of baby-blue luggage on her front porch, he'd muttered, "Well, Glo, see you around some time," and had driven away without so much as a goodbye kiss. "What was that all about?" her mother had asked, and Gloria had answered, "Oh, nothing, Mom. Just a little difference of opinion." Leaving her things for the brats to carry in, Gloria had walked past her mother, closed herself in her bedroom, thrown herself on the bed, and had lain there for an hour waiting for the tears to start, but she hadn't cried. She'd just been depressed out of her mind, and she'd stayed depressed out of her mind for days. Her timing, she had to admit, had been atrocious. Why had she been so stupid as to tell him after a wedding—especially a wedding as lovely as Susie's? But she hadn't said, "I won't marry you." She'd only said, "I won't marry you *yet*."

That morning in church she'd felt a shift inside herself; instead of thinking, as she had been, "What on earth am I supposed to do from now until September?" she'd thought, "Wow, I've got the whole rest of the summer and I can do *anything I want*," and she'd finally allowed herself to feel pleased—with her Phi Beta Kappa key, with her straight-A average and her honors BA, with having been a darn good president of her chapter of Delta Lambda, and even with having been May Queen. In the fall she would be going to Columbia to begin her graduate work, but, in the meantime, there were no more classes, no more deadlines, no more exams, no more house meetings or Panhellenic Council meetings, no more planning sessions for Susie's wedding, no more rituals or ceremonies or parades or dances or smokers or parties—no more anything. There were some dozen books she'd planned to read, and she looked forward to reading them, but not quite yet. And if Rolland was going to go on being so mean to her, well, there would be lots of boys in New York, and so, fully conscious that she'd been killing time—savoring every lovely, useless, wasted moment of it— she'd just spent the afternoon painting her toenails and fingernails to match the red piping on her black maillot; the piping was, in turn, an exact match for the broad red stripe on her black bathing cap.

Ted Cotter opened his eyes behind his sunglasses and saw his daughter arrive at the wall, bob up in an incandescent spray transmuted to gold by the low sun, turn, kick off, and glide. He did not think of her as athletic, but he had to admit she made a hell of a pretty picture in the water. In the summer, Gloria's naturally dark skin deepened nearly to the color of mahogany; now, wet and gleaming in the golden light, she looked burnished, and her figure was every bit as good as her mother's had been in her twenties—maybe even a little bit better with her long, Betty Grable legs and tiny waist. Gloria swam with a tidy, fastidious stroke he saw as typical of the way she did everything; her brothers, intent on speed, thrashed through the water like outboard motors, but she swam carefully, held each hand carefully, pointed like a dart, her gleaming red fingernails leading the hand, the angled hand slicing neatly into the water with no splash whatsoever. Laney, when she was mad at Gloria, liked to call her "Princess Priss," and it was apt, he supposed, but he rather liked his daughter's prissiness (there were a hell of a lot worse things your daughter could be). He had no worries about Gloria. She was sure to marry well.

Then Ted saw that Billy was hunched forward, his muscles tense, his elbows on his knees, his cigarette hanging forgotten in one slack hand, as he stared at Gloria. His head turned to follow her. If Ted were to guess what his old exec was thinking, he was pretty sure he'd hit it bang on the money, and he didn't like it one damn bit.

Billy and his dumb, little round-heels of a wife, Dottie, after a couple years of spectacular split-ups and melodramatic reconciliations, had finally gotten themselves divorced, and Billy was one of those guys—Ted supposed he would be much the same—who went crazy as jack rabbits the minute they didn't have a woman around. Billy had moved out of the house just after Christmas and pitched camp in a little bachelor apartment in Meadowland; he was still living out of his suitcase and eating all his meals at the club or at other people's tables.

Billy had dropped in right after they'd got back from church "just to say hi," but he was still there, just as they'd known he would be from the moment they'd heard his silver Porsche come purring up the driveway.

"Another hot one," Ted said to let Billy know he was watching him.

"Yep, a real scorcher," Billy replied with an embarrassed laugh.

We're going to have to get the poor son-of-a-bitch laid, Ted thought, or he's going to start humping chair legs. But, in the meantime, if he keeps on looking at my daughter like that, I'm going to knock his ass straight into the swimming pool.

The men's voices woke Laney. "Oh, dear," she said, removed the sun shield and sat up. She wasn't sure how long she'd been asleep, but she'd dropped off listening to her daughter's steady churning in the water, and she still heard it. "What's she trying to prove?" she asked and immediately wished she hadn't said it.

There was nothing to hear but Gloria going splash, splash, splash; it was too damn quiet. Then Laney remembered that the boys had been dispatched to summer camp early that morning. From where she sat, Laney could see, strewn across the lawn, an archery butt, two bows, several dozen arrows, a collapsed badminton net, shuttlecocks and rackets, an astonishingly large number of comic books, a pair of jeans, a pair of white bucks, a scattering of pop bottles, a partially eaten sandwich (oh God, that had to be from yesterday!), an infinity of balls, and James' navy blue blazer—the little creep—wadded into a sodden lump. She'd been longing for the boys to leave, but they hadn't been gone a day and she already missed them. In the meantime, why the devil hadn't Mrs. Warsinski picked up after them? Laney wished things were as they had been in her childhood, when you didn't have a housekeeper, you had servants, and if they didn't do what you wanted, you fired them (or, if it hadn't been exactly like that, that's the way Laney thought it should have been).

She felt Ted's hand on her arm, saw that he had lit her a cigarette along with his own—a gesture that went all the way back to their courtship. She was so grateful for that small but unmistakable token it made her eyes sting. It isn't fair, she thought and felt like a petulant child—for the "it" that wasn't fair was life. She was forty-three. And there was her damned daughter, reminding Laney with every lap that she was young and Laney was not.

Gloria, however, was not feeling particularly young at the moment; she was not swimming very fast, but it was all she could do to maintain her pace. She had bet herself that she could still make forty laps, but it had stopped being fun, and now only her pride kept her going—and the knowledge that she was being watched. "What should I say?" she chanted in her mind, "since faith is dead," timing the words to her flutter kick, "and truth away—from you is fled—" She was at the wall; she bobbed up and clung to it a moment, her arms aching, and heard her mother's bitchiest voice: "For heaven's sake, Gloria, enough is enough."

Angry, Gloria turned and kicked off. "Can ye say nay—but that you said—" She got stuck on "but that you said." Said what? She couldn't remember—which was ridiculous, because, if she knew anything, she knew that poem, right down to Wyatt's sixteenth-century spelling. Stroking hard, she jumped ahead to what she did remember and used it to pick up her tempo: "And thus betrayed—ere that I wist—" Triumphant at the end of her forty, she slammed into the wall—"Farewell, unkissed!"—and she felt a small but exquisite epiphany because she knew now why that particular poem had appeared in her mind.

She heard her father and Mr. Dougherty applaud. She clambered out of the pool—too quickly, so it seemed, for the world went wobbly beneath her. She steadied herself on the ladder, closed her eyes.

Dancing, fiery swirls of sun blazed in her field of vision, turned themselves green as emeralds against a throbbing red blur. She felt the hot roughness of cement under her feet, smelled chlorine and suntan lotion and new-mown grass and the nasty, rubbery pungency of her bathing cap—and felt that she had been plunged into the very essence of summer: sensations and emotions blending in her like a complex symphony. Summer! Out of school, home again, and bored—a summer just as though she were back in high school—for it went with the promise of more and more and yet more time to waste.

She felt the world firm itself up. Still savoring her inner state—carrying it, she thought, like a diamond hidden in her mouth—Gloria opened her eyes, saw her mother and father and Mr. Dougherty watching her. Feigning total nonchalance, she walked to her lawn chair and picked up her towel.

"Good going, princess," her father said. Her mother said nothing but gave her a darkly inscrutable look. What, Gloria asked herself, is wrong with her?

"Gee, skipper," Mr. Dougherty said to her father, "I didn't know you had an Esther Williams in the family."

"Yeah, they're all good swimmers," Gloria's father replied and immediately launched into the oft-told tale of Gloria's brothers, both of whom held Ohio Valley age-group records—Bobby in the individual medley and Jimmy in the freestyle sprints. Surely Mr. Dougherty must have heard all of this before, and the brats were not at home to hear their praises being sung, and Gloria could have used a bit of praise herself, but it was obvious that she had received all she was going to get. As a girl, Gloria had not been expected to be a competitive swimmer, and so she had not been. *Sic transit gloria Gloriae*, she thought—not for the first time.

She pulled off her bathing cap, began to towel her hair, and caught Mr. Dougherty staring at her, his eyes fixed on the point where her bathing suit met the top of her thighs. He did not look away but gave her an ingenuous grin. Gloria averted her eyes, but she remained acutely conscious of him. He had a pot belly but was obviously strong as a bull; there was an anchor tattooed over his left biceps and his jaws were smeared with a five-o'clock shadow dense as Vice President Nixon's; he was covered from top to toe with curly black hair—even hair between his shoulder blades. Men, Gloria thought, should not be allowed to get that hairy; it was repellant—and fascinating in a sickly kind of way. When she'd first met him, he'd told her to call him Uncle Billy, but Gloria, who had been fourteen at the time, was not about to call any man who had suddenly appeared out of nowhere Uncle anything.

She lay back in the lawn chair and closed her eyes so she wouldn't have to see him. "Billy?" she heard her father say in what she thought of as his Lieutenant Commander's voice, "you want to do the honors?"

"Sure, skipper. Same again?"

"Make that two," her mother said, "you sweet man. Oh, Gloria?"

Gloria opened her eyes. "Could you please clear away your grandmother's tray and see if she needs anything?" Her mother was giving Gloria a get-lost look.

Allowing herself a deeply expressive sigh (she'd learned it from her mother), Gloria sprang to her feet and walked into the house in an abrupt, stiff-backed manner designed to let her mother know just how annoyed she was (she'd learned that from her mother too).

When Gloria had returned home, she had not been pleased to discover that her grandmother—her mother's mother, *the* Mrs. Alfred Merriman—had been moved to Raysburg and established in the guest room. During the four years her father had been away in the war, Gloria and her mother had lived in her grandmother's house in Providence, but even so, Gloria hardly knew her. Her grandmother's rooms had been off limits, and Gloria had only seen her briefly, every few weeks, by appointment only—like visiting a queen. Then she'd been outfitted in her daintiest dress and party shoes, lectured on good manners, promised an ice cream cone if she was good, and led into the presence of a frightening old lady who (Gloria had known it instantly and instinctively) did not like children. Now Gloria thought of her grandmother not as a person but as a stereotype—the aging society matron in an old movie, the one who is supposed to chaperone the irrepressible young heroine.

Gloria bounded upstairs to her grandmother's room and hesitated—her childhood distaste still with her—before stepping into it. "Excuse me, Grandmother," she said, "can I get your tray?"

"Yes, you certainly can, my dear. Come in."

The old lady was sitting bolt upright in her chair directly in front of the window, her back toward the door; the last of the afternoon sunlight poured around her, and she seemed disembodied inside a haze of brilliance. Gloria tiptoed across the rug and came to rest by the small mahogany table; it held the tray with the remains of her grandmother's dinner, three roses in a crystal vase, several magazines—Gloria saw *Vogue* and *Vanity Fair*—a box of white bond stationery, a gold fountain pen, and two decks of cards. "You're an excellent swimmer, Gloria," her grandmother said.

"Thank you, Grandmother," Gloria replied automatically. The window provided a panoramic view of the pool and the lawn beyond. Mr. Dougherty and her parents were laughing about something; their adult voices sounded as distant and meaningless as the buzz of locusts.

"In my day, girls were never taught to swim," her grandmother said. "In the costumes we wore, we would have drowned if we'd tried it— Gloria, do you know how to mix a martini?"

"Yes, of course I do, Grandmother. Are you allowed to drink martinis, Grandmother?"

"At my age, I'm allowed to drink anything I damn well please, and I would appreciate it if you were to stop calling me 'Grandmother' with every breath. I appreciate good manners, but the constant repetition is growing somewhat tedious. A good martini, Gloria, has only a whisper of vermouth, is stirred, never shaken, and must be served cold as death. The pleasure of a good martini is one that will last long after many other pleasures have faded, and a good martini, Gloria, is what I would dearly love to see appear before me." Gloria dutifully rose to go. "And Gloria?" her grandmother called after her, "Don't bruise the gin!"

Gloria carried her grandmother's tray downstairs and into the kitchen where Mrs. Warsinski was cleaning up. Willing herself into invisibility, Gloria filled a mixing bowl with ice cubes, floated into the dining room, slipped a bottle of gin from the liquor cabinet, poured the bowl full, and added a capful of vermouth. She knew perfectly well that her grandmother was not supposed to drink, and she felt a tickle of gleeful naughtiness as though they were putting something over on the grown-ups. Passing silently back through the kitchen, she picked up a jar of olives and a martini glass—then, on impulse, a second glass. It was not her grandmother's fault, Gloria had just decided, that her childhood had been so routinely miserable.

Gloria deposited the bowl on the table in her grandmother's room so quickly that the gin almost sloshed out. She was, she had to admit, still afraid of her grandmother. "Good heavens," her grandmother said with a faint smile. Intentionally playing a role—inviting her grandmother to laugh at her, and, therefore, like her— Gloria stirred the bowl gently with a teaspoon, filled the glasses and dropped an olive into each.

Gloria's grandmother sipped, frowned, considered, nodded. "Your methods may be unorthodox," she said, "but the results are excellent. Do you smoke, Gloria?"

"No, I do not smoke," Gloria replied in a voice that was dangerously close to being a parody of the old lady's.

"I am delighted to hear that. Smoking is a dirty and disgusting habit that has nothing whatsoever to recommend it. If you look in the top drawer of my dresser, you will find a silver box with a rosebud design on the lid."

Gloria passed over the box, and from it her grandmother extracted a Turkish cigarette; she fitted it to a long, green holder and ignited it with a tiny silver lighter. "Should you be smoking, Grandmother?" Gloria said.

"No, I should not. Nor should I be drinking martinis. Nor, for that matter, should I still be alive. Now tell me about yourself, Gloria."

Instead of replying, Gloria took a sip of her martini. She didn't know why she was drinking it; she hated martinis. It could not have tasted any worse, she thought, if she had filled her glass with her grandmother's lighter fluid. "That's what boys always ask," she said. "They seem to want a neat little summary in two or three sentences."

"You should prepare a speech then—but not for me. You are a splendid-looking girl, my dear, but other than that, I hardly know anything about you."

Gloria looked directly into her grandmother's eyes; they were pale blue, and watery, but focused and intelligent; Gloria resisted the adjective "birdlike" as too easy, but it was apt. Over the past winter the old lady had suffered two heart attacks; if she had not, she would have still been in Providence, drinking all the martinis she wanted and playing bridge with other old society ladies. Now Gloria was struck by the obvious: her grandmother was probably lonely and afraid of dying and might genuinely be interested in something more than small talk.

"You know I'm going to Columbia next year," Gloria said.

"I understand you've always been a good student, my dear." Her grandmother's tone was dismissive, as though she wanted to move Gloria on toward a more provocative topic—clothes or dances or *boys*—and Gloria could easily enough have told her grandmother all about Rolland (she still was engaged to him—well, maybe she was), but she didn't feel like it.

"No, you don't understand, Grandmother," Gloria said and was alarmed to hear the sudden passion quivering in her voice. "Nobody understands, really. It isn't just being a good student. I love it!"

Ted Cotter, fully aware that the old bag upstairs could see him from her window, rose from his lawn chair, accepted the Scotch Billy was offering him, knelt next to his recumbent wife—her eyes were closed—and kissed her full on the mouth. She emitted a startled squawk; her body went rigid; she giggled and tried to push him away. He probed deeply with his tongue until she melted back onto her chair. He kissed her for some time. "Teddy, what*ever* do you think you're *doing?*" she said in a smoky voice. He winked at her, walked to the side of the pool, and looked out across his property. He owned five acres.

Ted Cotter was, by his own lights—and, he was sure, by anybody else's—a roaring success; to measure that success, all he had to do was turn and look at Laney (she'd joined him at the side of the pool). Sometimes he still couldn't believe it: an honest-to-God high society deb had married him, and not only that, she had turned out to be a hell of a good wife—a real trooper. And he had three wonderful kids. And he had a home that would be the envy of anyone. And he was the number two man at Raysburg Steel and certain to be the number one man when Carl Eberhardt retired. And the snooty old bitch who had not wanted him for a son-in-law was living upstairs in *his* house, enjoying *his* hospitality. And, by God, there was no woman over forty anywhere near as lovely as Laney Merriman Cotter.

Why, then, was he feeling such a vague, itching dissatisfaction?

There was something ominous about the hot, red, slanting light of the setting sun. But there hadn't been anything ominous about it yesterday, or the day before that. So what the hell was bothering him? It was a strange feeling, a mixture of tension and boredom.

"What do you say, skipper?" Billy said. "Dinner at the club?"

"I'd say that's about right," Ted replied evenly. He'd been hoping that Billy had a date for the night, but no such luck. The war seemed a long time ago, and Billy was beginning to bore him.

Suddenly Ted knew when he'd felt like this before. It didn't seem such a long time ago at all, now that he thought about it; it might have been only last week when he'd been commanding *The Minnewaukan*. It had been near the end of the war, and, by then, everything had become a dumb, tedious routine. There'd been nothing to worry about, not really, except getting some new movies or connecting up with one of the big oilers so you could buy some ice cream—or the remote but ever present possibility that some demented kamikaze might come whining out of nowhere and blow you and your men straight to shit. He'd had direct, firsthand experiences with kamikazes—two of them, as a matter of fact—and one would have been more than enough. After the first kamikaze, he'd never rested easy again; after the second one, he'd said to himself, *OK, Cotter, three strikes and you're out.* But there hadn't been any third strike. So here he was, sitting pretty on top of the heap, and he wondered again if he shouldn't go ahead and have the bomb shelter built. He'd been thinking about it for a long time, but he hadn't been able to make himself part with the money. And why not? You couldn't spend the money if you were dead, and there was nothing, after all, more important than your family.

Ted handed his glass to his wife. "You know, old girl," he said under his breath, "we're drinking too much these days," and before she could answer, he dived into the pool.

Gloria hadn't known that you could get yourself blitzed on one martini. Maybe it was dumping it into an empty stomach after swimming forty laps, but she was certainly giddy—a not at all unpleasant sensation. The steady encroachment of evening as viewed through her grandmother's window—the sullen, jam-colored aftermath of the sun and the long velveteen shadows—felt resonant with some ancient, Robert Graves-like mystery and she thought that this summer might turn out to be just fine after all.

"Tennyson was our man," her grandmother was saying (she was sipping her *third* martini and appeared absolutely unaffected by it), "'To strive, to seek, to find, and not to yield!'—and Swinburne, of course. Ah, there was music! 'From too much love of living, from hope and fear set free, we thank with—' Oh, heavens, I can't recall it now. It must be sixty years since I read him. It doesn't seem possible."

Gloria was thoroughly enjoying herself; who would have thought that her grandmother had ever read poetry? Gloria was even willing to forgive her for liking Swinburne.

"Mother!" Gloria turned toward the sound of the voice and saw that her mother, still wearing her swimsuit, had arrived silently and was staring disapprovingly at Grandmother Merriman's martini glass and burning cigarette. *There are too many mothers here*, Gloria thought illogically, not sure what her mind had meant by that. "Gloria, I'm surprised at you," her mother said.

"Don't blame it on her, Marcelaine," Gloria's mother's mother said, "I am still, in spite of everything, the captain of my soul." And then, in an absolutely bland voice, the old lady added: "Gloria has just been telling me about her studies."

"How nice for you," Gloria's mother said, and then to Gloria: "Are you coming to the club with us?" Her tone meant: "I hope you're not."

Until that moment Gloria hadn't even thought about going to the club, but she had to make an appearance sometime, didn't she? And, if she was going to be stuck in Raysburg for the rest of the summer without a boyfriend, wasn't it about time she got back into the swim of things? "I don't know," she said. "Do you want me to?"

"Sure, princess," her father said. He too had appeared silently. It must be padding around barefoot, Gloria thought, that gave these people the appearance of having sprung inexplicably from behind the arras. He was looking at the women though the bedroom door and wore a peculiar smile Gloria couldn't read. "Do you need anything, Agnes?" he said.

"Thank you, no, Theodore," Gloria's grandmother said, "I am quite comfortable." She had pronounced his first name crisply, with emphasis, much the way he'd pronounced hers.

"Get dressed, girls," Gloria's father said, and that, she knew, was the law.

As Gloria rose to go, her grandmother gave her a conspiratorial wink.

Laney had stepped into the hall and paused, turned back, waiting for Gloria to come out—the damned fool girl knew better than to be giving Mother martinis!—and she'd seen the wink. It made her so mad she knew if she opened her mouth, she'd start screaming, and then, before she could pull herself together, Gloria was looking her right in the eyes. Since she'd been at college, Princess Priss had been cultivating an air of utter inscrutability, and Laney might as well have been staring into the face of a porcelain doll. Without a word, Gloria turned away. You little bitch, Laney thought—and despised herself for thinking it.

In their bedroom, Ted had already settled down with the *New York Times*—his Sunday treat. He looked up and, after a moment, said, "What's the matter, cookie?"

He's always been, Laney thought, pretty damned astute for a man. "Oh, just a teensy bit of a headache," she said.

The wink coming right on top of Ted's, "You know, old girl, we're drinking too much these days," was more than Laney could bear, and she knew she was going to cry. She hurried into the bathroom, but just as she was reaching for the tap in the shower stall, she heard the shower go on in Gloria's suite. "Damn!" she said and felt the tears splashing down.

"What's the matter *now*?" Ted called to her. He didn't sound the least bit sympathetic.

"Nothing!" she yelled back at him, "It's just—with all the goddamned money you make— why the hell can't we— have a goddamned water tank— big enough— so we could *take two goddamned showers at once!*" After that outburst, she leaned back into the wall, shut her eyes, and bit her lip so he wouldn't hear her crying.

"We're drinking too much," had really meant, "*you're* drinking too much," and maybe she *was* drinking too much, but she'd never made a slip in public, so what the hell was he talking about? She still hadn't shed the eight pounds she'd picked up over the winter, but did he expect her to have as good a figure as Gloria's? It wasn't fair. Careful not to slam it, she closed the bathroom door and locked it.

The horrible thing was that everything had been fine until Princess Priss had come home. Laney hadn't felt close to Gloria since she'd been little—and she felt terrible about that, and she kept trying to do something about that, but all

Gloria did was push her away. Imagine, Laney thought, sitting there for an hour talking to *Mother* about her studies, and Gloria never tells *me* about her studies — and her mother had never winked at Laney, not once, not in her entire life.

Now Laney wished the summer were over so Princess Priss would pack her bags and go off to Columbia — *Columbia?* How utterly ridiculous. Why was Ted letting her get away with it? Did Gloria really think she was going to get a degree from Columbia University? A PhD, for God's sake? And if she did get it, what on earth did she think she was going to do with it? What she should have done was marry that nice Rolland Spicer while he still wanted to marry her. What a shame — a fine boy, well mannered, one of our sort, not to mention the fact that he would inherit money from both the Rollands and the Spicers, and he was obviously just nuts about Gloria. What did the little fool think, that he was actually going to wait four more years? Did she think she'd get another chance like that? Well, maybe she would catch a husband at Columbia — and Laney hoped (it was mean of her, but she hoped it anyway) that Gloria would meet a boy there who was bright enough, and knew enough, to finally put Little Miss Know-it-all in her place.

The sound of the shower on Gloria's shower cap was like — like what? Don't be sloppy with words, she told herself; find the exact simile. Rain on a tin roof? Yeah, probably, if you've ever heard rain on a tin roof. She was still dizzy from her one lousy martini, and a dim voice in her mind was still rattling away idiotically: "Can ye say nay but that you said — "

And why was her mother mad at her again, as she so obviously was? It wasn't just the martinis; she'd been mad at her ever since she came home — and in return for the silent, angry, withering stare she'd received in the hallway, Gloria had made sure to beat her mother to the shower. Gloria was using the water to cool off, but she knew her mother liked it hot even in the summer, and she was tempted to turn the hot tap on full and use it all up, but no, she thought, that'd just be mean, and she should get out anyway or she wouldn't have time to dress.

Ted heard the shower in Gloria's bathroom stop and the shower in his bathroom go on. He looked at his watch. Yep, plenty of time. The girls needed a good hour, and he needed five minutes. He took a sip of his Scotch and looked back down at the *New York Times*. There was a lot of the usual hoo-ha about the rise in the price of steel, but what the hell did people expect? The industry had negotiated itself two years of peace, and the wage increases went into effect on the first of July, so of course the price of steel was going to go up; any idiot could have predicted that — but the goddamn Democrats would scream the way they always did. Big deal.

He flipped on through the paper, was stopped by a headline that read: GEN-

ERAL DEFENDS ATOMIC SHELTERS. He felt a sickly contraction in his stomach and imagined, as he had a million times before, a big map of the USA hanging on a wall in the Kremlin. It was stuck full of bright red push pins (did the Commies have push pins?) indicating where the missiles would fall. *Steel.* There was no doubt about it: Raysburg was a target.

"The American people are not being told enough about the destructiveness of nuclear weapons," he read. There'd been a big test named "Priscilla"—a hell of a name for an atom bomb, he thought. He lit a cigarette. ". . . six big concrete domes, built with materials of varying strengths, all were destroyed by the shock of the nuclear explosion. At the same time, soldiers in trenches that were covered to shelter them from debris lived through the blast. The distance of the soldiers from the point of explosion was not disclosed—"

Now that Laney was in the shower with the hot water pounding the tense muscles in her back and neck, she was beginning to feel a little bit better. She wished she knew what Princess Priss was wearing; the last thing in the world she wanted to do was compete with her wretched beauty-queen daughter. Stop it, Laney told herself, don't think of her like that. But she couldn't help it. She felt teary and out of sorts and hard done by.

Laney turned the water to cool; if she boiled herself like a lobster, she'd be sweating buckets by the time she got dressed. Gloria would probably wear the little pink dress she'd come home in, the one that made her look so damnably young and fresh—or if not that one, then one just like it. Ted hardly ever expressed an opinion about Laney's clothes, but she knew, nonetheless, exactly what he liked, so she should wear her new sheath. That's right, it would give her a mature, sophisticated look that Gloria couldn't match, and maybe it was a bit dressy for the club on Sunday night, but Gloria would probably dress down, so she should dress up—and, as Mother always said, you're not supposed to be comfortable after five anyway.

". . . the slightest defect in a structure would make habitation in it impossible if it were hit by a nuclear shock," Ted read. Well, suppose you spent all that money and there was still a slight defect in your structure? How the hell could you be sure that there wasn't a slight defect in your structure? Jesus, you'd practically have to supervise the job yourself.

Gloria studied the contents of her closet. What she should do, she thought, was throw on any old thing—her new little pink dress, for instance—and then run down to the kitchen and call Binkie, because Binkie was certain to be at the club, and, if Gloria hadn't called her, the first thing she'd say would be: "Hey, when did you get back? Why didn't you *call* me?"

Even though she sometimes bored Gloria silly, Gloria was genuinely fond of Binkie Eberhardt. She'd always been the most loyal friend Gloria could imagine, and the last thing she wanted to do was hurt her feelings. Well, Gloria

could say she'd been too depressed to call anybody—which was true enough—
but that wouldn't make any sense to Binkie, because, from her point of view,
what you were supposed to do if you were having boy trouble was talk to your
girlfriends about it. OK, Gloria thought, so I'll lie and say I've only been back
a day or two, but, in the meantime, what am I going to wear?

It was a hot night, and her mother would probably dress down. Gloria was
in no mood to do a mother-daughter act, so she should dress up, and, besides,
it would be the first time anybody at the club had seen her this summer, and
she had her reputation to maintain, didn't she? So, more than merely dressing
up, she should dress to the nines, and the perfect thing for that would be her
midnight-blue Traina-Norell. It was a classic, and, with its big big *big* skirt,
younger and sassier than anything her mother would have dared to wear.

Ted turned to the news of the week in review, and splashed across the entire
front page—it appeared that there was no escaping it—was a goddamn mushroom cloud. STOP THE TESTS? a headline read. Christ, no, Ted thought,
don't stop them. It's just another commie trick. "The U.S. has long maintained
that it can continue testing indefinitely without dangerously contaminating
the atmosphere," he read. And the U.S. was supposed to have a clean bomb now,
but, as everybody with half a brain knew, the Russians sure as hell didn't have
one. They probably didn't give a shit whether their bombs were clean or not.
They'd hit the mills all up and down the river. Oh, my God, he thought, we
might have to stay underground for months.

Laney stepped into her firmest all-in-one and worked it up over her hips. She
adjusted the shoulder straps to give herself maximum uplift, drew herself up to
her tallest, sucked in her tummy, and pulled up the zipper. Not bad, she
thought, looking in the mirror—but still, there's no doubt about it: cottage
cheese and rye crackers, starting tomorrow.

Ted looked up from the paper and saw his wife staring at herself in the full-
length mirror. She was wearing nothing but a long, sleek, black girdle, and she
was standing perfectly still, her small bare feet resting side by side on the silly ivory
carpet she'd insisted they have in their bedroom. She seemed to him, caught in
that fleeting moment, unaware that he was looking at her, like the absolute essence
of womanliness. *My wife*, he thought and felt a painful emotion that was nearly
overwhelming. It was the way he'd felt all the way through those boring, wasted
years in the South Pacific—missing Laney, wanting nothing big or grand out of
life, just for the war to be over, just to see his wife in a pretty dress across the table
in a nice restaurant, and he knew that he would give anything, make any sacrifice, to keep her safe, take care of her no matter what. No, he thought, those
years weren't wasted. We had to fight that damn war, and *this* is the reason we
fought it.

Expenses be damned, he was going to build that goddamn bomb shelter—

and the moment he decided, he felt his spirits lift. He jumped off the bed, walked over to Laney, turned her to face him, and kissed her full on the mouth. He didn't stop until he felt her body responding.

"Teddy, why do you always do this to me when I'm half dressed?" she whispered.

"I'm just feeling affectionate, hon."

"Affectionate? That doesn't feel very affectionate to me." She'd found his cock inside his swimsuit. She stroked it erect and held it. He kissed her again.

"Oh, Teddy," she murmured, "we're so lucky. After all the years we've been married, you can still get me hot as an alley cat in half a second."

She'd always been great with her hands. Stroking steadily, she said: "That's enough now, hon. Stop it—I mean it. We're going to be late— I really mean it. We've got to stop this right now." She bit him lightly on the lip, stepped away, and slapped his hand. "You're just going to have to wait for it, aren't you, sailor?"

He could have jumped her on the spot, and, for a second or two, he seriously considered doing exactly that. Then he laughed and said, "We've got a date, cookie. And I don't want to hear any bullshit about headaches."

Gloria had heard her mother's shower turn off, so she knew she had twenty minutes. Her bathing cap and shower cap hadn't preserved even a whisper of her last set, but she did her best with a hairband topped with a velvet bow that would emphasize her young look. The Traina-Norell was off the shoulder, so it required a strapless bra and a firmly boned waspie to emphasize her small waist. She opened a new box of nylons; they were the sheerest of the sheer, ran if you looked at them in anger, and, of course, that fatal inch of starched crinoline extending below her slip would rip them to shreds. It was a shame to sacrifice them to the club, but, if she were going to be stuck in Raysburg for the rest of the summer, where else was she going to wear them?

Gloria had never liked the way she looked. She saw herself as only minimally pretty—dark as a Gypsy with features crammed together into a small space like a big-eyed rat—but, after years of practice, she'd become an artist with makeup and could create a sophisticated image that was really quite presentable. The foundation and rouge went on automatically, but the lines around her eyes required fierce concentration—had to be as sharp and clean as if they'd been drawn with a fine-nibbed pen. She felt lucky tonight and knew she'd get them both right on the first try—and she did.

The martini was wearing off, but she still felt a curious, Alice-in-Wonderland disorientation as though, when she turned away from the mirror, she'd find herself not in her bedroom in Raysburg but somewhere else, somewhere totally unforeseen, somewhere as mysterious as Professor Bolton's living room with its beaded lampshades and pools of magical light and walls of old books and millions of antique whatnots and fantastic, impossible objects—even a human skull.

The feeling also had something to do with her grandmother, and she didn't know how or why. She told herself that she had to try to remember all the complexities of these interlocking feelings so she could write about them in her diary.

Gloria finished her second coat of mascara, and then, staring hard so she wouldn't blink and mark her eye shadow, began to draw her lip line. Now she was thinking of Rolland, feeling a sudden, sickly wave of missing him, and wishing he wasn't so mad at her, and wondering what she could possibly do about it, and—for a second or two anyway—she was totally convinced she should marry him right away and forget all about going to Columbia.

She separated her dried lashes and gave them each a quick, hard squeeze with the curler and then a tiny, final flick of mascara at the tips. She'd met Rolland at her first Delta Lambda White and Gold Invitational; he was—and she enjoyed describing him the way Hemingway would have—*very tall and very brown*, and when she'd caught him staring at her across the room, he'd walked directly over to her. "Hi," he'd said, "are you as icy as you look?"

She'd been shocked. She'd thought only blondes could be icy. But she'd answered: "Oh, yes, ten degrees below zero."

Using a sable brush, Gloria did her first coat of lipstick; she always wore a brilliant red. She had looked icy, she'd realized later, writing about it in her diary, and she'd decided that she liked looking icy—it went with being a Delta Lambda girl—and she would cultivate it.

Gloria powdered her lips to set the lipstick, whisked off the excess with a complexion brush, and did the second coat, adding a bit of gloss for shine. She slid on a nylon petticoat and then a set of crinolines. Almost out of time, she slipped quickly into her dress, added pearls and her favorite patent pumps, finished herself with dabs of Miss Dior—her signature scent—at her throat and wrists. Into her evening bag went a small cosmetic case, a spare pair of stockings, and a pair of soft ballerinas in case she might decide to walk home. Following the old rule "the lower the neckline, the longer the glove," she chose a three-quarter-length pair and laid them on her bag.

The only question remaining was whether or not to wear her Delta Lambda pin, a question complicated by the fact that it was still chained to Rolland's Beta Theta Pi pin, and cutting the chain was out of the question. But, if she wore the pins together, she might as well be wearing the collar in Wyatt's poem that said in diamond letters: "Don't touch me." So did she want to be touched? No, probably not—certainly not by anyone at the Raysburg Country Club, but she and Rolland had agreed that they could date other people—or at least Gloria *thought* that's what they'd agreed. Oh dear, it was all just too ambiguous! Well, there were other ways to say "don't touch me" without wearing a sign pinned to one's dress.

She surveyed herself in the mirror: hair passable, makeup perfect, no loose threads; no lint, smudges, or wrinkles; no imperfections to be seen anywhere. She tried out her most aloof, go-jump-in-the-lake look. Yes, she *was* icy. But beautiful? If Gloria was seen as beautiful—and she'd gradually accumulated so much evidence that she'd come to believe that some people really *did* see her as beautiful—the effect had to be based on sheer artifice. True beauty was something you were born with—like, for instance, Gloria's exquisite room-mate Susie who'd been a runner-up for Miss Pennsylvania, or, for another instance even closer to home, Gloria's mother with her fine-boned face, peaches-and-cream complexion, and perfect little turned-up nose.

But what Gloria could achieve was exactly what she was seeing: discipline, style, polish. She didn't care if other women liked it better than boys did. And other women did like it—those with enough fashion sense to appreciate the effort—like the batty society editor for the *Raysburg Times*. There were a dozen other Raysburg girls whose parents had as much social clout in the Ohio Valley as Mr. and Mrs. Theodore R. Cotter and a few whose parents had even more; many of them were more beautiful than Gloria, and many of them were *blondes*; yet it was Gloria who kept getting her picture splashed across the society page.

The crazy lady from the *Times*—Gloria dreaded hearing that hoarse, pene-trating, gin-soaked contralto come honking suddenly out of nowhere—"Yooo, hooo! Gloo-riii-aaa!" Usually it was at the club, a dance, or a party, but last summer Gloria had been merely walking down Market Street, doing nothing more remark-able than window shopping. Gloria always turned toward the voice, took a deep breath, and dutifully smiled her best beauty-queen smile. The society page lady always had a little man with her, and the little man always had a big camera—*flash!*—and there she'd be in the paper again: "On vacation from Briarville Uni-versity, our own lovely Miss Gloria Cotter, daughter of Mr. and Mrs. Theodore R. Cotter of Highlight Park, enjoys the summer sunshine—"

The last time she'd been splashed across the Raysburg society page—the biggest, most ostentatious, most utterly tasteless splash of all—had been two Sundays ago when Gloria had still been at Briarville. Her mother had left the paper prominently displayed on Gloria's vanity table, presumably as a wel-come home present, but Gloria hadn't been able to tell if her mother had meant the present seriously or ironically; her mother didn't exactly *approve* of things like Prom Queens and May Queens. The society page lady had somehow man-aged to get her hands on the picture from the *Briarville Bugle*, and the society page lady had used it to fill up the entire top half of the society page. The head-line—GLORIA COTTER CROWNED MAY QUEEN!—was set in letters only slightly smaller than might have been used to announce the beginning of the Third World War. The story, which took up most of the remainder of the page, listed every one of Gloria's accomplishments all the way back to high school; it even provided the dubious information that she was engaged to Rolland Edward Spicer, son of Mrs. and Mrs. Emmory J. Spicer of Scranton, Pennsylvania. It did not, however, mention the fact that she was going to Columbia University in the fall.

The picture, Gloria had to admit, was an excellent one. She was bending her head demurely to receive the circlet of flowers that had traditionally crowned Briarville's May Queen since 1922. Susie had put a massive amount of makeup on her—even false eyelashes so unabashedly artificial they could have been lifted straight from a Betsie Wetsie doll—and, in the flesh and from three feet away, she must have looked about as charming as a Pittsburgh showgirl, but, in the photograph, she looked sweet and dewy and doe-eyed and young, and, best of all, not even remotely like what she really looked like. As appalled as Gloria had been when she'd first seen the society page, as utterly tasteless as she'd thought it, she'd also been maliciously pleased and had wished she could send a copy to every one of those rotten girls who'd tormented her at boarding school. Nobody she'd known at Fairhaven would be able to believe it: Gloria Cotter—whose school nickname had been "Worm"—was now, by golly, the veritable Queen of the May. Most of the time Gloria had trouble believing it herself. While researching her honors thesis, she'd felt a growing identification with another stylish, highly publicized, well-dressed brunette, the one who might have worn the don't-touch-me collar in Wyatt's sonnet—pretty enough but no knock out, with lots of brains and a tongue a little too ready, a little too sharp, for her own damn good.

Watch out, Gloria told herself (just as she often told herself in her mind and in her diary): one day you can be at the very top of the heap—the very Queen of England—but then, with no warning, the great Wheel of Fortune turns—*zing!*— and you're falsely convicted of sleeping with half the guys in town and they're going to cut your head off for it. The horrible detail Gloria wished she could forget but couldn't forget—she sometimes woke in the night, sweating and sick with fear, and then she always remembered it—was that poor Anne Boleyn had glanced nervously behind her, afraid that the headsman would strike before she was ready.

In the dining room of the Raysburg Country Club it had become late enough so that any qualms anyone might have had about drinking too much had long ago been forgotten. There was, after all, a good dinner under one's belt, and, arriving upon the table at this very moment was an excellent brandy to nail it down. The muggy, tedious, even desperate day was only a memory. Quite soon one could signal the waiter for another Scotch, but, in the meantime, it was almost enough to sit quietly, surrounded by familiar faces, chatting about nothing important, listening to the band play the lovely old swing tunes that always sounded like the best years of our lives. Soon one might awaken, as if from a bad dream, to realize that it has become the very shank of the night: that delicious moment when it seems possible—well, more than possible, absolutely inevitable—that we're going to have one hell of a good time before it's all over.

A strong breeze had sprung up, was blowing in through the doors that opened onto the terrace that looked down over the swimming pool, and the shrill voices of the children as they splashed in the water sounded both absolutely ordinary and heartbreaking. Ted Cotter, his wife at his side, was sitting at the table always reserved for him, the one that commanded a full, panoramic view of the dining room and the terrace beyond it. Facing Ted were his old pal, Billy Dougherty, and Ted's impossibly mature daughter. (How did she grow up so fast? Only a few years ago she would still have been in the pool.) The plates had been cleared away; everyone but Gloria was smoking; no one had spoken for some time. Then, looking out across the room, Ted was struck by a sudden, happy thought: except for the waiters and the boys in the band, every man he could see worked for him.

"What do you say, skipper?" Billy said, "Good roast tonight, huh?"

"You bet. One of the best in a long time," Ted said.

"Sure is nice to see them get it rare enough for a change," Laney said.

Laney was not in a mood anywhere near as good as her husband's. The warm, sexy sensations she'd had back in their bedroom had melted away, leaving her tense and jittery. To try to make herself feel better, she'd drunk far too much, and the only thing she wanted now was about twelve hours of sleep, but Ted— she knew from the meaningful glances he kept directing at her—would want to make love the minute they got home, and she'd have to go through with it just as though she were having a peachy-keen time. Damn, they should have done it before they left the house. As hot as they'd been, it would have been over in ten minutes, and instead of feeling sour and uncomfortable now, she'd be euphoric. It was Gloria's fault, she thought. If Princess Priss hadn't been home, they would have done it.

Gloria knew that her mother was still mad at her, but she'd given up trying to figure out why. Unlike most everyone else at the Raysburg Country Club, Gloria was sober, and that was exactly the way she liked it—she couldn't imagine any social situation in which she would not need all of her wits about her— but, if she *had* been a bit tipsy, everything might not have felt so stale. The same old, wheezy band was playing the same old, wheezy tunes from the war, and dancing to them were exactly those kids you'd expect to see on a slow, hot Sunday night in the summer. A lot of Gloria's crowd must have been out of town, but, just as Gloria had known she would be, Binkie was there—with a boy she'd brought back from Columbus—and Judy Staub was there with her parents. Janice Stewart and Lisa Phillips didn't seem to be with anyone, but they were flirting with the guys who were permanent fixtures at the club—Mike Clark and Lee Hockner and Jack Farrington—and each of those three clowns had, by now, made something resembling a pass at Gloria, so she probably should have worn her chained pins after all.

When she'd first arrived, Gloria had been horrified to find herself greeted by a standing ovation. Mike Clark had set it off. He was one of those boys who could shove two fingers into his mouth and emit a whistle as loud as an air raid siren, and that's what he'd done. "The Queen of the May, the Queen of the May!" he'd yelled, and the other kids had taken it up, and then, gradually, everyone in the club had risen, applauding—even the grown-ups!—and the leader of the band had finally clued in and signaled the drummer to launch into a roll, and there had been absolutely nothing Gloria could possibly have done but what she did: attempt her very best impersonation of Miss America and walk alone into the middle of the dance floor and curtsy—and then, as the kids had continued to whistle and shout and applaud, curtsy again. Binkie had rushed up and seized Gloria's hands. "Gloria! When did you get *back*? Why didn't you *call* me?"

Binkie was a very tactile person, far too tactile for Gloria's taste, but she'd become used to her over the years, so she'd allowed Binkie to smother her in a big, sweaty, perfumed embrace. "I've only been back a day or two," she'd whispered. "Rolland and I had the most *terrible* fight and I've just been *so* depressed."

The strangest thing was that the moment she'd laid eyes on Binkie, she'd actually wanted to talk about it—would have thoroughly enjoyed talking about it—but Binkie seemed to be hot for the guy from Columbus, so, if Gloria went over to their table, she would be expected to smile sweetly and bat her eyelashes while he went on and on about whatever fatuous, boyish things he had going around in his little pea brain. But she supposed she would have to put up with him, at least for a while, and then she'd probably dance with Mike or Lee or Jack, and one of them, or even all of them, would ask if she wanted to go for a ride, and she would sweetly decline—or, if he, or they, were pushy, she'd turn into the Ice Queen. Then she and Judy or Janice or Lisa—or some combination thereof—would have a nice, long, girlish chat about clothes that would begin with, "Oh, Gloria, I just adore your dress!" and Gloria would be required to tell the story of how she'd got to be May Queen and every little thing that she, as May Queen, had done and experienced, and there was not—there never had been and never would be—a single soul at the Raysburg Country Club who would be interested, even remotely, in a discussion of English literature.

Oh, save me from this! Gloria thought. She remembered the first night she'd been there: she'd been fourteen, wearing heels out in public for the first time in her life, and she'd been so nervous she'd practically wet her pants. Then the band had sounded sweet as heaven, the candle-lit dining room had looked like a hall in a fairy castle. Over the years, the club had stayed the same, but Gloria had changed, and now, the longer she sat silently at her parents' table, watching, the more she felt like the stereotype of the utterly, utterly bored society girl in some big, sloppy, popular, pointless novel—maybe by John O'Hara. But the worst of it was that she also liked the country club, liked the staid predictability of it, liked the fact that she was known there, accorded her rightful place there—a standing ovation!—and if she weren't at the country club, she didn't know where else in Raysburg she might have gone to show off her dress. And then, finally, there was the subtle and quite intense pleasure in knowing that, if she appeared to be the perfect, stereotypical country club girl, she had succeeded in fooling everyone.

Gloria had by now more than done her duty to her parents. "Excuse me," she said, "I'm going to go talk to Binkie."

Ted watched his daughter walk across the dance floor. In her pearls and dark blue dress with its big, swinging skirt—walking in her heels with an elegance she must have learned from her mother—she exemplified for him everything that was admirable about being female, and he told himself, once again, that he was a lucky man. He signaled the waiter: "Ask the band, please, to play 'String of Pearls' for my daughter."

"Well, skipper," Billy said, looking significantly at the waiter, "is it that time?"

"I'd say that's about right," Ted replied, and Billy ordered a round of Scotch.

"Excuse me a minute, folks," the band leader said through the mike, "some sentimental sap out there has just asked for a request. OK, this next one's for the Queen of the May. Where are you, Gloria? This one's from your dad."

The band began to play; everyone over thirty knew the name of the tune; there was a scattering of applause. Feeling dreadfully alone—utterly abandoned—Laney watched her husband stride across the room and sweep his daughter away from Binkie Eberhardt's table and onto the dance floor. In her damnably perfect dress, Gloria looked like she'd just fox-trotted out of a Fred Astaire movie.

Gloria, having spent countless Sunday afternoons with a dozen other country club girls and their sullen, unhappy little brothers fox-trotting around an empty room in the Pythian Building to old swing music on the dancing teacher's tinny vic, could have, when she was being led by someone as self-assured as her father (she wouldn't have called him a good dancer, but self-assured he certainly was), fox-trotted in her sleep. She never knew how to respond to one of his rare shows of affection. How typical of him, she thought, that he should do it in public; if they'd been alone together, she couldn't have got a word out of him. "So, Daddy," she said to make him laugh, "how's everything at the satanic mills?"

"What do you say, Lane, old girl?" Billy was saying, "You want to give it a whirl?"

Billy was drunk, but Laney had seen him drunker, so she rose automatically to her feet, smiled, and let him wrap his meaty arm around her waist. A powerful smell, masculine as a tomcat's, emanated from him—sweat and Vitalis and cigarettes and Scotch—and he gave her a discreet squeeze, and she knew exactly what that squeeze was supposed to mean—a reminder of the naughty, little secret they shared—and Laney, as usual, didn't respond at all, and, as usual, she wished to God she hadn't done it.

She still didn't know what she could have been thinking about that night—if much of anything. She'd been loaded to the gills, and she and Billy had mysteriously ended up in the back bedroom at Carl Eberhardt's with the door locked—yes, at Teddy's boss's house, for Christ's sake! And all she'd done had been to allow Billy to unzip her dress and take off her bra, to kiss her and stroke her breasts while he rubbed up against her. "Jesus, you got beautiful tits, Laney," he'd murmured over and over—and then the goddamned pig had finished himself off right in front of her. They'd got themselves back down to the party before anybody noticed—thank God—and Teddy had been exactly where Laney had left him, sitting in a corner deep in conversation with Carl Eberhardt and a couple other VPs, and Laney had fixed herself another drink and surveyed the party, and then the full, sickening impact had hit her: for absolutely no reason whatsoever she'd just done something unforgivably stupid, something that could have ended her marriage and lost Teddy his job. And where the hell had Billy's wife been the whole time? Laney had never found out the answer to that one.

Now she was stuck with Billy and his damnably discreet little squeezes. He steered her ponderously past Ted and Gloria; he was putting so much weight on her that she felt like a coat rack. "Some girl," he murmured in her ear, "your little Gloria."

"Yes," Laney said, "she is *that* all right."

When the tune ended, Laney found herself standing in the middle of the dance floor facing her husband and her daughter. Billy was still wrapped around her as though they were back in one of those rent-a-girl dance halls of the thirties and he'd paid a hard-earned nickel for the privilege; she gave him a firm nudge, and he undraped himself. She saw that he was directing his man-of-the-world grin at Gloria. "Hey there, princess," he said with a wink, "come on and take a spin with your Uncle Billy."

All of Laney's sympathies instantly went out to Gloria, and she was delighted to hear her daughter say in a cool, Katharine Hepburn voice: "No, thank you, Mr. Dougherty. I've had enough dancing for the moment—and please don't call me 'princess.' Only my dad's allowed to do that."

Gloria gave her father an affectionate pat and floated away, her crinolines rustling. Ted took Laney into his arms, smiled his wonderfully boyish smile at her, and she thanked God that human beings had never learned to read each other's minds.

"We still got a date?" he said.

"Of course we do, sailor," she answered automatically and gave him a sideways look she hoped would appear appropriately lascivious.

When the tune ended, Laney let Ted guide her to their table. Glancing back, she saw Billy still standing on the dance floor, a distressed expression on his face; then, as he remained stuck there—weaving slightly like a boxer who has been knocked out but whose body hasn't told him about it yet—Laney saw that he was more than distressed: he was in a rage. He was breathing hard and had actually gone white. Whoops, she thought, and said, "Teddy!" under her breath.

Ted looked over at Billy, got Laney's message immediately, sang out in a cheery voice, "Come on, old man. Get back over here. Your ice cubes are melting."

Billy didn't respond immediately. Then Laney saw him turn away from the dance floor. He was forcing his usual amiable grin back onto himself. "He's really loaded again," she whispered. "Poor slob. He's had such a rough time since he and Dotty split up."

"Oh," Ted said, laughing, "he's always had a rough time."

When Billy sat down at their table, he knocked the ashtray onto the floor in a single, brilliant gesture as unlikely as a magician's; he couldn't have done it any more deftly if he'd been practicing for weeks. "Well, damn my soul," he said, assuming a phony Southern accent, "I seem to be a bit pissed." He shook his head and smiled at them—first at Laney and then at Ted—and his puppylike expression seemed to be begging their indulgence, even their forgiveness. Laney's heart did go out to him then: he was a man who should have stayed married.

"Hey," Billy said with a sly wink, "have you heard the one about the colored boy in Korea?"

"Can't say as I have," Ted replied and winked back; he nudged Laney under the table.

"Well, there's this colored boy, see," Billy said, "and he's got a big problem. It's really a *big* problem, you know what I mean? His—ah, excuse me, Laney— his *organ* is a heck of a lot bigger than usual. You might even say it's gigantic, and our boy's never been able to find a girl who could take the whole works—"

"Billy," Ted said, still smiling, "maybe this isn't the best story for mixed company."

"Oh, it's all right," Laney said, "let him tell it."

"So, anyhow," Billy went on, "this poor colored boy's got this thing that— well, when it's ready to go, you know, it's as long as a fence post and thick as a boot— and so, back down where he comes from— some crap-hole down in Georgia, you know, all he could do was—excuse me, Laney—well, you know how the song goes: 'Many brave hearts are asleep with the sheep—" Billy stopped to chuckle, and Laney saw Ted give her a look of sympathy. She sighed.

"So anyhow," Billy said, "this colored boy, he gets himself to Korea, and, naturally, he gets to wondering if there isn't some Korean gal—you know how those Oriental gals are, skipper—wonders if there's maybe some Korean gal who could, you know, do the job right, so to speak. And the first time he goes on leave, he goes straight off to a— well, you know, one of them houses they've got there, and he gets this little, tiny Korean gal, you know, no bigger than a minute, and he thinks, Christ, not a chance. But then he thinks, well, she *is* one of them inscrutable Oriental gals and all that, so maybe— So anyhow, they get going at it, and he puts just the first little bit in, and—"

"Billy," Ted said, a note of warning in his voice, "this doesn't sound much like it's going any place very interesting."

"Ah, come on, skipper, we're all adults here. Ain't that right, Lane? Bear with me, OK? So anyhow, the little Korean gal, she yells out—excuse me, Laney— 'Mora Cocki!' Oh, my God, the nigger thinks, this is amazing—"

Laney saw that Ted's face had gone blank as a mask—which meant he was getting angry. Billy, however, was absolutely oblivious; he bent toward them, laughing. "So he shoves a little more in, and she yells out even louder than before—she sounds like she's being skinned alive—'Mora Cocki!'"

Laney felt herself blushing—not because of the story (she'd heard worse)— but because of the truly embarrassing situation that had suddenly descended upon them—well, not so suddenly, for they should have seen it coming: now that Billy was so far along in his smutty story, it appeared that all they could do was wait for him to finish, and Laney could see, out of the corner of her eye, that Gloria was on her way back to their table.

"So," Billy went on, "our boy thinks everything's going great, you know, and he shoves it on in—the whole works, you might say, right up to the hilt—and the whole time she's yelling to beat the band, louder and louder, just screaming her head off, 'Mora Cocki, Mora Cocki!'"

Laney stared hard at Billy to let him know he was offending her; he gave her his most winsome smile—and then a quick, sly, shifty, guilty look. Laney was the mother of two boys, and she'd seen exactly that smile and exactly that shifty look a million times before, and she knew, now, exactly what Billy was doing. He's decided to be *a bad boy*, she thought, and he wants to see if we'll let him get away with it. She was furious.

"So that's that," Billy was saying, "and he thinks Korea's the greatest place on earth. Well, some time goes by, and he's at a track meet, you know, just walking around and looking at everything, and he stops by the pole vault pit, and this Korean pole vaulter goes sailing over the bar easy as pie, and then he jumps up and he yells out, 'Mora Cocki!' So the nigger's really dumbfounded, you know, and he says to one of them Koreans who speaks English, 'Hey, what's Mora Cocki mean?' and the Korean says, 'Oh, that just means: *move it up another hole.*'"

Gloria arrived at the table in time to hear the end of the joke and see that neither of her parents were laughing at it. Mr. Dougherty, however, was killing himself, laughing so hard that people were turning to stare. Gloria's mother, stony-faced, stood up abruptly and said, "I believe it's time for the girls to powder their noses— Gloria!" and Gloria felt herself gathered up and walked away just as though she were ten years old. "Mom!" she said before she could stop her-self—and *sounded* ten years old.

Gloria did not actually see them, but she was keenly aware that Judy Staub and her parents, and Binkie and the boy from Columbus, and Janice and Lisa and Mike and Lee and Jack must all surely have been watching as her mother marched her out of the dining room. "Hey? Mom?" she said, "what's going on?"

"Nothing."

They stopped in front of the wall of mirrors in the ladies' room. Her mother threw her purse down on the pink-tiled counter and, with deft, choppy, angry motions began refurbishing her makeup. "Lend me some lipstick, OK?" Gloria said.

"Use your own damned lipstick, hon."

"I can't, Mom. You waltzed me in here before I could get my bag."

Laney slapped the lipstick tube into her daughter's open palm. "All right. You asked for it. But it's not a good color for you."

"Oh, come on, Mom. It's practically the same color as mine." Gloria bent toward the mirror and began applying it. "So," she said, "just why *are* we girls powdering our noses?"

"Gloria, don't be insufferable."

"Insufferable? I'm just asking a question, OK?"

"Just for once, will you please not give me a hard time."

"I don't get it," Gloria said after a moment, "they had track meets in the Korean War—? There's supposed to be something funny about that? What's the point?"

"There's nothing to get—believe me. Absolutely nothing."

"Then why are we in the ladies' room?" Gloria asked sweetly. Her mother didn't answer her.

"I think I'll go home," Gloria said after a moment.

"Well, you'll just have to wait, won't you?"

"I'll walk." The Cotters' house was so close to the club that Gloria could hear the band playing from her bedroom window but so far from the nearest bus stop that it took her a half hour to walk there—a perfect metaphor for her life, she'd always thought.

"In those?" Laney said, glancing down at her daughter's patent pumps.

"I brought ballerinas with me."

"Oh, did you? What a good little Girl Scout—always prepared."

"That's right, Mom," Gloria said, walking out, *"semper paratus."*

The moment that Gloria and Laney left, Ted said to Billy: "Where the hell do you think you are—the locker room at the Y? Jesus Christ, Billy!"

"Sorry, skipper. A little out of line, huh?"

"About a hundred miles— Get out of here, Billy. You've had too much to drink."

As Billy continued to sit at the table, unfolded into a slack heap, his hand wrapped around his glass and a sappy, apologetic smile plastered across his big, ugly mug, Ted thought that he'd had just about enough of his good old exec to last the rest of his life. "I mean it," he said, "clear out."

"Aw, come on, skipper."

"Out, Billy. Now. If you want to keep drinking, go down to South Raysburg. They'll appreciate your sense of humor down there."

"Hey," Billy said, turning red, "it's a free goddamn country the last I heard. You can't throw me out of here."

"The hell I can't. And if you ever tell an off-color story anywhere near my wife or daughter again, you'll be looking for a another job. Got that? Now get your ass out of here."

"Aw, come on, skipper. Who the hell you think you're talking to? It's me, Billy Dougherty. Why, goddamn it, I saved your ass a million times—"

"That's right, Billy," Ted said in his best Lieutenant Commander's voice, "you saved my ass a million times. The war's over. Get out of here."

Ted slid his chair back from the table and rose to his feet; he'd thought for a moment that Billy was actually going to try to take a poke at him, but Billy had only levered himself upright, and now he was simply standing there, hunched forward, his face red, puffing like a steam engine. Ted waited.

"Fuck you, skipper," Billy said and headed for the door.

Gloria felt better as soon as she left the club. The sky was clear, brilliant with stars, and the lovely moon was new—thin and poignant as an afterthought. Still wearing her pumps (she could still be seen), she walked across the parking lot and came abreast of Mr. Dougherty's silver Porsche before she was aware that he was in it. He was sitting in the driver's seat, looking straight back toward the front entrance, and he must have been watching her from the moment she stepped outside. There was something about his posture—slumped in upon itself but also tensely contracted—that made him look somewhat less than human, like a crude jack-in-the-box with the lid pressing down. Her eyes met his momentarily, and she expected him to say something, but he didn't.

Ordinarily, Gloria would have spoken—it was obvious that she should speak; she even wanted to—but, in the moment when her eyes had met his, she'd felt an obscure movement in her mind—a snap and then something falling irrevocably away from her like a penny flipped down a mine shaft—and she couldn't bring herself to say even a simple goodnight. Although she disliked this man, it was not her intention to snub him; she had no intention at all. It was as though, having missed the first opportunity to make some automatic, mindless remark, she wouldn't get a second chance. She kept on walking (she hadn't even broken stride). She knew he was watching her.

As soon as she was safely on the other side of the big hedge, out of sight of the parking lot, Gloria slipped her pumps off and her ballerinas on. Seeing Mr. Dougherty had destroyed the pleasure she'd been anticipating, and all she wanted now was to get home as quickly as possible. She couldn't—she thought, taking a cool and ironic tone with herself—arouse her imaginative faculties even sufficiently to turn the new moon into a convincing pathetic fallacy. When she heard the Porsche coming after her, she knew she'd been expecting it.

The car slowed to a stop; the door to the passenger's side swung open; she saw Mr. Dougherty draw himself back from it. A shadowy space had been left for her to fill. "Hey, Gloria, honey," he said, speaking with the deliberate, concentrated effort of a man who's had years of practice in talking while drunk, "you shoulda said something when you went by. I thought you was just getting a breath of air. I didn't know you was going home." He laughed.

She couldn't see his eyes. She hesitated, wondering what she would have to say to make him go away. Then, simply because it was polite, and, therefore, the easiest thing to do, she was just on the point of getting into his car when he said: "Come on, princess, I'll give you a lift home, and you can give me a nightcap."

He'd spoken quickly, in a low, wet voice, and something about his tone, the way he'd swallowed half the words, made her skin prickle before she'd analyzed his meaning. He was a good friend of her father's; he and her father had served together in the war; yet she knew instinctively that her father would not want her to invite this man in for a nightcap any more than she wanted to invite him in, and it had been a deliberate insult for him to call her "princess" after she'd asked him not to, and there was also something more, something truly unpleasant.

A shadowy personage lived at the back of Gloria's mind; it had begun to talk to her while she'd been at Fairhaven, and she called it "the secret watcher." She'd never told anyone about it because she was sure that most other people didn't have secret watchers at the back of their minds, and she didn't want anyone to know that she did. Now the secret watcher said, "*Gloria, don't get into that car.*"

"No thanks, Mr. Dougherty," she said brightly, "I'll have to take a rain check." She didn't want him to see that he'd frightened her, so she gave him her most brilliant smile and walked away—briskly, but not too briskly. She forced herself not to look back.

She couldn't hear anything but the steady swish, swish of her crinolines; it was astonishing how loud they were. Her underarms were burning, and she knew that her dress would have to go straight to the cleaners in the morning. She was almost at the top of the hill when she heard the purr of the Porsche. She resisted a nearly overpowering desire—almost a physical need—to look behind her. The worst of it was that she couldn't put a name to what was happening; she'd become so apprehensive she couldn't think straight and was actually getting sick at her stomach. If anything else were to happen—although she couldn't imagine what else might happen—she could dart into the woods where he couldn't drive his wretched car; she knew he was too drunk to follow on foot. If she ruined her dress, that was just too damned bad.

With its discreet, expensive, throaty murmur, the Porsche was gradually drawing closer. She was afraid that it was going to bump into her—oh, ever so gently—but hard enough to knock her sprawling. Then she saw, out of the corner of her eye, the low-slung, gleaming silver nose emerge directly below her left shoulder—moving only slightly faster than she was walking. She hadn't thought of it before, but the car was shaped exactly like a scarab beetle.

For an eternity, the Porsche floated along next to her, so close she was almost crowded off the road. She refused to look directly at it. Still not in a hurry, it pulled away. She watched it arrive at the turn-off to her own driveway, hesitate, and then make the turn and vanish behind the trees—headed straight for her house. You son-of-a-bitch, she thought.

Instead of continuing to follow the road, she took the shortcut through the woods. She couldn't see a thing in there, but she'd walked it so many times she could have done it blindfolded. Abandoning any effort to protect her dress, she ran as recklessly as a little kid. She emerged through the apple trees, darted across the lawn, and stopped, out of breath, in a shadow at the corner of the house. She saw that he'd parked in the driveway near the front door where he must have expected her to go in.

She ran up the back steps, let herself in through the kitchen, locked the kitchen door, checked to make sure the French doors and the front door were locked, then, taking the stairs two at a time, ran upstairs to her parents' bedroom. Now that she was safe inside, she was so angry she could hear a steady pounding that must be her heartbeat; it sounded as though it were coming from watery caverns just behind her ears. She paced back and forth in the dark, panting.

She would call the club. She would say to her father in her most ironic voice: "Oh, hi, Daddy, sorry to bother you, but that old pal of yours—oh, yes, Mr. Dougherty—he's obviously had too much to drink, and he's followed me home, and now he's parked right out front. I can't imagine what that absurd man thinks he's doing." She pushed back the Venetian blinds, looked out, and saw the Porsche drive slowly away.

Gloria sat down on her parents' bed. She couldn't remember having ever been so angry; the intensity of it frightened her, and the more she came to understand how impotent she was to do anything about it, the angrier she got. She couldn't tell anyone about what had happened; no one would sympathize or even understand her point of view. Mr. Dougherty could, she was sure, create a story so plausible it would make anything she might say sound hysterical. She'd breezed by his car without speaking, he might well say; in spite of that, he'd offered her a ride. When she'd refused, he'd followed her home to make sure she was safe.

That version of events was so convincing that she could, in the right frame of mind, use it to convince herself—except for the simple fact that it wasn't true—but she was glad now that she hadn't called her father and made an utter fool of herself.

Gloria's anger died gradually away like a fire going out, and she was left not knowing quite what she was feeling—not frightened exactly, but—well, "upset" wasn't subtle enough, so she settled for "disquieted." Her mind sounded like several radio stations playing simultaneously, none of them quite in tune, and she sat in the dark, listening to the blurry voices until one of them said, "Some time I fled the fire that me brent"—which was Wyatt, of course—and she wished she could go back to Briarville and stay there forever.

She wanted to live in the Delta Lambda house forever. She wanted to tell Susie about what had just happened so they could laugh about it. She wanted to wear crisp, white linen and sit with the brothers—every one a gentleman— on the back porch of the Beta Theta Pi house and drink a Miller's High Life. She wanted to wear her sexiest underwear and go out for a drive with Rolland; she wanted to kiss him and taste fresh toothpaste. She wanted to wear the dress she was wearing right now—with her pearls and patent leather and her perfectly painted nails—and sit in Professor Bolton's living room surrounded by his millions of books and talk about Lionel Trilling and the high moral purpose of the novel.

But she was going to Columbia— Fleeing? That didn't make any sense. "By sea, by land, by water and by wind, and now—" and now, and now, and now? She was truly terrified of going to Columbia. Maybe she *should* marry Rolland right away. She heard a soft ululation and felt a pinching at her heart, an ache, as though something in her might burst apart, and she completed the lines: "I follow the coals that be quent, from Dover to Calais against my mind." That was it—somehow, obscurely—but *what* was against her mind?

Then Gloria realized that she'd been hearing her grandmother's TV set; it must have been playing the entire time. Not knowing why she was doing it, she stood up and followed the sound. The door to her grandmother's room was ajar; she looked inside and saw a pocket of yellow radiance inside which her grandmother was sitting, propped up in bed on a half-dozen flounced pillows. She thought that her grandmother must be asleep, but then she heard: "Come in, Gloria."

Gloria gathered her crinolines under her and sat in the chair next to the bed. "Are you all right, Grandmother?" she said.

"I'm having some pain, but it's actually quite mild tonight. Are *you* all right, Gloria? You're home early. You don't look well."

"I'm fine," Gloria said (except that there's something against my mind).

"Do you like Steve Allen?" her grandmother asked her. "I watch him every night. I find his sense of the absurd utterly delightful."

2

The Cotters of Briarville, Pennsylvania, were, like most Americans, nobody in particular—"good yeoman stock" Ted always called them, although he didn't know anything about them beyond a handful of vague childhood memories of his grandparents' run-down dairy farm, and he didn't give a damn, really, what kind of stock the Cotters might have been.

Ted's father never talked about his family. He had been pronounced unfit for the Great War and worked his entire life for the same employer—pretty much the only employer in town, Briarville College—and he was the only one of the five Cotters in his generation who had not left Briarville at the first possible opportunity. "You can always count on Jimmy Cotter," people said. "Honest as the day is long," they said. In spite of these sterling qualities, Jimmy had few friends; he was not a man neighbors invited to take a glass of lemonade on the front porch glider, let alone into the house for dinner; he was a man who always seemed to have too much to do and not enough time to do it in, yet he'd never been known to hurry. Stolid and methodical, he shouldered his burden each day with the air of a convict sentenced to life at hard labor who has, nevertheless, determined to make the best of things. Ted was in his twenties before he found the words to express the pinched, sad ache he felt for his father: the poor bastard stinks of failure, he thought. Yet, by Briarville standards, Jimmy was a success; the college had taken him on as a general handyman when all the other boys were over in France; they'd kept him on because they'd discovered they couldn't do without him; by the time he retired, he'd risen as high as he could get, to the rank of Manager of Buildings and Grounds. He built his own home on weekends, every plank and nail of it; by the time the Crash hit, the bank had been paid off, and all the Depression meant to the Cotters was that they were a little poorer than usual. His father taught Ted to plane wood and turn it on a lathe, to drive nails and level beams, to paint cabinets and walls, to rewire lamps, to shingle a roof. "If you want something done right," his father told him, "you've got to do it yourself."

Ted's mother—she'd been Myrtle Greene, the Methodist minister's youngest daughter—was "no beauty," people said, putting it kindly. Although she'd never been trained as a librarian, she ran Briarville's tiny Carnegie library forty years without ever betraying the slightest doubt about her qualifications to decide exactly what should or should not be included in its collection, and she supervised her son's reading with the same firmness, chucking *Tales from Dead Man's Gulch* into the furnace when Ted was a boy and *The Sun Also Rises* when he was a teenager. The Cotters never missed church; strong spirits, strong language, and tobacco in any form were never permitted in their home. In Sunday School, Ted learned that Jesus had been the first businessman and that the sacred duty of every good Christian was to make pots of money.

Ted's father, in an uncharacteristic moment of self-assertion—probably the only time in his life the sorry son-of-a-bitch ever insisted on anything, Ted thought—had named his only child "Theodore Roosevelt." When they were off in the woods fishing or hunting and there were no "damn meddling women" around, Jimmy smoked the briar pipe he kept hidden in the garage (along with a jug of hard cider) and told his son tales of the republic's greatest president—that weak, sissy boy who'd made a man's man of himself. "Get the hell out of this fool place," Ted's father would say. "There's a big, wide wonderful world out there, son. Don't marry some dumb little local girl and spend your life under her thumb. Make something of yourself the way our greatest president did. When you see something you want, get up and go after it. For a boy like you, the sky's the limit!"

Ted always referred to Briarville as the heartland of America, but once he'd left, he hardly ever went back. When he'd been twelve, his dad had helped him build a crystal radio, and it had been his most treasured possession. All through his teens he'd listened to the sounds of "the great wide wonderful world out there." Every year he could find more stations; late at night he could get New York, and New York always sounded as though there was a constant party going on. When Ted felt nostalgic about his boyhood, that's what he remembered: the bittersweet feeling of lying in his bed high up under the eaves of the house, the headset over his ears, listening to a dance band hundreds of miles away in a place where he'd never been but knew he'd go someday. And then, as he'd drift into sleep, childhood stories would run together in his mind, and he'd feel like Teddy Roosevelt planning to be great, like Lincoln reading by candlelight, like Dick Whittington (or maybe it was Ben Franklin) walking into town, the poorest of poor boys, with a loaf of bread sticking out of his pocket, and nobody could possibly know (but Ben or Dick or Ted) that he'd be a great man someday, a famous man. He kept pictures of film stars hidden under a loose floor board; thirty years later he could close his eyes and see Clara Bow with her pouting, painted mouth and big, dark, wild eyes. He'd be half asleep, and he'd be in love with a phantom girl like Clara Bow who had fallen in love with him at first sight when she'd seen him walking into town with bread in his pocket, and the music in New York would turn into a bell that was calling to him: "Turn again, Teddy Cotter, Lord Mayor of London town!" These memories were so sacred to Ted that he never told anyone about them; even as a happy, successful man in his forties, he couldn't have stood it if anyone had made fun of them.

Because his father worked there, Ted got his tuition free at Briarville College. "I've done all I can for you, boy," his father told him, "now it's up to you." Ted played football—left half—as though he'd rather die than lose, and they made him captain of the team his senior year. He lived at home, didn't join a fraternity, and got straight As. Any girl on campus would have gone out with him, but he didn't know that; he thought they'd despise him because his father was the sour old guy who painted the classrooms and changed the light bulbs. He didn't have time for girls—that's what he told himself—although his longing for them was fierce and fiery. He earned his Phi Beta Kappa key and won a modest scholarship to study business administration at the University of Pennsylvania. As soon as he left Briarville, Ted stopped being Theodore Roosevelt Cotter and became Ted R. He never again told anybody what the R. stood for.

Ted would always remember his years at the university as the worst of his life—worse even than the endless, nerve-racking tedium of the South Pacific. Penn had awarded him only a partial scholarship so he had to work five shifts a week in the dining hall; he had a room and his meals and tuition but no cash beyond the few sweaty dollars his mother slipped into his pocket whenever he went home, and still he was lucky (he kept trying to convince himself he was lucky; thousands of guys his age were on the bum or standing in bread lines, weren't they?), but it felt ridiculous—painfully, bitterly ironic—to be devoting his entire energies to the study of the intricacies of commerce and control accounting while there was a depression on.

Nothing in the outside world seemed particularly reassuring. In Germany, Hitler had proclaimed himself "Der Führer"; in Spain, war was raging. FDR appeared to be bent upon dismantling not only the Constitution but the very Republic itself, yet at least he was doing *something*—but, by God, how long would it take for that *something* to have any effect? And Ted still didn't have time for girls; he would have died on the rack before admitting it, but he was still a virgin. He kept telling himself that he had to make the best of his opportunities, but sometimes he got so down in the dumps he considered quitting. If he quit, however, he'd have to go home and live with his parents and maybe plant trees for the CCC, and nothing could be any worse than that. Forget Lord Mayor of London town, he thought; at the rate he was going, he'd be lucky to wind up as the Dog Catcher of Briarville, Pennsylvania. The odds, Ted would often say, against a poor boy like himself meeting a Vassar girl—let alone marrying her—had been at least several million to one. Obviously, the hand of fate must have been at work.

There was in Ted's class a guy named Chuck Nightingale; he was a Philadelphia blue blood, and he'd got his undergraduate degree at Princeton. Chuck always wore his Princeton tie, and he always wore, for whatever occasion, the right outfit with it, and he always wore that right outfit with such a lazy, to-hell-with-it insolence that Ted wanted to strangle him. While Ted sweated for every A, Chuck drifted along on gentleman's Cs; he called Ted by his last name (which Ted hated) or "old man" (which Ted hated even more), but the worst thing he'd ever done to Ted was buy him dinner. Chuck's hand—nicely but not excessively manicured, sun-tanned from a summer spent on a sailboat—had gracefully fallen over the tab, and when Ted had protested, Chuck had said, "Oh, don't be silly, old man. I'm flush at the moment."

You do not, Ted told himself repeatedly, hate someone for buying you dinner. If you hate someone for buying you dinner, you are a petty, churlish, uncultured, mean-spirited, envious jerk with a chip on your shoulder the size of a telephone pole, and so, because Ted did not want to be someone like that, he went out of his way to be friendly to Chuck. He did such a good job of it that Chuck had come to regard him as one of his best friends. On a lovely Friday afternoon in October, Chuck said, "Tell you what, Cotter, why don't we pop over to Princeton for the game tomorrow?"

Philadelphia to Princeton, Ted thought, wasn't exactly a pop, but, on the other hand, it wasn't that much of a drive either, especially not in Chuck's Oldsmobile—that is, if you didn't mind being in the Oldsmobile with Chuck. Even though he loved football and would have loved to see a Princeton game, Ted was right on the point of saying, "Sorry, I've got too much work," when something stopped him. Maybe it was the autumnal tang in the air—the smell of leaves burning, that crisp October sun—and, besides, he didn't want Chuck to know that he hated his guts. So he found himself saying, "Sure. Why not?"

When Ted first laid eyes on Marcelaine Merriman it was, as he always put it, "hate at first sight." She was so over-dressed for a football game—suit, hat, and gloves—that all the guys were staring at her, and Ted had never seen anything quite like her outside of a movie. She was with a boy, and the boy had thrown up all over himself and passed out at her feet; all she was doing was standing there with a faintly distressed look on her delicate, fine-boned face. She seemed incapable of doing anything—incapable even of asking for help—and Ted's first thought was that nobody as helpless as all that, as obviously stupid as all that, had any right to be the most beautiful girl he had ever seen in his life.

Looking at her, you'd never know there was a depression on; every inch of her said money. What Ted would remember vividly were her tiny, prissy, high-heeled shoes—gleaming white and navy—without a scuff mark on them. He couldn't understand how he could loathe a perfect stranger with such intensity; if he could have done anything with her he wanted, all he could imagine doing was throwing her into a manure pile and then, when she tried to get out, pelting her with cow plops.

Ted hadn't been able to stop staring at her, and Chuck had obviously been watching Ted staring at the girl: "Go on, old man," he said with a wink, "why don't you give her a hand before somebody else does?" and Ted had felt a devastating blast of murderous, icy, self-righteous anger—at Chuck Nightingale and every other idiot who'd ever gone to Princeton, at that gorgeous little rich bitch and her slobbering simpleton of a boyfriend, at Franklin Delano Roosevelt and the stinking Depression, and, while he was at it, at the whole damned universe. He was on his feet before he had a chance to think about it. He half dragged, half carried the drunken oaf to his car—it was a Stutz, of course—while the girl, with a wan smile, trailed behind, saying in her phony, upstage voice, "Oh, dear. What do you suppose I should do with him now? He's my cousin, but I hardly know him—"

Ted dumped the jerk in his car. "If I were you, lady," Ted told her, "I'd leave him there."

For the first time she looked directly at him instead of off to one side. "What a novel idea," she said. Her smile was brilliant. Her deft, little hat framed a perfectly waved cap of lustrous brunette. She wore more makeup—"paint" Ted's mother would have said—than any girl he'd ever known, but an artist couldn't have applied it to any better effect, and Ted, having been warned against them his entire life, had a weakness for painted ladies. Her eyes were sapphire blue and sparkling; as he gazed into them, they corrected his impression that she had no sense of humor. And what she did then astonished him: she executed a deep, honest-to-God curtsy. No one had ever curtsied to him before.

"I'm Marcelaine Merriman," she said, offering a small hand in an immaculate white kid glove. "How can I ever thank you?"

The curtsy had done it; Ted's feelings executed a one hundred and eighty degree flip, and he thought: *this is the one*. When he dared to speak again, he said, "You could watch the rest of the game with me." She took his arm, and they'd been together ever since.

That was Ted's version of how they'd met. Every year or two, on a night when everything had gone perfectly and they were lying in bed together afterward, sharing a Scotch and a cigarette, he would tell it again, and Laney would agree with everything and corroborate every detail. She would agree that the odds against their meeting had been several million to one—as indeed they had been—and she would agree that it must have been fated. "Oh, Teddy," she would say, "after all these years, how can you remember those shoes?"—although she would never forget her Schiaparelli spectators. "If I hadn't looked like that," she would say, "we wouldn't be here now," and, laughing, he would have to admit she was right. "Of course I curtsied," she would say. "My English nanny taught me when I was four, and I'd spent my whole life curtsying. It was," she lied, "absolutely automatic."

Laney's memory of how they'd met was somewhat different from Ted's, and she kept it to herself. The fellow who'd passed out at the Brown-Princeton game had, indeed, been a distant relative of hers, a second or third cousin, and she'd met him for the first time in bed that morning—well, that wasn't quite right; she must surely have met him years before at some social function or other, and even if she hadn't, she must have met him the previous afternoon at the wedding reception for her cousin Prudence Merriman, but she couldn't remember anything about it. She couldn't remember anything much beyond the fifth highball. She couldn't remember if she'd disgraced herself (and the Merriman name) in public; she couldn't remember who this man was (let alone getting in bed with him); she couldn't remember what, if anything, they'd done in the bed—although she couldn't find any evidence that they'd done much of anything.

She had the worst hangover of her life, and all she could think to say was: "Do I know you?" Instead of laughing—if he had laughed, she would have got up and walked out even though she wouldn't have had the remotest notion where she was walking out *to*—he said in a muffled voice of affronted dignity: "Well, I should hope so, Marcelaine. I'm your cousin, Ronald Whittock." Then, right there in bed, he offered her his hand. They were, she discovered, in a hotel in Princeton—which Laney found quite disconcerting, considering that her last memories were of drinking highballs in Providence. She'd been drinking too much over the last year—she was painfully aware of that—and she'd blanked out before, but this memory lapse was so magnificent and unfathomable it truly terrified her.

"Don't cry, Marcelaine," Ronald said. "Everything's all right. We're in the best hotel in town."

"How did I get here?" she wailed. "Did I walk in?"

"Of course you walked in," he said, patting her in a vague, ineffectual way. "You were a little wobbly on your pins, but nobody noticed."

Then a spasm of panic hit her; it was so sudden and intense it was like having a cramp. "Oh, God, *what name* are we registered under?"

"We're registered as Mr. and Mrs. Roger Williams," he said with a high-pitched giggle.

They had, apparently, driven down for the Brown-Princeton game. "You thought it was a great idea last night, Marcelaine," he said. "Don't you remember? We were just driving around so you could get some fresh air, and you'd started feeling better by then—"

"Better than what?" It was hard for Laney to get words to come out; she had a headache that started at the base of her skull, continued over her head like a massive steel band, and ended in two thick spikes piercing her eyeballs.

"Well, better than you'd been at the wedding reception. Don't you remember? Your brother helped me carry you out to the car."

"Which brother?" Tiny flickers of memory were coming back. "Oh, God, not Alfred!" She burst into tears again.

"We couldn't very well leave you there, now could we?" Ronald said. "Somebody might have found you— Oh, please don't cry any more, Marcelaine. I hate it when girls cry!"

"Where was I?"

"In the foyer—out cold as a cod. Please stop crying. Nobody saw you. I'll drive you back to Vassar right after the game."

She couldn't believe that he actually expected her to go to a football game. She crawled out of bed, and when she saw her Schiaparelli suit lying in a crumpled heap on the floor, she started crying even harder. "Oh, God, I can't wear that!" She found the bathroom and threw up. Then she drew herself a hot bath, climbed into it, and lay there trying to figure out what she could possibly do next.

It's not fair, she thought. She'd always done what she was supposed to do— well, maybe not all the time and not exactly to the letter, but you were supposed to have fun sometimes, weren't you? You weren't supposed to be a little goodie two shoes, were you? She'd been one of the most popular girls at Fairhaven. She'd always dressed beautifully—better than beautifully, *exquisitely*. She was a good dancer and a good conversationalist, and she knew that boys enjoyed her company. Her deb year, she'd been the acknowledged beauty of Providence. But, since then, her life had been steadily unraveling, and she couldn't seem to locate the thread that had gone awry or to do anything to stop the unraveling. Maybe it had all started when she'd lost her virginity. *He* (which was how she always thought of him, although he certainly had a name, and one that would have been instantly recognized by anyone in Providence society) had given her neither a social disease nor a baby, and she had not enjoyed it—although it hadn't been really all *that* bad—and now she couldn't quite remember why she'd allowed him to do it, but the worst thing was that it hadn't seemed to make any difference to anything whatsoever. Once he'd done it, he'd never called her again (at first she'd been hurt to the quick—later, she'd felt a pure, cold relief), and now he was somewhere in Europe; the best she could tell, he'd told no one about it (or, if he had, they weren't letting on), and she didn't feel any difference in herself—she certainly didn't feel as though she'd been made into *a woman.* So losing her virginity couldn't have been when things had started to go wrong—and everybody drank (her *mother* drank, for heaven's sakes!), but you weren't supposed to pass out in the foyer at Prudence Merriman's wedding reception, and you weren't supposed to wake up in a hotel in bed with a boy you hardly knew—cousin or not—and you weren't supposed to flunk out of Vassar, which Laney was just on the edge of doing. Lately she had been dreaming that she was floating away.

Her roommate, Babs, who was in analysis, told her: "Floating dreams are always about sex. It must be your repressed libido." Laney didn't think so; the dreams just seemed to be about *floating away*—as though she could drift anywhere, swept by any wind whatsoever, and there was nothing to hold her down, and no one would care. "It's probably your Electra complex," Babs said, but Laney didn't know her father well enough to have any kind of a complex about him, let alone an Electra one. He was so distant, he might as well have been Zeus.

Laney carried around in her veins some of the most refined blood in Providence ("condensed like soup," Ted would say later). When the Whittocks and the Merrimans had followed Roger Williams out of the Massachusetts Bay Colony to the Providence Plantations, they had already married each other once, and they'd married each other many times since, most recently when Laney's father, Alfred John Merriman the Third, had married her mother, Agnes Gertrude Compton Whittock. The enduring fondness of the Merrimans and the Whittocks for each other, and the persistent inclination of the Whittock and Merriman men to marry not only their cousins and other close relatives but the sisters of their deceased wives ("It's a wonder there aren't even more idiots in your family than there are already," Ted would say), made for an obscure and densely knotted family tree understood in its entirety only by Miss Isobel Jane Merriman Whittock—Laney's ancient Aunt Issy—who had devoted her life to genealogical pursuits. The tangled web of Merrimans and Whittocks had always felt to Laney like a net wrapped around her, holding her down, but now she was floating away.

As merchants trading out of Newport (in rum and slaves, as they preferred not to remember), the Merrimans and the Whittocks had amassed enormous fortunes; now they were bankers, brokers, and lawyers, and their fortunes were even more enormous. Every time Laney saw her parents these days, they told how they had to *economize*, but if they were economizing, Laney couldn't see where they were doing it; the only way she knew there was a depression on was by reading about it in the papers. Last spring, her parents, not giving a damn who might be ruling Germany at the moment, had been taking the waters at Bad Hartzberg; after that, they'd stopped for a few weeks in Paris, and, ordinarily, Laney would have accompanied them, but she had not wanted to encounter *him* — as she almost certainly would have done, given that their sort always went to the same places. Her mother, knowing that Laney must be sorely missing her annual visit to Elsa Schiaparelli — as indeed she had been — had brought her back a consolation prize: a pair of Schiaparelli glass slippers. How in God's name did they expect her to wear glass slippers when there was a depression on?

Her headache had receded slightly, and she was beginning to entertain the notion that she might be able to live through the day. When she emerged from the bathroom wrapped in towels, she discovered that Cousin Ronald had sent her suit and shoes out; they had just returned, restored to their original beauty by the hotel staff; it was a thoughtfulness she would never have expected from a boy. "Oh, you're a dear," she said, and he peered at her owlishly. He'd begun drinking again, and he was already tiddly. She dressed, put her tea ring on her left hand, turned it around so only the band showed, and made him take her down to the dining room for poached eggs.

Laney felt like an utter ass in the Schiaparelli suit; she looked like Mrs. Simpson, for Christ's sake! Everywhere she went, people stared at her — especially at the football game. Ronald had eaten nothing; he was thoroughly pissed by then and had picked the wrong side of the stadium; they were on the Princeton side, surrounded by Princeton boys and their dates, while Ronald cheered for Brown and squealed about "all those beautiful young gods on the field," and Laney finally understood why her stick-in-the-mud brother Alfred had entrusted her to the care of Cousin Ronald. She thought she'd die of mortification; she thought, oh, what the hell, and took a long pull from Ronald's hip flask. And then, shortly into the third quarter, Ronald threw up and passed out. The poached eggs and the large shot of rye had begun to make her feel reasonably normal again — but not quite normal enough to begin to know what to do with Cousin Ronald.

"You want some help, lady?" some man asked her in an angry voice. She couldn't remember ever being called "lady" like that.

Laney's entire life had trained her to be able to assess people in a matter of seconds — the assessment based on their clothes, speech, and manners — and she assessed Ted. He was wearing a brown suit, cheap but immaculately clean; his hair was short, neatly combed but badly cut. She guessed, wrongly, that he was a Princeton boy; rightly, that he was from some dumb, tiny town in the middle of nowhere, that he was on a scholarship, that he was sensitive about his background but would certainly be wildly successful in later life. She'd seen the way he looked at her, knew that he was exactly the kind of man who would fall madly in love with her—what a bore!—and she also knew he despised her, and she couldn't blame him even a teensy little bit for that—damn the Schiaparelli suit! It was odd that she thought of him as a "man"; she would have thought of someone his age who was, as her mother would have said, "our sort," as a boy.

She watched Ted hoist Ronald onto his shoulder. She watched Ted drag Ronald to the car and, with surprisingly little effort, dump him into it. She looked at Ted's broad, strong hands with short, flat, squared-off nails. The exertion had barely ruffled him; he shrugged, and she saw how broad his shoulders were. Then she saw him look her over again; for a moment he couldn't take his eyes off her feet.

Laney had always been vain about her feet; a series of English nannies had kept her in tight little shoes and had warned her to be careful or her feet would *spread*, and then, of course, she would look *common*. She'd never gone barefoot, and her feet were five-and-a-half, five in some styles. The glass slippers— why, in God's name, was she thinking about the glass slippers?—were a five. Oh, they weren't real glass—they wouldn't shatter—but they were something like glass, a first cousin to it, and they were extraordinarily fragile and had to be worn with nerve-racking care. They had delicate, girlish baby-Louis heels, fit tight as gloves, were not even remotely comfortable, and she'd never felt about any article of clothing as intensely as she did about the Schiaparelli glass slippers: she adored them and she loathed them. Wearing them made her feel like one of her mother's display dolls—the ones you could admire from a distance but weren't allowed to play with. The evocation of Cinderella had not been lost upon Laney, but she couldn't see quite how it applied to her. She'd never in her life been asked to wash a cup, let alone clean a hearth. If this guy thinks I'm just too, too something-or-other-for-words in my Schiaparelli spectators, she thought, he ought to see me in my Schiaparelli glass slippers.

When Laney curtsied, the beginning of the gesture was (just as she would tell Ted later) instinctive, but no one in Laney's set ever did such a deep, Southern-belle curtsy; Laney had never in her life done one so mannered. She saw, instantly, that it had worked and felt a savage rush of power. Once again, she turned the full force of her smile upon him and said, "I'm Marcelaine Merriman. How can I ever thank you?" She offered her hand and saw his eyes drop to her gloves. His face flushed, and he was suddenly at a loss for words. The poor sap's never seen a girl like me in his life, she thought, and then she looked into his eyes. She felt her knees go weak, and she knew she would never again think of him as a poor sap.

If I married a man like this, she thought, Mother would never speak to me again and Daddy would cut me off without a penny. We'd have hardly any money, so I couldn't have servants. I'd have to learn to clean a house. I'd even have to learn to cook. A man like this would want to have babies, and I'd have to take care of them myself. My God, I'd have to be *useful!*

"You could watch the rest of the game with me," he said.

"What a delightful idea," Laney said and took his arm. What do you know? she thought. I'm still a virgin after all.

Ted and Laney were married in the Methodist Church in Briarville, and the only member of her family in attendance was her brother Alfred. By Merriman and Whittock standards, it wasn't much of a wedding; by Briarville standards, it was a showy affair indeed. Laney's parents had been even worse than she'd expected. Her father had summoned Ted to Providence for a man-to-man in his club and offered him ten thousand dollars to get lost; Ted had been so astonished ("I couldn't believe it, Laney! It was like something out of a movie.") that it had taken nearly a week for him to realize how angry he was. Laney's mother had called her long distance, and, in a voice so cold that Laney was sure the phone lines must have been icing up all the way from Providence to Poughkeepsie, informed her that not only should she expect no financial support for this ridiculous and ill-conceived venture but she should also understand that the doors of Providence and Newport would be closed to her forthwith. "Forthwith?" Laney had said. "Oh, Mother. Really." Her mother had hung up on her.

Aunt Issy, who was so old that she didn't care what anybody thought, had given Grandmother Whittock's wedding dress to Laney. Beautifully preserved, it was watered silk with the elaborate gatherings and flounces that had been stylish in the seventies; according to Aunt Issy, it had originally been brilliant lavender, but time had bleached it out to a deep, nostalgic ivory, and it was perfect as Laney's "something old." The "something borrowed" was a French corset lent by Babs' mother so that Laney could get the dress on and actually fasten it up; the "something blue" was a whimsical pair of panties the color of a robin's egg; the "something new" were the Schiaparelli glass slippers—Laney had decided to be married in them and never wear them again.

Babs was Laney's maid of honor, and her brother Alfred gave her away. Ted's best man was a pleasant fellow from Philadelphia named Chuck Nightingale. Ted's parents, wearing the same pathetic expressions of sad-happy puzzlement they'd worn ever since Laney had turned up in Briarville, wept. Every penny counted now, so there was no honeymoon; Alfred drove them to New York where they had rented a tiny apartment. Alfred had got Ted a junior position at Merriman, Henderson, Frankhauser, and Smith; Laney knew that it galled the hell out of Ted to take a job at her brother's firm, but she had to have some security, didn't she? And besides, as Ted himself had said, "Oh, what the hell, a job's a job, and there's a depression on."

Laney lost her virginity again on a cheap iron-framed bed in Manhattan, and, within weeks, their bodies were fitting together like the lost pieces—suddenly rejoined—of an ecstatic jigsaw puzzle. Laney's world shrank to the size of their apartment, and that was exactly how she wanted it. Neither cleaning nor cooking turned out to be as difficult as she'd thought they would be; she cleaned every day until the apartment gleamed, skimmed ladies' magazines for recipes, discovered that there were an infinite number of things one could do with hamburger and canned soup. Ted didn't seem to mind how badly anything was cooked just so long as there was a hunk of meat and a big pile of potatoes.

They made love every day as soon as Ted came home from work, and sometimes did it again before they went to sleep. She lost herself completely sometimes, clawed Ted's poor back bloody without knowing she was doing it, howled so loudly he stuffed a pillow into her mouth—which made her even more passionate, because then she got to bite as hard as she wanted. Her body was utterly shameless and would do things her mind could never have conceived: she flipped over onto all fours and invited him to come in from behind; she jumped on top and—arching, screaming, clinging to the bedposts—impaled herself on him and rode him at full gallop; they even did it when she was having her monthly and got blood all over everything—even in her mouth, for God's sake! and she didn't care. They both agreed that it was too soon to consider children, but sometimes they were in too much of a hurry, and then Ted, who seemed to have more control over himself than she did, would pull out at the last minute.

One morning she woke up after Ted had gone to work. Usually she woke up when he was shaving, but that morning she hadn't; she'd slept so long and so soundly she felt utterly rested and relaxed, and her first thought was about sex. She got up, washed Ted's coffee cup and cereal bowl, and wandered around the apartment thinking about sex. It was as though she were in a drugged stupor and all that mattered in the world was sex. There was an odd, sloshy, wet, heavy ache in her tummy, and she vaguely remembered that it had been about two weeks since her last monthly, but then she promptly forgot it. By the middle of the afternoon, she discovered to her astonishment that she was so wet she had to change her underwear, and she almost went back to bed to relieve herself, but she thought that wouldn't be fair to Ted, so she didn't. When he came home from work, she met him at the door wearing nothing but a black peignoir and as much makeup as a prostitute.

They were in bed so fast Ted still had his socks on, and Laney didn't want to do anything exotic; she just wanted to lie on her back with her legs spread wide open while he pounded her good. She heard herself howling like a banshee, but she refused the pillow he offered her; she just wanted to howl. When she felt him starting to climax, she grabbed his lean buttocks with both hands and pulled him into her with every ounce of force she could muster, and she climaxed right along with him. They fell into a deep sleep for a few minutes, and when she woke up, she was delighted to find that he was still on top and still inside her. He stayed like that, lit a cigarette, dragged on it, pressed it between her lips. The smoke tasted delicious.

With a laugh, he said, "I didn't think we were ready to have kids."

"It takes two to make one," Laney said and held her breath.

"Oh, hell, honey," he said, laughing again, "why bother to get married if you don't have kids?"

Laney got so big near the end of her term they were both sure she was carrying a boy. She was delighted when old ladies on the street came up and patted her tummy; it made her feel—as she realized she never had quite before—as though she were an integral part of the human race. Doctors in those days drugged women in labor up to the eyeballs, and Laney couldn't remember much about it, but she'd given birth to a tiny girl. Laney couldn't get enough of looking at her daughter's fingers and toes and perfect, miniature nails.

Gloria was, as all the nurses said, "a good baby." She only cried when something was wrong, and if you fixed it, she stopped. A few days after Laney came home from the hospital, on an afternoon when Gloria was sleeping, Laney called her mother; she hadn't talked to her since the "forthwith." She listened as the operator told the butler that it was long distance; she wasn't at all sure her mother would accept the call; then she heard her mother's sharp, loud voice: "Marcelaine?"

"Hello, Mother," Laney said carefully, "you've got another granddaughter."

In the long silence, Laney heard the lines hum and crackle between New York and Providence. "We named her Gloria Merriman," Laney said. "Mother? Are you still there?"

Again Laney listened to the long silence. Then, suddenly, her mother began talking frantically in the way she always did whenever she was deeply embarrassed: "Well, Marcelaine, I hope you're going to breast-feed her. That really is the best way after all. The doctors are all against it now, but what do they know? Nothing, if you ask me. Do you remember the Spanish influenza? No, of course you don't, you were too young. Oh, no, you weren't. What were you? Four or five? You must remember, you ran a very high fever and talked constantly. But the point I was trying to make, we had an Italian family working for us, and every single one of us got sick, but none of those Italians got it, not a single one of them, and I asked old Mrs. Carlotti, she couldn't speak much English, but she could make herself understood, and she said it was the garlic. Well, I thought, why not give it a try? So the next time I felt a cold coming on, I ate a clove and the cold cleared right up. Can you imagine that? And I've done it ever since. I just peel a clove and eat it right up. Oh, I know I must smell as though I just got off the boat, but it works, believe me, and I told that to Doctor Conroy, and he said, 'Mrs. Merriman, that's the most ridiculous thing I've ever heard in my life. Garlic has no medicinal effect whatsoever,' and that just shows you how much they know. When your little sister died, they said they'd done all they could, good heavens, quacks every one of them. I don't know why I said 'your little sister,' she was born before you were born, and she passed on before you were born. If she'd lived, she'd be older than you are. It's hard to believe the passage of time. And then you wouldn't be the only girl. Marcelaine, are you all right?"

In the midst of this, Laney had begun to cry. "Mother," she said, "I've never been better in my life."

Even as a baby, Gloria appeared to be thoughtful and self-contained; she learned to talk before she learned to walk, and she looked at everything fixedly, as though trying to memorize the world; she had huge, dark eyes the color—Laney thought—of the sea at night. The Merriman blood was said to have a very dark streak in it that surfaced at least once in every generation—"pure Castilian," Aunt Issy always claimed; "a leftover from the slave trade," Ted suggested, offending Laney so deeply she didn't speak to him for days, and that dark blood sprang out full force in Gloria. Laney was a true brunette, but Gloria's hair came in black and glistening as a crow's wing; by the time she was two, Gloria's deep blue eyes had turned to obsidian, and her skin was not only darker than anyone else's in the family—she always looked as though she'd been out in the sun even when she hadn't—it also had an exotic olive tint that, indeed, could have been Spanish. Laney called her "my little Gypsy girl" and thought: poor dark thing, she'll just have to make the best of it.

Many of Laney's Vassar friends had married men who worked in New York, and, like Laney, they were learning to clean and cook and take care of babies. No one was making much money, and there was a jolly feeling of we're-all-in-it-together. The girls visited each other in the afternoons, children in tow, and swapped gossip, recipes, and housekeeping tips; on weekends they had pot-luck dinners and proudly drank cheap Italian wine. Ted was well liked—he fit right in—and Laney never lost her wonderment at how magnificent her luck had been; she felt as though she had narrowly escaped some obscure disaster (floating away), that she had been blessed far beyond anything she deserved. Marrying Ted had been the perfect thing for her to do, and, given how different their backgrounds were, how little she'd known about him, really, it could just as easily have been, as her parents had predicted, the worst mistake of her life. Tough as things were, she was happy; for the first time since her deb year, she was proud of herself.

Gloria was such a delightful child she made Laney want to have a dozen more. She was so dark and tiny and delicate she looked like a Rackham drawing of a wood sprite; her hair was dead straight, and Laney cut bangs in the front and brushed it until it gleamed like jet. Gloria talked all day long and fell asleep talking; she had a small, precise voice, and Laney was amused, and somewhat embarrassed, to hear a perfect reproduction of her own upper-class New England, Providence debutante, Vassar, la-dee-dah accent. By the time she was five, Gloria had lost all traces of her babyish lisp and had stopped making grammatical mistakes—"goed" had been replaced by "went"—and she appeared to have mastered all the tenses of English. Her vocabulary was astonishing; one night at dinner she stopped her father dead by saying: "You know, Daddy, I've just had a singular idea."

"What did you say?" he asked her, and she repeated it word for word. "Where the devil did she hear that?" he asked Laney.

"I didn't hear it," Gloria insisted, "I read it." Ted and Laney laughed, and Gloria burst into tears. Gloria liked to pretend she was reading; whenever Laney sat down with a book or a magazine, Gloria did the same thing. How cute, Laney thought, but Gloria always insisted that she really *was* reading. Ted gave his daughter a sharp, hard look and said, "OK, honey, if you're reading, read something to us."

"Oh, Teddy," Laney said, "don't be mean to her." But Gloria, who was obviously offended, picked up a magazine—it was a *Ladies' Home Journal*—and read them a recipe for cheese balls. Ted and Laney were too astonished to speak. "Mommy," Gloria said, "what's walnuts?"

"I don't believe this," Ted said. "Have you been teaching her?" Laney shook her head. He picked up a copy of *Gone with the Wind*, opened it to the first page, handed it to Gloria, and Gloria read it to them. She stumbled over the big words, and they could tell from the inflection of her voice that she didn't understand it, but she read it none the less. "Honey," Laney said, "why didn't you tell us you could read?"

"I did tell you," Gloria wailed. "I told you over and over and over again!"

Laney gradually became reconciled with her family. She'd vowed never to go back to Providence until she was invited; the year Gloria turned five, she was invited. Her father had suffered a stroke, and his health was failing; it hurt her to see him in a wheelchair with a plaid blanket over his legs like an old man— and then she realized that he *was* an old man. Her parents loved the *idea* of a granddaughter, but they could bear the presence of a real flesh-and-blood one for only a few minutes, and so, even though Gloria was behaving like a miniature Edwardian lady, she was sent off to play with the cook and the maids while Laney was left to make stiff, difficult conversation in the upstairs drawing room.

Her father offered Laney a small allowance; her first impulse was to refuse, but when she looked into his sad, dignified, watery eyes, she knew she couldn't do that to him. She used the money to buy clothes for Gloria.

Laney would always remember those years as the happiest of her life; while she'd been living through them, they'd felt quite ordinary, sometimes even dull and grim, and she had no way of knowing that they were special, precious, perfect years—that when they were gone they'd never come back—but when they were ending, she knew it, and she wept for the loss of them. She was six months pregnant, and she had instinctively wrapped her arms around her tummy; it was a Sunday afternoon early in December—she'd already begun to buy Christmas presents—and she and Teddy and Gloria had run to the radio when they'd heard the terrifying interruption in the regular broadcast. "Oh, God, Teddy," she said, sobbing, "what does it mean? Tell me what it means! Where the hell's Pearl Harbor?"

The year Gloria was six, her whole world was turned upside down. Her daddy went off to fight the war, and she missed him every day. She and her mother left their dear, little apartment in New York and moved to the big, strange house in Providence with Gloria's mean grandmother, and then Gloria's grandfather died, and everybody was sad, and everybody went on being sad for months. And Gloria's nasty little brother Robert was born, and he was so horribly cute, and nobody any longer thought Gloria was the least bit cute, and Gloria's mother started yelling at her for no reason at all and spent hours lying in bed with a cloth over her eyes, saying, "Please don't bother me, sweetie." Gloria had promised her daddy that she'd take care of her mommy, but her mommy wouldn't let her, and all she heard was: "Mommy doesn't feel good. Go find yourself something to do." But the worst thing of all was the first grade.

Surely Gloria had not cried *every* morning—but that's how she would remember it. Her teachers—ancient spinster ladies, every one of them—adored Gloria because she was everything a little girl ought to be: pretty, good, quiet, obedient, clean, neat, well-mannered, and unfailingly well-dressed. Gloria always colored inside the lines; Gloria did the neatest push-pulls and ovals; Gloria never got ink on her fingers; Gloria could read anything they put in front of her. "Children, look at what *Gloria* has done," her teachers would say, and Gloria would feel herself sinking into a hot, horrible pit of sickening shame. The other kids always got even at recess.

The other girls were bad enough—they teased Gloria mercilessly about how dark she was and the way she talked—but the boys were truly monstrous. They dragged Gloria through mud puddles, threw snowballs and dirt on her, flipped her skirts up and pulled down her underpants, tied her to a tree with her skipping rope, dipped her hair in the inkwells, poured sand and salt over her

head. Once they caught her and held her down; then, slowly and methodically, they rubbed her hair, face, neck, and even the insides of her ears, with a
peanut butter and jelly sandwich. Years later she would tell that story and always
get a laugh with it (she would send the entire dinner table at the Delta Lambda
house into hysterics with it), but when she'd allow herself to remember it—
remember the exact feeling of it—she'd always feel dizzy and sick.

When she'd been a little kid caught in the midst of it, she'd never been able
to understand why the other kids didn't like her. It wasn't fair; grown-ups always
liked her. She prayed to Jesus; she tried to be as good as Jesus had been ("be ye
perfect even as your father in heaven is perfect," she'd learned in church, and
she really *did* try), but nothing worked, and surely she hadn't cried herself to
sleep every night, but that's how she would remember it—and she would
remember wandering around the big, draughty house, bored and scared and
cold and afraid to bother anyone—and she would remember reading.

The children's books were all kept together on the bottom shelf in the library,
and Gloria read nursery rhymes and fairy tales and all of the Elsie Dinsmore
books, and all of Louisa May Alcott, and all of Frances Hodgson Burnett. She
ran out of children's books and read Twain and Dickens; she read her mother's
grown-up novels; her grandmother had been fond of the weird tales of Fu
Manchu, and Gloria read every one of them; she read her grandfather's Philo
Vance books; she read every magazine that came into the house. She read furiously; she read until she was bleary-eyed. When she was reading, she was in a
different world, but the sad thing was that when she stopped reading, she always
found herself right back where she had started—alone in the cold, scary house—
and then she'd remember that she'd have to face another day at school.

Years later, when Gloria would remember it, she would get furious at her
mother. What could her mother have been thinking? If you have half a brain
in your head, you don't tell the literal-minded Irish maid to put sausage curls
into your daughter's hair every morning (it took an hour). You don't send your
daughter to a public school in a chauffeured limousine. And then, just about
the time she's beginning to get the first dim inkling of how she might possibly
be able to fit in, you don't suddenly insist that your daughter be skipped a
grade, and then, when she has to start all over again with a new bunch of kids
who hate her—and she's the youngest and smallest of any of them—you don't
send her to school in petticoats and patent leather, in velvet or white lace, in
Alice-in-Wonderland dresses or Victorian pinafores. You certainly don't send
her in the middle of a grim, slushy winter in a pale pink snowsuit and tell her
not to get it dirty.

Laney knew that Gloria was miserable, but there was little she could do about
it; she was miserable herself. Her father had died six weeks after Pearl Harbor,

and her mother was, as the stock phrase went, prostrate with grief—except that it wasn't a stock phrase; she really was *prostrate with grief*. Laney had always thought of her garrulous mother as the world's most sociable woman, but now there were no dinner parties or bridge games; her mother turned away visitors, never left her room, and her sorrow drifted throughout the house like the pungent smoke from her Turkish cigarettes. And then Laney hadn't been able to bounce back after Bobby had been born. All she wanted to do was lie in bed; some days it took every ounce of energy she had just to get up and get dressed. They'd hired a nursemaid for Bobby, but Laney tried to spend a few hours a day with him so he'd know who his mommy was, and the effort left her totally spent.

Some days Laney couldn't stop crying. For three months, Ted had been at Midshipmen's school in New York, and sometimes he'd been able to get home on leave; then they'd sent him to Florida for advanced training. She'd seen him one more time, but after that he'd been shipped off without further ado to the South Pacific; because of the wartime secrecy, she never knew where he was until after he'd been there. Life didn't seem worth a damn without a man around, and she despised herself for being so weak and feminine. A good wife should have been able to keep up the home front, but all she could do for Teddy was write him silly, optimistic letters full of lies. She'd forgotten how demanding babies were; a good mother should have something left over for her daughter too, but all she could do for Gloria was dress her beautifully—at least I can do *that*, she'd thought, trying to make herself feel better, but nothing made her feel better.

Laney lived in constant dread that Teddy would be killed; she imagined, obscurely, that it was what she deserved—that she'd been too happy and so had it coming. She'd hoped that it might be possible to escape her fate, but maybe there was no escape, and then she hated herself for being so swamped by her petty, personal problems—good God, who did she think she was even to think she had any problems at all? She was living in the lap of luxury with her two beautiful, healthy children while the entire world was engulfed in the most terrible war in all of human history.

When Ted came home, Laney met him at a hotel in New York. She'd never dressed more carefully for any event in her life, wore a crisp navy suit and under it her sexiest French underwear and a precious pair of silk stockings saved from before the war. She felt numb and stiff and stupid; she couldn't even talk. Ted had a bottle of Scotch; he ordered dinner from room service. The South Pacific sun had tanned him dark as mahogany; he was leaner than when he'd left; there were unfamiliar lines around his eyes and mouth (she wanted to kiss them). He'd developed a strange habit of stopping what he was saying right in the middle of a sentence and staring off into space, and she kept thinking: Oh, God, does he still love me? But their bodies fit together as beautifully as they always had.

They got drunk together afterward. He must have said a hundred times, "Christ, Lane, we've got to make up for lost time!" She was surprised—and frightened—to hear that he wasn't going back to her brother's firm. He hadn't been out of the Navy a week, and he'd already had an offer from some new company— the Xenon Corporation—in New York; he thought he'd better take it, "get in on the ground floor," he said. "We're going to have a hell of a boom now the war's over," he said, staring into space. "The sky's the limit, cookie," he said, "just got to make up for lost time, that's all."

Ted started at Xenon, and they bought a house in one of the new developments that were springing up; it was near the train station, and Ted could get into town in a little over an hour. Laney was pregnant again, and she had morning sickness—except that it was morning, noon, and night sickness—and Gloria was driving her mad. The minute her father had reappeared in her life, Gloria had turned into a whiny, nasty infant. She wet the bed, sucked her thumb, talked baby talk. She kept appearing in their bedroom in the middle of the night and tried to crawl in bed with them—*in between them*, to be exact. "Dadda, Dadda," she'd wail, "Me had a bad dweam!" Once, when he was trying to leave to catch his train, Gloria clung to her father's legs and screamed in a perfect imitation of her little brother at his most vile: "Don't go, Dadda. Oh, pwease, pwease, pwease, Dadda, don't go!"

Ted had never said it in so many words, but he obviously thought that whatever had gone wrong with Gloria was Laney's fault, and Laney tried not to, but she thought so too. Ted was working six days a week; he never got home till after ten. The only time Laney was alone with him was the twenty minutes or so as they were drifting off to sleep, and it was on one of those nights that he came right out and asked her: "What the hell's happened to Gloria?"

"The same thing that happened to the rest of us," Laney snapped back at him, "Pearl Harbor!"

Ted fell asleep, but Laney didn't. She lay there for hours, her arms wrapped around the new, tiny baby growing in her tummy, and thought, I don't deserve this. When Laney had been younger than Gloria, she'd been sent to boarding school, and she'd liked it—loved it, actually. Maybe Gloria would like it too.

Fairhaven Hall was situated in the charming village of Fairhaven, Connecticut; Gloria's mother and her mother's mother had gone there, but Gloria was sure her mother wasn't really going to make *her* go there. She's just doing this to scare me, Gloria thought during the long drive; she's just doing this so I'll be good. Then they got to the school, and her mother really did leave her there. Gloria was sure it would only be for a few days, and she promised God that when her mother came to take her home, she'd never talk baby talk again.

After several weeks, Gloria woke up one morning and knew that her mother wasn't coming back. They've sent me away, she thought, and felt a pain shoot through her worse than anything she'd ever felt in her life. It was such a huge, black, awful pain she knew it wouldn't even help to cry. Whenever she said the words in her mind—*they've sent me away!*—she felt that pain. She wondered if she'd die from it.

She didn't die. Looking back on Fairhaven Hall, Gloria could never find the right words to describe it—probably because (as she decided years later) she didn't *want* to describe it. "It started out as hell but gradually turned into purgatory," she'd say, employing a wryly deadpan tone. "I was in a trance the whole time," she'd say, knowing she was lying. "I remember the girls in *Little Women* better than my classmates, the moors of *Wuthering Heights* better than Connecticut, Jane Eyre's childhood better than my own." But the truth that she'd never told anyone—had not even written into her diary—was that she'd transformed hell into purgatory by learning her lessons well: don't be a smartypants, don't show off in class, don't talk back, don't be a teacher's pet, don't rat no matter what, and—the most important lesson—every chance you get, make yourself into a laughing stock because the only way you can get them to let you alone is if you can get them to laugh at you. By twelve, she'd carved a niche for herself at Fairhaven: she was Worm Cotter, the class clown.

As soon as she left there, Gloria made a conscious decision never to think about Fairhaven Hall ever again, but her mind wouldn't entirely cooperate, and stuck in her memory were dozens of hideous moments she could never forget no matter how hard she tried; some she could turn into funny stories, and some she couldn't. Among the incidents that would not become funny were the times she'd been physically hurt (and those neutral, emphatically non-descriptive words "physically hurt" were the closest she'd ever come to writing about what had happened), the things left in her bed: sand and stones, chicken bones, a frog, and, worst of all, a rubber rat that meant, "you ratted, so you're really going to get it," (and she *had* really got it); her first nickname, "Tar Baby," and the way the other girls hummed "Mammy" whenever they passed her in the halls; her second and permanent nickname, "Worm," and the time one of the bigger girls stole her diary and read it out at recess to gales of laughter. Everyone especially enjoyed the passage that began, "Why is it that no one ever likes me?" She still, at twenty-one, had nightmares that she was back at Fairhaven. After one of these, she'd written into her diary: "What I learned at Fairhaven is that there's no limit to cruelty."

Among the stories that Gloria *could* make funny was an incident that had taken place one afternoon the year she was twelve. She'd been in deportment class when one of the older girls had popped in to say, "Hey, Worm. Miss Devon wants to see you." Miss Devon was the Head Mistress.

Gloria climbed the winding staircase to the second floor, tapped at Miss Devon's door, was told to enter. Miss Devon was a large woman with a single, huge shelf for a bosom; she wore her glasses on a chain around her neck. Miss Devon began to speak, looked up at Gloria, and stopped; she settled her glasses on her nose and looked at Gloria again. "Gloria," she said firmly, "you have a bean bag on your head."

Gloria felt herself blushing; this was the sort of thing that was always happening to her. "I'm sorry, Miss Devon."

"Why do you have a bean bag on your head, Gloria?"

"I was in deportment class, Miss Devon."

"So it appears. Why didn't you take the bean bag off your head before you left the class, Gloria?"

"I guess I forgot, Miss Devon," Gloria said hopefully.

"How could you forget a bean bag on your head, Gloria?"

"I don't know, Miss Devon." Gloria wasn't kidding; she *had* forgotten the bean bag on her head. Now that Miss Devon had called her attention to it, it didn't seem possible that she could have forgotten something like that. She felt like an idiot. It was a familiar feeling.

"You certainly have excellent posture, Gloria. You may take the bean bag off now, Gloria."

"Yes, Miss Devon."

Miss Devon sighed and looked out the window. "Gloria," she said, "what do you enjoy doing?"

Gloria wondered if it was a trick question. "Reading?" she said.

"Yes. Reading. What are you reading at the moment?"

"Sir Walter Scott."

"Very good. What of Sir Walter Scott?"

Gloria began to chant: "Ill fared it then with Roderick Dhu, that on the field his targe he threw—"

"Very good, Gloria."

"Whose brazen studs and tough bull-hide," Gloria continued. She was just getting warmed up. "Had death so often dash'd aside—"

"That's enough, Gloria. What do you like doing other than reading?"

Gloria searched her mind. She couldn't think of a thing.

"I gather that horses make you sneeze," Miss Devon said.

"Yes, Miss Devon."

"And break out into hives—"

"Yes, Miss Devon."

"And now I have just received a note from your mother asking me to excuse you from 'team sports played with balls'—I believe that's what the note said."

That, apparently, had been her mother's response to Gloria's last letter—the one she'd done her best to make truly and deeply tragic so they'd bring her home. It obviously hadn't worked. "Yes, Miss Devon," she said.

"That pretty well eliminates our athletic program, Gloria. Is there anything else you like to do?"

Gloria took the question seriously and searched her mind. She'd loved her ballet classes in Providence, but ballet wasn't athletics, was it? And she'd always wanted to be a baton twirler, but every time she'd mentioned it, her mother had said, "Oh, sweetie, that's not something you *really* want to do," and, besides, Fairhaven didn't even have a band. Suddenly inspired, Gloria said, "I like to swim." She'd learned at summer camp. It was something she could do alone.

Miss Devon sighed. "This," she said, "is the middle of November, and we at Fairhaven Hall are not blessed with access to an indoor pool."

There was a long pause. Gloria could hear the piano tinkling in the deportment class. She longed to be back down there walking around to music with a bean bag on her head.

"*Mens sana in corpore sano*—isn't that right, Gloria?" Miss Devon said.

"Yes, Miss Devon."

"You're not giving me much help, Gloria."

"Archery?" Gloria blurted out. She wasn't at all sure she liked archery, but at least she'd tried it.

"Archery," Miss Devon said and clapped her hands, sharply, once. "Excellent."

When Laney drove up to Fairhaven to take Gloria home for Christmas that year, she watched from Miss Devon's office window as Gloria—utterly alone—stood on the wintery, dun-colored lawn and shot arrow after arrow into a straw target. Gloria's hair had never been cut; she wore it as many of the younger Fairhaven girls did, in two long pigtails tied with ribbons. Gloria stood with her back toward the window, unaware she was being watched. She wore her navy winter coat with a quiver of arrows hanging over the back; she wore a small brown glove on her right hand. She reached behind her, drew an arrow from the quiver, settled it into the bow string, drew the bow back, held it a moment, and then released it. The bow uttered a single, resonant, harplike note; the arrow sailed off into a high arc and landed with a solid thwack in the bull's eye—where all of Gloria's other arrows had landed. Gloria paused a moment with her right hand in the air, gracefully posed, her wrist languidly arched, her pinkie raised above the other fingers; then, with the dreamy grace of a sleepwalker, she reached behind her for the next arrow. Her movements were so repetitive she looked like a mechanical doll from a Christmas display in Macy's window. A faint dusting of snow was falling on the lawn, on the target, and on Gloria.

"Well, Marcelaine, what do you think of that?" Miss Devon, at Laney's shoulder, boomed out so loudly that Laney jumped. "She's doing splendidly, isn't she?"

Laney turned and looked at Miss Devon—who had not changed in any noticeable way in twenty years. Laney reminded herself that she was a grown and married woman with three children, yet she still could not bring herself to call Miss Devon "Edith." She looked into Miss Devon's proudly gleaming eyes and thought: This woman is quite mad. Did I really go here for eight years? This place is a nut house. Oh, I must be a terrible mother.

When Laney got Gloria home, she bought her a black velvet dress with a sparkling white Peter Pan collar, black patent shoes with baby-Louis heels, sparkling white ankle socks and shortie gloves. From her knees to the tops of her neatly folded socks, Gloria's legs were covered with delicate whirls of hair that looked—maybe it was the contrast to the sparkling white—black as coal dust. Oh, God, Laney thought, she's turned out to be a hairy little thing just like me!

"You've got to start shaving your legs, honey," she said.

"Sure, Mom," Gloria said. "I don't know how, Mom."

"Come on, dopey," Laney said; she drew a bath, put her daughter in it, and shaved her legs. Kneeling on a towel by the side of the tub, drawing the razor up in short, careful strokes—rasp, rasp—Laney felt an uncanny pang, and her eyes stung. This is ridiculous, she thought. "Here, you try it," she said. "Be careful, hon. Don't cut yourself." I *am* a terrible mother, Laney thought. But she sent Gloria back to Fairhaven because she couldn't think of anything else to do with her.

Laney always regretted that she hadn't used all her skill and energy and feminine wiles to talk Ted out of taking the job at Raysburg Steel. She'd never quite known exactly what it was Ted did at the Xenon Corporation (any more than she'd known what he'd done at Merriman, Henderson, Frankhauser, and Smith), but whatever it was, he must have been good at it because he'd become the youngest vice-president there. Raysburg Steel, he told her, was offering him twice what he was getting. He wasn't kidding, he said: *twice* what he was getting at Xenon.

West Virginia? Laney thought, oh, good Christ.

She imagined West Virginia as a wild, densely forested region slightly to the north of Mississippi, inhabited by grim-faced coal miners with bombs in their lunch buckets and sinister, in-bred, drawling mountain men toting ancient rifles

left over from the Confederate army as they skulked through the woods to tend
to their moonshine stills. But when she looked on a map, she was astonished to
see Raysburg located on the Ohio river on a narrow slice of West Virginia stuck
up between Pennsylvania and Ohio. "It looks like you could drive down there
in a day," she said.

"Sure," Ted told her, "easy."

Laney always regretted that she'd first seen Raysburg on such a beautiful
weekend. Everything fitted in around the river, and the series of knobby hills
piled on top of each other were rioting with a spectacular blaze of autumn
leaves. Her first impression of Raysburg was that it was a quaint little *Saturday
Evening Post* town, not without a certain seedy charm. The temperature was
in the high sixties, and there was a good, steady breeze—so she had no warning
of how oppressive the heat could be in the summer or how the whole valley
could be clogged for weeks on end with smoke from the steel mills.

While Ted was closeted with Carl Eberhardt, the president of Raysburg Steel,
Carl's plump, blonde wife Patsy showed Laney the sights. They strolled through
an old mansion, now a museum, that had been built by Carl's great-grandfather,
and Laney admired how cleverly everything had been restored. They drove
around Waverley Park, which was built on land donated to the city by Carl's
father, and Laney oohed and aahed and said it was exquisite. They drove down
the river on the Ohio side and came back up on the West Virginia side so
Laney could see the steel mills, and Laney was tempted to say, "Oh, what
lovely steel mills," but instead she told Patsy she found them utterly fascinating.
Patsy coasted into the parking lot of yet another one—a huge, dirty building with
dim, little windows. It emitted a steady, ferocious banging so loud that Laney
imagined that everybody who worked inside had to be deaf as the dead. "What
do they do in this one?" she asked.

"Oh, I'm not really sure," Patsy said, wrinkling her nose.

Then, luckily, they discovered a mutual interest in clothes; after that, the
conversation was easy as pie, and, without any effort whatsoever, Laney found
out exactly what Patsy was going to wear out to dinner that night.

Laney was nothing if not adaptable, so she told Patsy she wouldn't mind a
teensy bit of a nap, and then, as soon as she was alone, rushed out of the hotel
and up the street to the Eberhardt department store where she bought the
most tasteless cocktail dress in the place—a shirred navy-blue taffeta with a
grotesque pink flower on the bodice. That night they dined at the Raysburg
Country Club. They sat on the terrace that overlooked the sadly empty swimming pool already drained for winter and were waited on by colored boys in
tuxedos.

The men ordered Scotch; that's what Laney would have liked too, but she
ordered what Patsy ordered—a gin fizz. Carl Eberhardt was a red-faced, balding,

middle-aged man in a bland, gray banker's suit; he had a wonderful, broad smile, and whenever he said anything at all, he laughed so heartily it took Laney most of the evening to realize that nothing he said was ever funny: "Well, folks, welcome to the good, old West Virginia hills! Ha, ha, ha!" And whenever Carl laughed, Ted laughed right along with him. Laney had never seen Ted playing up to somebody before, and it made her miserable.

"It's lovely here in the summer," Patsy told Laney. "Do you play tennis?"

Laney didn't play anything more strenuous than bridge, but she said, "Oh, a little."

"Let's leave the men to their boring old business," Patsy said with a girl-to-girl wink and led Laney away to show her the tennis courts.

They were both wearing long, black gloves; Patsy had left hers on, so, gauche as it was, so did Laney, and she did exactly what Patsy was doing—lit and smoked a cigarette with her gloves on. Patsy introduced her to dozens of grinning men and their plump, over-dressed wives, many of whom sat drinking cocktails with their gloves on, and there was so much perfume in the air it was like walking through a funeral parlor. Laney's wretched shirred taffeta cocktail dress was exactly like what everybody else was wearing; without flattering herself in the least, she could see that she had the best figure in the club that night, and the men were looking at her with expressions that were absolutely avid. She felt her heart sink. She already knew that Teddy was going to take the goddamned job.

Now with her gin fizz in her (she'd belted it down like water), Patsy was talking so fast that Laney could only answer in monosyllables. Patsy talked in a bright, strained, breathy voice with a funny twang to it that wasn't quite Southern—wasn't quite like anything that Laney had ever heard before. "Yep, so here's our good old country club," Patsy said, grinning with pride, gesturing expansively with her black-gloved arm hung with a big rhinestone bracelet. (Laney was not wearing a rhinestone bracelet; she had to draw the line somewhere.) "Oh, you'll spend half your life here!" and she asked if Laney liked riding—there were wonderful opportunities for it—and she asked how old Laney's children were. Raysburg had a military academy where she could send her boys, but all of "our girls" went to Canden High; it was "out the pike" (Laney had already figured out that was the classy part of town), and it was a public school, but it was, Patsy said, a perfectly nice school.

The first Gloria knew that she was never going back to Fairhaven Hall was when they were twenty miles away from it, well on their way to the mysterious state of West Virginia. In the novels Gloria read, people often had "mixed emotions," but this was the first time she understood fully what that phrase meant; she felt enormously sad because she hadn't said any real goodbyes to anyone—and there were two girls and at least one teacher she would have liked to say a real goodbye to, and now she'd never get a chance. But, at the same time, she felt wildly happy at the thought that she'd never set foot in the Fairhaven Hall again—never, ever, ever again in her entire life. *My heart leaps up,* she said to herself—like Wordsworth seeing the rainbow.

Laney glanced over at her daughter and had a sudden, vivid memory of a tiny two-year-old who used to skip along behind her chanting: "Baa, baa, black sheep. Wool! Yes, sir, yes, sir. Bags! Full!" The silent fourteen-year-old in the passenger's seat had no expression on her face whatsoever, and, to Laney, no expression always meant unhappy. "Are you going to miss your friends?" she tried.

Gloria thought about it. Despite the two girls she would have liked to have said goodbye to, she had no friends at Fairhaven, so she answered honestly: "No." But then, quoting *Jane Eyre* (she'd read it four times), she added with a suitably dramatic quiver in her voice, "But I shall have new people to dread."

"Oh, honey," Laney said, "that's ridiculous." *Shall?* she thought. Is that what they teach those poor girls to say?

Another ten miles unwound in silence. She's going to talk to me or I'll kill her, Laney thought. "So how was your year, hon?" she asked.

"Fine."

"Anything interesting happen?"

"No, not much—" but then, brightening, Gloria said, "I won the class literary prize."

"Oh, did you? How did you do that?"

"I wrote a poem."

"Oh. Will you read it to me some time?"

"I can say it for you— Do you really want to hear it?"

"Of course I do, sweetheart."

Gloria stared straight ahead through the windshield. She took a deep breath and began:

> Sweepingly, surgingly, drifting and blanketing,
> Cleansing the sins of all men of the race,
> Falls the rain, sings the rain, battering windowpane,
> Clearing all debts in a goddess embrace.
> Kissing the street where it falls like a blessing,
> Soaking the passerby, woman or man,
> Falling alike on both saint and on sinner,
> It cools me and thrills me as nothing else can.

"Oh, that's wonderful, honey!" Laney exclaimed, putting lots of expression into her voice.

"There's another stanza," Gloria said, annoyed, and continued:

Foggy and wispy or wrathful and angrily,
Misting from heaven or pelting from high,
Nothing so clears my soul as a good downpouring
Chilling, refreshing, both me and the sky.
Look at the poets the same rain has blessèd,
Look at the artists, Modigliani and Klee,
Milton and Chaucer and Pope and old Wordsworth
Shakespeare and Dante and Virgil and me.

Laney almost laughed but caught herself in time. "Good heavens, Gloria," she said, "that's really—quite special."

Gloria had thought that the ending was hysterical; it had—just as she'd hoped it would—got a big laugh when she'd read it in assembly, but her mother hadn't even smiled. She felt let down. "Oh, it isn't really anything," she said. "Keeping in meter was the hardest part."

They stopped for lunch. Gloria had a cheeseburger and a milkshake just like a normal teenager, but her hair was so long she could have sat on her pigtails, and, in her sensible, scuffed oxfords and pleated uniform skirt well above her knees, talking about something or other she'd read but Laney hadn't—quoting in Latin, for Christ's sake—she was exactly like the monstrous misfits Laney remembered from her own days at Fairhaven—those obnoxious, little bookworm girls Laney and her friends had tormented relentlessly day and night until they'd broken down into hysterical sobbing and begged to be sent home. (She didn't know that Gloria had often been tormented relentlessly day and night until she'd broken down into hysterical sobbing and begged to be sent home—and that it hadn't done her any good.) The kids at Canden High will eat her alive, Laney thought.

Gloria, however, was not fat and pudding-faced; nor was she scrawny and twitching. She did not wear glasses, and her skin was not covered with pimples. Her figure was perfect for a girl her age, and her legs—once you got past the black stubble and the thick wool kneesocks that kept falling down—were fairly spectacular. Gloria was—you could see it if you studied her carefully—actually quite pretty, and she could be, with some work, some discipline, even better than pretty. When Gloria was relaxed, and smiled, and looked directly at you, her eyes were exquisite. Yes, those enormous, black, sloe-berry eyes could drive the boys wild, but, of course, the wildly bushy eyebrows would have to go.

"What are you looking at, Mom?" Gloria asked.

Raw material, Laney thought, but she said, "It's just nice to see you again, hon."

Laney drove straight on through to Pittsburgh, checked into a hotel, and called Ted to tell him they'd be a day late. "Why are we staying in Pittsburgh?" Gloria asked over dinner.

"We're going to buy you some new clothes, hon," Laney told her.

Gloria made no comment on that, but after they were settled into their beds in the hotel room, she said "Mom?"—pronouncing that single word in a way that filled Laney with dread.

"Yes, sweetie," Laney said carefully.

"Do you remember the pale pink snowsuit?"

"What pale pink snowsuit?"

"The one you sent me to school in—in *the third grade.*"

It took Laney a moment, but then she did remember it. "Oh. OK, hon, yes, I remember it. What about it?"

"Please don't do that to me again, OK?"

Laney sat up; she was suddenly—unreasonably—so angry at Gloria she could have cheerfully strangled her. But then a voice in her mind said, "You're a terrible mother, Marcelaine." The voice sounded unpleasantly like *Laney's* mother. Laney lit a cigarette. It wouldn't do at all to tell Gloria how cute she'd looked in the pale pink snowsuit. "You can't go to public school in your Fairhaven uniforms," she said.

"I know that," Gloria said.

It felt spooky, eerie—and vaguely confusing—to be talking to her daughter in the dark; Laney almost lit the bed lamp, but then she thought, Good heavens, what's the matter with me? It's just Gloria. I used to change her diapers.

"Hon," she said in her Mother-knows-best voice, "it's time you started looking like a young lady."

"That's fine with me, Mom. Just don't do anything to me like the pink snowsuit, OK?"

"I won't. I promise."

Laney couldn't sleep. She sat stiffly upright in her bed until she heard Gloria drop off; then she got up, quietly poured herself a double shot of Scotch and lit a cigarette. She felt like crying—she didn't know why—and she remembered buying the pale pink snowsuit. It had taken every ounce of energy she'd had just to get up and get dressed and get out of the house the day she'd bought the pale pink snowsuit, and she'd fallen in love with it the minute she'd seen it because it had looked so Christopher Robin—just so damned cute—and she remembered that if Gloria hadn't been so tiny for her age, she couldn't have got her into it. It didn't make sense. Was she really crying about the pale pink snowsuit?

Gloria's mother got her up at eight the next morning so they could get a good start, and Gloria quickly stopped worrying that her mother was going to make her look too young and began to worry that her mother was going to make her look too old. She got her first nylons and her first girdle. She got an under-wired bra that made her breasts stick straight out in a way she knew would be impossible to hide. She got her first handbag and her first real heels and her first lipstick. She would have been happy with a girlish pink, but her mother said, "You're quite dark complected, hon. You can stand a lot of color," and picked one that was red as cherries.

Gloria tried on so many skirts and dresses she lost track of them. Her mother's favorite words for what she liked were "clean" and "crisp." Gloria got lots of clean, crisp clothes. Then they had lunch, and her mother took Gloria to what was reputed to be the best salon in Pittsburgh—she'd asked in the stores—and had Gloria's hair cut and permed, her eyebrows plucked, and her nails done. Gloria felt like crying when they cut her hair, but at Fairhaven she'd learned how to stop herself from crying, so she stopped herself. Back in their hotel room, Gloria stared at herself in the mirror. She felt like Cinderella after the fairy godmother had waved the wand over her, and now she knew exactly how Cin-derella must have felt when she went to the ball—scared to death.

Gloria turned away from the mirror to discover that her mother was going through her suitcases and throwing all her Fairhaven uniforms, her old under-wear, and every single pair of her oxfords into the wastebasket. Gloria felt like somebody had rubbed ice cubes down her back. "Mom!" she said.

"Don't worry, sweetheart," her mother said, "you're going to do just fine."

They had dinner in Pittsburgh and started to drive south in the twilight. By the time night had fallen, they were following the Ohio River, and they kept passing what looked like whole towns made of sparks and fire—towers and explo-sions of fire—flames pouring out of thickly moving, strange shadows—"steel mills" her mother said, and Gloria heard them pounding and huffing like metallic giants. Gloria kept glancing down at her nails; she'd never worn nail polish before, and it made the tips of her fingers feel heavier; she loved how her nails gleamed in the mysterious, fiery light flickering through the car win-dows. Oh! Gloria thought—and again felt her heart leap up like Wordsworth's—*this must be real life.*

The next day she wrote in her diary: "I am going to become an entirely dif-ferent person."

3

Ted Cotter's house had originally been built by Carl Eberhardt's father, Maynard, in 1931. Hardly any new construction had been done in Raysburg during
the early years of the Depression, but the Eberhardts had survived the crash
better than most, and Maynard had taken advantage of the plentitude of cheap
labor to build himself a big, solid, five-bedroom colonial along a high ridge
less than a mile from the Raysburg Country Club. Ted had hated the house
when he'd first seen it.

The arrangement of the bedrooms—lined up like compartments on a train
down the length of the upstairs hallway, three to one side, two and the bathroom
to the other—had shaped the structure exactly to the proportions of a Velveeta
cheese box. Near the south side, a three-car garage repeated the cheese box proportions in miniature; on the east, the land fell away sharply, taking first the
driveway, then the main road down with it; on the west, the land descended
more gradually in a graceful arc to the apple trees. In a painfully rigid sym-
metricality, four oak trees huddled tightly to the corners of the house where they
shed leaves and acorns into the gutters every fall.

Ted had been astonished at the asking price—even with five acres, it had
been, by New York standards, dirt cheap—and he'd wanted to tear the whole
thing down and start over, build something more to his taste—a modern, convenient split-level rancher that would utilize the natural contours of the land—
but Laney wouldn't let him. "Aw, come on," she'd said, "just look at those
hardwood floors."

They had compromised: she could keep her hardwood floors, but he, by God,
was going to have a swimming pool. It didn't matter to him that they could
drive to the club in two minutes or walk there in fifteen, and he didn't care how
much it cost or if anybody thought it was corny: a pool in the backyard meant
success to him—meant that he, Theodore R. Cotter, had, by God, arrived. And,
while he was at it, he figured he might just as well do a few more renovations to
make everything really nice and livable. He had the plumbing and the electrical wiring ugraded; he had bathrooms added to the two big bedrooms. A broad
porch had originally run around the entire house, but Ted had it replaced in
the back with a flagstone terrace and steps that led down to the pool; in the
basement he had a recreation room built—complete with a bar and a conversation pit—and, to go with the pool, a change room and a small bathroom with

a shower. Laney, of course, had the final say on the kitchen, and she chose convenient Arborite counter tops in a brilliant yellow; easily accessible cabinets with narrow shelves, sliding doors, and plenty of toe room at the bottom; low-hanging light valances over the counters; and a high-quality linoleum flooring in a bright, contemporary pattern of interlinking yellow and turquoise rectangles.

There was nothing Ted hated more than dark, gloomy houses like the one he'd grown up in, so he had a huge picture window built into the master bedroom and the entire western wall in the kitchen ripped out and replaced with windows that looked down over the pool. Now, at six-thirty in the morning, the kitchen was cool and pleasant as could be at a time when nobody ever did any cooking in it, while the window above the bed where Ted and Laney were sleeping caught the full force of the rising sun. With most of his face mashed into his pillow to try to escape the fierce light, Ted was dreaming that he was asleep on *The Martha C.*

Ted had never served on a ship called *The Martha C.* and, for that matter, had never even heard of a ship called *The Martha C.*, but in his dream it made perfect sense. He was somewhere in the South Pacific, and he couldn't remember whether or not he was in command, and that was the one thing he should have known with absolute certainty, and it made him very unhappy that he didn't know. He was also hearing a distant, nasty buzzing. It was, he decided, either 1) a mosquito; or 2) a piece of power equipment like a table saw or a lawn mower (in his dream, there were lawns in the South Pacific); or 3) an approaching kamikaze. If it was 3), an approaching kamikaze, then Ted should wake up immediately and do something about it, so Ted woke up immediately. Ted never remembered his dreams, and he didn't remember this one.

The bedroom was so bright it made Ted's eyes water; as usual, he was awake a good half-hour ahead of the alarm. "Yep," he thought grimly, "going to be another scorcher." The dream he didn't remember had left him with the firm conviction that something, somewhere was badly out of kilter, and he lay there a moment, trying to figure out what it could be. Then he remembered that it was Monday, that the goddamn weekend was over—thank God—and he felt cheered up by that. Following his routine of years, he slipped out of bed, shaved, showered, and dressed quietly so he wouldn't wake Laney.

He always intended to eat breakfast at home, but, every morning as he strode through the cool shadows of the kitchen, he was in too much of a hurry to bother—and, anyway, he knew his secretary would have doughnuts and a fresh pot of coffee waiting for him. On the terrace he broke his routine and paused a moment to look out across his property. *The Commies*, he thought—yeah, that's what was bothering him. The bomb shelter could take up a whole hell of a lot of space under the lawn; it could be like a whole damn little house under there, but if it was done right, nobody would even notice it.

He jumped into his Buick Roadmaster, fired up the engine, and lit his first cigarette of the day; just as always, it tasted wonderful. He shot down his driveway and onto the twisty road that led to Route 40; he always took it fast; this morning he took it even faster than usual. He'd made it through another long, dull, tedious weekend, and if he hadn't had exactly what he'd call a hell of a good time, at least he'd had a reasonably pleasant one, but now Ted Cotter was a truly happy man: he was on his way to work.

Ted was the most senior of the vice-presidents of Raysburg Steel—the admiral of the fleet, as he liked to think of himself—and his only boss was Carl Eberhardt, the president and chairman of the board. For several years now Carl had been shifting an ever increasing weight of responsibility onto Ted's shoulders; when Carl retired—it could be any day now—Ted was sure to replace him, and it was damn well about time. Ted might not have known an ingot from an ice cube when they'd hired him, but, after seven years, no one in America understood the steel industry any better than he did, and he wanted Carl's job so bad he could taste it.

Ted had a lot of enemies—guys who resented the fact that he'd been brought in from the outside and had shot right by them on his way up—but Ted didn't give a shit; one thing in life was certain: if a man didn't have any enemies, he wasn't much of a man. Ted's first assignment had been to streamline middle management, and, within a few months, he'd retired a good ninety percent of the old duds—that sorry multitude of Eberhardt cousins, uncles, nephews, and brothers-in-law. They'd gone out howling bloody murder, but Carl had backed Ted to the hilt: "Better *you* can them than *me*, ha, ha, ha." To replace them, Ted had hired keen, young veterans—guys like himself who were in a hurry to make up for the lost war years and weren't afraid of a sixty-hour work week.

"You're doing a great job," Carl had said. "Keep it up. Just see if you can get us somewhere near the twentieth century, ha, ha, ha!"

When Ted had first arrived, Raysburg Steel had been a crazy quilt of mills and plants spread out for miles up and down the Ohio River, slapped together not for any rational reasons but because, back in the good old buccaneering days, the Eberhardts had simply bought or stolen everything they could get their hands on. Even the war, with its big push for efficiency, hadn't solved the problems of cross-haul, and many of the mills badly needed modernizing, but, during the freeze of the Truman years, there hadn't been enough capital, so Ted had been forced to go at it cautiously, in a piecemeal fashion, adding new equipment where he could, building onto existing facilities—"rounding out" they called it in the industry. And, of course, he'd continued to streamline management. Ted ran the corporation like the Navy—or rather the way the Navy *should* have been run. He'd learned control accounting at Penn, and it was his religion;

he demanded a constant flow of hard data into his office, and he could spot fudging a mile away. He paid his boys top dollar, and every six months or so he fired one of them just to keep them all on their toes.

The last seven years had been one hell of a ride. Korea had meant a boom in the industry, and Ted had ridden that boom right up through the ranks of the VPs. Then in '52, when that son-of-a-bitch Truman had thought he could get away with seizing the steel mills, Ted had really come into his own; he'd been the only guy at Raysburg Steel who'd understood the crucial importance of public relations, and he'd been at Carl Eberhardt's side the whole time. Now that Ike was in the White House, they were finally, thank God, expanding—not quite fast enough to suit Ted, but expanding nonetheless. The old farts kept grumbling about how risky it was, but Ted knew better: steel was essential to every sector of the American economy; no matter how fast they expanded, capacity would never outstrip demand. Ted had big plans for Raysburg Steel, but, in the meantime, he'd just have to sit tight and wait for Carl Eberhardt to retire.

So every day Ted sat in his office on the top floor of the Eberhardt building and waited and watched the numbers go by: the graphs and charts and tables he needed to make sure that Raysburg Steel kept on expanding, and kept on making money, so he'd be ready when it was *his* turn. This was going to be a damned good year for Raysburg Steel, and this year he was sure to make *Fortune's* list of the best paid executives in the good old U.S. of A. (Not bad, he thought, for a poor boy from Briarville, Pennsylvania.) So he watched the numbers go by that stood for the raw materials Raysburg Steel gobbled up by the ton: mainly coke and limestone—and iron ore, of course, thousands and thousands of tons of iron ore. And he watched the numbers go by that stood for pigs of iron and blooms and ingots of steel and streams of continuous rolled steel passing through the mills; he watched the numbers go by that stood for galvanized steel and tin plate, for rods, pipes, tees, channels, I-beams, for rivets, machine parts, steel castings, spring wire, ball bearings, and those good old Raysburg Steel garbage cans—and all the numbers translated into money.

Each furnace at Raysburg Steel sucked up air at the rate of four to five hundred tons a day, but Ted didn't have to pay for that, and the mills slurped up about a hundred and fifty tons of water from the Ohio River for every ton of finished steel, but Ted didn't have to pay for that either. And he didn't have to watch any numbers that stood for the tons of crud pouring out of the smokestacks of Raysburg Steel.

Ted had inquired about the tons of crud and had been told, "Oh, nothing much to worry about—mainly sulphur dioxide and particulate matter." He'd had a study done to see if there was any recoverable iron going up in smoke and had been told that yes, indeed, there was recoverable iron, but when he'd seen figures for the cost of recovering it, he hadn't even bothered to present the scheme to the board. So, for the moment, no one would pay Ted for what was pouring out of the smokestacks of Raysburg Steel, and it sometimes turned the sky over the valley white as milk, and it sometimes made fogs so thick you couldn't see from one side of the river to the other, and it sometimes fell back to the earth in rain more acidic than battery acid, and (yes, Ted had to admit it, although, just like everybody else in the valley, he laughed it off) it sometimes made the air just a little bit hard to breathe. Ted, like all the board members and executives of Raysburg Steel, lived ten miles out of town on the highest hills that money could buy.

For years Laney had been listening to her husband get up and go to work, and most mornings she fell back to sleep as soon as he was clear of the bed, but this morning she didn't do that. Her temples were throbbing, and the inside of her mouth tasted like a million ashtrays, and she had—there was no use denying it—another hangover. Oh Christ, she thought, maybe today I'll do it—rye crisps and cottage cheese and water. Lots and lots of ice water.

Feigning sleep, she waited until she heard the door close; then she got up, filled the toothbrush glass to the brim with water, and drank it all. She took three aspirin. She got back into bed and waited to drop off, but nothing happened. Her stomach was on fire, and her mind was churning away as fast as an egg-beater, and everything she was thinking was making her feel utterly wretched. Now she was thinking about her eldest brother; to be exact, she was remembering that goddamned photograph in Vogue last summer.

Laney had been raised to believe that *our sort* did not allow themselves to be photographed for newspapers or fashion magazines, and part of her still believed it. Yes, there was something crass and vulgar and simply just not very nice about the way these new-money people kept getting their photographs splashed all over the place, and so, when she'd discovered that her very own brother had allowed himself and his family to be photographed for Vogue, she should have felt an amused and superior disdain, but she hadn't. It had been a full page photograph, and it had filled Laney with such envy it had made her literally sick at her stomach. There was Alf, leaning on the back of the couch with a self-satisfied smirk on his big mug, and there was his tasteless, pretentious, over-dressed little wife sitting on the couch with their two wan, droopy daughters—and there they were in Vogue.

And the lovely, tasteful living room in the Alfred Merrimans' lovely, tasteful home on Long Island was nowhere near as lovely and tasteful as Laney's living room, and Laney had just as much Merriman and Whittock blood in her as stupid old Alf did, and Ted made as much money as stupid old Alf did, and Alf's wife (his second wife, actually) was an absolute little nobody, and Alf's daughters were as dumb as two stones and had no more personalities than a pair of Angora cats—and there they were in *Vogue*.

No, it didn't matter how tasteful and lovely Laney's living room was or how much Merriman and Whittock blood she had in her veins or how much money Teddy made or how damned stylish and clever Gloria was. There was not a goddamned thing that would make any difference. No family who lived in Raysburg, West Virginia, was ever going to get its picture in *Vogue*.

Gloria heard the sound of her father's car and considered getting up, but she'd been so upset the night before she hadn't gone to bed until after two, so she turned over and told herself to go back to sleep. It should be easy; she was drifting away already. But if her mind was unfolding downward toward sleep, then the flow of memories and images must be running against it—her ruined stockings and her ruined evening, the swish of her crinolines and the ugly beetle nose of the Porsche purring by her left shoulder—and what was that steady throbbing? She was lying on her left side, so it must be her own heartbeat reflecting back from the mattress; she should turn over, but she was back in her parents' bedroom, her heart hammering with anger; something said, "Do it again, and do it right this time," and she didn't know what that meant, although it seemed to mean something very important. The throbbing was like a dull, wet drum behind her ears—almost like a voice—and now she was dreaming that she had a date with Rolland. They were sure to have a heavy make-out session, and the thought of it was getting her hot. She wanted to get dressed quickly, but none of her clothes were where they ought to be.

She was in the attic. She pushed through the secret door that opened into a vast storage area she'd forgotten. Now she was wandering through dozens of closets, each one leading into the next like a maze, but she couldn't find the dress she wanted. She stopped in front of a rack of formals with big, Scarlett O'Hara skirts. She seemed to remember that she'd been chosen for something really important—even more important than Prom Queen or May Queen— and she knew she had to pick the right dress. There were dozens to choose from but all in various shades of yellow, and Gloria couldn't wear yellow; it made her skin look sallow and dead. But she knew she had to pick something. It was important that she look exactly right.

She kept sliding the formals along the rack until she got beyond yellow and found a sparkling white one trimmed with blood-red ribbon. Oh, she thought, perfect. Then she saw that right behind the enormous skirt, wedged tightly into the wall, was Ken Henderson—the *other* boy who'd asked her to marry him. He looked absurdly young—like a Norman Rockwell kid—the cowlick in his carrot-red hair sticking straight up and his freckles glowing hotly. His eyes were streaming with tears, and he was glaring at her. She didn't want to notice him, so she pretended she hadn't seen him, slid the white formal right back where she'd found it and covered him up with it.

She was in her bedroom, looking at herself in the mirror. She had on a tight merry widow and the too-high heels she'd worn for the May Queen candidates' party, which was exactly what she *should* be wearing, although she couldn't remember why. But something wasn't right, and she couldn't see what it was. Now the dream began coming apart—or Gloria began coming apart: for a moment there were two of her; one was a girl standing looking at herself in a mirror and the other was something—it didn't have a body—looking at the girl looking at herself in the mirror. The secret watcher said, "This is only a dream. Nobody's going to see you but yourself, so you can wear anything you want," but the girl looking at herself in the mirror didn't know what she wanted. Gloria, watching, thought that maybe the heels were too high, but the girl in the mirror wouldn't know for sure until she knew what dress she was going to wear with them. By then the secret watcher had disappeared, so Gloria forgot she was dreaming. She saw what was wrong—it was absolutely obvious—she'd forgotten to put her nylons on.

She got a new pair out of the box and sat down on her bed. Her legs were covered with thick, black hair, growing right in front of her eyes. The hair shafts were swelling up to the size of plant stems—like weeds growing out of her legs. She grabbed a handful of it and tugged. It made a sucking sound and tore out with little pops like corks being pulled from bottles. The hairs she'd torn out left deep holes in her legs; the holes were seeping with blood and pus. The hair kept growing, and she kept tearing it out, making more and more holes. She knew she was going to be sick and wondered if she could make it to the bathroom in time. You've got to wake up, she told herself.

Gloria sat straight up in bed. She heard herself making a strangled sound in the back of her throat. She wrapped her arms around her stomach and bent forward, gagging. It's only a dream, she thought and took a ragged breath. She was drenched in perspiration, and her head was pounding. Oh, help, she thought. She'd hoped she was done with throwing up. She hadn't thrown up since the night of the May Queen candidates' party.

Gloria did what she always did when she didn't want to throw up: sat firmly upright, wrapped her arms around her chest, breathed slowly and deeply, counting her breaths. "Eleven, twelve—" she counted now and imagined herself as someone cool and controlled. The secret watcher—who *was* cool and controlled—said, "Keep going, Gloria, you're doing fine."

Yuck, she thought, another hair dream. Since reading Freud in high school, she'd made notes on her most significant dreams, so, if she looked through her diaries, she'd be able to count the number of times she'd had the hair dream. She'd never figured out what it meant, and she told herself once again that she must be hopelessly neurotic.

Gloria had always loathed her body hair. The advent of her pubic hair had upset her far more than her first menstrual blood, and when it had first begun to appear, she'd ripped it out by the roots. She'd been at Fairhaven then, and she'd known that there was something wrong—something dirty and nasty— about tearing out her pubic hair, so she'd always locked herself into a toilet stall to do it. She'd kept on doing it until it had grown in so fast she'd given up in despair. Since she'd been fourteen, she'd shaved her underarms and legs every morning—even her toes—and buffed the hair off her arms, and, for special occasions, shaved them too. If science had offered her a way to do it—she imagined it as a bland, white cream you could smooth on your skin and then wash off in the shower—she would have joyfully rendered her entire body as permanently smooth and hairless as a dinner plate. Now only one thing would make her feel better—clean!—so she drew a bath and put a fresh blade in her razor. A chimpanzee, she thought, couldn't have much more body hair than I've got.

Every summer when Gloria made her annual visit to her aunt and uncle in New York, she and Sandra, the younger of her two pleasant, blonde, stupid cousins, had their legs waxed in a snooty salon in Manhattan that catered to snooty debs like her stupid cousins. Waxing was not, as it was supposed to be, relatively painless—far from it—but Gloria didn't care. It was supposed to discourage hair growth, but only once a year obviously wasn't much discouragement. And now Gloria promised herself that when she was at Columbia, she'd get waxed once a week. She'd discourage her hair roots, all right; she'd murder the little black bastards right down in their little black pits.

When, at nearly noon, hunger drove Gloria downstairs, her mother greeted her with a thin smile. "Well, good morning, sleeping beauty." Oh, no, Gloria thought, here we go again. "You seem to have an admirer," her mother said. A blue florist's box was lying in the middle of the kitchen table.

"For me?"

"Is there another Miss Gloria Cotter living here?"

In the box Gloria found a dozen perfect red roses and a card inscribed with a big, clumsy, masculine hand. It said: "Here's a dozen long-stemmed American beauties for the most beautiful long-stemmed American beauty of all." There was no signature.

"Made a new conquest, have we?" Gloria knew that her mother was burning up with curiosity.

"No," Gloria said, "they're from Rolland." She was deliriously, absurdly, ridiculously happy. Rolland must have forgiven her. The summer was going to turn out all right after all.

Gloria had the roses arranged in a crystal vase on her bed table before it occurred to her that they might not be from Rolland. She looked at the card again. Rolland wrote a big, clumsy, masculine hand (Gloria had seen plenty of it; she'd rewritten all of his papers his senior year), but she wasn't absolutely certain it was *this* big, clumsy, masculine hand. And, although the silly message was something Rolland could easily have written, it was surely not what he would have said if he were trying to make up. Even if he had decided to ignore their fight, not refer to it at all, the note still didn't have the exact Rolland touch. He would have said something even stupider, like: "Roses for my little rose," or "Hi, Glo, don't let this give you a swelled head." And he would have signed his name or at least used the cavalier R. that always ended the notes he'd left for her at the Delta Lambda house.

The roses had come from Klemmer's downtown, but that didn't mean anything; they could have been sent long-distance. People did that all the time. Gloria had even been with Rolland when he'd sent flowers to his mother, so she knew that he knew how to do it.

Gloria called Klemmer's. "I'm sorry, Miss Cotter, I didn't take the order," a female voice said in a deferential tone (there were certain advantages to being Ted Cotter's daughter). "I'd be glad to ask around though. Can I call you back?"

While she waited for them to call back, Gloria remembered Rolland dictating a message to go with the flowers he'd sent to his mother; if somebody at Klemmer's had taken the message, then it made sense that the handwriting wasn't Rolland's. And she remembered that Rolland had once called her a "long-stemmed American beauty"—or at least she was pretty sure she remembered that—but, at any rate, she was certain now that the roses had come from Rolland. Who else could have sent them?

How sweet of him, she thought, even if he hadn't mentioned their fight or said he was sorry. She'd been dreaming about him—well, sort of, although he'd never quite appeared. Maybe he'd been dreaming about her. He was a sweet boy, and she both liked and trusted him, so why didn't she forget all about going to Columbia and marry him? She wasn't in love with him, but she'd never been in love with anybody, and she sometimes wondered if she was capable of love. She'd had a heck of a crush on Ken Henderson, but it certainly hadn't been love (although at the time she'd called it love), and look how *that* had turned out.

She hadn't seen Rolland as handsome when she'd met him, but he'd grown on her. She'd become quite fond of his big, square, amiable face. He spent so much time in the sun that it bleached his hair out and his nose was always peeling; he had just enough body hair to be manly, but not too much hair, and she loved his height: in her highest heels, she still had to look up to kiss him. When he'd been playing tennis, she could taste the salt on his lips, feel the heat of the sun on his skin. He glowed with it. And if he'd forgiven her, she wouldn't have to spend the rest of the summer in a state of itchy, unrelieved chastity. She imagined his clever fingers sliding under the band of her panties—

Stop it, Gloria, she told herself, but she knew immediately that she didn't have the least inclination to stop it. She felt as though she were in a trance. She locked her bedroom door, lay down on the bed and pulled the sheet over herself. She'd been making out with Rolland for months before the obvious had occurred to her. It had been like a little devil whispering in her ear—she thought of it as the little devil on the ham can—*Hey, Gloria, you can do that yourself.*

She tried not to do it herself very often. It wasn't a topic one could discuss with one's Lamb sisters, so Gloria had no idea if other girls did it, but she had a hard time imagining other girls doing it, and she was afraid she'd been cursed with an abnormally high sex drive.

She was still trying to talk herself out of it. Get up right now, she told herself, put on your swimsuit and go jump in the pool. But the idea was preposterous. She heard the phone ringing downstairs; "shut up," she said to it, pushing the sound away. She touched herself. She was already experiencing the usual splitting in her mind: she was both herself—or a somewhat more beautiful version of herself—and the boy who wanted her, was touching her. Today she was so hot she barely had time to get a good fantasy going, and then—suddenly, absolutely out of nowhere—the boy who wanted her, was touching her, wasn't Rolland at all but was Susie's older brother Rick. Within seconds, it was over, and she fell sound asleep.

When Gloria woke up, her time sense had come back, and she knew she'd been asleep for close to an hour. She was so depressed she could barely move. What was she doing having sexual fantasies about Rick Steibel? And—even more depressing—what if the roses weren't from Rolland?

At this time last year—she thought in bitter retrospect—she'd been in the midst of an achingly perfect summer she would remember forever. Right after school was out, she and Rolland had gone to Roanoke for Morgan's wedding. Then Rolland had come to Raysburg three times, and she'd gone to Scranton twice. She and Susie had each spent a week at the other's home, and Gloria loved showing off Susie at the country club just as much as she loved visiting Cloverton and flirting—in a perfectly innocent way—with Susie's cute, sexy brother Rick. When she'd had free time, she'd spent it with Sir Thomas Wyatt and Anne Boleyn, and they'd been fascinating company. Yes, last summer had been, as she'd described it in her diary—somewhat coyly, even *she* thought—"Gloria's glorious summer," a summer made glorious by good friends and sun and swimming pools and lovely dances and parties (and, of course, by lots of lovely make-out sessions with Rolland), but last summer Rolland had still believed they were going to get married after she graduated, and this summer he knew better because she'd told him. Well, she thought, I had to tell him sometime, didn't I? But why on earth did I wait till after Susie's wedding to do it?

Susie had been a mess the night before—such a mess that Gloria had seriously wondered if there were going to *be* a wedding—but then, as though to make up for Susie's dark night of the soul, everything had gone so well that Norman Rockwell could have painted it for a *Saturday Evening Post* cover. Susie always looked fabulous, but, walking down the aisle on her father's arm, she'd looked more than fabulous—so eerily, stunningly beautiful that even Gloria, who, until a half hour before, had been one of the girls working on all the tiny details required to dress and coif and make up the bride, had burst into tears.

The reception had gone beautifully too, and then the wedding party had piled into a convoy of cars to drive twenty miles to the Briarville Country Club for the dinner insisted upon (and paid for) by the groom's genial father because a bone-dry reception on the lawn of the Christian Church in Cloverton might be all well and good, but, by God, you've got to drink champagne on the day your only son gets married. Gloria had still been wearing her baby-blue bridesmaid's dress, and—because she loved costumes and they were part of it—her baby-blue kid gloves, and she remembered thinking that it was fitting for her to spend her last night in Briarville with Rolland at the club where they'd spent so many other nights, but she didn't remember very clearly what happened after that because she'd been so upset and angry—and stupidly drinking champagne on an empty stomach and hardly any sleep.

She must have said something about how beautiful the wedding had been, and Rolland must have asked her when *they* were going to do it, meaning when *exactly*, and she must have blurted it out somehow—that there wasn't going to be any wedding, certainly not this year—and then he actually yelled at her. He'd never yelled at her before, not once in all the time they'd been going together. "When the hell'd you decide *that!* Jesus, Gloria, it's just not fair, you know? It's just not. How the hell long you expect me to wait for you anyhow?"

He'd hardly ever sworn in front of her, had certainly never sworn *at her.* She did her best, by her frosty tone of voice, to convey just how offended she was. "Only until I get my PhD."

"Oh, great. Oh, just terrific. How long's that going to take?"

"I don't know. I could do it in two years, but I probably won't. Four years maybe—"

"Four years!" He stared at her a moment and then simply turned and walked away—walked only a few feet away, but *away* nonetheless—and lit a cigarette.

The perfect sunset was flooding perfect pink and golden light over the freshly mown and perfect golf course, and she should've had enough sense to keep her mouth shut, but she was too angry. "OK, Rolland," she said, "you want to marry me this summer? Do you really? All right, we'll get married this summer. But then you come to New York with me."

"That's not funny." He snapped his cigarette onto the golf course and then, after a moment, lit another one. "Christ almighty, Glo, I just can't believe you sometimes. You've just been stringing me along the whole time."

And she'd said, no, that was ridiculous; she hadn't been stringing him along, and, oh, by the way, she would appreciate it if he watched his language. And she'd said, yes, she really loved him and of course she wanted to marry him, but even as she'd been saying it, she'd been asking herself if she really loved him, and now she thought she probably didn't love him—or at least didn't love him enough, because if she did, she'd be willing to sacrifice herself for him. Oh, she thought, *I'm so depressed* — And they'd talked and talked and talked about it, talked it to death, and always before she'd been able to talk him around, but not that time.

"OK," he'd said, "have it your way. I should know by now—no matter what I say, you always get your own way in the end. But if it's going to be four more years, I just— Well, damn it, Gloria, I just think we should both be able to date other people, OK?"

And that had been the signal for her to give him his pin back, and she'd tried to give it back, but he'd refused to take it, and now she was sure they both had been terrified of that final, irrevocable step: actually cutting the chain that bound her pin to his—which would have meant that everything was off. So they were still pinned, and she supposed they were still engaged, in some vague, ambiguous way—but he'd gone back to Scranton, she knew perfectly well, fully intending to date other girls—well, not really other *girls*, some abstract horde of them, but *a particular girl*—and the last thing in the world she wanted to do was think about that particular girl because if she did, she just might as well go and drown herself in the swimming pool.

What finally got Gloria out of bed an hour later was the decision to read all her diaries over again and make yet another set of notes on them, but once she was on her feet, she assigned herself forty laps in the pool as penance. She put on her suit, bobby-pinned her hair up, put her cap on, and slouched downstairs. Even walking was an effort. Passing the phone in the kitchen, she saw that her mother had left her a note: "Gloria—florist returned your call—a man came in and sent the roses this morning, but Mr. Klemmer didn't know him!"

Just as she knew she'd been meant to, Gloria felt pierced by her mother's exclamation point. She felt a sharp, answering stab of anger, and her depression lifted as quickly as if someone had whipped away a thick, stifling eiderdown that had been covering her. Her mother lay in her lawn chair, tanning; Gloria walked by without speaking and dived into the pool. She was so mad she swam ten laps before she began to calm down.

She's just doing that to get my goat, Laney thought, listening to the maddening sound of Gloria churning steadily through the water. And immediately, having had that mean thought, Laney, as usual, tried to talk herself out of it: Don't be ridiculous, Marcelaine, she's swimming because she likes it. It doesn't have anything to do with you, and besides, if you were a good mother, you'd be proud of her for getting some exercise.

But Laney was obviously not a good mother because now she was thinking: *I* used to have a figure every bit as nice as that. And then whatever part of her was carrying on the other side of the argument said: No, you didn't. Don't kid yourself. You had an excellent figure, but you never had quite such a cute little derriere, and you certainly never had legs like that— But my feet were smaller, Laney thought, loathing herself, and I was prettier. I was actually beautiful— everybody said so!

But that wasn't the point, was it? The point was that however beautiful Marcelaine Merriman might have been her deb year, however picture-perfect, peaches-and-cream porcelain her skin might have been her deb year, she was now over forty, and, therefore, no unknown, mysterious man was going to send *her* a dozen long-stemmed roses out of the blue, on impulse, for no occasion whatsoever. Laney had been out in the sun so long she was beginning to feel like a link sausage and she should go in the house (and do what?) or maybe even swim a few laps herself (trail along after Princess Priss? Oh, sure), and what she wanted was not the rye crisp and two ounces of cottage cheese that had vanished into her stomach without any noticeable effect whatsoever, but a thick corned beef sandwich with hot German mustard and one of Ted's ice-cold beers. Right, Marcelaine, start drinking at two in the afternoon. On a Monday. Swell idea.

God, she felt wretched. Was it just her hangover, or could it have started to happen already? Even the *word* was terrible; even the *thought* of the word gave her the creeps right out there in the full sunlight; it was like "cancer," a word you didn't want to hear spoken, a word you didn't want to say even in the privacy of your own mind, and Laney knew better, or at least she tried to convince herself she knew better—which was hard considering the fact that she'd never discussed it with anyone, and who the hell was she going to discuss it with anyway? Patsy Eberhardt? (And embarrass poor, thick, dumpy Patsy half to death, because the assumption would be, of course, that Patsy had already gone through it.) Her doctor? (But how could she be expected to discuss such a thing with a man?) Oh, dear God— And in her worst flights of imagination,

Laney feared that the moment her monthlies stopped, her waist would thicken and she would grow turkey wattles, a dowager's hump, and a mustache. She would have hot flashes—whatever the hell they were—and need naps in the afternoon. Her voice would go deep and mannish, and all her interest in sex would instantly vanish. Then Ted would stop sleeping with her and take a lover—maybe one of those little gum-chewing idiots they hired right out of high school to do the filing—and Laney's life, for all intents and purposes, would be over. And that, of course, was totally ridiculous, and anyway she had years to go— She wished she had a bridge game or even a committee meeting that afternoon; she even wished the boys were home—and a single beer with a late lunch wasn't really drinking.

Her penance completed, Gloria climbed out of the water and flung herself onto a lawn chair. Her mother looked at Gloria with an expression that was just about as warm and expressive as a lizard's. Guessing what might be on her mother's mind, Gloria said in a casual voice, "You know, Mom, I just can't imagine who the man might be."

"Oh, can't you?"

"Maybe it was one of the boys we saw at the club last night—Mike or Lee."

"Oh? The first thing you said was that they were from Rolland."

"Well, that was my first thought. You know, it was kind of an obvious."

"Obvious," her mother said, pronouncing the word meditatively as though it were the key to the secrets of the universe. She looked out across the lawn and lit a cigarette.

"Mom? Are you mad at me?"

"Oh, no, sweetie, why would I be mad at you? But could you— Do be an angel, Gloria, and please pick up all that junk the boys left behind."

Oh, for Pete's sake, Gloria thought. "Sure, Mom."

By the time Gloria had picked up most of the brats' crap—including a vast number of balls of various sizes, bats and rackets and several wadded-up articles of clothing and even two mouldy, half-eaten sandwiches—she was so angry she felt like screaming. She turned back toward the house and saw that her mother had vanished. I won't be able to survive the summer, Gloria thought. I'll go mad!

She couldn't go to New York and stay with her stupid cousins because they were in Paris, the lucky things. Maybe she could go stay with Morgan. When she'd been Morgan's bridesmaid last summer, both Morgan and James had said, "Oh, you'll just have to come for a nice, long visit!" But Morgan had a new baby, and the last thing she needed was a house guest, and Susie, of course, hadn't even been married two weeks— Oh dear, Gloria thought, pretty soon every Lamb's going to be married but me! She heard herself sigh. She was standing in the middle of the back lawn holding her wretched little brother's bow. He was so irresponsible he'd left it strung.

It wasn't a light, finicky recurve like the one she'd shot, dutifully, day after day, at Fairhaven; it was an American longbow, a hunter's bow—as Bobby had explained to her in some detail, not caring whether she'd wanted to hear about it or not. In the quiver lying at her feet were hunter's arrows with sharp triangular points designed to hurt an animal—a deer—to bleed it to death. She bent, picked up the quiver, and hung it over her shoulder. Then she drew an arrow out and looked at it; just as Bobby had said, the point was as sharp as a razor blade. How ridiculous, Gloria thought, annoyed at her brothers, at her father (and at all the males in the world). Why is he allowed to shoot this lethal thing right in the middle of our backyard? He could kill somebody.

I used to be good at this, Gloria thought. What an odd thing to be good at—but she'd even won half a dozen ribbons she'd been so good at it. She fitted the arrow to the string and tried to draw the bow. It felt impossible—as though the string were attached to a concrete wall—and her anger blazed up. If Bobby can draw this, so can I, she thought, took a deep breath and pulled. Her skinny little brother must have been something of a brute; it took every ounce of her strength to draw the bow and hold it, the string pressed lightly against her lips. Her arms were shaking with the effort.

Then Gloria realized that she was already well along into one of those intense experiences she had labeled in her diary as "mental flooding." The term was not an adequate metaphor to describe what happened to her, but Gloria had never found a better one: she felt as though she were being flooded with a tidal wave of images and associations. She'd never been able to make these strange states happen on demand; if they went on long enough, they left her exhausted—empty as a zero—and when she tried to write about them, it took her hours to sketch even the barest outline of what had been in her mind *for only a minute or two*. Some of her best papers were the result of mental flooding, but it wasn't an easy way to write them; if the experience took hours to sketch, the imposition of scholarly coherence upon the sketch took days of hard work.

This particular flooding had begun when Gloria had caught herself—become fully aware of herself—holding Bobby's bow and had made the easy, obvious association to Wyatt: "Whoso list to hunt, I know where is an hind—" and the moment her mind had given her that opening line, she'd had the entire poem available—every word of it—and it had continued to sound underneath the profusion of more associations, each association a stream flowing to other associations: the deer of the courtly love tradition, the lover as hunter and hunted, Petrarch's Laura, Wyatt's "Brunette" (with whom Gloria had always identified) evoking Shakespeare's dark lady of the sonnets and then the dark Gypsies of nursery rhymes and fairy tales, and on into the Matter of Britain—

to Nimue, Vivienne, Morgan la Fey—reminding Gloria of her own Morgan who was not dark but shimmery ash blonde, and Morgan reminding her of Susie who was blonde as sunlight—and Gloria saw Susie strutting across the football field in her sparkling white majorette's uniform, and saw the silvery sparkle of Susie's spinning baton, and that made her see the sunlight refracted through the crystal vase, see the roses on her bed table and feel their associations—the mystic rose—and that stream led away to glass and rose, Rose Red, Snow White in her glass coffin— and flowing into her, simultaneously, more and more of them, other deer images and associations: Cummings' deer, his lean hounds "low and smiling," and Acteon, Artemis-Diana the Huntress, the virgin moon goddess, and Britomartis, who kept the hounds of Artemis, transformed into Spenser's chaste Britomart, which, of course, took her to Amoret and Florimell and the False Florimell and the evil enchanter, Busyrane—and Gloria had already been hearing Pound before she felt the connection; she'd heard the repeated feminine endings—amphibrachs—sounding throughout his dense, subtle music—ta DUH dum—caught one, "before her"— What was it? Something about clouds, eyes—and throughout all of this, there had been no decision to let the arrow go; she had simply run out of strength.

She loved the sound—the deep, single-minded note—and then the string smacked hard into her wrist; she gasped, and her eyes stung with tears, but years of archery had trained her, and she held her stance—her follow-through—and watched her shot. The bow had a terrific cast; she'd totally misjudged it. Gloria had never shot a bow with that much cast; she felt her heart leap, and the physical experience of shooting the bow (her wrist still stung) had staunched, for the moment, the brilliant images flowing into her mind, but, as she watched the flight of the arrow, as it sailed high, a good four feet above the butt, and continued out in a sweet, silvery arc into the luckily empty space of the lawn and fell to earth not far from the apple trees, she heard the line from Pound: "with the veil of faint cloud before her . . ." then something in Greek and "something, something . . . pale eyes as if without fire." Oh! she thought, hearing the slant rhyme of "fore her" and "fire," seeing the veiled moon goddess, her pale eyes— Oh, how lovely!

Bobby's wrist guard was lying a few feet away. She put it on and drew out the next arrow. Breathe, she told herself just as Miss Devon had always told her; she was surprised at how satisfying it felt to draw a bow that massive. "Who list her hunt, I put him out of doubt," she thought—said it in her mind like a prayer ending with "amen"—and kissed the string. She willed the arrow home to the bull's-eye as she had done a million times before. The bow sang; the string snapped hard onto the wrist guard; she felt her right hand floating in the air. The arrow struck the butt with a loud WHAP!

She shot all the arrows—and put all of them in the butt and the last three in the bull's-eye. She stood, still poised from her final shot, and heard an odd sound—a distant, dry, mysteriously slapping sound. She turned to see what it was—and laughed. The completion—it felt like a couplet—was perfect: her grandmother, sitting behind her window upstairs, was applauding her.

"I arched too," Gloria's grandmother said. "Is that the word for it?—at Newport. It was considered quite the proper sport for a young lady."

"Really?" Gloria said. "Did you like it?"

"Oh, I couldn't even hit the target most of the time. I wasn't a very sporting girl."

"I'm not either," Gloria said. She'd brought her grandmother's lunch tray, had stayed behind to chat. Now she was sitting in the wingback chair with her knees drawn up to her chin. She could smell chlorine on her skin; she should take a shower, but she didn't feel like it. The mental flooding had left her feeling, as usual, empty and quiet. She wanted to get her grandmother talking so she could sit passively and listen. "What was it like?" she asked.

"What was *what* like?" her grandmother said, laughing.

"You know, when you were a girl—Newport and everything."

"Oh, we didn't think Newport was all that grand. It was just where we went in the summer."

As Gloria listened to her grandmother, another part of her mind was wandering away on its own. Whenever Professor Bolton had talked about her academic career, he'd used the phrase "your languages," and Gloria had never been courageous enough to ask just how many darn languages he thought she ought to know, but one of them was certainly Greek. Well, if she wanted to read Ezra Pound, she was going to have to take Greek at Columbia—

"I had a little trap with a pony," her grandmother was saying, "and we went on picnics—walked a lot—much more, I think, than you girls walk. After I came out, of course, there were the balls and the flirting. It was the happiest time of my life—that and the first years of my marriage—until my poor, dear Cicely died, oh, but that's another story. It's so long ago, Gloria, it's like another age. It's really quite unbelievable how the times have changed. You would have found it all quite stodgy, I'm sure."

"Maybe not. Sometimes I think I don't fit into this age. Maybe I would have liked yours better."

"Oh, no, dear. You belong right here."

Back in her room, Gloria sat at her desk and stared at the enigmatic roses on her bed table. Something about Pound was still nagging at her mind, so she dug out her copy of *The Pisan Cantos*. As she always did whenever she picked up the book, she looked at the title page so she could be amazed all over again that Ezra Pound himself had actually written his name there.

Maybe now was the time to have another go at Pound, and, for a moment, the prospect of spending the summer on serious scholarship made her giddy with delight. Then, just a few seconds later, she couldn't imagine anything she'd less rather do. She felt deflated, irritable and sour; what on earth had she been thinking? She didn't have to write a paper on Pound, for heaven's sake—at least not yet. She slammed the book back onto the shelf and stared out the window. As though it were reluctant to let Pound go, a wispy voice in her mind said, "pale eyes as if without fire."

"Gloria, you think too much," Susie used to say. Over their years together, that line had become one of their standard shared jokes—and Gloria often thought that Susie was right; she'd probably be a healthier person if she were not quite as introspective as she so obviously—and so exhaustively—was. Gloria had begun keeping a diary at Fairhaven; since then, she had filled fifteen volumes, was well into the sixteenth, and she thought of these little books simply as "my life."

She used her diary not only to record current events but to engage in page after page of self-analysis—this year's self-analysis contradicting much of what she'd said in last year's self-analysis—followed by page after page of pep-talks and stern advice to herself. In the last few years she'd begun annotating her diaries, writing marginal notes, and then, when she ran out of space, inserting new pages. In an attempt to maintain a thread of clarity though what could easily have become a sprawling, crazy-quilt chaos, she'd drawn a huge chart of her life keyed to the diaries. Certain crucial times had pulled her back again and again; about these, she'd written not only annotations, but annotations of annotations, creating a mul-tilayered text with as many as a dozen different times folded in upon each other. Working on this project that was, by definition, endless, made her feel like a detached scholar—her own serene biographer, the world's leading authority on Gloria Merriman Cotter.

Now she felt another serious bout of annotation coming on. Not sure exactly where she should start, she chose the diary from the summer when her family had moved to Raysburg. The mere appearance of the book was enough to bring back a shiver of the stomach-knotting anxiety that had characterized her years at Canden High; she'd still been using genuine diaries from the stationery store, and this one was bound in pink, had pink unlined paper, and she'd written in it with a deep mauve ink using a tiny, excessively neat script that transformed all the dots into tiny circles. Looking at it seven years later, she cringed with embarrass-ment.

She turned to the first page and read the single, momentous sentence: "I am going to become an entirely different person." As admirably concise as that sentence was, she had always wished she'd written more, filled in the details— because she *had* become an entirely different person. She thought now that she should write an account of exactly how she'd done it. Who knows? Maybe someday she'd have to become an entirely different person again.

She turned the page and saw that her next diary entry was a set of step-by-step instructions for giving herself a manicure—something she'd copied from a magazine. She'd spent a huge amount of time that summer sitting in the Ohio County Public Library reading back issues of *Seventeen*, and *Vogue*, and every advice-to-girls book they had on their shelves. The opening quarter of her diary contained hardly anything but carefully copied excerpts from what she'd been reading; not until Christmas had she written a single entry about what she'd been feeling. Now she remembered that *fear* had been the main thing she'd been feeling at Canden High—sometimes more than fear, sometimes utter terror—but, as terrified as she'd been, she'd also felt, for the first time in her life, truly alive.

The contractors had assured Gloria's father that the renovations would be finished by April, but they dragged on throughout most of the summer, so Gloria had to dodge workmen, walk around ladders, and wake up every morning to the sound of hammering. Her room was one of the few in the house that was completely finished, and, if she wouldn't have picked the exact wallpaper her mother had chosen for her—tiny, pink, girlish flowers on a field of ivory—she thought it was nice enough. She sat alone in her room for hours, planning where to put things, thinking: I don't have to share it with anybody; it's mine!

Gloria had been spared camp that summer, and she was not—she could finally allow herself to believe in the joy and the wonder of it—ever going back to Fairhaven Hall. She was going to live with her family like any normal girl. But she still felt like a stranger, a not entirely welcome guest in what was supposed to be her own home. The brats did not like her any better than they ever had, and she didn't like them. Her father left early every morning and never got home before nine or ten at night; he worked most Saturdays; some Sundays he went in "just for an hour or two"—which meant most of the day, so she hardly ever saw him. Her mother did the shopping, supervised the renovations, chose the new carpeting, wallpaper, drapes, blinds, paint, and furniture; she pulled the brats out of the muddy hole in the backyard that should by then have been a finished swimming pool; at least once a day she shut herself into one of the rooms where no one was working and wept. Gloria heard her mother weeping through the closed doors and wondered if she should do something about it. Even if she could have thought of something, she wasn't sure she wanted to do something about it.

They'd already had three housekeepers. Gloria's mother had fired the first, the second had quit, and the third was Mrs. Warsinski. Each morning Mrs. Warsinski arrived chewing an enormous wad of gum—it had to be two sticks—

removed it from her mouth as soon as she stepped through the door, and stuck it on the sleeve of her house dress where it rode around all day waiting to be crammed back into her mouth when she left. Mrs. Warsinski thought nothing of picking the brats up bodily to move them out of the way, or of grabbing them by their ears and hauling them screaming in to lunch—but they adored her. Mrs. Warsinski tied the garbage up with string and brown paper into neat little bundles (Gloria's mother had opened one, thinking it was Ted's shirts back from the laundry). Mrs. Warsinski used so much cleansing powder and disinfectant that the shiny, new kitchen smelled like a hospital—except when she was cooking; then it smelled, as Gloria's mother said, like the kitchen in a refugee camp, for everything Mrs. Warsinski cooked seemed to have garlic in it (yet the brats loved her food and ate huge mounds of it). "Oh, God, I loathe that wretched woman!" Gloria's mother said every night after Mrs. Warsinski had gone home, yet she lived in mortal terror that Mrs. Warsinski would quit on her.

Gloria was the only member of her family who talked to Mrs. Warsinski, so she was the only member of her family who knew that Mr. Warsinski had been killed in a terrible accident at the Indian Works a few years ago, that Mrs. Warsinski's son Frank had gone through Raysburg College on the G.I. Bill and her other son Eddie was in Korea, that both of her daughters were married, and Shirley, who worked in the five-and-dime, was about to give birth to Mrs. Warsinski's third grandchild. Mrs. Warsinski taught Gloria how to make spaghetti and sloppy joes and cole slaw, how to roast a chicken and mash potatoes, how to iron pleats as sharp as knife edges, how to polish her shoes, how to starch her dresses to crisp perfection, how to use just the right amount of bluing to make her blouses come out white white white.

That summer Gloria met the girl who would turn out to be her best friend in Raysburg: Binkie Eberhardt. The main thing Gloria liked about Binkie was that Binkie liked *her*—although she didn't know why Binkie could possibly have liked her, and, seven years later, she still hadn't figured it out, but maybe it was the cherry-red lipstick her mother had bought her in Pittsburgh (Binkie was allowed to wear only pink) or Gloria's first pair of heels: "Does your mom let you wear heels that high? *Neato!*" Binkie was a real blonde (even then Gloria had been able to spot a bottle blonde a mile off), and, at fifteen, had the best figure she would ever have. Her picture frequently graced the society page of the *Raysburg Times*. ("Miss Barbara 'Binkie' Eberhardt, daughter of Mr. and Mrs. Carl Eberhardt of Eberhardt Place, takes a welcome dip at the Raysburg Country Club.") "Daddy says I have to look out for you," Binkie announced at their first meeting, and, before she left that day, made sure that Gloria's mom was going to sign her up for dancing class and junior membership in the Raysburg Cotillion.

Gloria wrote Binkie's fashion advice into her diary: "All the girls in our class will be wearing lipstick and nail polish this year, so you should too. Don't wear nylons on the first day or the kids will think you're stuck-up; wear bobby socks and saddle shoes. After people get to know you, you can wear nylons sometimes, but not too often. You can wear heels to the club or out on formal dates, but if a girl our age wears heels to school, the boys think she's fast, so don't do it. Don't wear your skirts too short or the boys will think you're too young to date, and if you ever ever *ever* again wear ballerinas with ankle socks the way you did on Sunday, not a single boy will ever ask you out, so don't say I didn't warn you."

No matter how many unkind thoughts Gloria might have had about Binkie Eberhardt over the years—"shallow" was the mildest—she vowed that Binkie would always be her friend because, on the first day of school, when Gloria was standing on the sidewalk looking up toward the huge main doors of Canden High so terrified that her vision was blurring, standing on a spot not ten feet from where she'd climbed out of her mother's car, frozen, unable to take another step forward, unable to think anything but the idiotically repeated phrase, *I can't do it*, Binkie walked up to her, took her by the hand (Canden High girls most definitely did not walk around holding hands), and led her up the steps and through the doors and down the hall to their home room, saying to everyone they met: "This is my friend Gloria. She's just moved here from New York."

Margaret Mead in New Guinea couldn't have studied a primitive tribe with any more scholarly care than Gloria studied Canden High. She memorized the names of her fellow sophomores and spoke to everyone. As she'd learned to do at Fairhaven, she sat at the back of the classroom and volunteered nothing. At recess and in the cafeteria, she stuck with Binkie and the other country club girls, but she talked with anyone who seemed interested in talking to her. By the time she came home every afternoon, her face ached from smiling.

Gloria couldn't believe it: here she was in a *real* high school that had all those mysterious and wonderful things she'd been reading about: clubs and a school newspaper, a home economics room with sewing machines in it, a marching band with majorettes, boys who played sports and cheerleaders who cheered for them. Fascinated by the idea of cheerleaders, she went to watch the try-outs, and, while she was standing there minding her own business, Sally Wright, the head cheerleader, walked up to her and said, "Hi, Gloria."

Gloria said hi and smiled and wondered how on earth an upper classman could possibly know her name. "Are you going to try out?" Sally said.

Try out! Gloria thought. It had never crossed her mind that she could be a cheerleader—well, on second thought, maybe it had and she hadn't wanted to admit it. "You won't get anywhere just watching," Sally said. "Come on, give it a try. We've got three places, and you've got the perfect figure for it."

I do? Gloria thought, and, before she could talk herself out of it, found herself walking down onto the field with the other girls.

The cheerleaders did a cheer, and then the girls trying out were supposed to imitate them—luckily not alone, but in a group—and Gloria stared with a terrified, single-minded intensity and tried to memorize every move the cheerleaders made. They weren't doing anything particularly athletic, but they stepped and kicked and swung their pompoms and jumped and yelled beautifully in unison. Why am I doing this? Gloria asked herself, and the secret watcher appeared to say, "Don't think about that now. Just throw your whole heart into it," and she watched her body as it managed to make a reasonably good attempt at imitating what it had just seen.

They kept doing more cheers and sending girls away. Gloria couldn't believe it, but, after a half hour, she was one of the ones still left. She saw Sally conferring with Miss Wilson, the gym teacher. They gestured for her to come over. "Are you willing to put a lot of work into this?" Miss Wilson asked her.

"Oh, yes!" Gloria said.

"OK, Gloria," Miss Wilson said, "we're going to take a chance on you. You have such a pretty smile, we just can't say no."

"Oh, thank you." As soon as she could, Gloria fled into the girls' room and threw up.

At home that night, her mother said in her driest, most sarcastic voice, "A cheerleader? How charming of you. I'm surprised you didn't decide to be a drum majorette."

"I couldn't, Mom," Gloria said, "I never learned to twirl a baton." Her father laughed his head off at that, but Gloria hadn't meant to be funny.

Gloria's parents hardly ever had a serious disagreement—at least not in front of the children—but they did that night. "Oh, Teddy," her mother said, "it's not something that— Well, *our sort* don't usually do things like that."

"Don't be so stuffy, cookie," he said. "Gloria just wants to fit in. Isn't that right, honey? Well, I say more power to her."

Gloria adored her cheerleader's uniform; she wouldn't trust the nifty, swingy skirt even to Mrs. Warsinski but ironed every pleat herself. She liked the other girls on the squad and they seemed to like her. As soon as she'd memorized the names of the boys on the football team and learned how to follow the plays, she actually enjoyed the games. She never missed a practice at school, not even when she had a bad cold, and she practiced at home for hours; eventually she blended right in with other girls. Being a cheerleader was her first success at Canden High, and she was pleased with herself.

By the end of football season, Gloria was astonished to discover that she was considered "date-bait." Because she'd skipped the second grade, she was a year younger than everyone else in her class; by the time she'd realized that she should have kept it a secret, it was too late, and everyone knew she was only fourteen, but the boys didn't seem to care. She even had seniors calling her up.

"I think she's a little young for all this running around," her mother said.

"Isn't that what girls are supposed to do in high school?" her father said. "Run around? Come on, cookie, you're only young once."

At first, so people wouldn't think she was stuck-up, Gloria went out with almost any boy who asked her, but she quickly figured out that a girl's social status depended—not exclusively, but to a large extent—upon the boys she dated, and going out with certain boys could be disastrous to her reputation. No one, for instance, would ever consider going out with fat, moronic, pimply-face Jerry Wishgerber or brainy, goofy Eddie Holcomb, the president of the chess club. Whenever Gloria had any doubts about whether to go out with someone, she always asked Binkie first.

Boys were not nearly as frightening as she'd thought they'd be. They were no longer the stupid, dirty, violent animals Gloria remembered from grade school in Providence; a lot of them were even more nervous than she was. All the advice-to-girls books Gloria had read agreed upon one point: when out on a date, you should "be yourself." That was all well and good if you were a normal girl, Gloria thought, but for her that advice was not merely wrong, it was incomprehensible, and she knew she had to invent a girl the boys would like. In her diary she wrote a description of that phantom person: "Bouncy and bright. Cute, cheerful, optimistic, friendly, kind, self-assured, but not egotistical or stuck on herself. Knows how to have fun, interested in others. Kind, sympathetic, a good listener." She wrote out and memorized lists of questions she could ask boys if they weren't talking. Boys, she discovered, when they did talk, usually delivered monologues—and usually about sports, cars, or Korea. She'd been dreading her first kiss, but when it arrived, delivered by Bill Ewing, a tall, inarticulate basketball player, it excited her so much she immediately excused herself and hid out in the ladies' room until she could stop shaking. He actually kissed me! she kept thinking. He wouldn't have kissed me if he didn't think I was a normal girl.

All boys wanted to make out, so Gloria learned to make out, and, of course, she learned the first commandment of making out—it was as inflexible and unquestionable as if it had been given by God to Moses—that the girl decides how far to go. That natural, fundamental law left the boy free to try to go as far as he could—and any healthy, normal boy was going to go as far as he could. A girl who allowed a boy to go too far was labeled "fast"—which was fatal to her reputation—but if she didn't allow him to do anything at all, she got labeled "tease"—which was also fatal. It was sometimes excruciatingly difficult to know exactly where to draw the line, and making out required all of Gloria's concentration. Whenever she made out with a boy she couldn't control—and she didn't care how cute or neat or popular he was—she never went out with him again, but she could afford to do that; she never lacked for dates.

By the fall of her junior year, her parents had reversed positions. "Don't you think we'd better clip her wings a bit?" her father said. "Her social life's kind of frantic."

"Well, if you remember, sweetheart," her mother said, "you were the one who wanted her to be Miss Popularity."

School work was easy; she got it done in study hall, and, just as she always had, she got straight As. She joined the Future Homemakers of America, the Classical Club, and the Journalism Club. She worked on the school newspaper and the yearbook committee. Her weekends were booked a month in advance, and she spent hours on the telephone every school night. "I want people to like me," she wrote in her diary. "I want to have lots of friends. I want *boys* to like me. I want everyone to think I'm just an ordinary, perfectly nice girl. I want to be *popular*." The best she could tell, she was succeeding, but, no matter how many boys took her out or how many girls seemed to be her friend, she didn't *feel* popular. She still had nightmares of being back at Fairhaven, and she always expected disaster: that ghastly moment when she'd say something or do something unforgivable and her entire painstaking construction would come tumbling down. Being an entirely different person was horribly hard work; it required a constant effort, a constant watchfulness.

The boys had outside interests—sports or school work or hobbies—but the girls were interested in only one thing—dating—and the girls, however friendly they might appear, were actually in fierce competition for the cutest boys. Gloria knew that if she wanted to stay in the game, she had to compete too, but the game itself was far from fair: girls could only date boys their own age or older, but boys could date younger girls, so Gloria was competing not only with her own classmates but with every younger girl all the way down to the freshmen. And just getting a boy to take you out wasn't enough; you didn't really "have" him until you were going steady, but then, even when you were going steady, you couldn't relax because other girls would be doing their best to take him away from you. It was like a fiendish game of musical chairs, and the worst possible thing was to be left without a boy when the music stopped. By the end of her junior year, Gloria had gone steady with five different boys.

Gloria escaped from the pressures of Canden High the way she'd always escaped. Every Saturday morning she rode into town with her dad and spent most of the day in her haven—the wondrous, magical center of her interior universe—the Ohio County Public Library. She loved nothing better than wandering through the stacks, pulling books off the shelf at random, and reading anything that struck her fancy. She read dozens of old novels and all the recent ones. She told herself that she should read the classics, and so read Plato and even some Aristotle. Feeling deliciously daring, she read Freud. And, of course, she read poetry.

The most recent poetry in the library at Fairhaven Hall had been Matthew Arnold's, but now she discovered—it felt like an explosion in her brain—an entire world of new poetry. She wept over Yeats, read Pound and Eliot, wept over *Prufrock*, read the *Preludes* over and over until, without trying, she'd memorized them. (This is about *real life*, she kept thinking; "Wipe your hand across your mouth, and laugh"—oh wonderful, oh perfect!) She read Auden, cummings, William Carlos Williams, Marianne Moore, Elizabeth Bishop, Richard Wilbur, Robert Lowell, Theodore Roethke, Louis MacNeice. In her senior year she stumbled upon the great warlock of words, Dylan Thomas; why hadn't she found him before? she kept asking herself, drunk on his language. She'd always needed less sleep than other kids, and most nights she stayed up until midnight with a book. Her reading, and the pages of notes and comments she wrote in her diary about what she was reading, created an entirely separate, entirely inner, entirely secret life. Kids at Canden High who read anything outside of school assignments were considered "queer," and Gloria would have died before admitting to anyone that she actually read, and loved, poetry.

Canden High was dominated by cliques ("clicks" the kids called them); most kids were lucky to be in one, but Gloria managed to be in several. She was automatically in the country club clique; because she was Binkie Eberhardt's friend, she was a member of the inner circle of country club girls. The cheerleaders formed a tight, little clique of their own, and it was lots of fun to be in that one. In her senior year she was the editor of the school newspaper and was elected to the student council, so that made her a wheel. To her constant surprise, the other kids really did seem to like her.

She would never have admitted to anyone that she wanted to be Prom Queen; it took her a long time to admit it even to herself. Why Prom Queen? Because it was an out-and-out popularity contest: every student in the school voted. And if you were elected Prom Queen—or at least a Prom Princess—what better confirmation could you have that you'd succeeded in making yourself into an entirely different person? So what do you do if you want to be Prom Queen? Gloria set out to answer that question in the same methodical way she did everything.

She read through piles of old school yearbooks. She'd wised up a lot, so she wasn't surprised at what she found. The kids were certainly aware of social distinctions—you were pegged at once by where you lived and what your father did—but you were still expected to make your own place in the school, and country club girls were far more interested in club and cotillion dances than they were in anything going on at Canden High, so they were not especially popular, and not a single Prom Queen for the last ten years had been a country club girl.

When Gloria had first arrived at Canden High, she'd thought that the most popular girls must surely be the majorettes, but she'd learned by now that they weren't; majorettes were often Prom Princesses, but almost never Prom Queens. Most of the kids liked and admired the majorettes, but—she wasn't sure how to put it—there was something not entirely respectable about them. It wasn't that they were thought to be "fast"—no, everyone knew they were nice girls— so maybe it had something to do with their skimpy uniforms. But no, that still wasn't it—or at least not all of it. Maybe it was that majorettes always seemed to have fathers who did things like selling Alcoa Aluminum Siding door to door.

Clearly the most popular girls at Canden High were the cheerleaders; for the last ten years, all the Prom Queens but two had been cheerleaders, so getting onto the cheerleading squad had been the best thing that could possibly have happened to her, and it still seemed something of a miracle—although, on second thought, maybe it hadn't been that much of a miracle. The final decision to put her on the squad, she'd come to suspect, might have had less to do with her pretty smile than with the fact that her father was a VP at Raysburg Steel.

So, Gloria asked herself, what were her chances at Prom Queen? Well, she was not merely a cheerleader, and not merely a *good* cheerleader, she had just been elected (in a fair and democratic vote!) as *head* cheerleader, so that was a darned good start—so long as the other kids didn't think of her primarily as a country club girl. And then all Prom Queens were—it went without saying—cute, and Gloria had learned that with the right clothes and makeup, she could fool a lot of people into thinking she was cute.

Prom Queens always had popular boyfriends, and one of the most popular boys in Gloria's class was a sunny, friendly, goofy guy named Tommy Englewood. He lettered in three sports, was tall and quite good-looking in an innocuous, scrubbed, athletic way, and, of course, he was going steady—with Sandy Caldwell, the cute, blonde head majorette. Gloria had nothing against Sandy; she was, in fact, somewhat in awe of her, as she was of all the majorettes, and she thought Sandy was a perfectly nice girl, and she wasn't sure she really *wanted* Tommy, but early in her senior year she made a play for him just to see if she could get him. By Thanksgiving she was going steady with him, and she managed to hang onto him right through graduation. (Then he went down to the state university at Morgantown, and she never saw him again.)

When the results of the College Boards were announced, Gloria was astonished to hear that she'd achieved an eight hundred—a perfect score—on the

English Boards; she was the first student at Canden High ever to get an eight hundred in anything. Her first reaction was: whoops, there goes my chance at Prom Queen. But later in the week she overheard the captain of the football team saying, "Gloria? Oh, yeah, sure she's a brain, but she's a good kid too," so she thought that maybe she was still in the running.

She'd worked like a dog for it—and she'd been fully aware of what she was doing—so it shouldn't have come as such a profound shock to be nominated, but when she saw who else had been nominated, she was sure she didn't stand a chance. Her main competition, she thought, was her fellow cheerleader, Judy MacGee, and two majorettes, Sandy Caldwell and Lisa Metzger. Judy was a blonde, a genuinely sweet girl, and truly gorgeous (beauty pageant-gorgeous, lots of kids thought, including Gloria). Sandy was head majorette; after Tommy had dumped her for Gloria, she'd snagged a boy who was both a basketball star and the president of the student council—a boy easily as popular as Tommy— and Lisa was going steady with the captain of the football team. If the Canden High kids voted the way they had for the last ten years, Judy would be Prom Queen and the best Gloria could hope for was to beat out one of the two majorettes for Prom Princess.

When Mr. Clements, the principal, announced the result of the vote, Gloria couldn't even stand up until Binkie pushed her. She was shaking so hard she was afraid she was going to fall before she got to the stage, and, once up there, she was afraid she was going to throw up. Everybody was applauding. She stood at the lectern with the mike in front of her and looked out over the auditorium— at all the kids in Canden High who were grinning up at her—and then it sunk in: they'd elected *her*; she was going to be *their Prom Queen*; that must mean *they liked her*. All she could say, her voice breaking, was, "Thank you," and every- body applauded and stamped and whistled.

Later that day she told Mr. Clements she wasn't feeling very well, and he said, "That's understandable, Gloria. It must have been a tense day for you. Why don't you just go home?" Her mother was, thank heaven, out. As soon as Gloria locked herself in her bedroom, she started to cry. At Fairhaven she'd learned so well how to stop herself from crying that she'd hardly cried at all since she'd been ten, but now she was having, as she thought of it, a "real crying jag," and she couldn't find any way to stop it. She lay on her bed, hugging herself and rocking and wailing. The secret watcher said in a detached voice: "Gee, Gloria, you're sure making a lot of noise," and then later it said, "I wonder if you can hurt yourself by crying too much." She cried until she was totally exhausted. I'm a fake, she kept thinking. I fooled everybody, and I don't deserve it. Then, when she was finished crying and was, strangely, drifting off to sleep, she thought: so I fooled everybody, what does that mean?

"Whether you fooled everybody or not," the secret watcher told her, "it's a true honor. So now you've got to be the very best Prom Queen Canden High has ever had."

Gloria closed her diary and slowly became aware of herself sitting at her desk, staring across at the sunlight blazing through the window. She had, she remembered, cried for hours—from the middle of the afternoon till dinner time—almost as though she'd stored up every tear she hadn't shed since she'd been ten and they'd all had to come out. The experience, painful as it had been, had restored her ability to cry. Since then, she'd been able to cry easily, just like any normal girl.

She didn't know whether or not she'd been Canden High's very best Prom Queen, but she'd thrown her whole heart into it, and she still had the formal she'd worn to the prom—a true baby-pink with a skirt so big, requiring so many crinolines, that she'd had to sit alone in the back seat of Tommy's Chevy; she'd worn it again to her first Delta Lambda White and Gold Invitational, and she'd promised herself she'd keep it forever. She remembered feeling awkward and embarrassed and scared at the prom, and absurdly happy—and guilty because she knew she didn't deserve it—and the secret watcher had said, "You're doing a fine job, Gloria, but isn't all of this just a little bit silly for a girl who got an eight hundred in English on the College Boards?" No, she'd replied firmly, it's *not* silly. Doesn't every girl deserve to be Cinderella at least once in her life?

Her room was like an oven, but it would be worse outside, and the roses were almost certainly not from Rolland, and so he must still be mad at her, and there was nowhere to go except to the country club, and it was barely July, and she was already bored to death, and in September she'd have to go to Columbia where she would have to meet, and try to impress, Lionel Trilling. It never stopped, did it?

4

The big Independence Day barbecue was one of the most popular annual events at the Raysburg Country Club. The rolling lawns were transformed into one gigantic backyard cookout, and the members got to eat as much as they pleased, and the kids got to splash in the pool as long as they wanted and were allowed to run around wild on the golf course—the only time they were ever permitted to do so—and the younger members did a lot of flirting, and the grown-ups got to drink—oh, perhaps just a bit more than usual, and, of course, the fireworks were always a big hit.

The Fourth fell on a Thursday that year—a nice break near the end of the week, everyone was saying—and it turned out to be blistering hot with a high, sopping humidity and not a breath of air, but that just made the club members all the more determined to have themselves a hell of a good time. The big boxes of sparklers had been popped open, and the children, squealing, were drawing squiggles of sparks against the fading light; pinwheels were spinning madly on trees, and the pungent smell of burning metal blended with the chlorine tang of the pool and the sizzling odor of the burgers and hotdogs and steaks to create a perfect memory of midsummer in mid-America—a memory that could lie in wait for years so that suddenly, out of nowhere, a sudden whiff of the same mixture of smells would nail you dead with nostalgia. But now, not knowing how good they had it, all these good folks were barely hanging on, their patience wearing dangerously thin, for the Parada brothers of Staubsville—the Firework Kings of the Ohio Valley, they billed themselves—to really do their stuff.

The Cotters arrived late, just at twilight—a half hour, at the most, before the fireworks would begin—and Gloria walked away from her parents the moment they got out of the car. An unspoken protocol at the club required that girls who were graduated from high school but not yet married—"debs" and "post-debs" Gloria supposed they'd be called in some larger city where girls actually came out—dress to the nines on the Fourth, which meant, no matter how hot and muggy the night, nylons. It was a barbaric custom, she thought; viewed from an anthropological point of view, it probably had to do with displaying oneself to the males who were potential mates, because, the moment one married, one could show up in shorts and a halter top. Nothing if not respectful of custom, Gloria had worn her favorite opera pumps, but she intended to walk no farther in them than she had to, so she stepped out onto the terrace and took up a position where she could see nearly everyone—and, of course, where she could best be seen.

Gloria had spent the last few days sinking back into her old, familiar Raysburg summer routine that consisted simply of finding one thing after another—nearly anything would do—to kill time. She'd been swimming every day and had taken to watching Steve Allen with her grandmother; she'd written into her diary a detailed account of her years at Canden High, had finally unpacked all of her clothes, had done several loads of laundry and even some ironing. She'd caught up on all the news about Mrs. Warsinski's children and grandchildren, had read her mother's latest mystery novel, had begun to unpack her books and sort out the ones she wanted to take to New York with her, had made an appointment to have her teeth cleaned. She'd sweetly declined Jack Farrington who'd called up to ask her out to a movie, and she'd driven into downtown Raysburg where she'd bought a box of nylons and had a manicure. Twice she'd had lunch with Binkie and watched her play tennis, and three times she'd talked herself out of calling Rolland (the last time, it had taken a lot of talking). She was, by now— just as she should have been able to predict if she'd been thinking clearly— utterly bored out of her mind, and, no less than any other member of the Raysburg Country Club, she was more than ready for a rousing good time, and, if that were not possible, then an evening of pleasant distraction would certainly do.

Husbands and wives were required to split up and, as anyone would have put it, "circulate" (if they stayed together, they'd be labeled "standoffish"), so, after the crucial first visit to the bar, Ted had given his wife a quick, affectionate pat on the arm and strolled down toward a knot of men—steel VPs—standing around the barbecue at the edge of the golf course. And Laney was looking around for some place to settle by the pool. Although barelegged—she was well tanned and could get away with it—she was wearing dainty white summer sandals and had to stay on the concrete.

Laney was expecting the curse at any minute; her nerves were so raw she could have spit carpet tacks, and her breasts were swollen—heavy as two cats, she thought of them, not to mention hot and painful. She was wearing a simple sundress, so simple it looked as though she'd done nothing more than whip it off a hanger and step into it; the dress, however, had been cleverly designed to keep one's little secrets: the swinging, sweetly feminine skirt covered her derrière and thighs; the ribbed, elasticized bodice hid the super-pushup waspie that nipped her waist and displayed her breasts like two cantaloupes in a serving dish. She had, without any help, the best figure of any woman her age at the country club; tonight, *with* help, she looked absolutely spectacular. She could gauge her success by the way the men were staring at her. Even Teddy, who'd watched her getting dressed and so knew exactly how she'd achieved the effect, had been impressed; he'd kissed her in a way that had told her they had a date later. It was just too damned bad she felt so lousy—certainly in no mood at all for sex—but she was working on a double Scotch to try to remedy that.

With the suddenness of an apparition—or maybe, Laney thought, like the emergence of the Creature from the Black Lagoon in full 3-D—a big, hairy man vaulted out of the pool right in front of her and shook himself like a Great Dane; Laney stepped back to avoid getting splashed. Of course it was Billy. "Hey, Lane, old girl," he said. She didn't know whether to speak to him or not; she hadn't seen him since Sunday night, and she knew that Ted was still furious with him. "Jeez!" he said, his small, yellow eyes focused on her chest; she saw that he'd intended to say something more, but he laughed instead.

She couldn't very well cut him dead, now could she? "Billy," she said.

"Ah, sweet Jesus, you are sure some *girl*, Lane." His lop-sided grin and the path his eyes were tracing over her body told her exactly what he was thinking. Without a moment's hesitation, she walked away. "Hey, Lane," he called after her—it had come out as an anguished yelp. "Wait. Listen. I, ah— I was out of line the other night, huh? Yeah, I know I was. I'm sorry, kid, OK?"

She turned back to look at him. He'd assumed a sorrowful, hangdog expression exactly like that employed by her boys when they'd been abominable and were trying to make up. "It's just this thing with me and Dottie, you know? It's driving me nuts. I know I been screwing up royally. Gotta do something about it, huh?"—hapless shrug—"I'm really sorry, kid, OK?"

"OK, Billy, just—" Just what? Just go jump back in the pool and drown yourself. "Oh, find yourself a girl or something, good grief! No, I'm not mad any more, but—look, if you've got another apology in you, try it on Teddy. He was mad enough to kill you."

"Yeah," he said. "Yeah, I know he was. Thanks, kid. I mean it."

She gave him a dismissive gesture—not an unfriendly one—and kept on walking. Patsy Eberhardt, in a gaudy floral print dress that did somewhat less than nothing for her, was sprawled all over a deck chair. She'd been trying to get Laney's attention; now that she had it, she sent her an extravagant yoo-hoo wave, pointing at the vacant chair next to her. Laney sank into it.

"Marcelaine Cotter," Patsy said in the voice a spinster school teacher would have employed upon a girl who's been very naughty indeed, "how could you do this to me? Why, I'd murder for your figure. I mean it literally. I'd murder ten people for it."

"Oh, Patsy."

"My God, you never age. I swear you don't. It's like that silly old rhyme: 'When to the age of forty they come, men turn to belly and women to bum.' All except for you. You're going to look the same when you're ninety, you lucky thing."

"Oh, Patsy, stop it. You want to see great figures, look at our kids."

"Now ain't that the sorry truth? I always say to Binkie, 'Enjoy it while you can, honey-bun. At your age, it's easy as pie.'"

Having invoked their daughters, the women turned to look for them. (It felt nearly involuntary to Laney, like turning toward a brass band.) Binkie was not ten feet away; she'd inherited her mother's large, theatrical gestures and was waving her arms extravagantly—Laney could hear her bracelets jangling—as she talked to Mike Clark and Jack Farrington; she'd also inherited her mother's tendency to run to flesh—although, on Binkie, still in her twenties, it did nothing worse than give her a sleek, sexy, well-fed look that boys seemed to find quite fetching. Binkie was wearing an off-white little-nothing dress and looked like a big, pretty, friendly, healthy, happy, well-turned-out country club girl—which was exactly what she was. Binkie would have no problems marrying. Princess Priss, however—

Gloria was standing at the far end of the terrace so that anyone who wanted to talk to her would have to walk thirty feet to do it; she was leaning on the balustrade gazing pensively down over the golf course, and (could she have actually done it intentionally?) she was perfectly placed between two balusters so that anyone passing below would get a load of her stunning legs. The pumps she was wearing tonight were so high Laney's back ached in sympathy, but any boy looking up from below was sure to go absolutely berserk—for all the good it would do him. If he could bring himself to raise his eyes above her legs, he would see that Princess Priss, perfect though she might be, did not look even the least bit friendly. She did not look as though she were waiting for her prince to come; she looked as though she were waiting for the photographer to come. Was *I* that bad? Laney couldn't help asking herself.

Then Laney saw Gloria turn and smile; Lee Hockner was walking across the terrace toward her. Lee Hockner? Laney wondered. No, not in a million years—and a good thing too. There was, after all, no one in Raysburg suitable for Gloria, and Laney had to admit, however grudgingly, that she admired her daughter's performance. Go ahead, sweetie, she thought, give them all the brushoff.

Gloria—in a crisp, disciplined red dress with a big, big skirt—had, indeed, posed herself between the balusters intentionally. She had, almost immediately, caught Lee Hockner; he'd fetched her a Coke. "Sure you don't want something a little harder?" he'd said with a grimace she supposed had been intended as a wink. "You're a big girl now, you know." Great line, Lee, she'd thought, shaking her head and giving him her sweetest smile.

Now Lee was slurping a beer and sucking a cigarette and looking her over. He was five or six years older than she was and so he must remember her best in her *jeune fille* persona, and the easiest thing for her to do was revert to it. "So how's everything at the bank these days?" she said and looked at him like the dog in the RCA Victor ad.

"Oh, you know," he said.

Ted, standing around with several of his boys by the barbecue, was, out of the corner of his eye, watching his daughter talk to that stupid Hockner kid. The sooner she goes off to New York, the better, he thought. Laney's ridiculous stuffed-shirt brother and his little social-climbing wife would make sure that she was running with the right crowd.

Ted turned back to watch the hotdogs cook. He had the familiar, thoroughly enjoyable tingle at the back of his neck that told him he'd had a bit too much to drink on an empty stomach and should eat something fast; what he wanted was a hotdog, but he couldn't bring himself to ask for one. Right beside the hotdogs were big slabs of prime beef; they were coming off the grill perfectly cooked, dripping blood, and they were what you were supposed to eat if you were the senior vice-president of the Raysburg Steel Corporation. Ted could eat a steak later—would even enjoy eating it—but ever since he'd been a kid, he'd always loved hotdogs. Damn, he could almost taste the relish. But if he ate a hotdog, the boys might think he was a dumb old farmer with no class. Or maybe not. Maybe they'd just think it was a funny, endearing quirk, just like he'd thought about Admiral Delrick and his fondness for licorice.

Ted felt a tug at his elbow, turned and confronted the improbable sight of Billy Dougherty, wet, in swimming trunks. "Hey, skipper, can I bend your ear?"

"Sure," Ted said and allowed himself to be led away, down onto the golf course.

"Hey, look, I don't know how to say this, but—shit, I'm real sorry about the other night, skipper. I just wanted to tell you it won't happen again, OK?"

Ted looked straight into Billy's face, and all he could see was a sorry man, but that didn't necessarily mean anything; he'd seen Billy Dougherty lie like a rug and practically weep with sincerity while he was doing it. Don't let him off too easy, Ted told himself. "Yeah, you were a fucking pain in the ass all right," he said.

"Shit, don't I know it! Jeez, woke up the next morning, thought, fuckin' A, Dougherty, now you've really torn it. Christ, skipper, I just don't know. But I'll tell you one thing, I've never fucked up on the job—never, not once, and you can ask anybody, swear to God. I've been busting my ass for you over there, and you can ask anybody. Skipper?" He took a hold of both Ted's arms just above the elbows; he stared straight into Ted's face.

"Listen," he said, "if it wasn't for you, I wouldn't be here. Who? Me? Billy Dougherty in a goddamn country club? Who the fuck you kidding? But here I am, and it's all on account of you, and believe me, skipper, I'll never forget it. Never. I may be an asshole, but I'm an asshole that loves to work—and, by God, if you want a loyal man, skipper, you're looking at him."

"I know that, Billy."

"I just hope to God you do, Ted."

Billy gave Ted's arms a final squeeze and let go.

"Let's just forget the other night, OK?" Ted said. "Let's just start over, OK?"

He offered his hand. Billy grabbed it; just as suddenly, he dropped it, strode ahead several paces, and then turned back, his mouth hanging open. "I don't give a fuck about Dottie any more. It's the boys."

"Oh, Christ, yeah," Ted said. "Look, you'll get through this all right, you sorry son-of-a-bitch. We got through the war, didn't we?"

"Yeah, we sure as hell did!"

"Billy?"

"Yeah, skipper?"

"Go put a shirt on, will you?"

"Aye, aye, sir." And Billy brought his bare heels together, drew himself upright, and saluted. Ted had to laugh. He'd never before been saluted by a man wearing nothing but wet swimming trunks.

Ted watched Billy walking up the hill, maybe to get a shirt, but definitely for another Scotch, showing off his hairy Tarzan chest and the big hunk of salami between his legs just like some horny teenager on the prowl—a man in his forties, for Christ's sake, the ignoramus, the goddamn jerk—but likable too, as much fun as the Three Stooges. No matter how deadly dull and boring and stupid the routine had been, Billy had always been able to get a laugh out of the guys. Even Ted had laughed at him plenty. Some days near the end of the war, Billy Dougherty had been just about the only laugh you were likely to get.

Ted lit a cigarette, stood a moment savoring his distance from everybody, looking over the rest of his boys. They were doing what men ought to be doing on the Fourth of July: having good, clean, honest fun with their families. Yeah, he thought, they were what Raysburg Steel executives ought to look like—in shorts and nice shirts, clean-cut, presentable—not a one of them parading around in goddamn swimming trunks. A great bunch of guys, he thought. A great bunch of wives and a great bunch of kids.

It wasn't accidental, of course, that they were a great bunch of guys with great wives and great kids. Raysburg Steel had high standards for its executives, and Ted ought to know, because he was in charge of hiring them. It was pretty damn simple, really: when looking for an executive, Raysburg Steel was not interested in a single man over thirty (what was wrong with him?), a divorced man, a man with personal problems or screwy opinions, a man who runs around on his wife—or whose wife runs around on him. The fellow Raysburg Steel wanted was a veteran and a regular churchgoer (but hardly ever a Catholic and never *boring* about his religion); he was a good family man—a mature, stable, responsible guy with a couple kids, or maybe three—and, by God, Raysburg Steel wanted him happily married.

The final decision on applicants was made over dinner in the country club. Ted and Carl might have liked the guy, might have even been impressed with him, but they'd always wait to see what their wives had thought of *his* wife. Last fall there'd been a terrific young fellow in from Chicago; he'd come highly recommended, and, on paper, he'd looked like a dream; Ted and Carl and the other VPs had gone at him a whole damn weekend, and he'd fielded everything they'd thrown at him; the congratulations letter had been as good as written—but then, during dinner, Carl had asked of no one in particular: "Gee, I wonder why they don't have any kids? My God, they've been married—what? three, four years? Suppose there's any *medical* reason?"

"Oh," Patsy had said, "I did ask her—and you know what she told me, hon? I couldn't believe it. She said she wasn't quite *ready*."

"Quite ready?" Carl had said. "Ready! Ha, ha, ha. That's a good one. When are you ever ready?" And so the poor son-of-a-bitch had not been hired.

Ted knew that Laney didn't like to get involved in these things, but occasionally, when she felt impelled to voice them, her opinions were invaluable, and if she said about an applicant's wife: "Well, Teddy, it's probably not much of anything, but, ah, did you get a look at that cheap, trashy dress she was wearing? I'm just not sure she'd—you know, really *fit in*," then that was all the information Ted needed to scratch the guy's name off the list.

Sometimes you made a mistake when you hired them—given human fallibility, it was unavoidable—and then you'd have to can them later. Sometimes it was tough. There'd been that young Clarkson fellow, just out of the Marines, and he'd looked like he was going to be absolutely perfect. He'd jumped right in, was working his butt off, Saturdays and Sundays, the whole shot, but his wife had strong ties to the Democratic Party (her great-uncle had been a Democratic senator from Ohio), and that could certainly have been overlooked (it was a free country, after all), but she'd had the gall—or stupidity, which is probably more what it had been—to volunteer in the Stevenson campaign office right in downtown Raysburg where anybody could see her. Firing that guy had been one of the most unpleasant tasks Ted had ever had to perform, but, just like old Give-em-hell-Harry used to say (speaking of Democrats), "If you can't stand the heat—" And besides, it didn't matter how good a job a fellow was doing for you at the moment, because, just as sure as you know the sun's going to rise in the morning, you know that a man's going to screw up eventually if he can't keep his wife in line.

And the upshot of all this rumination had been—just as he'd known all along—leading Ted to the gloomy question: apology or no apology, just why the hell was William Parnell Dougherty still on the payroll?—divorced and on the prowl and drinking like a fish and telling slimy jokes in the presence of ladies (not to mention the "Fuck you, skipper") and wandering around the country club in swimming trunks. The answer was simple. He was still on the payroll because he was a personal friend of Theodore R. Cotter. But how long, Ted thought, do I have to go on fighting the war anyway?

One thing you learned in the navy, however, and that was, when dealing with superiors, you always cover your ass, and if Ted was having doubts about Billy, that meant that Carl must be having them too. Well, Ted thought, better I say it to him before he says it to me.

Up on the terrace, Gloria was still trying to carry on a conversation with Lee. The Hockners were an ancient family in the valley and had been bankers as long as anyone could remember, so, as Lee J. Hockner the Fourth waited for his number to come up at the Draft Board, he spent his days in the First National Bank of Raysburg doing whatever it was that first sons with fourth names of ancient banking families did in first banks; in his free time, he could usually be found in the country club with one hand on a beer glass and the other on a girl, and Gloria knew that if he got what he wanted, she'd end up in his little green MG parked by the lake in Waverley Park with her crisp, disciplined dress undone to the waist, her bra off, his tongue down her throat, one hand kneading her breasts and the other delving into her panties—which she wanted to do about as much as she wanted to swim the Ohio River with lead weights on her feet (if he'd been Rolland, however, it would be a different story—sigh). Lee was—there was no escaping it—utterly boring, but she'd forced herself to talk to him because he might have sent the roses, and, if he had, he was sure, eventually, to mention it. "So, Glo," he was saying, "you having a good summer?"

"So far."

"I hear you're going— Where's it you're going?"

"Columbia."

"Cool. What're you going to take?"

"English."

"Cool—So where's your little blonde roommate?"

It was inevitable: the boys always remembered Susie. "Oh, didn't you hear? She's married."

"Oh, yeah? Well, good for her—but too bad for the rest of us guys, you know what I mean?"

He took a long drag on his cigarette, and, in the ensuing pause, she knew he was working himself up to the next line: "You want to go for a drive?" She looked into his vacuous eyes and thought, no, it would never occur to him to send me roses, not in a million years—and then it dawned on her that Jack Farrington had probably sent them. That's right; he was the one who'd asked her out, and he was exactly the sort of guy who would send somebody roses. Well, maybe she'd go out with him after all.

"Oh," she said, in a Corliss Archer voice, "there's Binkie. *Hi, Binkie!* Excuse me, will you, Lee?"

Laney, still trapped by Patsy, tried to catch her husband's eye, but, munching a hotdog, he passed within ten feet of her without even looking her way. He was one of the few men who managed to look presentable—even dashing and sexy—in Bermuda shorts. Jerk, she thought fondly; then she saw that he was deep in thought—lost in what she called his "Sherlock Holmes mood"—and, with a little tickle of foreboding, she wondered what was up. Well, if there was something wrong at work, she'd hear about it in bed—after (as Mother would have put it) he'd had his way with her, and, meanwhile, Patsy was yammering about something or other: "And you know, the way they're tampering with our water—I mean the very water *we drink*—" She gave Laney a dark, significant look. She dropped her voice a notch and leaned closer. "They're already putting in that damn fluoride—in violation of our constitutional rights—so who's to say that they'll *stop with fluoride?*"

Laney did her best to produce a properly horrified gasp. Oh, God, she thought, this woman's got a brain like a Swiss cheese.

"We'll never know the full extent of what's going on," Patsy said. "It's just a crime all the information that's withheld from the American people."

"Oh, Gloria, love your dress!" Binkie was chirping. "It's an Ann Fogarty, isn't it? I just adore her things. Did you get it in New York?"

Gloria sighed. Well, after all these years, she should be used to Binkie by now. "No, Philadelphia," she said. "Love yours too. And cute shoes, wow." Gloria wasn't kidding; Binkie always looked great, but, given that Binkie never thought about anything other than clothes, she ought to look great. "Oh, I wish I could wear ivory," Gloria said. "It's so summery."

"Oh, come on, Glo, you can wear ivory, for Pete's sakes. It'd look great on you."

"You'd think so, wouldn't you? But all I can wear is absolutely *pure* snow-white with a blue note under it. The slightest hint of cream, my skin goes dead. I just adore off-whites on other people. They're great for blondes like you—but ivory just *destroys* me—and it's so darned hard to get things that are really pure *pure* white."

"Isn't that the truth? Well, I wish I could wear *red*."

"You kidding? Of course you can wear red. Red's just devastating on blondes."

"Really? I always think I look cheap in red."

"Oh no, Bink—with your hair? And you can wear orangey reds, which I can't. Of course you'd have to pick up the same tone in your lipstick—" And the horrible thing was, Gloria thought, that they could go on for hours like that without even taking a breath. Out of the corner of her eye she saw that Lee had walked away, which is exactly what she'd wanted him to do.

Now, out of the blue, Binkie said, "You know, I just can't imagine you as a school teacher."

For a moment Gloria was startled speechless; then she realized that Binkie must not be able to imagine a girl going on to graduate school for any other reason. "I can't either, Binkie," she said—nor could she imagine herself as a university professor, which is, presumably, what one becomes when one has a PhD from Columbia—and now Binkie was giving her a baffled look that was an accurate representation of the question Gloria had often asked herself. "Why the heck are you doing it then?"

"I don't know, Bink," Gloria said. "I've always been a good student. Maybe that's what they'll put on my gravestone: She was a good student. I guess I don't know what else to do with myself."

Gloria felt a hand on her shoulder; she was about to pull away (don't touch me, you idiot, whoever you are!) when she saw that the hand belonged to Binkie's father; his other hand was on Binkie's shoulder. "So how are my favorite girls tonight?"

"Great, Daddy," Binkie said, giggling.

"Just wonderful, Mr. Eberhardt," Gloria said, giggling. Oh, why was she so good at this? And the secret watcher answered her, "Because you *wanted* to be good at it, that's why."

"Well, well, well," Mr. Eberhardt said, beaming like a carved pumpkin.

Gloria saw that her own father was standing down on the lawn looking directly up at Binkie's father; she saw their eyes meet. "Enjoy yourselves, girls," Mr. Eberhardt said, gave them a final grin, and sauntered away, down the steps. Then, with a boom, a sizzle and a hiss, a rocket went up, rose into a fiery arc, and splattered a fat magenta flower across the sky; the Superman POW! followed a fraction of a second after, and the whole works trailed away into green and gold glitter to a chorus of "ooohs" from the crowd.

"Hell of a fine night for fireworks, huh, Ted? Ha, ha, ha," Carl winked at his number-one man. "I'm just so damn proud of our little girls I could bust," he said.

"Yeah, me too, Carl, me too. We're lucky, all right." They took a moment to grin at each other, and then, with no further words required, strolled down onto the golf course just as though they'd planned it.

"Going over to Gettysburg next week," Carl said, "do a little golfing."

"Oh, is that right?"

"Yep. Glad of the opportunity."

A second rocket went up, and the air stank of gunpowder. "Give me a chance to explain a few things to the president." Carl said. "The goddamned Democrats, you know—"

"Yeah, I do know. It's got me worried. Might be a rough ride this time."

"Maybe so, and maybe not. Seems to me that Ike's pretty sympathetic. Just want to be sure, that he—ha, ha, ha—understands certain key factors in the industry."

Ted laughed too, and then they grinned at each other again. Carl did indeed have a wonderful smile; although he'd never held public office, he had a real politician's smile ("the ole shit-eater," they'd called it in the navy). It was an enormous, disarming, ingenuous smile. It was a smile as promising as a sunrise. It was a smile that was—you couldn't really avoid the comparison—a hell of a lot like Ike's, and Ted imagined those two wily, steel-hearted old sons-of-guns grinning away at each other on the golf course like a couple of Cheshire cats in the cream dish. Oh, yeah, Ted thought, if anybody could explain things to the president, it would be Carl.

"You just can't be too careful," Patsy was saying, "you really can't, and if your colon's full of poisons, you're just asking for trouble. Now they're—"

Another round of fireworks exploded over the golf course. "Hey! That's a pretty one!" Patsy yelped, and then, without a pause, went right on: "But now they're grown up, so naturally, stupid old Mom doesn't know diddly-squat. 'Binkie,' I tell her, 'keep your colon clean, for God's sake! It's just part of normal hygiene.' 'Oh, Mom,' she says, 'that's disgusting. I don't even want to talk about it.' 'Yeah,' I say, 'and polio's pretty disgusting too, sweetheart.'"

Oh, Christ, Laney thought, hasn't she ever heard of the vaccine? Am I stuck with this loony woman for the rest of my life—in this crude, ugly, stupid town? Why couldn't Teddy have stayed at Xenon? We were so happy in New York. Oh, God, I'm so miserable! And a shower of purple and red sparks slithered down with handfuls of golden pixie dust skittering along behind them.

"You know, Carl," Ted was saying, "I've been thinking about, ah, my ole pal Billy, and—well, he's been kind of a disappointment lately."

"Hey, it's a funny thing you should say that. I've had a very similar thought. Of course I didn't want to mention it—with him being a good, close, personal friend of yours and all—an old navy buddy."

"Yeah, he was my exec. Damn good one too. But, ah, since he and Dottie split up—"

"Yeah. Point well taken. So how is everything at Old Reliable these days?"

"Well, nothing wrong that you can really put your finger on." That was a safe thing to say; so far as Ted knew, everything at Old Reliable was just dandy.

"Might be a good time to take a good, hard look, wouldn't you say that, Ted?"

"That's exactly what I was thinking."

Then both men fell silent; they had walked in a semi-circle, were now headed back toward the pool, and they both had seen Billy Dougherty walking toward them under a fountain of copper-green fireballs. "Speak of angels," Carl said under his breath, and then aloud: "Well, Dougherty. Great to see you again. How you doing?"

"Just great, sir, couldn't be better."

"It shows, Billy. Yep, sure does." Carl slapped Billy on his biceps. "A man ought to keep fit. That's what I always say."

"Well, you're right about that, sir."

"Enjoy yourself, Billy, enjoy yourself."

"Yes, sir. Not much doubt there, I can tell you that, sir."

A huge, slamming explosion warned everyone that the Parada brothers had shot off a truly big one this time. It exploded into a stuttering cannonade that hammered back sympathetic thumps from the hills, and all the children squealed. Carl leaned to Ted's ear to ask: "So who would you put in his place?"

"Al Connely."

"Good choice. Gee, Ted, I'm sure glad you talked to me about this. But then—hell, I know I can always count on you."

Jesus, Ted thought, why did I tell him all that stuff? For all I know, Billy's doing a great job just the way he always has.

Gloria and Binkie were leaning over the balustrade looking up. The sky had divided into three distinct arenas of fire, each a different color. "Wow," Binkie yelled along with everyone else, and then, as the sparks filtered down, she said, "You don't really want to split up with Rolland, do you?"

"Oh, I don't know, Bink. Half the time I think I should just marry him and forget all about graduate school."

Gloria had not been unaware that Mr. Dougherty had draped himself over the balustrade on the side of her that was vacant. Her entire body had gone rigid; she'd resolved to ignore him, but she could almost feel the weight of him as though it were mysteriously transmitted through the balustrade. She heard the deep, heavy boom of another sky-rocket, and, in the pause as the crowd waited to see what unforeseen thing would appear this time, she heard a deep, cottony voice not more than a foot from her ear: "So, princess, did you like the roses?"

Gloria was so angry she still couldn't sit down; she kept pacing back and forth from the bed to the TV set. "Do you mean that loud, vulgar person who works for your father?" her grandmother asked in an incredulous voice, "the one who was here on Sunday?"

"Yes, yes, yes," Gloria said, "Mr. Dougherty."

"Good Lord, how appalling."

Gloria hadn't spoken to the wretched man, of course; she'd immediately walked away from him. She'd gathered up Binkie by the elbow, whispered to her, "Oh, I've just got the most terrible cramps!" Overhead the fireworks had continued to smear themselves idiotically across the sky, and Gloria hadn't even turned back to see if he'd still been watching her.

"You must tell your mother immediately," her grandmother said.

In Binkie's car, Gloria's mind had kept repeating, "men's eyes, men's eyes," like a stuck record. "Oh, Gloria, what a shame," Binkie had said several times. Words, sounds, the boom of the fireworks had been reverberating inside her, stupidly—*men's eyes*—*what a shame*—*so, princess*—and not until she'd been stepping out of the car had the rest of the line clicked in: "When in disgrace with fortune and men's eyes—" Why disgrace? She hadn't been disgraced, but she'd fled just as though she had been.

So angry she hadn't paused, as she usually would have, to take off her heels, she'd marched straight through the hall, and banged her heels down on her mother's precious hardwood floor in the hall, and straight up the stairs, and banged her heels down hard on her mother's precious runner, and straight into her grandmother's room—with never a doubt that her grandmother would be awake, never a doubt that her grandmother would want to hear all about it. Now she knew that she shouldn't have said a word.

"I can't tell Mom," Gloria said. "I really can't."

"Oh? And why ever not?"

"I don't know—exactly—but I— Mom's really mad at me. She's been mad at me ever since I came home. I don't know why, but I know she is, and I can't do anything right as far as she's concerned. She'd turn it around somehow so it would come out my fault."

Gloria stopped pacing; she'd come to rest at the end of her grandmother's bed; she stood, looking down at her grandmother; she heard, behind her, the TV blatting away. Gloria hated being impulsive, and she'd just been impulsive. Her grandmother was giving her a cold, fishy-eyed look; if Gloria had been six years old again, it would have scared her to death. She stepped out of her pumps. She wanted to go and lie down. "I'm sorry," she said. "I'm really upset."

After a moment, her grandmother said, "Well, if you don't want to talk to your mother, you must go straight to your father."

Oh, great, Gloria thought. "That doesn't feel right either. Mr. Dougherty's Dad's old navy buddy—his best friend. He didn't sign the darned card, and he could deny it, and— I don't know. If Daddy did believe it, I'm afraid of what he'd do—and I just don't want to make trouble."

"Gloria, believe me, it's not *you* who's making the trouble. Well then, if you're not going to tell your parents, what do you propose to do?"

"Nothing." The moment she said it, Gloria felt the unfairness of it. She'd just been driven out of the country club—her own country club—and she wasn't sure she could ever go back there. Through the open window she could hear the band playing, and it wasn't as though she were missing some fabulous and delightful event—it was, after all, just another predictable club dance—but she would've liked to have a choice in the matter. Damn him, she thought. "I don't know what to do," she said.

"Well, my dear, you could start by making us each one of your excellent martinis."

"Oh, sure," Gloria said, laughing, "and don't bruise the gin!"

This time she made the martinis properly, in the cocktail shaker, arranged the glasses on a silver tray with folded napkins and, as an afterthought, added a dish of peanuts. She set the tray down on her grandmother's bed table. Without being asked, she handed her grandmother the cigarette case and lighter from the dresser drawer. "Turn that damned thing off," her grandmother said, nodding toward the TV. Gloria turned it off.

"Grandmother," Gloria said, "will you please keep all this to yourself?"

"Oh, I certainly will, my dear—and seeing as you're the only person who ever talks to me, it won't even be that difficult."

Her grandmother lit a cigarette, tested her martini and nodded to Gloria: well done. Gloria sank into the wingback chair, lifted her glass, and sipped; she appreciated the formal, ritualized aspect of this nonsense with martinis, but the blamed thing still tasted like iced lighter fluid.

"Maybe it's not serious," Gloria said. "Maybe it didn't really mean much of anything. Maybe he just thought—I don't know—maybe he just thought he was teasing me—"

"Teasing you? Good heavens. A man of that class. A man your father's age? An *employee* of your father's? A married man? And I gather he's divorcing his wife, or she's divorcing him—it doesn't really matter, now does it? And you think he might have been *teasing* you? Is that considered proper behavior nowadays?"

"Oh, probably not—I don't know."

"You keep saying that—'I don't know. I don't know.' But of course you know. You were raised properly, Gloria. You know what's right and what's wrong."

"Oh, sure. What he's been doing is ugly—really ugly. But I'm just trying to— What on earth could he be thinking about? Why is he doing this to me? What does he want?"

"What does *he* want?" her grandmother said. "That doesn't matter. Why should anybody give a damn what that person wants?"

Gloria didn't have any good answer to that. The martini was so horrible—so cold and metallic and damnably *persistent*—that she began to see how someone might eventually grow to like it.

"In a proper country club," her grandmother said, "a man like that wouldn't be admitted through the front doors, let alone to membership. There's far too much familiarity with the lower classes these days, if you ask me." She sipped her martini, gave Gloria a thin smile. "I know I must sound like a terrible old snob, but that's how I was raised, and there's something to be said for it. Indeed there is."

They sat in silence a while, and then her grandmother said in a meditative voice, "I suppose that times have changed since I was a girl. Oh, indeed they have. We're making progress, so they say. What rot! There was a time, my dear, and not that long ago either, when a lady was always treated like a lady. But, I gather, this is no longer the rule. Well, so much for progress."

Although Gloria had certainly learned how to impersonate a lady, she was far from sure she *was* one, not deep in her heart, but she loved her grandmother's rock-hard certainty. "I wish I knew what was right," she said.

"Oh, poppycock! You know what's right. Just follow your conscience."

"I do. It just gets me into trouble."

"Gloria?"

"Yes."

"Throw those damned roses away."

Was it really that simple? "OK," Gloria said.

She didn't hesitate; she walked into her room, picked up the crystal vase with the roses in it, and carried it down to the kitchen. Her father was a great lover of gadgets; last summer he'd bought one that was supposed to eat up the garbage. He'd gathered everyone into the kitchen and delivered a lecture on the use of the strange, scary thing; if you were stupid or careless, he'd said in his best Lieutenant Commander's voice, it could take your fingers off, but if you observed a few simple precautions, it was perfectly safe—but nobody ever used it, not even Mrs. Warsinski, and certainly not Gloria's father who never did anything in the kitchen except eat. Gloria remembered exactly what he'd said to do.

Maybe it *is* this simple, she thought. She removed the plug from the drain, turned on the cold water, and pushed the button. She heard the motor snarl into life. Then, with a growing sense of satisfaction, she fed the roses, one at a time, blossom first, down the drain.

The next morning Gloria lay in bed wide awake until noon. She kept telling herself to get up, but she couldn't make herself do it. She'd had a rough night— every hour or so had popped straight out of a sound sleep to go over it all again—and, as she remembered Mr. Dougherty's voice in her ear like the sibilant issuance of a talking snake ("So, princess, did you like the roses?"), she wished, fervently, that she'd been born into her grandmother's time so she could have been simply a Providence-Newport society girl who'd never heard of Freud or T.S. Eliot—and then she thought, as she often did, that she probably should have gone to Vassar.

Of course it was silly to be thinking about Vassar after all these years, but a hard kernel of herself remained convinced that if she had gone to Vassar—that is, if she'd done everything right, the way *our sort* were supposed to do things— she would have been transformed into that perfect, mystical being, *a lady* (exactly the way her grandmother used the term), and then no jerk like Mr. Dougherty would have dared to send her roses, or, if he had, she would have known exactly what to do about it. But that notion was more than merely silly; it was grotesque. She should stop thinking about it. But she couldn't stop thinking about it.

Her English courses had trained her to nothing if not to a hypersensitivity for irony, and she could fully savor this one: that she should resent having not gone to Vassar—resent it just as intensely as if it had been something *done to her*—when *she* had been the one who'd refused to go there. And what, really, was bothering her? If she had gone to Vassar, she never would have met Professor Bolton or Rolland, never would have been in Delta Lambda, never would have met Susie. Except for the wretched spring of her sophomore year, her years at Briarville had been the happiest of her life, so why couldn't she just stop thinking about what might have been? But she still felt gypped, short-changed, tricked. Try as she might, she couldn't pin that feeling down; it was far more complicated than simply a matter of where she'd gone to school—and, somehow, the most ironic thing of all was that, if her mother hadn't tried so hard to talk Gloria into being a debutante, Gloria might very well have allowed herself to be talked into going to Vassar.

In her mother's mind, it must always have been as much of a given as the sun rising: *of course* Gloria was going to come out, preferably in Providence, but, if not there, then in New York with her stupid cousin Sandra. But the only thing Gloria wanted was to fit in at Canden High—simply to be accepted as a normal girl—and she had been accepted; better than that, she seemed to be—wonder of wonders—popular, and she couldn't imagine anything worse than calling attention to herself with something as pretentious and old-fashioned and downright *undemocratic* (she'd recently decided that, unlike her parents and most of her friends, she was a political liberal) as *coming out*. She didn't want to be presented to society; she wanted to be Prom Queen.

She was hoping her mother would listen to reason. "Raysburg girls don't come out," she told her. "Even Binkie. She's from the best family in town, and nobody ever talks about Binkie coming out."

"You're not a Raysburg girl," her mother said. "Don't you *ever* think of yourself as a Raysburg girl."

"Mom! That's ridiculous. What am I supposed to be, a Providence girl? I haven't lived in Providence since I was nine. And I'm not really a New York girl either. I don't want to come out."

"I'm sorry, sweetie, but you don't have any choice in the matter."

But it turned out that Gloria did have a choice: her father didn't want her to come out any more than she did—and he proved to be utterly inflexible on the topic. "Oh, for God's sake, cookie," he said to his wife, "I'm not going to dump thousands of dollars into something as stupid as that." Then, when pressed, he admitted that it wasn't the money, it was *the principle of the thing.*

"Laney, honey," he said in the voice of infinite patience he used when he was explaining something so obvious it shouldn't have required explaining at all, "if she wanted to be a debutante, I'd be all for it, but she doesn't. Why do you want to force her to do something she doesn't want to do?"

When they were having a serious discussion, Gloria's parents usually retired to their bedroom and shut the door; that night they were so mad at each other they couldn't make it out of the living room. They'd been having a nightcap—which turned into several good, stiff drinks—and they both told Gloria to go to bed, but she knew that if she pretended to be cleaning up the kitchen, they'd forget all about her. Her parents hardly ever disagreed about anything, but now they were having the worst fight she could remember—a fight so savage it frightened her. Holy cow, she thought, and it's all about *me!*

As her mother's voice got louder, her father's voice got softer—until he finally blew up: "Jesus Christ, Laney, look at me. Where else but in America, huh? I make more money that most of those stuffed shirts in your goddamn family—and I'll be damned if I served four years in the goddamn South Pacific so some bunch of idiots can go around thinking they're better than everybody else!"

That night Gloria's mother slept in the guest room, and she continued to sleep in the guest room for several nights after that. She didn't speak to either her husband or daughter for well over a week. Then, gradually, things settled back to normal, and no one ever mentioned coming out again.

A year later, Gloria's mother announced that Gloria was going to Vassar. Oh, no, I'm not, Gloria thought. Her father had saved her the last time, so she was pretty sure he'd save her this time too. (It didn't occur to her that she might actually want to go to Vassar.) "Daddy," she asked in her sweetest and most daughterly voice, "can't *I* decide where I want to go to school?"

"Sure you can, honey. You can go anywhere you want."

With her straight As and spectacular Board and SAT scores (and her father's money), Gloria could, indeed, go anywhere, and she wanted to go to a good state university—Pennsylvania maybe, or Michigan—anywhere but to a snobby all-girls school.

"Gloria, you're just being ridiculous again," her mother said. "You'll probably marry somebody you meet in college—and you have to have *the right sort of boys* to choose from. That's why you're going to Vassar—or to one of the Seven Sisters."

"At Vassar there's *no* boys to choose from, and I have no intention of getting married for ten years at least."

"Don't be so naive, Gloria,"—there was nothing Gloria hated more than to be called naive, and Gloria knew that her mother knew it—"when I was at Vassar I was practically drowning in boys, and you'll be married before you're twenty-one."

The heck I will, Gloria thought, and was tempted to say, "How about you, Mom? You didn't pick one of *the right sort of boys*, did you?" But she knew enough to keep her mouth shut on that particular topic.

This time the fight between her parents was not loud and dramatic and over in a night; it was slow and dogged and dragged on for days. Her father couldn't see any reason why Gloria shouldn't be allowed to decide where she would go to school. She was an award-winning student, wasn't she? True enough, her mother said, but did he really think that a sixteen-year-old—no matter how damned smart she was—was mature enough to make a decision that would affect the rest of her life? He had to admit she had a point there, but what was wrong with a big, modern, progressive school like Penn? It was a great school, and he ought to know. Yes, she said, but you got your MBA there and not your undergrad degree. The state universities are so big the kids get lost in them, but at Vassar or Smith or Wellesley the girls get individual attention and lots of it. They really give their girls a good, solid education. Isn't that what he wanted for his daughter? Well, of course he did—and then, eventually, he had a wonderful idea: "Hey, cookie, maybe she'd like it at Briarville."

"Oh, Teddy, don't be absurd."

Gloria needed her father on her side no matter what, and she wasn't about to tell him that she thought the idea of going to Briarville was just about as absurd as her mother did. One sunny weekend in March, she found herself being packed into her father's Buick so he could drive her back to his old hometown to see if she might like his old *alma mater*. The last thing her mother said to her before they left was, "You know, sweetie, it's not too late to get you into Vassar. I can get you in with one phone call."

After she'd been alone in the car with him for an hour, Gloria discovered something she hadn't known before—or at least hadn't known quite this fully: she was shy with her dad. Then, because the long silence between them was forcing her to think about it, she tried to remember the last time she'd been alone with him for longer than a few minutes, and she had to go all the way back to their New York apartment before the war to find it. That isn't the way it ought to be, she thought; you're not supposed to have to work to make conversation with your father, are you?

He wasn't helping matters. He obviously enjoyed driving; he drove very fast, and he didn't say a word. He smoked and threw the cigarette butts out the window; she worried that he might start a forest fire, but she didn't want to say anything the least bit critical. Both her parents smoked, so she was used to being around smokers, yet that day the smoke was nauseating her. The longer they rode in absolute silence, the more anxious she felt, so she said: "Dad? Maybe I *should* go to Vassar. Mom really wants me to. What do you think?"

He gave her a quick, startled look as though he'd forgotten she was in the car with him. "I didn't think you wanted to, honey."

"Well, I don't. Not really."

"OK, princess. Then you don't have to."

They had just repeated what they'd said to each other already dozens of times; after that, the conversation seemed to have died. To try to resurrect it, she said, "Mom seems to have her heart set on— Well, if I don't go to Vassar—or to one of the Seven Sisters—I just don't think she'll be very pleased."

"You know how your mother is. She has strong opinions, honey. But she just wants the best for you, believe me. Wherever you decide to go, she'll be perfectly happy about it." Gloria knew that was a lie, so she abandoned the idea of having a serious heart-to-heart with her dad.

"I don't know why she wants you to go to Vassar anyway," he said after another thirty miles. "She didn't even like it all that much." Oh, she didn't, did she? Gloria thought. She'd stopped being nauseated. Now she was angry. She turned on the car radio, tuned across the dial and found the Andrews Sisters; they were singing a silly, bouncy tune about hot chocolate.

Neither Gloria nor her father spoke again until they turned off the main highway. She'd seen the sign: BRIARVILLE. "Here it is, princess," her father said in a voice as strange and artificial as the radio announcer's, "the heartland of America."

Gloria barely remembered Gram and Gramps Cotter. They lived at the crest of a quiet, tree-lined street in a charming, old Queen Anne house straight out of a Booth Tarkington novel, and, the moment Gloria and her father stepped through the door, she saw him transmogrified into someone she didn't know. With his face drawn into a tight grin, he paced up and down and slammed his right fist into his left palm in exactly the way Gloria's rotten little brothers did when they were waiting for a softball game to start, and he talked in such a loud, deep, cheerful voice he sounded exactly like the Canden High football coach. "Well, Dad," he bellowed, "how you keeping?"

"Oh, can't complain, Teddy," Gramps Cotter bellowed back, "can't complain."

"Well, you can always complain, but it never does you much good, now does it?"

"Nope, not much." Then her father and grandfather laughed and slapped each other on the back.

"Oh, and just look at little Gloria," Grammy Cotter said. "She's all grown-up—quite the young lady, aren't you, honey?"

Gloria felt her face stretch into a grin just as fake as her father's. "Yep, my little girl's all grown-up," her father said in his huge, deep, resonating stranger's voice and tousled her hair—something he hadn't done since she'd been four—and she played right along with him: "Oh, Daddy," she said and giggled. This is so strange, she thought.

"Teddy, you're so thin," Grammy said. "Doesn't that high society wife of yours feed you?"

"To tell you the truth, Maw, she doesn't," her father said. "We got a Polack lady who comes in, cooks most of the meals. Real Hunky cooking, ha, ha, ha. Cabbage, garlic, the whole works!"

"Well, Teddy, I never—good grief, sit down!"

"That's the ticket, son, take a load off!" Gloria's grandfather shouted.

"No garlic in my kitchen, believe you me," Gloria's grandmother said, and everyone got a good laugh out of that one.

Later, after the fried chicken dinner and a restive evening spent sipping tea in front of the enormous, old-fashioned Philco radio in the living room, Gloria lay between Grammy Cotter's freshly ironed sheets—they felt stiff as tin—in the hard, narrow bed in her father's old room in the attic and tried to think things through. She wished she'd brought her diary with her—writing things out always helped—but she hadn't, so she was stuck inside her mind going around in circles. She'd applied at the University of Pennsylvania, Ohio State, and the University of Michigan, and she had, of course, been accepted by all of them, but her father obviously wanted her to go to Briarville. He was giving up not only his entire weekend for her but even the following Monday—he was actually missing a day of work!—so of course she felt grateful (and guilty), and she was prepared to give Briarville a chance, but she felt like a ping-pong ball bounced back and forth between her parents. Why wouldn't they just let her alone to do what she wanted? But the longer she thought about it, the less she was certain that she really wanted what she'd thought she wanted.

When Briarville Farmers' College had been founded in 1858, it had employed one teacher, enrolled less than a dozen students, and crammed them all into an old, drafty farmhouse on a few acres of lovely, rolling, richly productive land in the middle of nowhere. In a period of rapid expansion after the Civil War, the school added an everincreasing number of faculty, students, buildings, acres, and cows, and became first the Briarville Agricultural College and later, with the addition of a baccalaureate program, simply Briarville College. By the time Gloria's father matriculated there, the gentry of dozens of Pennsylvania towns were sending to Briarville those of their children whose high school careers had been somewhat less than luminous; for daughters who should have gone to Bryn Mawr, they wanted a finishing school; for sons who should have gone to Princeton, a taste of higher education with a practical bent; and the administration did its best to oblige them.

In the years following the Second World War, the massive influx of serious young men on the G.I. Bill pushed the college into the most rapid growth in its history; the new president—himself a veteran—actively recruited new faculty, beefed up both the arts and sciences, raised new money to pay for it all, and applied for university status, but only the president and a few of the deans could ever pronounce the word "university" with a straight face, and everyone else continued to call Briarville what it had always been called: the college.

By the time that Gloria and her father were strolling around the campus, the college employed nearly a hundred and fifty faculty to teach its eighteen hundred students, and the population of Briarville during the academic year was the largest of any town in the county. The heart of the college was still the ag school (Briarville operated a model farm second only to that of the University of Pennsylvania); the college owned a hundred acres of land and scores of buildings, and—although it had yet to do so—was empowered to grant the degree of doctor of philosophy; and now, nearly a hundred years after its founding, the college was still located in the middle of nowhere.

"Hey, it's really grown," Gloria's father kept saying, but Gloria—remembering that for the last hour of the drive into the town she'd seen nothing but cows—had a powerful sense of being in the middle of nowhere. The campus was lovely, however; with its mock-Colonial architecture, it looked like an artist's idealized illustration of the golden college years, and she had the same feeling she'd had when she'd first arrived at her grandparents': that she'd gone backward in time, that at any moment she might run into Penrod and Sam. The coeds were dressed, by Canden High standards, quite conservatively—she saw lots of bobby socks and long, droopy skirts—and she wondered what the girls wore when they went out on dates.

Her father was in a fabulous mood—so fabulous that he was oblivious to her mood, which was far from fabulous—and he was talking about some football game he'd played back in the good old days at good old Briarville, but she was giving him only enough attention so she could smile or laugh at the right moments. She followed him into a drug store, and he ordered lime phosphates.

The state universities, she was thinking, are big big *big*—just like Mom keeps saying—and I'd have to start all over again from scratch, be an absolute nobody all over again. So I was head cheerleader at Canden High in Raysburg, West Virginia, big deal—that's going to cut ice at the University of Pennsylvania? And there was something about Briarville that felt small and safe, like an overgrown high school. "But do you want to stay in high school forever?" the secret watcher asked her, and Gloria didn't have an answer to that. Her stomach was knotting up, and she was afraid if she drank the whole lime phosphate, she'd throw up. She'd wanted more than this, she thought; she'd wanted a heck of a lot more than this—and she could, of course, always change her mind and go to Vassar, but that would really disappoint her father, and, besides, she owed him for saving her from coming out. "But what about *you?*" the secret watcher asked her. Gloria didn't have the answer to that one either; she no longer knew what she wanted— if, indeed, she ever had—and she was sick of everything being up in the air. "Well, princess?" her father said, grinning at her.

"Oh, Daddy," she lied, "I love it." Freshman girls were never, under any circumstance, permitted to live off campus, but Gloria's father went to see the Dean of Women and got the rule waived.

"How'd you do that?" she asked him, and he just winked.

All the way back to Raysburg, Gloria was dreading the moment when she'd have to tell her mother, but, when she did, the news didn't provoke the expected explosion. "Oh, you little nitwit," her mother said in a quiet, resigned voice. "Well, you'll be sorry."

When Gloria returned to Briarville in September, she found that her grand-parents had redecorated her father's old bedroom in the attic for her. The wood-work had been painted pink; the sloping walls had been papered in a hectic floral pattern like that on a Victorian valentine; a Briarville pennant had been tacked over her bed; an ancient doll had been set on a tiny flounced pillow high on a shelf. The doll was wearing pantaloons under her dress, had blond sausage curls and big, round, brilliant, idiotic, glassy, pale blue eyes. Gloria wanted to hide the doll in the wardrobe but knew she'd better not. And then, when she was unpacking, she found—it was the only object in the top drawer of her dresser—a brand-new, big, black Bible.

Gloria met with her advisor and signed up for a slate of freshman courses leading toward the Bachelor of Arts degree. Because of her eight hundred in English on the College Boards, she was exempted from English 100 and placed in a sophomore survey course popularly known as "From Beowulf to Virginia Woolf." If it had been expressly designed for the purpose of discouraging stu-dents from majoring in English, it couldn't have done a better job: each of the professors in the department taught his specialty, demanded a paper, and gave an exam. Gloria survived old Doc Thompkins who wheezed and snuffled his way from the dim beginnings of English literature up through Chaucer, and she was more than ready to move on to someone the catalogue called "Bolton, T." who was to do the Tudors and the Elizabethans.

When Professor Bolton appeared in the enormous lecture hall, Gloria's first thought was: oh, what an ugly man. Then, as she watched him, she took it back; "ugly" wasn't the right word, but she couldn't find another that would do any better. At seventeen, she lumped everybody over thirty into one big, general category, so, if asked, she would have said that he was "middle-aged," of a "normal" height, but nothing else about him was middle or normal. He had a gangly, knobby body that should have belonged to a thin man, but pasted onto the front of it was a perfectly round beach-ball stomach that looked detachable, as though he'd stuffed it under his shirt as an afterthought when he was getting dressed. He wore a conservative, crisply pressed blue suit, but the pasted-on stomach forced him to fasten his belt below it, at his hips, so the seat of his pants ended up halfway down his thighs and the cuffs piled up at the bottom like collapsing accordions. His shoes were tiny, black, highly polished, and improbably pointed; his suit jacket obviously would not fasten over the stomach; a narrow striped tie swung loose from a tight collar that forced his neck out above it into an alarming circle like a layer of pink modeling clay. His hair was black streaked with silver and might have looked distinguished, but the entire top of his head was bald except for one moist, errant tuft. He walked with a splay-footed waddle; once he'd set his briefcase down, he carried his hands (they were very white with inky black hairs on the wrists) thrust loosely out in front of him, high in the air—a performance that made him look like a big, homely dog strutting on its hind legs. Throughout his entrance—and it had most certainly been an *entrance*—he'd been talking steadily in an impossibly plummy British voice, and Gloria had not understood a word he'd said.

The students were tittering, but Professor Bolton did not appear to be put off by it. Gloria finally managed to make out something of what he was saying—nothing particularly important: "Oh, dear me, dear me— Good heavens, wherever could I have put it?" He arranged his notes, then looked out, surveying the room. He had surprisingly appealing eyes—a deep chocolate brown.

"Ah, dear children," he said in his ridiculous British voice, "how delightful to see you this morning gathered so dutifully before me. I am your instructor, Trevor Bolton. Please do not call me doctor—professor will do. I welcome you. The Tudor poets welcome you. May we have—oh, a jolly, jolly month together!"

That speech—not the words themselves but rather the way he'd delivered them—prompted, as he must have known it would, a laugh. He waited for it to subside. Then he inhaled.

When Professor Bolton spoke again, his voice was totally transformed. All the silliness was gone from it, and it rang out like a deep, rich bell. "Whoso list to hunt," he declaimed, "I know where is an hind, but as for me, alas!, I may no more—"

Gloria had never heard these words: she'd never read Wyatt. She stared at the preposterous figure behind the lectern, astonished that such a deep, glorious, ringing sound could be coming out of it. And then—as suddenly as if someone standing in Professor Bolton's place had shot an arrow straight through her—she was pierced by a profound, sweet, inexplicable emotion. She couldn't breathe; her eyes flooded; she was oblivious to the students around her. She hung, suspended in an ecstatic, timeless state, as the silent tears continued to pour steadily down her face, as she waited for each perfect word to unfold and follow after the last perfect word—until the perfect music unwound to a perfect end: "*Noli me tangere*, for Caesar's I am, and wild for to hold, though I seem tame."

She could breathe again. She remembered where she was, felt herself blushing with embarrassment, fished about in her purse for a tissue, blew her nose—and, by then, had already missed the opening of the lecture, for Professor Bolton had sprung into action like a marionette pulled by some frenzied madman. The blackboard was already filling up; she couldn't believe how anyone with such a sappy, syrupy accent could talk that fast. "DON'T TOUCH ME!" he'd written in capital letters. She whipped open her notebook and started taking things down—anything at all—while she did her best to follow him. She'd just managed to figure out that the poet's name was Wyatt and that what he'd written was a sonnet when Professor Bolton switched to a language even more foreign than his brand of English: "*Scritto avea di diamanti e di topazi!*" he sang out gleefully, "*Nussun mi tocci!*"

"Petrarch," Gloria dutifully transcribed from the blackboard, "Courtly Love Tradition—Laura as Muse"—and found, to her amazement, that now he was talking about Anne Boleyn, Henry the Eighth, and the politics of the Tudor Court—all of which, somehow, related to the poem, but, before she could figure out exactly how, he was quoting Chaucer.

The only thing that stopped him was the bell. "Oh dear, oh dear," he said, looking around as though he'd just awakened from a dream. "I had so much more I wanted to tell you, but I suppose it must keep—"

Until that morning, Gloria had held a high opinion of her intellectual abilities: she was the eight-hundred-on-the-Boards girl, the read-everything-under-the-sun girl, the whiz kid who could, at a moment's notice, whip off an essay on any topic and get an A plus on it. Now she had some idea of just how deeply ignorant she must be. Poetry had always been the great love of her life, and so, of course, she'd cried over it before, but she'd never before heard music like Wyatt's, and now she understood what she must surely have always known: that poetry was far more than a bunch of pretty words—it was, of all the works of man, the most beautiful and profound and eternal.

Gloria's first paper for Professor Bolton came back without a grade. All he'd done was correct her punctuation, and his only comment —scrawled in the margin with a blood-red pen—referred to her frequent use of ellipses: "Please do not do this any more. It: 1) indicates a failure to think through your argument, and, therefore, to find the proper way to punctuate it; 2) lends a breathless, girlish quality to your prose, which many might find charming but I do not; 3) creates

a visual solecism, as though you had attacked your pages with a pepper shaker."
On the last page he'd written: "See me. T.B."

"Ah, Miss Carter, how lovely of you to drop by," he said when she tapped at
his office door.

"Cotter," Gloria said.

"Ah, yes," he said, "come in. Sit down, please." He looked around with a
startled expression as though he'd just discovered that the entire contents of his
office had been foisted upon him in some dubious and underhanded fashion.
The only vacant chair was the large leather one behind his desk; he considered
the three others, which were piled high with books and papers. He shot a dark,
accusatory look at Gloria, sprang into action, swooped down upon the chair
nearest the desk, and swept everything onto the floor.

She tiptoed over the debris and sat down. He settled opposite her, took up a
short, blunt briar pipe carved into the face of a bulldog, seized a kitchen match
from a box resting on top of the thick stratum of books and papers that covered
every available inch of his desktop, lit the tobacco, and then murmured, through
gouts of blue, heavily aromatic smoke: "Yes, yes, yes. Now what can I do for you,
my dear?"

"You said to come and see you."

"I did? Good heavens. What ever could I have been thinking?"

She thrust her paper at him; he took it reluctantly, peered down at his own
writing, then back at her with a magnificent smile. "Ah, yes, yes, the pepper
shaker girl— I do so appreciate your feelings—that you responded so enthusiastically, so *bravely*, to Wyatt's love poetry—but I would be remiss in my pro-
fessorial duties if I failed to mention, my dear, that we would normally expect
a scholarly work to take a somewhat less encomious tone."

Encomious? Gloria thought.

"And there's another matter— Well, you see, my dear, I would like a modest
rewrite, actually."

It took Gloria a moment to understand what he meant. He must not have
liked her paper. This had never happened to her before. Her eyes stung, and
she had to look away.

The space on the bookshelves must have been used up years ago: books
were piled on top of books; books were stacked in the corners; books were
lying in heaps on the floor. The thick, sweet pipe smoke—like something out
of *The Arabian Nights* —was making her queasy, and then she caught another
scent behind it; oddly enough, Professor Bolton reeked of lilacs.

"What do you want me to do?" she asked.

"Oh, just answer a simple question—and only about the poem that appears
to be your favorite—'Whoso list—' Please tell me how much Wyatt got from
Petrarch."

"Excuse me?"

"I want you to compare Wyatt and Petrarch," he said, "word for word. They both, as you must know by now, wrote poems about deer with 'don't touch me' written on their collars. I want you to compare the two poems."

Gloria was dumbfounded. "How can I do that? I can't read Italian. Should I get a translation, or—"

"Oh, good heavens. You've had your Latin, haven't you? You get your Petrarch, and you get your Italian dictionary, and you get a good translation or two, and you lay them all out before you, and you set to it. Oh, and be sure to check Wyatt's usage in the OED. Don't assume that even the most ordinary word meant quite the same in his time as it does to us."

As she rose to go, he said, smiling, "Miss Carter—? If you're not conversant with Petrarch and the courtly love tradition, you may have to do just a tad of background reading."

For a month Gloria stayed up until two in the morning while she did just a tad of background reading. Then she wrote up her findings in eighteen careful pages with no ellipses in them. This time, having looked up "encomious" in the OED, she kept her feelings about the poetry to herself.

Except for the "don't touch me" collar, there was absolutely nothing she could find in common between Petrarch's deer and Wyatt's. Petrarch's sonnet— Gloria wrote—is like a mystical vision or a sadly poignant dream; his white hind must not be touched because her lord has seen fit to set her free; she is, of course, the unobtainable Laura—and, on a deeper level, she symbolizes Christ. Wyatt's sonnet is an extended metaphor in which hunting a deer stands for hunting a woman; his tone is cynical and bitter, and his hind is, obviously, a naughty court lady; she must not be touched because another man has already put his collar on her. Some historians suggested that she was Anne Boleyn claimed by Henry the Eighth.

Her new paper came back bleeding red ink from every pore; the margins were crammed with comments; she'd never been treated so roughly by a teacher. It would take her years to read everything that Professor Bolton had suggested. Filled with dread, she turned the paper over to find the grade. When she saw the A plus, she felt a strange stuttering in her chest as though her heart had literally skipped a beat. But even better than the A plus was the comment: "This, my dear, is graduate work."

5

After she'd finished her paper for Professor Bolton and had time to think about something other than Petrarch and Wyatt, Gloria began to wonder if she hadn't made a mistake in living off campus. (She didn't dare ask herself if she'd made a mistake in coming to Briarville.) Her grandparents' house had at first seemed so cozy and nice and homey—or at least that's how she'd wanted to see it: like a Currier and Ives print—but winter was coming, and it was raining a lot, and, no matter how much the radiators banged and hissed, the house never got warm and there was a spirit to it that felt mean and sorrowful. Despite the fact that they'd been married to each other a million years, Gram and Gramps didn't appear to be very fond of each other; Gramps was retired and spent his time puttering around in the garage or fixing things that didn't need fixing, and, if Gloria never knew what to say to him, he appeared to know even less what to say to her; he never looked her in the eyes, and it made her feel creepy. And Gram seemed to expect Gloria to get up every Sunday and go to church with her; if Gloria slept in, Gram didn't say anything about it, but Gloria could feel a chill for days afterward, and, no matter how much school work Gloria had, Gram expected her to help around the house—which was obviously what girls were supposed to do—and Gram had a way of pursing her lips and sniffing that was beginning to drive Gloria absolutely mad. But, worst of all, Gloria felt entirely left out of college life. She'd bought a cute English bike, and, whenever she climbed onto it and began her long ride back to her grandparents' house, she felt her heart sink, and she longed to be in the dorm with all the other freshman girls. Every day after her last class she went to the Student Union, got herself a Coke, and tried to study in the midst of all that cheery noise—just so she could put off as long as possible the dreadful moment when she'd have to get onto her bike and pedal off campus.

If she'd fully realized just how much Briarville really *was* like an overgrown high school, she would have tried out for the cheerleading squad—she badly missed being a cheerleader—but she'd stupidly thought that going to college meant getting an education and so had decided not to get involved in any extracurricular activities until she was sure she could keep up with her studies. She went to every football game when the team was at home, and she usually found some girls from her classes to sit with, but all the games did was remind her of what she was missing; in high school she would have known the football players and the kids in the band and the majorettes, and she would have been out on the field herself, leading cheers, and everybody would have know her. She'd worked like a dog to make herself popular at Canden High, but at Briarville she was anonymous again, and she felt nearly as shy and unsure of herself as she had at Fairhaven. Once again she was ready to do anything to fit in, and it was obvious that the best way to fit in at Briarville was to join a sorority. It was forbidden at Briarville to rush freshmen until their second semester, so the first week in January was "rush week," and all through her Christmas vacation, she worried about it. Would anybody rush her? Would she get into a good sorority? And even if she got in, would she like it?

On Monday afternoon her first week back, Gloria was sitting alone at a table in the Union. She'd just come from her English Lit survey course, and they'd made it up to Wordsworth, and she was trying to read "Intimations of Immortality," and it was, depending on how you looked at it, either the perfect thing for her to be reading or the worst possible thing. She'd started several times, and each time she'd arrived at the line, "To me alone there came a thought of grief," her eyes had filled and she'd had to stop. It was ridiculous; she didn't even like the poem that much—but the light was fading away at the big windows, and the other kids were beginning to leave, and by the time she got home (and it wasn't really home), she'd be wind-burnt and half frozen, and then she'd have to sit through another silent dinner with Gram and Gramps (it was always overcooked meat and watery potatoes and soggy vegetables), and she'd have to help wash up, and then she could escape to her wretched little valentine room in the attic and curl up under her two eiderdowns, but she never would get warm enough, and the wind would be whistling through the eaves and rattling the loose windows, and Wordsworth would be telling her "there hath past away a glory from the earth." Oh, just great, she thought.

She looked up from Wordsworth and saw that the two grown-up ladies she'd seen earlier (she'd been too lost in her inner misery to pay much attention to them) had stopped chatting with some freshman girls Gloria knew from her rat-psych class and now were walking across the room in her general direction. As they came closer, she decided that they weren't really grown-up ladies after all but just college girls, probably juniors or seniors, and she must have thought of them as grown-up ladies because they were dressed to the nines in suits and heels. Now they appeared to be walking directly toward her table. She was sure there must be some mistake.

As they approached, Gloria saw that they had great figures, that their suits were very good suits indeed. They were wearing sorority pins, and they emanated a complex air of womanly sophistication that was quite unusual for Briarville. They were definitely headed straight for her. Maybe they just wanted her table.

"Hi," the strawberry-blonde said, "do you mind if we join you?"

"Oh, no," Gloria said, "please sit down. I'm Gloria."

"We know. Gloria Cotter. We're *so* very glad to meet you, Gloria. I'm Mitsy Thorton, the President of Delta Lambda. We're practically neighbors. I'm from Pittsburgh."

Thorton? Gloria thought. The coal and steel Thortons?

"And I'm Morgan Clendenning, the Rush Chairman," the ash-blonde said in a dry, drawling, stagey, Southern voice. "We're having an open house at Delta Lambda tomorrow evening, and we'd be just delighted if you could come."

Oh, my gosh, Gloria thought, *I'm being rushed.* She felt her mouth go dry and couldn't say a word.

Mitsy and Morgan had mysteriously managed to arrange themselves on either side of her, and they took turns talking. "You've probably heard all about us by now. Delta Lambda is an old sorority at Briarville, the second oldest on campus—"

"That's right. We have *years* of tradition behind us. And we've always gone out of our way to make sure that we have the *very best* girls—"

"And your reputation has preceded you, Gloria—"

My reputation? Gloria thought. What reputation? "And we knew that a girl like you would want to give *very serious* consideration to Delta Lambda—"

"So, Gloria, I bet you have lots of questions about Delta Lambda."

Gloria was caught with her mind totally devoid of any questions about Delta Lambda. She had indeed heard of it—both pro and con. She'd heard the Lambs called "the ladies of the campus"; she'd also heard the sorority referred to as "Rich Bitch House." "Gee, I don't know. It's—really nice of you to invite me—"

"Oh, but it's our *duty* to find the very best girls," Mitsy said.

"Delta Lambda friendships last *a lifetime*," Morgan said, "and we try very hard to make sure our girls are congenial—"

"You know, Gloria, from *a similar background* — I think you'll find our girls— well, *congenial.*"

"And then, of course, there are the intangibles—the ideals of the Panhellenic movement. We believe that sorority builds *character*—"

"And we've always had the *cutest* girls on campus—"

"So, naturally, when we heard that you'd been *Prom Queen* in high school—"

"Oh, but we don't want you to get the wrong idea. We expect our girls to be *well-rounded*—"

"You might have some reservations about us. Oh, we know all about the campus gossip, and—well, it's true that in the past we haven't been exactly *known* for academic achievement—"

"But we're working very hard to correct that. Believe me, we are. It's one of our major projects this year, you might say, and seeing as you're on *the Dean's List* —Well, we feel that would be quite an asset—"

"We really *need* a serious intellectual in the house—"

"Ye gods, do we ever!" A strand of cool, shimmering hair had fallen over one of Morgan's eyes; she brushed it away with a graceful gesture, and Gloria was sure that Morgan must have rehearsed that achingly coy gesture in a mirror.

As protective coloration, Gloria had adopted the standard Briarville coed uniform—long, droopy skirt and bobby socks—and, next to the Lambs, she felt considerably less than nothing special. They were sitting so close to her that Gloria could smell each of their distinctive, subtle perfumes; since she'd been at Briarville, Gloria hadn't bothered to wear perfume. Their nail polish was perfect, and hers was chipped. They were beautifully made up, and she was wearing only lipstick—if there was any left; it had been several hours since she'd checked. She knew she was expected to say something, but she couldn't think of a thing.

"You know, Gloria," Mitsy said, "it really *is* a small world. When we were preparing our rush list, I just happened to mention your name to my mother, and she said, 'Oh, not Ted and Laney Cotter's girl? From Raysburg? Why, Mitsy, she's a lovely girl. She must be *exactly* the sort of girl you want."

"Oh, gee, that's nice of her," Gloria said.

"We do want you, Gloria," Mitsy said. "We think you'd be *perfect* for Delta Lambda."

"And Delta Lambda," Morgan said, "would be perfect for *you*."

Right from the beginning, Gloria felt a sense of fatality about Delta Lambda. She was reasonably sure that if she visited all the open houses, other sororities would rush her, but she felt strangely reluctant to do that. Always before, she'd had to work to make herself wanted; never had anyone said to her in such a straightforward way, "We want you, Gloria." If the Lambs want me, she thought, then they should probably have me.

The major sororities at Briarville had distinctive personalities. The Dee Gees were real Betty Coeds: they were bouncy, perky, and bright; they wore sweaters, skirts with kick-pleats, bobby socks and saddle shoes; they were always smiling, and they reminded Gloria uncomfortably of the persona she'd cultivated in high school. The Alpha Gams were the intellectuals, and Gloria didn't even consider them. What she valued least about herself—perhaps because it had never required any effort on her part—was her intellect; she'd always much preferred to be told that she was pretty, or kind, or loyal, rather than smart, and the last thing she wanted was to be defined by her intelligence. Then there were the Thetas, and they appeared to be drowning in good works; they were always throwing parties for orphans or collecting things for charity, and Gloria had nothing against good works, but still— That left the houses that were fairly nondescript, the ones whose letters nobody remembered—every girl's second choice. But Gloria had been rushed by Delta Lambda—the most exclusive sorority at Briarville.

If you were walking across campus and passed a cool, self-possessed sorority girl (she was always wearing her pin), and if her every hair was in place, and if she was wearing far more makeup than was generally the custom, and nylons— almost no one wore nylons to class—she was certain to be a Lamb, but, from Gloria's point of view, this was no drawback; Gloria loved clothes and dressing up ("my major vice" she'd written in her diary). And the Lambs were big city girls, but that was OK too; Gloria thought she'd feel more at home with girls from Pittsburgh or Philadelphia than with girls who'd grown up on farms. The annual Delta Lambda spring ball—the White and Gold Invitational—was touted as the most glamorous event of the year, and the Lambs were notorious for snapping up the most attractive girls at Briarville (Briarville's Homecoming Queens and Valentine Queens and May Queens were Lambs more often than not), so of course Gloria was flattered. But they also had one of the lowest grade averages of any Greek letter society, and, several years ago they had, briefly, lost their charter because of certain "irregularities"—whatever that might mean. A sophomore in Gloria's English survey course—someone Gloria respected— said to her: "*Lamb!* Come on Gloria, you've got to be kidding. No girl with a brain in her head would consider Lamb for even half a second."

Gloria decided to go to the open house and make up her own mind. She didn't have to pledge if she didn't want to—and despite what the Lambs had told her, she was not at all certain that they would bid her. They bid only twelve to fifteen girls a year.

She owned several suits every bit as good as either Mitsy's or Morgan's—actually, some of her suits were a bit better than either Mitsy's or Morgan's—and she wore a superbly tailored Ben Zuckerman. Her grandfather drove her onto campus. She was worried that she was over-dressed until she walked into the Delta Lambda house. "Oh, Gloria," Mitsy said, clapping her hands, "you look terrif!"

Morgan and Mitsy showed Gloria around; the house was old, had window seats and leaded glass and a huge circular staircase and lots of dark wood and a nifty recreation room in the basement, and Gloria liked it—although she was too nervous to take in more than a general impression. The Lambs had obviously been primed to meet her: every sister called her by name. She could see by their smiles that they loved her suit. She was invited back for tea the next day which meant that she'd made the first cut—and fairly easily at that.

She stood on the sidewalk outside the Delta Lambda house and found herself caught in an existential dilemma. (She thought of it exactly like that: I'm caught in an existential dilemma.) Right across the street was Delta Gamma; a steady procession of cute girls was walking in, and every time the door opened, Gloria could hear a record on the vic—it sounded like Bing Crosby—and she could easily walk in too and introduce herself, but she'd never seen a Dee Gee in heels (although she supposed they had to wear them sometimes), and she was sure they'd find her suit pretentious. She could walk over to the ice cream parlor on Main Street, call a cab (*the* cab, she should say, as there was only one in town), go back to her grandparents', change her clothes, and come back again. She could visit all the open houses, which is exactly what she should do if she were being sensible—although, other than Lamb, the only one that really appealed to her *was* Delta Gamma; it was like the sorority in a girls' novel, and Gloria knew that she could easily, even happily, spend four years in kickpleats smiling at everyone she met; she'd already had lots of practice doing exactly that. It was— she'd been reading Sartre—a matter of self-definition, and if, along with the Lambs, she got the Dee Gees to rush her, then at least she'd have a choice.

She walked over to Main and called the cab. Back in her bedroom, she studied herself in the full-length mirror; she liked the way she looked in her Zuckerman suit, and she liked wearing it. If she pledged Delta Gamma, she'd probably never wear it again, but if she pledged Lamb, she might get to wear all of her New York clothes. That's right, she thought, if I pledged Lamb, they'd polish me up to a high shine like Mitsy and Morgan—and a little imp in her mind said, "Gloria, you'd polish up even *better* than Mitsy or Morgan." The question was: did she want to be polished?

When she woke up the next morning, Gloria discovered that she must have decided in her sleep: she did indeed want to be polished. She was sure that tea meant white gloves, and once again she was right. She was introduced to blue-haired Mrs. Donner, the house mother, and then she was deposited in the living room. The rushees sat unmoving—knees together, ankles crossed—and tried to drink tea while the Lambs, one at a time, knelt at their feet and introduced themselves. Every sister was required to say a few words to every rushee, and they quickly began to blur in Gloria's mind; she couldn't remember which had been Debbie or Nancy or Linda or Betty, and they all said approximately the same thing: "Hi, Gloria, I've heard *so* much about you from Mitsy, and we're *so* glad you're interested in Delta Lambda—oh, just love your dress—heard you were Prom Queen in high school. Gee, bet that was fun! So, you like the house? Oh, isn't it though! Decided your major yet? Been out with any neat guys? Thanks for coming, Gloria. Good luck." As Gloria was leaving, Morgan, with a wink, handed her an envelope. She hadn't seen any of the other rushees getting an envelope. It was—just as Gloria had known it was going to be—an invitation to dinner on Thursday night.

Gloria wore a black, princess-length cocktail dress with a prim Peter Pan collar; once again, she'd made exactly the right choice. At candle-lit tables laid with real silver, with linen napkins monogrammed with the sorority's letters and symbol—a stylized sun—as carefully balanced as if they had bean bags on their heads, thirty rushees were doing their best to eat creamed chicken without dumping it down the fronts of their lovely dresses. They had already—as Gloria had done—counted each other, and now they must all be considering—as Gloria was—the alarming fact that half of them would be cut before Monday. Delta Lambda was living up to her reputation for rushing the cutest girls: Gloria saw two of the freshman cheerleaders and one of the freshman majorettes, and many of the rushees were pretty enough to be *Seventeen* covers. She wondered how on earth the Lambs had managed to find so damn many blondes.

After dinner, Mitsy rose and delivered a speech on the traditions of the sorority, emphasizing Virtue, Service, Achievement, Sisterly Love, Divine Guidance, and the Spiritual Values of Ritual; Gloria found it both silly and true—and true things, she thought, often sounded silly when you stood up in public and made a speech out of them. At the end of the evening, the Lambs serenaded the rushees with a medley of sorority songs; most of the sisters had reasonably good voices, and some had splendid ones, and the songs—sweet and tender as hymn tunes—seemed to have been designed for no other purpose than to invoke a mood of gently poignant, moist-eyed nostalgia, and Gloria imagined that the other rushees must have been experiencing a feeling similar to her own: a keen longing to be admitted to the charmed circle of Delta Lambda.

Then, as the rushees were leaving, the sisters formed a line outside on the lawn and sang to the tune of "Dixie" (Delta Lambda had been founded in Virginia): "Oh, I'm so happy that I *am* a—Delta Delta Delta Lambda; hoo-ray, hooray, hoo-ray, Delta *Lamb!*"—which was, Gloria thought, fairly silly but not any sillier than some of the things she'd sung as a Canden High cheerleader. Until then she'd been reasonably certain that the fix had been in for her right from the start, but all it would take to keep her out was one black ball. She was astonished at the intensity of her feeling: she desperately wanted the Lambs to bid her.

Over the weekend, the Greeks picked their final choices. Gloria kept telling herself it was a sure thing—good grief, how often do you get a former prom queen with straight As whose father is the senior vice-president of a major steel corporation!—but by Sunday night she was a nervous wreck. She'd thrown up once; she couldn't eat, couldn't study, couldn't do anything but lie on her bed, her stomach in a knot, trying to remember if she'd said anything gauche, or had, even for a moment, been too much of a smarty-pants. I'm too dark, she finally decided; they obviously only want blondes. When Mitsy and Morgan appeared to tell her that Lamb was bidding her, Gloria burst into tears—and hated herself for it—but, as they hugged her and congratulated her, she could see by their smiles that bursting into tears had been exactly the right thing to do.

The Delta Lambda house, when Gloria arrived on Monday night, was ominously quiet; she was ushered into the common room and told to wait. Just as every other girl must have been doing, Gloria counted the rushees; of the thirty at dinner, only fourteen were left—and yes, a high percentage of them were blonde. One at a time, each girl was led out. When her turn came, Gloria was escorted into a small room. The only light came from a single white candle resting on a table draped in black. Mitsy and the two other senior officers of the sorority were standing behind the table. They were wearing long black robes decorated with white and gold, the colors of the Delta Lambda.

Mitsy, in a voice as solemn as a Methodist preacher's, asked Gloria if she accepted the invitation to pledge Delta Lambda. Gloria quickly said, "Yes." Then Mitsy read the sacred oath, and Gloria repeated it after her: "I, Gloria Merriman Cotter do hereby declare myself to be pledged of Delta Lambda Sorority—"

Back in the common room, the sisters formed a double line through which the rushees passed on their way out to murmurs of "Congratulations— So glad you made it— Good night, good night—" On the sidewalk Gloria felt disoriented; as consistently as if they had agreed upon it beforehand, the rushees drifted away from each other without speaking; good night, sweet ladies, good night, Gloria thought, echoing Ophelia and Eliot. The perfectly ordinary view of Briarville's Sorority Row looked as unfamiliar to her as if she'd never seen it before—unreal city!—or had never seen it in precisely this way; she stared at the tree-lined street, the patches of snow on the lawns, the yellow cones of light from the street lamps, the deep, nostalgic indigo of the sky. It wasn't even ten, and she had nowhere to go in her hat and gloves and beautifully tailored suit except back to her grandparents' house; yet she could sense—like a wisp of perfume in her mind—some other destination. I made it, she thought. Delta Lambda, good grief! What she was feeling was as sweet as icing sugar, but she also knew that it could be treacherous: she'd had moods like this one turn on her before. Watch out, she told herself.

Gloria was thankful she'd had Professor Bolton in the fall semester and not in the spring one: being a Lamb pledge took so much time she could barely keep up with her courses. Once a week there was a formal dinner followed by a "pep session" (the pledges stood in a row and sang sorority songs); every Sunday afternoon there were "hash sessions"; these were, in theory, supposed to give the pledges "a chance to hash things over," but, in practice, gave the Pledge Training Committee a chance to make hash out of the pledges. Sisterly criticism was offered—"in a constructive spirit"—of everything from clothes, makeup, and manners to attitudes, aspirations, and choice of friends outside the sorority. The pledges were also expected to criticize each other—and themselves. "What's your worst trait?" they were asked, "the one big thing you really want to change?" Gloria confessed to being shy—which was perfectly true—but she could see that they didn't believe her. She wondered if she should make up some other worst trait.

Each pledge was assigned to a Big Sister, and Gloria was assigned to Morgan Clendenning. Horrors! Gloria thought. Morgan's thin, ironic smile and stagey, pretentious, Southern voice—and, of course, her shimmering, ash-blonde hair—affected Gloria like fingernails on a blackboard. "You must have some Greek or Italian blood in you," Morgan said at their first meeting, "you're so dark."

Gloria felt her stomach knot. "It's Castilian," she said, "you know, from Spain."

"Spain, huh? That's neat. So why don't you cultivate a sultry look—you know, like Gina Lollabrigida? Anybody can go blonde, Gloria, but you can do something blondes can't do—" and this was said with a wink, "you can *smolder*."

Gloria decided she might like Morgan after all—and, back in her bedroom, she stared into her mirror and wondered what, exactly, it would look like to smolder.

They met on Tuesday nights in Morgan's room. Gloria always sat in the chair by the window; she felt as carefully balanced as the half-empty teacup Morgan usually left perched on the windowsill. Morgan kicked off her shoes, stretched out on her bed, lay back on her flounced pink-and-white pillows, blew smoke rings at the ceiling, and played the role of the infinitely more sophisticated older woman. She's having a whale of a good time, Gloria thought—but she was ready to do anything to make sure that Morgan went on having a good time. Gloria knew she was being patronized, but she didn't mind. She was having a good time too.

"OK, Gloria," Morgan told her, "now that you're a Lamb pledge, you've got to spruce up a bit. You've looked simply splendid at the house functions, but on campus—well, let's say we've got some work to do."

"Oh, but—I was just trying to, you know, fit in."

"Gloria, I'm going to tell you something really important. Lambs don't *fit in*. Lambs *stand out*."

Nothing in the complex social code of Canden High School had been spelled out clearly, and Gloria had been forced to observe and analyze as carefully as an anthropologist; she'd learned the hard way that the most important rules and taboos were far from obvious—and yet were never clearly formulated. What she liked about Delta Lambda was how clear everything was, how simple and direct and unambiguous. If you wanted to know, you asked. If you wanted to fit in, all you had to do was what you were told.

Morgan took Gloria shopping for makeup. Gloria had never worn foundation except at formal dances; Morgan told her to wear it every day. "It'll even out your skin tone," she said. "It's like painting. The foundation gives you the ground for your canvas. Don't stop at your jaw line. Carry it right down onto your neck or you'll look like you're wearing a mask." She showed Gloria a basic daytime makeup that could be augmented for evening; she showed her the best way to put on mascara (three coats), how to use an eyelash curler, how to taper her eyebrows down to a pencil-thin line at the outer margins, how to contour her cheekbones like a model with two shades of rouge, how to use eye shadow (just a hint for daytime, lots and lots for evening), how to apply eye-liner and feather it outward to make her eyes look wider, how to use a lip-liner and a sable brush for lipstick, how to set the whole works with a dusting of translucent powder, and, if she really wanted it to hold, a bit of steam.

The first time Gloria tried the whole works, it took her an hour and a half; she made sure to apply the foundation right down onto her neck, but still, to her own eyes, it looked like a mask—an overdone Halloween impersonation of a movie star—and, when she looked at the final result, she didn't have the remotest idea who that elaborately painted grown-up lady in the mirror could possibly be, but Morgan said, "That's it, Gloria, utterly terrif. Now all you've got to do is stop grinning all the time. You've got a smile that's—I don't know quite how to put it. Well, it's kind of pathetic. You know, sort of an oh-please-like-me smile. Cut it out. Cultivate an air of mystery. Be cool and distant. If you've got to smile, give 'em the ole Mona Lisa."

While wearing her pledge pin and her new makeup and "the ole Mona Lisa," Gloria was asked out twice. She had to refuse one boy —pledges were not permitted to date non-Greeks—but the Pledge Dating Committee approved the other, so she went out with him. He was in ag school, an Alpha Gamma Rho, and dull as dishwater, but at least she'd had her first date at Briarville.

Just as it was supposed to, the constant round of shared activities was giving the pledges a growing sense of group identity; even Gloria felt it—although, she suspected, to a lesser degree than the others; she was afraid she'd never feel entirely comfortable in any group, no matter how congenial, but at least (as she lectured herself) she could do her best to *look* comfortable just as she had at Canden High. What she really needed, she thought, was a genuine friend—one would be enough—and then, just as she was trying to decide upon a likely candidate, Susie Steibel, the majorette in her pledge class, said to her, "I like you. Why don't we do something tomorrow—have a Coke or something?"

Gloria had been struck speechless by the simplicity of "I like you." Susie was looking at her with cool, clear, impossibly blue eyes. "OK, sure," Gloria managed to say and then flagellated herself during the bike ride back to her grandparents because it hadn't occurred to her to say, "I like you too"—which is obviously what she should have said even though she didn't know Susie well enough to know whether she liked her or not, and might never have known because she was so in awe of majorettes that, left to her own devices, she probably would never have said a word to her.

What was it about majorettes anyway? She'd always been fascinated by them, and she'd often thought she'd get a kick out of doing what they did—but she never could, not in a million years. Cheerleading had been as much of a public spectacle as she'd ever wanted to make of herself—even that had not been easy— and, try as she might, she couldn't imagine herself wearing a skimpy uniform with a teensy skirt, marching across a football field, twirling a baton, displaying her charms in that relentlessly cute way required of a majorette. The awe she'd always felt toward girls who could do that was precisely because they *could* do that—and, apparently, without embarrassment or self-consciousness or even a second thought.

From the gossip in their pledge class, Gloria had learned that Susie Steibel had been her high school's head majorette and prom queen; she was also a championship twirler and had won several beauty pageants. She was a natural blonde and so pretty—in a wholesome, scrubbed, girl-next-door way—she looked too good to be true, like a mannequin in the window of a junior miss shop. Given her looks and talent, she could easily make head majorette her senior year and was sure to win one or more of Briarville's many queenships— possibly even the prestigious May Queen—and that was almost certainly why the Lambs had rushed her.

Gloria had agreed to meet Susie at Sneaky's, the campus juke joint. When she got there, she found Susie already waiting for her—oddly enough, outside on the sidewalk. "Oh, here you are," Susie said with a tense smile and an impatient gesture, her fingers fidgeting on the front of her open coat.

"Am I late?" Gloria said, sure that she wasn't.

"Oh, no, you're right on time."

It was crowded inside, and Gloria had almost resigned herself to standing up when a couple left a booth and Susie shot instantly into it. Gloria followed. Susie was carrying a plaid satchel exactly like something from grade school, and she plunked it on the table. "You glad you got into Lamb?" she said.

"Sure. Are you?"

"I guess so."

If Lambs were supposed to stand out, then Gloria was doing a good job; as far as she could tell from a quick glance around, she was the only girl in the whole place wearing nylons, and she felt unpleasantly conspicuous. If anyone had told Susie to spruce up, however, she hadn't paid the least bit of attention: in her droopy skirt and bobby socks, she was dressed much like every other freshman girl on campus, but she was so pretty she made even that dumb co- ed uniform look good.

They ordered milkshakes. Susie seemed incapable of sitting still; Gloria watched her making innumerable skittery movements: drumming her fingers on the table top, shifting back and forth, picking up her book bag and putting it down. "The Dee Gees really wanted me. It would of been real easy for me to pledge Dee Gee."

"I thought of Dee Gee too," Gloria said.

The comparison was inevitable: Susie's small, heart-shaped face, huge blue eyes, and deftly sculpted features really *did* look like a doll's. Oh, Gloria thought, irritated at her own cattiness, she's so blonde—a real beauty queen, so *conventionally* pretty.

"Who's your big sister?" Susie asked her.

"Morgan."

"You like her?"

"Oh, yes. I like her a lot. Who's yours?"

"They gave me to Mitsy. I guess they figured—you know, when they got *me*, they must of figured they really had their work cut out for them. So they gave me to the prez herself."

"You like her?"

"Oh, sure. I drive her nuts though, I can tell—I mean I don't mean to drive her nuts but—it just, you know—I've sure got a lot to learn. Are you really shy?"

Gloria was startled, but then she remembered the hash session. "Yes, I really am."

Gloria tried to remember what Susie had said *her* worst fault was, but Susie saved her the effort: "Yeah, and I really do shoot off my mouth too much. It's like my dad always says, 'Engage brain before operating mouth.' Yeah, and I thought you were—kind of standoffish—but when you said that about being shy, I thought, oh, *that's* what it is. She just wants somebody to come over and talk to her."

Gloria was taken aback, annoyed that this stranger—fellow pledge or not—had been able to read her so accurately. "How very astute of you," she said.

Susie was drumming lightly on the table top again; she was looking down at her fingertips. "You know, Lamb didn't rush any of the girls I know in the dorm—" she said, her voice trailing off inconclusively.

Susie had unusual hands: white, literally, as milk, and narrow, with clearly defined pale blue veins; instead of tapering, her long fingers ended in blunt, squared-off tips, which might not have been so noticeable if she hadn't worn her nails so very short. They were nicely manicured though, with clear polish on them. Then—why had it taken her so long to notice?—Gloria saw in those drumming fingers just how nervous Susie was. What on earth did she have to be nervous about?

Come on, Gloria told herself, say something; anything will do. But Susie took a deep breath and said, "So what's Morgan making you do?"

That was an odd way to put it. "Oh, dress up more. Wear more makeup. How about you? What's Mitsy making you do?"

"She said if I said any more bad words, she'd wash my mouth out with soap. She meant it too!"

"Good gosh, what did you say?"

"Oh, just, you know—I slipped and said the F word."

Gloria was shocked. She, of course, knew what the F word was, but she couldn't imagine any girl actually saying it.

"I thought it was like when you've got a best girlfriend—how you can say *any-thing*? Well, I must of thought a sorority was like that—but I guess it's not, huh?"

Susie's question had sounded entirely rhetorical, but Gloria guessed that it hadn't been, and she tried to find an answer to it. She'd never had a best girl-friend to whom she could say anything, and she never would have expected a sorority—even the most wonderful of sororities—to be filled with best girlfriends like that, but to say so would make her sound cynical, or worse, would imply that she'd found Susie naive—which, indeed, she had. After another moment of silence—the silences were beginning to become quite uncomfortable—she said the first thing that popped into her head: "Do you like being a majorette?"

Susie laughed. "I don't know—do you like being on the Dean's List?"

Gloria felt a wave of prickly irritation but forced herself to smile. "Of course I do."

"Yeah, well, it's the same thing. Sure, I like being a majorette. It's kind of— I've got a scholarship for it."

"Oh, really?"

"Yeah. I wouldn't be here if I didn't. So, you picked your major yet?"

"English. How about you?"

"Either primary ed or phys ed, I'm not sure."

Oh, Gloria thought, it's no wonder we can't find much of anything to say to each other, but then Susie glanced over at her with a quick smile that made her look, momentarily, like a wicked little fox. It was almost as though she were inviting Gloria to share—she wasn't sure what, a joke maybe. Well, it *was* kind of funny how hard a time they were having.

"Hey," Susie said, "you want to see a magic trick?"

There was nothing Gloria could possibly answer but, "Sure."

Susie took a silver dollar out of her book bag. "Call it," she said.

"Tails."

Susie tossed the coin into the air, caught it, and showed it to Gloria. It was tails. "Call it again," she said as she flipped the coin again.

"Heads." It was heads.

Susie flipped the coin four more times, and, each time, whatever Gloria called, that's what it was. "You want to know how I do it?"

"Sure."

"It looks like it's turning over in the air, but it's not really. It's just wobbling real fast."

Gloria thought about it. "Wait a minute," she said. "That can't be right. I've been calling it while it's *already* up in the air."

"Hey, you're real smart! Here's the secret, OK? I flip it up, and I know it's tails. So if you say 'tails,' I just catch it like this." She caught the coin in the palm of her hand. "But if you say, 'heads,' then I catch it and slap it on my wrist like this—so it turns over. See."

"Hey, that's really wonderful," Gloria said, and meant it, although what she'd found wonderful hadn't been the trick itself—it was, after all, fairly puerile—but that a girl, someone her own age, could do something so adroit, so uncannily fast, with her hands. Gloria couldn't even catch a beach ball. "Where'd you learn to do that?"

"It's just something my brother showed me." Susie shrugged and dropped the coin back into her satchel. "There's nothing to do in Cloverton, especially in the summer. Nothing. If you have to, you'll play with mud."

Whenever Gloria was in strange social situations, her natural tendency was to keep her mouth shut and watch, and that's what she'd been doing. Now she sensed that Susie was getting over her nervousness—but, no, there was something more than that. It was as though an obscure impediment—an immense block that had been standing between them—were crumbling. She watched Susie take a compact and a tube of lipstick out of her book bag and redo her lips. Mitsy must not have told her that ladies didn't put on makeup in public. Gloria wondered if she should tell her but then decided not to.

"I was the only majorette the Lambs rushed," Susie said. "It seems kind of funny to me. The other majorettes are real nice girls."

The lipstick was too bright for Susie's pale skin; such a vivid red made her look cheap—even a bit tough—like the blonde, wise-cracking girl reporter in a movie. But why was Gloria surprised? Of course a majorette would want lips that were red red *red*, wouldn't she?

Susie folded a paper napkin in half, slipped it between her lips and pressed them down on it. "Better?"

"Yes. That's better." Gloria felt a tiny, internal shiver. How had Susie known what she'd been thinking?

"I guess Lambs are supposed to be glamorous or something," Susie said. "I love how you do your eyes."

"Thanks." Gloria thought she might actually get to like Susie. How very strange.

"When I got bid, the girls in the dorm said, 'Oh, Susie, how'd you ever get into Lamb? It's so *exclusive!*' So I went around on cloud nine for about a week—"

Susie sighed. "Mitsy says I've got a chip on my shoulder. She says I've got to stop talking about how much money the other girls have. She says I'll just make trouble for myself. She says ladies don't discuss money—but—oh, I don't know. The rest of you girls are all from big cities, and I'm from this tiny, little town nobody's every heard of—just a bend in the road with a gas station, and my dad owns the gas station—and I keep thinking maybe I should have pledged Dee Gee."

Gloria's sudden insight felt exactly like the "ah-ha" experience she'd learned about in rat-psych: Susie was just as worried about fitting in as she was. "Well, I'm really glad you didn't pledge Dee Gee."

For the first time Susie gave her a wholly ingenuous smile—a smile as spontaneous as a child's. When she smiles like that, Gloria thought, she isn't just pretty, she's truly beautiful—and she decided to give Susie one of the lectures she gave herself late at night when she was tossing and turning, sick with worry. "You know what they say: the hardest thing with fraternities is staying in, but the hardest thing with sororities is getting in. Well, we got in, didn't we? If they hadn't wanted us, they wouldn't have bid us."

"Yeah, I guess that's right."

"Sure it is. We've made it. The hard part's over. We just have to do what they tell us. That shouldn't be too hard, should it?"

"Huh-uh."

"I worry about fitting in too, but we're going to do OK. Pretty soon it'll be all over, and we'll wonder what we were so worried about."

Again Susie gave her that stunning smile. "Yeah," she said, "we'll show 'em, won't we?"

In the next few weeks Gloria worried about that "we." Looking for clues, she kept going over their conversation; if she'd said or done anything to make Susie like her, she couldn't figure out what it could possibly have been, but Susie seemed to think they'd become the best of friends. They paired up automatically at house functions; wheeling her bike, Gloria walked Susie back to the women's dorm every night; by spring, Gloria realized that she looked forward to seeing her, that she did enjoy her company—that she'd come to rely on her.

Gloria was flattered that someone as pretty and successful (and blonde!) as Susie had picked her for a friend, and she liked Susie's irreverent sense of humor. Susie was a natural mimic; when they were alone together, she could reduce

Gloria to helpless laughter with her imitations of the girls in their chapter. Susie made fun of everything; her version of the Lamb "Dixie" song went: "Oh, I'm so happy that I am a—snooty, rich, and bitchy Lambda!" But, oddly enough, she could also be the most gung-ho of the pledges. "We shouldn't ever forget," she told Gloria, "when we're out in public, we're representing Delta Lambda," and Gloria knew that she meant every word of it. Gloria still thought that she and Susie had hardly anything in common, but, as long as they talked about their sorority, they had plenty to talk about, and Susie, after all, wasn't much more of an unlikely a friend than Binkie Eberhardt had been.

Over spring break Gloria got her hair cut. In high school she'd worn a versatile pageboy that converted quickly to a bouncy, *Seventeen* ponytail that went perfectly with a letter sweater, bobby socks, and a cheerleader's skirt—but she had, she was sure, outgrown her cheerleader persona (or at least she hoped she had), and she returned to Briarville with a shorter, more mature and sophisticated style that, if not exactly like Morgan's, had at least been inspired by it. Morgan said exactly what Gloria wanted to hear—"Devastating!"—and took Gloria out for a pitcher of beer at the Blue Cellar. Gloria didn't like beer but drank it anyway and got tipsy for the first time in her life. Morgan got somewhat more than tipsy and gave Gloria advice on making out: "If he's losing interest, just stick your ole tongue in his ear—"

Gloria had gone out with twenty-two different boys in high school (she'd kept exact count in her diary) and had gone steady with six of them, but the most she'd ever allowed any boy to do was put his hand on her breast (*over* her bra, absolutely never *under* it), and the farthest she'd ever gone with anyone—even with her steadies—had been kissing with her mouth open. And she had never intentionally teased a boy—yet this was apparently what Morgan was telling her to do. "In *his ear?*" Gloria said. She wasn't absolutely sure that Morgan wasn't kidding her.

"You bet. Believe it or not, it's an erogenous zone. Just slip your tongue on in that little ole hole and squish it around. He'll go right through the roof!"

Morgan ordered another pitcher of beer. "You know," she said, her eyes sparkling, "when you're really getting to him—the way it gets all stiff down along his pants leg—?"

"Uh-huh," Gloria said, hoping she didn't look as wide-eyed as she felt.

"You just let your hand rest on it, real light, just like you don't quite know what you're doing."

"Uh-huh. But what if he, ah—" Gloria wanted to say, "gets too rough," but she couldn't make the words come out.

"Well, sure, Gloria, if you keep on going, he's going to, ah—you know," Morgan said. She must have totally misinterpreted Gloria's question.

Gloria's head was spinning; she didn't know whether it was the beer or the conversation. She was dying to ask, "You mean you actually let a boy *ejaculate?*" (That was the word used in the medical books she'd secretly read hiding in the stacks of the Ohio County Public Library.) But she couldn't possibly ask that; what if that wasn't what Morgan had meant at all? She'd be so mortified she'd die on the spot. "Yes, but—I mean, do you really, ah—" She gave up and just looked at Morgan across the table.

Morgan leaned closer to whisper. "Only if you really like him, and not too often or he'll think you're cheap. Most of the time, you stop him. You can tell when he's just about there, and then you stop him. You've always got to leave him wanting more, you know? Then you can be darned sure he'll call you up again!"

Morgan told Gloria how to get out of a car with a boy she liked. "Let him open the door for you, then you swing your legs around, and you slide out of the car so your skirt stays on the seat for just a second—you know, so he gets a real good look—not all the way to Dallas, mind you—and then, zip, you stand up and smooth it all down, and you pretend nothing's happened. Ye gods, girl, with legs like you've got, you'll drive them absolutely nuts!"

"Really?"

"Natch. Boys are suckers for that stuff. If you've got a full skirt on, you can tease a guy half to death with it—but you've got to be real cool and icy, like butter wouldn't melt in your mouth, you know what I mean?"

"Uh-huh."

"You can sure tell you were a cheerleader," Morgan said, "but you're in college now, so stop bounding around like a little kid—or like somebody's puppy dog. Wear heels. Boys love heels. When you walk in a room, take your time. Make people notice you."

Gloria didn't think she was quite ready to start teasing boys with a full skirt (and, as to sliding her tongue into their ears or letting her hand rest lightly on their erect penises—well, those things could wait even longer), but she practiced walking in heels like Morgan—as arrogantly as Morgan—with her head held high and her breasts thrust forward, with a self-assured, womanly swing to her hips. When she walked into a room, she paused and counted to five.

The other pledges complained constantly. Because she didn't want to be different—or, more accurately, didn't want to *be seen* to be different—Gloria complained too, but her heart wasn't in it. How could it be? She'd gone from having to decide what to do with every hour of her spare time to having her entire life organized for her. She'd gone from being sad, scared, and lonely to having an instant circle of friends—or at least friendly people. Her only real friend was Susie—if she could call her a friend; she still didn't know her very well and wasn't sure she ever would.

Gloria was, as she wrote in her diary, "happy enough," but she added: "I'm not exactly sure why I'm doing this. Is there a real *me* somewhere inside? Sometimes I think I must be the most outer-directed girl in all of America." And sometimes when she was falling asleep, the secret watcher said things she couldn't bear to write down: "You may look like you fit in," it said, "you may look like a normal girl, and you may fool Morgan, and you may fool Susie, and you may fool all the other pledges, and you may fool every single Lamb, but you'll never really fit in, not in your heart, because you're irrevocably different from those girls. You're a strange, dark Gypsy girl. No one knows you, and no one ever will."

On the Sunday night before the opening of "Hell Week"—as the Greeks themselves still called it even though the president of the college had, several years before, changed the name to "Greek Week"—the pledges were assembled in the recreation room. Delta Lambda, they were told, did not practice hazing. For one thing, hazing was unladylike, and, therefore, no sorority ever practiced hazing; for another thing, the president had expressly forbidden hazing on campus, so now even the fraternities had given it up. ("You bet," Susie whispered to Gloria, "and pigs fly.") So Hell Week at Delta Lambda—that is, Greek Week—had nothing do with hazing, but rather with the ancient rituals and traditions of the sorority—as had been carefully explained several years ago to the Dean of Women when the Briarville chapter of Delta Lambda had, briefly, lost its charter. Therefore, following these ancient rituals and traditions, pledges were required to report to the house for inspection each morning at seven-thirty; they were to take all their meals at the house and, except for classes, were not permitted to leave the house, where they would be given special duties. Throughout the week, they were to wear suits with all the proper accessories. (There was a collective groan from the pledges.) For dinner, they were to change into cocktail dresses. During the week, they must enter the house through the back door; they were not permitted to speak to each other and could speak to the sisters only if spoken to; they were to address the sisters by their last names as "Miss so-and-so," and they must request permission—by raising their hands—to be allowed to pass through doorways and archways. Were there any questions?

By then the pledges knew what was what, so there were no questions. Out on the street afterward, Susie said to Gloria, "Gee, I'm sure glad Delta Lambda doesn't practice hazing."

Gloria could not imagine riding her bike in a suit while carrying a cocktail dress, so she was forced to beg her grandfather for a ride onto campus every morning during Hell Week. On Monday morning the pledges were inspected at seven-thirty by several yawning sisters in pajamas. One pledge, Julie, flunked the inspection and was sent back to the dorm to try again. Then, after breakfast, Gloria walked to her history class in suit, hat, gloves, and heels; she felt wildly conspicuous. Fraternity boys whistled and applauded and yelled at her: "Hey, Lamb, how's it going?"

"Just great," she answered them. Her class over, she rushed back to the house and was assigned her duties for the day: organizing and color-coordinating Morgan's wardrobe and shining her sorority pin. Gloria's afternoon class was the big English Lit survey; they were doing Eliot, and Gloria usually had something to say in that class and certainly had a lot to say about Eliot, but when she walked in, Dr. Stauffer, who was arranging his notes at the lectern, bowed to her and said: "Do mine eyes deceive me, or has our own Miss Cotter pledged fair Delta Lambda?" The other students laughed and applauded; they were all staring at her. The only thing Gloria had ever liked about being so dark was that she could blush without it showing; she felt the blood blazing in her face, forced herself to smile faintly (the ole Mona Lisa) and carefully removed her gloves, folded them, and laid them next to her purse; that performance had used up every ounce of her courage; speaking, she knew, was an impossibility. She sat through the class staring straight ahead at the blackboard; she took notes, but she knew they would prove to be meaningless. She would, she was sure, learn something important from this experience, but she didn't have the faintest idea what it might turn out to be.

After class she hurried back to the house, finished her work on Morgan's wardrobe, and changed into her cocktail dress for dinner. The elegantly attired pledges served dinner to the sisters and then filed out to eat their own dinner in the kitchen; sophomore Lambs took turns monitoring them to make sure they didn't speak. After dinner they cleared the main table, and their own table, and were led back into the recreation room where they sang sorority songs. By the time Gloria called her grandfather to pick her up, it was nearly eleven. She was exhausted—but so tense and restless she knew it would take her hours to get to sleep; all she could think about was that she'd have to get up and do it all over again the next day.

By Friday, the pledges were stumbling around the Delta Lambda house with all the *joie de vivre* of freshly disinterred zombies. Gloria estimated that she'd been averaging four or five hours of sleep a night; when she did sleep, she kept dreaming that she was late for obscure classes she'd forgotten, or that she was trying to get dressed for some extraordinarily important event but couldn't find the right clothes. Her eyes burned and watered; she couldn't concentrate; her feet and legs and lower back ached from wearing nothing but heels; she was so exhausted she'd actually fallen asleep standing up while stuck in the hallway waiting for a sister to appear so she could request permission to walk through the archway into the living room, and she knew that she was only a breath away from a serious, uncontrollable crying jag. The rule against the pledges talking to each other, she thought, was truly demonic; she felt isolated inside a cage of numbing misery, and she was afraid that she was losing her ability to carry on even the most moronic of conversations. And, no matter how often she told herself that it was just a little thing—something that shouldn't bother her at all—she found it humiliating to have to call Morgan "Miss Clendenning." It's only a week, she kept telling herself; we're not actually being tortured or anything like that; compared to what the fraternity boys go through, this is nothing—but her mind kept conjuring up lurid, melodramatic images of the Red Chinese brainwashing techniques from the Korean War.

That night, after dinner, the pledges were lined up in a row in the living room. "Tomorrow is the most solemn and important day of Hell Week," Mitsy told them, reading from prepared notes. Since the sorority had been founded, she said, the pledges had always, on the evening of the sixth day, undergone the Trial of the Three Questions. Over the years, many of Delta Lambda's rituals had changed—been updated—but the sorority had never permitted even the teensiest change in the Trial of the Three Questions. "You will perform that ritual tomorrow exactly as it was performed by the founding mothers in 1887. Think of all the sisters who have gone before you, and do your best to be worthy to follow in their footsteps."

Then Morgan consulted her notes and told the pledges that if they thought things had been rough up until now, they were sadly kidding themselves. The Trial of the Three Questions, she said, would be the most terrible ordeal they'd ever faced in their lives, and if any pledge failed, her pledge pin would be taken away and she would be escorted out of the house and never allowed to enter it again. "You must not speak—not a word, not to anyone—until you face the Trial of the Three Questions. Any pledge caught talking won't be allowed to continue. What we want tomorrow, girls, is your very best. Nothing less will do."

Weeks ago they had been told to buy plain white dresses with high necklines, skirts to the ankle, and long sleeves that covered their arms—and matching white flats to go with them. They were to wear these initiation dresses tomorrow. They did not have to be at the house until ten, but they were to bathe in the morning. "Wash your hair, girls," Mitsy said, "and don't set it. Don't do anything at all to it, just towel it dry and brush it straight back. No barrettes or ribbons. Scrub your face, get every speck of makeup off. Take your nail polish off. No foundation garments. Except for your pledge pin, don't wear any jewelry, not even a watch. You're to be absolutely *unadorned*."

Gloria was so apprehensive she didn't get to sleep until nearly dawn and then woke up promptly at six-thirty. She was too nervous to eat; she soaked in the bathtub for an hour and wondered if the Delta Lambda sisters knew that what they'd assigned the pledges was a purification ritual. She hadn't been told to shave, but she did anyway (her *soul* wouldn't have felt purified unless she had). Dressed, she saw in the mirror a scrubbed, scared, tired little kid with circles under her eyes, an angry pimple on her chin, a pinched weasel face, and flat, short, dead-black hair. So much for the idea that the Lambs are the cutest girls on campus, she thought.

When her grandfather dropped her at the house at ten, she found all the curtains closed and no lights lit; she couldn't hear anyone talking; it was spooky—a timeless twilight and a dead quiet. Debbie, a sophomore sister she didn't know very well, handed her an envelope and whispered in her ear: "Walk away from the house until you're sure you're alone, then open the envelope and follow the instructions. Don't forget, you're not allowed to speak today—*not a word!*"

Gloria walked a block up Sorority Row. After a week in heels, her flats made her feel oddly unbalanced. She turned left, looked back, and saw no one. She felt as though she'd entered into a state far beyond mere exhaustion; she was a walking oxymoron: giddy, inconsequential, and nearly weightless, like one of those elusive gases she'd created in the Canden High chemistry lab; at the same time, her body was made out of lead, or mud, or some other sullen, recalcitrant substance, and even walking the block away from the house had required a monstrous effort. She opened her envelope. "Go to the vacant lot behind the Admin building," she read, "and pick a bouquet of wild flowers. Bring your bouquet back to the house and go directly to your Big Sister's room."

Gloria was surprised to find daffodils growing wild in the vacant lot; it was too good to be true: daffodils were Delta Lambda's flower. Thinking of Wordsworth, she picked a dozen of them—and some small blue flowers to set them off, and ferns and grasses, and made an exquisite bouquet. It was a lovely spring morning. If you were about to face the most terrible ordeal of your life, she thought, you couldn't ask for a nicer day to do it.

When she returned to the house, she expected Morgan to be in her room but instead found another note: "Write your full name on the card and bind it to your bouquet with ribbons. Place your bouquet on the floor of the living room and kneel in front of the wall." A pen, a white vellum card with a hole punched in it, and two lengths of ribbon, one white and one gold, had been left for her. She followed the instructions.

Susie and Sharon and Julie were already kneeling in front of a wall in the living room when Gloria came in; she placed her bouquet on the floor with theirs and knelt next to them. She didn't know whether she was allowed to look around—no one had told her not to—so she watched the rest of her pledge class come in, place their bouquets on the floor, and kneel. Then Mitsy suddenly appeared; unlike the pledges, she was perfectly made-up and as formally dressed as if she were going to church; her expression was grave. She gestured for the pledges to rise, led them into the basement, and told them to kneel in front of the brick wall by the furnace. A row of towels had been neatly folded for them to kneel on. "You don't have to stay perfectly still," she told them, "but don't look around."

It was dark and chilly in the basement, and even with the towels, the concrete floor felt monstrously hard. They can't possibly leave us here for longer than a few minutes, Gloria thought; this isn't a fraternity, so they wouldn't do something like that to us—but, after an interminable amount of time had passed, she had to fight down a horrific, irrational panic. She felt her heartbeat getting faster, and she thought, I can't stand this; in another few minutes I'll jump up and run out—and then I'll have to de-pledge. "Yes, you can stand it," the secret watcher told her. "You've had a lot of practice at standing things, remember?"

It wasn't too bad if she shifted her weight every few minutes—forward onto her knees then back to rest on her heels—and she began playing some of the games she'd taught herself at Fairhaven. Reciting poetry in her mind usually worked; as a grim joke, she tried to see how much of "The Prisoner of Chillon" she knew off by heart (two full stanzas and parts of several others). She ran through "Prufrock" and some Auden and Yeats. Then she began to play games with the patch of brick wall directly in front of her. Her eyes had adjusted to the dark, and she could see lots of details. She'd close her eyes and draw her patch of wall in her mind; when she thought she had it—every chip in every brick, every discoloration and oddly shaped bit of plaster—she'd look to see if she'd forgotten anything. She must have done this exercise a dozen times when she began to fall asleep. She'd nod off, begin to fall, and catch herself. They can't possibly leave us here much longer, she thought. This isn't just hazing; this is honest-to-God sadism. She leaned carefully forward, pressed her forehead into the bricks, and promptly fell asleep. She woke several seconds later when she heard one of her fellow pledges sobbing. Oh, for Pete's sake, Gloria thought—and was surprised at how angry she was—stop it! It's not that bad yet.

"Come on, girls," Mitsy said, her voice sudden and loud (had she been standing behind them, waiting?), "you can get up now. Follow me."

In the living room they were told to take off their shoes and stockings, pick up their bouquets, and line up in the downstairs hallway. Then Mitsy arranged them by height, and they were left alone standing in a row. Gloria had seen Susie sending her a significant look, but she hadn't dared to return it, and now she didn't dare to look anywhere but at the wall directly in front of her; she felt sick with apprehension. Somewhere far away in the house a small bell began to ring slowly—and continued to ring as steadily as a metronome. At first the sound was annoying, but then Gloria became so used to it that when it stopped, she felt her skin prickle. She heard footsteps, saw that Mitsy was coming back—

was now wearing a long, black ceremonial robe and a circlet of gold leaves in her hair. She passed down the row of pledges, giving each a slender white candle.

"You are about to perform a very solemn ritual," she said. "Hold your bouquet cradled in your left arm and your candle in your right hand. I'll lead you. Carry yourself with dignity, and don't smile. Don't look to the right or the left. Don't look up. Look directly at the feet of the girl in front of you. Try to keep in step with her. We're going to be going quite slowly. If you concentrate on the girl in front of you, we'll all end up in step—and remember, *never look up*."

The pace was even slower than Gloria had expected—even slower than a wedding march. Susie was in front of her, so she stared hard at the heels of Susie's bare feet under the hem of her long dress and fell into step with her. It took so much concentration that Gloria only gradually became aware that Mitsy was leading them down the hall and into the common room. Gloria was amazed at how much she could see with her peripheral vision—well, not exactly *see*; it was more like a blurry visual intuition. The common room was dark, the windows draped with what seemed to be black velvet, and the Delta Lambda sisters, all in black ceremonial robes, were standing in a large circle facing into the center of the room. Each sister was holding a lit white candle, and the candle light was the only illumination in the room. Mitsy was leading the pledges in a clockwise circle just inside the circle of sisters.

Gloria suddenly imagined the pledges as the Lambs must be seeing them: the girls in their long white dresses passing in single file, scrubbed and unadorned, looking very young. Since January, two of the original fourteen had de-pledged, so there were only twelve now, walking in step with each other in a stately, artificial way, their eyes staring fixedly forward and downward, carrying fresh bouquets of spring flowers—"like lambs to the slaughter," she couldn't help thinking, or even "lambs of God"—twelve virgins (were they all virgins? she wondered; surely they must all be virgins), fertility maidens, corn maidens—but were they going to be sacrificed to make the crops grow?

Mitsy led them in a complete circle around the room and then stopped. "Let us pray," she said. Gloria closed her eyes. "Dear Lord, we ask thy blessing upon this chapter of the Delta Lambda Sorority and upon the solemn rituals we are about to perform. We pray that these pledges here assembled will be found worthy to be received into this circle of sisters, that they will be found worthy to add their light to our own. And we, the sisters of Delta Lambda Sorority, ask that our hearts be purified by the grace of thy Holy Spirit so that we may be worthy to receive them. We ask these things in the name of Jesus Christ, your only son, our Lord. Amen."

Oh, help, Gloria thought, *this is serious*. She opened her eyes and saw that the sister nearest her, a junior named Barbara, had stepped forward and was lighting Gloria's candle with her own. Then Mitsy led the pledges through another complete circuit of the room.

The small bell began ringing again; now it was much closer, but Gloria, her eyes still glued to Susie's heels, couldn't see where the sound was coming from. "Pledges," Mitsy said, "turn toward the pledge behind you." Gloria turned around so that she was facing Julie's back, and Mitsy led them in a third circuit of the room; this time they were going counterclockwise; as Gloria knew from fairy tales, that was the direction against the sun called widdershins—an ominous, sinister direction. When Mitsy had completed the circuit, she led the pledges out of the circle of sisters. As each pledge left the circle, Morgan, with a long, gold candle snuffer, extinguished her candle.

Gloria didn't dare to look up at Morgan; she saw her own flame extinguished; the air was thick with the stink of snuffed candles. Gloria followed Julie through the door and into the hall. Since they'd been there, someone had draped all the windows, and the hall was so dark that all she could see ahead of her were shadowy shapes. Someone reached out of the darkness and took her candle from her.

The pledges were led first into the living room where they left their bouquets behind, then into the dining room. Gloria was crying, although she couldn't have said why. She saw that some of the other pledges were crying too. Places had been set for them at the dining room table. Sophomore sisters, still in their long black robes, escorted them to their places and held their chairs for them. Each pledge received two slices of plain bread and a cup of hot water. Gloria wondered if the water had been heated as a bizarre punishment, but when she began to sip it, she was grateful for the warmth. Susie was sitting opposite her, and their eyes met. Neither of them changed expression, but they looked at each other for a long moment. Gloria was as grateful for Susie's level gaze as she was for the warm water, and she imagined Susie saying, "Hang in there, Gloria. We'll show 'em."

After lunch, each pledge was given a work assignment; Gloria's was to make all the beds in the house. The drapes were drawn everywhere, and all she could hear were the furtive movements of the other pledges going about their jobs. Either most of the sisters had left the house, or they, too, were obeying a rule of silence. Gloria made forty-two beds. She tried not to think about the Trial of the Three Questions, but she couldn't help it. Whatever it was, she desperately wanted it to be over.

At what should have been dinner time—Gloria had been famished hours ago, and now she had a throbbing, sick headache—another sophomore sister, Linda, told Gloria to get her bouquet from the living room and to kneel on the window seat just off the landing on the second floor. "If you have to go," Linda whispered, "you know where the bathroom is—but come right back.

Don't look around. Hold your bouquet. Don't put it down. Stay kneeling there till we come and get you for the Three Questions."

In comparison to the towel on the concrete floor of the basement, the cushion in the window seat was so soft that Gloria felt absurdly grateful. She settled her weight back onto her heels and prepared to wait. When this is over, she promised herself, I'll never, ever again, not in my entire life, not for any reason whatsoever, spend even five seconds kneeling.

She watched the daylight fade away through the crack at the edge of the drapes, and her mind—she'd had it under reasonably good control most of the day—began to run away with her. Everything she'd read about the human personality described it as *resilient*; but she didn't feel particularly resilient; she felt as fragile as an egg shell (and even more fragile than that, but she didn't want to search for a more effective metaphor). She was sure that if she'd been a POW in Korea, they could have washed her brain in no time at all, lickety-split. But what about her inner core? That was what was supposed to be so resilient it could survive almost anything, but did she *have* an inner core? Sometimes—like right now, for instance—she wasn't sure she had any core whatsoever.

This is only a sorority initiation, she kept telling herself. They do not torture people in sororities; if they did, they'd lose their charter. But she couldn't convince herself; she felt as though she'd been tortured *already*; they'd been torturing her all week, and they'd tortured her all day, and the Trial of the Three Questions was supposed to be the worst of all—oh, God!

She thought about the founding mothers of Delta Lambda. Their pictures hung in the living room—four old ladies looking utterly harmless and benign; the pledges had been required to memorize their biographies. Their maiden names had been Bedelia Raines Cox, Mary Alice Coughlin Stuart, Elizabeth Lee McAndrews, and Frances Grubner Oglethorp, and the Lambs commonly referred to them as "Del, Mary, Betsy, and Fran." Two of them, Mary and Fran, were still alive; the Briarville chapter had actually received a note from Fran (framed, it also hung in the living room). And Del, Mary, Betsy, and Fran, when they'd been hardly more than girls—in fact, Fran had been exactly Gloria's age—when they'd been attending their small, sappy women's college in Virginia in 1887, had founded Delta Lambda Sorority—and had invented the Trial of the Three Questions. Del, Mary, Betsy, and Fran had married, had produced children and grandchildren and great-grandchildren; they were model Christian ladies and had devoted their lives to Service and Good Works, and so surely Del, Mary, Betsy, and Fran would not have invented anything in which pledges were tortured, would they?

Gloria imagined them like the characters in a girls' novel. "Hey, you know what we ought to do?" Del says one night when they're sitting around bored out of their minds. "Let's found a sorority."

"Terrific idea," Mary says, "and we can dream up some strange, scary, secret rituals and *put ourselves though them.*"

"Wow, right," Betsy says, "what kind of rituals?"

"Hey, I've got a great idea, girls," Fran says. She's the youngest, and she still loves playing dress-up. "We'll put on long, white gowns and walk around with candles."

"Yeah, and we'll carry spring flowers, so we'll be symbols of spring and rebirth."

"Good idea, and then after that we'll have to do something really awful and spooky."

"Yeah, a real *ordeal.*"

Gloria shifted her weight onto her knees. She couldn't imagine what that real ordeal could possibly be. What had Del, Mary, Betsy, and Fran been *reading?* She couldn't remember if Frazer had been published by 1887, and probably nice girls in a Virginia women's college wouldn't have read Frazer anyway. It was amazing actually: when Del, Mary, Betsy, and Fran had founded Delta Lambda, it had been, she thought, an act of self-creation practically *ex nihilo.*

Gloria heard movement behind her; she forced herself not to look around. Someone—she had no idea who—without saying a word, was wrapping a blindfold over her eyes and fastening it. She heard the person leave—or she thought she did. Her entire body was rigid; she realized she'd been holding her breath and exhaled slowly. When she was absolutely sure she was alone, she risked touching the blindfold; it wasn't anything as simple as a folded scarf; there were large, round pads over her eyes. She couldn't see even a suggestion of light. Somewhere a clock was ticking; it didn't seem possible that she could be hearing the grandfather clock down in the living room, but that was the only clock she remembered. She coaxed her body to relax, but it didn't obey; she bent forward until she felt her face pressed into the curtains. She wished she could fall asleep again, but she knew she couldn't.

Her time sense wasn't working right; she had no real estimation of how long she'd been left there, blindfolded, clutching her bouquet, when she thought she heard someone crying. Without any prompting from her mind, her body had jerked upright; she forced herself to settle back into a kneeling position, her weight on her heels. The hair on her arms and neck was standing up; her stomach had clenched into a fiery fist, and she felt as though her hearing had expanded out to the size of a football stadium—every inch of her was listening; then, when she was ready to tell herself that she'd imagined it, she heard it again; it was far away, muffled through closed doors, but unmistakable—a sound that could not possibly be faked—a girl crying. Oh, God, she thought, *what are they doing to her?*

Gloria had never fainted, but now she was afraid she might do it. Her mouth had gone dry; she was sweating; her head was pounding; she couldn't think straight. She began to recite the multiplication tables—a trick that went all the way back to grade school. Breathe, she told herself. When she could think clearly again, she realized that she was going to have to throw up. But she knew she couldn't find the bathroom blindfolded—and what if they came to get her and she wasn't there? She tried to swallow, but her mouth was too dry.

Without any warning, she felt hands touch her, and, before she could stop herself, she'd allowed a small, strangled scream to escape. Was that enough to fail me? she thought. They wouldn't fail me for that, would they? It wasn't really *speaking*.

She couldn't tell how many people were around her; there seemed to be one on each side, helping her to stand, guiding her as she walked. She could hear them breathing, but no one was saying a word. She could feel by the pressure of their arms around her waist what they wanted her to do. They stopped, and she guessed that they were just at the top of the front staircase. She felt with her bare foot and found the first step. They guided her down to the main floor. She couldn't tell where they were going, although it seemed to be far into the back of the house. They helped her onto her knees, then pushed her gently over until she was lying face down on the rug, turned slightly to one side as she tried to protect her bouquet cradled in her left arm. Someone pressed a piece of thick string into her right hand.

She had no idea whose voice was whispering to her; she could feel the lips only an inch or so away from her ear. "Crawl. Don't stand up. Follow the string. It'll lead you where you have to go. Don't squash your bouquet. Now *go*."

Gloria crawled away. She wanted to get it over with, and she was hoping she only had to crawl a short way, but the string didn't follow a straight line. Again and again, she was led to a wall; then the string would follow the wall for a few feet and turn to send her back the way she had come. She wondered if there were lights on, if people were standing around silently, watching and grinning and enjoying the show. If they were, she'd be damned if she'd cry—although she *had* cried when they'd made her crawl around the room at Fairhaven. "Crawl, Worm," they'd yelled at her, and every time she'd tried to get up, they'd knocked her down. The biggest girl, the ringleader, Sally—"Sal" the big girls called her—had said, "Shut up, Worm. If you yell, you'll really be sorry. Now crawl, Worm, crawl." Gloria had crawled, sobbing, trying not to make too much noise. "Tell us your name," and when Gloria had said, "Gloria," Sally had stepped down hard on the back of her hand. "No. Wrong. Come on, nigger baby, tell us your *real* name."

Gloria was crying now, crawling. The string had led her to yet another wall, and it was so frustrating it made her cry harder—and she'd completely broken down; she would have told them anything. "Worm! My name's Worm."

Gloria was crying so hard she had to stop for a moment. You're not at Fairhaven, she told herself. You're not, you're not, you're not—and then the secret watcher reappeared at the back of her mind and said, "OK, Gloria, don't be melodramatic. You never once *really* thought you were back at Fairhaven, did you? Calm down. If you keep on crawling, you'll get to the end."

The string was leading her in a straight line now. Her knees and elbows were burning. She scrabbled forward, felt hands on her shoulders. Someone had stopped her. Someone unfastened her blindfold and took it away and pushed her forward. She could see flickering light. She crawled toward the light.

A nasty smell—sickly sweet and smokey—nearly choked her. "Rise, pledge," a voice said. It had sounded like Mitsy, but Gloria couldn't be sure. "Approach the fire," the voice said. Gloria stood up and forced herself to stop crying.

High screens on either side of the fireplace cast the light from the burning logs directly forward—toward Gloria as she approached—and blocked it off at the sides. She didn't know how far she was supposed to go, so she walked directly up to the fireplace and stopped only a couple of feet in front of it. Even though the light was dim and ruddy, it seemed impossibly brilliant after the darkness in the blindfold. "State your full name, pledge," the voice said. It was coming from behind the screen on Gloria's left.

She had to clear her throat several times before she could get the words to come out: "Gloria Merriman Cotter."

"Will anyone come forth to stand with this pledge before the fire?" the voice said.

"I will."

Gloria heard a rustle, and then she saw Morgan walking around from behind the screen. She was so glad that her eyes filled again. Morgan, wearing a long, black robe, stood next to her facing the fire.

"Who stands with this pledge?"

"Morgan Louise Colfax Clendenning."

"Do you swear that this pledge is of good character?"

"I do so swear."

"You may now administer the oath."

Morgan held out a book toward Gloria. "This is a Bible," she whispered. "Put your right hand on it, and repeat after me."

Morgan whispered the oath in phrases, and Gloria repeated them: "I, Gloria Merriman Cotter—swear on this holy Bible—before these witnesses here gathered—that I will look into my heart and hide nothing—and that I will speak only the truth—and the whole truth—so help me God."

"Pledge, you will now undergo the Trial of the Three Questions," the voice said.

"I'm here to help you, Gloria," Morgan whispered. "Don't answer immediately. Let me explain the questions to you first. Then think about them—and take your time."

"This is the first question," the voice said. "What evil hast thou done?"

The biblical language pierced Gloria like an arrow, and she began to cry so hard she knew everyone could hear it. She felt utterly humiliated. "Think of the worst thing you've ever done in your life and tell us about it," Morgan whispered. "You know, like the thing you're most ashamed of—"

Gloria's mind was filling with images and ideas so fast she couldn't begin to catch them all. One of them—a big and important one—was that she had not so much done evil in her life as had it done to her; the things she was most ashamed of had been forced upon her: the pale pink snowsuit, Fairhaven, Worm— Then she knew—and knew without a doubt—the worst thing she'd done, and she couldn't tell them about *that*; it was just too ugly. But she'd sworn to God to tell the truth. Now she understood why this was the worst ordeal of all: she *had* to tell the truth.

She tried to speak, but all she could do was sob. "Take your time," Morgan said.

"I went to—" Gloria started. She couldn't do it. Breathe, she told herself, and she breathed.

She started again: "I went to boarding school, and I was— I didn't have any friends. Oh, later on I did, but not for the first couple of years, and—everybody made fun of me, and I was—really miserable. And then another little girl came, and she was even more of—more of an outcast than I was. She only lasted a couple months. A little fat girl. And they called her 'pigeon.' And it was—like a lot of their nicknames, it was absolutely perfect, because she looked *exactly* like a pigeon—a little beak nose and a big, round, fat stomach sticking out and little, skinny match-stick legs—

"And they really tormented her. Wherever she went, people would coo—like a pigeon—coo, coo, coo. And I was the only one who was nice to her, and she thought I was her friend. And one day we were all outside, and there weren't any teachers around, and a bunch of the girls made a ring around her and started cooing—and—I don't know, I was just so glad they weren't picking on me for a change, and one of the bigger girls looked at me and went 'coo,' and it was— You know, like she was saying, 'Come on, Worm—' That's what they called me. So it was like, 'Come on, Worm, you do it too, *or else.*' And so I went 'coo.' And that girl, that little fat girl, looked at me—she gave me one look, and it was so hurt—so hurt—so betrayed—"

Gloria could see the little fat girl clearly in her mind—that single, awful betrayed look—and she felt shame; she hugged her bouquet and bent forward, crying. "I'm so sorry," she said.

"Pledge," the voice said, "cast thy flowers into the fire."

Gloria wasn't sure she'd heard right. Her bouquet? The one she'd picked so carefully and carried around most of the day and tried her best not to squash as she'd been crawling all over the damned house? She looked at Morgan, and Morgan made a gesture: yes, into the fire. Gloria threw in the bouquet. She saw that others had gone ahead of her; she could see the shreds of their burned ribbons. She saw her flowers wither in the flame; she saw her name burning on the white vellum card; she saw her name extinguished in the fire.

"This is the second question," the voice said. "What lovest thou?"

"That doesn't mean a boy," Morgan whispered, "or even your family. It's not a who, it's a what—you know, in your life. The really important things—what you live for."

The moment she'd heard the question, Gloria had known what the only possible answer could be. She froze; she was mute—because she could never possibly find the words that would make them understand, and, even if she did, then they'd know how strange and abnormal she was, and she'd be an outcast again. They certainly wouldn't want her in their sorority. What can I make up? she thought desperately. Will they know I'm lying?

"It's OK," Morgan whispered. "Take your time," and then, as though she could read Gloria's mind, she added, "just tell the truth."

The truth. What was that anyway? And Gloria was hearing—had been hearing for several seconds—a strange, annoying sound. It was beginning to frighten her. It was a nasty, pulsing sound like dry grain being shaken in a coffee can—and then she realized that she was making that sound herself; it was her initiation dress rustling—she was shaking that hard. She had to say something. "When I was at boarding school—" she said, "When I was at boarding school—"

She closed her eyes. She had a peculiar illusion: she could still see the fire. "I used to run away and read all the time—" She couldn't control her voice. It sounded small and strangled. "It was the only time I was happy." She opened her eyes. The fire burning in the fireplace looked exactly like the one that had been burning behind her eyelids—how positively bizarre! She was shaking so hard by now she was afraid she might fall down.

"I liked poetry the best," she said in a small, flat, stupid, child's voice. The worst thing was that she wasn't talking to anyone at all; Morgan was just a shadow on her right, and there was nothing in front of her but the fire, and if other people were listening, they were invisible, so how could she go on talking to nobody? Especially when she was saying such ridiculous things? Dear God, she prayed, please, at least let me stop shaking.

Instantly something in her mind spoke Roethke's line: "This shaking keeps me steady—" and, with that, she was flooded with words, with poems and fragments of poems—and Morgan was whispering, "We can't hear you," so Gloria must actually have said something out loud, and before she had a chance to wonder what it was, she heard herself saying: *"This shaking keeps me steady. I should know —"*

"That's Roethke," she said. "It's a poem. It's—" and, mysteriously, she had the entire poem in her mind at once. "Oh God!" she cried out because an enormous wave of something—it was like an electrical shock—had swept through her, and she was crying so hard she thought she would drown in her tears.

She kept trying to breathe. She did breathe. "It's *for me!* I never saw it before. 'The lowly worm climbs up a winding stair'"—and, as she saw that poem, whole and blazing, she understood it, whole and blazing; Roethke's poem was all the poems, and she was the poem, whole and blazing: "That's what I love," she cried out, "It's all in the poem. It's the heart, it's the fire, it's the center, it's everything! Nobody understands. It's 'the foul rag and bone shop of the heart' and it's 'the nightingales singing near the Convent of the Sacred Heart—' and it's 'what falls away is always, and is near—' and it's 'wordless as the flight of birds—' and it's 'nothing is left of the sea but its sound—' and it's 'the word outleaps the world, and light—' It's light, it's light—"

She didn't know how long she'd been speaking or even exactly what she'd said; she'd come back from a strange, blazing place, and she knew she'd utterly disgraced herself. She was just her ordinary self again, and all she could do was cry in an ordinary way.

"Pledge," the voice said, "turn thee unto the darkness."

"Turn around and face the room," Morgan whispered. Gloria turned, heard a scraping noise and a heavy, metallic slam behind her; the light from the fire was cut off and she was truly facing darkness. "This is the third and final question," the voice said. "What wouldst thou ask?"

"This is like a prayer," Morgan whispered. "If you were praying to God, what would you ask for?"

Gloria had to scream to force her voice up through the sea of her tears: "there's a—there's a—" She was trying to say that there was another poem, but she gave up and cried out to God in the words Richard Wilbur had given her: "Please give me—yet another sun to do the shapely thing I have not done!"

"Kneel, pledge," the voice said.

Gloria fell to her knees, let her head drop all the way to the floor. She felt the carpet on her forehead; then she felt Morgan's hands on her shoulders, lifting her up. Through the blur of her tears, she saw lights blazing up everywhere; Morgan was putting something on her head.

"Rise, sister," the voice said. Gloria stood up. She wasn't sure how long she could go on standing; every fiber in her body was shaking. She saw Mitsy walking toward her. Other sisters were walking toward her from behind the screens; they were wearing long black robes and carrying white candles. She felt her head;

Morgan had crowned her with leaves—real, honest-to-God leaves from a tree. She looked at Morgan and saw tears on Morgan's face; an infinitely sweet, searing pain passed through Gloria's body like a ray of light through crystal, and then, for a fraction of a second, she was obliterated.

Gloria must have fallen. Morgan and someone else were helping her up. She couldn't stop crying. "It's OK, Gloria," Morgan said. "You made it. You're in. It's *all over*. Come on, girls, help her. Get her downstairs. She's in shock."

Later, Gloria wouldn't remember how she got downstairs; she would remember sitting in the kitchen, shaking, her teeth chattering, wrapped in a blanket, crying, while they fed her cocoa sip by sip. She kept trying to tell them that she was all right—just fine, as a matter of fact—but she couldn't get the words to come out. Debbie drove her back to her grandparents and helped her into her house.

Wrapped up in her bed, with three blankets over her even though it was a warm night, Gloria kept thinking: I did it; I made it. And then, as she was drifting off to sleep, she thought: *what* shapely thing haven't I done?

The next day the pledges were initiated into Delta Lambda—a procedure that took all afternoon. They were told the secret Greek motto for which the letters Delta Lambda stood, the significance of Delta Lambda's colors, white and gold, of Delta Lambda's symbol, the sun, and flower, the daffodil; they were taught the secret hand clasp; they were told the hidden meanings of the morning bath, the gathering of flowers, the unadorned gowns, the ordeal in the dark chapel, the circle of sisters, the descent into darkness, the mystic meal, the humble work, the twisting path, the ascent toward light, the cleansing fire, the aid of the true sister, the act of repentance, the death of the old spirit and the rebirth of the new. Nothing she heard surprised Gloria; it was as though she'd known much of it already. The pledges took their secret vows, and then they were declared full members of the sorority.

The initiation was followed by a festive dinner. Each new sister received a commemorative crystal goblet etched with the sorority's crest. Mitsy stood and banged her knife on her wine glass to get their attention. "Here's to the new sisters," she said, lifting her glass in a toast. "You girls are just terrif, just great, just super. You're all wonderful girls, and real dolls—and we just couldn't have asked for a better bunch. We're so very glad to have you as sisters, and— What else can I say? Here's to the best darned pledge class we've ever seen!"

After dinner they elected next year's officers. Morgan succeeded Mitsy as president. To her astonishment, Gloria was nominated as the sophomore member of the Pledge Training Committee and won by acclamation.

The new sisters were asked to submit lists of the girls they'd prefer for roommates, and the House Chairman said she would do her best to put friends together. Gloria hadn't lived with roommates since Fairhaven, and she liked her privacy, but there were only a few singles in the house — most of them reserved for seniors — and, besides, she lectured herself, you don't join a sorority to live alone, do you? She liked every girl in her pledge class, but she still didn't know any of them very well. Susie was her obvious choice because they'd spent so much time together and all the other girls seemed to regard them as the best of friends, but she still didn't feel entirely comfortable with Susie and couldn't quite imagine having a blonde majorette beauty queen for a roommate. The only girl she would have preferred over anyone else was Julie Sanhoeven who was quiet and shy and, like Gloria, a straight-A student and an English major (and had brown hair), but she couldn't simply put one name on her list, could she? That wouldn't look right. She didn't, however, want to end up in one of the big, four-girl rooms, so she wrote: "Anybody is fine with me, but I'd like a small room if possible." When next year's room assignments were posted, she found that she'd been paired with Susie. She wasn't surprised; something about it felt inevitable.

"Hey, isn't that great?" Susie said, and what could Gloria possibly do but agree? Susie couldn't wait to check out their room. It overlooked Sorority Row and was, Gloria thought, one of the loveliest in the house. "Which bed do you want?" Susie asked.

Gloria badly wanted the bed by the window, but she said, "It doesn't matter to me. You choose."

"I'd better take the one by the door. I spend half my life in the shower. Oh, isn't this wonderful, Gloria? We're going to have so much fun next year."

We are? Gloria thought.

For days after the initiation Gloria felt a sweet melancholy she couldn't define; it was, as she described it in her diary, "a mixture of exhaustion and relief, a diffuse sorrow and a fragile happiness," and then she added, "those still aren't the right words."

She didn't know why she had to tell her mother, but she knew she did, and she also wanted her Prom Queen gown for the White and Gold Invitational. She'd intended to sound bubbly and excited — the way she thought a daughter who's just become a member of the most exclusive sorority on campus ought to sound — but when she got her mother on the phone on Monday night, she heard herself saying in a voice as flat as a pancake: "Well, Mom, I made it."

"Made what? Oh, the sorority. What's it called? Lamma Lamma something?"

"Delta Lambda."

"Right. Well, congratulations are in order, I suppose. You did want in, didn't you?"

"Yes, Mom, I did want in."

"Well, good for you then," her mother said dryly. "Congratulations, sweet-heart."

"Thanks, Mom. I, ah, have to go to a ball. Could you send me my Prom Queen gown?"

"Oh, for crying out loud, Gloria, how the devil—? The skirt's the size of a sofa. Oh, I suppose I could take it to Eberhardt's and they'd find a way to pack it. They're in the business. They must do that all the time. You want the crino-lines and everything?"

This always happened to Gloria on the phone with her mother: she suddenly felt as though she were ten years old. "Sure, Mom," she said in a petulant voice, "of course I want the crinolines. And there's a merry widow I wore with it—it's probably still in my lingerie drawer. And the pumps? You know, they were dyed to match?"

"Oh, God—OK. I'll have to put it all on the Greyhound, I suppose. Oh, wait a minute, your father wants to say something."

Without even a second's pause—he must have been standing right by the phone—Gloria's father's voice boomed out in his best football coach imita-tion: "Well, princess, you did it again, huh?"

Did what? Gloria thought. "I guess so, Daddy."

"Well, good for you. Congratulations, hon."

She was wondering what to say to him, but, before she could think of a thing, she heard her mother again: "What kind of a ball? Is it a big deal?"

"A *very* big deal, Mom. It's the biggest deal we've got here. You wouldn't happen to have, ah, long evening gloves?"

"Of course I do, but you *have* evening gloves, don't you? I distinctly remember, we bought—"

"Yes, but I want, you know, old-fashioned—"

"You didn't lose them, did you? I thought you had two or—"

"No, Mom, I didn't lose them. But I mean like—" Like what? Gloria thought. Like Cinderella? She could see in her mind exactly what she wanted, but she couldn't seem to find the right words to translate that image into language that would be readily understood by her mother. "You know, Mom, *old-fashioned*, really good quality French kid, all the way up to—"

"Oh! Well, yes, I've got a pair of your grandmother's like that. Little pearl but-tons—is that what you mean? Right up to your armpits?"

Gloria laughed; the strain of talking to her mother long distance was making her feel giddy. "Yes, that's it, Mom. Right up to my hairy armpits."

Her mother laughed too. "Well, *shave*, silly. OK, I'll send them. It'll take you an hour to put them on, hon, and I'm not kidding. You want a dog collar to go with them?"

"Pardon?"

"You know, sweetie, a choker."

"Oh, sure."

"It was Mother's too. You can have it, if you want it. I'll never wear the damned thing again. You've got to have a neck like a swan, and these days I'm a bit more of the turkey persuasion. But, ah, Gloria—don't lose it. Those pretty sparkly things aren't rhinestones."

"Oh, Mom, I won't lose it."

"Gloria?"

"Yes."

Gloria waited. Eventually her mother said, "Oh, nothing, sweetheart. Just be happy, OK?"

Her grandmother's evening gloves were exactly what Gloria had wanted; they fit as tight as paint—slightly tighter actually, Gloria thought; paint doesn't have to be stretched to go on—and each glove had twenty-four buttons. No one in the Delta Lambda house owned anything resembling a button hook, so Morgan—she'd volunteered for the job—had to work each pearl through its button hole with the aid of a nail file. "Ye gods, Gloria," she said, "I sure hope you don't decide you have to take these things off halfway through the night."

"Nope. Once they're on, they're going to stay on. They look all right?"

"Are you kidding? Fabulous! Especially with the choker."

"Morgan? Do I look all right *really?*"

"Of course you do, silly— utterly devastating."

"Really?"

"Really!"

"Not too much makeup?"

"Of course not—but you know what I'd do if I were you? I'd wear some jewelry over your gloves—a bracelet. A ring."

"Oh, come on, Morgan, that would be pretentious."

"Gloria," Morgan said with her thin smile, "go on. Here's your big chance. *Be pretentious.*"

Gloria met Morgan's eyes in the mirror; they both laughed.

"Morgan," Gloria said, "hey, ah, thanks for everything, OK?"

"Oh, Gloria," Morgan said in a voice that sounded to Gloria annoyed—or even angry. For several seconds of awkward silence, Gloria didn't understand what was happening; then Morgan said, "I went to boarding school too. Did I ever tell you that? Oh, they ought to outlaw those damn places." She slipped off her diamond tea ring and tried it on Gloria's right hand; with a bit of wiggling, it settled perfectly over her glove. "There," she said, "I knew it would fit. You're such a darned tiny little thing."

• • •

The White and Gold Invitational was held in the Briarville Country Club, and the Lambs were driven there in shifts by fraternity boys. As Gloria and Susie stood outside the house, waiting for their ride, Susie said, "Wow, Glo, you look like a dream."

They were both wearing pink. "So do you," Gloria said and meant it. She couldn't imagine what it must be like to have skin as white as Susie's, a face so magazine-cover pretty. "Well, here we are," she said, "Full-fledged Lambs. Amazing, isn't it?"

"Oh, yeah, I guess it is," Susie said. "So what'd you think of the Three Questions?"

"I don't know. Are we allowed to talk about it?"

"Nobody told us not to."

"Yeah, but—it still feels kind of— I'm not sure I *want* to talk about it. It was very intense for me—like a mystical experience."

"Oh, yeah?" Susie said. "I guess that's what it's supposed to be. I was just scared and tired. I just said the first thing that came into my head. I cried a lot. But—I don't know, it was kind of like when I was baptized. I kept waiting to feel something big, you know, really spectacular, but then it's over, and you're still waiting, and it's all a blur. And then you think, oh, maybe it doesn't matter what I felt. Maybe that's not the point—"

Susie looked away, her eyes narrowing. She's a lot smarter than she lets on, Gloria thought. Then, giggling, Susie said, "But you know, it's just like they say—a sorority's like a sewer: you only get out of it what you put into it."

Gloria laughed so hard she was afraid she was going to run her mascara.

By the time that Gloria and Susie arrived at the country club, dozens of people were there ahead of them, and the band had already begun to play. "You like wearing a formal?" Susie asked Gloria.

"Of course," Gloria said. The question had taken her by surprise. "I love it actually. Don't you?"

"Oh, I wouldn't say I love it, but it's fun. I grew up on the stage, so I'm kind of used to costumes."

Costumes? Gloria thought. She'd never before thought of a formal as a costume, but she supposed it was.

"A lot of girls don't really like wearing formals," Susie said. "You can tell just by looking at them—how stiff they are. Look at Julie and Sharon—"

"Hey, you're right. You can see how uncomfortable they are."

"Not like us," Susie said, laughing, "natural-born prom queens."

Gloria would never have called herself a natural-born prom queen, but she did feel perfectly at ease, and it was, now that she thought about it, certainly a costume—and she loved how artificial that costume was, how mannered. It was like an elaborate disguise; she could use it, oddly enough, to hide behind.

For the next few hours, there would never be a doubt in her mind who she was, because she would be exactly what she looked like. She was suddenly ecstatically happy. "And *this*," the secret watcher told her, "is exactly what you wanted."

A Sigma Chi asked Susie to dance, and Gloria was, for the moment, left alone. She surveyed the room. If a lot of girls looked stiff and awkward in formals, the boys were worse; you could see it by the way they stood around like so many ducks or suddenly burst into big, clumsy, thrashing movements as though to demonstrate that they really were *men*, after all, even if they were, for the moment, got up in these silly monkey suits. Then she was sure she saw—of all people!—Professor Bolton, standing among a cluster of boys on the other side of the room. But that didn't make the least bit of sense. Why would he be at the White and Gold Invitational?

"Hey," she said to Mitsy who was rustling past, "that isn't Professor Bolton over there, is it?"

"Oh, yeah," Mitsy said. "We always invite him, and he always comes. He only stays for about an hour though, and he never dances."

Gloria looked across the room again to see what Professor Bolton could possibly look like in a tuxedo, but now she couldn't find him. Instead she saw a very tall boy staring at her. She looked away, then looked back, and the boy was *still* staring at her. He was one of the tallest boys at the dance; he was wearing a midnight-blue tux so beautifully fitted he must surely own it, and he wore it with an easy, self-assured grace she'd never seen in a male short of her father's age. She looked straight at him so he'd know that she'd caught him staring at her, and she wasn't surprised when he walked directly across the dance floor toward her. It was only the end of April, but he was already tanned. Don't smile, she told herself, not even the ole Mona Lisa. You're not in high school anymore, and now—yes, you are—you're a Delta Lambda.

"Hi," he said, "are you as icy as you look?"

"Oh, yes. Ten degrees below zero."

They read each other's pins; he was a Beta Theta Pi; that is, he was in the fraternity that was the male counterpart to Delta Lambda—the rich boys' house. He had a slow, sunny smile, and he didn't seem the least bit nervous. "I'm Rolland Spicer," he said in a tone implying that she ought to know who he was (she didn't).

"Gloria Cotter," she said and repressed an impulse to curtsy.

"New sister, huh?"

"That's right. Brand new."

Then, suddenly, for the first time since she'd noticed him, he did something awkward: he glanced away and rubbed his neck under his collar. Oh, she thought, he really likes me.

"So," he said after a moment, "are you glad to be a Lamb?"

"Oh, yes!" Gloria said.

6

Gloria dreamed that she was back in her room in the Delta Lambda House. She was sitting at her desk by the window that looked out over Sorority Row, and she was trying to write a paper on Ezra Pound so Professor Bolton could send it to Lionel Trilling as a letter of introduction for her. The paper was weeks overdue, and she couldn't manage to write even the first sentence because she couldn't remember anything she'd planned to say. Several majorettes had stopped by to see Susie; they were standing just inside the door, chatting, and they were driving Gloria crazy. Feeling a numbing despair, she looked up, out the window, and saw that someone was balanced on the power line.

The image was so unexpected and horrifying she caught her breath. A man wearing a long, ragged coat and a slouch hat was standing on the power line as carefully balanced as a circus acrobat. He must have seen her looking at him; with tiny, quick steps he skittered away along the wire. His hat was tilted down and hid his face, but she knew that it was Mr. Dougherty, and she felt her stomach contract. Susie and the other majorettes were still chatting as though nothing strange were happening; maybe they couldn't see him from where they were. He's spying on me, Gloria thought. He can't get away with that—not here at the Delta Lambda house. I'm *safe* at the house. She drew the blind down so she wouldn't have to see him.

She could sense his movements out there even though he was hidden; the moment he'd seen the blind go down, he'd begun to tiptoe toward her. She knelt and looked through the crack at the bottom of the blind. She could see his feet balanced on the power line just outside her window. He was wearing—of all bizarre things—old, beat-up saddle shoes, and she knew that he was in disguise. There was something strange about the saddle shoes. They had white soles, and only girls' saddle shoes have white soles, and then she recognized them: they were hers. She'd worn them the summer of her sophomore year at Canden High, and her mother had thrown them out three times, and three times Gloria had retrieved them from the garbage. The fourth time her mother had said, "Enough is enough of these damned things, Gloria. I mean it."

"All the girls wear them like that, all beat up like that," Gloria had said.

"I don't care what all the girls wear."

"*Binkie Eberhardt* wears them like that!"

"I don't care what Binkie Eberhardt wears—my daughter's not going to look like a rag picker!" And that had been the end of the saddle shoes. Mr. Dougherty must have picked them out of the garbage; that's what he was disguised as: a rag picker.

He can't fool me, Gloria thought. How dare he wear my saddle shoes? What a creepy, rotten thing to do, and I'm not going to put up with it, not for another minute—and, with a bang, she shot the blind all the way up to the top. The man skittered backward so quickly he almost lost his balance and fell off the power line. Then he teetered to a stop; even though the brim of his slouch hat still hid his face, she could feel him staring at her. He tilted his head back, and she saw that he wasn't Mr. Dougherty. He was Ken Henderson.

Gloria inhaled—made a sound like a long, shuddery gasp. She wanted to pull the blind down again, but she couldn't make herself do it. The girls seemed to have left the room; she couldn't hear their voices. She couldn't look away from Ken's eyes. She tried to scream, but she couldn't make a sound, and she knew she was dreaming. "Wake up!" she told herself, but nothing happened. Oh, help, she thought, I'm stuck here forever.

Gloria sat up so violently that the entire bed jerked. She was as wide awake as if she'd never been asleep at all. She wrote the dream into her diary, then took a bath and shaved off every nasty black prickle. She dried herself, powdered herself, and looked at her diary again. She read the last sentence she'd written: "I've got to get out of here." Now she added below it: "Where the devil am I supposed to go?"

The obvious answer was the country club. It was nearly ten on a Saturday morning, and Binkie was sure to be there playing tennis in a crisp, white tennis dress. Gloria had always wanted to wear a crisp, white tennis dress, but, unfortunately, she didn't play tennis. The girl in Scranton, however— Gloria had been doing her best not to think about the girl in Scranton. Her full, ridiculous (and fully ridiculous) name was Heidi Bronwyn Smith, and she'd been Rolland's childhood sweetheart. Heidi not only played tennis, she won cups and ribbons for playing tennis, and she played mixed doubles with Rolland. I can't believe it, Gloria thought, when he suggested that we should be able to date other people, I actually agreed with him!

To her surprise, Gloria found that she was so angry she could have broken something—a plate or a pencil or maybe Rolland's neck—and she was suddenly afflicted by a truly demonic idea: if Rolland could date other people, so could she. She could put on something just a teensy bit trashy and go over to the club and let Lee Hockner pick her up. They could go park somewhere— Gloria, for heaven's sake, she told herself, not Lee Hockner. Well, if not him, then why not Jack Farrington? He was more her speed, and she really should have gone to the movies with him, so why hadn't she? Maybe because he'd tried to put the make on Binkie about a million times and Binkie had told Gloria all about it, or maybe because he had to be at least thirty-five and wasn't married yet, so what was wrong with him? He might, however, turn out to be amusing enough to get her through the rest of the summer, and she could wear her really tight pink skirt if she could still get into it—but then she'd have to wear a girdle, which would, of course, be utterly delightful when it's eighty-some degrees in the shade. OK, a little sundress she could wear with heels so he'd get the point, and he might take her to the Pine Top for a late dinner, but then she'd end up in his apartment at midnight, and he'd surely try to get her to go all the way—

"Stop it, Gloria," the secret watcher told her. "There's not a boy or a man at the Raysburg Country Club worth thinking about. Wait till September. You're going to be going out with lots of interesting boys in September."

Gloria dressed as carefully as if she had an important luncheon date, borrowed her mother's station wagon, and drove into town. She didn't have the faintest idea where she was going until she got there: her old haven, the library. She went straight to the poetry section. Just as she should have known, they hadn't added a single book to the collection since last summer.

Then, just the way she'd done in high school, she crept into the forbidden section, and, yes, right there in front of her was the big, fat, brown medical book that had been her first tutor on matters sexual. The librarian had caught her once—"Gloria Cotter, I'm surprised at you!"—and she'd nearly died of shame, but that hadn't stopped her; it had just made her sneakier. She'd read standing, her ears tuned for the slightest hint of a sound that would be her signal to shove the book back onto the shelf and walk quickly away. She'd stood there and memorized the line drawings of the male reproductive organs; she'd learned what "engorgement" and "ejaculation" meant; she'd learned why she got wet between her legs; she'd even learned—at least approximately—how to *do it*. She put the book back on the shelf. She was feeling something obscure and alto-gether unpleasant. She had to get out of the library.

She'd already crossed the little bridge over the creek before she began to feel better. Yes, it was good to be outside, surrounded by people. She was wearing heels, but they weren't too high, and she didn't mind walking in them. Market Street was jammed with Saturday shoppers, and they made her feel safe. She was hearing—had been hearing—the soft murmur in her mind that always turned out to be a poem; it was Delmore Schwartz: "What am I now that I was then / Which I shall suffer and act again—" Why on earth was that poem in her mind?

People were looking at her curiously—she'd caught a number of them doing it—and she didn't blame them; all the other girls were wearing sandals or tennis shoes, and, if not halter tops and shorts, at least sundresses; she didn't know any of them (they must have gone to Raysburg High). In her nylons and crisp linen, she was, of course, wildly over-dressed for Raysburg in July, and ordinarily she would have thought that it was her duty to be over-dressed—but now she caught up with that idea, spun it around and looked at it: duty to *whom?* To Delta Lambda? To the society page editor of the *Raysburg Times?* To *our sort?* She wished she were, for once, inconspicuous.

So that her trip downtown wouldn't be utterly pointless, she went into Eberhardt's and bought a lipstick. She came out on the Main Street side and kept on walking toward Tenth; she thought she'd have a Coke in the Howe-Ferris pharmacy, and, by then, would've killed enough time to go home (and get this damned girdle off and jump in the pool). Just as she was passing Rossiter's Hardware, she heard a wolf whistle; she ignored it the way she always did such things.

"Hey, snooty, can't you say hi?" It was Mr. Dougherty—*of course* it was Mr. Dougherty—appearing at this moment without the faintest possibility of coincidence. (God hates me! she thought.) He was wearing Bermudas and the gaudiest of Hawaiian shirts. He was also wearing two little boys; one was hanging onto his shoulder and swinging like a monkey; the other was clinging to his big, hairy forearm and yelling, "Flip me, Daddy. Flip me, Daddy. Flip me!"

"Hey, knock it off!" Mr. Dougherty yelled to no effect whatsoever. Gloria still had said nothing, although she had stopped walking. "Hey, princess, how you doing? Can we, ah—talk a minute? The reason I sent the—those darned roses, OK? I was just trying to say I was sorry—"

"Flip me, Daddy, flip me, Daddy, flip me—"

"Oh, for crying out loud— *Shut up!*"

Gloria had yet to find a single word, but she didn't seem able to walk away either. She'd never seen him with his kids, and it changed her perception of him; to these little boys he was "Daddy," and that humanized him, turned him back into what he'd always been until a few days ago: a big, hairy, harmless goof of a grown-up. But in her dream he'd been mixed up with Ken Henderson, and she didn't know why or what it could mean. "Hi, Mr. Dougherty," she said, and heard her voice—flat and metallic.

He shrugged off the older boy, allowed the younger to grab his hands, walk up the front of him, and execute a somersault off his belly. "That's it," he yelled. "No more flips! Gloria, honey—can we talk?"

What is there to talk about? she thought, but she said, "I was going to Howe-Ferris."

"Hey, great idea. What do you think, kids? Banana splits all round?"

Howe-Ferris was like a time capsule; surely nothing much could have changed in thirty years. It had the distinctive pharmacy smell that was as unmistakable as it was unidentifiable; glass jars were filled with wildly colored fluids, meant, Gloria supposed, to advertise the fact that medicines were compounded there; yellowed posters with "great moments in medicine" lined the walls, and a huge ceiling fan turned slowly and stirred the torpid summer air. She and Mr. Dougherty sat on high, wire-backed stools at the marble-top counter; he'd seated his boys at a table on the far side of the room where they were wolfing their banana splits. Mr. Dougherty looked at Gloria, rubbed the back of his neck and grinned. "Got the monsters for the whole damn day," he said, "Jesus, what a handful. Sure you don't want a banana split?"

"Yes, I'm really sure I don't want a banana split, thank you."

He really is just an ordinary guy, Gloria thought. That's all he is. He's just a jerk who works for my dad.

Directly in front of Gloria was an advertisement so old that all the reds had been bleached out of it. A girl who resembled Betty Grable was grinning mischievously over her shoulder as she bent to pick up a tray of glasses brimming with Coke. She was wearing platform heels and a straight skirt so tight that if she'd been a real girl and not a painting, she couldn't have walked a step in it. She made Gloria think of old newsreels images of battle ships with their guns firing, grinning sailors with Luckies hanging out of their mouths—

Her father had never told Gloria much about the war, so these cliché images were the best she could do; the last time she'd asked him, he'd said, "You've read *Mr. Roberts,* haven't you? That's exactly what it was like." But she didn't care about Mr. Roberts' war; she cared about her father's, and she would probably never know anything about it—

Mr. Dougherty was staring straight at her. He'd taken off his dark glasses and laid them on the counter, and the harsh light from the windows facing the street had shrunk his pupils to the size of pencil points; it gave him an avid, tigerish, but somewhat stupid look. As usual, he needed a shave, and the masses of curly black hair on his arms made him look faintly soiled—even straight out of the bath he would probably look faintly soiled—and the anchor tattooed on his left biceps was peeking out from under the neatly rolled sleeve of his shirt. She wondered if he'd intentionally sat her down in front of the old Coke poster— but no, he didn't have the wit for that kind of game; it was only another nasty coincidence that wasn't really a coincidence.

"Jeez," he said, "I can't seem to do anything right, you know what I mean? I shouldn't have sent you the roses, huh?"

"No, Mr. Dougherty, you shouldn't have," she said in a voice that would have done justice to a grade school teacher, and the secret watcher said, "Be careful, Gloria."

"Listen, princess, the other night at the club— you know, Sunday night— I was way out of line, huh? I'm sorry, kid, OK?"

Gloria looked into his yellowish brown eyes—into the tiny pencil points with the hot, white light on them—and thought: I can't read this man.

"Jeez, Gloria," he said, finally turning away from the light, "I woke up the next morning, thought, my God, Dougherty, now you've really torn it. I just don't know what happens to me sometimes. I get drinking and the devil gets in me, you know what I mean? About the only thing I'm proud of these day is I always do my job—and you can ask anybody about that, swear to God, and they'll tell you the same thing. Dougherty always does his job."

What on earth is he talking about? Gloria thought.

"Listen, princess, if it wasn't for your old man, I wouldn't even have that job—wouldn't have diddly squat, if you want the truth. You know who I am? Just a big, dumb mick from Tacoma—but there's one thing you can say about me is I'm loyal. You can ask anybody, and they'll tell you the same damn thing. I'm the best friend your old man ever had."

A dark spasmodic motion passed across his face; he pawed the cigarette pack out of his shirt pocket—not Luckies, Gloria saw, but Camels—pounded one out and lit it. "You know what's been getting to me, princess?" he said without looking at her. "It's my marriage going down the tubes, that's what. And it ain't even Dottie any more—it's those two little devils over there. Goddamn, I sure miss 'em—every damn day, you know what I mean? And then I start hitting the bottle and—well, there you go. Really got to straighten out—

"So anyhow, that's the long and the short of it. I'm real sorry about Sunday night. That's why I sent the roses. So anyhow, will you forgive me, princess? Can we be friends?"

He stuck out his hand. Gloria took it automatically, but nothing he'd said had carried the full emotional force of an apology, and the roses, and their unsigned card, also required an explanation and an apology.

She thought about what to say. Use simple words, she told herself; just talk like the Dick and Jane reader. "Mr. Dougherty," she said, "what was it you *did* on Sunday night?"

He stared at her a moment with his mouth hanging open like a bad actor mugging amazement. "What're you saying, Gloria? I wasn't out of line? Is that what you're saying?"

Simple words or not, he was having just as much trouble understanding her as she was having understanding him. "Yes, of course you were out of line. I just want to know how you saw it."

"Well, jeez, kid, I was pretty well pissed—excuse my French—but feeling no pain, if you follow me, and you walked by me without saying hi or nothing, and it just ticked me off, you know what I mean? And I thought, who's that snooty little thing think she is, the queen of Sheba? Why don't I just give her a good little scare?"

Gloria felt the enormous relief that comes with clarity: that was exactly what she'd thought had happened. "Well, you succeeded," she said. "You scared me—

Listen, Mr. Dougherty, I'm sorry I didn't speak to you. My mind was elsewhere. That's *my* apology, OK? But if you ever do anything like that again, I'll tell my father."

"Of course you will, princess. That goes without—"

"Don't call me princess!"

"OK, OK, OK."

"Now what about the roses—the *card* with the roses?"

"Oh, hell, honey, I was just trying to be cute—a joke, you know—"

"It wasn't funny. It was an anonymous card. What was I supposed to think? It wasn't in good taste."

"Good taste? Haw. That's something I never learned much about. Don't teach it where I come from, you know what I mean? Why don't you call me Billy?"

"I think I should be going," she said, sliding off her stool.

"You *have* got the finest damn legs I ever saw in my life, honey, and that's the goddamn truth." He winked at her.

A million hot little needles prickled her freshly shaved armpits. "I don't think you should have an opinion about my legs, Mr. Dougherty, and if you do have one, I don't want to hear it."

"Aye-aye, skipper," he said and saluted her, grinning. "See, there I go again, putting my foot it. Can't do anything right—just trying to give you a little compliment, but— Hey, look, Gloria, I just want everything to be OK between us, you know what I mean? There must be something I can— Hey, I got it! You want to drive my Porsche?"

The idea was so preposterous that all she could do was stare at him. What did he think—that he was talking to some dumb little girl who worked behind the lunch counter at the five-and-dime, somebody whose idea of heaven would be to drive a Porsche? And what was it with males and their cars? The whole universe seemed to revolve around their cars.

"Some days it's the only thing keeps me from going down and jumping in the river," he was saying. "Take the ole silver bullet out in the country and really let her rip. Cheers me up, every time. What do you say, Gloria honey, give her a shot?"

She still couldn't find a response. A million miles away, in the part of her mind apparently reserved for amusing quotations appropriate for bizarre occasions, a smarty-pants voice was rattling away: "'It grieves me much,' replied the Peer again, 'Who speaks so well should ever speak in vain.'"

"What do you say, Gloria? How about tomorrow?— Then everything'll be squared away."

Her mind was running full gallop as she tried to make sense of what was happening. "Squared away," he'd said; how would letting her drive his silly car square anything away? And what was there to square? It wasn't as though they'd been friends—or were about to become friends—

But then, with a sudden mental "click," everything fell into place. The whole idiotic chain of events had not begun when she'd walked by him in the parking lot; it had been earlier, when she'd refused to dance with him. She'd forgotten it, and he hadn't mentioned it, but that surely must have been the start of it. She'd said, "No, thank you," and he'd felt snubbed, and from his point of view, she owed him, so it wasn't really driving the car, *per se*; it could be anything at all—accepting an invitation to walk around the block—because all he really wanted was a yes to cancel out the no and make him feel good again. That's what "squared away" meant. But it still didn't seem fair: shouldn't she be allowed to say no if she wanted to?

She sensed in this man a stupid bulldog tenacity, and she didn't want to make an enemy of him, and there was also something else going on she couldn't quite define. Up until Sunday night he'd simply not existed in her world in any significant way, and she felt vaguely guilty about that even though she couldn't find any sufficient reason why he *should* have existed. Her guilt, she decided, had something to do with the way she'd regarded him as little more than a piece of ugly, familiar furniture in a room through which she'd been passing on her way toward somewhere else far more interesting, and she did not want to become, genuinely, what she already appeared to be (what he almost certainly thought she was): snooty, selfish, spoiled—what Ken had called her: a rich bitch. "Well, it might be fun," she said.

"Yeah?" he said with a grin. "That's the ticket, Gloria honey, you bet. Tell you what—tomorrow, about the time when the day starts to get ugly, you know what I mean? When you just can't wait for it to start to cool off—let's say at four? You just walk down the hill like you're going to the club, and I'll swing by and get you? How's that? And we'll take her out in the country and just blow her right out, how's that?"

Gloria's armpits now felt as though the points of hot steam irons had been forcibly pressed into them; she shivered involuntarily. He'd slid neatly over it, but it had been unmistakable, nonetheless: "like you're going to the club," had meant, "don't tell your father."

"Stop this stupid nonsense right now," the secret watcher told her. "There's nothing in this for you, absolutely nothing. Just say, 'I'll have to ask Daddy,' and that will end it, you know darned well it will. So what if this guy doesn't like you? It shouldn't matter what he thinks of you." But, in some nasty, undefined, darkly knotted way it did matter.

Maybe I do owe him, she thought. Maybe I owe him the small decency of briefly regarding him as a human being. "OK," she said.

Gloria wasn't even halfway home before she knew she'd made a mistake, but she couldn't think of any way to correct it without making things worse. She'd said she'd meet him tomorrow, and so she would, but the prospect of riding around in Mr. Dougherty's Porsche filled her with—"anxiety" wasn't a strong enough word; it filled her with the emotion of her dream: that densely clotted, utterly paralyzing sense of dread.

In her dream she'd mixed up Mr. Dougherty with Ken Henderson, and she felt as though she were mixing them up now, although she couldn't quite see how she might be doing it. The only thing she could imagine that they had in common was a love of driving and a love for the things they drove; Ken had loved and babied his old, beat-up truck, whatever it was (a Chevy, she thought), probably just as much as Mr. Dougherty loved and babied his Porsche. And she had a clear—actually fairly happy—image of Ken driving, chanting his poetry to her: "So many nights we pick-up-trucked it through / the living streets, living only in darkness, / never in the light—"

It was a memory from early on, when they'd first started dating (if that's what they'd been doing), when she'd thought she was in love with him. Why had she dreamed about him?

Since she'd begun to write them down in high school, Gloria had gradually come to believe that her dreams were smarter than she was—smarter in that sneaky, indirect, multilayered way things were when they were *true*, as opposed to the neatly formulated things she *thought*, which were never entirely true no matter how much effort she put into thinking them. She hardly ever understood her own dreams until she read them in her diary a year or so later, and then, of course, it was too late to do anything about them—but this morning's dream felt as though it was just on the edge of making sense. Ken had been just *out there*, watching. Out where? Out in the world, of course—as in, "I've got to get *out* of here"—and he'd been wearing her shoes as though he'd taken the old saying literally—"put yourself in my shoes"— which is exactly what she'd always wished he'd been able to do—which he'd never been able to do—and he'd been disguised as a rag picker. Oh! And she got it, or got *something*: Yeats' foul rag and bone shop—the place where all the ladders start—the foundation of poetry.

Gloria pulled the station wagon over by the side of the road. Yeats' rag and bone shop had suddenly connected to Eliot's notion of the poet's mind forming new wholes out of disparate experiences, and she saw Ken rummaging around in the garbage, pulling out her old, cracked saddle shoes and putting them on, and then she saw herself putting them on in high school—so she could look like Binkie—but looking like Binkie hadn't been good enough for her mother who had wanted her to look like— And she saw herself walking through downtown Raysburg in her crisp linen dress and saw it as emblematic—in the Yeatsian sense—but emblematic of what?

At the same time the feelings of her sophomore year at Briarville—the wretched spring of her sophomore year—were coming back so strongly that her

teeth were chattering and all she wanted to do was turn off the tap in her mind
so the images would stop flowing into her. She hugged herself, shivering in the
heat. She was feeling again that awfulness of being hurt, and the awful secret of
being alone with being hurt. Stop it, she told herself, breathing. But the feeling
was like that in the dream when she'd thought: I'm stuck here forever. And
then, just the way the dream had ended, this experience—whatever it was—
ended as abruptly; she was her ordinary self, sitting in her mother's station wagon
parked safely by the side of the National Road at the foot of Raysburg Hill. It
wasn't even two in the afternoon, but she felt as though she'd been awake for
ten years. She'd been sweating so hard her nice linen dress was soaked through—
how embarrassing—and she could, once again, think clearly. She was afraid—
and she allowed herself to put this old fear into words—she was terribly afraid of
going crazy.

At home, Gloria was grateful to find that her mother had gone out. She swam
forty laps and emerged from the pool famished; she ate a cottage cheese sandwich and an apple; she stepped into her grandmother's room to see how she was
doing. "Very well, today, thank you, my dear. Why don't you come in and sit
with me a while?"

Once Gloria was settled in the wingback chair, her grandmother said, "Well,
have you talked to your mother yet?"

"Not yet," Gloria said, "but I will," although she had no intention of talking
to her mother. She considered telling her grandmother the latest installment
of the Mr. Dougherty saga but decided that was out of the question; her grandmother would find it absolutely incomprehensible.

She picked up her grandmother's *Vogue* and began to flip through it. Her
feeling of dread had receded so far by now that the memory of it felt as ludicrous
as cheap melodrama. Going crazy? she thought, how utterly ridiculous—but
she asked, punctuating the question with a small laugh, "So, Grandmother,
has there ever been any insanity in the family?"

"I suppose it depends on how you look at it. Do you mean the kind that gets
you locked up? There was a distant uncle on the Whittock side, but I never knew
him."

The exercise and the food and the afternoon heat had combined to make
Gloria sleepy, even dreamy, and she found it calming, peaceful, to sit next to
her grandmother's bed even though they weren't saying much of anything to each
other. How odd, she thought; Grandmother used to scare me half to death, but
now she makes me feel safe. And her grandmother seemed to be as drowsy as
she was; Gloria looked over and saw something that looked like a milky film
over her grandmother's eyes. Oh, she thought, she's really old. How sad.

Vogue had a big spread on weddings, so Gloria lost herself in it. She imagined picking her trousseau and honeymooning in Paris; she studied the dresses and fell in love with one of them—"for a very young girl," it said. Could she, at twenty-one, be considered "a very young girl?" Probably not, but how young was *young?* Girls didn't get married at twelve these days, so what could that possibly mean? But it didn't really matter, because, "very young" or not, she knew she could wear that dress; as a matter of fact, she'd be absolutely spectacular in it—"circle after circle of lace-ruched organdy," it said, and there were obviously four million crinolines under it, probably even hoops, and she imagined a grand wedding with all the trimmings—the bridesmaids from Delta Lambda identically dressed, and two cute little flower girls, and a page—

"Hey, stop it," the secret watcher told her. "You're not getting married *yet.*"

Gloria borrowed the *Vogue* and took it back to her own room. She'd thought she might read awhile and then take a nap, but as soon as she stretched out on her bed, her dreamy state deserted her and she felt wide awake and alert. She was thinking about her sophomore year at Briarville; to be exact, she was wondering again how it could have gone as wrong as it did. She'd been happy; her life had been complete, nearly perfect; she hadn't needed Ken Henderson in it.

Since she'd been fourteen, she'd always begun a new diary for every school year; now she pulled out the one dated 1954–55. Flipping through the earliest entries, she found a long account of her first date with Rolland and a painstaking record of her worries about Delta Lambda and Susie. She'd spent the summer worrying about the same things she always worried about: once she was actually living in the Delta Lambda house, could she continue to fool everyone into thinking she was a normal girl, and could she even manage to make the Lambs *like her?*

She hadn't been too worried about her fellow sophomores; having been pledges together, they shared a sense of camaraderie, and most of them had seemed to like her well enough—but the older sisters had seen her bare her soul in the initiation ritual, and every time she thought about it, she felt exposed and embarrassed. She trusted Morgan—Morgan was true blue, all right—but she wasn't sure she trusted any of the others. Her biggest worry, however, was Susie. She was sure she'd made a mistake in asking for a two-girl room; in a four-girl room she'd be able to fade into the background, but she was trapped alone with Susie for a year at least. She liked and admired Susie—or at least she thought she did—but, no matter how hard she tried to talk herself out of it, she was also scared of her.

Susie was the epitome of the successful normal girl: a blonde majorette who'd won two beauty pageants. Susie had a chip on her shoulder about being a poor girl in a rich girls' house, and Gloria didn't think of herself as rich, but from

Susie's point of view she certainly was, so why on earth should Susie like her? Her worst fears were that Susie would turn out to be boy-crazy, sloppy, and irresponsible—that she would make a mess of their room, leave her clothes everywhere and her nylons draped over the light fixtures, use Gloria's makeup, stay out half the night, drink too much, play stupid popular music too loud, invite the most empty-headed girls in the house into their room at one in the morning, never study and make fun of anyone who did—and worst of all, that she would quickly see through Gloria's carefully constructed surface to the real person beneath: a queer, neurotic, terrified, hollow, poetry-reading priss— the biggest misfit in Delta Lambda.

When Gloria had first arrived on campus, Susie had already been there most of the week for band practice; she'd put her things neatly away and made her bed, so, when she walked in at dinner time, the mess in the room was all Gloria's. "Wow, Glo, have you ever got a lot of clothes! When'd you get here? Hey, it's good to see you. No, don't get too close,"—Gloria had tried to give her a hug— "I'm lathered like a horse." Susie raised one arm to demonstrate. The simile was uncannily accurate: her unshaven armpit was covered with white froth. How distasteful, Gloria thought.

"I sure wish the weather would break," Susie said. "It's too darn hot for this." The "this" was her baton; she leaned it against the wall by the head of her bed.

Susie's hair was up in a ponytail; she had no makeup on, and she was wearing a bizarre outfit: sunglasses, a broad-brimmed straw hat, a halter top, gym shorts, and old, battered majorette boots. She threw the hat and sunglasses onto her desk, plunked down onto her bed, pulled off her boots and her thick athletic socks. Her feet were as pink as carnations, her face flushed and shiny with per-spiration. "I bet you didn't know what you were letting yourself in for—the B.O. kid. Did you have a good summer? What'd you do?"

What *had* Gloria done? Worried mainly. "Oh, not that much," she said. "It was kind of boring, actually. There were some nice dances. I swam a bit."

"Yeah, I can see that. Boy, are you tan!"

I'm not *that* tan, Gloria thought, just a shade darker than the color I was born with. And Susie had obviously *not* been tanning; with her skin, she probably was incapable of tanning, but the summer had turned her ivory to pale gold.

"Yeah, mine was kind of boring too. Cloverton's dullsville in the summer— well, it's dullsville any time. But I taught in twirling camp. That was just great. Wow, you should see some of the little girls coming along—eight, nine years old, doing fabulous stuff—" As she talked, she shed the rest of her clothes. Gloria was not used to seeing girls strip themselves naked in an abrupt and unselfcon-scious way, and, in spite of herself, she was shocked, but Susie, grabbing a towel, was already gone, calling from the hallway: "Hey, I'm really glad you're back."

Gloria heard Morgan's voice: "Susie Steibel! Don't run around the house like that, you jerk."

"OK. Sorry."

Good grief, Gloria thought, she's so *physical!* Susie reminded her of—of what? Of a camp counselor she'd had a crush on when she'd been eleven—a tall, blonde, athletic college girl named Patty. Gloria had been so shy with her she hadn't been able to say a word, but she'd so badly needed Patty to like her that she'd allowed her to do what no one else had been able to do: teach her to swim.

After dinner, Susie helped Gloria unpack. Her books took up all the shelf space, but Susie didn't seem to mind. "Gee, you must read a lot. Whenever I try to read for very long, I always fall asleep."

Gloria had been worried that when she and Susie were alone in their room, they'd have nothing to say to each other, but, so far, Susie had been chattering away non-stop. "I'm going crazy, Glo," she was saying. "Mr. Allen decided I was going to be the featured twirler this year, and some of the other girls are really mad at me. Donna especially—"

"Donna?"

"You know, Donna Mason, the Head Majorette. I went to Mr. Allen and said, 'Hey, it's just not fair. I'm just a sophomore, and Donna and Marilee are seniors,' and you know what he said? He said, 'Fair's got nothing to do with it, Susie. I want to have the best marching band in Pennsylvania.' So I said, 'Look, Donna and Marilee can really twirl, you know,' and he said, 'They'll get their chance,' so anyhow, I've got a solo at our first game—Penn State—and Donna and Marilee hate my guts— Hey, wow, do you ever have some nice things!"

It was rapidly becoming obvious that Gloria had far more clothes than were going to fit into her closet. "Use part of mine," Susie said, "I've got space."

"Oh, I don't want to do that."

"Why not? You can't just leave your things piled on the floor— And you know what else? The other majorettes are all Dee Gees. Well, almost all of them. Marcia's a Gam, but the rest of them are Dee Gees, and so of course they're going to gang up on me. Why am I the only majorette in the house? Why do they all think they've got to go to Delta Gamma? They've got a bigger house than us, but still— I thought we were supposed to rush the cutest girls on campus, so why don't we rush all the freshmen majorettes, sort of, you know, automatically? I was the only one Lamb rushed last year. I'm going to talk to Morgan about it— Hey, I've got an idea. Why don't you get a wardrobe? Yeah, we could fit it in right here— Come on, help me."

Within a matter of minutes, Susie had rearranged the furniture to create enough space. "There's a place over on Main sells second-hand stuff to students," she said. "I bet you could get one real cheap, and some fraternity boys would move it in for you."

"Well, maybe," Gloria said dubiously.

As they began to get ready for bed, Gloria heard Susie's constant stream of chatter gradually drying up, and that was the last thing in the world she wanted. Looking around for something—anything—that might make for the next topic of conversation, she saw, on Susie's bed table, a framed photograph: Susie and another blonde—slightly taller and more buxom—in majorette uniforms, holding batons, standing side by side in identical, cute poses, each leaning backward, balanced on one leg with the other raised and bent, toe to knee. The other girl wasn't as pretty as Susie, but she looked enough like her for Gloria to ask, "Is that your sister?"

"No. I don't have a sister. Just four brothers. That's my cousin, Tommie Jean."

Susie studied the picture as though Gloria's question were making her see it as brand new. "That was in the dumb, little Jordanstown paper. She was a senior, and I was a sophomore. 'Susan Jane and Tommie Jean, the fabulous twirling Steibel girls'—that's what it said. We did all the solos for two years— I guess you wouldn't call them solos if there's two of you, would you? But we were so in unison we must of looked like twins on the field. She graduated and quit twirling, and I went on and won the Teen Majorette Championship at the Nationals—and then there was just me doing the solos."

She turned and looked directly into Gloria's eyes; she was as expressionless as that lovely mannequin in a junior miss shop Gloria had always thought she resembled. "I was so happy in that picture. You can probably tell."

Gloria felt as though she'd suddenly been plunged into one of those dark passages in a Dostoyevski novel in which something is going on that's acute, urgent, and momentous, but neither the characters nor the reader has the faintest idea of what it is. Clearly a response was demanded of her, if only the next line to keep the dialogue alive—any stupid thing would do. Possibilities included: "Oh, I can see that," or, "Yes, you do look happy," or, even better, "Why were you so happy?" but Gloria seemed to be incapable of making any of them. Before she could choose one at random and proceed with it, Susie had turned away from the picture, yawning, and Gloria knew that her opportunity had been lost.

"I go to bed early," Susie said, "but you don't have to. I grew up in a big family, so nothing bothers me."

"I go to bed early too—although I read sometimes."

Susie slept in striped cotton pajamas like a little kid. Feeling self-conscious in her pink baby-dolls, Gloria got into her bed with a mystery novel she'd filched from her parent's bedroom the night before she'd left Raysburg. Whoever had occupied Gloria's bed last year must have read in it: the lamp was perfectly positioned.

Susie knelt by the side of her bed, folded her hands, and rested her forehead on them. She remained that way for at least ten minutes while Gloria tried, without success, to lose herself in the ominous world of Philip Marlowe. Then Susie slipped into bed and pulled the sheet over herself. "Good night, Gloria," she said in a firm voice.

The next day Gloria went to Briarville's best furniture store, bought the biggest wardrobe in the place, and paid to have it delivered. She filled it up, used a bit of Susie's closet, and still couldn't make everything fit. She was separating out her winter outfits to pack and store in the basement when Morgan popped in to say, "Rolland Spicer's here to see you."

"Rolland Spicer?" Gloria heard her own voice as though somebody else had spoken; she'd sounded as though she didn't remember quite who he was, which was really stupid; she had no doubt in the world who he was. She was wearing what she'd thrown on when she'd first jumped out of bed: a plain blouse and a tartan skirt. She hadn't even combed her hair. "He could have called first," she said, annoyed.

"But it's *Rolland Spicer*."

Gloria took a moment to ponder the problem. "Gloria," Morgan said with a warning note in her voice (it said, "I am, and don't you forget it, your president"), "some guys you can make wait and some guys you can't."

"OK, OK. Do I look all right?"

She read the answer in Morgan's face, but all Morgan said was: "Put some lipstick on."

Gloria walked into the beau parlour and again heard her own voice from a stranger's observing distance; it sounded exactly like her mother's: "Well, good heavens, Rolland. How very nice to see you again."

He'd risen immediately. He was wearing the standard fraternity uniform of chinos and dirty white bucks; the sun had bleached his hair nearly to the color of straw, and he was deeply tanned—nearly as dark as she was, and she liked that. She was wearing loafers, and he was so much taller that it gave her an unpleasant moment—like existential vertigo—of feeling like a grubby little schoolgirl confronting a grown man. "Hey, nice to see you too," he said, and then, after they'd settled, "I've been thinking about you all summer."

"Oh, have you? How very flattering."

He offered her a cigarette, and she shook her head. "Mind if I—?" he asked (most boys wouldn't have asked). "Of course not," she said. Grinning, never taking his eyes off her, he tapped his cigarette sharply several times on the coffee table, then, with a metallic click of his lighter, lit it. "I checked you out, you know," he said.

"Oh? How did you do that?"

"You know, asked around."

She didn't like that. "And what did you find out?"

"You're a steel brat," he said, laughing.

Oh, Gloria thought, is that what I am? "Really?" she said in a cool voice.

"Yeah. And I'm a coal brat."

"Is there some profound conclusion I'm supposed to draw from that?"

He laughed again, then stopped; he looked puzzled. "You know, everybody told me you were too smart for me."

She didn't know what to say. "What else did they tell you?"

"Gloria," he said, suddenly grave, "it doesn't matter what they told me." He'd spent so much time in the sun that even his eyebrows had been bleached blonde. She remembered him as a good dancer, but did he have a brain in his head?

She looked directly into his eyes and saw—she didn't know how to put it except in the language of a silly, old-fashioned novel—that he was quite smitten with her (with boys, she could always tell). It didn't surprise her; he'd been smitten at the White and Gold. But then she'd been Cinderella polished to a high shine, her hair and makeup perfect, her hairy-monkey arms covered by her grandmother's elegant kid gloves, and here she was in knee socks and loafers, her hair a mess and no more makeup than her hastily applied lipstick, and he was still smitten. How could she not like him?

That night he took her to the Briarville Country Club for dinner and dancing. They ate rare steaks, and his table manners were impeccable. He was the accomplished, self-assured dancer she remembered—he could even do the rumba!—and, wearing her highest heels, she was a perfect height for him. He was exactly the kind of boy her mother would have described as "our sort," and that, in itself, was almost enough to make her decide not to go out with him again, but there was something else—something hard to define—she found appealing. He wasn't the least bit nervous; he talked easily, but nothing he said ever quite transcended what she called "state-of-the-weather conversation." He was an avid tennis player. He was majoring in business administration. He had a job waiting for him at Spicer Coal as soon as he graduated; when his dad retired, he'd take over the company. He talked about it as though it had never occurred to him to want to do anything else.

"Beta Theta Pi's the best thing that ever happened to me," he said, and she could tell that he assumed she was just as big on Delta Lambda, which, in her own way, she was. They exchanged the usual clichés about the Panhellenic Movement. He wasn't stupid, she decided, revising her opinion; no, it was as though his intelligence were located somewhere other than in words—or even in ideas. He would never, she was sure, lose any sleep pondering the meaning of life; she would never, she was sure, have to wonder what he was thinking. He felt solid to her. She felt safe with him.

They danced another slow dance, and then he guided her out onto the terrace overlooking the golf course—guided her with such an air of command it never crossed her mind not to go. (She thought wryly of Wyatt's adjectives: gentle, tame, and meek.) In a shadow thrown by a huge, hoary tree (how corny, she ordinarily would have thought), he kissed her. Gloria never kissed boys on first dates, but, after all, this wasn't a first date; they'd danced till one in the morning at the White and Gold. And ordinarily she would never have kissed a boy with her mouth open unless she knew him very well indeed, but his tongue brushed her lips as though asking a friendly little question—Do you mind?—and Gloria didn't mind.

He hadn't grabbed her the way most boys did; he held her in a gentle, respectful way, but his tongue was thrust deeply into her mouth, and, for the moment, she couldn't find any desire to get it out of there. She could taste smoke from his cigarettes and the dinner he'd just eaten, and she was surprised that she wasn't repulsed. Gee, she thought, I wonder what would happen if I played with his tongue with my tongue? She tried it. The kiss was going on an amazingly long time, and it had far more variety to it than any kiss she'd ever known before. Oh, she thought, so *this* is why people do it. Then Gloria felt a strong twinge somewhere below her waist; it scared her, and her body stiffened. He stopped kissing her immediately, stepped back, his manner utterly deferential and gracious—and thoroughly in control. What a gentleman! she couldn't help thinking—and it had been, she would decide later, the first genuinely sexual kiss of her life.

Now he was offering her a cigarette. She shook her head. He lit one for himself, looked out over the golf course, then back at her. "You're a sweetheart," he said.

Her smarty-pants mind was not helping her out; she didn't know what to say to him. She looked into his eyes and saw the level, direct gaze of someone who was looking at her and *really seeing her*, and she knew—it was one of her sudden, wordless moments of insight—that he was a kind boy, that he had a good heart.

"Want to do something Friday night?" he said.

"Can't. It's the first big, formal dinner at the house."

"Saturday?"

"Sure."

"Play hard to get, why don't you?" he said, grinning.

"Why should I? I like you."

He laughed. There was nothing in his laugh implying that he thought he'd scored on her. "Yeah, I like you too," he said. "I think you're super."

They stepped out from under the shadow and walked toward the music. "You've got my lipstick all over you," she said. He slipped a clean linen handkerchief out of his pocket; without saying a word, she took it from him, unfolded it, and wiped his face with it. "How about me?" she asked. It was lovely moment—as though they were sharing a delicious secret.

"I'd stop in the little girls' if I were you."

The next morning at breakfast the Lambs were dying to hear all about it, and Gloria found herself using for him the same word he'd used for her: "He's a sweetheart."

"Oh, Gloria," Morgan said, "we're so happy for you!"

"Oh, come on. He hasn't pinned me yet."

It seemed ironic to Gloria that her social life should have been clarified so quickly and simply in the person of Rolland Spicer while she still wasn't comfortable with her roommate. Susie was always pleasant enough, but she was turning out to be a far more complex person than Gloria had expected, and Gloria's "sixth sense" as she thought of it—her ability to make sudden leaps into other people's minds—wasn't working with Susie. She began to suspect that Susie was being just as careful and guarded with her as she was being with Susie. We can't go on the whole year like this, she thought. I should be able to let my hair down in my own room, shouldn't I?

Feeling like a detective in one of her mother's mystery novels, Gloria began collecting clues that might make her mysterious roommate add up to a comprehensible, accessible person. All Susie talked about was the band and the other majorettes and her halftime routines. She got up every morning at six and practiced twirling in the back yard. She was the most limber girl Gloria had ever seen, and she was always stretching; right in the middle of a conversation, she'd plunk a foot on the back of a chair and stretch, or she'd get down on the floor and do the splits. She did sit-ups and leg raises and toe touches and exercises Gloria remembered from ballet.

Never in her life had Gloria met anyone as worried about body odor as Susie was—or, as Gloria amended it, she'd never met anyone so ready to talk about it (most girls wouldn't). Susie took two showers a day, wore no perfume whatsoever, and did have a smell sometimes, Gloria had to admit, but it wasn't a bad smell; it was like—Gloria wasn't sure what, maybe like a big, clean, short-haired dog. But the thing that was really getting to Gloria was Susie's praying, and it bothered Gloria that she was bothered. People should be allowed to pray in peace, shouldn't they?

One night near the end of their first week together, Susie knelt by the side of her bed for so long that Gloria began to feel creepy—as though she were witnessing something far more intimate than she had any right to see—so, even though she wasn't nearly ready to go to sleep, she turned her light out. She heard Susie slip quietly into bed.

"Gloria?" Susie whispered after a minute or two, "are you still awake?"

"Yes."

"Can I ask you something?"

"Sure."

"Do you go to church?"

"Yes, sometimes."

"Which one?"

"Presbyterian. How about you?"

"Oh, our church is just called the Christian church. Our pastor says that God didn't intend to have all these denominations—just Christians. Hey, Glo, do you think I'm—you know, queer—because I pray every night?"

"No. Do you think I'm queer because I don't?"

To Gloria's relief, Susie laughed. "No, of course not. Do you ever pray?"

"Yes. Sure."

"Do you believe in Jesus?"

Oh, good grief! Gloria thought. "I guess so," she said. "Do you?"

"Oh, I believe in Jesus—"

Gloria waited; she could feel that there was more coming. "I'm just not sure I believe in my church anymore."

"Why is that?"

"Well, I don't know, it's hard to— I just don't believe that the only people in the world who are saved and going to heaven are the congregation of my church. I'm not even sure that half the congregation of my church would know Jesus if he walked right in there and sat down in a pew. Do you know what I mean?"

"Yes, of course I know what you mean."

"Do you ever read the Bible?"

"Sometimes."

"Well, there's something in Luke—you remember when Jesus talks about how different he is from John the Baptist?"

"No, I don't remember that. Remind me."

"OK. It's in Luke, Eight." Susie cleared her throat and then continued on in a small, embarrassed voice: "It goes like this: 'For John the Baptist came neither eating bread nor drinking wine, and ye say, He hath a devil. The Son of Man is come eating and drinking, and ye say, Behold a gluttonous man, and a winebibber, a friend of publicans and sinners! But the wisdom is justified of all her children.' Do you remember it now? And it's right after that a woman comes, and she washes Jesus' feet with her tears and she's a great sinner—"

Gloria was trying to recover from her surprise that Susie could quote Scripture; she heard Susie sigh. "You don't really want to hear all this, do you?" she said.

"Sure I do. Come on, tell me what you're thinking."

"Really?"

"Yes, really."

"OK. So anyhow, that part of Luke—I must of read it over about a million times. That's why I've got it memorized. I don't go around saying, hey, now I'm going to memorize the Bible, you know?"

Gloria laughed as she was sure Susie wanted her to. Susie laughed with her but immediately fell back into her serious, anxious voice: "OK, so I thought, what would it be like if John and Jesus were here today? John would be off in the woods somewhere, living all by himself, maybe hunting rabbits or something, and telling people to repent, and the people in our church would say, 'Don't pay any attention to him. That guy's a nut.' And Jesus would be hanging out in the tavern, drinking a beer, and talking to anybody who wanted to talk to him, and people would say, 'Don't pay any attention to him. That guy's just a goof-off.' And if some girl who'd got herself in trouble came in, people would say to Jesus, 'Hey, buddy, don't talk to her. She's just a tramp,' but Jesus would tell her, 'Go in peace. Your sins are forgiven.'"

Gloria couldn't even begin to think of anything to say.

Susie sighed again. "I feel funny talking about this," she said, "but sometimes I just get so filled up— I feel like I'm going to bust, you know what I mean?"

"Oh, yes."

Susie turned the light on. For a moment Gloria was dazzled; the first thing she could see was the blue brilliance of Susie's eyes. "I'm sorry I'm keeping you up," she said.

"It's OK. I wasn't ready to go to sleep anyway. This is really interesting, Susie."

"You're not just saying that?"

"No, I'm not just saying that."

"Oh, Gloria, I don't know—Yeah, there's the broad gate and the strait gate, but do you think that God's—? I just don't think that God's picked this tiny bunch of people to be the only—"

"The only ones saved?"

"Right. Tell me what you think. Really."

It had never occurred to Gloria to think about who might be saved, so she said the first thing that came into her mind, "Oh, I don't think God's exclusive. It's not as though heaven's a sorority."

"Hey, that's funny—but you're right. 'Wisdom is justified of *all* her children.' No matter who they are. There's good people everywhere. Do you see what I mean?"

"Of course I see what you mean."

"Oh, Gloria, I'm so glad you're religious. It's such a relief!"

Gloria was frightened by that. If she didn't tell the truth now, she'd be stuck trying to live up to lies. "Wait a minute, Susie, I don't know whether I'd call myself religious. I guess I am in a funny sort of way. Back in high school I tried to be an atheist for a while. I tried it on, you know, like trying on a dress, and it didn't fit. So I guess I am religious, although I'm not sure that what I believe matches what they teach in anybody's church."

Choosing her words carefully, Gloria tried to tell Susie what she did believe— that much of what was in the Scripture was metaphor, that many other religions were just as true as Christianity. "I went through a period when I believed it all literally," she said. "When I was a kid— Well, there were a couple years when I was really religious—"

"Oh, yeah? How old were you?"

"Oh—twelve, I guess."

"Really? Me too! I don't think I've ever been as religious—"

"That's right, you believe *everything*, don't you? I went to church every Sunday even if I was sick. I got confirmed—"

"Yeah, and I stood up in church and accepted Jesus Christ as my personal Lord and Savior. And after that, I got baptized. They dunk you in our church. Everybody was so proud of me. Pastor Harris told me I was a model Christian girl— I knew I wasn't, but it was nice he thought so."

"I don't know if anybody was proud of me or not," Gloria said. "I was in boarding school, and I just hated it. But going to church and confirmation classes at least got me out of there a couple of times a week—"

The maddening tension between them had vanished, and they were talking freely, easily. This is what a conversation should be, Gloria thought: you don't have to plan what you're going to say; the words just tumble out of you. She told Susie about Fairhaven—at least something about it—and Susie told her about growing up in Cloverton: "just a bend in the road with my dad's gas station and three churches—and you *had* to go to one of them."

Susie had been the youngest, and the only girl in a family full of boys, "and Mom had always wanted a daughter, so she finally got to do all the girly things with me she'd always wanted to do." Starting when Susie was four, they drove over to Jordanstown every Saturday morning to see Miss Laverne who taught tap and toe. "I was a pretty good little dancer. I did my first solo performance when I was five; can you believe that? I can't quite believe it. But nothing fazed me when I was a kid. I was in the Jaycees' talent show every year for fourteen straight years."

When she was nine, Susie saw a majorette leading a band at the county fair. "I took one look at her, and I knew that's what I wanted to be, so I got my first baton. I loved it so much I slept with it like a doll. And I turned into a real fanatic twirler—just, you know, nuts. And then I got my cousin interested, so there were two of us. There's nothing to do in Cloverton—I mean, absolutely *nothing*— so we just twirled all the time."

One Sunday afternoon in July the year she was twelve, Susie heard God's voice clear as a church bell. "Gloria?" she said, "did you feel Jesus in your life? You know, walking by your side?"

Absolutely nothing last year had prepared Gloria for this; when they'd been pledges, Susie had not said a single word about being religious, and Gloria felt disoriented and strangely apprehensive. Looking into them, she was amazed again at how blue Susie's eyes were; it was an ultramarine that really took the light, and, in this particular light, it proclaimed itself unabashedly like the bluest of lobelia—and then she suddenly got what she'd been looking for—that intuitive leap—and she knew that Susie presented a carefully constructed and utterly misleading mask to the world just as she did. "Oh, I don't know, Suse. I don't think so. But I've felt the presence of God sometimes—at least I *think* I have."

"The grace of God—"

"Maybe. Or maybe it was just all in my mind."

"No, it wasn't. God's really with us all the time, Gloria. Even though sometimes—well, you know, sometimes He's closer than others. Oh, I'm so glad you're religious. I was worried about that. I was afraid to talk to anybody about it. There's a lot of people in college who make fun of religion, and I was afraid the other girls in the house would make fun of me."

Gloria was momentarily annoyed at Susie for calling her religious again after she'd gone out of her way to deny it—or at least to qualify it—but then she thought, OK, I've told her what I believe; if she wants to call me religious, she can call me religious. "You shouldn't worry about the girls in the house," she said. "Most of them go to church. I sort of thought you had to, to be a Lamb."

"Yeah, I guess so— But I don't mean just going to church. How many of them—? I mean, how many of them could I just go up to and say, 'I heard the voice of God'?"

"I don't know."

"I don't know either."

"What did He say?" Gloria couldn't help asking.

"It's kind of hard to put into words. It wasn't like He said sentences, you know—and the feeling I had was that I shouldn't tell just anybody about it—"

"Well, you don't have to—"

"Oh, I can tell *you*, Glo. It was like that thing in the Old Testament where God says, 'I am who I am.' He told me He was there and He was with me and He had something for me to do."

"That's wonderful!"

"Yeah, but you can see how I don't want to go around talking about it to everybody. Glo? Do you, ah, do you feel OK in the house?"

"Oh, sure—Well, actually, I'm still a little nervous."

"Why?"

"I'm just afraid the other girls won't like me."

"How could anybody not like you?"

"Gee, it's nice of you to say that."

"Well, it's true. Everybody likes you. You're pretty, and you're smart, and you're a big city girl—you know, sophisticated—and you've got money, a lot of nice clothes, and—I don't know. I feel like such a hick."

"Oh, Susie, come on."

"Well, I do. Just this little dumbass jerk from Cloverton, and— Gloria, I'm sorry I've been such a drip since you got here. I haven't been any fun at all, have I? I'm just so scared."

"Scared? What are you scared about?"

"Well, the same as you, about people liking me—and about screwing up. I'm the only majorette with a full scholarship. And I'm getting solos, and I'm only a sophomore. And when I'm out on the field, I'm representing the school, and Mr. Allen's really counting on me. Everybody's counting on me. And a lot of the other girls are really jealous, and if I'm not good—oh boy!"

"Gee, that must be hard."

"Yeah, it is. Well, I am the best twirler at Briarville. I'm one of the best twirlers in the country, if you want to know the truth. I just wish I didn't have to *prove* it. The next time you pray, Glo, pray for me, OK?"

The next day, while Susie was off at band practice, Gloria began looking through Susie's things. She'd always been fascinated by majorettes, and she'd never had a chance to study one up close, and she told herself that all she wanted to do was look at Susie's majorette uniform, but, once she started, she couldn't stop herself, until—careful to put each item back exactly as she'd found it—she went through everything Susie owned. It didn't take very long.

She found Susie's two good cashmere sweaters and one good pair of heels. She noted the Sears Roebuck and J.C. Penney labels in Susie's dresses. She found Susie's one and only cocktail dress; it was as blue as Susie's eyes and beautifully made by hand—the finish work was exquisite—and Gloria remembered it from last spring. If Gloria remembered it, then the other girls in the house must remember it too, and Susie couldn't very well go on wearing it at every formal occasion all year, could she? What was Susie going to wear to the formal dinner on Friday? She'd have to buy something new or the girls would start talking. But could she afford to buy something new? Oh, the poor thing, she thought, she has hardly *anything*—and Gloria was ashamed.

After dinner that night, Gloria said—she'd tried out various ways to say it, and this was the most casual she could find—"If there's anything of mine you ever want to wear—you know, like on Friday night for the dinner—just feel free, OK?"

"Thanks, Gloria, but I couldn't do that."

"Oh, come on, why not? We're sisters, aren't we?" She'd meant, of course, Delta Lambda sisters, and it had been an easy, almost automatic, thing to say, but Susie sank down onto the edge of her bed as suddenly as if someone had knocked the wind out of her. Her gaze was fixed on the far wall, and Gloria knew exactly what she was doing because she'd done it so often herself: she was stopping herself from crying. "You're a little thinner than I am," Gloria said, "but I bet we both wear ten petite."

Without looking at Gloria, Susie nodded.

"What size are your feet?"

After a moment, Susie said in a small, expressionless voice, "Six and a half."

"Hey, that's great. So are mine."

Gloria waited, but Susie said nothing. "Look," Gloria said, "it's not like I went out and worked to get all these things. And when we took our vows, we said we'd help each other and share—"

Still Susie said nothing. Oh, help, Gloria thought, why did I start this? I'll bet she's really proud. Why didn't I just let well enough alone? What is she thinking? Why can't I ever tell what she's thinking? "I'm sorry," she said. "I didn't mean to hurt your feelings."

Susie turned and gave her a shining smile. "Oh, Gloria, you didn't hurt my feelings."

During registration week, Gloria declared herself an English major and was assigned Dr. Stauffer as her faculty advisor. Dr. Stauffer was small, wan, disheveled, and watery-eyed; his specialty was Lawrence, and he looked to Gloria like the Tenniel illustration for the dormouse in *Alice in Wonderland*. Dr. Stauffer had a knobby, horse-faced wife who was taller than he was; when Gloria had met her at a student-faculty tea the year before, Mrs. Stauffer had been wearing lavender slacks with tan golf shoes. Dr. Stauffer was also the father of three small children; from time to time, Gloria saw, pressed against the windows of Dr. and Mrs. Stauffer's passing station wagon, perfectly round zeroes in the centers of their small, red, screaming faces.

Gloria gathered from English Department gossip that Dr. Stauffer and Professor Bolton were bitter enemies. They had, apparently, in the spring of 1948, during a panel discussion on the critical theories of T.S. Eliot, discovered a divergence of scholarly opinion between themselves so profound that they had not spoken a word to each other since. Forewarned, Gloria was not surprised when Dr. Stauffer questioned her choice of Dr. Bolton's seminar: "Critical Problems of Contemporary Literature."

"That's a fourth-year course, Gloria," Dr. Stauffer said, staring at her breasts.

She was wearing a crisp, white blouse over a sassy push-up bra. Dr. Stauffer had not been able to take his eyes off her chest since she'd walked into his office;

it was making her feel itchy. "It says,"—she attempted to shift his attention to the college catalogue—"or with permission of the instructor."

"Dr. Bolton will never give you permission," Dr. Stauffer replied in a gloomy tone.

"He gave me an A plus last year. Everybody says he never gives A pluses."

"That's extraordinary. I've never heard of him giving an A plus," Dr. Stauffer replied like someone half asleep as he leaned out from behind his desk to get a good look at Gloria's legs.

"Why don't I ask him?" she said, standing.

"Certainly. Go ahead and ask him," Dr. Stauffer said, staring at Gloria's skinny patent belt, "but he's sure to say no. He never takes girls in his seminars."

"Oh, really? Why's that?"

Wearing a faint, sickly smile, Dr. Stauffer looked, for half a second, into her eyes, and then his gaze skittered down to caress the lines of her hips. "I don't know. I suppose that, ah—he doesn't like girls."

Oh, but *you* do, don't you? she thought. "Thank you, Dr. Stauffer," she said, intentionally using a voice so girlish it was practically infantile—a voice she instinctively knew would drive him nuts. A faint flush spread across his face; he stood—ostensibly to usher her out, but actually so he could gorge his eyes, greedily, one last time, on the dramatic curves created by her Maidenform bra. You horny little rat, she thought.

She stopped Professor Bolton in the hallway. "No, no, no, no, no, no, no, Miss Carter," he said, waving his hands in the air as though shooing flies, "it's a fourth-year course."

"Cotter," she said firmly. "I'm the pepper shaker girl, remember? The one you made go and read Petrarch in the original. You gave me an A plus on Wyatt last year and said it was graduate work."

"Oh, yes, yes, yes," he shouted, grinning wildly, and looked her over from top to toe. He studied her in a way entirely different from Dr. Stauffer—as though she were a curiously ingenious mechanism, perhaps a Swiss clock mysteriously brought to ticking directly in front of him—and then he looked her straight in the eyes. "Why on earth do you want to take my seminar?"

"You're the best teacher I've ever had in my life."

"Oh, good heavens," he exclaimed with an odd falsetto titter. Then he patted her shoulder—or at least that's what she thought he was doing—but, no: she saw that he'd removed a bit of lint from her blouse. "Why don't you stop by my office tomorrow morning?" he said. "Around nine, hmmm?"

She wasn't sure what to wear for the interview; for safety, she settled upon the dutiful schoolgirl look: jumper, knee socks, and penny loafers. She checked herself carefully for lint and arrived at nine on the dot.

"Ah, Miss Cotter!" he boomed out. He'd actually cleared a chair for her: that, and his getting her name right, made her immediately apprehensive. As she was sitting down, she saw a folder spread open on his desk: there, so it appeared, was everything Briarville University knew about her. He must have borrowed her records from the Registrar; she hadn't known that professors could do that, and she felt obscurely violated.

"Eight hundred on the Boards," he said with one eyebrow raised. She nodded. "Very clever of you. Of course American standards are not what they could be—but nonetheless, very very *very* clever. And look at that IQ score, good heavens! You Americans are so terribly dead keen on measuring things, and it's always eluded me what it is exactly that those tests measure, but whatever it is, you must have it in spades—that's the highest IQ score I've ever seen. And you're carrying straight A's—my, my, my—and a Prom Queen, to boot, and of course you're a Delta Lambda. You must have an active social life, hmmm?" His smile was as enigmatic and sinister as a crocodile's.

How terrible, she thought, *he doesn't like me at all!* And, while she was trying to absorb that dark thought, he said in a sleek, pussycat voice: "Now tell me, Miss Cotter, why does a Lamb want to take an upper level seminar on literary criticism, hmmmm?"

If you cry, she told herself, it'll be fatal. Time dragged by while she searched for something to say; then she realized that the smarty-pants part of herself was telling her what to say—something that ordinarily she never would have dared to say—but this did not appear to be the time for half measures, so she said it: "Hath not a Lamb eyes? Hath not a Lamb hands, organs, dimensions, senses, affections, passions?— Fed with the same food, hurt with the same weapons, subject to the same diseases, healed by the same means, warmed and cooled by the same winter and summer? If you prick us, do we not bleed? If we study, do we not learn?"

Just as she was beginning to wonder if she hadn't laid it on a bit thick, he threw back his head and brayed several times. That, so it appeared, was the way he laughed. "Well done, Miss Cotter," he said, chuckling, "well done!" and snatched up a pen and signed her permission form.

During her first few weeks at the Delta Lambda house, Gloria had been so careful, discreet, and watchful she'd felt like a ghost of herself, but she seemed to be getting along OK, so she gradually allowed herself to relax. Then, after the first month, she decided that Delta Lambda had been—just as Mitsy and Morgan had predicted—a perfect choice for her.

Morgan was an excellent president. Her fiancé—the suave, Rhett Butlerish James (no one could possibly have called him "Jimmy")—had graduated and was working in Philadelphia, and Morgan had never been known to cheat on

him. Whenever he couldn't make it back to Briarville for the weekend, she
stayed home, so she was around the house a lot, and, even if Gloria didn't have
anything important to say to her—didn't necessarily even want to talk to her—
just knowing that Morgan, her big sister, was there, presiding over everything,
made her feel safe.

Gloria liked the house mother, the kind and loopy Mrs. Donner who sipped
sherry in the evenings and delivered pronouncements on the proper behavior
of young ladies that would have been entirely appropriate if the young ladies
had been living in 1910—and, like the rest of the Lambs, Gloria particularly
appreciated Mrs. Donner for her highly developed ability not to notice things
that shouldn't be noticed: girls crawling into the house through the kitchen windows an hour after curfew, for instance. And Gloria didn't mind it a bit that the
chapter employed not only a cook, but two maids who did all the housework.

Gloria knew that a lot of the kids on campus saw Delta Lambda as an exclusive club for pampered rich girls, and, at least partially, that's what it was—but
only partially. Although the girls from wealthy or socially prominent backgrounds
like Mitsy and Morgan set the tone of the chapter, a lot of them—she estimated
nearly a quarter—were far from the social elite; they'd been rushed because,
like Susie, they had demonstrated that they fit into that elastic, hard to define,
but crucial category—"cute"—and they provided the chapter with, as Gloria
thought of it, a democratic balance. And then there were the rituals; in her
diary, Gloria had described her initiation as "one of the most intense and moving
experiences in my life," and she felt that having experienced it bound her to Delta
Lambda in a deeply mysterious way that defied categorization.

Gloria liked the house meetings—however silly the topics under discussion—
liked having a vote the same as everyone else, liked the feeling of being a part
of a larger whole, and, of course, she liked the formal dances and dinners and
parties for which she and all the other Lambs were expected to dress to the nines.
With forty-two sisters in the house, she certainly couldn't be friends with all of
them, or even with very many of them, but she felt quite friendly toward
everyone (well, maybe not *everyone*; there was that serpent-tongued Laura Myers
with her too-tight skirts and her penchant for making passes at other girls'
boyfriends), and she didn't know if Susie liked her as much as she liked Susie,
but they were getting along great. She still couldn't guess Susie's thoughts, but
if she wanted to know what she was thinking, all she had to do was ask, and
Gloria found, to her surprise, that she could tell Susie—well, if not *anything*,
then certainly more than she'd told any other friend she'd ever had.

The first football game was a revelation. Gloria had gone to games the year
before, but she'd been so lost in her own miserable loneliness she hadn't been
able to look outside herself and really *see* the band or the majorettes. This year,
sitting with Rolland, with other Lambs and their boyfriends, she saw why Bri-

arville's marching band was one of the best in the state and why Susie had a full scholarship. When she was in the majorette line, Susie moved in perfect unison with the other girls—did nothing to stand out from them—but when she began her solo, she was instantly transformed into a heart-stopping virtuoso. She made that strange, highly artificial movement—the majorette's high-stepping strut—look relaxed and easy and sexy; she did things with her baton that didn't seem humanly possible. She twirled it between her fingers, on the top of her wrist; she passed it behind her back, between her legs; she threw it up a dozen times and caught it almost casually—and while she was doing these impossible things, she smiled radiantly up into the bleachers as though there were nothing in the world she would ever enjoy as much as this. Gloria was afraid to look directly at her, afraid that if Susie met her eye, it would jinx her, but, as Susie marched by at the forty yard line where the Lambs were sitting, she looked directly up at Gloria and winked.

Gloria had always thought that Canden High's majorettes were pretty good, especially the two in her class—Lisa and Sandy—in fact, she'd thought you couldn't get much better, but now she realized that comparing Lisa Metzger or Sandy Caldwell with Susie was like comparing the authors of the verses that appear in the *Woman's Home Companion* with T.S. Eliot.

None of Gloria's worries about Susie had turned out to be true. Susie was just as compulsively neat and orderly as Gloria was; she went to bed earlier. When she borrowed Gloria's clothes, she always returned them washed and ironed. The boys went crazy over Susie, but she was far from boy crazy; she only dated once a week during football season, and never on the night before a game. Studying was hard for her, but she had to maintain a C average or she'd lose her scholarship, so she worked every night. (She sprawled on the floor with her books, chewed the ends of her pencils, and sometimes, to Gloria's amusement, twirled them between her fingertips.) And it wasn't, she knew, a particularly praiseworthy thing to be feeling, but Gloria thoroughly enjoyed being the roommate of someone who was rapidly becoming a campus glamour queen.

The only thing Gloria had left to worry about—she had to worry about something, didn't she?—was that the sorority would take so much of her time she wouldn't be able to do anything else, but what she hadn't taken into account was the regulation imposed several years before by the new president of Briarville: any Greek letter society whose members' averaged grades fell below a B lost its charter. Every reporting period Delta Lambda came out with barely enough to get by, and the chapter was kept afloat by less than a dozen girls who were carrying straight As, a fact that was not lost upon the officers of the sorority—just as it was not lost upon them how much Susie's halftime performances were doing to maintain Delta Lambda's reputation as the most glamorous house on campus. And so the big booker, as Gloria was called, and the star twirler were ideal roommates. If they were alone in their room with books open and anybody dared to bother them, Morgan or one of the other seniors was sure to appear, saying: "Come on, girls, get out of here. Can't you see they're *studying!*"

The entire English Department was astonished that Professor Bolton had admitted Gloria to his fourth-year seminar; he'd occasionally permitted a sophomore to take that course, but never before a girl. Alarmed at what she'd done, she found herself in a class with seven boys, most of them seniors and all of them English majors.

In the big survey course the year before, Professor Bolton had played the dotty British professor; now, in his own domain, he took his bizarre performance even further. To indicate his disagreement with ideas under discussion, he'd leap up, seize one of his voluminous pantlegs, hike it up, and shake his foot as though trying to dislodge some noxious substance. "Deeper, deeper," he'd intone in a voice like a profound organ note, "it's getting ever deeper." (And if one were similarly "deep" on a paper, he'd draw a spade in the margin.) When one of the duller boys hazarded the opinion that, "I, ah, like the kind of poetry that has a moral to it—that, ah—well, you know, you can apply to your own life," Professor Bolton uttered a piercing operatic shriek, clutched at his heart, and fell straight to the floor where he lay kicking like an overturned beetle. Whenever he reduced his class to helpless, hysterical laughter, he'd stare about balefully, his eyes popping, and roar: "Good heavens, you don't think that's funny, do you? *Nothing* is funny. This is *English literature*—and English literature is bloody well *not funny!*"

It took Gloria several weeks to figure out exactly what the seminar was all about. "English 407, Critical Problems of Contemporary Literature," was Professor Bolton's ferocious one-man war upon his arch enemies, The New Critics. He styled himself a "simple, old-fashioned British scholar—the last of a dying breed." He taught the class to chant his own central doctrine along with him while he beat time with his fist on the table: "A poem is NOT—an independent TEXT—that somebody FOUND—in a BOTTLE!"

He employed standard nicknames for the authors they were reading: F.R. Leavis was always styled "The Divine Doctor," (and, whenever his name was mentioned, Professor Bolton would sink to his knees, cross himself, and intone in the music of the Roman liturgy: "I believe in The Great Tradition and His only Son, the Divine Doctor, world without end, Amen!"); T.S. Eliot was "the Possum," Pound was "Uncle Ez," R. P. Blackmur was "I.P. Quagmire," and Empson was "My learned colleague, the Eminent Willie Enema." The only critic who did not have a silly nickname was Lionel Trilling; he was also the only critic with whom Professor Bolton agreed—at least some of the time—and he was referred to simply as "Lionel."

Professor Bolton called the boys by their first names but always addressed Gloria as "Miss Cotter"; he also, oddly, called the boys "ladies." Gloria, hypnotized by his performances, often, without being fully conscious of what she was doing, transcribed him verbatim into her notebook. Later, when studying for exams, she would read: "Now, ladies—and Miss Cotter—let us eschew ignorance and proceed upon the arduous path to the higher wisdom. Let us consult Professor Dimwit's excellent tome, *The Verbal Moron*. (Wimsatt's *The Verbal Icon*.)"

Gloria loved the seminars, and she also had never worked so hard at anything (except, perhaps, fitting in at Canden High). It had never occurred to her before that scholars might have differing opinions, and the discovery exhilarated her. If differing opinions were possible, then there might be, someday, room for *her* opinion—if she ever knew enough to have one. In the meantime, when Professor Bolton looked her in the eye and asked, "What do *you* think, Miss Cotter?" she knew that she must have thought something, and thinking something required a massive amount of effort—but, mysteriously, it didn't feel like work. She'd never had so much fun in her life.

Rolland had yet to give Gloria his pin, but they were, nonetheless, behaving just as though he had: neither was dating anyone else; they spent all their free time together. He obviously thought that playing tennis while she watched him do it made for a perfectly fine date—and, oddly enough, so did she. She could sit on the side of the court and read; and she enjoyed being outdoors, and she liked seeing his lean, brown body leaping about the tennis court—especially when she thought about what she would be doing with that lean, brown body later in the evening. She read all of Empson's *Seven Types of Asininity* (as Professor Bolton styled *Seven Types of Ambiguity*) while watching Rolland play tennis. She would always remember those fall afternoons as perfect: sitting by the court in a pretty dress, reading slowly, savoring Empson's extraordinarily subtle distinctions; taking a moment to think about them, looking up to see Rolland in a lithe, sinewy flow of movement, leap, stop, pivot, backhand the ball—*smash!*— a white blur over the net; looking down at Empson, preparing to follow the next sinuous line of argument; imagining Rolland's tongue in her mouth, his subtle fingers exploring her breasts.

In the late afternoons, they'd stroll back to the Beta house where they'd drink a pre-dinner beer with Rolland's brothers. Gloria liked the Betas; unlike a lot of the other fraternity boys on campus, they were gentlemen ("If you didn't know your manners when you were a pledge," Rolland said, laughing, "they beat them into you."), and the brothers treated her with an exaggerated deference she found charming. As the ruddy sun was sinking behind the wildly colored trees, they'd sit on the lawn chairs behind the Beta house, and Gloria would drink enough beer to feel her mind gently blur (one Miller's High Life was usually enough), and she'd think: I'm happy. How strange, how extraordinary, but it's true: *I'm happy*. Rolland was just wonderful, and she adored Susie, and she felt as though she genuinely belonged in Delta Lambda—which was especially wonderful, given that she'd never before felt that she belonged anywhere.

Rolland drove a 1950 steel-blue Cadillac; she thought it a pretentious car for a college boy, but it had big, comfortable, roomy seats, and he kept it immaculately clean. They never talked about what they were doing, but they made out every time they saw each other. She always sat perfectly upright (nice girls don't lie down) with her knees glued together (nice girls don't open their legs) while she let him do pretty much anything he wanted except put his hand very far under her skirt. The second Saturday in October (the date was noted in her diary), she let him take her sweater and bra off; he petted her until her nipples were transmogrified into smoldering coals, and when she undressed that night, she was alarmed at the state of her underwear. Oh, how embarrassing, she thought, and rinsed her panties out immediately.

She went to bed at midnight but tossed and turned until two in the morning; she couldn't stop thinking about what she'd been doing with Rolland, and every time she thought about it, she got hot all over again. She could hear from the sound of her breathing that Susie was sound asleep. Susie had so many boys asking her out that she could have dated every night of the week if she'd wanted to, and so, model Christian girl or not, she must know *something* about making out—maybe even a lot—and Gloria wanted to wake her and say: "Hey, Suse, when you've been making out, do you ever get so hot you can't sleep?" but she couldn't bring herself to do it.

After only a few classes, Gloria knew that the star of Professor Bolton's seminar was a kid named Ken Henderson. He was a senior, in honors English, and obviously very bright. A redhead—a genuine carrot-top—he had the longest hair Gloria had ever seen on a boy: it curled over his collar and around his ears. He never wore anything but blue jeans, motorcycle boots, and plaid flannel shirts; he had a clear, translucent complexion—on a girl it would have been called "peaches and cream"—and a winsome scattering of freckles; his rough clothes made him look like a little boy escaped from a *Saturday Evening Post* cover playing dress-up as a lumberjack.

Ken was the first boy Gloria had ever known who seemed to have read as much as she had, and he talked constantly—Professor Bolton had to shut him up so other students could get a few words in—and she was sure that Ken disliked her as much as she disliked him; whatever opinion she expressed, he always took the opposite one, and then, when she tried to argue with him, he'd slither away by saying, "Oh, I don't think we disagree with each other really—it's all just *semantics*." He called *The Catcher in the Rye* "the greatest novel of the twentieth century," and his favorite words were "passion" and "madness," and he was always quoting Blake (his honors thesis topic), dropping out of nowhere such gnomic maxims as, "If the fool would persist in his folly, he would become wise," or "Sooner murder an infant in its cradle than nurse unacted desires." Professor Bolton was obviously quite fond of Ken and allowed him an astonishing latitude in the seminar—far more latitude than he allowed Gloria. If anybody was headed for an A, Ken was. Gloria decided she'd go for an A plus.

"Let us consider a certain dictum," Professor Bolton said one afternoon, "which issueth from the mouths of those learned pundits, Cleanth Brookth and Rabbit Pen Warren. Metaphor, they tell us, is not *ornamental* but *structural*. Would any of you care to elucidate on that? Ah, Miss Cotter."

Pleased with herself that she'd got her hand up before Ken, Gloria said, "If a poem is well built, then metaphor operates inside it structurally. It's an integral part of the poem. It isn't just added decoration, like icing on a cake."

"Ah, yes. And how do we know if a poem is well built?"

"Well, we do a close reading of it, see if all the parts fit together, work well together"

"Very good, Miss Cotter. But do we need to consider anything *outside* the poem?"

Here we go again, Gloria thought, right back into the old quagmire. "Brooks and Warren seem to consider the poem to be an independent, self-contained text," she said.

"And *is* the poem an independent, self-contained text?"

"*They* seem to think so."

"What do you think, Miss Cotter?"

"Well, no. A poem was written by a specific person at a specific time in a specific place and was intended to be read by a specific audience."

"Ah, you quote me back to myself very well, Miss Cotter, but what do *you* think?"

Gloria was having trouble thinking anything because, out of the corner of her eye, she saw Ken Henderson wildly waving his hand in the air. "I think there's more than one way to read a poem," she said.

"Ah—yes—I'm inclined to agree with you, although it is a position fraught with difficulties—to which we shall return momentarily. Kenneth? There appears to be something on your mind."

"Metaphor is its own truth," Ken said.

"Oh? Would you care to expand upon that pronouncement?"

"It's like a—like a fire burning in the poem. If the poem gets you, the fire in the poem will set your heart burning with your own fire. You'll ignite and burn right along with it."

"It resembles a religious experience, then, would you say?" Professor Bolton asked.

"Oh, yes. Absolutely," Ken said.

"Are there any of the eminent gentlemen we've been reading who hold something like that position?" Professor Bolton asked the class.

"Yes," Gloria said, "Ransom—Brooks too."

"Right you are, Miss Cotter. But what if we're not amongst those readers who ignite? Are we to be cast into the outer darkness? How do we know what the poem *means*?"

"A poem should not mean, but be," Ken said.

Gloria didn't wait to be called on. "Right," she said—she was so keyed up she had to fight to keep her voice under control—"'palpable and mute' and 'dumb' and 'silent' and 'motionless'—and all those other oxymorons used to describe a *written text*. But MacLeish wrote that particular poem for a specific purpose. It's didactic, an argument. It doesn't completely make sense unless you see it in its own time. It was written in the nineteen-twenties. It's an argument against certain literary attitudes that were—"

"It doesn't matter when it was written," Ken broke in. "It's a timeless statement. All true poetry exists outside time—"

"Ah," Professor Bolton said, "*true* poetry. Please, dear Kenneth, could you elaborate on that? True poetry?"

"I mean by it exactly what Eliot means by it."

"Very good. What does the Possum mean by it?"

"It's like Louis Armstrong said about jazz: 'If you've got to ask, you'll never know.'"

Professor Bolton was grinning ear to ear. "I am, unfortunately, one of these thick-headed fellows totally devoid of such profound mystical insights, and I *must* ask. What will you say to me?"

Ken didn't have a ready answer, so Gloria jumped in: "That's why they've got all those rules. They look to see if the poem is complex and unified and—"

"True poetry cuts through all that crap," Ken yelled. "It burns away the mind-forged manacles—"

"Yes, dear boy, but how do we know what the poem *means?*"

"It means anything you want it to mean!" Ken said.

"Oh, indeed?" Professor Bolton said. "Then why are we wasting our time in this classroom?"

Everyone laughed, and Gloria saw Ken's face turn red. "It can't mean anything you want it to mean," she said.

"Oh? And why not?" Professor Bolton asked her.

"There may be a wide number of interpretations, but they're not infinite. The text imposes it's own limits—and also it's *not* self-contained and independent. It's part of a wider context."

"Excellent, Miss Cotter, excellent. And, alas, true poetry may exist outside time, but our little seminar does not, and I see that we have used up our allotment yet once again. We will consider these deep matters at our next meeting. Oh, yes, and as pleasant as it is to listen to Miss Cotter and Mr. Henderson, I would be delighted if others of you developed some informed opinions of your own, hmmm? And Miss Cotter? Could I see you a moment after class?"

Gloria waited, breathing slowly to try to calm herself; these arguments got her as worked up as if she'd been in phys ed; she was sweating, and her heart was racing, and she felt like a fraud. She wasn't sure she believed anything she'd just said; she'd been doing her best to defend the position she knew Professor Bolton held—the safest thing to do, after all—but she, as much as Ken Henderson, believed in *true* poetry: that fiery, mystical arrow that burns straight through to the heart. And what could Professor Bolton want with her? Had he detected the insincerity in her arguments?

"I should have mentioned this to you before, Miss Cotter," he was saying with his crocodile grin, "I get together with some of the better chaps, and we have what might be styled a literary evening over at the Blue Cellar on Thursday nights. So, if the demands of fair Delta Lambda are not too onerous, perhaps you might care to join us. Around eight, hmmm?"

Gloria was thunderstruck. She'd just been invited to Professor Bolton's notorious Thursday night bull sessions where the wit was said to be razor sharp and the beer to flow like water; only his favorite students were ever invited, only honors English majors, most of them seniors, and *never girls*. "Thank you," she said automatically, "I'd love to." Oh my gosh, she thought, what will I wear?

"Wear something pretty," Susie told her, "just don't try to be one of the boys," and that, Gloria thought, was excellent advice. She was too nervous to eat dinner, used the time to redo her nails; she wore a tight sweater with her Delta Lambda pin, a straight wool skirt, and heels. Although she had nothing in her stomach but tea, by the time she was walking down the stairs into the Blue Cellar, she was afraid that she was going to have to stop in the ladies' and throw up.

"No, you don't have to do that," the secret watcher told her, "breathe!" She took several deep breaths and then threaded her way through the students crowding the main room of the bar; she looked into several of the side rooms until she saw Professor Bolton's back. He was sitting at a circular table—as big as King Arthur's—with some dozen boys; it sounded as though they were all shouting at once. She heard Ken Henderson's high-pitched voice cut through the hubbub; "We're *all* in rat's alley," he yelled, and someone yelled something back at him—Gloria couldn't make out the words—and a great storm of raucous male laughter rose up. This is terrible, she thought as she crossed the room; *why do I have to be the only girl?* She tried her best to walk like Morgan; it must have been working because several boys were staring at her.

"Ah, Miss Cotter," Professor Bolton said—standing, turning—"how lovely of you to join us." He had his jacket off, was red-faced and sweating and drinking beer from a glass that must have held a quart when it had been full. He introduced her around the table; most of the boys were, indeed, seniors; she knew only a few of them.

Gloria was settled at the table; she refused the offer of beer, accepted a 7-Up, did what she always did in difficult situations: watched and smiled and kept her mouth shut. The beer was, indeed, flowing by the gallon, but, except when Professor Bolton said something, the wit was nowhere near as sharp as it was reputed to be. They were deep into *The Waste Land*. "—far less telegraphic before Uncle Ez got a hold of it," Professor Bolton was saying.

"Did he cut a lot?" someone asked.

"Cut a lot? Oh, ho; oh, ho—"

"—don't know what the big deal is"—this was Ken Henderson—"it's still clear as a bell, you know, line for line—"

Feeling like an outsider—even something of a voyeur—Gloria watched the boys showing off. It was as though they were in a private club with a private language and they were keenly delighted to be carrying on a conversation that anyone who was not a member of the club would have found utterly incomprehensible. "What was it originally called?" someone asked, "something about the police—?"

"He Do the Police in Different Voices."

"Yeah, really? That's perfect. He should've kept it."

Gloria imagined how this chatter would sound to any of the Lambs—to Morgan or Susie, for instance—probably deep and profound and mysterious, but Gloria had begun reading Eliot in high school, and she'd been reading him ever since, and she'd read piles of Eliot criticism, and she knew that what was being said was neither particularly insightful nor particularly original. It would have been better if they'd all kept their mouths shut and listened to Professor Bolton.

"Rat's alley—unreal city," a tall kid with acne was saying, "to hell with Dante, you don't have to know the references—"

"But if you haven't read Dante, haven't read Webster—"

"Yeah, right," Ken Henderson was shouting, "Webster's goddamned wolf—couldn't possibly be a wolf these days, don't you see it? A wolf would've been too big, too dramatic, too—just too damn *heroic*, right? In the unreal city, it's just a scruffy dog—you know, the one that's always in your garbage. That's what our life's become. We're all down rat's alley with some pain-in-the-ass dog digging up our garbage."

"No," Gloria said, "that's not right." She saw Ken stopped in midstream; she saw his face flush and darken.

She'd waited for a tiny opening and had found it; she'd hoped that when she finally said something—imposed the sound of her voice, a girl's voice, upon this table full of boys—they'd pause for her, and they did; they were all looking at her, silent for the moment, but she also knew that she only had a second or two left. "It's the dog that's *friend* to men," she said. "He digs up what's been hidden, what's been buried. He digs up the truth."

When she was nervous, she had to work to control her voice, so it had come out cold and prim; she'd hated the sound of it.

Ken Henderson was the first one to react; laughing, he toasted her. "Hey," he said, "an informed opinion. I'll bet you've read all the footnotes—haven't you, Grishkin?"

Even before she got the reference, Gloria knew that she'd been grievously insulted; once she did get it, she was furious. She hadn't intentionally memorized that particular poem, but now she had every line and every word of it as available to her as if she were reading it off the page. She didn't know what was more insulting, Grishkin's pneumatic bust or the *smell* of her in a drawing room.

By now even the dimmest wit at the table had caught up to the reference— all the seniors must have been doing Eliot in one of their courses—and Gloria was hammered by waves of coarse, stupid male laughter. She was so angry she felt as icy as the center of Dante's hell, and her mind was going so fast she felt as though everyone else were in slow motion; she knew exactly what she was going to say—of course it had to be in images from the poem—and all she needed was enough of an opening to say it. She saw it dawn on the boys that they were not behaving like gentlemen to laugh so hard at a lady; she saw guilty schoolboy looks pass across their wretched faces; she knew they were going to give her plenty of room—

In the silence after the laughter had died, she gathered up all their attention; she looked directly into Ken Henderson's eyes across the table; she smiled faintly (the ole Mona Lisa). "If my bust is promising bliss," she said firmly, clearly, "it's not for *you*, my little marmoset."

She was astonished to hear a bull's huge and resonant bellow followed by a prolonged air raid siren; both unlikely sounds had issued from Professor Bolton; he was laughing so hard he'd spilled his beer. Chuckling, giggling, mopping his eyes with his handkerchief, he said: "There you have it, ladies. Don't tease *this* little jaguar," and he did to her what she'd seen him do to his male students— what he'd never before done to her—slapped her lightly on the shoulder.

For the next hour, Gloria was acutely aware of Ken's eyes on her, acutely aware of the fact that he'd stopped talking altogether. She hadn't meant to silence him, and she wasn't surprised that when she rose to leave, he decided to leave too. Out on the street, he asked in a small, muffled voice: "Hey, want me to walk you back to campus?"

"If you'd like," she said, her voice so lofty and cold it had sounded exactly like her mother's. They walked down Main Street, turned off toward the campus, and neither said a word. She didn't feel like giving him any help whatsoever.

"A Lamb," he said, "whew."

She wouldn't have thought he was the kind of boy to notice a sorority pin let alone attach a name to its letters. "That's right," she said, "Delta Lambda."

"Amazing."

"What's so amazing about it?"

"Well, you know what they say, don't you? If brains were dynamite, there wouldn't be enough in the Delta Lambda house for one of the girls to blow her nose—"

"Oh, go to hell!" Gloria said and walked away from him.

He caught up to her easily. "Hey, I'm sorry—I didn't mean to—"

She was astonished at how angry she was. "Don't you dare say a word about Delta Lambda," she said, "not a single word!"

"Look, all I was going to say was—well, you know, what they say is wrong—because if brains were dynamite, they could've dropped *you* on Hiroshima."

Gloria thought the image was appalling, but she was somewhat mollified by it, nonetheless—but not mollified enough to talk to him. They walked in silence all the way to the foot of Sorority Row.

"Hey," he said out of nowhere, "you're really cruel, you know that?"

"Me? Good grief, you started it!"

They both stopped walking. He looked at her without speaking. He was a senior and, therefore, at least two years older than she was, probably three, but—with his smooth, pink cheeks, messy red hair, cowlick and freckles—he still looked like a little boy.

"*Grishkin*," she said, "that wasn't cruel?"

"Hey," he said, "let's be friends."

She was taken aback by his simplicity, but she wasn't sure she believed it. "Look, I'm not the one who was—"

"Shhh," he said, pressing his fingertips against her lips. "Be *nice*, Grishkin. Besides, I didn't mean your friendly bust—although it *is* fairly spectacular. I meant your 'Russian eye underlined for emphasis.' You do have wonderful eyes—Russian eyes, Gypsy eyes, Cleopatra eyes, the most beautiful eyes I ever saw in my life, wow. Do you have a first name? Uncle Bats never calls you anything but Miss Cotter, and I sure as hell can't call you that."

"My name's Gloria," she said, laughing.

"It's perfect. *In excelcis Deo.*"

Now they were both laughing. *"Uncle Bats?"* she said. "Who's that? Is that what you call Professor Bolton?"

"Yeah, sure. Batty Bolton. Uncle Bats, the king of cats—haven't you heard that? Where've you been, gorgeous Gloria? Don't they let you out of the Delta Lambda house? Do little lambs eat ivy? Hey, why don't you have dinner with me sometime?"

Gloria was no longer a pledge, so she wasn't required to ask permission from the Dating Committee, and the Lambs did not have a rule forbidding sisters from going out with non-Greeks, but she knew, nevertheless, that no one in the house would be pleased if she went out with Ken Henderson. She arranged to meet him at the library.

He picked her up in an old, rusty, dented truck, and she was glad she wasn't wearing nylons. He drove off campus, crossed a little bridge over the creek, and parked in a seedy residential neighborhood where she'd never been. The houses were old, had once been grand, but had been allowed to run down, and it looked like a highly unlikely location for a restaurant. It hadn't occurred to her that "having dinner with me" had meant at *his place* until they'd practically stepped inside it. "Ken, for Pete's sake," she said, "what are you thinking about? I can't go into your apartment."

Leading from the sidewalk toward a ramshackle Victorian house was a little archway where they'd stopped; it was overgrown with morning glory and ivy; it was, what?—an arbor? No, there was a fancier word for it, she thought, and found it after a moment: a *pergola*. Inside it, she was—she was glad to see—invisible from the street. "You know I can't go into a boy's apartment," she said.

He was frowning. "Oh, for God's sake, of course you can. Girls go visit guys all the time."

"If I got caught, I'd get expelled."

"Oh, sure, that's the rule, but— Jesus, Miss Cotter, don't be so damn square!"

They stared at each other, deadlocked. "Listen," he said. A radio somewhere was blaring so loudly it must have been on at full volume. "My landlady's eighty years old, and she's deaf—"

"Is she blind too?"

"Come on, take my word for it, she's one hundred percent out to lunch, hasn't had a coherent thought since nineteen twenty-seven." She was still hesitating. "Look," he said, "even Lambs go into guys' places. It's true, Gloria. It really is."

"Don't tell anybody?"

"Oh, for Christ's sake."

The pergola intersected a path that circled the house. Ken led her around the back and down concrete steps and into a basement apartment. It was a mess, but that didn't surprise her (she would have expected any boy's apartment to be a mess), and it was a fascinating mess.

Off to one side was a minute kitchen; most of the space in the small living room was taken up by an old, upright Hi-Fi and an easy chair with the stuffing coming out. Book shelves built of planks on concrete blocks lined the lower halves of the walls; above them were a Picasso print (one of his sad clowns), a Blake print (several of his strange angels), and three bullfight posters. The bedroom was visible through an open door; a picture of Ernest Hemingway hung above the bed. Half a dozen candles burned in Italian wine bottles. "You didn't go out and leave these burning, did you?"

"Oh, I was only gone ten minutes," he said and, with a winsome smile, added, "I wanted everything to look nice for you."

It was, Gloria thought, the most Bohemian apartment she'd ever seen, and she was delighted with it. She hesitated at the bedroom door. "Go ahead," he said, "look around."

There was no closet in the bedroom, but, instead, an old, battered wardrobe so big it took up an entire wall, and an equally old dresser, and, of all strange things, a girl's vanity table that once, long ago, had been painted pink; Ken's Remington typewriter sat directly in the center of it where the makeup should be, and he'd covered the mirror with brown paper. Taped to the brown paper were dozens of notes written on small scraps of paper—some even on napkins. "She usually only rents to girls," he said, "but I charmed her with my boyish smile. I love this place. It's so damn cheap. Beer or wine?"

"Do you have any pop?"

"Good God. Well, I've got some RC, I think."

A boy had never cooked dinner for Gloria before; amused, she sat at the tiny Formica-topped table and watched him do it. "We're just having spaghetti," he said. "I was going to get some bread, but I forgot." He'd poured himself both a glass of beer and a glass of wine and alternated between them; he'd started smoking the moment he'd walked in the door, and he never stopped (there were overloaded ashtrays everywhere). He played Alfred Deller for her on the Hi-Fi ("I'll bet you like this guy, don't you?") and then switched to Negro folk music—the "real stuff" he called it—and she'd never heard anything like it; the sound was raw, and rough, and exciting. To see if the spaghetti was done, he threw a strand against the wall; dozens of strands of dried spaghetti clung to the wall above the stove. "If you like it really well done," he said, laughing, "you use the ceiling." His spaghetti sauce was thick with meat and rich with spices; it had so much red pepper in it, her nose ran. There was no salad. She loved the spaghetti.

From her experience of watching her parents and their friends do it, Gloria had always thought that drinking slowed people down, made them sentimental and blurred and stupid; Ken had drunk the entire bottle of red wine and opened another, and he appeared to be speeding up. He leapt about, flinging dishes into soapy water; he paced in circles around the living room, sat down, jumped up, waved his arms in the air, pounded on the table, leaned directly into her face to make a point, sprang back and circled the room again. He was shedding cigarette ash everywhere; he was talking constantly. His voice was not the least bit blurred but hard and loud and fast; the words poured out of him in a great torrent. He quoted Blake, of course — "Energy is eternal delight!" — and Rimbaud in an appalling accent — "ay le joor on fo!" "In my work," he kept saying. What work? she thought, his thesis? Now he was yelling about "gray, repressive, bourgeois America!" Good grief, could he be a communist? "You've got to feel the energy in every vein, every fiber, ever pore," he yelled. "Feel it, feel it, feel it. Get it down fast, burning on the page. Never revise, never look back — like Blake. It comes to you in a fiery, burning vision, spewing up out of your guts, out of the deepest bottom of your very soul, and you've got to let it come out, damn it, got to let it burn. Blake never rewrote a goddamn word, he never — "

"Hey, wait a minute, Ken. Blake revised."

"Bullshit! Bullshit! He never rewrote a word, he just — "

"Yes, he did. He really did. What you're saying about inspiration's right, but of course he revised. He — "

"How the hell would you know?"

"I read it in Eliot. It's in a footnote."

He burst into laughter. "A footnote! Oh, Grishkin, see, I knew you read the footnotes. Oh, Jesus, you're such a good girl. Stop reading the fucking footnotes — Hey, you want to hear something? I'll show you what I mean."

Hear what? Gloria thought. She was still trying to recover, not only from *good girl* but also from *fucking* footnotes; that's no way to talk to a lady, she thought — but he'd already run into the bedroom, was back again, waving a notebook. "Wrote this one in an hour," he yelled, "swear to God. Just came blazing up out of my guts, and I got it — " He stopped, gave her a quick sideways look; he'd been suddenly transformed into a shy little boy. "You really want to hear it?"

Oh, Gloria thought — finally cluing in — *he's a poet.* She'd never met a poet. She couldn't have imagined ever being so lucky as to meet a poet. She was so thrilled she couldn't speak; when she could, she said, "Of course I want to hear it."

He began slowly, in a deliberate voice:

> I sometimes think I see a tribe of demons
> ride the night, grinning wolf-like at
> a driving rain that somehow swiftly sweeps

them on their way. I sometimes think I see,
with burning sight, a way of life. And sometimes
when I walk the flowing streets that street-lit
seem to fire (cool, yet hard and frightening)
a sudden gust of wind between the trees,
a sudden sound of singing in the breeze,
stops me dead to wonder—

He paused and looked at her; at first she thought that he'd been stopped dead to wonder, but then she saw that he wanted to see how she'd liked it so far. She'd been hanging on every word; she was delighted with the poem, and she did her best to express her delight with her eyes. He smiled, began to read in a faster, more rhythmical, more energetic voice:

—and somehow, somewhere
in the thunder-rumble, pitch-black morning an engine
bellows into second gear, winds out
a sound as vibrant as a rainstorm, and off
the buildings sounding blazes light to cut
the grasping darkness and ride the night without a rein.

These devils know no answer but are looking.
Beer and whiskey blaze them on their way.
And times are I ride with them. And when the sun's
down dry and dusty, I know no answer but
mere living to break this sudden savage loathing,
then nothing frees me but to seize the night
myself a bit and goad it till it turns to day!

And on and on the poem swept, going faster and faster. Isn't it a bit long? Gloria couldn't help thinking; wouldn't it be more effective shorter?—as the poet joined the tribe of demons and found, as promised, beer and whiskey—and also darkness, night, speed, danger, passion, madness, sex, death, and utter transformation. She knew that it was coming to an end because Ken's voice slowed down, became sad and meditative:

I look for words and sometimes think I catch
a hidden strain or see a tribe of demons
ride the night, grinning wolf-like at a driving
rain, cast up mute—before a fading light.

He'd been pacing as he'd been reading; now he sank into a chair, let the note-book fall to his lap, his chin fall onto his chest. The poem had been far too long and frequently out of control, even overwrought, but Gloria didn't care; she'd loved it. I could help him, she thought, if he'd let me, I could show him how to make it truly magnificent—but that could wait. She knew what he needed to hear now. "Oh, Ken," she said, "that was wonderful. Just wonderful. Truly, truly won-derful."

By the time Ken started on his third bottle of wine, Gloria decided it was high time to go back to the house. For a couple hours she'd forgotten that she was in violation of one of the most dire regulations at Briarville, but now she couldn't stop thinking about it—*expelled!* She suggested that they walk back across the creek to the foot of Main where she could call the cab. "What?" he said with an unpleasant grin, "think I'm too drunk to drive, huh?"

He drove her back to the house. He drove far too fast for her liking and didn't respond to her attempts at conversation. "Sorority Row, Jesus!" he said. "Do they really lock all of you girls up in chastity belts, or is that just an ugly rumor?"

He parked directly in front of the house. "I'll tell you something, Grishkin," he said. "You know what poetry is? It's the energy of life, that's what it is—no more and no less. And you know what the energy of life is? It's sex. Yeah, that's goddamned right. *Sex.* It's the foundation of everything, every goddamn thing under the sun."

She didn't have the faintest idea how she was supposed to respond to that, and he obviously had no intention of getting out and opening the door for her. "Thank you, Ken," she said, "I had a lovely time."

"Oh, well, Miss Cotter," he said, laughing, "the pleasure's all mine."

There was something in his eyes she hadn't seen there before; she didn't know what label to put on it, but it was pinched and nasty. He's just drunk, she thought. "See you in class," she said, climbed out and walked quickly away without looking back. Behind her, she heard his engine rev, his tires scream. Oh, for crying out loud, Ken, she thought, not here right in front of the house!

When they were getting ready for bed, she said to Susie, "Gee, I had the most marvelous time. Hey, can you keep a secret?"

Susie wasn't impressed. "Ken Henderson? Oh, Gloria, he's so darn scruffy."

As Gloria fell asleep, she kept thinking, a poet; oh, a poet; how wonderful, *a poet.* And then she thought, what if I fall in love with him?

7

Without knowing quite how it had happened, Gloria slipped into the routine of seeing Ken once or even twice a week; they weren't really *dating*, she told herself, they were *studying together*, so there was no reason why she should mention it to her Delta Lambda sisters—and Susie, thank heaven, was keeping her mouth shut. On Friday and Saturday nights she went out with Rolland; in the middle of the week she went out with Ken. Rolland picked her up at the house, took her to the Briarville Inn, to the country club, to Panhellenic dances, to dinners or parties at the Beta house. She met Ken at the library; he cooked her spaghetti, or hot dogs, or hash and eggs—or they went Dutch to Sneaky's and had cheeseburgers and graham cracker milkshakes. When she went out with Rolland, she dressed to the nines; with Ken, she wore skirts and loafers. She and Rolland chatted about what the Greeks were up to—and made out; she and Ken continued the arguments they'd begun in Professor Bolton's seminar or read poetry to each other—and he never touched her.

It was no longer only occasionally that Gloria came home from a date with Rolland to find herself too hot to sleep; now it was every time she went out with him. She was terrified of losing control and allowing him to slip his hand all the way up between her legs as he was always trying to do; if he ever felt her there, she'd be utterly humiliated. She pressed her knees so tightly together the inner bones felt bruised; the moment his hand reached her stocking tops, she seized his wrist and held it. With his free hand, he stroked her bare breasts; with her free hand, she caressed the back of his neck. It was astonishing how many things one could find to do with one's mouth and tongue, and, in her kisses, she allowed herself to be entirely wanton. Morgan had been right about the ear being an erogenous zone; "into the porches of his ears," her smarty-pants mind said, as she thrust her tongue in; when he did it back to her, she thought she'd die. On weekend nights she could never go to sleep until three or four in the morning.

Ken didn't even try to kiss her goodnight, but he talked about sex—"the energy of life"—and quoted Blake:

> What is it men in women do require?
> The lineaments of Gratified Desire.
> What is it women do in men require?
> The lineaments of Gratified Desire.

Gloria wondered what it would feel like to have her desires gratified; she wondered what her desires *were*. "Why don't we make love, Grishkin?" he kept saying. "It'd do us both a world of good."

Gloria liked all of Rolland's little attentions; he was a master of little attentions. When they walked into a room, he let his hand rest lightly on the small of her back, guiding her; when she was out with him, she never had to open the car door; when it was raining, he opened an umbrella and held it over her head; when she wanted to sit, he pulled out the chair for her; when she wanted something—like the Coke on the other side of the table, for instance—all she had to do was look at it. She liked the way he always noticed what she was wearing and complimented her. "You're the best-dressed girl I've ever met in my life," he said. She liked it when he stared at her with his big, sunny smile and open admiration in his eyes. She liked asking him if her slip was showing or her seams straight; she felt as though they were sharing some lovely, naughty intimacy— as though they were married. She liked catching his eyes on her breasts or her legs and then, with her most deliberately suggestive smile, looking straight back into his eyes. Rolland made her feel cherished and pampered; Rolland could get her hot in ten seconds flat. "Every time they see you," he said, "the guys tell me I'm a real lucky dog." So am I, Gloria thought, if only he weren't so—well, so darned pleasant and predictable.

One night in November when Rolland slipped his hand up to her stocking tops, she didn't seize his wrist; instead she thought: why shouldn't I let him? For the first time she allowed him to slide his hand all the way up between her legs; her breastbone—as her mind somewhat melodramatically put it—was cut by a cold blade of shame, but nothing terrible happened; he just went on kissing her. Then, much to her surprise, he began to massage her gently— almost, she would have said, discreetly. She understood him well enough by then to know that he could never have learned about sex the way she had—from a book—but he'd gone straight to the right spot just as accurately as if he'd memorized a diagram of female anatomy, and his touch was quite delicate—almost, she would have said, solicitous. What he was doing felt simply lovely, but she knew that a nice girl should have stopped him instantly, and then— Well, even if she didn't stop him, a nice girl, no matter how lovely it felt, should at least have kept her knees locked tightly together, but Gloria seemed to have run out of the will to do that; it would have been sheer torture to go on doing that, and she felt she'd been tortured long enough. Her bra was off—it always came off when they were making out—and her nipples were on fire. He was French-kissing her.

He made a slight withdrawal motion with his hand; she knew him, and it meant, "Do you want me to stop?" That was the last thing in the world she wanted, so she made a slight movement with her hips that said, "Oh, no, don't stop," and she slipped her tongue into his ear. She began to move gently with him, and he seemed to know exactly what felt good to her—clever boy!—and then it became difficult to tell who was doing the initiating and who the responding. Of course she couldn't let it go on forever; of course she would have to stop it fairly soon—but just not quite yet. He thrust his tongue deeply into her ear, and she heard herself gasp. Her chattery mind suddenly had nothing more to say. She pulled his face into hers, his open mouth onto hers, and did her best to inhale him. The first orgasm of her life took Gloria completely by surprise.

Gloria thought later that she wouldn't have been much more shocked if she'd been hit by lightning. After a moment, she understood what had happened; she pulled away and burst into tears. "What's the matter?" he said. "Come on, honey, what is it? Did I hurt you?"

"No, you didn't hurt me!" she yelled at him.

"What's the matter? Oh, don't cry, Gloria, please. Everything's OK."

"Give me a minute, let me alone a minute, oh, just shut up!"

She put her bra back on and buttoned up her dress. Her knees had automatically gone back to where they should have been all along. She gathered her skirt under her and smoothed it out. What could she say? She couldn't very well say, "I just had an orgasm, you idiot!" Although she was still crying, her mind felt clear—even cool and brisk—and the secret watcher said, "That was extraordinary, terrific, wonderful, superb, fantastic, amazing, phenomenal, magnificent, and now you know why people do it, don't you?"

Then she had a disturbing thought: of course Rolland hadn't learned how to do it from a book; he'd learned how to do it from *doing it*, and, therefore, there had to have been other girls. She felt absurdly jealous of them—whoever they were.

"Are you all right?" he said. He'd lit a cigarette. She looked into his eyes and saw that he knew perfectly well what had happened.

She took a deep breath and stopped herself from crying. "I'm fine," she said, "just dandy."

He didn't lose respect for her; the following night he offered her his pin. "Oh, Rolland," she said, looking at it in the palm of her hand. The Beta Theta Pi pins were truly handsome, and Rolland's was set with diamonds.

Gloria was not, at the moment, feeling like a particularly good Delta Lambda girl—a good Lamb wouldn't have been keeping Ken a secret—but she'd taken vows and she'd meant them, and she believed in her sorority and in the ideals of the Panhellenic movement (however much she'd been avoiding doing anything useful for her chapter), and she couldn't accept his pin unless she meant it—that would have been sheer hypocrisy—and, if you took a boy's pin, you were one step away from being engaged; you certainly could not go out with another boy. And even though she'd yet to use it on anybody but herself, Gloria could no longer make that little white lie—studying together—work; if she took Rolland's pin, she'd have to stop seeing Ken, and she didn't want to stop seeing Ken. Gee, she thought, Ken must be really important to me. Maybe I *am* in love with him.

"Oh, Rolland, sweetheart," she said, "I'm really honored, but—and this doesn't mean forever, but—well, look, you know as well as I do how serious this is, and— Oh, Rolly, I'm just not ready!"

He took it very well. "Can I ask you again sometime?"

"Oh, yes!"

Gloria always trusted what her mind told her in the first few minutes after she woke up, and some mornings she was sure she was in love with Ken Henderson and others she was just as sure she wasn't. She tried it out on Susie: "Sometimes I think I'm falling in love with him."

"Oh, Gloria, for somebody as smart as you are, you can be such a dope. What is he going to do? Is he going to teach English somewhere?"

"Well, he's a *poet* —"

"Oh, great. A poet. And we all know poets make just gobs of money."

"He's going on to graduate school."

"Yeah? So he'll end up teaching somewhere, right? And we all know teachers make just gobs of money."

"But if I'm in love with him, none of that—"

"Hey, don't kid yourself. You've always had gobs of money, you're used to having gobs of money, and you like it. What's the matter with Rolland Spicer? Half the girls on campus would give their left arm for a date with Rolland Spicer. My gosh, Glo, you can be so darn smart when it comes to books and so darn dumb when it comes to life. Don't you want to have a nice house and all that—and nice things and all that—and babies?"

Gloria did want to have a nice house and nice things and all that and babies— isn't that what all girls want?—but just not yet. No matter how well she'd learned to impersonate a sophisticated young lady, inside she still sometimes felt like a little kid (and she'd barely turned nineteen, after all), and someday she'd want to get married, but that was years and years and years away, and, in the meantime, she'd never, before Ken, met a boy she could talk to—and not merely talk to but talk about all the things that fascinated her. They continued Professor Bolton's seminar in Ken's living room; they were so far ahead of the other students by now that they might as well have been in a different universe.

She learned to watch carefully the amount of wine Ken was drinking. The best time for her to leave was while he was still excited and talking nonstop; if

she waited too long, he became gloomy and quarrelsome. Although it frightened her, she loved his intensity. When he read poetry to her, he broke down
and wept. "If I'm not a major poet by the time I'm thirty," he said, slamming
his fist down on the table, "I'll commit suicide!" He took everything personally. "Fuck Eliot," he'd shriek. "Fuck his goddamn Christianity. They're trying
to kill us, Grishkin, you know that, don't you? *Fuck literature!*"

As the term was ending, Ken finally kissed her. At first she thought he'd
bumped into her by accident, but then she found herself trapped by his arms.
Their noses collided, and then their lips met; his were cold and dry. She opened
her mouth, but he didn't take advantage of it. She'd been imagining what it
would be like to kiss him, and the actuality wasn't—well, not even an anticlimax;
she'd felt nothing, neither excited nor repulsed. He hadn't kissed her for very
long; he'd let go of her, turned away, and had continued talking about whatever it was he'd been talking about before. She'd felt, oddly, that he'd done it
not for himself but for her—to demonstrate something to her. But had that
clumsy, cursive, emphatically non-passionate gesture been intended to demonstrate *sex, the energy of life?*

"When I don't get laid," he said, "it hurts my poetry."

"Oh, really?"

"Yeah, things kind of—well, you know, get all blocked up and—"

"It just doesn't come up out of your guts," she said, teasing him.

He'd missed her tone entirely. "That's right. That's exactly right."

"What you need, Grishkin," he told her repeatedly, "is a good, hard, long,
therapeutic fucking." The first time he said it, she was shocked—just as she
was sure he'd meant her to be—but she got used to hearing it. He still didn't
do anything more than kiss her good night; when he did, she kept waiting to feel
something, but she didn't. The only time she was genuinely excited was when
he read her his poetry.

"Why don't you ever have me over to your damn sorority house?" he asked.

"Why? So you can play bad boy and try to shock everybody?"

"Oh, I wouldn't do that."

"Oh, yes, you would."

"Jesus, Grishkin, forget it. I understand, believe me. You're just ashamed to
be seen with me."

One night as they were studying for the end-of-term exams, he said, suddenly,
out of nowhere: "Why don't you take me to the Christmas dance?"

The idea was so preposterous Gloria couldn't say a word. "I can rent a
tuxedo," he said. "Believe it or not, I even know how to dance."

"It's a Panhellenic dance, Ken."

"Panhellenic. Shit. You mean to tell me they wouldn't let a GDI in the door?"

They would, of course, let a God Damn Independent in the door—if the

GDI had been invited by a Greek. Even a Greek girl could take a GDI boy. It just wasn't done very often, and it wasn't exactly the way to win a Panhellenic popularity contest. "I already have a date," she said, which wasn't exactly true. Rolland hadn't asked her yet, but he didn't need to; they always went to the big dances together.

"Well, you just go with your goddamn asshole rich dumbass fucking pea-brained boyfriend, OK? Panhellenic, Panhellenic, *Panhellenic*— Oh, Jesus! You know what all that Greek crap is, don't you? Fascism. Yes, Miss Cotter, *fascism* pure and simple. They tell you what to wear and how to act and who you can go out with—and who you can't, right? They tell you what to *think*—"

"OK, Ken, stop it. I'm not going to listen—"

"Oh, yes you are, Grishkin. You're going to listen, all right, because I'm going to tell you the truth for once. I'm fucking tired of how you treat me. Fucking *tired of it*, you hear me? You just treat me like a piece of shit, and I'm fucking well sick of it, sick to death of it, you goddamned frigid rich bitch!"

If Gloria hadn't been so angry, the word "frigid" would have made her laugh. But he was so drunk she couldn't expect him to make any sense, and she'd had enough. She stood up, walked into his bedroom and grabbed up her coat and purse from his bed while he continued to sit at the table and scream at her: "You're never going to have an original idea in your whole fucking life, you know why? Because you're too fucking *repressed*, that's why! You're like some backed-up creek in the middle of the winter—shallow and cold and stagnant. You don't know life. You've never suffered. You think tragedy is when you get a run in your stockings. You haven't got any feelings—nothing but ice in your veins."

She'd walked past him to the door, was already opening it. "Gloria," he yelled. "Oh, God, please don't leave me! I love you."

For a second or two she felt as though she did, indeed, have ice in her veins— she was chilled to the marrow—but, as much as she wanted to leave, she could not possibly walk out on "I love you." She turned around, saw that he was slumped over the table, his face in his hands. She walked back to him; he reached out for her, and she took his hand. He began to sob loudly. "Life's shit," he said. "It's all just fucking shit. There's no hope. There's never been any hope."

"Oh, Ken, for heaven's sake! You've just had too much to drink." She held his hand and patted his head. He was crying so hard his shoulders were shaking. "You're like something out of a dream," he said, "infinitely beautiful, infinitely unobtainable—"

"No, I'm not."

"Oh, God!" He was choking the words out between great, heaving sobs. "I love you so much!— I can't write any more!—I'm all frozen up inside!" He caught her around the waist and buried his face in her chest just below her breasts; she stroked his head. "Do you love me, Gloria? Do you love me even a little?"

Oh, help! she thought. "Yes, I love you, Ken," she said. She hated having to say it.

"Oh, God, don't leave me," he said and clung to her, crying. "Everybody always leaves me."

"Everything's going to be fine," she said. "You've just had too much to drink."

"If you loved me, you'd take me to that dance."

For a moment she couldn't believe she'd heard him right. Then the secret watcher told her: "It doesn't matter how drunk he is, that's just not fair."

"I'll talk to you when you're sober, Ken," she said, untangled his arms, walked to the door, opened it, and walked through it.

"Bitch!" he yelled, "don't you dare walk out on me, you bitch."

She was halfway through the pergola when she heard him running after her. She walked faster. She was afraid he was going to grab her, but she heard his footsteps stop. "You dumb bitch," he shrieked, "you'll never know a fucking thing—never never never—" As she kept on walking, he continued to scream at her, his voice rising into an anguished, tear-soaked howl: "You'll never get it, never understand it. Jesus fucking Christ! Hey, you hear me? Hey, bitch—*learn to cry tears of blood!*"

When Gloria walked into the seminar room to take Professor Bolton's mid-term, Ken passed her and looked right through her as though she didn't exist. I can't believe it, she thought, I've just been cut dead like the cad in a nineteenth century novel. To hell with him, the little creep. She firmly aced the exam, but she couldn't stop feeling guilty.

Gloria's world had too few formal dances in it; she'd always thought that in a properly ordered society there'd be one a week, and she'd been looking forward to the Christmas dance, but she didn't have a very good time because she couldn't stop brooding about Ken. He'd been—as much as she wanted to deny it—absolutely right: she would have been ashamed to be seen with him at a Panhellenic dance; in fact, she would've rather died than take him to a Panhellenic dance, and she felt like a snob and a hypocrite. Frigid she was not, but *rich bitch?* Was there some truth in that with all its wretched connotations? And was she shallow and cold?—not sexually cold but emotionally cold? Did she genuinely love anybody? Was she capable of love?

"Are you OK, honey?" Rolland asked her. "You seem kind of quiet tonight."

"Oh—I guess I must be coming down with something."

Rolland gave her what he called "a pre-Christmas present": a Beta Theta Pi charm for her charm bracelet. "It's not a pin, so you're not *pinned,*" he said.

"No," she said, "but I am *charmed.*"

He got it after a moment and laughed. "Could we say we're engaged to be pinned?" he asked her.

"Oh, Rolly, how sweet." If he'd offered her his pin that night, she would've taken it, but she couldn't very well ask for it, could she?

On the Christmas break she took so many books home they had to be packed in a carton and shipped on the Greyhound. She'd decided that when Professor Bolton's seminar resumed, she was going to *devastate* Ken Henderson.

Unlike Gloria, Binkie Eberhardt didn't get to New York very often and so did most of her shopping in Pittsburgh. Her clothing allowance must have been every bit as generous as Gloria's, but she couldn't resist a bargain; right after Christmas that year they drove to Pittsburgh for the big sales. Binkie loved shoes and owned even more pairs than Gloria did, and she had huge feet—seven and a half, she claimed, but Gloria was sure they were closer to a nine—and when Binkie settled down in a shoe store, the entire world ground to a halt and shoes piled up around her as though she were one of those dizzy blondes in the comic strips. After forty minutes or so, Gloria said, "Take your time, Bink. I'll be back in a minute."

Gloria was feeling odd—as though she was not fully who she usually was, or not fully in control of what she was doing—and she wandered into a lingerie shop intending to buy stockings but, instead, bought a pair of the wispiest possible black lace panties with a matching garter belt. They were something only a married woman would wear—or maybe a high-class courtesan (they were French and quite expensive)—a far cry, she thought, from her usual plain white cotton. She stuffed them into the bottom of one of her shopping bags so Binkie wouldn't see them.

How silly of me, she thought; I'll never wear them—but she wore them for her first date with Rolland in the new semester, and the thought of what she was wearing—what he would eventually find—made her hot before he even put a hand on her. By the time they were parked and making out, she felt as though everything below her waist had turned into one enormous mass of warm, flowing pancake syrup, and she was sure if she tried to stand up, her legs wouldn't support her.

Eventually—why was he taking so damned long!—his hand slid up under her skirt; he caressed her thighs just above her stocking tops; he played with her garters (boys always seemed to be fascinated by garters), then meandered on up between her legs. She'd allowed her right hand to slide discreetly down onto his lap; when he found the whisper-thin panties, she simultaneously—strictly by accident, of course—located his penis. It was stretched out along his pantleg like a big sausage; she saw in her mind the drawing in the medical book, the one labeled "fully engorged," and she let her hand rest lightly on it just the way Morgan had told her to do. She could feel it throbbing. With an eerie thrill—part pleasure, part terror—she felt his fingers slip *inside* her wispy panties; instantly his penis got even harder and thicker. With his usual accuracy, he found her most sensitive spot; she heard herself moan involuntarily and was horribly ashamed, but it didn't seem to matter—to her, to him, or to anything—and, suddenly she couldn't *think* about anything, and then, just as suddenly, she clamped her thighs shut hard, trapping his hand. "Oh, God!" she heard herself cry out between clenched teeth.

Her mind came back as quickly as if somebody had flipped a switch. I just had another orgasm, she thought. What's wrong with me? Girls aren't supposed to have orgasms that fast. That's what the books say. But it must have been less than two minutes. Good grief, she'd let a boy touch her *there!* "Frigid," Ken had called her; that was a laugh. Nymphomaniac was more like it.

Rolland was sitting upright in the driver's seat, and she was half-lying across him, her dress unbuttoned to the waist, her bra off, and her legs wide open. All the rules about what nice girls did and didn't do seemed to have gone entirely out the window quite some time ago. Her hand was still on his penis, and now it felt like something carved out of sun-warmed stone. He bent and kissed her; she left her hand where it was; he moved his hips, moved his penis against her hand. "Ah," he said in a distant, hissing voice, "Gloria." She actually felt it when he ejaculated. Wow, she thought.

After a moment, she sat up. He already had his pack of cigarettes out and was offering her one.

"Rolland," she said, "what makes you think I started smoking over Christmas?"

He fell back in the seat and laughed and laughed. "My gosh, Gloria," he said, "you're funny, you know that? You're a real riot."

She tried to be offended, but she couldn't; after a moment, she laughed right along with him. Then they both fell silent and looked at each other. "Gloria," he said, "I love you."

"Oh, Rolland," she said—spontaneously, easily—"I love you too!" and immediately panicked. "I mean sometimes I think I do," she said and turned away, blushing. When she looked back at him, she knew that he was about to offer her his pin again. She gave him a look she hoped he could read, one that said: no, please, not yet—although she couldn't understand why she didn't want to take his pin now when she'd been so ready for it at the Christmas dance. Astonishingly, he must have understood her. He held her eyes for a moment longer, then put the car in gear and drove away.

Gloria had been dreading seeing Ken; she was sure he'd never speak to her again, but, as she was studying in her carrel in the library on her first Monday back, a folded piece of paper was slipped over the page she was reading. She looked up, saw Ken standing in front of her with a faint, uneasy smile on his face. She unfolded the piece of paper and read: "I'm sorry."

"I really *am* sorry," he said. "I was just awful to you. Want to go to Sneaky's? I'll even pay for it."

"Gee, how could I pass that up?"

As they were walking off campus, he said, "All I needed was to get laid, you know. I feel a hell of a lot better now."

"Oh?"

"Yeah, drove up to New York. Stayed in the Y, hung around in the Village. A girl picked me up in a coffee house, a model from *Seventeen* magazine."

"Oh?"

"Yeah, I couldn't believe it. A model, Jesus. Longest damn legs I ever saw in my life. Wore, you know, like super high heels—and wow, did she ever like to fuck. Spent the whole weekend in bed, drinking wine, eating hoagie sandwiches from the deli on the corner, and fucking. Just fucked each other senseless. We'd, you know, fall asleep for a few hours and then wake up and start all over again. Jesus, she knew every trick in the book. I couldn't walk straight for a week, but it sure straightened me out. Wrote a dozen new poems."

"Oh, is that right?"

"Yeah, they're good too— Oh, and everybody in New York smokes reefer. That's what they call marijuana—and boy, can you ever ball on reefer! Heightens all your sensations, you know what I mean? Sometimes I felt like I was nothing but one enormous prick, shoved in up to the hilt, just pumping away like a stallion, in that beautiful, beautiful, tight, wet cunt. We did everything, and— Oh, God, did she ever love to suck me off! You know what she said? 'I must've been born with a dick in my mouth.'— Oh, sorry, didn't mean to shock you."

"You didn't shock me."

"So, anyhow I feel a hell of a lot better. How was your Christmas?"

Gloria didn't know what she was feeling—she'd have to sort it out later—and she wasn't sure she believed him. On the other hand, it could, every word of it, be true; how the devil would she know? She didn't know anything about people who lived in Greenwich Village and smoked marijuana.

"Here's something for you," Ken said and handed her a book. It was *The Pisan Cantos*.

"Oh, gee, Ken, how very thoughtful of you."

"Look inside."

She opened the book. On the title page was a black scrawl that appeared to say "Ezra Pound." Ken was grinning ear to ear. "Is it really?" she said. "You're kidding me. Is it really signed by Pound! Where on earth did you get it?"

"I saw him. I went to visit him."

Gloria stared at him. The *Seventeen* model had been easier to believe than this. "Scout's honor," he said, raising two fingers. "Uncle Bats wrote me a letter of introduction, so I just drove down to Washington. You know, to the booby hatch where they've got him locked up."

Gloria was speechless. "Uncle Bats said it wouldn't be any trouble to get in to see him, and he was right. Wow, Grishkin, it was just incredible! Pound kind of, you know, holds court right there in the nut house. He's got a little alcove off the ward where he entertains people, got a little screen to make it private, and the people that work there never bother him at all. He was wearing old ratty clothes, and his hair was a mess, and— Well, he's got a scraggly beard, you know, and all that hair, and— Wow, and he just talked, and talked, and talked in this really weird—I don't know, kind of—well, a *really weird* voice—and people sat around and listened to him. I got to see him twice. Two afternoons. And the second time, well, somebody had brought French wine, and we all drank French wine and ate caviar! Yeah, really! And listened to him. He's even got a girlfriend— well, I guess she must've been a girlfriend from the way he was patting her ass, you know what I mean? And— Jesus, I never saw a mind like that! He even knows more than Uncle Bats. He knows *everything*. What an experience! You know what? He told me to come back any time. Wow, it really affected my poetry."

Gloria ate her cheeseburger and drank her milkshake and let Ken talk. Even if she'd wanted to say something, she didn't have any idea what she could have said. The mid-term grades had been posted on Professor Bolton's door, and she'd got the A plus she'd wanted; in fact, she'd got the highest grade in the class, and Ken the second, and she'd beaten him by over ten points, but now it didn't matter in the least.

Back at the house, she sat in her room with the door shut and stared out the window. It was snowing, and she felt both dizzy and strangely numb. She knew perfectly well that the story of the model—colorful language and all—had been designed for no other purpose than to shock her right down to her toenails, and it *had* shocked her right down to her toenails. She'd grown up reading *Seventeen*, and she still read it, and she'd read interviews with models, and Ken's Greenwich Village model in her super high heels didn't sound like any model she'd ever read about, but what did she know? And she couldn't imagine any girl in the world saying, "I must've been born with a dick in my mouth," but maybe there were girls like that out in the world. But whether the model was an invention of Ken's or not didn't really matter; she was convinced that he had, indeed, visited Ezra Pound. He'd told her too many perfect details to have made it up, and she knew that Professor Bolton had been to see Pound; he'd talked about it in class. And Gloria finally identified what she was feeling: she was nearly dying of envy and trying to pretend she wasn't.

Gloria had never wanted to be a boy. She couldn't imagine any girl in her right mind wanting to be a boy (even though she remembered a few girls at Fairhaven who would have been better off as boys), and whatever complaints she might have made about her life, she'd always been glad to have been born a girl. Boys were so physical, always punching each other, like her wretched little brothers, not to mention loud and dirty and crude; boys were forced to be interested in profoundly boring things like sports, cars, drinking, business, politics, and steel mills; boys got drafted. But now, for the first time in her life, Gloria thought: *it's just not fair.* She would have loved to meet Ezra Pound—and that was putting it mildly—but a girl could not simply take off over Christmas break and drive to Washington and visit Ezra Pound, and the only reason she couldn't—at least it was the only reason Gloria could find—was that she *was* a girl.

And Gloria had returned, of course, to Rush Week. Now she was on the other side of the fence: she had become one of the sisters kneeling next to some terrified rushee who was trying to balance a cookie and a teacup. That's right, she thought, not without a certain wry humor, I have become one of the multitude of the fabulous, indistinguishable Delta Lambda sisters, saying in a bouncy, bright, breathy voice: "Hi, Karen, I'm Gloria, and I've heard *so* much about you from Morgan, and we're *so* glad you're interested in Delta Lambda—oh, just love your shoes—heard you were Head Majorette in high school. Gee, bet that was fun! So, you like the house? Oh, isn't it though! Decided your major yet? Been out with any neat guys? Thanks for coming, Karen. Good luck."

Every sister kept a score card on every rushee; discussions lasted until one in the morning.

"Do we really have to take her? She's such a horse!"

"Yes, of course we do. She's a legacy."

"Well, gee, we've got to cut somebody. I want to get to sleep sometime this year."

"OK, so what about Karen?"

"Did you see that trashy skirt she was wearing?" Gloria heard herself saying and wanted to bite her tongue.

"That's something we can teach her," Morgan said, "and you've got to admit she's got a spectacular figure—"

"Yeah, cute as a button, and she *is* a majorette—"

"She seemed really sweet—but kind of shy—"

Not shy, Gloria thought; she was so scared she was practically wetting her pants. "You should know her pretty well," Gloria said to Susie, "what do you think?"

Everyone turned to Susie to hear the definitive answer. "She's not the world's greatest twirler, but she works hard, and she learns fast—and she's a really *really* good kid. And the house sure needs some more majorettes."

"OK, let's leave her in."

"Sure, but then who do we cut? Ye gods, we've only cut six of them!"

Without thinking it through and consciously deciding to do it, Gloria slipped right back into her old routine of seeing Ken once or twice a week. Whenever she remembered that horrible scene they'd had before Christmas, she told herself that he'd just been drunk—disgustingly drunk—so the trick was to leave before he got too drunk. She was careful never to stay much beyond ten, and, for a while, things seemed to be much the way they'd been last term; then, by February, she and Ken began to have silly, overheated fights about, so far as she could tell, nothing whatsoever. There was, for instance, the one she labeled in her diary "the trailing clouds of glory fight."

Ken was preparing to write a paper for Dr. Stauffer. "I'm going to argue that sorrow over the loss of innocence is the central theme of contemporary poetry," he said. "What do you think?"

"I don't know— You could probably argue that it's one of the central themes, but *the* central theme?"

"Well, it is, isn't it? Of course it is."

"What? Like the loss of innocence after Auschwitz—after Hiroshima?"

"No, no, no. I mean the loss of innocence of *childhood* — You know, how the pure, natural, innocent child is gradually crushed by authority, by the entire weight of our rotten civilization—"

She laughed. It was the wrong thing to do—and she also knew better than to say, Oh, I see—like Holden Caulfield.

"That's not a particularly contemporary theme," she said, trying to sound conciliatory (although she had no intention of giving in to him on this one). "It's a romantic theme. The child comes—how's it go?—'Trailing clouds of glory do we come from God, who is our home—' and then 'shades of the prison-house begin to close upon the growing boy—'" He was giving her a blank look. What's wrong with him? she thought. He was writing his honors thesis on Blake; he surely must have read all the other romantics. "You know, Ken—Wordsworth."

"Oh, yeah. Right. Boring old Wordswords. Well, that just goes to show you how true it is, how universal—"

"Oh, come on, you don't really believe that, do you? *Trailing clouds of glory*? Children aren't like that. They're cruel, savage little animals. What they need is to be civilized."

"Gloria, you can't mean that!" He was so angry, his eyes were actually leaking tears.

"Why can't I?"

"I just can't believe it. *Cruel? Little children?* It's *you* that's cruel. You must have a heart like granite."

"Hey, what are we arguing about? Why are you so upset? Can't we have different opinions?"

He'd been pacing around; she stood up. They faced off and glared at each other. What the devil's going on? Gloria thought.

"OK, Grishkin," he said. "I'm sorry, OK? You're right, OK? Anything you say, OK?"

He often apologized like that when they'd had a fight; he didn't just say he was sorry, he pretended to give up entirely, and she never believed him even for a moment. "Why do you do this to me?" she said.

"You're absolutely right, Gloria. *You're always right.*"

"Oh, good grief!"

He paced several times around the room; then, turning toward her, his face flushed and tears still in his eyes, he yelled: "Why the hell won't you sleep with me?"

Gloria wasn't sure why, but she began thinking that maybe she should sleep with him. When she tried to examine that idea, all she found were words—words and words and yet more words going around in her head in an endless, inconclusive circle. Maybe she *was* repressed, and maybe she *didn't* know anything about life. And didn't she want to experience sex, the energy of life? And shouldn't her first experience be with someone who'd had as much experience as Ken, and someone she respected, a poet?

As hard as it was for her to imagine actually going to bed with him, that was easier to imagine than taking him to a Panhellenic dance—or even, for that matter, inviting him to the house for dinner—and she felt terrible about that, the worst and most wretched of hypocrites. And then sometimes she wondered if her real reason for considering sleeping with him wasn't simply to shut him up, make him stop hectoring her—but then, if that was the case, why didn't she stop seeing him? She didn't want to stop seeing him.

She knew that people were gossiping about her. One night Morgan said, "Gee, Gloria, I was sure Rolland would have pinned you by now."

"Oh?"

"Everybody knows he's nuts about you, and ah—" Morgan shrugged and let the sentence dangle.

"I don't know what he's thinking about," Gloria lied. "Some boys take it really seriously. Maybe he wants to be absolutely sure."

"Yeah, maybe you're right—but he isn't dating anybody else."

Morgan had not emphasized the *he*, but Gloria had heard it nonetheless—just as she'd been meant to. "Oh," she said and gave Morgan her most ingenuous, wide-eyed look, "I guess he isn't, is he?"

And Rolland, of course, did know about Ken. It was characteristic of him that he simply said it straight out: "I know you're seeing another guy."

"Oh, Rolly, he's just a friend."

"Look, Gloria, I don't want to tie you down, but, ah—I just want to know where I stand, OK?"

"There's nothing at all between Ken Henderson and me. He's really smart, and he's in my advanced seminar. We're just *studying together*." Well put, Gloria thought, *you hypocrite*.

And then, by spring, there was no time for reflection, no time to write in her diary, no time to try to figure out what it all meant, no time to sleep, no time for anything. At the house, she was the sophomore member of the Pledge Training Committee, and it wasn't a job she could avoid, and she wouldn't have wanted to avoid it even if she could; she was tired of paying fines to get out of things (she didn't care about the money, she cared about what the other girls must be thinking of her). In Professor Bolton's seminar, she'd become the undisputed star; if a final A plus were possible, she'd surely get one, but still she didn't feel safe. The critics they were reading kept mentioning writers whose names had whizzed by her the year before in the big survey course; now she tried to read them all.

Empson kept referring to Shakespeare; she read more Shakespeare. Because Eliot referred to them, she read big chunks of Marlowe, Webster, Donne, Chapman, Kyd, Nash, Johnson, Decker. She read all of Eliot, of course, and, because he mentioned them, she tried to read the critical works of Coleridge, Matthew Arnold, Swinburne, and Irving Babbitt; they, of course, referred to more people she hadn't read. It drove her crazy: there seemed to be an endless supply of people she hadn't read. She kept dragging enormous stacks of books into her room and piling them up on her desk, on her bed table, on the floor. "Why don't you just move your bed into the library?" Susie asked her.

When she'd lived with her grandparents, she'd discovered Grammy Cotter's extraordinary pantry in the basement; there were dozens of shelves, and on the shelves were hundreds of cans—canned soup, canned fish, canned meat, canned spaghetti, canned milk, canned everything. There were hundreds of jars of preserves; there were boxes stuffed with useful fabrics that could be made into all manner of useful things; there were boxes filled with hundreds of spools of thread, other boxes filled with quilts and blankets, still others filled with spare coats and shoes and gloves. At least once a week Grammy added something more to the pantry. No depression was going to take *her* by surprise—no, by God, not ever again! And the horrible thing about it was that Gloria understood her grandmother perfectly.

How could you ever feel safe? How much did it take? You couldn't read too many books, that was certain, and you couldn't get too many A's. You could get elected Prom Queen, and you still wouldn't feel safe (how about Miss America, would that do it?); you could get into the most exclusive sorority on campus, but, no, that wouldn't do it either, because you'd always know you were a fraud. You couldn't have too many combs and brushes, bobby pins, lipsticks, makeup pencils, fresh razor blades, nylons, girdles, slips, bras, panties, patent leather shoes, cashmere sweaters, pleated skirts, belts, "little nothing" dresses, cocktail dresses, or white gloves (especially not white shortie gloves; they vanished like snowflakes). You couldn't have too many friends because you'd never know for sure that some of them weren't going to dump you, so you had to be prepared with another bunch of friends in case that happened, but, of course you couldn't give much of yourself to any of them, because there were too many of them—like the forty-two girls in the Delta Lambda house, for instance—but you had at least to *appear* to be friendly to all of them because you never knew when you might need one. In high school, Gloria had thought she couldn't have too many boyfriends, and now she had two, and that was at least one too many—maybe, actually, two too many.

Get thee to a nunnery, she thought. "Oh sure," the secret watcher said, "you're marvelously well equipped to be a nun what with that sex drive of yours that's about the size and temperature of Mt. Vesuvius." She'd just learned how to give herself an orgasm, and she couldn't keep her hands off herself—the more orgasms she had, the more she wanted—and she felt sick about it, and ashamed. She kept thinking about how happy she'd been in the fall, how clear and simple everything had been; it had felt as though her whole life—and a damned fine one it would be too!—was ahead of her, but now what? She was so *in medias res*, she couldn't see the *media* for the *res*, and there was no sense of the sap or the sparkle or—oh, to hell with the metaphor! She was lying to Rolland about Ken and lying to Ken about Rolland and lying to her fellow Lambs about both of them, and she didn't any longer have any idea why she was doing anything, and she thought sometimes that all that really mattered was having orgasms in Rolland's Cadillac—they were much more satisfying than the ones she had alone—which is not what should matter to a nice girl, but it was fairly clear by now that she wasn't a nice girl (however much she could impersonate one); she was a sick, strange girl who never really fit in anywhere (however much she could pretend she did)—not to mention small, dark, and hairy (oh, stop it, Gloria!), and why the devil shouldn't she sleep with Ken Henderson?

Ken might not have kissed her, but he seemed to want her desperately—far more desperately than Rolland had ever wanted her—and Rolland was a kind, nice, gentle boy—but, oh yes, her standard word, a bit *dull* —and Ken was a *poet*, maybe even a genius, and he was obviously far more sexually experienced than

Rolland. And Gloria had gone so close to going all the way with Rolland she might as well have gone all the way, and what was virginity anyhow? If you've had an orgasm, and the boy's had an orgasm, are you still a virgin? Sometimes she caught Ken looking at her with a fiery intensity in his eyes, and then it felt cruel to withhold herself from someone who wanted her as much as he did. I suppose I could sacrifice myself to his genius, she thought—but always, when she got that far, something stopped her, and she thought, good grief, it's impossible. I can't go to bed with him. Why am I even thinking about it?

But while she was on the subject, she might as well consider—purely hypothetically, of course—what she would do if she ever got pregnant. She tried to approach the problem in a cool and rational way. She spent an entire weekend thinking about it. She even made notes. The conclusion she drew was that the only sane and logical thing to do if she got pregnant was to commit suicide—and it followed as the night followeth the day that, given the fact that she did not have even the most rudimentary desire to commit suicide, she should not, therefore, run the risk of getting pregnant.

The next time Ken said, "You know, Grishkin, you really ought to go to bed with me," she said, "Oh, really? What if you got me pregnant?"

The question appeared to have genuinely—as the stock phrase he liked to use in his poems put it—stopped him dead. He did nothing but look at her for what must have been a full minute; then he said, "Oh, Gloria, I wouldn't do that. What kind of a creep do you think I am anyway?"

After that, he stopped asking her to go to bed with him. Gee, she thought, was it that simple? Could it be that all he wanted was for me to admit that I might actually consider it? But, whatever the reason, she was certainly glad he'd stopped asking her; then, over the next few weeks, the nasty tension between them—that feeling of being utterly at cross-purposes and not knowing why—seemed to have faded away and she remembered why she'd liked him so much in the first place.

One Saturday when Rolland had gone back to Scranton for the weekend, Gloria invited herself over to Ken's for dinner. She hadn't planned to do it until the words were coming out of her mouth, and she felt herself blushing at having been so forward. She half-expected him to say, "Oh, your dumbass boyfriend's out of town, is he?" but he didn't. He gave her a small, ingenuous smile and said, "Sure. I'll cook something nice."

It was the most elaborate meal he'd yet prepared for her—not only spaghetti but an Italian salad and a fresh loaf of bakery bread and even Neapolitan ice cream. He'd cleaned up his apartment and lit it with a dozen candles in wine bottles. He put Beethoven's *Eroica* on the Hi-Fi and treated her with an uncharacteristic deference that made him seem almost gallant.

She'd made an effort too. From the none-too-subtle hints he'd dropped, she'd figured out that (in spite of his phantom nymphomaniac *Seventeen* model), he liked girls to look young and virginal—even childish—and one of his most recent poems had been a paean of praise to schoolgirls in petticoats, so she'd painted her nails baby pink and worn her most demure, full-skirted dress with flats—which was just about as young and virginal as she could get short of pigtails and ankle socks. She knew from the way he was looking at her that she was a hit.

They talked about Pound—or rather Ken talked and Gloria listened as she so often did with him. "When he's reading his poetry," he said, "he rolls his Rs. Kind of like this—" and he chanted in a resonant, nasal, oratorical voice: "Out of key with his time, he strove to rrrrrrresuscitate the dead art of poetrrrrrry—"

"Oh, no! Does he really?"

"Yeah. Exactly like that."

Whenever she was visiting, she usually, out of politeness, drank a little wine even though she hated it. She knew next to nothing about wine (her dad used to give her a little with dinner sometimes, that was all), but the stuff Ken bought was raw, hot, and acrid, and she usually drank it like medicine, a sip at a time. Now, much to her surprise, she saw him refilling her glass, and she realized that she must have downed the whole thing—and yes, she was feeling a bit of a glow. She knew she shouldn't drink any more—but it *was* such a lovely feeling.

"Is Pound really a Fascist?" she asked to keep Ken talking.

"Oh, I don't know. So what if he liked Mussolini? He couldn't be right about everything, could he? He knew there was something rotten in the state of America—even if he didn't know exactly what."

He got up to change the record; she followed him. "Play some Mozart," she said.

"OK," he said and turned toward her with a shy, awkward gesture, his hands half extended as though he'd stopped himself from hugging her. "Gee, you look nice tonight."

"Thanks." She stepped toward him, and then, as they bumbled into each other, they seemed to be kissing—if you could call it that: one of his hands had come to rest, ineptly, on the point of her right shoulder blade; his lips were firmly closed.

Moved by an obscure impulse—it felt as though the wicked, little devil from the ham can had leapt up unexpectedly to take over her personality—she licked his chapped lips. He gasped with surprise, opened his mouth, and she slipped her tongue in. She felt her tongue meet his tongue and was shocked at herself—how could she have been so forward? *Again?*—and she felt a shudder move down his hard, little body. She absorbed that shudder into herself, felt it as something deliciously naughty; her own body answered with a flushing, a warmth, with that familiar melting sensation. Oh, she thought, it might be fun to make out with him after all.

Just when it was beginning to get interesting, he stepped back. "Wow, Grishkin, what would your boyfriend say?"

"He's not here, is he?"

She looked directly into his eyes. She would have known exactly what Rolland was thinking, but, with Ken, she didn't have a clue. "You do like me, don't you?" he said.

"Of course I do. You know I do."

She thought he might be angry—was afraid, for a moment, that they were on their way into another fight. He turned away, pawed through his records, pulled one out, slapped it on the turntable. Instead of Mozart, it was a Negro whacking away on a guitar and singing words she couldn't understand.

Ken walked back to the kitchen table and sat down; so did she. He took several long drinks from his wine glass, and she took a sip from hers. He lit a cigarette. She wished he wouldn't smoke so much.

"You're in a cage, kid," he said without looking at her. "It may be a nice cage—you know, all trimmed with ribbons and lace—and you've got a lot of nice things in there with you, but it's still a cage. And you know the funniest thing about it? The door's standing wide open all the time. All you gotta do is fly through it."

She was, for a moment, mad enough to kill him and almost said, "Don't patronize me, Ken," but she saw him give her a furtive, assessing look, and then, with one of her intuitive leaps, she knew that he must have felt teased. But she hadn't been teasing— Oh, but, on second thought, if you were used to *doing it*, all this fooling around might just seem annoying.

She should make something of the gilded cage image he'd just given her, turn it around, say something cute and clever, but she couldn't think of a thing. Usually she liked the Negro music he played, but right at the moment she didn't. "Can you play something else?" He didn't answer.

"Do you mind if I change the record?"

He glanced at her, then away. "Go ahead."

The moment she stood up, she knew she'd had way too much to drink. She should stop. She *would* stop. Aware of his eyes on her, she crossed the room and lifted the tone arm. She'd been longing for silence, but what she heard was his landlady's TV upstairs—and then she sensed that he'd followed her, was standing right behind her. She turned around, and he seized her by the waist. She could feel his anger, so she gazed up at him with the classic kiss-me-you-fool look.

She was glad to learn that he did, after all, know how to French kiss—although he did it nothing like Rolland, which was probably why it felt so deliciously wicked. She opened her eyes and saw that he was kissing her with his eyes shut. How odd. She shut *her* eyes sometimes, but she'd never before been kissed by a boy with *his* eyes shut. When she shut her eyes, it was so she could feel the sensations more intensely, so that's probably why he was doing it too.

Again, he stopped before she wanted him to. "You know what Nietzsche says," he whispered into her ear.

Oh, shut up, she thought, but she said, "No. What?"

"What happens out of love, happens beyond good and evil."

She liked that. It was better than "I love you." It always made her uncomfortable when Ken said "I love you."

He'd stepped back to look at her. "God, you're beautiful," he said. "I can never get used to how beautiful you are."

"I'm glad you think so," she heard herself stupidly saying.

"Wow, do you ever have a small waist. It's the first thing I noticed about you."

"I thought it was my Russian eyes."

"Hey," he said gently, "do you have to be such a smartass all the time?"

"No, I don't," she said just as though it had been a serious question.

He wrapped his hands around either side of her waist. "I'm not a Victorian maiden," she murmured. "You won't be able to span me."

"Damn near." He squeezed so tightly it hurt. "See, it's really close," and then, oddly—when she thought about it later, it would seem very odd indeed—still squeezing her waist like that, squeezing it really hard, he kissed her. When he finally let go, she both did and didn't want him to.

Oh, great, some little voice at the back of her mind was saying, he likes teensy waists, does he? So now you've got to wear a waspie every time you go out with him—although you're not really going *out* with him, are you? You're just friends, aren't you? But maybe what's happening changes everything. Maybe you'll even have to split up with Rolland—but good heavens, don't think about that *now*—

Her knees were shaking. She could still feel it—a ghostly burning—where his hands had been squeezing her. She allowed herself to melt into him; she closed her eyes, opened her mouth, slipped a hand behind his neck, ran it through his long hair. His hair was so long she could feel little curls in it. She could tell from the way he was kissing her that he really wanted her—maybe more than anybody had ever wanted her. Oh, and she was hot. Really, really, *really* hot.

"Do you want to go to bed?" he whispered.

She felt an icy thrill behind her breastbone, and her eyes popped open. Well, of course, just standing around necking must seem childish to him. No, of course, he wouldn't want to do what she wanted to do: put something gentle on the Hi-Fi and sit on his couch and make out, oh, for maybe an hour or two,

until they were both satisfied. No, of course, that's not what he'd want to do—
someone as experienced as he was—and then she had to ask herself if she wanted
to go to bed with him.

The terrible thing was that the answer wasn't simple. She would have preferred it if he'd simply led her into the bedroom without saying anything. Now
that she had to think about it, she wasn't sure that any girl in her right mind
could say "yes" to a flat, straightforward question like that, but then, again—
then again, what?

She wasn't like other girls. She'd known her whole life she wasn't like other
girls, and she'd tried and tried to be like other girls, but she just wasn't, so why
should she keep on pretending? And she and Rolland had done everything but
go all the way, and, yes, Ken was a poet, and, yes, maybe even a genius, and,
yes, he really wanted her, and she knew he wasn't the kind of boy who'd tell,
and— Well, there was something else too, something decisive, but she wasn't
sure what. "OK," she said.

She'd been looking away from him; now she sought out his eyes. His face
looked closed to her, pinched; his lips were oddly pursed as though he were
about to start whistling. "This is a mistake," the secret watcher told her. "Say
something. Get out of it." But she couldn't say anything.

He turned abruptly away from her, carried several candles into the bedroom.
She didn't know what else to do, so followed him, sat down on the edge of the
bed. He went and got the bottle of wine and their two glasses. He held out hers
to her. She shook her head. He drank his own straight down. He lit another
cigarette. He still hadn't said a word. He kept looking over at her and then
looking away.

"We don't have to," she said. He didn't answer. There was nowhere she
wanted to be more than back in her bed at the Lamb house, alone, reading
Robert Lowell.

He hadn't even touched her, and she didn't know what she was supposed to
do. She didn't feel the least bit hot anymore—where had it all gone?—and her
mind was stupidly rattling away, saying, oh, why do I have to be dressed like this?
She wished she'd worn skyscraper heels like his wretched model or wispy French
underwear so he'd find it when he undressed her. But, no, she looked like a little
kid because *that's what she'd thought he liked*—and she found herself unaccountably angry with him, which was certainly not a nice feeling to be having
about someone with whom she was about to go all the way—well, *maybe* all
the way.

She badly needed to hear him say something. "Ken—"

"We aren't in any rush, are we?" he said. "We've got till—at least eleven.
We've got at least till eleven, don't we?"

"Yes, that's right. There's a midnight curfew."

"Good. That's lots of time."

As she waited for him to finish his cigarette, she realized that his landlady's TV was so fearfully loud that it must be right over his bedroom. How could he put up with it? "Ken—? Do you really want to?"

"Sure, I do. You know I do." He offered her his hand. It was cold and covered with sweat. He slid onto the bed and pulled her down so she was lying next to him. She kicked her shoes off, but he said, "No, leave them on. Girls are sexier with their clothes on," so she got up and put her shoes back on, although she couldn't imagine what could be sexy about them; they were just plain, black flats—and she finally admitted to herself how terrified she was. She was shaking all over. She lay down next to him; he put his arms around her, but she didn't feel comforted. She might as well have been held by a window mannequin.

If he was the least bit hot, he certainly wasn't showing it, and she sensed there was something he wanted she wouldn't be able to give him; she'd always before thought it was sex, but now she knew that it was something else entirely. "I'm scared," she said because she had to say something—because she badly needed help.

"Oh, come on, Grishkin, there's nothing to be scared of. It's the most natural thing in the world."

"Hey, Ken. If you're going to make love to me, *don't call me Grishkin.*"

He laughed, but she didn't believe the laugh. If she'd been lying on a bed with Rolland, they would by now, both of them, have been as hot as alley cats, but Ken still felt cold and rigid—scared—but what on earth could he have to be scared about?

But she couldn't deny it any longer; she knew now, without a doubt, how scared he was—she could feel it through her pores—and, with that, she wanted to be out of Ken's bed and out of Ken's apartment and maybe even out of Ken's life forever. If they lay there without moving for even another ten seconds, she'd start to cry. "Let's go to the Cellar and have a beer," she said.

"Are you chickening out?"

That was the perfect time to say, "Yes, I am. Let's stop this," but while she was still thinking about it, he jumped up, kicked off his motorcycle boots, pulled off his jeans and underpants and threw them into a corner. He took the pillow out from under her head, made a gesture for her to raise her hips. She arched up and felt really creepy about being in somebody's bed with her shoes on; he pushed the pillow under her pelvis, raised her skirt and slip, arranged them carefully around her, and began to tug at her panties. This is ridiculous, she thought; this is humiliating. She arched up again, and he pulled her panties off, with some difficulty worked them over her legs and feet, and threw them onto the floor.

Wearing his flannel shirt, T-shirt, and socks, he knelt at the end of the bed between her splayed legs. She wasn't sure what he was doing, but she heard the click of the lid coming off something—a jar maybe—and saw that his eyes were shut tight. He rose up—that was exactly how she described it in her mind: *rose up*—and she saw that he was frantically massaging his penis with his right hand. He'd smeared it with something—oh, it must be Vaseline; she could smell it. His penis gleamed wetly, but it didn't seem to want to get hard. It kept shrinking and flopping around in his hand. She felt sick.

"Ken? What about, ah—you know what we talked about—*babies?*"

"I've got something," he hissed at her. "*I'll* take care of it. At least let me get it *in* first."

Is that dangerous? she thought. She didn't know. She wished she knew more about birth control. He was kneeling over her again, and she felt him poking around down there between her legs. She couldn't tell if he was using his hand or his penis. "Where is it?" he shrieked.

"Where's *what?*"

"You know, your—the way *in!*"

"You're in the right place. I'm just—" A virgin, she wanted to say. Why couldn't she say it?

She felt his cold fingers between her legs. He seemed to think that the solution to his problems was more Vaseline; he was smearing gobs of it between her legs. He must be using half the jar. He was probably getting it all over everything. Then she saw him shut his eyes tight again and reach for himself. Gloria shut her eyes. Later she would ask herself how she could have allowed herself to be trapped inside such an inevitability—as though she had no say in the matter, as though she had no choice but to suffer and endure until it was over. Please, dear God, she prayed, make it fast.

Gloria felt a horrible stab of pain and screamed before she could stop herself.

"What's the matter? What's the matter?" Ken was yelling. He looked frenzied and bizarre; his eyes were bugging out, and he was shaking all over. "Am I in the right place?" he screamed, his voice high-pitched and desperate. "I can't get in!"

"Yes," she yelled back, "you're in the right place! I'm a virgin."

"A virgin!" He'd pronounced the word as though it were "leper." Then he said it again: "A virgin. A goddamned *virgin*. Jesus Christ, Gloria. Jesus fucking Christ."

"What did you think I was?" she screamed at him.

"Oh, God," he said and started to cry.

I can't stand this, Gloria thought. "Oh, please, Ken, don't *cry*," she said. "If you don't want to do it, then you don't—"

"Do you *want* me to?"

No, of course she didn't want him to. "Just tell him to stop," the secret watcher said. "If you tell him to stop, he will." But Gloria couldn't get the words to come out.

She waited while he screwed his eyes shut and cranked away at himself with his right hand. She knew now that it was going to hurt—that it was going to hurt a lot—so she took a deep breath and braced herself. "Just get up and push him away," the secret watcher told her, "or cry or do something. You don't have to go through this." But she couldn't move.

She felt him pushing, and the pain was worse than she'd expected. Dear God, she prayed, let it be over—please, please, please! He kept pushing, and she felt a horrible aching, a horrible burning, and she couldn't stand it. "Please stop," she wanted to say, "Oh, please, please, please stop." Later she wouldn't be able to remember if she'd actually said it or had only wanted to.

He sobbed once and suddenly heaved himself against her with the full weight of his body. She couldn't have yelled any louder if he'd just disemboweled her, and she heard him yell right along with her. She lay there panting, unable to think, tears flooding out and running down the sides of her face and absurdly into her ears. Her eyes popped open; she blinked to clear them and saw Ken recoiled back at the end of the bed, frozen. He didn't appear to be breathing, and he was staring at his right hand. His penis was collapsed into a small knob. His fingers were splashed with blood.

He started screaming—a rising crescendo of horrible, infantile shrieks and wails—and leapt off the bed. He ran straight into the bathroom. She heard him gagging and then retching into the toilet; she heard the wet splash of wine and then his dinner. She heard him sobbing: "Oh, God, no. Oh, God, no. Oh, God, no. Oh, God, no."

What about me? Gloria thought. Very gingerly she began to draw her legs together. It hurt. She sat up and looked down. She was bleeding between her legs. Yeats' word appeared in her mind: "rent." He'd rhymed it with excrement.

"Keep calm," the secret watcher told her. "Don't panic."

"Ken?" she called. "I need a towel."

She watched in appalled fascination at the trickle of blood. It was going to soil her slip and maybe even her stockings—but that was a ridiculous thing to be thinking about. All she could hear from Ken was sobbing. She stood up. It hurt to move. "Ken?" she said. "Hey. I need a towel."

"No!" he shrieked. "Leave me alone." He slammed the bathroom door in her face. She heard it lock.

You little bastard, she thought. She pounded on the door but stopped when she heard him throwing up again. Great, she thought.

The first thing to do was get out of his apartment; his landlady might be deaf as plaster, but other people in the neighborhood weren't, and what Gloria had just gone through was bad enough on its own without getting expelled on top of it. She jerked open the drawers in Ken's dresser, found a clean T-shirt, and wiped away the blood. She retrieved her panties from the floor, lined them with one of Ken's handkerchiefs, and put them on. It hurt to walk fast, but she made herself do it.

She stopped in the shadows of the pergola and looked out onto the street in the front. She didn't see anyone. She took a deep breath, drew herself up like a good Delta Lambda girl (cool, disciplined, and alert) and stepped onto the sidewalk.

She tried to look as though she was merely going for a stroll in the mild spring night. By the time she was a couple blocks away from Ken's, she let herself feel—fully—just how frightened she'd been. No, she wouldn't get expelled for it; so all that was left of the ordeal now was getting back to the house, and all that was left of the pain now was a dull ache, a steady throb; if she walked slowly, it wasn't too bad. She wondered if anyone could tell there was something wrong with her just by looking at her.

She was probably still bleeding, but nobody could see it. She didn't know why she was even thinking about somebody being able to see it, but, nevertheless, she stopped under a streetlight to check, and, no, of course nothing showed—and she'd learned at Fairhaven to blank out her face so no one could tell what she was thinking or feeling. If she had to, she could probably even smile and say, "Lovely evening," so there was really nothing to worry about.

If you called the number for Briarville's one cab, you'd get Joe Brewster in his living room, and if he didn't answer, that meant he was out driving somebody somewhere. Gloria thought of calling Joe Brewster, but the old man was a terrible gossip and knew everyone in town—including, of course, her grandparents. (Not that she was doing anything wrong; she was just out for a nice stroll.) She thought of stopping at the Cellar; there would almost certainly be some Lambs there, and at least one of them would be with a boy with a car—but what could she say? She couldn't think of a thing she could say, and, besides, she didn't want to walk into the Cellar in this little kid dress, and that shouldn't matter at a time like this, but it did. "You're doing OK," the secret watcher told her. "Just keep walking." She walked all the way back to the house.

It was still early, and Susie had a date—most of the Lambs had dates—so Gloria had their room, and even the second floor bathroom, to herself. She washed out her underwear with Ivory Snow. She soaked for a long time in a hot bath. It stung badly when she first got into the water, but, after she was in there for a while, it felt good. She was afraid to look at herself too carefully and wished she had that big, brown medical book from the Raysburg library; she wished now she'd paid as much attention to the detailed diagrams of female anatomy as she had to the ones illustrating the functions of the penis.

It was a warm night, but she put on a long flannel nightgown. She changed the sheets on her bed, climbed into it, and read "The Quaker Graveyard in Nantucket." She read through it slowly, savoring every line—feeling the surge of the great sea in every line—and then she read through it again. There were parts of it that had eluded her before, but now they were falling into place. Satisfied, she put the book aside.

Last year she'd bought all of Wyatt; she didn't know why she wanted to, but she felt like reading his Psalms, but then, instead of reading, she lay back on the pillows with the book open on her lap. She thought about everyone she knew—from her parents through her classmates at Canden High (even good old Binkie) to her Delta Lambda sisters (even Morgan, even Susie)—but she couldn't think of a single person she could tell about what had just happened to her.

She finally looked down at Wyatt. His music was calming—maybe that's why she'd picked him. Then, suddenly, his lines burned on the page, then blurred as her eyes filled. His words had released her tears, and she gave in to them, allowed herself to cry as she read his perfect words over and over:

> Temper, O Lord, the harm of my excess
> With mending will that I for recompense
> Prepare again, and rather pity me
> For I am weak and clean without defence.

Looking back several years later, Gloria would write in her diary: "The next morning, I was obviously in shock—or in *something*—but I didn't know it." She'd been congratulating herself on how well she was taking everything— how calm she felt, how rational—but she hadn't been calm, she'd been numb, and she'd been far from rational. If she had been rational, she never would have seen Ken again—not even for the one last time she'd thought was his due—and she wouldn't have taken his phone call.

He asked Gloria to meet him off campus. His voice on the phone had no expression whatsoever, and he did not say the only thing Gloria wanted to hear: "I'm sorry."

"I'm not going to meet you anywhere," she said and heard her own voice sounding just as expressionless as his. "I'll be here all day." She didn't care if any of the Lambs saw him coming to the house; she didn't expect that he would come to the house, and, even if he did, that was OK: whatever they'd had between them was clearly over, and nothing was left now, not even friendship. If he needed to hear that said plainly, she would certainly say it.

He turned up in the middle of the afternoon. It was sunny and warm, and they sat on the front steps. As soon as he'd arrived, she'd known it was a mistake. He hadn't said, "I'm sorry," and, if he couldn't say that, then all she wanted was for him to go away. He sat hunched in upon himself and smoked. After a long silence, he asked her, "Are you all right?"

"I'll live," she said.

He handed her a folded piece of paper. She unfolded it and read:

> Gloria, this life is strange as any dream,
> its protrusions as unreal as darkness cry—

Oh, she thought with a touch of the old thrill, *a poem*, but then she felt the emotion die. Ordinarily she would have been delighted, but not today. After thinking about it a moment, she realized that she didn't appreciate how quickly Ken had transformed life into art; it felt both cruel and stupid—but, nonetheless, she knew she had to read the rest of it.

> We thrust through pointed streets of sorrow, in rain,
> for meaning's life. Our shadow-echoes mock
> what river-returnings and dismal rain light knows.

Why *pointed?* she thought. What *do* river returnings and dismal rain light know? Does anything mean anything, or were all the words chosen primarily for their sounds? She'd never felt more keenly the lack of discipline—of form— in Ken's work.

Her eyes skimmed down the poem—it was a long one—and hit upon:

> You are mother darkness on which I move,
> skiff-chipped woodadrift, to what of light.

Gloria did not want to be mother darkness—and he had not moved on her *at all*, certainly not drifted on her like a skiff or a wood chip. She felt a growing sense of uneasiness. "Our plans are insane?" she read, "So is life—" She looked at him. He was looking away.

Life was not insane for Gloria. It was confusing, frustrating, painful, mysterious—but not insane. She could imagine situations that would feel insane— the one she was in at the moment, for instance—but not life itself. She tried to imagine how it must feel to think of life as insane. She looked back at the words on the page for a clue. *What* plans are insane? she wondered. Plans were mentioned nowhere else. But maybe close reading was not what the poem demanded; maybe it demanded what she'd always given before: unquestioning adulation. This time, she couldn't do it. Nowhere did the poem say, "I'm sorry."

> Gloria, our reality's illusions are
> as real as our illusion's destroying shears—

She didn't feel the least inclination to try to sort *that* one out. She stopped reading and looked out at the sunlight dappling the new grass. Oh, she thought with a quick rush of insight, he thinks I'm his muse. Why didn't I understand that before? I wouldn't have been so damned stupid if I'd understood that before. Without comment, she handed the poem back to him.

After a miserable interval, he said, "What do you think?"

"The same thing I've always thought. You're enormously talented. You should work on form and structure."

"Form and structure," he said.

Their eyes met. He was, she saw, just as angry with her as she was with him. "It's all a crock of shit," he said.

"What is?"

"Form and structure—and your goddamned T.S. Eliot—and Batty Bolton and your goddamned fucking English department—and all of your goddamn fucking English literature."

"Uh-huh," Gloria said and stood up to go back inside.

"Wait a minute," he said, leaping up.

"Why should I?"

"Gloria." She saw that he'd started to cry. She stopped and waited to hear, "I'm sorry."

He swallowed several times. "Gloria," he said, "will you marry me?"

For a moment her mind was a big, round nothing. Then she thought: oh, so that's the insane plan, is it?

"You don't have to marry me just because you deflowered me," she said.

"No," he said. "It's not that. I love you, Gloria. I love you."

She was suddenly very frightened. She knew that she could not allow him even the faintest degree of ambiguity. "I'm sorry, Ken," she said, "I don't love *you.*"

He took a step backward; his arms whipped tight into his body to arrive crossed in front of his chest in a tight V—as though she'd threatened to strike him there. He was sobbing. She almost reached out to him, but he shrieked at her: "Bitch! Bitch! Bitch!"

Later Gloria would think of Emily Dickinson's "zero at the bone"; for a terrible moment she couldn't move.

"You fat cunt," Ken howled, "you big fat filthy cunt—"

He was rocking back and forth, holding himself as though if he didn't, his chest would blow apart; his face seemed blind with tears as he chanted in a tortured, weirdly liturgical voice: "You big fat filthy cunt—you big fat filthy cunt—" Gloria turned and ran.

By the time she was inside, she was crying. She couldn't think at all. She ran up the stairs to the second floor, stumbled and fell. Then Susie was kneeling on the floor with her, holding her in her arms, murmuring over and over: "Shhh. Gloria. It's all right. It's all right."

Gloria had never been so glad to be a Lamb. The girls were wonderful; they put her to bed, told her to stay there until she felt better, brought her dinner on a tray. Of course they didn't know the full extent of what had happened; all they knew was that Gloria had been seeing Ken and he'd behaved abominably (several of them, Susie included, had heard what he'd been yelling), but, best of all, not a single sister—not even Susie who would have been fully justified—said what many of them must surely have been thinking: "I told you so."

Gloria dreaded going to Professor Bolton's seminar but went anyway; Ken didn't turn up. When she came back to the house, she discovered that her sisters had filled her room with daffodils. She felt like an utter hypocrite. She thought everything over yet again, resolved to take her medicine, and climbed the stairs to the large, single room on the third floor traditionally reserved for the president of the sorority—Morgan's room.

The door was open. Morgan was sitting cross-legged on the floor, chewing on a pencil, her back against the bed; papers were arranged in a neat row in front of her; they looked like student essays, but Gloria guessed that they were officers' reports. Morgan made her prototypical gesture—pushed back a strand of champagne-blonde hair—and looked up. She didn't smile. "I thought I'd be seeing you eventually," she said in a flat voice. "Shut the door."

Gloria shut the door. She felt a nasty buzzing at the back of her neck. "Listen, Gloria," Morgan said, "it's not just that I'm the president of your sorority, but I was your big sister, and I'm really, ah, kind of hurt, you know, that you didn't trust me enough to come and talk to me."

Gloria felt as though she'd been slapped. It would have been easy to cry; she was sure Morgan would have felt better if she did cry, but she was stubbornly stopping herself from doing it. The effort of not crying, however, was so intense she couldn't say a word.

"Everybody makes mistakes," Morgan said. "Ye gods, some of the things I did a few years ago—it makes my skin crawl just to think about it. Sit *down*, damn it."

It didn't seem right to sit on a chair, so Gloria lowered herself to the floor. She and Morgan looked at each other silently.

"Sarah Walker de-pledged," Morgan said.

Why is she telling me this? Gloria thought. "Oh?" she said. "That's too bad. She was a sweet girl. Why'd she do it?"

"She said she couldn't keep up with her studies. It's what everybody says when they de-pledge."

"Well, it does take a lot of time."

"Oh, come on, Gloria, you did it, and you stayed on the Dean's List."

Right, Gloria thought, but it's not hard for me to stay on the Dean's List. She didn't want to say that. Whatever it was that Morgan was going to say to her, she wanted to hear it, and she didn't want to hear anything else, so she simply waited. "Are you still glad you're a Lamb?" Morgan asked her.

"Of course I am! Look, Morgan, I'm sorry. I really am. It's just that—" That what? Gloria didn't have the remotest idea.

"Do you want to tell me what happened?"

Gloria had repeated the lie so often by now that she could deliver it with total conviction: "We were just studying together. He's really bright, you know."

"Yeah, so I've heard. But you were doing more than studying, weren't you? You had quite a crush on him, didn't you? So how far did you go with him?"

Gloria looked straight into Morgan's pale blue eyes. She's really ticked off at me, she thought—and this was her chance to tell the whole story. She considered it. "Not that far," she said—which was, she realized after a moment, pretty close to the truth.

"Well, thank God for that. OK, you're not going to see him any more, are you?"

"Oh, no. I couldn't—" Then the implication of the tone in Morgan's voice caught up with her. She wanted everything to be absolutely clear. "My dad was in the navy," she said. "Whenever he wanted us to be sure he meant something, he'd say, 'That's an order, kids.'"

"OK, Gloria, if you want me to say it, that's an order."

"OK."

"Look, we've given you plenty of leeway, haven't we?"

"Oh, sure, lots—"

"Have we ever interfered with your studies?"

"No, of course not. I couldn't have asked for any more—"

"Well, damn it, Gloria, grow up! Delta Lambda is a very conservative sorority. You knew that when you pledged, and if you didn't, you should have figured it out. Very conservative. And a Delta Lambda girl does not go out with a boy who stands and screams obscenities at her in front of the house. Have you got that?"

"Oh, for Pete's sake, Morgan, what do you think? Do you think I'd ever want to see—"

"Shut up. Listen to me. This is a small campus. People are talking. People have been talking for months. Ken Henderson has a really scummy reputation. You're not the first girl on campus who's had trouble with him, and— It's probably my fault, but we've pretty much let you alone, haven't we? Well, haven't we?"

Gloria nodded.

"OK," Morgan said, "but enough is enough. You're not special. You're just like everybody else here. And I'm not going to let you hurt the reputation of the chapter. Have you got that?"

This was, Gloria thought, exactly what she deserved; nevertheless, she was so angry she couldn't hold the tears back any longer. She hadn't intended to yell, but she heard herself yelling: "I'm sorry, all right! I really am. Oh, I never—" She was crying too hard to finish her sentence.

Morgan snagged a box of Kleenex from the bed table and offered it. "I know what happened," she said. "You've got a heart as big as a barn, and you just felt sorry for the sick little creep."

Well, that's a kind interpretation, Gloria thought.

"Listen to me, Gloria. You're never going out with him again. And you're not even going to talk to him. If you pass him on the street, you're not going to see him. If you've got a class with him, you're going to sit on the other side of the room, and you won't even know he's there. Have you got that?"

Gloria had never cut anybody dead in her life, but she imagined she could learn how to do it. Ken had certainly done it easily enough.

"Yes."

"Is there anything you want to say?"

"Oh, Morgan, just the same thing I've been saying over and over—I'm sorry, I'm sorry, I'm sorry. Yes, I'll do everything you want me to, OK? I just didn't know it was going to—"

"No, I'm sure you didn't. Listen, Gloria. When we rushed you, I thought you'd make a perfect Lamb, and I still think so. I just hope you don't, ah—"

Again Gloria looked straight into Morgan's eyes. My hair's styled like hers, she thought, and sometimes I dress like her; I try to walk like her, and sometimes I even catch myself talking like her; so am I going to hold it against her just because she chewed me out? No, of course not. And I deserved every word of it. Gloria didn't know what to say, so she offered her hand. Morgan looked surprised, but she took it. They sat a moment, holding hands; then they both let go.

"Wow, am I ever glad that's over!" Morgan said. For the first time since Gloria had walked into her room she smiled. "I don't like this part of the job, I really don't."

"Oh, Morgan, I'm so sorry."

"Hey, don't start crying again. Everything's going to be fine. You just take it easy, Glo. Pull yourself together. Finals are coming up."

Right, Gloria thought, and the chapter needs my GPA. Well, why not? It was the least she could do for Delta Lambda.

Ken appeared for none of his classes that week, and, despite herself, Gloria began to worry about him. The following week she found out what had happened—the entire English department was buzzing with it—he'd packed up and left Briarville, no one knew exactly when. He hadn't bothered to tell anyone—not the Registrar, not his faculty advisor, not even his landlady.

Ken had been less than a month away from graduating in honors English; he'd been carrying straight A's; he would surely have been nominated for Phi Beta Kappa; he'd been provisionally accepted at several graduate schools—even Yale!—but now he'd probably get drafted. If the administration had managed to track him down, the administration wasn't telling anyone, and the kids in the Department offered a variety of guesses where Ken might have gone; New York or California were considered the best bets. Gloria said nothing. She knew it was her fault.

Gloria didn't have time to brood about what had happened because Hell Week was beginning. On Sunday night, Morgan gave the final instructions to the sisters: "Don't be mean to the pledges. Remember what it was like when you went through it. Just stick to the rules, and don't let them get away with a darned thing."

As sophomore member of the Pledge Training Committee, Gloria took her turn at morning inspection. She thought that if the pledges had to be up and dressed at that ungodly hour, she should be too, so she didn't do what had been done to her: wear pajamas while she was inspecting them. None of them were what she would have called perfect, but she passed them all. Let somebody else, she thought, tell Karen Thompson to go back to the dorm and put a girdle on—as, indeed, someone did later in the day.

Gloria felt very tender toward the pledges. When, during the Trial of the Three Questions, they wept and revealed their terrible secrets—none, she thought, particularly terrible—she cried silently right along with them. She was crying a lot these days; anything the least bit sad could make her cry, and, at the same time, she felt numb and distant as though she were an inept actress hired to impersonate herself. When the Lambs elected next year's officers, Gloria was surprised to hear herself nominated for Rush Chairman, was even more surprised that it was Morgan who'd nominated her. Two other girls were also nominated, but Gloria won. The ballot had been secret, but she would have bet that it had been a close vote. She felt both annoyed (it was a heck of a lot of work) and grateful (at least a few girls in the house still liked her). I wouldn't have voted for me, she thought.

Gloria didn't feel fit for human company—not even Rolland's. She'd used Hell Week as an excuse not to see him, and then she used final exams as an excuse not to see him. She wouldn't have thought it possible, but she didn't want to go to the White and Gold, and, if she could have found any graceful way out, she wouldn't have gone.

On her last trip to New York with her mother, she'd been fitted for a new formal, one that was older and more sophisticated than she'd ever worn before; it was smoke and silver, princess length, quite low cut, and she didn't want to wear it— would have preferred to revert to her *jeune fille* Cinderella persona—but she didn't have any choice; she couldn't very well get another one made at this late date. Preparing to do her makeup, looking in the mirror at her freshly scrubbed, bare skin, she saw a sad, tired girl who wanted to stay home with a book. Maybe if I put on lots and lots of makeup, she thought, just gobs of it, nobody will be able to see *me* at all.

When Rolland picked her up, she could sense that something was wrong. Just as he always did, he told her she looked fabulous, but his words sounded automatic, formulaic. In the car, he said, "Are you all right?"

"I'm just fine— Oh, well, a bit tired, I guess. You know, exams and everything."

"Yeah, exams. How'd you do?"

"Oh, I aced everything. At least I'm pretty sure I did. How about you?"

"Well, I don't think I bombed anything. You *really* all right?"

At the country club, they danced several dances, then walked out onto the terrace. She couldn't understand what was happening. They might not ever have said anything especially profound to each other, but, always before, they'd been able to talk easily; now every word felt like an effort.

She thought he should be wanting to kiss her, but he didn't make any moves in that direction. He lit a cigarette, leaned on the balustrade, and stared out at the golf course. "Remember the White and Gold last year?" he said.

"Of course I do."

"When I first saw you, I was scared to death of you," he said.

"*You?* Rolland Spicer, big man on campus. Oh, come on."

"Yeah, I really was. That's why I just had to talk to you."

"The challenge, huh?"

"Oh, yeah. The challenge." After a moment, he said, "Yeah, you sure can look icy when you want to, Glo. You sure look icy tonight."

Oh, great, she thought. "What's the matter, Rolly?" she said.

"Oh, nothing. Nothing—really."

He snapped his cigarette off the terrace in a fiery arc; he took her in his arms, tilted her face up, and kissed her. His movements had been uncharacteristically stiff, and it was the first time he'd ever made her feel grabbed. Her mouth opened automatically, but the moment she felt his tongue, her stomach contracted. What's the matter with me? she thought, panicked. After a moment he let her go.

He was breathing hard. She saw a look on his face she'd seen before only on the tennis court: he was furious, barely able to control himself. He lit another cigarette. Oh, wonderful, she thought; everybody in the world's mad at me.

"Rolland," she said, "what's going on?"

"You tell me what's going on. Look," he said, "I'm trying to behave like a gentleman, but— Well, gee whiz, Gloria, I just want to know where I stand."

She still didn't know what to say. "Some of the guys at the house have been really riding me," he said.

"Oh?"

"Come on, Glo, you know what I mean. About *you*—you and that— Oh, hell."

"Rolly, we were only studying together. I told you that. I thought— I really thought we were just friends. He was—" Could she actually call Ken "crazy"?

"I never made out with him," she said. "Did you think I did?"

"I don't know what to think."

"He kissed me a couple times. That was it. You know, just good-night kisses. Just a peck. And that was it. We, ah— He's a poet, Rolly. He read me his poems."

"Read you his poems?" he said in a queer, strangled voice. Oh, she thought, he's really hurt.

Rolland Spicer was a human being with real feelings. Why was that so surprising? What was it she'd thought he was? A six-foot-tall teddy bear so cunningly designed that when you wind it up, it makes out? I'm a terrible person, she thought.

"I'm sorry," she said. How many times did she have to say it? Don't cry, she told herself, but she was already doing it.

"Oh, honey," he said, "don't," and put his arms around her.

He held her a moment, then kissed her again. She kissed him back desperately, and, just as she was beginning to feel something—that lovely melting sensation—she saw a picture in her mind, sudden and unexpected: Ken Henderson's long, dirty fingernails. Her stomach *turned over*— Professor Bolton had said once when they'd been reading Empson that clichés get to be clichés because they're *true*, and this one, however improbable, had turned out to be true: her stomach had felt as though it were a hard lump the size of a basketball, that it had rotated a hundred and eighty degrees. She pulled away, pushed

Rolland away, and leaned over the balustrade, trying not to gag—or at least trying to look as though she were doing something other than gagging. She took several deep breaths, then, terrified, turned to look at him again.

He was not someone who'd ever learned to disguise his feelings, and he could not disguise them now; she saw shock, confusion, anger. "Oh, Rolly," she said, "I'm not a nice girl!"

She was using every trick she'd ever learned to stop herself from crying; she felt herself splitting apart; it was a very familiar feeling. The secret watcher said, "Just keep breathing—easy, easy—and you'll be OK."

Rolland lit his third cigarette. "Why aren't you a nice girl?" he said quietly. She heard the danger in the quiet.

"I shouldn't have—shouldn't have done anything I did. I didn't know what I was doing. He really hurt me."

"Oh, you poor kid."

"Wait, Rolly. You don't understand. Wait a minute. I'll tell you what happened. I want to."

"I don't want to hear it. It's none of my business."

"Oh, Rolly, listen!"

Instead of listening, he put his arms around her again. "It's OK, honey," he said, "you're so tender-hearted, you probably felt sorry for him."

Gee, that's strange, she thought. That sounded exactly like Morgan.

Then she got it: of course it had sounded exactly like Morgan; *it had come straight from Morgan.* But when could he have talked to Morgan? Had he actually come over to the house on one of the nights when she'd been seeing Ken? She could imagine them deep in a little *tête-à-tête* in the beau parlour; Morgan is saying: "Don't worry, Rolland. She doesn't care about him, she just feels sorry for him. She's got a really soft heart, you know—a real sucker for misfits. Ye gods, she'd even take in stray cats if we let her."

Yes, that's what Morgan must have said, or something much like it; she'd been standing right next to Gloria during the Trial of the Three Questions when Gloria had told the story of the worst thing she'd ever done in her life—betraying the little fat girl at Fairhaven.

"You had quite a crush on him, didn't you?" Morgan had said, and it hadn't just been a lucky guess; Susie had spilled the beans. She'd probably thought it had been for Gloria's own good.

"People are talking," Morgan had said—well, that had been one heck of an understatement. Everybody must be talking, everybody in the whole darned house, and all the boys in Beta Theta Pi, and probably half the Greeks on campus.

Gloria's mind supplied her with another perfectly accurate clichéd image: it was as though she'd been standing at the edge of a sheer cliff; if she'd taken one more step—even half a step—she would have fallen a million miles to utter disaster. The ground was still crumbling away beneath her feet. "Save your-self," the secret watcher told her. "Do anything you have to. For starters, cry—and cry really hard."

It wasn't difficult to cry. All she had to do was hold her breath and think about how bad she felt; once she started, it was easy enough to keep it going, easy enough to make it really dramatic—complete with big, loud, painful sobs. "He really *hurt me*," she wailed between sobs. "Oh, Rolly, it was so *terrible*— I thought we were just *friends*, but he fell *in love* with me— He wouldn't let me *alone*— I couldn't *get rid* of him— He was so pathetic and *miserable*— I tried to be *nice* about it, but— Oh, Rolly, he was just so *crazy!*"

Rolland had melted into a great puddle of slush. He kept patting her, saying: "Shhh, shhh, shhh— Oh, Gloria— Oh, don't— Oh, it's going to be all right— Oh, you poor kid—"

When she was sure she'd cried long enough, she allowed it to run down. Just as she'd known he would, he kissed her. "Oh, sweetheart," he said, "I'm so sorry."

Great, she thought, now *he's* sorry.

"I tried to be a gentleman about all this," he said, "but Jeez, Glo, it's been hard! You know I love you. I've been in love with you all year. I'm just nuts about you!"

"Oh, I love you too, Rolland."

"Look, do you, ah— I'd be so happy, if, ah—"

"OK," she said, maybe a little too quickly.

"Do you mean it?"

"Yes, yes, I mean it. I really mean it. I'd be honored." Help, she thought. I'm trapped in an old, corny novel, and I can't get out.

He unfastened his pin from his tuxedo jacket. She stood unmoving—the most docile of Lambs—while he pinned his pin next to hers. Boys were so clumsy at that sort of thing, but she knew she had to let him do it.

Gloria spent a full half hour in the ladies' redoing her makeup; she wanted to look absolutely perfect. Julie joined her briefly at the mirror, saw Rolland's pin, squealed: "Oh, Gloria! Wow-eee!"

"Shhh," Gloria said, "don't tell anybody," but she knew Julie would.

When she returned to the dance floor, she was mobbed by Lambs. She was hugged a hundred times, and some of them were even crying, and Susie was so excited she actually jumped up and down in her full-length formal and heels. "Oh, we're so happy for you!" the girls kept saying, and the band leader intoned through his mike: "This next one's for Gloria from Delta Lambda and Rolland from Beta Theta Pi. They just got pinned. Congratulations, kids!" and everyone applauded. Gloria imagined Ken Henderson saying: "Oh, Grishkin, you're such a good girl."

Gloria and Rolland danced alone inside a ring of happy, smiling faces. Rolland's brothers seemed to be just as pleased as Gloria's sisters, and then, as Rolland swept her around to the far side of the floor, she saw, in a dark corner, the weird image of Professor Bolton in a tuxedo; smiling, he bowed to her—a slight but unmistakable gesture—as she danced past.

Throughout the evening the Betas kept cutting in until she'd danced with all of Rolland's friends; looking over their shoulders, she saw Rolland dancing with Lambs—with Debbie and Nancy and Betsy and Julie, and, of course, with Susie and Morgan. After the last dance, as Gloria was gathering her things together, Morgan drew her close and whispered in her ear: "See, silly, I told you everything would work out fine."

The following night after dinner the Lambs performed the ritual for girls who'd been pinned: a lighted candle was passed from sister to sister until Gloria, who received it last, blew it out. Gloria loved rituals, and she was touched by this one, but her feelings were mixed—that was putting it mildly—and, when she cried, it was certainly not from an emotion as simple as joy. Then, the next night, the Lambs performed the ritual for the sisters who were graduating—goodbye Morgan! Gloria thought, and cried again—and the school year was over.

The day before she was to leave for the summer, Gloria found herself wandering around the campus trying to think of something that might cheer her up. Rolland had left, and they'd promised to write each other once a week. Susie had left, saying, "Hey, Glo, good going. You've sure got the world by the tail!" Morgan had left just an hour before, and she was leaving for good; Gloria had vowed to keep in touch and be her friend forever. And most of the other Lambs had left; the house felt empty and strange.

Gloria was more than ready to leave, but her father wasn't coming for her until tomorrow (no, he'd said, he couldn't take Saturday off; he was far too busy), and today the sun was blazing, and the campus looked pretty enough to be photographed for the cover of the college calendar. She'd tried to cheer herself up by wearing a bouncy, sparkling, full-skirted summer dress with her new white sandals—an ensemble that should have made her feel young as Alice and fresh as paint—but it hadn't worked, and she might as well have been the only miserable girl on the face of the earth. She was tired of saying goodbye, and tired of smiling when she didn't feel like smiling, and she was just plain tired. She was fairly certain she'd got her A plus from Professor Bolton; if she knew for sure she'd got it, that might cheer her up just a little.

The secretary appeared to be the only person in the English Department, but Gloria looked down the hall and saw Professor Bolton's open door. "Oh, Miss Cotter," he said, "how lovely you should drop by. Come in, my dear, come in. Oh, and congratulations. I gather you've caught the biggest fish in the pond."

Riding his wheeled chair like a huge child on a wagon, he shot from behind the desk, rolled around to the side of it, and gathered up a stack of exam blue-books so she could sit down. "Ah, yes, I'm afraid the end of term does rather overwhelm one—" Gloria sat down.

"I won't keep you in suspense, Miss Cotter. You performed splendidly on your final—so splendidly that once again the rare garland of first-class honors will bedeck your fair brow." Gloria did her best to smile.

"Oh, I'm so terribly pleased with your work, my dear. I do so want to tell you how much I appreciate it. Why, your essay on Wretched Richards—a marvel, believe me—" To her utter dismay, Gloria felt silent tears running down her cheeks. She looked at the floor and hoped he wouldn't notice.

"Good heavens, Miss Cotter," he said and made a little clicking sound with his tongue. "Whatever is the matter? Have I said something to upset you?"

"Oh, no, of course you haven't. I'm all right, it's just—" and now Gloria felt her tears splashing down full tilt. "Oh, I hate this! I'm sorry. I'm really, really sorry."

None of her usual tricks for stopping herself from crying were working. She hung her head and sobbed. She hadn't known that she felt quite *that* bad.

"This surely can't be an academic problem?" he said.

"Oh, no. It's, ah—personal."

"Personal?" He gave her a long, dark, and intensely scrutinizing look. "Ah!" he said and mugged a then-came-the-dawn reaction. "I see. This has something to do with our errant bad boy, doesn't it?"

Afraid to speak, Gloria nodded. "Ah," he said again, "you must tell me all about it."

"I'm not sure I can— Oh, Professor Bolton— Has anybody heard from him? Does anybody know where he went?"

"No. No one has heard from him—the bloody, little twit."

"It's all my fault! He asked me to marry him—"

"Marry him? Marry him! Good and triumphant Christ!"

He began flinging papers about. "Marry him, marry him," he muttered, "Good God, Good God." He unearthed one of his pipes, got it going, stared hard at Gloria. "Nothing is your fault, my dear. Absolutely nothing. Really, my dear, you must tell me all about it—absolutely everything."

"I don't know if I can."

"Of course you can."

It appeared, however, that all Gloria could do was keep on crying. He regarded her a moment longer and then said, "Come, come— Let us go then, you and I—"

"Through certain half deserted streets—" she managed to say between sobs, and allowed him to guide her out of his office, down the stairs, and into the faculty parking lot. He drove a battered Nash Rambler; he opened the door for her, and she got in. It never once occurred to her to ask him where they were going.

She'd often pedalled her bike past Professor Bolton's little house; it was tucked away near the creek behind some thick and hoary maple trees at the far western edge of the campus; she'd gazed at it curiously, but it had never seemed a possibility that she would ever be invited inside (only his most favored students, all of them boys, were ever invited inside), but now she was being ushered in by the elbow. She had, thank heaven, stopped crying. "Ah, yes, yes," he said, "here we are in Kent and Christendom, where I read and rhyme." Her first thought was that Professor Bolton owned more books than Briarville University.

Gloria was being led through what must have been intended for the parlor when the house had first been built; it had been transformed into a what-not room, a cleaning lady's nightmare. Gloria had to pick her way among a dozen ancient tables, their surfaces cluttered with old glass, with pictures in silver frames, with enormous punch bowls, with porcelain and brass figurines, with vases holding peacock feathers and cat-tails and creepy dried flowers. The windows were so heavily draped she couldn't be certain that there really were windows back of the thick, dusty folds; on all sides, on shelves rising to within inches of the ceiling, were books and books and yet more books.

She followed through the partially opened sliding doors into the living room where she was greeted by a welcome burst of sunlight. "What is it that you drink, Gloria? That crucial fact appears to have slipped my mind."

"Gin and tonic?"

"Ah, yes, yes, how silly of me to have forgotten. I also have an excellent sherry that might interest you— No? Perhaps another time— but you really should, you know—yes, yes—branch out, extend your range. Oh, splendid! I'll have one with you. How lovely, how terribly lovely to have you here, my dear. We should have done this long ago."

All of the chairs—and there were many of them—were decorated with antimacassars, doilies, and embroidered throws; their seats were piled high with books and papers.

"Oh, oh, let me move these. Yes, sit right here where you can savor my baronial view."

One entire wall had been brutally cut away and replaced by modern French doors; the house had been spoiled as an example of turn-of-the-century architecture, but the doors revealed a breathtaking view of the little creek and the stand of woods and the rolling hills beyond, all bathed in late afternoon sunlight. Professor Bolton swung the doors open; a breeze swept in and made all the papers in the room rustle.

Gloria had been settled into a surprisingly comfortable over-stuffed chair;

she rested her feet on the camel saddle that had been provided for that purpose (she knew it was a camel saddle because her grandmother, in Providence, had one, and she wondered if there had once been a vogue for these screwy things); she admired the way a patch of sunlight made the worn leather of the saddle glow brandy-gold, the new leather of her white sandals gleam with a bluish edge like skimmed milk—and then, with a start, she remembered how miserable she'd been feeling; she'd been so intrigued by this exotic environment she'd forgotten it for the moment.

She watched Professor Bolton drift off through an archway. In contrast to the highly varnished, sludge-brown mahogany that proliferated everywhere else, the kitchen—that's where he'd gone—had been painted an unapologetic urine-yellow trimmed with a shrieking lime-green. It appeared, at least so far as Gloria could see through the archway, that Professor Bolton washed his dishes perhaps once a year.

The living room was lined with books (no surprise); crammed in between the books at various levels was an assortment of bizarre objects: a stuffed owl, a mandolin, several bell jars, old clocks (all of them ticking and proclaiming wrong times), the head from a cigar store Indian, an unidentifiable brass thing that looked like part of someone's boiler works, and what appeared to be an honest-to-God human skull.

Professor Bolton returned with sherry in two crystal glasses. "So the flaming little idiot asked you to marry him, did he?"

"I shouldn't have told you. I don't know. It was just—" Her resistance to talking felt as solid as if she were holding it like a physical object in her lap. "I'm not even sure he meant it."

Professor Bolton dug out a space for himself on the couch and sat in it. He crossed his legs and regarded her. She never would have guessed that he was capable of maintaining such a prolonged silence. "Did he ever show you his poetry?" she asked.

"Oh, yes. An enormously talented young man, no doubt about it. What did you think? You must obviously have read it."

"Talented? Oh, sure, he was really talented, but, ah—undisciplined."

"Exactly. I couldn't have chosen a better word."

"Did he really go see Pound?"

"Why, yes."

She saw that he was studying her. "That's not as remarkable as it seems," he said. "I wrote a little note for him, but it's not all that difficult. One simply goes and ingratiates oneself, hmmm? I suppose half the literate population of America has gone to sit at the feet of Uncle Ez by now—a brilliant man, a terrible old man—"

"Terrible?"

"Well, he is a bloody fascist, my dear, and don't you believe anybody who says he isn't."

"But you said— In class, I thought you said—"

"Oh, yes, he's one of our best, but being a great poet has never, in itself, saved anyone yet from being a damned fool. But we really don't want to be talking about Ezra Pound, now do we?"

No, she did not want to talk about Ezra Pound. She was feeling a dull ache in her chest; she set her sherry glass down so she could press her hands, hard, against her breastbone. She felt her lip quivering. What she was considering doing was, of course, impossible, and so, therefore, she couldn't do it. The worst thing that could happen to a girl was to lose her virginity; once that most terrible of things had happened, she could not, under any circumstances tell anyone, not a soul—certainly not her English professor.

"He wanted to make love to me," she heard herself, nevertheless, saying. There, she thought, that's the beginning. Now just keep going, step by step. She didn't know why she wanted to say the unsayable except, perhaps, to punish herself.

"I was a virgin. It really hurt. I bled all over the place." What a bald and unpleasant way to put it, she thought—but she knew that if she tried to find a more delicate way, she wouldn't say it at all.

She felt the shame in her face—her entire face was burning—and even her tears felt hot; they were scalding her. "He was scared to death," she said. "He couldn't do anything, he— He couldn't do it. He used his fingers." Oh, she thought, I've actually said that—*out loud!* "He went in the bathroom and threw up. The next day he asked me to marry him. When I said I wouldn't, he called me— I can't say it. I can't say what he called me."

She waited. She risked a look at him; Professor Bolton did not look angry, nor did he look even particularly shocked. He looked sad. "Oh, my dear," he said, "how terrible for you."

Then the tears began to pour through her so fast she bent nearly double in her chair; she heard herself wailing. She wanted him to stand, cross the few feet that separated them, and take her hand, pat her, touch her—but he didn't. After a moment she understood that it was right that he didn't—even if she didn't understand why it was right. She sat up and gasped for breath. The room was blurry. With a deft flick of his wrist, he threw her a handkerchief. It landed in her lap. It was clean linen, freshly ironed. She unfolded it and blew her nose. The unbearable knot inside her was gone.

She felt a qualitative change in the ambience of the room. She knew that it was more than merely her personal inner state—that it included Professor Bolton—and she didn't begin to know how to define it. Eventually she decided to call it a quieting—a huge settling. It was comfortable for both of them to sit without speaking; before the settling, it would not have been. She sipped her sherry slowly until she drained the glass.

"Speech after long silence—" Gloria said. She didn't know why that particular poem should be in her mind.

"It is right," he said, completing the line.

The colors in the room looked extraordinarily vivid. "It *is* right, Gloria," he said. "Listen. I will play decrepitude and wisdom to your youth and ignorance. The first thing I want to say—and please consider what I'm about to say, although I'm sure that for someone your age it will sound as though I'm recommending hypocrisy— Consider, my dear, that virginity is not so much a state of the body as a state of the mind. And the second thing I want to say— Well, poor dear Kenneth— You may, later in your life, attain some considerable sympathy for him, so, please, sweet Gloria, do not reproach yourself that you have so little sympathy for him now."

She was astonished: this most garrulous of men was having trouble finding words. He must have read her expression; he gave her a wry smile. "Well, to be frank—and painfully to the point—God made you a girl, and, therefore, He did not make you for Ken Henderson."

She couldn't say a word. "Don't pretend to be naive," he said. "You know exactly what I mean."

She stared at him in astonishment. What he'd said made everything make sense.

"Come, my dear, let me fill your glass again. Oh, it *is* a lovely sherry. I know a little place a few miles out of town—a roadhouse as they used to be called— where they do the most marvelous barbecued ribs. It's such a lovely night for a drive, and I would be so pleased if you would accompany me—will you? Oh, good!"

She liked the sherry, she decided. She liked the warmth of it. "So, my dear," he said, "when all the fury is done, there is left to us the supreme theme—"

"Of art and song," Gloria said and had the eerie sensation that the human mind was a poem—was just as formally structured. She felt that she had just learned something immaculate and vast, but she didn't have the words for it. She lifted her crystal glass into the sunlight. "Our thoughts aren't random, are they?" she said.

"Oh," he said, obviously startled. Then he smiled. "No, of course they aren't random. No, no, of course not. They're the farthest thing from it."

8

Talking to Professor Bolton had made Gloria feel better for a day or two, but, by the time she was settled at home again for the summer, she finally had to admit that any sense of well-being had been temporary, that what she still felt, down deep, was utterly ghastly. It was all well and good to say, as Professor Bolton had, that virginity is a state of mind, but virginity is also a membrane. She liked the quaintness of the old-fashioned "maidenhead" rather than the coldly medical connotations of "hymen," but, whatever you called it, hers was gone. As soon as she was back in Raysburg, she consulted the big, brown medical book in the library, and it told her that many modern girls lost their maidenheads by accident; that, she supposed, was all well and good too; nevertheless, she would no longer be able to present her husband on her wedding night with absolute, indisputable proof of her virginity, and that shouldn't matter, but it did.

She kept wondering if she'd healed properly, if there was anything more she should be doing about it. She kept wishing she could go to a doctor who would examine her and tell her she was all right, but she knew she couldn't. She kept going over the events of that painful and ridiculous night, and she couldn't understand what on earth she'd been thinking. She could have stopped it at almost any point, but she hadn't, and her stupidity—or whatever it had been—made her loathe and distrust herself. Being pinned to Rolland should have made her feel better, but it didn't; she knew she'd tricked him into it, and she punished herself with Pound's nasty word, "devirginated." That's right: Rolland had got himself pinned to a devirginated little hypocrite, and he didn't even know it.

She couldn't get Ken out of her mind. She still felt guilty. If she hadn't stupidly agreed to go to bed with him, he would have stayed in school and graduated—but sometimes she felt mad enough to murder him. If he didn't like girls, why did he pretend he did? He could have told her about it. She wouldn't have held it against him (or at least she was pretty sure she wouldn't have); they could have been friends. But, no matter how many times she went around it, she always arrived in the same place: he'd had no right to do that to her, *no right at all*— and then she hated him. She tried not to think about his dirty fingernails.

"Put it all behind you," she wrote into her diary. "No one knows." It was odd, but somehow it didn't matter that Professor Bolton knew. "Stop worrying about Ken and his fate," she wrote. "He can worry about his own fate, the rotten, little creep. And stop being so melodramatic. Nothing that bad happened to you. You're perfectly fine."

In the middle of the afternoon, as she was swimming or chatting with Binkie at the club, she could talk herself into believing she was perfectly fine, but at night she couldn't. "I can no longer trust my own mind," she wrote into her diary. "I'm afraid of going to sleep, afraid of passing through that eerie half-world between sleeping and waking. I can never remember much of what's in my mind then, but it's so terrible, I can't stand it. There's a feeling like a dark, sorrowful dread—like a prolonged inner shiver. Then, when I do get to sleep, I have awful dreams." Every morning she dutifully wrote her dreams down until she'd filled over twenty pages of her diary.

She dreamed that she was wandering around a deserted summer camp in the middle of a gray, rainy winter, trying to keep a date with Rolland. They were supposed to play tennis, and, just as was true in real life, Gloria had never learned to play tennis. When she took her racket out of the press, she saw that the strings were broken.

In several dreams she had to go back to Fairhaven Hall, and it was not filled with the girls she'd been dreading to see—the ones who had tormented her there—but silent and empty, and she walked down endless hallways looking for anybody at all, but found no one.

The only dream that was funny (or at least it would have become funny when, a year later, she would read it again) was of trying to bleach her hair. Knowing she shouldn't be doing it, knowing it was sure to hurt her, she used the big bottle of bleach from the shelf in Grammy Cotter's basement, poured it directly over her head, and her hair came out clumped into gummy, ropey, sludgy brown strands exactly like the mess she used to see in her brother Bobby's diapers. There was nothing she could do to make it look any better—she just had to live with it—and the head mistress (in the dream she was in charge of *heads*) summoned Gloria to explain herself, and she turned out to be, not Miss Devon, but Morgan. "I told you, Gloria," the dream Morgan said in a voice so proper and chilling it outdid even Miss Devon, "you are *never* allowed to be blonde."

The last thing Gloria wanted that miserable summer was a social life. She wanted nothing whatsoever to do with boys, not even casual conversation, and being pinned gave her the perfect excuse to refuse dates, but she knew she had to find something to occupy her mind or she'd go really crazy. Ever since the big English lit survey course her freshman year, she'd wished she had time to go back and read more of the authors who'd intrigued her as she'd whizzed from Beowulf to Eliot in nine months, so she poked about in a collection of Middle English lyrics, found some lovely moments (*Levedy, all for thine sake—*

Longinge is ilent me on), but nothing fully engaged her, and she began to have the feeling that there was something else she should be reading, something specific that would be exactly the right thing, and if she kept on looking, it would present itself clearly and unmistakably.

She dreamed she was in the attic looking for a dress. She had to go somewhere very important, do something very important; she couldn't remember quite what it was, but she did know that she had to look exactly right. She kept finding clothes she'd worn as a child, and she knew they wouldn't fit her any more. Then, by accident, she brushed against the wall and it swung open. How odd, she thought; there's been a secret door up here all the time, and I never knew it. She stepped through the door, and she was in Professor Bolton's living room.

Intensely dark, richly brown shadows obscured thousands of books, but some of their spines were printed with gold letters that caught glints of light. Gloria couldn't read their titles and wondered if they were all in foreign languages. Professor Bolton sat in a pool of light so brilliant it made her eyes burn; his feet were resting on the camel saddle; he was reading, and he didn't look up. She walked toward him quietly, afraid of disturbing him. She was sure he wasn't aware of her, but—still without looking up—he said, "Gloria," in an abrupt, testy voice, "come here," and offered her the book he'd been reading. She took it and felt the weight of it; she could feel the age of it through her fingertips, and it was very old. She looked down, saw that the author's name began with S, and woke up.

All the next morning Gloria read bits and pieces of old authors whose name began with S. She rejected Shakespeare at once; she'd been reading him since high school, and she knew that the author she was looking for was someone she'd neglected. Smollett and Sterne and Swift were too modern. She tried Sheridan and Skelton and Surrey and Sidney, and none of them were right. Then, when browsing through Spenser's *Faerie Queene*, she felt a growing excitement.

She was in Book III, the one subtitled *Of Chastitie*. Ordinarily, chastity would have been a faintly repellant concept to her—invoking images of ancient, unmarried aunts and Victorian prudes—but, given the mood she was in, she found it oddly appealing, and she was intrigued that someone could have written an entire book of poetry about it. She was flipping quickly through the pages, had skimmed enough of the book to know that the main character, the heroine, was the chaste warrior maiden Britomart, and she liked the idea of a girl knight—she'd never run across one before—riding around *Faerie Lond* beating all the boy knights in single combat. She knew hardly anything about Spenser except that his work was supposed to be an allegory (that's what her notes from last fall's lecture said) and his characters were, therefore, personifications. Britomart was obviously supposed to personify chastity, but she seemed to Gloria like a real person with real feelings.

Britomart's adventures begin when she sees in a mirror the vision of a comely knight. She falls in love with him, feels as though she's been afflicted with a bleeding wound, and suffers from insomnia and bad dreams (and that's probably what hooked me, Gloria thought, looking back on it). Her nurse takes Britomart to see Merlin, the wizard, who explains to her that the image she saw in the mirror was that of Arthegall, her future husband—that it is her destiny to seek him out. So Britomart lays aside her maiden's garments, dons armor, and rides off to Faerie Lond on a quest for Arthegall.

Meanwhile, an evil enchanter called Busyrane (that's right, Gloria thought, all fairy tales have to have an evil enchanter) has captured the beautiful Amoret, the personification of true femininity, and has imprisoned her in a dark dungeon where he subjects her to cruel torments because she won't give up her virginity. (Gee, Gloria thought, she's holding out better than I did.)

As she read Britomart's vows to rescue Amoret, Gloria became more engrossed in the tale; she slowed down and began to read the stanzas carefully, line for line. Approaching the dreadful house of Busyrane where Amoret is imprisoned, Britomart finds flames, smoke, and stinking sulphur, but she raises her shield, follows the point of her sword into the flames, and passes though them as a thunderbolt pierces the empty air. Once inside the house of Busyrane, she sees a huge, majestic arras woven with disturbing, obscene images of love and lust. Approaching the next room, Britomart sees, written over the door, "Be bold." Entering, she finds, sculpted in pure gold, a thousand monstrous forms of false love:

> And as she looked about, she did behold
> How over that same door was likewise writ,
> *Be bold, be bold,* and everywhere *Be bold,*
> That much she mused, yet could not construe it
> By any riddling skill, or commune wit.
> At last she spied at that room's upper end,
> Another iron door, on which was writ,
> *Be not too bold;* whereto though she did bend
> Her earnest mind, yet wist not what it might intend.

Gloria felt the hair on her arms and the nape of her neck stand up. Oh, she thought, *true poetry*! She knew that she'd found what she'd been looking for. Faerie Lond was exactly where she wanted to be, and, for the rest of the summer, Faerie Lond was where she lived.

For the first time since she'd been fourteen, Gloria didn't feel like wearing makeup; she washed her face with Ivory soap and let it go at that. She didn't feel like getting her hair done either, or setting it; thick and straight, it fell around into her face like an unruly curtain; when it got in her eyes, she bobby-pinned it out of the way. Trying to feel clean, she shaved scrupulously every morning; she wore nothing but shorts, tennis shoes over bare feet, and old shirts of her father's. "I know you're pinned, Glo," Binkie Eberhardt said, "but don't you think you're overdoing it?" Gloria shrugged, and Binkie never mentioned Gloria's appearance again—but her mother did: "What on earth's the matter with you? You're really letting yourself go. And for God's sake do something with your hair—you look like a sheep dog!" But Gloria didn't want to do something with her hair.

Every night before she went to sleep, and every morning when she woke up, Gloria read *The Faerie Queene*. She read all of it, and then she went back to Book III—Britomart's book. She read Book III over and over until she'd memorized long passages of it. On the surface, Spenser's allegories seemed transparent, even banal, but his images wound into each other in a curiously indirect way like the scenes in her dreams, and Gloria felt a dark, resonant magic that would not translate into simple allegory. *Of course,* she thought again and again— although she didn't know what hidden source of knowledge enabled her to feel the rightness, the accuracy of the images, that enabled her to say with such certainty: *of course.* Of course Britomart would see the image of her own true love in *the mirror* in *her father's bedroom* while she was trying to see *herself.*

Like Gloria, Binkie had come back to Raysburg pinned and so, by Greek protocol, shouldn't be dating (although she did sometimes), and, in Binkie, Gloria found a perfect companion. Binkie never talked about anything the least bit serious; Binkie didn't seem to care if Gloria said little more than three words in an hour; Binkie never noticed when Gloria had departed into Faerie Lond. They met at the club every afternoon; while Binkie paddled around in the shallow end, Gloria swam laps like a boy, like her little brother—or, she thought, like Britomart would have done had Britomart been a swimmer. As the fat, muggy days drifted toward evening, Gloria, with *The Faerie Queene* open on her lap, watched Binkie play tennis, and, afterward, they sat on the terrace and drank Cokes while Binkie gossiped about everyone else in their country club set. They ate late dinners together at each other's houses or at the club; they watched TV, went to the movies, wandered around Waverley Park.

One night when her parents were having a late night at the club and the brats were away at summer camp, Gloria and Binkie had the house alone to themselves. Feeling daring and naughty, they sat in the twilight by the pool and drank gin and tonic filched from Gloria's dad's liquor cabinet. They got mildly tipsy.

"How far have you gone?" Binkie asked, giggling.

"You tell me first," Gloria said, giggling too—impersonating a normal girl.

"Well, have you ever, you know, taken it out of a guy's pants?"

"No! But I've, you know—inside his pants."

"Jeepers, Glo, I just couldn't believe how much *stuff* comes out!"

"Oh, amazing, isn't it?"

Even thought they were alone, they had instinctively dropped their voices. "You ever let a guy," Binkie whispered, bending close to Gloria's ear, "put his hand in?"

"Well, sometimes."

"Did you like it?"

Gloria thought of Rolland, not of Ken, and she was tipsy enough to say: "Of course I liked it. Did you?"

Binkie was so fair that her blush was clearly visible even in the twilight. "You wouldn't do that with somebody unless you were *pinned* to them," Binkie said.

"Oh, no. Of course not."

"Hey, Glo, have you ever had a—you know, had a—?"

"Sure," Gloria said, "and I bet you have too, haven't you?"

After a long pause, Binkie said quietly, "Yeah, sure." Binkie's face by now had turned the color of strawberry jam. She looked out over the silent swimming pool. "Oh golly, Glo," she said, "I just can't wait to get married."

Can I tell her about Ken? Gloria wondered—and then wondered why she even bothered to wonder: no, of course she couldn't.

Since the night she'd been devirginated, Gloria hadn't touched herself; she had, in fact, felt no desire—it was as though she'd gone dead below the waist— but, whispering with Binkie in the sensual heat of the wide, incomprehensible summer night with fireflies winking around the margins of the pool like tiny question marks, with the taste of the berry-flavored gin still in her mouth, she remembered Rolland's kisses, the smell of the leather seats in his Cadillac, the careful, rhythmic motion of his fingertips, and she felt the hot breath of—well, "lust" was the only word for it. Am I all right? she wondered for the millionth time.

Alone in her room after Binkie had gone home, she wrote a letter to Rolland (she'd been writing to him once a week, as promised); this letter was no different from any of her previous ones—"Binkie came over and we drank a little gin and got silly, talked about our pin-men, and I had lovely thoughts of you"— but for weeks Britomart and her emblematic confreres had been far more substantial in Gloria's mind than Rolland Spicer, and now, writing, she remembered him clearly—sweet boy—and all of his little attentions to her; she did, in a ghostly, detached way, miss him. She lay down on her bed and touched herself lightly, experimentally. Just as she'd known—but had not wanted to know—she was hot. Why not? she asked herself and couldn't find any reason why not, so, as she'd done so many nights in her bed in the Lamb house, she imagined her fingers as

Rolland's fingers; then, as she began to sink down into a dreamy, compelling blur of sensation, a waft of dark sorrow struck at her from some unexpected corner—that dreadful inner shiver. "*Stop it,*" the secret watcher said.

Frightened, she stood up. She had to get outside—out from under the pressure of ceilings, out of the stale, steamy, enclosed space of her bedroom. She pulled on her bathrobe and ran downstairs. Her parents still weren't home. She walked in circles around the pool. She sensed something lurking deep in her mind like the glittering gold woven into the arras in the dreadful house of Busyrane: "It showed itself, and shone unwillingly; like a discolored snake, whose hidden snares through the green grass his long bright burnished back declares." Simply knowing it was down there—giving it a snake's body—was a curious relief. The night was clear, and the moon was reflected in the pool; the fireflies were so high they looked like sparks struck from the edge of the stars, and, for a moment, she saw the possibility of being all right again, and she thought, what if I decided to be as chaste as Britomart?

For the rest of the summer Gloria was as chaste as Britomart. In his scrawled letters—they were never more than half a page—Rolland began to drop hints that he'd like to "pop over to Raysburg some weekend" and meet her parents. She didn't want him to pop over to Raysburg; she liked the thought of him several hundred miles away in Scranton and wanted him to stay there. She wrote back saying how hectic things were, how busy everyone was, how much she was looking forward to seeing him again—back at school.

In mid-July Gloria's father said to her: "Your mother's asked me to have a little talk with you, honey."

"Oh? Am I in trouble?"

Gloria's father, dressed to go to the club, was standing by the pool with a cigarette in his hand. He was looking across the water, across the back lawn; with his free hand, he was shielding his eyes from the sun. He appeared to have become fascinated by the trees at the edge of the property line, and Gloria felt compelled to look at them too, but all she could see was the sun setting behind their topmost branches. "Get a hair cut," he said. "That's an order."

"Sure," she said after a moment.

Feeling an intense, icy fury, Gloria turned and walked into the house, picked up the sharp sewing scissors from their drawer in the kitchen, walked upstairs, passed her mother in the hall and didn't say a word to her, shut herself in her bathroom and locked the door. She thrust her head under the tap, soaked her hair, parted it in the middle, combed her bangs down over her face and cut them straight across just above her eyes. Her compulsion to precision had not deserted her, and she combed and snipped until her bangs were straight as the edge of a meat cleaver. Then she discovered that it was virtually impossible to cut the back of your own hair while looking in a mirror. Later that night, she asked Binkie to do it.

"Why don't you go in to Tony on Market Street?" Binkie said. "He's not too bad."

"Just cut it, Bink, OK?"

What emerged was a dead straight pageboy—much like Gloria had worn when she'd been four. Her mother said nothing about it but took to calling her "Cleo."

The Ohio County Public Library was not exactly a well-stocked repository of Spenser criticism, but Gloria read what it did have, and she found it profoundly boring. Everything she loved in Spenser was simply not mentioned; it was as though these authors had read an entirely different poet from the one she'd been reading, and so she decided to write a paper on him when she got back to Briarville. She used her diary to make notes. "Britomart wears her armour like a chastity belt," she wrote. "Everyone who meets her, takes her for a boy."

The brats came home from summer camp. Bobby had been swimming every day, and he wanted to keep it up; he bought himself an alarm clock, got up every morning at six-thirty and hit the pool. The rhythmic splashing of his stroke always woke Gloria; after three mornings of lying in bed wide awake and annoyed, she began to get up and join him. Soon it became a ritual; if she didn't turn up, he'd walk into her bedroom and shake her: "Up and at 'em, Glo."

It was an odd companionship; she'd never much liked her little brother, and she still didn't like him much, but she liked swimming with him. He swam a hundred laps, and she swam forty—then fifty, then sixty (he taught her to breathe on both sides); she swam again in the afternoon at the club. She was swimming so much she was wrecking her hair and the whole world smelled of chlorine. She was swimming so much her arms and legs ached like sore teeth. "You ought to enter some meets," Bobby said.

"Why would I want to do that?" she said.

Despite all the exercise she was getting, Gloria still couldn't sleep very well at night, but she began to sleep in the afternoons. After her second swim of the day, she'd lie in a lawn chair on the terrace or by the tennis courts, pull her sun hat down over her eyes, wrap her towel around her shoulders, and, without the least bit of effort or worry, fall into deep, untroubled sleep. Sometimes she'd sleep two or three hours like that. She knew if she tried it at home in the quiet of her bedroom, it wouldn't work. As long as they didn't try to talk to her, she liked having people around her as she slept; she liked drifting off to the sounds of voices, the thud of tennis balls. She liked sleeping outside, under the sky, at the height of the afternoon, with the feeling of life going on all around her.

Gloria kept thinking about Britomart's bleeding wound. It was a powerfully evocative image. One afternoon she woke up by the tennis court, lay there with her eyes still shut, fully aware of where she was yet not quite ready to meet the world, when the thought jumped suddenly into her mind: oh, it isn't just a metaphor— Britomart isn't merely wounded in her psyche; *she's got her first period!*

"Britomart is wounded three times," Gloria wrote in her diary. "With each wound, she gains knowledge. Her first wound is the onset of her menstrual cycle which is brought about by her vision of Arthegall, her ideal future husband."

After that, Gloria began to see images of blood and wounds everywhere in Book III. "Amoret," she wrote, "is wounded too—horribly—and is constantly bleeding."

Poor Amoret had been trained up in true femininity to be an example to all fair ladies—Gloria saw her as a frail, blonde, sixteenth-century beauty queen— yet she suffers the most dreadful wound of all. When Busyrane captures her, he chains her to a pillar, binds her small waist with iron bands, shamefully strips her white breasts naked, and cuts a wide wound in her chest. "It's an image of hell," Gloria wrote. "Amoret can't die but, in her enchanted state, has to suffer the most terrible, unrelenting pain." Amoret's heart is cut out and laid in a silver basin, transfixed with a dart, and soaked in her own steaming blood.

"Scudamour, Amoret's beloved, cannot rescue her," Gloria wrote. "The flames protecting the house of Busyrane will not part for him. Amoret can only be rescued, not by a man, but by another girl—the chaste maiden, Britomart." A day later, Gloria read over what she'd written and added: "What can this mean?" She had an intuitive sense of what it meant, but she couldn't yet find the words to formulate it.

For the first time in her life Gloria and her brother Bobby had something that resembled a conversation. They were sitting on the edge of the pool, side by side, with their feet dangling in the water. "I'm going to break a world record," Bobby announced in a matter-of-fact voice.

"Oh," she said, "what in?"

"I don't know yet—whatever's my best stroke, or maybe the I.M."

"That's great, Bobby. Do you really think you can do it?"

Like their father, Bobby had the habit of not looking at you when he was talking to you; he was, at the moment, looking at his feet paddling in the water. "Oh, yeah. I know I've really got to work. Most kids my age don't know how to work."

Gloria had always thought of the brats not as separate little boys but as a single, two-headed entity brought into the world for no other purpose than to make her life miserable; now she saw Robert as separate from Jimmy, as a distinct personality. Jimmy was nine and still a child—a sturdy, fair, slightly plump little kid who whined and had spectacular temper tantrums, but also a sunny little character, never in a bad mood for long. Bobby was thirteen; it had been, she thought, a year or more since she'd seen him cry, but he was moody, grave, taciturn, inward; sometimes he seemed prematurely grown-up. If he decided to do it now, she thought, maybe he could break a world record.

"So what are you going to do, Glo?" he asked, taking her by surprise.

"Do?"

"Yeah, you know, with your life."

She wished she had something she could offer him as clear and shining as a world record, but she didn't. "I don't know. Get my degree. Get married, I guess."

"Yuck," he said and dived into the pool.

Right, she thought. Yuck.

She watched him swim the width of the pool under water. He bobbed up on the other side and shook himself. He grinned at her, and, although she wasn't sure what there was to grin about, she grinned back. Oh, she thought, he looks like me!

It was amazing she'd never seen it before. He had a pinched, rodentlike face much like hers—and the same lank, black hair, and the same long, shapely legs. His eyes were a clear, brownish hazel much lighter than hers, but his skin was as dark as hers, and it had a strong hint of her distinctive olivish color. Well, she thought, so much for my childhood conviction that the Gypsies left me in a basket; they couldn't have left *two of us*—and, if he looks that much like me, maybe his heart is something like mine too. She didn't know why, but she found that idea deeply unsettling. For the next few days, she kept watching him, studying him. She didn't know what she was looking for.

"There's something unsubstantial, illusory about the house of Busyrane," Gloria wrote. "When Britomart defeats the vile enchanter Busyrane and frees Amoret, the dreadful flames are quenched and the rooms of the castle vanish utterly. Amoret is unbound, and the steel dart that pierced her heart falls 'softly forth, as of his own accord.' Her wound is closed, 'and every part' is restored 'to safety full sound, as she were never hurt.'"

Gloria had never known quite what to make of the image of Amoret chained to her pillar, her breasts exposed, her waist bound with iron, her heart cut out, pierced and bleeding. She'd been trying her best not to read it with a modern mind—it had been written, after all, some three hundred years before Freud—but now she thought: oh, it's not naive at all. It's *meant* to be excessive and obscene—just as the images in the arras, the monstrous forms of the golden statues, are meant to be excessive and obscene. It *is* unsubstantial, illusory— *it's all about sexual fantasy.*

"Had Britomart not been bold," she wrote, "she never could have entered into the house of Busyrane at all. But, if she had been too bold, she would have been drawn away into the multitude of illusions—into those images of love and lust—of 'a thousand monstrous forms such as false love doth oft upon him wear.' Once trapped inside those illusions, she could never have escaped."

In the oppressive, unrelenting, muggy heat of August, Gloria began to wonder how much longer she could go on. She knew that what she was doing was self-imposed, and, therefore, she should be able to stop at any time and do something else, but it didn't feel self-imposed; it felt as though she'd signed up for a course, that she couldn't simply withdraw, that she had to stick with it until it was over. But how was she going to know when it was over? She wasn't even sure she was doing the course right—and she wasn't even sure it *was* a course. Maybe she was on a quest like Britomart. If so, what was she searching for?

She was swimming a hundred laps in their home pool now; it had begun to feel as small as a bathtub (she was always turning); in the big pool at the club, she was swimming forty laps; she was always tired—more than tired, she felt as though she were piling up exhaustion like stones on her back—but now she couldn't sleep at night at all. She often woke from her afternoon naps at the club—the only sleep she was getting—so groggy she didn't know where she was.

Many of Spenser's images resonated for her with an uncanny magic, but she kept returning to one in particular. After Britomart has rescued Amoret from the dreadful house of Busyrane, Amoret is in a terrible bind; she owes Britomart "her love, her service, and her utmost wealth," yet she is married to Scudamour, and she would rather die than "to be false in love." Amoret, as do all the other knights and ladies, believes Britomart to be a boy. To demonstrate that she's a girl, Britomart removes her helmet and appears to the assembly wrapped in her hair.

When Gloria had first read that passage, it had brought tears to her eyes. She'd immediately seen Britomart as standing forth naked; then, reading it over carefully, she wasn't able to find any textual evidence for Britomart's nakedness. Spenser had left it ambiguous; the long hair could as easily have been wrapped around Britomart's armour as around her body, but, in her mind, Gloria continued to see Britomart naked, clothed only in her long, shining, golden hair.

Gloria couldn't sleep at night any more, and she couldn't think of anything to do except write the paper, the one she'd been preparing all summer—the paper no one had assigned to her, the paper for no reason whatsoever. She set up her Remington and began pounding away on it. Almost immediately her father burst into her bedroom. He hadn't bothered to knock. "Gloria," he said, "how goddamn inconsiderate can you get? Some people around here have to work for a living."

She looked at the clock on her bed table and saw that it was a quarter to four in the morning. "Sorry, Daddy," she said.

She switched to longhand. "The chastity proposed in Book III of Spenser's *Faerie Queene*," she wrote, "refers not, as one might expect, to a state of virginity, celibacy, or moral innocence, but to virtuous procreative love. In addition to her allegorical role as an emblem of chastity, Britomart exists as a psychologically whole and independent being. Before she can marry, Britomart must learn to accept her femininity, protect it from the external influence of courtly love conventions, and control her own, internal susceptibility to perverse fantasies, fears, and illusions. Her quest for Arthegall symbolizes the task faced by any sexually awakening young girl."

All right, she thought, there's your thesis. Now prove it.

She wrote the paper in nine nights. She didn't know if it were any good or not, but at least it was finished. Several days later a fierce thunderstorm broke the summer heat wave.

Gloria and Binkie watched from the terrace of the club. Lightning was striking so close they could hear it sizzle and the entire golf course was lit for astonishingly long instants by flashes of eerie, cold light. With every bolt, Binkie jumped and squealed; the accompanying thunder was almost immediate, then echoed off the hills to settle gradually into a giant's hoarse muttering. "Wow," Gloria said, "it's wonderful."

They watched the storm pass over and leave behind a steady, driving rain. The temperature had dropped nearly fifteen degrees in an hour. Back home, Gloria stretched out on her bed and listened to the rain buffet the house. She didn't want to read another line of Spenser; she was tired of living in Faerie Lond. What do I do now? she wondered—and while she was wondering, she fell asleep.

The rain kept winding itself into her sleep; it was a comforting sound. She'd wake briefly and hear it and think, "Oh, gee, sleep's wonderful. The rain's wonderful. I love sleeping," and she'd sink down again, burrow under her quilt, and sleep.

She dreamed she was back in high school; it gave her a bright, happy feeling to be back in high school, and she thought that tomorrow she could wear her favorite shiny red raincoat, and then she woke briefly into the present and wondered what had happened to that raincoat over the years. She'd always loved it. She must have been fifteen when she'd had it—and she fell asleep again.

When Bobby came and shook her at six-thirty, she said, "Not today. I'm taking the day off." She slept until noon.

There was no one in the house when she got up. The rain had stopped, but it was still cool. Pleased to be alone, she wandered around from room to room, yawning. She didn't feel like doing anything—not swimming, not going to the club, not seeing Binkie, not even getting dressed. She ate a bowl of corn-flakes, went back to her room, got out her high school yearbooks and flipped through them, looking at the pictures.

She fell asleep again and dreamed that she was back in high school. It was like a continuation of her earlier dream. Now she was wearing her favorite shiny red raincoat. With the majorettes and cheerleaders, she was climbing a steep set of wooden steps leading up a hill toward the football stadium. She knew that she was on the other side of the river—the Ohio side—and she was very happy. She heard a marching band playing, and she thought: oh, how myste-rious everything is. When she woke up, it was dinner time.

She wasn't hungry, but her mother made her get up for dinner. She pulled on shorts and a shirt of her father's, sat dutifully at the table, ate a little coleslaw and part of a chicken breast. "What's the matter with you, Cleo?" her mother said. "Are you coming down with something?"

"No," Gloria said, yawning, "I'm just fine."

"Binkie called twice."

"Oh, did she? I'll call her back eventually."

Since she'd been fourteen, Gloria had religiously read *Vogue* (her mother had a subscription), but she hadn't looked at a single issue since she'd come home. She retrieved the summer issues out of the magazine rack in the living room and carried them up to her bedroom. She didn't feel like reading any of the articles, but she looked at the pictures. She fell asleep by ten.

Again Gloria dreamed she was back in high school. The year was just starting, and all the Delta Lambda girls were in school with her, and she was really glad because she'd get to see Morgan again. Then she woke briefly and thought, oh, but Morgan's graduated. I'm on my own now.

Then, sometime after dawn, she dreamed for the fourth time that she was back in high school. It was football season, and she had just finished ironing her cheerleader's skirt. She held it up and examined it; every pleat was perfect. Good grief, she thought, that sure was a lot of work—but now it's finished. Now you can go to the game with your friends. She was filled with a pure, clear, cool hap-piness. She woke up and thought: *it's over.*

A few minutes later Bobby came in. "Not today," she said.

"Hey, come on, Glo, you missed yesterday."

"Well, tough. I'm going to miss today too."

He stood stiffly, his legs spread and his head lowered slightly—it was a stance exactly like their father's—and glared at her. "Well," he said, "I guess you don't want to be great, huh?"

He stomped out and slammed her door. She lay in bed laughing. She felt wonderful.

She was famished. Her father had gone to work, and Jimmy and her mother were still in bed, and Bobby was in the pool, so, with no one to watch her and comment on her lack of manners, Gloria stood in front of the open refrigerator door and gobbled the leftovers from last night's dinner. Then she had a long bath and shaved. Over the summer her eyebrows, hidden under her bangs, had grown into an unkempt, scraggly mess; she plucked them back into disciplined curves. She hadn't worn a skirt since spring (how odd!), but today she felt like wearing one; she put on her favorite red linen, and it hung on her so loosely it might as well have been her mother's. What's going on? she thought, have I lost weight?

Her scales told her that she was two pounds heavier than she'd been in April. That didn't make any sense. She got out the tape measure and checked her vital statistics. She'd lost almost a full inch around her waist and a good inch and a half around her hips; her bustline had actually increased slightly! I don't believe it, she thought; could all that be from swimming?

Naked, she examined herself in the full-length mirror. She was trying not to feel overly smug or self-congratulatory, but the gentle rounding of tummy she'd had her whole life had melted away, and her hip bones actually stood out. She'd never have a shape anyone would be tempted to call "boyish"—no, she was inherently too much of an hour-glass to make a good Britomart—but this was as close as she was ever going to get; in fact, she hadn't been so lean since she'd been at Fairhaven, but then, of course, her breasts hadn't been developed, and now, with the right bra, she'd look—well, pretty darned good. She still might be a little brown weasel, but at least now she was a little brown weasel with a great figure.

She called Binkie, woke her up: "Come on, Bink, let's go to Pittsburgh!"

Binkie called ahead to her favorite salon; Gloria borrowed her mom's car, drove like a fiend, and they made their ten-thirty appointments with time to spare. Binkie asked for a trim and a tight French twist—which is exactly what Gloria would have wanted, but her home haircut made that impossible. Beauty salons always shocked her into a panicked distance from herself, and she stared into the mirror, appalled.

At the beginning of the summer she'd wanted to deflect male attention; it had been a conscious decision, but until now she hadn't been fully conscious of how quaint, queer, out of style, and plain downright unattractive she'd made herself (her mother had been kind to call her "Cleo"). The dead-straight pageboy with bangs grown down to her eyes made the worst possible frame for a face like hers; it made her look like a bad impersonation of Little Lord Fauntleroy. "I think I'd like something short," she said.

"*Short* short?" her hairdresser asked.

"Sure, or even *short short* short, but very feminine, very, you know—" she hoped the hairdresser knew—"sophisticated."

While she was under the drier, she had her nails done in that good old stan-dard brilliant red she hadn't worn since April. Then, brushed out and sprayed, she stared into the mirror. She'd never had a cut that short; no, she told her-self, it wasn't a mistake — just give it a chance. The tiny wave of high, side-swept bangs was, indeed, very feminine; her forehead, neck, and ears were newly and thoroughly exposed — which was exactly what was in fashion at the moment — but, with her naked, shiny face, the total effect was considerably more *jeune fille* than she'd intended. It cried out for makeup.

It's like riding a bike, she thought; you don't ever forget how to do it — as she whisked on eyeliner, mascara, lipstick, and rouge for the first time in months, enjoying that old familiar sensation of vanishing behind her own artifice. She powdered herself and looked again at the total effect. Her face seemed to have changed over the summer; like her body, it was leaner, her cheekbones more prominent. Her features appeared less crowded — or maybe that was an effect created by the super-short hair. She dug into the bottom of her purse to see if she had some eyeshadow, found a smokey blue-gray from last winter and drew it on, feathered it out at the corners of her eyes, increasing the illusion of sep-aration. She looked again, and finally she was pleased; there, she thought, is Delta Lambda's Rush Chairman.

Binkie wanted to have lunch in a nice restaurant, but Gloria didn't. "Grab a hotdog or something," she said. "We've only got a few hours."

In spite of the fact that her father never seemed to care how much money she spent on clothes, Gloria had always been a cautious shopper — mulling over every purchase, looking for quality construction, classics that would last longer than one season, things that were *just right* — but she'd spent the summer in Faerie Lond, had passed up her usual shopping trip to New York with her mother, and in less than two weeks she'd be back at school, so the moment she saw something she liked, she bought it.

She bought three girdles, a waspie, and a dozen pairs of lace-trimmed panties imported from France. The Lamb Rush Chairman, she thought, would defi-nitely be a nylons girl, so she bought ten boxes and didn't bother with socks. She bought red satin evening sandals and black kid T-strap sandals, spectators in autumnal brown and black, pumps in the new sepia red lizard, pumps in leather printed to look like wood grain, pumps in white-dotted black calfskin, and opera pumps in her favorite black patent beautifully balanced on four-inch wine-glass heels. Even the Rush Chairman would have to wear flats sometime, so she bought cute walking shoes in russet, beige, and black. "Holy smoke, Glo," Binkie said, "your dad's going to kill you!"

"No, he's not," Gloria said. "The only time he's ever hit the roof was when I bought the Oxford English Dictionary."

The fall lines appeared to be either full bouffant or long, straight sheaths —

nothing much intermediate—so Gloria bought plenty of both. She was delighted to see that all the stores were showing plaids and reds; they were both great with her complexion—and then, with a start, she remembered Susie. She hadn't thought about Susie much over the summer, but now she remembered that plaids and reds were just as great with Susie's pale ivory complexion as they were with her dark olivish one, and, of course, Susie would be wearing some of these things, so she bought lots of plaid and red. She and Binkie had to keep carrying packages back to the car; they filled the trunk and started on the back seat.

She bought tweed suits in warm, deep fall colors, day dresses in dazzling varieties of blues and greens, a sophisticated black velvet evening dress, and a sexy black sheath. For the last of the hot weather, she bought a dotted swiss and an organdy and the perfect icy white skirt to show off her tanned legs—and *still* the stores hadn't closed. "We've got a little time," she said, "why don't we go look at coats?"

"Oh, golly," Binkie wailed, "my feet are killing me. *You're* killing me!" But they looked at coats and Gloria bought a slim one for sheaths and an A-line for bouffants. By now she was feeling a giddy sensation of—well, she wasn't sure what, but she knew she was allowing herself to go wickedly out of control, and she bought a ton of cosmetics and kid gloves and two purses and four berets because they looked just utterly terrif with her new hairstyle.

Binkie had, of course, bought a few things for herself, and the car was so crammed she had to ride with packages under her feet and more piled up on her lap. Not sure why she was doing it, Gloria drove back just as fast as she had going up, and it wasn't until they were nearly to Raysburg that she began to feel guilty—not about the money she'd spent (her father always said he liked his girls well dressed, didn't he?)—but about how much fun she'd had spending it. "Of course you had fun," she heard Ken Henderson's voice murmuring in her mind, "you spoiled little rich bitch."

She hadn't thought of him in weeks. "You're a great one to talk," she told him, "you lying little phony."

As Gloria saw the sign telling her that she had just passed from Pennsylvania into West Virginia, Binkie said, "Hey, let's stop at the Pine Top. I'm hungry as a horse." The Pine Top was a supper club out beyond the S-bridge—out in the Sheriff's jurisdiction beyond the city limits. It had a reputation for excellent food and a clientele of gangsters. Neither girl had ever been there, and Gloria didn't think they could get in—you were supposed to be twenty-one—and she would ordinarily have tried to talk Binkie out of it, but she was hungry too, and all day long everything had gone so well she felt lucky.

The man who intercepted them just inside the door (was he a bouncer? a gangster?—he sure looked big enough) didn't ask for ID but said, "I'm sorry, girls, there might be a bit of a wait."

"Could you tell the manager, please," Binkie said in a frosty voice, "that Miss Eberhardt and Miss Cotter are here." Gloria was shocked speechless, but, in a moment the manager himself appeared. "Sorry about the mix-up, ladies, right this way."

Gloria followed Binkie following the manager through the dark, crowded club. There was a good band playing, and the tables were lit with candles. The manager whisked away a reserved sign and seated them at an excellent table at the edge of the dance floor. "Well, here we are," Gloria said, "two steel brats, and everybody knows it. Wow, I've never heard you pull rank before."

"Sometimes you have to," Binkie said primly.

"Hey," Gloria said, suddenly inspired, "let's pretend we're society girls in a trashy novel. You know, spoiled rotten rich girls—beautiful and bored and bad."

Binkie laughed. "Sure, Glo. You want to be bored and bad, you go right ahead. You just smile at that guy over there and we'll have him at our table in two seconds flat. Yeah, the one who's been giving you the eye ever since we walked in."

"He isn't staring at me, is he? I thought he was staring at you."

"Oh, come on. He can't take his eyes off you."

Gloria risked a look. It was true: he was staring at her, and she was pleased, but she didn't want the man (he looked as old as her father) at their table—or any man, for that matter. "They're always welcome to look," she said.

The band began to play—Gloria couldn't remember the name of the tune, but she knew it was Ellington—and she was filling up with joy. It was a dumb, sappy cliché image, but she couldn't help it—that was exactly the way she felt—as though she were a tall, clear glass and joy were pouring into her like sweet fluid.

"Are you going to marry your pin-man?" Binkie was asking.

Good question. Was Rolland Gloria's Arthegall? In less than two weeks she'd be seeing him; how odd—she'd almost forgotten about him. "I don't know, Bink. He's a sweet boy, but I don't know. How about you?"

"I don't know either. Probably not. I don't want to leave Raysburg."

Gloria was surprised. She thought everybody wanted to leave Raysburg. "Why not?"

"Well, in this tiny, little pond, I'm a pretty big frog, but somewhere else, I'd just be—you know, just another blonde with money."

Gloria felt a sudden wave of affection (was it strong enough to call it love?) for her blonde, boring, and utterly reliable friend. She reached across the table and squeezed Binkie's hand. "You'd be a wonderful frog anywhere, Bink."

Binkie looked surprised. Then she said, "Hey, it's been a great summer, Glo."

It has? Gloria thought.

"We probably won't get to do it again," Binkie said, "you know, with the way life is and all—so it's nice we had the time together."

She actually likes me, Gloria thought. Self-obsessed, neurotic, little intellectual snob that I am—*and she actually likes me.* "We'll always be friends, Bink," she said, "no matter what."

It's not just me, she thought; *nobody's* simple; *everybody* has a complex and compelling and mysterious and valuable inner life—even if they don't read Spenser. And she *did* love Binkie; she loved her for standing by her, always, and for being her companion all summer and for being blonde as honey and for telling the doorman "Miss Eberhardt and Miss Cotter are here." She loved it that the band was playing Ellington and that there were candles on their table. She loved her own flat, hard stomach and her new short, sophisticated hairstyle and her shiny red nails and her sun-burnished legs and the way guys were looking at her—and she loved the thought of her mother's car out in the parking lot crammed full of clothes, and—wow!—she'd be glad to get back to school and back to Professor Bolton and wonderful Susie and good old Delta Lambda—*her* sorority. And then she remembered Rolland—not a disembodied abstraction, her pin-man, but Rolland in the flesh, tall and brown and sweaty from playing tennis—and she felt a painful lurch in her stomach. Was she really all right?

Gloria talked her father into driving her to Briarville a few days early. Susie was already there for band practice, and, when she walked into their room in the late afternoon wearing her old, beat-up majorette boots and carrying her baton, it was, Gloria thought, like a reprise of last year. "Hey, Glo, are you ever thin! And your hair! You look fab—right out of a magazine. Are all these things new? I just can't believe you. What'd you do, buy out the store?"

This year Susie allowed Gloria to hug her, sweaty armpits and all. "I've got some things that are going to look just great on you," Gloria said. "Look, try this—"

"Come on, Glo, I'm sweating like a pig— Hey, that really *is* cute. Oh, just wait a minute, let me take a shower, for crying out loud. Oh, have I ever got a lot to tell you! Not only did we lose our two seniors, but Cindy Arthur got married and dropped out, so we've got three—count them, *three*—freshman majorettes, and I want them all. And you're the Rush Chairman, get it?"

"Got it. But you know we can't do anything till—"

"I know, I know. Just leave it to me."

"Susie. Not till January. It's against the—"

"Oh, I'm not going to *rush them*, Glo. I'm just going to *talk to them*. There's two of us now, and I want them to know they don't just have to go to Dee Gee without even thinking about it. Hey, it's going to be a great year. We're doing some fabulous, complicated routines, and Lacey even likes me—"

"Lacey?"

"You know, Lacey Becker, the head majorette— Wow, I just know we're going to win the state championship this year. We really feel like a team— Just *let me take a shower*. I can't stand myself!" Susie stripped and grabbed a towel. "Hey, Glo," she yelled as she bounded out of the room, "I'm really glad you're back!"

Gloria was really glad too—and even more than glad. Oh, she thought, what a weird summer it's been.

Gloria expected Rolland to do what he'd done the September before: simply turn up at the house as soon as he was back in town, but he didn't do that; he called first. His voice sounded distant, even formal: "I didn't know if you'd want to see me right away."

"Of course I want to see you right away. You get over here right now, silly." It had come out all wrong, not teasing and kittenish as she'd intended, but just as stiff and awkward as he'd sounded. Her hands were shaking.

She'd planned exactly what to wear—her icy white skirt and under it, a pair of the lace panties imported from France. She'd always thought that wearing heels without stockings was cheap, something *our sort* didn't do (and she hated the feeling of bare feet against leather), but it was the sorority show-off-your-tan look, and she had lots of tan to show off—she hoped not too much—so she powdered her feet and worked them into white pumps. She was so nervous her mouth had gone dry.

He arrived before she was quite ready. A *boy*, her mind said stupidly. (What had she thought he was?) "Hey, Glo, you look great!" he said. "Wow, are you ever tan."

Where had his sunny grin gone?—his direct and open gaze? His eyes—grayer and cooler than she remembered—seemed abstracted, even shifty, as though he'd stopped by, briefly, on his way to somewhere else, and that secret somewhere else had all his hope and attention. "Do you like my hair?" she said.

"Oh, yeah. Wow, is it ever short."

They were alone in the beau parlor. Over the summer he'd grown taller in her mind—practically gargantuan—but heels made her a good height for him just as they always had. He kissed her. She opened her mouth, but he didn't take much advantage of it. "Sure missed you, Glo. Hey, you want to, ah, go for a ride or something?"

"Sounds great."

She took out her compact and redid her lipstick. He pulled out his hand-kerchief and wiped his mouth. They stepped outside into the fat Indian summer afternoon; it made Gloria think of a full cornucopia, and she tried to convince herself that everything was OK, but once he began to drive, he stopped talking, and his silence was making her chatter—oh, it was as bad as being back in high school!—and she was talking in a high-pitched, breathy, coquettish voice she couldn't seem to control, and everything she was saying sounded cheap and clichéd. She sounded—to use Holden Caulfield's word via Ken Henderson—utterly phony. (But the last thing she wanted to be thinking about was Ken.)

She knew exactly where they were going: up to the road that wound through the woods on the hills above the campus—to be exact, to *their spot*: a lovely little clearing at the edge of the woods that looked down over the river. He spread a beach towel out on the grass; they lay down on it and, without speaking, settled into a truly serious make-out session. That's better, she thought. Maybe *afterwards* we can talk.

Twenty minutes later (she shouldn't have been thinking about the time!) she was unbearably hot—and she also felt irritable, jumpy, prickly as a cactus. Before with Rolland everything had always been so relaxed and easy, but this didn't feel like pleasure; this felt like work. Maybe there was something seriously wrong with her after all.

But no, it wasn't all *her* fault. Why hadn't he taken her bra off? Why wouldn't he put his hand between her legs? She'd wrapped her legs around one of his, but it wasn't enough—she couldn't get the feeling right—and his tongue was deep in her mouth, and his fingers were playing with her breasts, but everything he was doing lacked conviction. And then, without any warning at all, he stopped, pulled away from her. She felt like screaming. "Breathe," the secret watcher said. She breathed and felt like crying.

"Say something," the secret watcher told her. "What's the matter, honey?" she said.

"Nothing's the matter."

"Come on, Rolland. Tell me."

"Jeez, I don't know." He sat up, lit another damn cigarette. She sat up too, smoothed her skirt down. Her legs were shaking. She watched him smoke the entire cigarette. He mashed the butt into the ground.

"Oh, hell, Gloria," he said, "you were acting so funny last spring— You know, at the White and Gold, and then—all summer— Oh, hell! Why didn't you want to see me the whole darn summer?"

Oh, so that was it—and Gloria was trapped. She could deny that she hadn't wanted to see him; she could swear that she'd been just *dying* to see him—but she'd been simply too busy. Of course he'd know she was lying, because just what the devil could she have been busy *doing*? What could she say? I was in training with my little brother? I was unfaithful to you with Edmund Spenser?

She couldn't possibly make him understand what she'd *really* been doing, but she had to tell him something he could understand and believe. "It was a test," she said.

He was giving her that hard, alert look he wore in tennis matches. "I wanted to be sure," she said. "I wanted to see if we could go all summer without seeing each other—if we'd still care. If our love was real."

She was cringing inwardly at what she'd just said—how melodramatic, how wretchedly, utterly phony—but she saw him thinking about it, and she saw that he believed her. "Why the hell didn't you tell me?" he said.

"It wasn't, you know, a fully conscious decision."

"Oh, jeez, Gloria. Girls are nuts. *You're* nuts!"

Oh, he's so transparent, she thought. He believes me, and he's still miserable. What's going on?

"Do you want to stay pinned?" he asked her. She guessed from his abrupt, angry delivery that the question must have been reverberating in his mind all summer.

"You know I do, silly."

"Are you sure?"

"Sure, I'm sure," she said even though she wasn't—not absolutely, not all the way to the end, not about *marrying* him—but she was sure about being *pinned*. Being pinned, especially if you were pinned to someone like Rolland Spicer, gave you enormous prestige in the world of the Greeks where Gloria lived. Being pinned meant that you didn't have to fend off the wolf pack, that you always had a date, that you actually had enough time to get your work done. But maybe *he* was the one who wasn't sure. She looked into his eyes and saw something wretched and guilty there.

Oh, she thought. "You went out with someone, didn't you?"

He nodded.

"Did you make out with her?"

He looked away. "I'm sorry, Gloria."

He can't bring himself to lie to me, she thought—and felt like an utter hypocrite: she'd just lied to him and got away with it. But, at the same time, a little clawing cat inside her was mewling with jealousy. It didn't matter that she'd hardly thought about him all summer. It still hurt. It hurt like hell, and she felt her eyes sting. "How far'd you go?"

"Oh, Gloria, it wasn't— We just, you know, played around and stuff. Nothing real serious." He looked her right in the eyes. "I didn't like it all that much. I mean— Well, I'm not going to lie to you and say I didn't like it at all, but—but I kept wishing she was you."

The little cat inside her wouldn't stop. "We're *pinned*, Rolland. Didn't that mean anything?"

"Sure, it did. It still does. It's just—you know."

"No, I don't know. Look at all the trouble I got into last year just trying to be friends with somebody." And that was wildly unfair, not to mention irrelevant, but she didn't feel like being fair or relevant. "Do you want your pin back?"

"No! Gloria, come on! You know I don't want my pin back. I don't care about anybody but you."

Oh, good, Gloria thought. "If you ever again— If you *ever* go out with another girl, I'll give you your pin back. Right on the spot."

"I won't. I promise."

"Even if all you do is take her out for a Coke."

"I won't, Gloria. I swear."

"I don't even want you *looking* at another girl."

"I promise. Honest to God!"

"OK, then."

"Really OK?"

"Yes, really. I forgive you, but— You can't start taking me for granted, Rolly!"

"That's enough," the secret watcher said. "Let up on him. Who are you to be taking the high moral ground?"

"Did you think I was playing around?" she asked him gently.

"I don't know. I guess so. I didn't know what to think. All I knew was you didn't want to see me."

"I'm sorry. I should have— I don't know what. I wrote to you once a week just the way I said I would. I didn't even *talk* to another boy. I was as chaste as a maiden in an old book. You can ask Binkie."

She could see that he was still really upset, and she didn't want him to be. They'd been so hot before; could it all have evaporated into nothing? Surely not. A demonic idea was forming in her mind; she wasn't sure she had the courage to do it, but then she thought: there's nothing wrong with it; we're pinned and we might even get married someday—and she felt immaculate. She felt as chaste as Britomart. She took off her blouse and then her bra.

He looked shocked, and she was embarrassed in spite of herself. "*Déjeuner sur l'Herbe*," she said out of embarrassment.

"What?"

"It's a painting."

"Yeah? You make me feel like such a dumbass sometimes."

"Oh, Rolland honey, it doesn't matter if you don't know about that painting. Listen, I want to—I just want to be sure that everything's clear. I just hate when things aren't clear. You know I want to be a virgin on my wedding night—"

"Sure you do," he said in an anguished voice.

"And we're pinned. And we're going to be faithful to each other—"

"You bet. Absolutely."

"But you're never *ever* going to try to get me to go all the way?"

He shook his head. "No. Never. I promise."

"But—well, *anything else* is pretty much OK—"

Their eyes met. He threw away his cigarette, took her into his arms, and kissed her. They stretched out again on the beach towel, and he stroked her bare breasts. No, all that heat had *not* evaporated. Her nipples were burning, were standing straight out. He was staring at them. She felt him getting hard against her leg. "Oh, God, Gloria. There's not a girl in the world as beautiful as you."

"Don't be silly. I'm just a plain, little brown weasel. But *you* make me feel beautiful." She tugged at his belt; he undid it, pushed down his chinos and boxer shorts. Shyly, she glanced down, saw his penis rising up to a jaunty angle, as self-satisfied as a rooster.

The sun was setting, suffusing the woods—and Rolland's penis—with a ruddy, Wordsworthian light. A faint suggestion of chill in the air, a nearly imperceptible stirring—not quite enough motion to call it a breeze—said that this was not high summer as it had seemed only an hour ago, but autumn. She saw goose bumps rising on his bare thighs. But she wasn't cold at all. She was hot, hot, hot. "I don't deserve you," he said.

"Of course you deserve me."

She welcomed his tongue with her tongue and took his penis into her hands; it was sweetly warm and felt like a living oxymoron: soft as velvet, hard as granite. He slid her panties off; she arched up to help him get them off. Then he slipped one hand under her bare bottom, the other between her legs, and she never would have guessed that his fingers under her skirt would feel so wonderful—so just plain downright naughty, sexy. She wanted it to go on forever, for hours and hours—

Her fingers felt him kick and throb and kick again and then burst—wet, spurting, and wonderful—and she answered him with a blinding inner flash, searing. Oh, heaven; oh, angel—and nothing, nothing, nothing, nothing, nothing—

Her mind came back—she could feel the snap of it like shook, wet linen— and she thought, wow, Gloria, you just had an orgasm that felt like the end of the world! Is that possible, is that normal, are *you* normal, *is everything OK?* She felt a delicious hurt in what she supposed was her womb. Her hands were covered with the stuff that comes out of boys, and she imagined a trillion jumpy sperm cells thrashing their tails. She wiped her hands on the beach towel.

"I love you," he said.

"Oh, I love you too."

Then, as strange as it seemed, they must both have drifted off, because she felt herself wake up, and she felt him in her arms breathing deeply—still half asleep. The sky overhead was turning the color of tarnished silver, and she invested it with the delicious, cooling gray radiance of satisfied desire. One of her legs was cramping, and she was hungry (they were having lamb chops and scalloped potatoes at the house, yummy), and she felt wonderful. Oh, it's true, she thought: I've been restored—to safety full sound, unbound and perfect whole, as I were never hurt.

As a third-year major in honors English, Gloria was required to choose a faculty tutor to supervise her honors thesis. Contemporary poetry was her passion just as it had always been, but if she chose to write on Eliot or Pound, she'd have to work with horny Dr. Stauffer, and she couldn't imagine anything worse. She'd decided to go back to Wyatt so she could continue working with Professor Bolton; she'd been looking forward to seeing him nearly as much as Rolland; she could hardly wait to give him her Britomart paper. She considered calling and making an appointment, but she was sure she could catch him in his office before classes started, and she didn't want their first encounter, however cursory, to be on the telephone.

She spent a ridiculous amount of mental energy worrying about what to wear, decided on her new plaid suit, did her nails to match the red in the plaid. As was the custom, she'd had a jeweler attach her Delta Lambda pin to Rolland's Beta Theta Pi pin with a little gold chain; she fastened both pins to her lapel a handspan away from her left collar bone. She put on a black beret at a jaunty angle. She looked in the mirror and liked what she saw: bright and chic, cute but not frivolous, Miss Gloria Cotter—pinned—Delta Lamb's Rush Chairman and the only student at Briarville College (whoops—University) ever to get an A plus from Batty Bolton.

Just as she'd expected, she found him in his cluttered office with the door open. He appeared to be reading an entire summer's worth of correspondence. He'd been throwing crumpled-up letters at the waste basket and missing. "Ah, Gloria!" he said and rose to his feet. "How splendid of you to drop by. Come in, come in, sit down, please, yes. And how have you been?"

"Just great," she said and lowered herself onto the edge of a chair. She had brought her Britomart paper—typed and bound—and almost offered it to him but thought it would be better to get the school business out of the way first.

"And you're feeling better?"

"Oh, yes."

"The last time we met, the circumstances were—so unfortunate. And I have thought of you, often."

"Oh, I'm just fine, Professor Bolton. I feel much better. Everything's OK."

"I'm delighted to hear that."

"And I was wondering— You know I'm in honors, and I have to—you know, do an honors thesis. And I thought if you didn't have too many students—"

She saw a dark look come over his face, and she stopped, studying him for a clue as to how to proceed. "Ah, dear Miss Cotter," he said.

She waited. He regarded her a moment longer, then said, "I'm afraid not, my dear."

She couldn't believe she'd heard him right. "I don't understand."

"Oh, I'm sure you will do quite well with my eminent colleague, the learned Dr. Stupor—"

"No, I don't want to do something contemporary. I want to do Wyatt."

"Ah—Wyatt— I'm not at all certain, my dear," he said gently, "but that you should not choose some other topic."

It took her a moment to sort out all the negatives. "Do you mean you really don't want to work with me?"

"As pleasant as it would be to continue our association, Miss Cotter," he said, smiling, "I'm afraid that it is not to be."

This, she could see, was supposed to be the end of the conversation; she had no intention of allowing it to be the end. "Why?" she said.

He considered a moment before he answered. "I'm sorry, Gloria," he said quietly, "but I don't ordinarily do tutorials with girls."

Gloria had never been so angry in her life. Her eyes filled with tears; she tried to blink them away, but they kept on flowing. "That's not fair!" she yelled at him. Before then, she wouldn't have thought it possible to yell at a professor.

He leapt up, crept past her and, with a quick, furtive movement, shut his office door. "I worked like a dog for you!" Gloria shouted at the back of his head. Her tears were continuing to pour down, and she didn't care. He turned toward her, regarded her solemnly, then fished out one of his clean linen handkerchiefs and handed it to her. She unfolded it and pressed its immaculate whiteness over her burning face; she was pleased to see that she'd marked it with wonderfully intense—if she were really lucky, utterly *indelible*—streaks of mascara. Everything in the room looked different—as though suffused with a hot, red light—and her entire body was shaking. This is what "fury" means, she thought, and, at the same time, the secret watcher said: "You should have been more careful. See what happens when you think you're on top of the world."

"I've always done everything you asked me." She was barely able to control her words, make them into intelligible speech instead of a strangled, inarticulate boo-hooing. "I did *more* than you asked me—"

"Heavens, Miss Cotter, I can't fault you there."

"I came to your Thursday night bull sessions, and I held my own, didn't I? I contributed, didn't I?"

"You were splendid."

She wanted to remind him of what had happened between them when she'd told him about Ken—good grief, she'd told him more personal stuff than she'd ever told anybody!—and he'd even taken her out to dinner, and they'd had a lovely time. They'd talked about literature, and she hadn't said anything too stupid—at least she didn't remember saying anything too stupid—and she'd thought there was some kind of understanding between them. She wanted to remind him of all that, but she couldn't think how to do it, so she just looked at him and cried.

"Well—*why*, then? Just because I'm a girl? I don't understand. It's not fair. It's really not fair. You've got to see that it's not fair."

"Gloria," he said in a somber voice, "there's nothing wrong with your work. It's extraordinarily promising. You are— Yes, I do have to say it because it's true: you are the best student I've ever had."

The next burst of words were already half out of her mouth—a childish repetition of "It's not fair!"—when she realized what he'd said. Best student? *Best student!*

"*Why?*" she said.

"Gloria, just look at you. A veritable fashion plate, as always. Perhaps if you were a mousy, nondescript little thing with thick spectacles—or, perhaps, one of these enormous, earnest, pimply-faced fat girls from the midwest one sees from time to time—then you might make a scholar, but you, unfortunately, do not have the remotest chance of that— No, no, no, do not say a word. Please, just listen to me for a moment.

"You're an extraordinarily beautiful young woman, my dear, and your breeding is obvious to anyone, and I have never seen you anything other than perfectly turned out. What do you spend a year on clothes? No, no, I don't expect you to come up with a figure, but please do consider it— And consider *everything* that has been spent on you, has been given to you. All the advantages, as the expression goes. How much would you say it costs to produce a girl like you?"

She didn't know whether she were expected to answer or not, but she didn't have an answer. When it was put in such a crass way—no, she'd never thought about it like that.

"To take only one instance, how many girls on campus could afford to live in the Delta Lambda house?"

It had never crossed Gloria's mind that it cost a lot to live in the Delta Lambda house, but now that he was making her think about it, she supposed that it did. Gloria never thought about money; the closest she'd ever come to thinking about money was thinking that money bored her silly. Now she realized that money bored her silly because there had always been plenty of it. Poor Susie, she thought, how cruel of me not even to notice; her family must be really *sacrificing!*

Professor Bolton reached out and lightly tapped the linked pins on Gloria's sweater. "Are you planning to marry this lucky fellow? This scion of two fortunes?"

"I don't know." Her anger had died away; now she felt bewildered and heart-broken.

"Well, if not he, then some other much like him—because, my dear, there is nothing you could possibly be but a well-kept wife. Oh, yes, yes, let us consider the evidence—not only how much it has cost to produce a girl like you, but how much it will cost to maintain you. So you *must* marry, and you must marry a young man who can maintain you properly—as you know perfectly well, having chosen a Rolland Spicer."

"I don't understand."

"Oh, yes do. You will marry some—I am sure—absolutely splendid young man. You will settle down to raising your babies. From time to time you will feel some nostalgia for your student days here at dear old Briarville, this fair Athens of the new world. You may even remember with some fondness a certain eccentric British professor, hmmm? And you will perhaps become an active patron of the arts. You will certainly imbue your children with a love of literature. You will have a happy and productive and useful and entirely praiseworthy life. But one thing you will not be, my dear, is a scholar. And so, you see, all the work that I would have done with you would have gone for nought."

Gloria was devastated. It was horribly, horribly unfair. It was also absolutely true. She didn't want it to be true. Her mind was racing as she tried to find a way—any way—so that it wouldn't have to be true.

"I don't have to dress like this," she said, "I don't. I really don't. It's just what I'm used to." How stupid and trivial and childish, she thought. Try something else. And suddenly she knew exactly what to do: she placed her Britomart paper on his lap.

"What's this?"

"It's a paper. I wrote it for you. I spent the whole summer on it."

"Good heavens!" He flipped it open, glanced down at it, then looked at her, surprised. "Spenser? We haven't done Spenser together."

"I know. I just— I don't know, I just got interested."

He began turning the pages. "Hmmm. Book III, yes, yes, yes— 'psychologically whole and independent being'— Yes, how clever of you. Britomart *is* unlike any of Spenser's other figures—yes, precisely in that way— 'Sexually awakening young girl'— Oh, indeed. Ah, 'menstrual imagery'—"

He looked up, looked out his office window. He tapped his teeth with his index finger. Then he turned back to her with his beamish, pussycat smile. "You know, Gloria, you could very well be right. Menstrual imagery—good God, it does appear to be plain as day! And I can't recall—I'll have to review the literature, but I can't recall having seen anyone take quite this approach."

He looked down at the paper again. "Wounded three times. Yes, yes, yes, three times— the holy Trinity— Yes, *yes* — Have you read much Spenser criticism, my dear?"

She shook her head.

"No, of course you haven't. Well, well, well. I am *so* looking forward to this. I shall peruse it at my leisure. But it appears quite original, my dear. I'm sure there will be problems, but yes, quite remarkable. The entire summer?"

"Professor Bolton," she said.

"Yes."

"I, ah, I don't want to marry young. My mother wants me to. Everybody expects me to, but I don't want to. Oh, sure, I'll probably get married someday— Yes, you're right, I'm *certain* to get married someday. But I want to get a—*a PhD!* That's right, I really do. I want to teach. English literature's the only thing I really care about. I want that more than anything in the whole world."

She was making it up as she went—had certainly never before thought of getting a PhD—and she didn't know if she believed a word of it. She had, however, delivered her speech with conviction, and, the best she could tell, she'd sounded painfully sincere. That she was still crying a little probably helped.

Professor Bolton stood, pulled his chair out from his desk, pushed it directly up in front of her, sat down in it, and stared into her eyes. "*Are you serious?*" he asked her in a voice that could not have been more serious.

Oh, God, Gloria thought, *if I say I am, then I have to be.* She took a deep breath. It felt as though she were about to jump off the high dive. "Yes," she said.

Professor Bolton sat back and appeared to be pondering this revelation. Then he kicked the floor and shot his big chair back to the side of his desk; he seized one of his pipes and lit it. He produced several fierce blasts of smoke. "Well," he said. "Well, well, well—Very well, Miss Cotter, you may write your honors thesis with me. Yes, indeed, I would be delighted to have you as a tutorial student."

"Thank you."

"Miss Cotter, have you an engagement tonight?"

She did, but she knew that whatever was coming, she didn't want to miss it. "No," she said.

"Excellent. You will now return to that fair bower of bliss wherein you dwell, and there you will recover your usual equanimity and estimable poise. You will dress yourself, my dear, even unto the eye teeth. And I will appear promptly at seven to escort you to our squalid excuse for a faculty club. Such a celebration is, I hasten to assure you, the way I always begin work with my tutorial students, but you, my dear, will be the first of your fair sex to be so honored. And we will dine in a civilized manner, and my colleagues will be astonished at your presence—but you, of course, will not deign to notice them—and we will discuss your future. Is all of this acceptable to you, my dear?"

She nodded dumbly and rose to her feet. He walked her to the door and opened it.

As she was stepping into the hall, he winked at her. "It would have been enough," he whispered, "if you had said a master's degree."

"Uncle Bats is taking me to the faculty club!" Gloria yelled at every Lamb she passed as she ran into the house and down the hall and up the stairs to her room—and to Susie: "He told me to dress *to the eye teeth!* What on earth am I going to wear?"

"A cocktail dress," Susie said as though the answer was obvious—which it had been. Gloria called and cancelled Rolland, took a shower, set her hair, considered redoing her nails—but if they weren't dead dead *dead* dry, her gloves would mark them, and she couldn't possibly *not* wear gloves, and she'd done them that morning anyway so they were *close* to perfect, but the red was just a teensy bit not quite blue enough—but, oh, to hell with it. She brushed her hair out and put on as much makeup as if she were going to a ball.

She chose her new black velvet because it was full bouffant and wore her new patent opera pumps with it—the four-inch heels made her feel deliciously dressed up—and white kid shorties which she was just tugging on when, through her window, she saw Professor Bolton's tiny Nash pulling up in front of her house. Boys you could make wait, but a professor?—she didn't think so. "Am I all right?" she said to Susie.

"*All right?* You're Cinderella!"

Professor Bolton was wearing a tuxedo which, instead of making him more elegant than usual, only succeeded in making him more ridiculous than usual; like the tweed suits he taught in, the tux seemed to have been made for a thinner man—well, if not exactly thinner, then certainly for a man who did not have that dismaying paunch secured to his front—and his sharply pressed pants collapsed, as usual, into a wrinkled heap over his absurdly tiny feet. "Ah, Miss Cotter, you are truly magnificent," he said as he held the car door open for her, "but from you, of course, one expects no less." She resisted the impulse to pirouette for him.

Getting into a Nash Rambler while wearing a full bouffant cocktail dress was something of a feat. Professor Bolton kept poking ineffectually at her skirt as though trying to pat it down like rising bread dough. "I couldn't resist another peek into your Spenser paper," he was saying, "and you know, Gloria, it could be worked up into something publishable."

"It could?"

Gloria was drowning in the stink of lilacs, and then, to make matters worse, he hunched forward so he could guide the car with his elbows—luckily they couldn't have been going much over ten miles an hour—while he stuffed a pipe with tobacco and lit it. She was afraid she was going to sneeze. "Certain gaping lacunae would have to be plugged, but it's remarkable work, my dear—for an undergraduate."

The faculty club was easily within walking distance, but it seemed to be taking forever to get there, and Professor Bolton was talking steadily in that silly, ebullient, inexorable voice he used when he was lecturing. "I wouldn't attempt any more work on it at the moment, my dear. Put it away. Yes, let it settle. It could well be the core of your PhD thesis—and speaking of that, you will, of course, be going to Columbia."

"I will?"

"There's really no other place for you, my dear. Lionel is there."

Lionel? she thought. *Lionel Trilling?* They had finally arrived; Professor Bolton *sprung* (yes, that was the right word) out of the car, raced around to the passenger's side, and opened the door for her. Together they coaxed out her skirt. She took a moment to smooth herself out. "But, ah, my real interest is contemporary poetry," she said, "and Trilling doesn't write about poetry very much, does he? I mean, doesn't he usually write about fiction? What is it you said?— 'The high moral purpose of the novel—'"

He took her by the elbow and guided her up the steps. "Indeed. But there's a basic rule of academic life that you should know, my dear. It never fails. Do not choose *the course*, choose *the man*— Ah, Harry, good evening—and Mrs. Thompkins, yes, yes, yes. A truly splendid evening. You surely must know Miss Cotter, one of our very best!"

Gloria had been whisked into the dining room before she knew quite where she was, and now she was being introduced to the wife of the head of the English Department. She'd hadn't found even a moment to take her gloves off, and this shrunken, white-haired monkey of a lady with benign, watery eyes had taken one of Gloria's hands between both of hers and was petting it like a cat. "Oh, such a beautiful young girl! Harry, you naughty boy, you never told me you had such beautiful young girls in the department."

Now what am I supposed to do? Gloria thought. Curtsy? Say something witty? ("Oh, I'm not *really* beautiful. It's all just a cunning illusion.") But Gloria, to her horror, was utterly tongue-tied; she felt her face burning, then hardening into a ghastly prom-queen smile. Most of the faculty of the English Department was there, and other men who must have been professors from other departments, and most were accompanied by ladies who presumably were their wives, and the professors were wearing the same slouchy, exhausted suits they always wore, and, among the wives, there was not a single one dressed as formally as Gloria. Oh, help! she thought.

Of course everyone was staring at her—and at Professor Bolton in his tux— and of course he had to walk her around and say a few words to every one of his colleagues (except for Dr. Stauffer who was gazing stonily elsewhere), and of course he had to choose a table in the center of the room where everyone could see them. "Professor Bolton," she whispered, "I'm grotesquely over-dressed."

"Oh, nonsense," he said, shooing away the concept with one hand. "What is it Chesterton said? Never— Ah, yes," to the waiter, "a sherry, I think? And will you have a sherry, my dear? Excellent— Now as to Columbia— Lionel is one of the few men in America who would not ruin you."

What was she supposed to say to that? A glass of sherry appeared in front of her, and she drank it.

"Columbia?" she said. "It's funny I never thought of Columbia." It wasn't that funny, actually: before this afternoon she'd never thought of graduate school at all—but now she thought: Columbia in *New York!* Wow, the stores, the clothes, the snooty salon where her stupid cousins got their legs waxed—and the night-clubs and dances and plays and foreign movies and the New York City Ballet. But then, of course, it might be a little bit hard to take full advantage of New York City if one were getting one's PhD—

"Now, my dear, what are you taking this year?"

"You know—all the requirements. I'm in honors, so I don't have a lot of choice—except for, ah, Contemp Lit with—"

"No, no, no, you don't need to take *anything* with the learned Dr. Stupor. A bloody waste of time, and— Well, as Wystan used to say when we were at Oxford, we don't need anyone to teach us our *own* literature, now do we?"

Wystan? she thought. Oh, that's *Auden.*

"George," Professor Bolton was saying to the waiter, "leave the bottle."

"But, Professor Bolton," she said, "don't I get to take anything contempo-rary? I really— Why don't *you* teach contemporary poetry? You know more than Dr. Stauffer."

"That's hardly a compliment, my dear." They both glanced over at Dr. Stauffer and caught him staring at them.

Professor Bolton chuckled. "You must understand the politics of the Depart-ment of English here at this great Athens of the new world. I must not—no, never, never—tread upon another man's domain. I was hired to teach the Tudors and Elizabethans, and teach them I shall!"

They sipped their sherries. She was so nervous she'd already drunk most of hers. "Now, as to your languages, how is your French, my dear?"

"I don't know. OK, I guess. I've had two years. I got A's."

"And your Latin?"

Latin! she thought. "Oh, just fine. I had four years in high school. I did Virgil."

"Excellent, excellent. And Catullus, Horace, Ovid?"

"Ah—no."

"And what is your elective this year?"

"Poli Sci. Introduction to—"

"Oh, no, no, no. If one wishes to know about governments, one simply reads about them, hmmm? And one never has too much Latin. You don't want it to slip away, now do you?"

"No, I suppose not." Gloria was appalled. The last thing in the world she would have considered was another year of Latin.

"Be sure to do your add-drop the first thing in the morning—not that there will be a great rush on advanced Latin. Then there's the matter of your Greek, but we can't cram everything into two years, now can we? You can do your Greek at Columbia. Hmmm, yes. And when were you planning to do your Old English?"

Gloria just looked at him.

"Best to get it out of the way as an undergraduate. I'm sure you'll find a spot for it next year. Dr. Thompkins, dull fellow though he may be, but, perfectly adequate for our purposes, and— How old are you, my dear? That crucial fact seems to have slipped my mind."

"Nineteen. I'll be twenty in February."

"*Indeed?* Good heavens. Well, there it is. Yes, you may catch up yet, my dear."

Catch up to *whom?* Gloria thought. She'd drunk too much sherry too fast, and she was getting blitzed—except maybe it wasn't entirely the fault of the sherry. She felt as though she had sailed off the edge of the known world to arrive in—or, to switch metaphors (she wasn't writing a paper; she could switch metaphors any time she pleased), as though she were suddenly in a late Henry James novel, right smack in the middle of one of those dense and maddening passages riddled with those things that one was being trained to ferret out and was rewarded with an A plus for finding: irony, ambiguity, complexity. And yes, this situation was just as ironic, ambiguous, and complex. That afternoon he had told her that she couldn't possibly make a scholar because she was—and he'd been too kind to say it plainly, but it had been obvious what he had meant— *a spoiled rotten rich girl*. But now here she was wildly overdressed for the faculty club because he'd told her to be wildly overdressed, and she couldn't have been any more on display if they were sitting in a glass case on a raised dais in the center of the room—so here she was in her fifty-dollar opera pumps and God-knows-how-much (she hadn't bothered to look at the price tag) black velvet evening dress and pearls (real ones, which went without saying), while he told her where to go to graduate school and exactly what to study—Latin, Old English, and Greek, for heaven's sake!—so she could catch up and become what? And then, after a moment, she knew what: *an old-fashioned British scholar just like him.*

And she was also managing to ferret out (the sherry fizzing in her brain was somehow helping) yet another layer of irony, ambiguity, and complexity—for, however much anyone might see her that way, she had never been, and, in fact, was incapable of being—not at that level which somebody or other (was it Erich Fromm?) called *authenticity*—a spoiled rotten rich girl, and even if she accomplished everything Professor Bolton set out for her, and accomplished it so well that the whole world saw her as a genuine scholar—a monster of erudition, as the cliché had it—that isn't what she would be either. The girl who had written the Britomart paper had not been interested in scholarship, and the girl who had been swimming over a mile a day had not been trying to improve her figure—

She looked across the table at this ugly middle-aged man—but no, that's not what he was. There was something quite appealing about his shiny, lined, puffy, grinning, utterly preposterous face. His dark brown eyes were glittering with amusement. Well, she thought, it *is* funny. The whole thing's funny.

"Speaking of your eminent colleague," she said, bending closer to him and speaking under her breath, "he just can't believe you're in here with me."

"Oh, yes, yes. There will be a fierce buzzing around the departmental coffee pot tomorrow morning, I assure you."

"Oh, he's such a horny little rat." The moment it was out of her mouth, she couldn't believe she'd said it, but Professor Bolton, instead of being shocked, uttered an explosive, high-pitched titter.

Now he was bending even closer to her—their foreheads were almost touching—and he rested two fingers lightly on the back of her wrist. "Well, he's a Lawrence scholar, you know—poor fellow."

"Oh, right," she said, "the dark coursings of the blood—"

"Oh, yes, yes. But with that wife of his—" Professor Bolton said, grinning madly, whispering, and they both risked a look at her.

"Lavender pants," Gloria said.

"Oh, my dear, *yes!* As lavender as a bloody powder box—the poor horse-faced woman—and that hideous—"

"*Mustard yellow*," Gloria said, giggling. "Oh, we're being terrible!"

Professor Bolton laughed so hard he had to take out his handkerchief and mop his eyes. "Oh, how very lovely it is to be here with you, my dear," he said, "how very lovely. Will you have the duck or the roast?"

PART TWO

9

"Why then would an infinitely wise, infinitely just, infinitely good and merciful God subject the souls of men to an eternity of misery, torment, and suffering?" this egg-faced stranger in the pulpit was asking.

Why, indeed? Gloria thought.

The Cotters went to church whenever Gloria's father decided they would; this morning he had announced his decision the way he always did: by appearing in the upstairs hallway shaved and dressed, drinking his second cup of coffee, and, in the long-suffering, self-righteous voice of a man who has been up for hours while everyone else has been asleep, barking at his wife and daughter, still in their beds: "Church, girls!"

The Cotters usually attended church once every four or five weeks; that this was the second Sunday in a row might have meant that Gloria's father was feeling more than usually devout, but if so, she would never hear about it, for religion was a topic he did not care to discuss. Once she'd asked him straight out if he believed in God. It had been during her senior year in high school when she'd been reading Freud and wondering if the God she'd believed in all of her life might be nothing more than an illusion—a personification of her own childish need to feel some magical power at work in the universe, a benevolent power that cared about her personally—and she'd really wanted to hear what her father believed. After a somber and protracted silence, he'd said: "Any man who's been in combat *knows* if there's a God."

The Cotters were sitting where they always sat: in the fifth pew from the back on the left-hand side. Gloria's father was wearing one of his identical gray flannel suits with one of his nearly identical striped ties. Gloria and her mother had costumed themselves like grown-up ladies—in small, deft hats, in kid gloves that were now removed and folded neatly and laid on the tops of their purses, in summer-weight gabardine suits, bought in New York and immediately recognizable by other grown-up ladies as models of classic tailoring (Gloria's was pale burgundy, her mother's blue-gray), in undecorated white blouses and smooth leather pumps. As much as Gloria enjoyed dressing up, she did not enjoy dressing for church; she hated being dressed exactly like her mother, and, when she regarded the multitude of blue-rinsed heads in the pews in front of her (they, after all, were the *real* grown-up ladies), she felt like an imposter, and then, of course, just like all the other grown-up ladies, she was suffering—if not the full torment of the damned, then at least the mundane miseries of those consigned to some mild-mannered, mediocre purgatory. The doors to the church had been shut when the service began, and the only ventilation was through the partially open side windows; the air was stale, wet, and dead, and the temperature in the pews must have risen well into the nineties. On the surface, the grown-up ladies might look as crisp as iced lettuce, but next to the skin where they were wearing their mandatory girdles, they were moist as sea urchins.

Almost all of the country club crowd was Presbyterian, and the country club crowd did not worship at the big First Presbyterian Church downtown; they attended the quaint, little Edgewood Presbyterian Church that was only a short drive from the country club. For nearly twenty years, the Reverend T. Charles Acker had presided over the Edgewood Presbyterian Church, and, although he was far from what anyone would call a good preacher, he was considered to be a first-rate minister because—as was readily apparent from any of his awkward, lopsided sermons punctuated with frequent phlegmy throat clearings or even from five minutes of strained conversation with him—the Reverend Acker believed with every scintilla of his soul that Jesus Christ had been a real person who had been the son of God, that He had risen from the dead, and, if you believed in Him, you could do it too. Now isn't that what you want from a minister? Gloria thought. *You* might not believe it—or you might not believe all of it all of the time—but you certainly wanted *him* to believe it.

Unfortunately, the Reverend Acker was not preaching this morning. The pulpit was occupied by this guest minister who was speaking in a sincere, mushy, pleading voice, and he did not believe it—or he did not believe as much of it as the Reverend Acker did. "No, we should not consider Hell to be a real place filled with flames and engines of torture and devils with pitchforks," he was saying. "Hell is a metaphor—a symbol for the absence of God."

The young man took a moment to look out over the congregation to see how he was going over—were they buying it?—and Gloria looked too. In the very first pew directly below the pulpit, old silver-haired Lee J. Hockner the Second—the largest single contributor to the Edgewood Presbyterian Church— was sitting as upright as if he were at a board meeting, but his massive, dignified head was sinking, and his soft, slow, murmurous breathing was beginning to sound dangerously like snoring. Ordinarily his wife would have roused him with a sharp dig to the ribs, but today she must have decided that the sermon did not merit his consciousness, a conclusion obviously shared by the rest of the congregation—the bankers, lawyers, doctors, and, of course, Raysburg Steel executives who were waiting with polite, stony, disapproving faces for this nonsense to be over. No, they weren't buying it, and neither were their wives. No, they did not want some pink-faced, watery-eyed, thin-haired sissy straight out of minister school telling them that hell is not real. If hell has been declared fictitious, mythical—a mere metaphor—then what's the next to go? Sin? Redemption? The resurrection and the life everlasting? Oh, come on, Gloria thought, give us real hell: "A Dungeon horrible, on all sides round / As one great Furnace flam'd, yet from those flames / No light, but rather darkness visible . . ."

Living for three years with a believing Christian had changed Gloria's attitudes toward religion—had made her more tolerant of other people's beliefs, less ready to label them naive or childish—and she never went to church now without thinking of Susie. They'd both been devout girls. Like Susie, Gloria had prayed and studied and searched her heart, had imagined herself a missionary, a minister's wife, and sometimes even a saint; she'd been confirmed. But Gloria's religious fervor—unlike Susie's—had burned itself out in a little over a year, and she'd come to see it as one of her many vain attempts to escape the hell of Fairhaven Hall, a hell that had not been in the least metaphorical. She'd been left with huge chunks of the King James committed to memory and vaguely Christian sentiments that, as the years had passed, had grown progressively less religious and more literary. But not *entirely* literary, she thought; just as she'd told Susie, she still had a faith, small but persistent as a pilot light, and a faith in— Well, she could not have said exactly in *what*, but she'd felt— or at least she thought she'd felt—the presence of God, and when she prayed, she prayed to that, however mysterious and distant it might be.

As Gloria listened to the guest minister bringing his well-wrought sermon to an appropriately fulsome close—hammering home his point that none of it should be taken literally, that it was *all* metaphor—she imagined John Calvin spinning in his grave, and, even though, in her midnight chats with Susie, she'd often argued for just such a metaphorical interpretation of Scripture, she found herself longing for something more substantial. If there were not, in religion, something you could use in your ordinary, daily life, then what was the point of it? And she found herself wishing—not for the first time—that she could share Susie's literal faith in—well, if not in Jesus Christ as her personal friend and savior, then at least in someone, or something, just as tangible.

She found herself remembering the only time she'd attended a service at the Christian Church in Cloverton. It had been during that Thanksgiving weekend of her first visit there, and, after everything that had gone before, the church service had been something of an anticlimax. She and Susie had dressed identically in jumpers, plain white blouses, and flats. Susie had worn no makeup, so neither had she (well, a touch of lipstick, but that hardly counted), and they'd blended right in with the congregation. Pastor Harris had not turned out to be, as Gloria had been imagining him, a figure larger than life—a tower of wrath, a raging Jonathan Edwards—but rather a middle-sized, balding man in a surprisingly dapper navy-blue suit. He'd radiated a beaming amiability and had a personality, she'd thought, like an insurance salesman's.

It had been an interminable service in which earnest, frightened children stammered their way through the Bible readings and half a dozen good old hymns were belted out by the congregation—she remembered "Rock of Ages" and "Take it to the Lord in Prayer"—and, in the longest sermon Gloria had ever heard, Pastor Harris preached on "true thankfulness." He'd taken for his text the story of the ten lepers who were healed but only one of whom turns back to give thanks, but, instead of elucidating the Scripture, or expanding upon the metaphor implicit in it, he'd immediately jumped away from it to go leapfrogging through the Bible from Deuteronomy to Corinthians and back to the Gospels in a motion that seemed entirely random, and Gloria had quickly lost the thread of his argument. Then, eventually, she'd realized that there *was* no argument; his sermon was not an intellectual construction like anything she'd heard in the Presbyterian Church but an emotional statement rising in pitch and fervor—a free association on the concept of "thankfulness."

Pastor Harris did something Gloria had never seen in church; he left the pulpit, wandered into the midst of the congregation, strode up and down the aisle, and addressed himself directly to this person or that: "Now Paul says, 'Thanks *be* unto God for his unspeakable gift, so let me ask you, Floyd—and you too, Mary—*why* is the gift unspeakable? That's a funny word to use, now isn't it? Well, Paul also says, 'for now we see as through a glass darkly,' and he talks about the peace of God, which passeth all understanding. Yes, sir, that's a hard one! You know, if we can't *understand* it, if we can't *see* it, then we sure can't *speak of it,* now can we? But with God all things are possible, and every little child in this church today knows exactly what that unspeakable gift is— Oh, yes, you do, children, I know you do! And every one of us here must become as little children, isn't that right? And doesn't every little child here know John Three, Sixteen? Come on, children, say it with me—" and, indeed, they did, all of the children and many of the adults: "For God so loved the world, that he gave his only begotten Son, that whosoever believeth in him should not perish, but have everlasting life."

After the service, Susie led Gloria into the church hall for coffee and introduced her to a bewildering number of neighbors. Gloria was hoping that she wouldn't have to meet, and talk to, Pastor Harris, but, as they were leaving, he intercepted them just inside the door. He gathered them up, one arm wrapped around each of their waists, and, not letting them go, told Gloria how wonderful Susie was: "She was just a little thing. I guess she was twelve. Isn't that right, honey? And she came to me and said, 'Pastor Harris, I've been reading my Bible just the way you told us to, and Jesus wasn't a baby when he was baptized, he was a full-grown man. And John the Baptist didn't put a little tiny spot of water on his forehead, he dunked him right there in the river Jordan. Isn't that what it means, Pastor, to get washed clean of your sins? So how can you get washed clean of your sins with a tiny little spot of water on your forehead?' And I said, 'Thank your God in heaven, child, for the Holy Ghost has flowed right into you and showed you the way.' Oh, she knew what she wanted, all right! She wanted the truth and the way and the life, and not some counterfeit."

Gloria hadn't said a word, but she'd been grinning idiotically up at him. He released his hold on their waists but took one of Gloria's hands in both of his. "Now, Gloria— You don't mind if I call you Gloria, do you?"

"Oh, no."

"What faith were you raised in, if you don't mind my asking you?"

"Presbyterian."

"Yes. John Calvin there in Geneva, Switzerland, preaching that some were saved and some were damned before they even had a say in the matter. Do you hold to that doctrine, Gloria?"

"No, I don't think so."

"Well, good for you. That's what I have to say. And I'll say it again. *Good for you, Gloria.* You're nobody's fool. Because Christ will redeem *anyone* just as he promised us. Now let me ask you something else, Gloria. You don't mind standing here talking to me a minute, do you?"

"No, of course not."

"I didn't think you did. Now tell me this. Do you love your roommate here?"

The question took Gloria completely by surprise. She answered honestly: "Yes."

"I can see that, Gloria. I can see how close you girls are. And isn't she easy to love, Gloria? This beautiful, sweet-natured girl? Well, of course she is. Who wouldn't love her? Well, I just want to remind you of something, Gloria, which you may have figured out for yourself— You're a smart girl, I can see that— When you love Susan Jane here, what you love is the Grace of the Lord Jesus shining straight through her like light through a windowpane. And I'm sure that Susan Jane loves you too, and nothing would make her happier than to know you were saved. Isn't that right, Susan Jane?"

"Yes, sir."

"Well, I know it is. Now I'm not going to keep you standing here jawing with me much longer—but to make a long story short, here it is in a nutshell. If ever you want to accept Jesus Christ as your personal lord and saviour— And I can't begin to tell you the *relief* of knowing your sins have been washed away! Oh, the *joy!* Oh, the *peace!* I can't begin to describe it to you, honey— When you know in your heart that wherever you go, you'll have a friend right there by your side, and that you'll never die *but live forever in glory.* Oh, yes, then you'll be just like your name—*Glo-ri-a*—glory be to God! So if you ever want to

come back here, honey, you just say the word and I'll baptize you in water—
for I'm only a man—but Jesus Christ Himself will baptize you in the Holy
Ghost."

Gloria had been struck more than speechless. He squeezed her hand and
then let go of it. He winked at her. "You think about it, honey."

Driving back to Briarville that afternoon, Susie had been silent at the wheel
for a good ten minutes, and then, with no preamble, had said: "That son-of-a-
bitch." A moment later she'd added, "May God forgive me—what a terrible
thing to say about your pastor," and, a moment after that, "Maybe he's not my
pastor."

After another long stretch of brooding silence, Susie had said, "He had no
right to do that to you."

"Oh, I didn't mind," Gloria said, although, of course, she had.

"If you're not saved, then I'm not saved either—and that's the truth, and I
know it in my heart, and I can't pretend I don't know it. Oh, Gloria, I've prayed
and prayed for guidance on this—"

Gloria waited to hear more about it, but nothing more appeared to be
coming. Just when she was about to ask, "Guidance on what?" Susie said, "Why
should people expect me to drive back to Cloverton every Sunday morning?"

"I don't know. Why should they?"

"I think I'll try the Baptist Church," Susie said.

From Gloria's point of view, switching from the Christian Church in Cloverton
to the Baptist Church in Briarville was hardly a change at all, but Susie couldn't
have struggled with it more if she'd been contemplating conversion to Zoroasteri-
anism. By spring, however, she was attending the Baptist Church every Sunday,
and, by their senior year, she was teaching Sunday school there and had become
a stalwart of the youth group.

Now the Reverend Acker, to the palpable relief of his little flock, had resumed
control over the service and was leading the responsive reading, and Gloria,
however much she might envy Susie her faith, found herself thankful that she
had been raised in the good, old, boring Presbyterian Church and not in some
wacky fundamentalist sect like Susie's. Then, because that morning was the first
Sunday in the month and, therefore, a communion day, the organist, hidden
from the eyes of the congregation, began to poke around to no great effect in a
minor key—she had chosen an improbable organ stop that sounded to Gloria
like warblers singing with their heads under water—while being passed down
the pews were silver trays loaded with Munchkin-sized cubes of bread and large
wooden trays drilled with holes, each hole containing a tiny glass filled with
grape juice—and Gloria was delighted to discover that, upon this hot Sunday
morning, God in His infinite wisdom had sent unto the congregation of the

Edgewood Presbyterian Church a bee. It was buzzing so brazenly that every Christian soul in attendance must surely be aware of its presence, but not one of them was about to acknowledge it—they were *Presbyterians*, after all.

As she always did when she took communion, Gloria closed her eyes and tried to imagine Christ in the upper room with His disciples saying, "This do in remembrance of me," and she tried to transubstantiate the tiny, prissy morsel and sticky, sweet gulp she was consuming into a fragment of a large, dense peasant loaf broken in Christ's strong hands and a swig of the harsh, red rotgut she imagined Him pouring into a crude clay cup. The organist had fallen silent, and the congregation was, presumably, deep in prayer; the only sound was the honed buzz of the bee, rising and falling, as it searched for a way out of this strange, hot, breathless situation.

"Dear Lord," Gloria prayed, "give both Mom and me more charity toward each other. It sure would be nice if we resembled from time to time a normal mother and daughter. And be good to all of us, and give us not what we think we should have, but what we really should have. And help me to put up with Mr. Dougherty for a couple hours no matter how boring or stupid he is," and then, moving from the particular to the general, she added, "and help me to like people, and care more about them, and stop being such a spoiled, self-centered little bitch."

She surely had more to pray for than that, but nothing was coming to mind. If the service went on much longer, she would sweat right through her dress shields and into her nice, crisp gabardine suit and it would have to go to the cleaners, and as soon as she got home, she was going to strip off the whole tortuous works and jump in the pool, and what on earth was she going to wear for her absurd rendezvous with Mr. Dougherty?—and she should stop thinking about these trivial things because she was supposed to be praying ("What, could ye not watch with me one hour?"), and Gloria tried to find the small, still point of quiet inside herself, and had almost found it, when the bee came sizzling by, inches from her right ear.

Gloria opened her eyes, looked up, and saw the bee floating in a shaft of sunlight, and, for one sharply etched moment, she saw it as nothing but a bee—not a symbol or metaphor but just a bee—a big fat honeybee, yellow and black and smacked into brilliant clarity by the light, and she felt an answering clarity in herself: spontaneously, unplanned and unbidden, she offered up a genuinely fervent prayer: "Oh, God, give me something *real* to do!"

Right after church, Ted had himself a good, long swim. Then he made a Dagwood sandwich, drank a beer with it, and fell sound asleep in the lawn chair by the side of the pool. He woke now feeling thoroughly out of whack. He'd felt like that so often in the last couple weeks it was beginning to seem familiar; it was that old feeling of nothing being right but nothing being wrong either, *except there was a war on*—but, of course, there wasn't any war on, and it had been twelve years since the war. Ted had met plenty of guys who'd never stopped fighting the war and would probably go on fighting it until the day they died, but he'd never thought he was one of them, and it wasn't as though he was thinking about the war anyway. Oh, hell, maybe he was just getting old.

At forty-six? No, that couldn't be. Yeah, but then what was he doing falling asleep in the afternoon like an old fart? He'd gone for years with no more than five or six hours of sleep a night, but now he just couldn't keep up the pace. What? At forty-six? Come on, he told himself, that's ridiculous. But there was no doubt about it: he was slowing down. Those days when he could give Laney a good, stiff poke every night come hell or high water were long gone, and lots of times now he was asleep before she was. Jesus, since the war, the years had been zipping by too fast, and there was never enough time to stop and think about anything, and four more years zipping by made fifty, and, damn it, he didn't like the sound of that at all. *Fifty* was ten years away from *sixty*—

A wave of sickening fear swept over Ted so powerfully he sprang to his feet to get rid of it. As though confirming his worst suspicions, that sudden movement made him so dizzy he was afraid he was going to have to sit down, but he willed himself to continue standing until his head cleared. He lit a cigarette. It tasted like shit, but he smoked it anyway. Have to get my heart checked one of these days, he thought, and then he felt like praying. What was the matter with him?

Ted hadn't liked the guest minister or his sermon any more than anybody else had, but he was glad he'd gone to church and taken communion. He'd never been able to make up his mind whether God was really *there* or only a story you told children when they asked you, "Daddy, what happens when you die?" Despite the fact that dozens of times during the war he'd prayed as fervently as the most simple-minded Baptist slob under his command, Ted had never arrived at any firm conclusions about God. After praying—and after he'd survived whatever had been scaring the shit out of him—he'd always felt embarrassed; what if he'd been praying to *nothing*? But he certainly wanted his wife and daughter to believe in God—and to act accordingly—and sometimes he believed in God too, and lately he'd wished he knew for sure that God was really there because he wouldn't have minded a little helping hand from Him.

What's going on? he thought. Am I going to turn into one of these sanctimonious old farts who all of a sudden get religion when they think they're getting old? And if he was going to start praying, he should have prayed in church, but that mealy-mouthed guest minister had put him off, and so he'd stubbornly refused to pray. But if God was really there, He knew everything, and so He could very well be watching Ted R. Cotter standing by the side of the pool once again *talking himself out of praying*, and that wouldn't look very good, now would it? And besides, if God wasn't there, who was going to know? So Ted closed his eyes, and then he couldn't decide what to pray for. After a moment, he said, "God help me." That should do it, he thought, and opened his eyes. He did feel better. He butted his smoke out, walked into the house, and, carefully avoiding everybody, picked up the *New York Times* and fled with it upstairs.

Ted liked the bedroom in the afternoon; after the fierce sun down by the pool, it was a pretty, little, shaded nook, and he liked all of Laney's feminine touches — the sheer curtains on the windows and her white vanity table with her makeup on it and the lace on the edges of the sheets and the pillow cases. Ted liked women — which was, he thought, kind of amazing considering he'd never much liked his mother — and he was still very much in love with his wife, and, even though she wasn't any farther away than the kitchen, and even though the last thing he wanted to do at the moment was talk to her, he liked being reminded of her.

I just needed to get out of the sun, that's all, he thought and opened the paper. Almost immediately he saw the headline: SENATOR ATTACKS STEEL PRICE RISES, and he sat up as abruptly as if he'd just been shocked. "Senator Hubert H. Humphrey, Democrat of Minnesota," he read, "said today that the steel industry was talking 'plain unadulterated nonsense' in asserting that recent price increases had been caused by higher wages."

Oh, shit, Ted thought, here we go. "The $6-a-ton rise first announced by the United States Steel Corporation amounted to a 'flouting' of President Eisenhower's plea for self-restraint in an inflationary situation," he read. Jesus, this could be real trouble. "The steel industry is enjoying record profits this year..." Well, didn't the industry deserve it? — after the war years, after the Truman years — but no, the goddamn Democrats didn't understand the first thing about the American economy. The main thing the steel industry needed was exactly what every other business in the country needed: no more government interference.

Looking for anything else about the industry, Ted continued to flip through the paper until he saw another headline that made him laugh out loud: PRESIDENT HAPPY OVER GOLF SCORE. Ike was quoted as saying he'd played "the best nine holes I've ever had," and Ike's golfing companions had included "Carl W. Eberhardt, West Virginia steel company executive."

Good old Carl, Ted thought, grinning. If anybody could talk sense to the president, it'd be Carl, and if anybody could pry out of Ike an educated guess as to what the goddamn Democrats might have up their sleeves, that'd be Carl too, and tomorrow Ted would hear all about it — but, if you knew how to read between the lines, one thing came through loud and clear: if the President of the United States was playing the best golf of his life with Carl Eberhardt, that surely meant a damn good day for the steel industry.

It was funny, Ted thought, how much business was conducted on the golf course. Ted couldn't imagine golfing with the President of the United States. Well, on second thought, he *could* imagine it, and the picture was enough to make his hair stand on end.

A man in Ted's position was required to golf—it was impossible to get out of it—and there was not a man at the Raysburg Country Club who could drive off the tee any farther than Ted R. Cotter; unfortunately, there was also not a man at the Raysburg Country Club—or in America, for that matter—who had a slice as bad as Ted's. The ball didn't merely go looping off to the right; it appeared to be defying the laws of physics. It always shot away with a deeply soul-satisfying CRACK!, but then, once airborne, it began to describe not merely a curve but something that looked suspiciously like the beginning of a perfect circle—as though he had magically converted that demonic little white bastard into a boomerang and it was on its way straight back at him to arrive like a bullet between his teeth. The harder he hit it, the worse his slice got, and his drive had become a thing of legend. No matter how much work he did with the pro, it never got any better. He'd stopped seeing the pro.

The last time Ted had seen the pro, the son-of-a-bitch had made him drive off the tee for an hour—ball after goddamn ball for an hour, every one of them slicing madly. "Don't worry, Teddy," the pro had said (only Ted's wife and the pro ever called him Teddy; it appeared to be a prerogative attached to the position of golf pro to be able to call him Teddy), "we'll lick this thing yet." At first the pro had thought it was Ted's elbow. But nope, correcting the elbow hadn't helped. Fiddling around with Ted's wrists hadn't helped either. Then, for a few drives, he'd thought it was something in Ted's hips. Finally he'd turned Ted bodily toward the left. "Aim that way," he'd said, "and hit it just the way you've been hitting it." He'd aimed Ted directly at the club house. Ted had slammed the ball with all his might and drilled it straight as a plumb bob through the club house window.

Yep, Ted thought, glad it was Carl at Gettysburg and not me. Yep, dumbass Billy Dougherty, the king of divots, is more my speed—and this was going to be quite the weekend for golf. Last night at the club, Billy had said, "Well, skipper, the old man's off whacking balls with Ike, is he? Can you beat that? Who would've thought I'd ever know somebody who'd know the president? So anyhoo, what do you say, skipper? Why don't we whack a few ourselves?"

"Not on your life, Billy."

"Oh, why not? I've got a few things I want to get off my chest, if you follow me, and it's kind of, you know, real pretty out on the golf course. We don't have to make a big deal out of it. Just a hole or two. Tell you what—tomorrow, about the time when the day starts to cool down a bit, you know what I mean? Let's say at four-thirty or five? Come on, skipper, we haven't had us a real shit session for a hell of a long time."

And because— well,yes, he might as well admit it: because he was considering giving Billy the boot and felt guilty as all hell about that, and because that very same night he was having Al Connely over to dinner to sound him out about replacing Billy, and because only the most cold-hearted, evil son-of-a-bitch would play a couple holes of golf with a guy he was planning on firing and then go home and have dinner with the guy who was going to replace him, and because he didn't want Billy to have a clue about what was going on, Ted had said yes. Now he felt like a shit and wished he could get out of it.

Sometimes Ted thought that Carl Eberhardt was such a straight arrow he made the Boy Scouts of America look like the Comintern. When McCarthy had been in the saddle, Carl had required that every non-union employee of Raysburg Steel all the way down to the lowliest file clerk sign a loyalty oath, and Ted had been in charge of making sure that everybody signed, and, by God, everybody *had* signed, but Ted had thought that Carl was naive—more than naive, stupid even. A real, committed, card-carrying, dyed-in-the-wool commie wouldn't have hesitated half a second before signing a loyalty oath, and anybody who knew anything at all about communism ought to know that. And besides, what was wrong with the country—and all you had to do was spend four years in the navy to know it—was not treason in high places; it was stupidity in high places. It had not been the commies who'd ordered all of the officers of *The Minnewaukan* from the skipper on down to dine with their neckties on, nor had it been the commies who'd steamed the Third Fleet directly into the middle of a typhoon. But, be that as it may, another thing Ted had learned in the navy was that no matter what happens, your commanding officer is always right, and if Carl wanted Billy fired because he was divorced and drinking too much, then, by God, he was going to get fired, and who was Ted to object? Guys had been fired for less, and, on the night of the Fourth, Ted had wanted Billy gone just as much as Carl had. But Ted had turned Charlie Edmonds and his boys loose on Old Reliable, and the final report wasn't in yet, and so far Charlie hadn't been able to find a damn thing wrong with how Billy was running Old Reliable—and Carl Eberhardt was turning sixty-six in the fall. Good Christ, wasn't it just about time for that sanctimonious, cold-hearted, evil old son-of-a-bitch to retire?

After church Gloria had tried to hang onto her moment of clarity, of religious epiphany—if that's what it had been—but, as the day had worn on, it had become progressively harder to do that. Her mother was, *mirabile dictu*, entertaining at home, and, although it was only a small dinner party with only one other couple, her mother was crackling with anxiety and doing her best to pass it on to everyone else. Gloria had changed into her swimsuit, but she'd never made it into the pool. Mrs. Warsinski had come out right after Mass, and she and Gloria had vacuumed and dusted and tidied. Gloria had made her grandmother's lunch and delivered it, had set the dining room table with the best china and crystal, and then had helped Mrs. Warsinski make the shrimp and lobster canapés and the tiny rolled sandwiches that her mother always served.

By mid-afternoon, Gloria was just as jumpy as her mother. Why on earth had she agreed to meet stupid Mr. Dougherty, and, with this darned dinner party, how was she going to get out of the house to do it? "Hey, Mom," she tried, "I've got a date with Bink this afternoon, and—"

"You *what?*"

"Well, you know, Binkie's parents are out of town, and I was supposed to meet her at the club, and—"

"Not today, Gloria. There's just too damned much to do here."

"Oh, Mom, I'll only be gone for an hour or two." And that was met with a frosty silence which Gloria translated as: "If you want to be that irresponsible, go right ahead, but if you do, I'll make your life miserable." So what she should do was call Mr. Dougherty and cancel, but there were only two phones: one in the kitchen, occupied by Mrs. Warsinski and her mother, and the other in her parents' bedroom, occupied by her father.

Maybe she could just stand Mr. Dougherty up. Hey, there was a wonderful thought. She even had a perfectly good reason for doing it. But then, no matter how hard she tried to talk herself into it, she simply couldn't. What she wanted was for everything to be hunky-dory with Mr. Dougherty—"squared away" to use his own phrase—so he would fade back into that position in her life he never should have left: utter nonexistence. It was after three by now, and Mrs. Warsinski had the potato salad made and the ham stuffed with cloves, so there really wasn't much left to do. "Mom," Gloria said, "it's only for an hour. Binkie's parents are—"

"I know damned well where Binkie's parents are. They're dining with the President of the United States! All right, Miss Priss, but you be back here by six."

"Sure, Mom."

Gloria ran straight up to her room and into the shower. Now all she had to worry about was what to wear. She wanted to remind that jerk she was some-body's daughter—his *boss's* daughter, to be exact—and so she decided on camp shorts, tennis shoes, a halter top, and a ponytail. Then, dressed and looking at her freshly scrubbed face, she couldn't do what she'd been planning—wear no makeup at all—so, with girlish pink lipstick, a flick of mascara, and a touch of rouge, she created a pretty good impersonation of a wide-eyed schoolgirl.

Her father was still lost behind the *New York Times*. "Hey, Dad, I'm going down to the club for a bit, OK?"

"Sure, hon."

"I'll be back in plenty of time."

He lowered the paper and gave her a long, hard look. "Did you talk to your mom about this?"

"Oh, yes. It's OK with her. I'm meeting Binkie."

As he continued to look at her with that alert but expressionless face he often wore—she thought of it as his navy face—she was afraid that she had, somehow, given herself away, but he surprised her: "You look nice, hon."

At exactly four Gloria was walking down the road toward the club. Maybe he won't show up, she thought—or he forgot, or he never meant it in the first place; now wouldn't that be a treat? But no such luck. Mr. Dougherty's low-slung, silver dung beetle had already appeared below her, at a bend in the road. The top was down. He reached over and opened the door for her. "Got your driving duds on, huh?" he said with a wink.

She got into the car. "I have to be back by six."

"Don't even say, hi, huh?"

"Hi, Mr. Dougherty. I have to be back by six."

He laughed. "You look good with your hair up, princess. You should wear it like that more often."

"Thanks," she said automatically.

Even with the air moving through the open-top car, she could smell bay rum, Sen-sen, and whiskey. She looked over at him. He was wearing sunglasses and a godawful Hawaiian shirt with the short sleeves rolled up and the buttons undone halfway down his chest; he'd slicked his hair back with brilliantine like a teenager. She wouldn't have thought he'd drive so slowly.

He was lounging back in the driver's seat, his left arm draped over the door. He gave her a boyish grin, and the anxiety she'd been feeling all day was suddenly focused into a painfully hot point—it was roughly the size of a cherry— at the top of her stomach just below her breastbone. "You don't have to say much of anything," the secret watcher told her. "Just put up with him for an hour, and then it'll be over, and, after that, never, never, *never* get yourself into this ridiculous position again."

"So what's going on at six?" he said.

"My mom's having guests for dinner."

"Oh, yeah? Who?"

None of your damned business, that's who, she thought, but she said, "The Connelys."

"Oh, yeah, that figures—and where you supposed to be?"

She was tempted to side-step the question, pretend she hadn't understood it or answer with something ambiguous—but why bother? "At the club. I'm supposed to be meeting Binkie."

"Oh, yeah, old man Eberhardt's daughter, right? OK, so we just keep our story straight, that's all. Don't worry, you'll be walking in the door long before six."

Now it was clear as clear could be: she was lying to her parents, and Mr. Dougherty knew it.

"Great day, huh?" he said, "if you like it hotter than the hinges of Hades." He pulled over to the side of the road. "OK, princess, take over."

For a moment she didn't know what he meant. Then she remembered: *she* was supposed to drive. She didn't want to drive his damned Porsche. "You look worried, honey," he said in a soft, coaxing voice. "Hey, don't worry, OK? I'm just a little bit tight— Yeah, and so what else is new, right?— But everything's under control, if you follow me. We get out in the country, get rolling along, always clears my mind. Come on, princess, why don't you give her a shot?"

Gloria got out of the Porsche and walked around it. Mr. Dougherty stepped out, opened the door for her, and bowed like someone doing an after-you-Alphonse routine. "There you go, honey," he said.

She sat waiting for him to tell her what to do. He threw himself into the passenger's side, opened the glove compartment, and took out a bottle of whiskey— not a pint, which is what she'd sometimes seen in boys' glove compartments, but a fifth. Although the bottle was already open, hardly any of it had been drunk. He unscrewed the top and took a long drink. It was Four Roses. "Know better than to offer *you* a snort, huh?" he said with a laugh, "but you're welcome to some if you're so inclined— OK, put the clutch in and shove her into first. You know where first is? Here, I'll show you— Now easy, easy, easy on that ole clutch. Just smooth her on out. Yeah, that's it."

Gloria shifted into second, and then into third. She could feel the power of the car; she was giving it hardly any gas at all, but she was already doing fifty— and Mr. Dougherty was leaning close to her so he wouldn't have to yell over the wind. "Oh, yeah," he said. "Good old Al Connely. Yeah, sure, I could of guessed it. He wants my job, good old Al Connely."

"Mr. Dougherty, I don't know anything about my father's work."

"Oh, hell, princess, I didn't think you did. I'm just thinking out loud— Hey, don't be afraid to boot her down. Yeah, that's better. Like the feel of her, huh? You bet."

Gloria had no idea where they were; she was just following the road. She wasn't comfortable driving that fast—over sixty now—but Mr. Dougherty kept egging her on: "That's it, kid. You're doing great. Let her rip."

He took another long drink. "Yeah, Al Connely. Great guy. And then there's

Charlie Edmonds. You ever meet him? No? Well, there's another great guy. Bunch of great guys working for your old man. And you know what Charlie does for your old man? He snoops. And you know where he's been snooping around? Old Reliable. Doing his damndest to get something on me. But I'll tell you, princess, you know what he's going to get? The big fat goose egg. Because your uncle Billy runs a tight ship, and you damn well better believe it."

"Mr. Dougherty," she said—and she had to yell now over the wind—"I don't think we should talk about my dad's work, OK? It doesn't feel right to me."

"OK, OK, I was just thinking, that's all."

She could sense something different about him—maybe that he'd been drinking. But no, it was more than that. The man she'd met downtown with his kids and characterized as a big, harmless goof was gone; he'd been replaced by the man who'd followed her in his car, the man who'd almost pushed her off the road. Now she was driving that ugly silver car that had almost pushed her off the road. How very strange.

"Hey, princess," he said, "you brake in the wrong place. You should be braking going into the curve, and then you accelerate out. You with me? Give her a try— Hey, there you go. That's it. Now try the next—no, no, no, *not yet*. OK, *now*. Brake. Yeah! Now off, and boot her! Hey, shit, we'll make a race driver out of you yet."

He leaned closer to her; his mouth was only a few inches from her ear. "Don't be scared of her, honey? You see anybody else on the road? Just wind her on out. You'll never find her top end, swear to God."

The road, for the moment, was straight, and—just as he'd said—there wasn't another car in sight. Gloria pushed the accelerator down; she risked a glance at the dash and saw that they were over eighty. A curve was coming up. "Not now," he yelled at her, "wait!" Sick with fear, she kept her foot off the brake. "Now!" She braked hard, and the car fish-tailed, tires screaming. "Kick her!" Mindlessly, Gloria slammed her foot onto the accelerator, and the car straightened out. Mr. Dougherty was laughing. "See. You're getting the feel of her."

Gloria had forgotten that the entire purpose of this clandestine rendezvous— at least from Mr. Dougherty's point of view—was for her to drive his car, but, even if she had remembered, no amount of mental rehearsal would have prepared her for what she was doing. It was all happening too fast: he'd appeared on the road by her house too fast, and she'd found herself behind the wheel of the Porsche too fast, and now she was driving too fast.

"Move it, move it, move it, honey. Got to make up that time— Don't hug the right side of the road, honey. You're losing time. You look ahead, right? And you see the road's clear, right? Then you use the whole damn road, right? Like drawing a straight line— Yeah, that's it, that's it—no, no, *no*, don't touch that brake!

"Hey, ass kisser coming up. Ready with the brake, ready, ready, ready—now! And *kick* her, hard, hard, hard. Brake! Off! Kick!" The tires were howling, and, for a moment, Gloria had the car sliding sideways. "Whip her over," he yelled, grabbed the wheel and did it for her. "Yeah! Back! Yeah! Don't you *dare* take your foot off the gas. Yeah, boot her, boot her good."

She would rather risk her life, she thought, than risk making this man mad at her, and that surely couldn't be right— "No, it's not right," the secret watcher said.

The car was suddenly dead still—motionless—but the world outside was roaring by too fast to comprehend; in an attempt to keep up with the vanishing world, her mind was accelerating. For a moment she was lost in a blur of panic, but then—as though bursting through something thickly occluded and coming out the other side—she had plenty of time. Now it was the car that was moving, not the world, and she was controlling the car. It was something boys did—something she never would have chosen and never wanted to do again—but she *was* doing it. She felt saturated with her own competence. Now if only she weren't so scared, if only she had enough time to really think things through—

"Keep the speed up, keep the speed up, make up time, make up time. When I say brake, I mean *lock it*. Here she comes. Ready, ready—*brake!* Yeah, yeah, yeah." Again the Porsche was sliding sideways, but this time she knew what to do. Out of the corner of her eye, she saw him reaching, but she'd already turned the wheel before his hand got to it. "Kick her!" he yelled, but Gloria had already kicked the accelerator down. They shot around a curve, and the road was straight.

"Yow!" he howled. "To the floor, honey. *To the floor.* Yeah! All right! OK, ease her off. You got a mile or two, but ease her on down. Good girl. Yeah, that's it. See that little gas station up there? You pull her right in there, sweets."

The car was stopped. Something in the engine kept on ticking. Her legs were shaking. Sweat was pouring down her sides; she could smell the stink of herself. "Aw, shit, honey, you're all right," he said. "Damn good reflexes on you. The next time we go out, I'll show you how to use the gears. You got a lot more control if you're using the gears right, you with me?"

She turned and looked at him. She couldn't have said exactly how she knew it—his manner hadn't changed; his speech wasn't slurring—but she knew that he was quite drunk. He'd been a little bit drunk before, but now he was plastered drunk. He lit himself a cigarette. "You're a damn good kid, Gloria," he said, grinning. He took off his sunglasses and mopped his face with his handkerchief. He winked at her. "Kind of gets your heart going, don't it? Yeah, I take the ole silver bullet out and, you know—clear my mind."

He took another drink, and then he began to speak in a leisurely, conversational voice as though they had hours to talk about anything at all. "You know what? The war started, they took them college boys like your old man and they just cranked them through like cans of soup, come out the other end, put them in command of a ship, and they didn't know their ass from a teacup. But me, I weren't no ninety-day wonder. Eight years, count 'em, eight goddamn friggin' years in the merchant marines— You got to excuse my French, princess, because it's a subject I got strong feelings on. Yeah, I should of had my own command, and that's the sorry truth of it. But ole Billy Dougherty, he's never been to college, right? He's never even seen the inside of a high school. Might of had eight goddamn years in the friggin' merchant marines, but you know what you can get for that, don't you? That and a nickel gets you a cup of coffee— Oh, well, hell. It's just life, right?"

He looked at his watch. "Shit, I knew it. I was supposed to call my damn wife an hour ago. You just wait here a sec, sweetheart, and I'll be right back."

She watched him walk toward the little store. "Hi, Fido," he said to the mongrel dog lying by the door, and the dog thumped its tail on the ground. The store and gas station were perched on a ridge looking down over a valley. The day was still and hot, and the sky was a featureless stretch of blue with only some high, feathery cirrus clouds. She was still sweating. Her mouth was dry, and she would have loved a Coke, but she hadn't brought any money with her, and she didn't want him to buy her anything, not even something as trivial as a Coke.

Inside the store, Mr. Dougherty picked up the telephone. He turned directly toward her. He was looking at her through the store window. Her mind had been twisting and turning and doubling back, trying to articulate something that felt obscure and complex. Now, suddenly, she understood how simple it was: she was afraid of him.

"Call for you, Mister Cotter." Ted looked at his watch: twelve minutes after five. He walked back into the club house and grabbed up the phone. Of course it was Billy; who else would it be? "Jeez, skipper, I'm really sorry."

"Where the hell are you, Dougherty?"

"You know that little gas station on the top of the hill on the road out to Little Washington—?"

"What the hell you doing out there? We're supposed to be having a golf game."

"Now just give me a chance, skipper, OK? I know you're steamed, and believe me, I don't blame you. But— Well, shit, I can't even make up a good story. It's the same damn thing, skipper. Had a couple drinks and got to feeling like dog shit, and—well, you know, just had to take the old silver bullet out and clear my mind. It's the only thing that keeps me going some days, you know what I mean?"

"Billy, this is getting really boring."

"Shit, don't I just know it. You think you're bored, skipper, you ought to try walking in my shoes."

Ted was nowhere near as mad as he was about to pretend to be. He was annoyed, all right, but he was also relieved. A day without Billy Dougherty in it was better than a month in the country. "Listen to me, you sorry son-of-a-bitch. Don't you ever do this to me again."

"Aye, aye, sir."

"And if you don't straighten your ass out, one of these days you're going to be looking for another job. Do you read me?"

"Loud and clear, sir."

There, Ted thought, I've said it. Now he's got some warning.

Billy wasn't saying a word, and Ted was feeling guilty as all hell. "Come on, you old bastard, I know you've got it in you. Yeah, I know you do. Just lay off the sauce for a while, and if you need some help, go to AA. Yeah, I mean it. They've helped thousands of people. And get yourself a girl, for Christ's sake, and quit stewing over Dottie. Come on, you sorry son-of-a-bitch, I'm pulling for you."

Ted locked his clubs and golf shoes back in his locker and walked up to the swimming pool to find Gloria. As annoying as it was, he thought, everything had turned out for the best.

Laney had been furious. "Teddy, I don't believe it," she'd said. "The Connelys will be here at seven, and you're the one who asked me to invite them, and now you're going golfing!" It hadn't done any good to point out that he'd be back in plenty of time or that his presence wasn't exactly essential to the dinner preparations. "You and *your daughter*," she'd said. "Well, you make sure both of you get back up here. I need you."

There was no sign of Gloria, but Carl's daughter was sprawled in a lawn chair. She was impossible to miss—big, blowsy blonde in her bright magenta swimsuit—and, as Ted got closer, he saw that the fellow in tennis whites who was smoking his pipe and leaning over her was John Farrington's boy, that queer duck. Ted did not like either of them; John's boy should have been married years ago, and Carl's kid, like her mother, was dumb as six cows. Ted hated it when girls used cute, ridiculous names—Muffy or Fluffy or Flopsy or Popsy—and he could never bring himself to call her Binkie. "Hi, Mr. Cotter," she was chirping at him.

"Hi, Barbara," he said. "Where's Gloria?"

"I don't know," she answered immediately, "haven't seen her today." Then she looked up, looked right into his eyes, and he saw her face turn pink. "Oh. But maybe she was here a little bit ago. Yeah, I think I *did* see her. Didn't *you* see her, Jack?"

"Oh, yes," Jack said, "I'm sure I did."

Good try, Barbara, Ted thought, but just not quick enough, and he winked at her to let her knew she was fooling no one. "Well, if you do see her, send her home, OK?"

Barbara nodded and gave him a wide-eyed look. It was a look that probably hadn't changed since she'd been four. She was getting a little bit over-ripe, and somebody better marry her pretty damn soon—but John Farrington's boy wouldn't, not in a million years—and, married or not, she'd go on playing the little girl forever. If she weighed an ounce, she weighed a hundred and fifty pounds, and she still climbed onto Carl's lap; Ted had even heard her call him "daddykins." Good God, he thought, if Gloria ever tried that with me, I'd drown her in the pool. And Barbara had always been Gloria's very best friend in town. What on earth could she see in her?

But it wouldn't do him any good at all if Barbara knew he disliked her, so he had to say something, so he said, "When are your mom and dad getting back?"

"Oh, they're back already. Got in about an hour ago. They're simply exhausted. But they had a wonderful time."

Oh, I bet they did, he thought. He winked at her again and continued walking around the pool. No one had seen Gloria.

Just so that Laney—or Gloria herself—couldn't say he hadn't tried, Ted checked every square foot of the country club. If Gloria had been there, she certainly hadn't impressed herself upon anyone's memory, and if she was hiding out somewhere—however improbable that might be—the only place left was the golf course, but Gloria had never been known to golf, and he seriously doubted that she'd taken up the game that very afternoon. There was, of course, the woods by the golf course—that's where the kids went to pet—but Gloria, he thought, was well beyond that stunt. And then he finally figured it out: a boy with a car.

But what boy? Not Lee Hockner, that lame-brained idiot. And Ted did a quick mental run-through of the people he'd just seen, and, yep, Lee J. Hockner the whateverith he was (the third? the fourth?) was nowhere to be seen. So that's it, he thought. But then, just to be sure, he walked though the club again, and he found Lee Hockner shooting billiards in the game room. Thank God for small favors, he thought, but whoever she's with, she better get herself home on time or Laney will kill her. Damn, she's never lied to me before.

And then he had a thought so disturbing he had to take a moment to consider it. Gloria was a hell of a lot smarter than either of her brothers, and Ted even had to admit that Gloria was also a hell of lot smarter than either of her parents. So maybe it wasn't that Gloria had never lied. Maybe Gloria had just never been caught.

• • •

Gloria was bracing herself with both hands—one against the dashboard, the other clutching the seat. She was holding her entire body so rigidly that if she were to be thrown from the car—as was not entirely unlikely—she imagined she would shatter into a million pieces like one of her mother's antique vases. There was, she'd discovered, a limit on fear—or at least she'd reached one; she could no longer continue to make accurate assessments of the danger she was in, minute by minute, and she'd entered a state she'd labeled "numb terror." Mr. Dougherty had just sent the Porsche screaming sideways around another blind curve. If there'd been a car on the road, they'd be dead.

Now they were on a straightaway. He was accelerating. The needle on the dash had drifted up well above a hundred. "Stop it!" she yelled at him, and he didn't pay any more attention to her than he had the other times she'd yelled at him.

Back at the roadside store where he'd called his wife, Gloria had watched through the window as he'd slammed down the telephone. He'd come striding back to the car radiating an anger so intense it had seemed a physical emana-tion she could feel in her body like the vibration from an airplane taking off. She'd still been sitting behind the wheel. With a jerk of his head, he'd signaled for her to move. She'd climbed into the passenger's seat and watched him take the fifth out of the glove compartment, tilt it up, and drink. She'd seen frater-nity boys drink beer like that, but she'd never seen anyone drink whiskey like that: holding the bottle straight up and chugging. She'd watched his Adam's apple bob. "Mr. Dougherty, I've got to get *home*," she'd said.

"Jesus," he'd said, "that fucking bitch."

They were approaching another blind curve. She didn't dare close her eyes. If she were going to die, she wanted to see it coming. The road snaked sharply off to the right around a rock face. To the left was a drop-off. She couldn't see how steep it was or how far down it went. Mr. Dougherty wasn't braking soon enough. The tires howled hideously. Through the windshield, she saw the rock face whipping by, then the road behind her, then the drop-off, then the road in front of her. A pickup truck was coming down the road right at her. Then she saw the rock face again, and, with an enormous slam, they were stopped. The pickup truck's brakes were screaming. She heard a man yell, "You goddamn idiot!"

The pickup truck pulled around them and shot away. Mr. Dougherty stared at her bug-eyed. "Mary, mother of God," he said, "I nearly lost her there."

They had spun entirely around. The front tires were off the road in a ditch. She looked at her watch. He'd been driving away from Raysburg for nearly fif-teen minutes. "Mr. Dougherty," she said in what she hoped was a firm, calm voice, "I have to be home in half an hour."

He pounded a cigarette out of his pack and lit it. "Shit," he said, "shit, shit,

shit. You see what that goddamn woman does to me? She makes me so god-damn mad I can't see straight."

The engine had stalled. He started it again, backed slowly onto the road, and pulled out. Everything she saw had a pinched or squashed feeling to it, and she knew that her mind wasn't working right. "You're still going the wrong way," she said.

He drove slowly for another mile or two, then pulled off the road into a small, clear area on a hill overlooking a corn field. Roughly the shape of half an egg, the area wasn't big enough for a car to turn around in; it was more like a space set aside for an historical marker, but there was no historical marker, only a large, lone maple tree. It didn't make any sense, she thought, unless the space had been provided for the lone maple tree.

Mr. Dougherty picked up his fifth of whiskey and climbed out of the car with it. The wind had whipped his brilliantined hair into a greasy mess. He drank, then walked around the Porsche, inspecting it from every angle. He was stag-gering in a wide, splay-legged stance as though he were rolling a barrel between his thighs. "Wheww. Goddamn. Your uncle Billy sure had his guardian angel looking out for him today all right, all right."

He lurched over to the tree, leaned against it, and drank again. She didn't know what she was supposed to do, if anything, so, after a moment, she got out of the car and walked to the edge of the hill. Her arms and legs ached, and she was still shaking. "Mr. Dougherty—?"

"Shit, princess," he said without looking at her, "you don't know nothing. Not a goddamn thing. Just let me tell you something, OK? Not everybody grows up in a goddamn country club, you know what I mean? Good old yours truly sure as hell didn't grow up in no country club. Jesus, when I think about it, it's a goddamn bad joke. You with me, princess? Yeah, you betcha. Bunch of dumb micks living in a little rat-trap house at the height of the Depression. Shita-rooski. Yeah siree, shit on a shingle."

She'd come to rest several feet away from him. She had no idea what he was talking about. "Goddamn place should of been condemned," he said. "Back porch fell right off the son-of-a-bitch. My sister Marg on it, and she just went right on down with it, *kaboom*. God knows why she didn't break her goddamn neck. Think the landlord give a shit? There's another joke— They had, you know, a big box over at Saint Pat's where they'd leave canned goods for the poor people—and that was us, the poor people—and a million times I went sneaking in there, hoping nobody would see me, going through that box looking for my dinner. Yeah, 'the poor ye have always with you,' ain't that the way it goes? Yeah, you bet."

The words were clattering out of him quickly, with a hard, mechanical sound as though from a badly built machine. Gloria had no sense that he was talking *to her*, and she wondered if it mattered who she was—if he would have said the same thing to anybody at all. It was hard to think about it. It was hard to think about anything. Maybe she was in shock.

"And the old man— He was like that song, you ever heard it? 'Clancy lowered the boom.' Well, shit, when old man Dougherty lowered the boom, it weren't no joke, believe you me. Five of us kids. He didn't give a shit, he'd slap the girls around same as the boys. But he wasn't a bad sort when he was sober. And the old lady— I don't know, there was something wrong with her. Never drank. Not a drop in her life. Just, you know, not right in the head."

"Mr. Dougherty? I have to go home."

"Sure you do, princess. Yeah, you bet you gotta go home. But not just yet— So anyhow, soon as I could, I got the hell out. Lied about my age. Got on at the shipyards. Michael went into the priesthood, the sorry son-of-a-bitch. Joined that order where you sleep in your coffin and you don't talk. Writes to me. Probably should write back, but you know. Always says he's praying for me. Well, shit, I'm glad *somebody's* praying for me. And my sisters— Well, Marg's big as a house, real Barnum and Bailey stuff, three hundred pounds if she's an ounce. Never married. The other two married. I don't know. Hell, I don't keep in touch. It's just one thing after another."

"Mr. Dougherty, please."

"Just shut the fuck up, OK? Aw, shit, sorry about my French, princess, but just bear with me a little bit longer, OK? So anyhow, my crazy mother, you know, she'd take it into her head to go somewhere and— Like one time right in the middle of making lunch, can of soup on the stove, and she just puts the spoon down, walks out, and it takes my old man a week to find her. Can you beat that? Five kids. Michael still in diapers. And she just puts the spoon down and walks out the door. 'Your mother's gone wandering again,' that's what the old man said. Shit, he used to lock her in the bedroom, but she'd climb out the window. And the funny thing was, she was always happy as a lark. Always singing, always smiling, just—one time—shit, I'll never forget it. One time I come home from school, and there she is, stretched out on the front lawn, and she's got her purse under her head, and her feet crossed at the ankles, and her hands folded, and she's just laying there like she was in bed. 'Mom,' I said, 'what are you doing?' And you never in your life seen anybody as happy as she looked right then. Peaceful. I was just a little kid, and I remember I thought she looked just like the Blessed Virgin, and she says— the sweetest, happiest voice you ever heard—she says, 'Oh, Billy, I'm just looking at the clouds.' Can you beat that?"

"That's an amazing story, Mr. Dougherty, but I have to go home."

"When the old man died, Michael put her in an institution—some Catholic institution, you know what I mean? I didn't think that was right, but what the hell do I know? He's the priest, not me. 'She's a danger to herself,' he says. Yeah? Well, maybe she was. 'Oh, Billy, I'm just looking at the clouds.' Jesus."

He hung his head and began to weep loudly. He jerked his sunglasses off and threw them down. He drew his handkerchief out of his pocket and mopped his face with it. "All the times she went wandering, nothing ever happened to her. It was different back then. If somebody was crazy, people knew it and kind of looked out for them, you know? Ah, well, shit, life's funny— Wouldn't you say that, princess? Life's pretty funny?"

He turned and stared directly at her. His small eyes were red, wet, and blazing with anger. "Hey, wouldn't you say that, princess? Life's funny? Wouldn't you say that?"

He took a step toward her, and she backed up. For a moment she'd been sure he was going to hit her. "So what *would* you say, huh? Anything? You got any opinion at all? Jesus fucking Christ on a crutch, you goddamn dumb little girl."

"Mr. Dougherty—?"

He sprang at her, and she leapt back. He staggered, fell to one knee. "Hey!" he screamed at her, "who let you out of your playpen? Huh?"

He straightened up, lurched back to the tree, steadied himself against it, and stared out over the corn field. She could hear him muttering, but she couldn't hear what he was saying. "You can kiss my fucking hairy ass!" he yelled. He raised the whiskey bottle in a toast to the sky. "Yeah, up yours." He tilted his head back, took a deep breath, and yelled: "Kiss my fuckin' ass!" He drank.

He turned and glared at her again. "My wife—my goddamn friggin' wife— my goddamn friggin' *ex*-wife—you know what the fuck she does? She stands up there in court and she lies. She gets all dressed up in her little friggin' blue suit and she lies. And she lies and she lies and she lies. 'Your Honor, he beat me up.' Yeah, that's what she said, the fucking bitch. 'He beat me up on a regular basis.' How you like them little green apples? *On a regular basis.* Shit. You think I'd raise my hand to a woman? Jesus, I never even raised *my voice* to that woman, and that's God's own truth. Rugs don't lie any flatter than that bitch. Jesus, I could of told a story or two of my own, you know what I mean? The number of guys that was dickin' her—"

He stopped abruptly, bent forward, hugging himself. He was weeping in great, wracking spasms. "Oh, Jesus, Jesus! My little boys. My *sons.* How the fuck could she do that to me? I did the best I could, I swear to God. That goddamn, rotten, fucking cunt!"

He turned and smashed his fist into the tree—once, twice, three times. He stepped back with an astonished look on his face. He sucked his bloody knuckles. "Jesus," he said in a stupid, slurring voice, "I'm drunk as a skunk."

In some mysterious way she couldn't begin to analyze, his admission of being drunk allowed her to get angry— Well, that wasn't right; it was more like a line

in a play that allowed—or even predicted—a certain response in another character, so now she could pretend to be angry rather than what she was: numb and
terrified. She knew that being numb and terrified would get her nowhere. She
would, therefore, treat him exactly like a drunken fraternity boy.

"You've had enough," she said firmly. "Give me that." She reached for the
whiskey bottle, and, with a sly, guilty smirk, he jerked it away from her. He was
falling over. He grabbed the tree with his free hand; she stepped up to him and
caught the neck of the bottle. He wouldn't let go, and, for a moment, they
were playing tug-of-war with the damned thing. Then he released it, and it
shot back against her chest, spraying her with whiskey.

The shock of it was like being slapped. She recoiled, wailed: "No!" She had
whiskey up her nose, even in her eyes. It burned. And her bra was soaked with
whiskey. She couldn't believe it. *Her bra!* It wasn't something she could very
well take off.

Mr. Dougherty suddenly snatched at the bottle, and she let go; it sprang from
her hands, hit the ground, and began rolling toward the edge of the hill. He
lurched after it, stumbled and fell. He pursued the bottle on his hands and knees.
It rolled over the edge. On all fours like some big, stupid animal—his backside
stuck up in the air—he sent her a betrayed, accusatory look over his shoulder.

Later, when she would be able to think again, she would ask herself why, after
everything he'd done, had that absurd, little farce been the last straw? She didn't
plan to do it, and, if she had planned it, she certainly couldn't have done it,
but she heard herself shrieking at him in a high-pitched, hysterical, harridan's
voice: "Damn you, damn you, damn you, damn you! Take me home, you idiot.
Take me home *right now!*"

She never would have guessed that something as crudely melodramatic as
that would work, but it seemed to be working. He pushed himself up onto his
haunches and said like a shamed little boy: "Aw, hell. Hey. I'm really sorry, OK?"
He stared at her with his mouth hanging slackly open. "Aw, good Christ, I've
had too much to drink."

He crawled over to the tree and used it to claw his way back onto his feet.
"I'm sorry, OK?" He offered her his hand as though he'd just met her; when
she didn't take it, he made a hapless, shrugging gesture. "God*damn*, am I ever
drunk! Yeah, I'll get ya home. Just wait. Just give me a minute, OK? I gotta—"

He managed to extract a cigarette, press it between his lips, and light it. She
was nowhere near him, but he pushed at her just as though she were. "Just
wait. Just wait a minute. Just wait a fucking minute. Yeah, you just wait one
fucking little minute."

He began slowly to slide down the tree. He slid all the way to the ground,
his legs splaying out. His head hit the dirt. The lit cigarette jumped out of his
hand. Oh, just great, she thought.

She knelt over him and did what she'd seen done in the movies: slapped his face. Absolutely nothing happened. She slapped him again, so hard his head rolled. His eyelids fluttered partially open, but all she could see were the whites. A thin line of drool dribbled out of the corner of his mouth. He began to snore. "Damn you," she said.

She stood up. What do I do now? she thought, and the secret watcher said, "You get in his car and you drive home in it."

Gloria had been born with no sense of direction whatsoever, and she'd often thought that a low-grade moron could find his way around better than she could, and all she knew about their current location was that it was somewhere in Pennsylvania. Don't panic, she told herself; just stop and think about it. OK, they had to be east and slightly north of Raysburg. The sun told her where west was—directly over the corn field—and, therefore, neither of the ways the road ran was the right one, although, if she had to choose, northwest was probably better than southeast—or was it? Well, at least northwest would take her to the Ohio River, or, if she ended up north of Pittsburgh, to *some* river—but it was ridiculous thinking about it anyway, because, no matter how mad she was at Mr. Dougherty, she could not simply drive away and leave him there.

A narrow dirt road ran west through the corn field, and there was a farmhouse near the end of it, and a farmhouse would surely have a telephone, and she was certainly mad enough at Mr. Dougherty to call her father and tell him exactly what had happened. So how far away was the farmhouse? She was terrible at estimating distances, but she could *see it*, couldn't she? So it couldn't be more than a mile or two.

She scrambled down the embankment, walked around the edge of the corn field to the dirt road, and began walking toward the farmhouse. The dust from the road was making her itchy, and the low sun was hitting her full in the face, and she was sweating in torrents, and now that she was down at the same level with it, the farmhouse looked a million miles away. Oh, God, she thought, I'm such an idiot! Why didn't I take the car? She looked at her watch, and it was two minutes after seven. If the Connelys were on time, they'd already arrived. Her mother was complimenting the wife on whatever she was wearing, and her father was asking them what they were drinking, but Gloria was not there to serve the drinks.

Why is this happening to me? she thought. What have I done to deserve this? She burst into tears and sank to her knees in the middle of the road. She heard herself wailing. Her pretty white tennis shoes were filthy; even her socks were filthy, and how could she possibly care about anything as trivial as that?—but she did care, and she was going to be good and late, and her dad was going to kill her, and she didn't know how she was going to get home anyway, oh, God! And she hadn't brought anything with her—no purse, no money, no hankie, not even a tube of lipstick—and how could she possibly be thinking about lipstick at a time like this? She stank of sweat and whiskey; she didn't have the remotest idea where she was. You little jerk, she thought, how did you get into this awful mess? Outside of a sorority house or a country club or a library, you're totally helpless. You pathetic moron—

"Stop that," the secret watcher said. "That's not going to do you any good. Stand up and breathe. Then keep walking. You're going to call your father, and he's going to come and get you. Now stop crying and stand up."

She wiped her face with her hands and wiped her hands on her shorts. She would have killed for a Coke. She started walking again, and she was nearly at the farmhouse when she heard the quiet, throaty rumble of the Porsche behind her. Then the ugly silver snout drifted up next to her. She was so angry she didn't even look over at it.

"Get in the car, honey, OK?"

"You shouldn't be driving, Mr. Dougherty."

"Honey, I can drive. Look, I'm sorry. I'm real sorry. I can't tell you how goddamn sorry I am. Hey, princess, will you please just get in the goddamn car?"

She got into the car. He must have left his sunglasses back under the tree; he was squinting against the sun. He looked like hell, but then she must have looked just as bad. He drove to the end of the dirt road and turned left. "Mr. Dougherty? I want to stop somewhere and call my dad, OK?"

"Please don't do that, honey."

"He's going to be really worried about me."

"Don't worry. Have you home in no time."

He was driving slowly, and that was just fine with her. She couldn't remember ever having been so exhausted. She lay back in the seat and closed her eyes. She felt numb again—numb and stupid—and there was nothing she could do that would get her home any faster, and so there was nothing left for her to do but give up.

"Jesus, princess," she heard him saying, "I'm just so goddamn sorry, you know. I gotta do something. But what? Can you tell me that? Shit, maybe AA. Went to a couple meetings, you know, but—just, you know, too much dumbass diddly-shit. *Hi, I'm Billy, and I'm an alcoholic.* Yeah, sure, right. But honey, I really am sorry."

"OK," she said, and that was the best she could do.

After a few minutes, she heard him asking her, "Are we in Pennsylvania or West Virginia?"

She opened her eyes and looked. The road they were on looked like every other road they'd been on. "I don't know."

"Gloria, honey, I'm so goddamn sorry, I can't tell you."

They were passing a gas station. "Hey, can I stop there and call my dad?"

"Come on, kid, you're almost home."

To hell with it, she thought. I'll get home when I get home. She closed her eyes again, and Mr. Dougherty was saying something. Did she have to pay attention to it?

"Tried to do it cold turkey," he was saying. "Jesus, I got the shakes like, and—and *I had to go to work*. Hold down a job, you know what I mean? Gotta pay that bitch her fucking— There goes the French again, sorry, honey. But I swear to God, I can't see any way out. Pink elephants, Jesus, that's a joke. I would of been glad for a pink elephant or two. A hundred and fifty million bugs crawling all over you, that's more like it. Anyhow, princess, I'm just as sorry as I can be. Damn my soul, I didn't want none of this to happen. Just thought we'd have us a good time. Gloria? Will you accept my apologies?"

Oh, he was so pathetic. Why wouldn't he just let her alone? "Yes, yes, yes," she said. "I accept your apologies. Please stop telling me how sorry you are and just get me home."

She tried to drift off into her own thoughts, but she couldn't get beyond an utter conviction that everything was hopelessly wrong and could never be made right again. Even doing nothing at all—merely lying there in the seat, feeling the movement of the car under her, listening to the sound of the tires on the road—was exhausting; she opened her eyes and pushed herself up. She knew where they were now. They were on the road winding down toward the country club and her house. She wanted to know the worst, so she looked at her watch. It was twenty minutes of nine.

He didn't turn into her driveway, and she didn't want him to. When people brought you home, you were supposed to say, "thanks," but it was impossible to say that, so she simply opened the door and started to get out. He reached over and caught her wrist. She tried to pull away. It was amazing how strong he was. He wasn't even holding her very tightly, but she couldn't even begin to free her hand. "Gloria, honey— Please, please, please don't say anything to your old man, OK? I could lose my job over this."

Until that moment, it had never occurred to her that she would tell her father anything but the truth. Oh, but she was so tired. "OK," she said.

"Promise?"

"OK. I promise."

The Connelys were still there; Gloria had seen their car parked in the driveway. They were probably down by the pool having dessert. She'd crept into the house as quietly as she could, but it hadn't been quietly enough. She was halfway up the stairs when she heard her father's voice behind her: "Gloria!"

She turned and looked down at him. "Oh, Dad, I'm so sorry."

She saw the color drain out of his face. "Where the hell have you been?"

Where the hell *had* she been? "I met Binkie at the club, and we went back to her place, and— Oh, it's all really silly."

He climbed the stairs and stopped one step below her. Their eyes were level. "Have you been drinking?"

"No."

He'd just put on his Lieutenant Commander's face that betrayed no emotion whatsoever. "Go to your room," he said. He turned, descended the stairs, and walked away. She tried to remember the last time she'd been sent to her room. She was pretty sure it had been during her sophomore year in high school.

She studied herself in her full-length mirror to see what her father had been seeing: her shoes and socks were covered with red-brown dirt; she had dirt on her knees and her shorts and even on her face; there was a huge, blotchy whiskey stain on her halter top; her ponytail had come down, and her hair was a wind-whipped tangle. Oh, just great, she thought. What could I have possibly been doing with Binkie to come home like this?

She took a long shower and changed into a crisp, white blouse and Bermuda shorts. She was so exhausted—so thoroughly drained of emotion, of energy, of thought, of *everything*—that all she wanted to do was sleep. She stretched out on her bed, but whenever she'd start to drift off, she'd see the road whipping by through the windshield of the Porsche. Then, even though it was a hot night, she began to feel chilled. Her teeth were actually chattering. She got a blanket out of the closet, and that seemed to help, but after a few minutes she was too hot again. The back of her neck felt as though it were in a vise. I drove a sports car at over a hundred miles an hour, she thought, and I kept it on the road. How utterly bizarre.

It was nearly eleven by the time the Connelys had left and her father knocked on her door. She forced herself to her feet and let him in. He'd brought an ashtray with him. She sat at her desk; he sat on the French wingback and lit a cigarette. "OK, honey, where were you?"

She'd gone over it and over it in her mind, so she knew what to say, but actually saying it took monstrous effort. "I told you, Dad. I was with Binkie. She wanted to go back to her place because her parents weren't home, and— I didn't do anything. Really, I didn't. *I* wasn't the one who was drinking. It was just—just a big, silly mix-up. Binkie kept saying she'd bring me back any minute, but—you know."

Oh, I hate this, she thought. This is truly horrible. And if I'm not careful, I'm going to get Binkie in trouble. "I'm sorry. I'm really *really* sorry. Please don't say anything to Binkie's dad, OK? She wasn't drinking either."

"All right," he said evenly, "so who were the boys?"

"Lee Hockner and Mike Clark," she said automatically. Oh, help, she thought, I've got to stop. I'm going to get everybody in trouble.

He didn't say anything. He finished his cigarette.

"OK, Gloria," he began in a quiet, deliberate voice, "I was down at the club, and I saw Barbara Eberhardt there, so you were not with her. You were not at the club. No one saw you at the club. Carl and Patsy got back sometime in the afternoon, so even if you met Barbara later, you were not raising hell over at *her* house. Lee Hockner and Mike Clark were both at the club when I was there, and I didn't leave till damn near six. So you want to try the truth this time?"

Gloria felt as though she'd been thrown into a deep pool of ice water. For a moment her mind had nothing in it whatsoever; then she thought, well, that's it, the game's over. She'd been caught, but good, and it was almost a relief. She hated lying to her father, and now that he'd caught her, she wasn't responsible any more, and, yes, that really was a relief. Now she could tell him the truth and let *him* worry about everything—

She'd thought he'd wait as long as necessary until she answered him, but he must have been reading her silence as a refusal to speak. "Listen, Gloria," he said, "you know that old saying, he who pays the piper—? Well, so long as I'm paying the bills around here, I'm calling the tune. You got that? And if you want to miss dinner when we're having guests—and not even make a phone call to tell us where you are—and if you want to come home hours late smelling like a distillery and looking like a—looking like you've been rolling around in a barn—and if you want to lie to us about where you've been—well, then you can damn well move out of this house and rent your own damn place. You got that? And you can buy your own damn clothes, and pay for your own damn education. You got that? OK, *now you tell me where the hell you were.*"

Gloria was furious. How dare he say that to her? She'd been ready to tell him the truth, and if he hadn't said that, she would have told him, and she'd done absolutely nothing to be ashamed of. To hell with him. If he put her on the rack, she wouldn't tell him—and she was just on the point of saying, "No, I won't tell you," when the secret watcher said, "Hey, hold on. Think about it."

To think about it, Gloria needed time. Her father always thought things over before he said anything, so he should understand it if she did the same thing, but he'd misinterpreted her silence before. "I *am* going to say something, Dad, " she told him. "Just give me a minute, OK?"

She stood up and walked to the window. It was the first time she could remember—yes, probably the first time in her life—when her father had not trusted her, and she was so hurt and angry she felt like screaming. "That's all well and good, Gloria," the secret watcher told her, "but you just lied to him. What did you expect?"

"I'm sorry I lied to you, Dad," she said without looking at him. "I just hated it. If I could have figured out any way not to do it, I wouldn't have done it."

He didn't say anything. She heard him light another cigarette. And she was caught in a genuine ethical dilemma just like the ones they'd studied in Philosophy 100, but the things they'd talked about in Philosophy 100 didn't seem to be much help: she'd just discovered that she didn't give a damn about the greater good. Maybe she could tell the story in a way that wouldn't make Mr. Dougherty look quite as bad as— But no, even if she left out most of the details, Mr. Dougherty was going to look pretty darned bad, and her father would fire him; she had no doubt about that.

OK, so Mr. Dougherty was a stupid, crazy, foul-mouthed drunk who'd scared the living daylights out of her. He was also utterly pathetic. She couldn't even begin to imagine what it must be like to come from a background like his, so who was *she* to get him fired?—especially when the reason she'd been out riding around with him in the first place was because of her own unparalleled stupidity. And he'd said he was sorry, and he'd begged her not to tell, and she'd promised not to tell. She'd certainly done lots of things in her life to be ashamed of, but she'd never broken a promise—at least never a big, important one.

Then, finally, she arrived at the crux of the matter. As much of a relief as it would be to turn her ethical dilemma over to her father, that would be chickening out—because it was *her* ethical dilemma. Mr. Dougherty might be a creep, but he was also a fellow human being, and if she didn't accept her own responsibility for what had happened, she really would be exactly what he thought she was: a *princess*—a pampered, naive little rich girl. Well, OK then, no matter how hard it was, she was going to have to keep her promise. Her father was going to have to trust her, and that was all there was to it.

She turned around to look at him and said in her most conciliatory voice, "I'm sorry, Dad, but I just can't tell you."

She saw the color drain out of his face; he was expressionless, but Gloria knew that she'd never seen him that angry.

"Daddy," she said, "now it's my turn. Now you have to listen to *me*, OK? I didn't do anything you'd be the least bit ashamed of. I swear to you that's the truth. And you've always trusted me before, so you've just got to trust me now. What happened isn't a big deal, really it isn't, and I'd tell you if I could, and— Believe me, I'd love to be able to tell you. But I just can't. There are other people involved, and I made a promise. I gave my word. It's just, you know—personal."

She could see that he wasn't buying a word of it. Help! she thought, I've been a good girl, really I have. "I'm *twenty-one!*" she said and was ashamed to hear the tears in her voice. "Shouldn't I be allowed to have things in my life that are personal?"

He didn't answer.

"I guess not," she said. "I'm sorry."

"I'm sorry too, princess."

It was incredible. He still expected her to tell him. He was sitting there waiting for her to tell him. She walked past him into her bathroom, shut the door and locked it. She pressed a wash cloth into her face so he wouldn't hear her crying.

His knuckles rapped sharply on the door. "Gloria. Clean up the kitchen."

10

Ted Cotter was a man of routine; he was fully aware of this trait in himself and heartily approved of it. There was, he would have said, no better way to waste time than to do things differently from the way you usually did them, and he never thought of himself as habitual, but rather as efficient. Every night in the summer, no matter how late it was when he got home, he had himself a nice, refreshing swim. Then his wife brought him a Scotch, and the two of them sat by the pool while he smoked exactly one cigarette; the last of the Scotch was always downed precisely with the last puff of the cigarette, and then, by God, it was dinner time. "You don't have to wait dinner for me," he liked to say. He didn't mean it. He expected that the boys, when they were at home, would have been fed and got out of the way, but he wanted his girls to wait for him, so dinner, whether it was at home or at the club, was always late.

Since Sunday, however, Ted—to the consternation of both his wife and daughter—had changed his routine. On Monday, he'd called Laney from work (he never called her from work) and told her to meet him at the club; he hadn't mentioned Gloria, but Laney had known, nonetheless, that their daughter was not to be included. Now, on Tuesday, he'd done the same thing again, and Gloria would have been a dull girl indeed not to get the point: she'd been banished. And it was even worse than that. For the two or three minutes when she'd seen him on Monday night, he'd looked right through her. Her mother had certainly given her the silent treatment before, but her father never; she'd always thought him incapable of such a nasty, petty, *feminine* tactic—and, as she was sure she was meant to be, Gloria was filled with dread. "I'm in disgrace with fortune and men's eyes," she wrote in her diary.

Swimming had been her salvation during her Britomart summer, so she had, both yesterday and this afternoon, swum forty laps; then, tonight, when it had become apparent that she was being excluded from dinner yet again, she'd been so angry she'd swum twenty more. She was sitting now drying off in a lawn chair, watching the hard-edged shadows of evening creeping across the lawn toward her. What if her father had meant what he'd said? What if he wasn't going to pay for her to go to Columbia? She'd won a scholarship, but that surely wouldn't pay for everything. She wished she understood money better than she did; she didn't even know what a year at Columbia cost, and even if she did know, there was nothing she could do about it. "He who pays the piper—" her father had said. Right. But he was only bluffing, wasn't he? He'd never in a million years *not* send her to Columbia, would he?

She thought sometimes that she lived her entire life to please other people, and Columbia hadn't been her idea; it had been Professor Bolton's idea—like advanced Latin and Old English, both of which she'd suffered through for his sake—and she asked herself again, did she *really* want to go to Columbia? Even though all she could remember of New York was their dear, little apartment before the war, she'd always thought of New York as her real home—her authentic home, her spiritual home—so why was she so scared? She knew the answer to that one too (she wasn't thinking anything new; she was merely going around in circles): she was afraid that once she got to Columbia, she'd be revealed, not as a genuine scholar, but as an imposter, a society girl dabbling in scholarship. Her stupid cousins actually were in New York society—not at a very high level but high enough to get their picture in *Vogue*—and she liked and even admired her stupid cousins in the circumscribed way one might like and admire a pair of marmosets for being particularly splendid examples of their species, and she really should stop thinking of Binkie as shallow, because, compared to Sandra and Elizabeth Merriman, Binkie Eberhardt was so deep as to be positively *abysmal*, and the horrible thing was that Gloria fit right in with Sandy and Lizzy; whatever they were wearing, she wore the same thing, and, after only a few days with them, she began to talk like them in a breathy, teensy-weensy debutante voice—oh, she really *was* as adaptable as a chameleon!—and she genuinely liked all the things they liked: *of course* she would love to go to balls on Long Island and dance with all the nice boys from Ivy League schools who trailed around after Sandy and Lizzy, and there wasn't anything stopping her from doing that, even though, of course, she wasn't a debutante because she'd never come out, and so she'd never really be in with their crowd, would always be a second-class citizen. And it was ridiculous to be thinking about the fall when what she should be thinking about was the mess she was in with her father and how to get out of it, but she'd already thought about that plenty, and she still hadn't found anything remotely close to a solution. She really should, however, go inside and make herself a sandwich, but she couldn't force herself to get out of the lawn chair.

At the same moment, Ted, like his daughter, was facing the setting sun and brooding. Laney, hoping that he would finally talk about what was so obviously on his mind—he usually did if she had the patience to wait long enough and not push him—had reserved the small table at the end of the terrace overlooking the pool; it was most definitely a dinner-for-two table, and she was counting on their friends to take the hint and let them alone. Ted was drinking a *second* Scotch before dinner, and Laney was fairly certain that he was right on the edge of opening up. Modulating her voice carefully so that what she was saying would sound like gentle encouragement and not a push, she said, "Oh, Teddy, I'm sure everything will sort itself out."

Without looking at her, he said, "Oh, hell. She's never lied to me before."

The last thing in the world Laney felt like doing was defending her pampered, spoiled rotten daughter, but she knew that if she played devil's advocate, she stood a good chance of getting Ted to open up, so she said, "You know, honey, I'll bet there's a perfectly good explanation. There has to be."

Grimacing, Ted turned to look at her. At first she thought she'd said the wrong thing, but then, following the direction of his exasperated gaze, she saw that Billy Dougherty was walking toward their table. She'd never seen Billy wearing a more miserable, hang-dog expression, and her heart sank. "Oh, no," she said under her breath.

"Lane," Billy said, "skipper." He stared first at Ted, then at Laney—quick, sharp, interrogative glances—and immediately away, off into the far distance of the sky as though he'd just discovered a flying saucer there. He squeezed the back of his neck with his right hand. She could see that there was something wrong with him, and her first thought was that maybe—God help the poor slob—he'd stopped drinking and was suffering from a bad case of the jimjams. The skin on his face was stretched and gleaming: he was sweating buckets. "Excuse me, skipper," he said, "can I have a word with you?"

"Not tonight, Billy. I'm out on a date with my wife."

Billy stepped closer, and Laney could smell him: no, he obviously was *not* sobering up. "Skipper," he said, "I can see you don't want to be disturbed, believe me. But look. If it wasn't real important, I wouldn't, ah— Look, it's real important."

"Oh, I'll bet it can wait till tomorrow," Ted said with a murderous smile.

"Well, to tell you the truth, Ted—no, it can't."

"Oh, for Christ's sake, *what?*"

"Look, skipper, this'll only take a minute or two, swear to God. And we don't want to, ah—bore Laney with it. It's about, you know, cross-haul."

"Cross-haul," Ted said evenly. He stood up, gave Laney a dark look that said: I'm going to kill the son-of-a-bitch. She watched as they walked down the steps toward the pool. Cross-haul, she thought, my ass.

"This better be good," Ted said.

"Uh, skipper—Sunday, you know?"

"Oh, for Christ's sake, you already apologized for that. I've forgot all about it."

"No, it's not that."

"OK, what is it?"

"Aw, Jesus, I feel like shit about this." Billy stopped, turned back and looked up at the terrace as though to assure himself that Laney really was well out of earshot.

Ted was getting madder by the second. "You feel like shit about *what?*"

Billy was taking so long to answer that Ted felt like kicking him.

"Skipper? Anything, ah—well, you know, kind of funny—happen on Sunday night?"

Ted froze. Then he took a deep breath. Stay calm, he told himself. "Dougherty, if you've got anything to say to me, you say it, OK?"

Billy sighed windily. "Well, it's none of my damn business, but ah—where was your little Gloria on Sunday night?"

When Ted finally spoke, it was in a calm, flat, noncommittal voice: "She said she was with Carl's daughter."

"Oh, yeah? Well, there you go. I must of seen somebody else, looked a lot like her, you know? But if she was with Carl's daughter, then everything's OK. I just seen—must of been some other girl. Sorry to bother you, skipper."

Ted took out his pack of smokes, offered one to Billy. He lit Billy's cigarette first. "All right," he said, "let's hear it."

"There's nothing to hear, skipper, really— And anyhow, the girl I seen had a ponytail."

For the first time since they'd been talking, Billy met his eyes—gave him a miserable, complicated, supplicating look—and Ted knew that if he wanted to hear any more of it, he was going to have to meet the son-of-a-bitch part way. "This girl you saw," he said, "what'd she have on?"

"I didn't get that good a look at her, you know, because it was kind of—a blouse I guess you'd call it. Except real short. No sleeves."

"You mean a halter top?"

"Yeah, that's it. Yeah, that's what they call them damn things. Yeah. It was pink."

"OK, Billy, maybe you did see Gloria. So where was she?"

"I thought you said she was somewhere with Carl's daughter."

"I didn't say that. *She* said it."

"Oh. Right. Jeez. You know, I feel like shit about this, skipper. You know. Really like shit."

"Come on, Billy, spit it out."

"Well, I was out—I don't know where exactly. It was after I called you. Some-where out around Little Washington, but I was just driving, you know, trying to clear my head. And nobody much on the road, so I was booting her along pretty good, and I hear—well, shit, tires screaming to beat hell, so I slowed her right down, and a—well, there's a long, straight stretch, and I seen this car come barrel-assing right at me, all over the road. An old Chevy convertible, 'forty-eight or 'forty-nine, something like that. You know how them cars looked, with the big—"

"Come on, Billy."

"So anyhow, here comes this old blue Chevy junker, top down, big guy driving it. No shirt on. Looked like a big, dumb Polack, you know what I mean? And he's got one hand on the wheel and the other wrapped around this girl, and she's cuddled into him, and Jesus, he must be doing a hundred. So I pull right over, you know, to give the son-of-a-bitch lots of room, and I think, hey, if I didn't know better, I'd think that was the skipper's girl. Big brown eyes and dark complected like your girl, skipper, and a young, sweet face. A lot like Gloria. And they go burning right on by me, and they're laughing and yelling, and damn if they ain't passing back and forth what looks like a fifth of whiskey, so I think, shit, that can't be little Gloria. Not in a million years.

"And as soon as they're by me, I check my rearview, so I seen them coming and I seen them going, and I thought, goddamn my soul, if that wasn't Gloria Cotter, it was her twin sister. And I worried about it all the way back in town. Should I say something or not? What if it wasn't Gloria? Wouldn't that be the shits, if I went and told the skipper about it, and it wasn't Gloria. I mean— You know, skipper, I still can't make up my mind if it was her or not. I mean, I couldn't swear to it."

Ted felt like a mule had kicked him in the stomach, but he forced himself to say in the same flat voice he'd been using: "What time was that?"

"Oh, hell, I don't know. It was a while after I called you. Maybe an hour after that."

"And it was out in Pennsylvania somewhere?"

"Yeah. But I couldn't tell you where exactly. Funny thing is, skipper, I keep thinking I know the guy. He looked a lot like a guy used to work for us, you know, at Old Reliable. Not steady. Day labor. Polack. Real nice guy though. Guy in his thirties—name of Malkovitch or Malovitch or some damn thing. I don't know if it's the same guy, but damn if he didn't look familiar. Must be over six feet, muscles on him like an ape, got them little beady Polack eyes, you know what I mean? Kind of slanty— Aw, shit, it's probably not the same guy."

Ted's mind was racing, but it wasn't arriving at any conclusions. "Dougherty? If this is one of your little jokes, you're going to be sorry you were ever born."

"Come on, Ted. You know me. You think I'd joke about something like this?" He was giving Ted a tragic look of man-to-man sympathy.

"Let me alone, Dougherty. Give me a chance to think."

Billy hesitated a moment, his mouth hanging open. Then, shrugging, he said, "Yeah, sure. But it's— You know—" He turned and walked back up the hill.

Ted knew that Laney could see him and must be wondering what in hell was going on, but, doing his best to look like a man with nothing more on his mind than some dumb, minor problem at work, he continued to stroll on down to the golf course. He hadn't cried since the war, but he was afraid he was going to cry now, and if he did, he sure as hell didn't want anybody to see him. He couldn't even think straight—couldn't have been any more upset if he'd just been told that Laney had been unfaithful to him. But, at the same time, he was mad enough to break bones, and he knew exactly whose bones he wanted to break, and he had half a mind to go straight home—dinner be damned—and have it out with her.

He lit another cigarette. He knew that the last thing he needed was to go off half cocked. And then, as suddenly as if someone had flipped over a page in his mind so he could see an entirely different story, he just didn't believe it. Billy must have seen Gloria *somewhere*, doing *something*—that much was obvious— but not riding in an old junk Chevy with some dumb jerk drinking whiskey straight from the bottle. Gloria had always been an overly impressionable kid— he knew that—and her sympathies always went out to the underdog; give her a whole sorority full of nice, ordinary girls to choose from, and who does she pick for a best friend but that tough little baton-twirler with a grease monkey for an old man—typical—and a girl like Gloria, no matter how smart she is, most of what she thinks she knows about life comes straight from a book. So Ted could imagine Gloria meeting some working stiff somewhere (although God knows where she could have met him) and being intrigued by him and telling herself a whole romantic story about him, and Ted could imagine that she might go out with a guy like that and not want her parents to know about it—Laney would drop dead!—and he could even imagine that Gloria might take a drink of hard liquor, but he couldn't imagine her drinking whiskey straight from the bottle—no, not the girl who always kept an extra pair of stockings in her purse in case she got a run. And Gloria drove a car the way she swam, the way she did everything—he wished he had a nickel for every time he'd heard, "Daddy, would you please slow down!"—so he couldn't imagine her riding in a car at any speed much over forty miles an hour and laughing about it. And he couldn't imagine that his Phi Beta Kappa daughter could ever have been so lamebrained as to get caught as easily as he'd caught her. No, she never would have planned a rendezvous with some guy on a night when they were having people in to dinner.

But then the page flipped over again, and he thought: wait a minute, don't be too sure. Don't lots of men have blind spots about their daughters? Sure they do; he'd met plenty of them—the poor dumb clucks. And hadn't she smelled like a whole goddamn distillery? Yeah, she'd positively reeked with it. And why would Billy make it up? That's right, why would Billy take a risk like that? It didn't make any sense. But none of it made any sense, on either side of the page. So she'd smelled like whiskey? He still could have sworn that she hadn't been the least bit drunk.

He smoked another cigarette and thought about it, but it didn't feel like a problem he was going to solve very quickly. So what would you do, he asked himself, if it wasn't a personal problem but a management problem? And he had no trouble at all answering that one: he wouldn't make a move until he knew the facts. Yep, that was right, and the funny thing was that usually, if you kept your mouth shut and your eyes open, the facts had a habit of falling right into your lap. And when he did have the facts, well, then somebody was going to pay. And that, he suspected, was as far as he was going to get with it tonight; if it didn't make him exactly happy, it did make him feel somewhat better — almost good enough, with another Scotch under his belt, to make it through dinner.

He turned and walked quickly back up to the terrace. As he approached their table, he saw that Laney was burning up with curiosity. He forced himself to smile. "I couldn't believe it," he said. "It really *was* about cross-haul."

Gloria had moved one of the lawn chairs far enough away from the pool so that her grandmother, if she were sitting by the window, couldn't see her. Gloria felt guilty about not wanting to talk to her grandmother, but she simply didn't. She'd eaten a tuna sandwich, and she'd brought her diary outside with her, but she wasn't writing in it. The sun had sunk well below the tree tops, and the entire back of the house was shadowed, and, in that subtle, creepy, interval between day and night, she felt oppressed by a not altogether unpleasant — although, she suspected, somewhat morbid — melancholy like that which might have afflicted a minor Romantic poet (James Elroy Flecker, perhaps?), and her mind, running away entirely on its own, had brought her through a series of tedious circumambulations leading her to the somber consideration of Lionel Trilling.

When Gloria had received her letter of acceptance to Columbia's graduate program, Professor Bolton — as he'd told her with his lunatic's grin — had written "a long, chatty letter to Lionel" all about her. *Oh, no,* Gloria had thought, and then, as though pursued by the Furies, she'd promptly read, if not every word Lionel Trilling had ever written, at least every word available to her in the Briarville University Library, and the more she'd read, the more terrified she'd become. It was apparent why Professor Bolton liked Lionel: neither of them talked about "verbal icons" or "ideal readers," and neither seemed to give a damn about the intentional fallacy; they both placed literature in an historical context — as a cultural, social activity — but, whereas Professor Bolton saw literature as a series of styles and influences and borrowings and developments, beginning with the Greeks and continuing on forever, each style relating to past styles, and all styles changing and growing and transforming into the next styles, Trilling was primarily interested in literature for its moral implications. And Trilling had none of Professor Bolton's irreverence or zany sense of humor; witty Trilling might be, but funny never, and, as she read his essays and even his stiff, philosophical fiction, Gloria began to see him as the high priest of seriousness. Oh, help, she thought.

And then there was the matter of Freud. Professor Bolton hardly ever mentioned Freud; of the copious red-penned notes he'd written onto the margins of her Spenser paper, one had said: "Come come, Miss Cotter, you aren't proposing to *psychoanalyze* Britomart, are you?" (Italics, Gloria's.) But Trilling was big on Freud, which, at first glance, might not be too bad because Gloria had read a lot of Freud and her world view was, at least to some degree, Freudian. She fully believed in the subconscious mind and sensed her own like an enormous, dark lake (or maybe a swamp) lying beneath the tiny, hectic, busybody chatter of her daily consciousness; she believed that most people were not fully—or even remotely—aware of why they did anything; she knew from firsthand experience that her dreams were meaningful even if they rarely contained the symbols Freud talked about. But Trilling's Freudian bent made him seem even scarier—as though he would be able to take her most innocuous comments and easily read them for their deep and loathsome subconscious messages.

Gloria had never seen a picture of Lionel Trilling, but she imagined his eyes burning with the pure, brilliant flame of intellectual passion, and she imagined those flaming eyes staring straight into her own. Briarville's English department had encouraged her in her gutless, unauthentic, chameleon-like habits; she'd had no trouble at all doing the most finicky and nit-picking of New Critical close readings for the new young professor they'd hired—Doctor James T. Ealing; BA, Kenyon College; PhD, Yale University—and then walking out of his seminar and into Professor Bolton's and switching her entire set of methods and opinions like a traitor switching coats, but she was afraid that Trilling would not let her get away with that. "Your reading of this text is excellent, Miss Cotter," she imagined him saying, "but what are its moral implications for *you, personally, in your own life?*" He would stare deeply into her soul, and she would be revealed as hollow as Kurtz in *Heart of Darkness.*

"I'm sorry, Professor Trilling," she imagined herself saying, "but my life doesn't have any moral implications whatsoever because there's no authentic core to my personality, so could you please just tell me what opinions you want me to have so I can get an A? You see, I'm one hundred percent outer-directed, and my only goal in life is to fit in and fool people into thinking I'm normal. And I'd love to chat longer, but I simply can't because I have to go to dinner with my stupid cousins at the Stork Club."

And that, she thought, really was enough of that; she was indeed getting morbid. She bounded up the steps and into the kitchen. Once inside the house, she stood, listening, as though she expected to hear—she wasn't sure what. A prowler? A ghost? But she couldn't hear anything at all except those common-place, unidentifiable house noises—the creakings and bumpings of the *Lares* and *Penates*—but then she could sense (or maybe she couldn't at all, but was only talking herself into it) her grandmother's presence upstairs.

Her grandmother was, exactly as Gloria had imagined her, sitting in her chair by the window; when Gloria stepped into her room, she laid aside her maga-zine. "I thought I'd be seeing you," she said with a thin smile.

"Would you like a martini, Grandmother?"

"Not tonight, dear, thank you. I'm having some pain—enough to remind me to be good. But what are you doing at home again? Aren't you feeling well?"

Gloria shrugged. "I'm OK. Well, I'm not, really I'm— I don't know. Kind of blue, I guess." Their eyes met. Gloria couldn't remember now quite why she'd been so reluctant to see her grandmother.

"Do you play bridge?" her grandmother asked.

"Sure. All sorority girls play bridge."

Her grandmother gestured toward the cards. Gloria picked them up and passed them over. "Don't we need two more people?"

"We can make do in a pinch."

Her grandmother dealt four hands. Gloria's was distinctly odd: void in spades, diamonds forever, but jack high.

"Two spades," her grandmother said.

Gloria sighed. "Is that a demand bid?"

"*Of course* it's a demand bid. Don't you play Goren?"

"Well, sort of. When I can remember. Three diamonds."

"Game in diamonds." Her grandmother laid out her hand. She only had three diamonds, but they were the missing honors. She picked up the other two hands, sorted them, and led a heart.

"No fair," Gloria said, laughing, "You know what everybody's got."

"You don't want things to be easy, do you, Gloria?"

Just before eleven Gloria heard her parents come home. She heard them walk past the open door of her grandmother's room; she heard them moving around in their bedroom; she heard water running in their bathroom. But neither of them came in to say goodnight, and neither Gloria nor her grandmother com-mented on that strange omission. Gloria and her grandmother played two-handed bridge until nearly midnight.

Gloria was exhausted, but so restless she knew she didn't stand a chance of getting to sleep any time soon. She picked up Pound, read a few lines, and put him down again. She tried her favorites—Lowell and Roethke and

Wilbur—but tonight their words were nothing more than black marks on paper. She lay on her bed with her radio turned on low, but all she could get were stations playing the sad, whiny country music that Susie adored and Gloria hated. She looked through her current diary, decided that everything she'd written in it was thoroughly inane but didn't feel like adding anything—even if she could have thought of anything that wasn't thoroughly inane. She turned out the lights, stretched out on her bed, and waited. The last time she looked at her clock, it was after four.

Gloria slept right through the sound of her father's car driving away, but the front doorbell woke her sometime in the mid-morning. Groggy and disoriented, she heard her mother and Mrs. Warsinski talking in the kitchen. She tried to remember the dream she'd been having, but it slithered away as soon as she went after it, leaving her with a wearying sense of duration—hours and hours of muddled, inconclusive, repetitive dreaming—and only one memory: herself standing in front of her open closet wondering what to wear.

She looked out her bedroom window, saw her mother sunning by the pool, and thought about the doorbell. Feeling an ominous sense of fatality, she got up and crept downstairs where she found another florist's box waiting for her. She knew exactly what she was going to find—a dozen long-stemmed American Beauty roses—and this time she knew that the masculine scrawl on the card was Mr. Dougherty's; all it said was, "Thanks."

She tore up the card, but she didn't feed the roses down the garberator. She didn't want to call any attention to them whatsoever, so she did what one is supposed to do with roses: arranged them in a nice bouquet in a crystal vase in the center of the dining room table. Then she fled back upstairs and closed herself into her bedroom. Thanks for what? she wondered. Thanks for going for a ride with me? Thanks for putting up with me when I was drunk and behaving abominably? Well, yes, he could have meant those things, but it was more likely he'd meant *thanks for not telling your father.*

She sat in the chair by the window wondering how to get through the day. She was wearing pink baby-dolls; she'd put them on the night before without thinking of them as anything but something *cool,* but now, with a detached and dour clarity, she saw them as just about the most ridiculous garment ever invented.

She felt dimwitted and slow, as though her brain had been poured full of glue. She had a bath and put on a baby-blue sundress. It looked just about as ridiculous as the pink baby-dolls; well, the mood she was in, probably anything would look ridiculous—but, no, it was more than that. Why was she bothering? There was nobody around to appreciate her, and there wasn't anything to look forward to; if she went to the big club dance on Saturday night, she'd have to go alone, so she might as well stay home and play bridge with her grandmother.

Just about this time last year in July—that's right, it had been the week after the Fourth—Rolland's sisters had given a truly lovely lawn party like something out of Scott Fitzgerald. The entire back yard had been strung with Japanese lanterns, and Gloria had worn her dotted Swiss with white sandals, and she and Rolland had been teasing each other for hours—kissing in the shadows—until, at some time around one in the morning, he'd led her into, of all unlikely places, his father's study.

He'd tilted back the big easy chair where his father watched television, stretched out in it, and guided Gloria onto his lap as though she were riding a horse. Wow, she'd thought, if we were married, and naked, we could *do it* exactly like this. She hadn't been able—alas—to relax enough to lose herself; she hadn't been able to stop thinking about how easy it would be for someone to walk in on them, but her mounting panic had intensified her awareness into an excruciating hypersensitivity, leaving her with memories so compelling she'd incorporated them into her sexual fantasies ever since.

If they'd been guaranteed privacy and time enough, she was sure she could have climaxed in that position without any help from his fingers, but, whenever she heard footsteps in the hall, her heart jumped into her throat—or missed a beat, or did some damned thing that made it feel perilously detached—and she began to hear a sealike roaring in her ears. Eventually all she wanted was to get Rolland finished so she could get herself out of danger. Her rider's position might have been perfection for her, but it was obviously somewhat less than perfection for him, and she stopped moving when she realized she was hurting him. He gave her a small, guiding push, and off she slid; in an urgent, ungainly scramble, he leapt to his feet and began to unfasten his belt—which she badly both did and didn't want him to do—and she dragged him behind the chair so that if anyone walked in, he'd be hidden for maybe a second or two. "Put your gloves back on," he whispered, and it didn't occur to her to wonder why or to do anything other than what she'd been told.

His pants fell to the floor with an alarmingly loud sound—she heard his wallet and his change and his keys in that sound—and he pushed his underpants down like a little boy in a fierce hurry to go to the bathroom. His penis jumped straight up, and she took it into her gloved hands. She wanted him to kiss her, but he didn't; he was staring down at himself, so she stared down too. For one spooky moment, she couldn't have been any more inside his point of view if she'd jumped into his brain and were looking out through his eyes: she watched her own dainty hands in smooth, tight, snow-white, immaculately clean kid gloves stroking his tense, muscular thighs, his hairy, dangling testicles, his emphatically erect penis; it was a potently, deliciously, overpoweringly, perversely sexy pic-

ture—and, almost immediately, he made a sound like a ragged sob and filled
her gloved right palm with a prodigious glob of egg white. (It was only later she'd
think: boys are such saps; sometimes it's almost *too* easy.)

A normal girl would have been disgusted, but Gloria hadn't been disgusted;
she hadn't even felt like pretending to be disgusted—although her fine, French
gloves had most certainly been ruined—"I'll buy you another pair," he'd said,
laughing, (and the next day actually did it); smiling sweetly, she'd cupped her
gloved left hand over her gloved right hand and had walked demurely to the
nearest bathroom— And now, suddenly, with no warning at all, a truly revolting
thought invaded her mind: *Does he do the things with her that he does with
me?*

Oh, God, Heidi Bronwyn Smith!

Heidi's family and Rolland's family had known each other since the beginning of time, and, when Rolland had first taken Gloria to Scranton and had
been proudly showing her off—pinned!—she'd met Heidi Bronwyn Smith
who'd introduced herself by firmly enunciating all five syllables of all three of
her ridiculous names. Elaine, the younger of Rolland's sisters, had said to Gloria,
"This is really hard for her, you know. She and Rolly were childhood sweet-
hearts, and *everybody* thought they were going to get married." So Gloria had
been very nice to Heidi Bronwyn Smith.

Heidi Bronwyn Smith was—what else could she possibly be?—blonde as
a cover girl for the Hitler Youth. Heidi Bronwyn Smith was the sort of person
who used the term "top-drawer" with no sense of irony whatsoever, and Gloria
had heard Heidi Bronwyn Smith describe her private girls' school as top-
drawer, and now Heidi Bronwyn Smith, having been (as Gloria had most
emphatically *not* been) presented to society, was going somewhere equally
top-drawer—to Bryn Mawr, to be exact—and Philadelphia was a heck of a
lot closer to Scranton than New York was.

Heidi Bronwyn Smith was quite lovely—if you liked girls with washed-out
blue eyes, aristocratic noses, and no chins. Heidi Bronwyn Smith was very tall
and very lean and very athletic; she skied and rode and played tennis and golf,
and she'd won a zillion cups and ribbons. She owned four horses, and she did
dressage, and Gloria had actually watched her doing it and had noted that Heidi
Bronwyn Smith looked utterly spectacular in a riding habit. Until she'd met
Heidi Bronwyn Smith, Gloria would not have imagined that shorts worn with
golf shoes and knee socks could be sexy, and Heidi Bronwyn Smith wore the
tightest ski pants known to Western civilization. Heidi Bronwyn Smith and Rolland often teamed up to play mixed doubles and thrashed every other couple
in the Scranton Country Club, and it went without saying that little white
tennis dresses were simply *made* for girls like Heidi Bronwyn Smith. Gloria had
always liked wearing heels—although she rarely wore anything higher than a

tasteful, classic three inches—but Heidi Bronwyn Smith, when she wasn't doing something sporting, wore veritable skyscrapers, and Rolland, like most boys, had a high-heel fetish. When Heidi Bronwyn Smith was wearing her skyscrapers, the top of her beautifully coiffed hair was exactly level with the top of Rolland's brush cut, and any idiot could see that they made a handsome couple. Heidi Bronwyn Smith adored children—as she said quite often, usually *à propos* of absolutely nothing—and she could hardly wait to have, as she said with a cute wrinkling of her doglike, freckle-strewn nose, "a whole passel of them." Heidi Bronwyn Smith, although she was too tall ever to make a dancer, had taken ballet since she'd been four, and when she was relaxing on the floor in her obscenely tight ski pants, she sat with her legs spread as wide open as a contortionist's. Whenever Gloria and Heidi Bronwyn Smith ran into each other, they hugged and gushed like long-lost sisters—

Gloria had been sitting in the chair by the window for ten minutes not doing anything but making herself sick with what she'd been thinking. She badly needed to escape, to think about something else, but she couldn't manage even to think of something else to think about. She sprang up and walked quickly into her parents' bedroom, shut the door, picked up the phone, and said to the operator in her best Ted Cotter's daughter's voice: "I'd like to make a long distance call to Scranton, Pennsylvania, please."

The Spicers' maid answered the phone; unlike Mrs. Warsinski, she really *was* a maid. "Hi, Louanne. This is Gloria Cotter. Is Rolland there?"

"No, I'm sorry, Miz Cotter, he's not. Young Mr. Spicer's *at work*."

How could she have forgotten that? Maybe it was because she had a hard time imagining Rolland working. "Oh, I'm sorry. How silly of me. Could you tell him I called, please?"

"Now you hold on there, Miz Cotter. I see if Miz Spicer is *available*."

Gloria had no desire in the world to talk to Rolland's mother, but there didn't seem to be any way out of it, and, in a moment, she heard Mrs. Spicer's smoke-cured, Lauren Bacall voice: "Gloria. How nice to hear from you. Is everything all right?"

"Oh, everything's fine. Just dandy. I just wanted to have a chat with Rolland. I completely forgot he'd be at work," and Gloria attempted an appropriately girlish and empty-headed giggle.

"Oh. Well, call him over at the plant. He'd be delighted to hear from you, I'm sure. Do you have his number there?"

"Oh, no, I wouldn't want to disturb him at work." Gloria was killing herself giggling. "It's really all right. Could you tell him I called."

It took her several minutes to extract herself from Mrs. Spicer's cheery solicitude; then she lay back on her parents' bed and tried to fight off a soupy fog of self-loathing. Why was I giggling like a fourteen-year-old? she thought. I should have been polite and gracious and cool and sophisticated—and I shouldn't have called him *at all*. She must think I'm awful—that's right, exactly the sort of pin-brained, giggling, aggressive, *not our sort of girl* you'd never want your son to marry in a million years.

She was still lying there, immobilized, when the phone rang. Ordinarily she would have let her mother or Mrs. Warsinski get it, but she grabbed it before the first ring was over. "Hi, kitty," he said.

"Holy smoke, that was fast."

"Mom called right after you called. How you doing, Glo? You having a good summer?"

"Oh, sure, it's been— No, not really. It's been pretty awful, actually. Oh, Rolland, I can't believe it's you. I really miss you. I feel just terrible about— you know, how we left everything. You were so *mad at me!*"

What she'd said had been a condensed version of what had been rattling around in her brain—which is why it had come out in a rush—but now she'd have to slow down, and pay attention, and actually *think*. He seemed to be thinking too. She couldn't hear anything behind him that sounded like a plant; well, maybe he was in an office with the door shut. "Rolland?"

"Yeah, I'm still here. Yeah, everything seemed kind of—I don't know— screwed up to me too. It's funny you called because I was thinking about calling—"

She waited. "Yes?" she said eventually.

"Well, you know, we love each other and all— Well, it should make everything simple, but nothing seems very simple." And that must have been the condensed version of what had been rattling around in *his* brain, and she quickly subjected it to a close reading which told her that he hadn't shifted his position even slightly since she'd seen him last; he had, however, found a way to express himself that sounded wistful instead of angry, and what he'd said allowed for a tiny degree of ambiguity—enough ambiguity to give her room to maneuver.

Her first maneuver was a side step. "Oh, honey," she said, "telephones are terrible. I wish I could see you."

"Yeah? You mean it?"

"Of course I mean it, you silly."

"I'll be there by dinner time."

"Tonight?" Gloria's mother said, springing to her feet, "Oh, my God," and the dinner Mrs. Warsinski had been planning was instantly abandoned. "Where are we going to put him? Bobby's room, I guess. Ethel, could you start on the vac- uuming— And Gloria, strip the boys' beds. Get it all in the wash— Don't just stand there, hon. We haven't got all day."

Gloria bounded upstairs to Bobby's room and began to strip the bed. "Why does she do this to me?" her mother was saying so loudly that Gloria had no trouble hearing her. "Not even a day's notice. My God, who does she think she is?"

Gloria had her arms full of linen from both boys' beds and was on the way out of Jimmy's room when her mother appeared in the doorway, blocking her way. "It smells like a kennel in here! Open the windows, for heaven's sake." Gloria put the linen down and opened the windows. Her mother lit a cigarette and paced, surveyed the room with a look of anguish. "Oh, I could kill him, the little creep— What does he drink?"

"Who? Jimmy?"

"No, you idiot. Rolland."

"He usually drinks beer."

"What kind?"

"Oh, I don't know, Mom. *Cold* beer."

"Don't be facetious. Men are really finicky about their brands."

"Duquesne, I think."

"And what does he eat for snacks?"

"I don't know. He's a boy. He eats what boys eat. You know, sandwiches."

"Does he like cold cuts?"

"He's *a boy*, Mom. He'll eat anything."

"I should have known better than to ask. Get that stuff in the wash, hon."

Gloria started the wash, ran back to the kitchen and poured herself a bowl of cereal. Mrs. Warsinski was on the phone trying to locate her nephew who did the gardening. "She wants *the lawn* done today," Mrs. Warsinski said to Gloria under her breath and rolled her eyes toward the heavens, and, from upstairs came the sound of heavy objects crashing to the floor. "Gloria. I *need* you," her mother yelled.

"Mom, I haven't even had breakfast!"

"Come on, Gloria, he's *your* boyfriend!"

Gloria ran upstairs. Her mother had been throwing things from one side of Jimmy's room to the other and imposing no order whatsoever that Gloria could see. "Here, get this crap."

"What crap?"

"This crap. Don't just stand there looking. It's *garbage.*"

"Marcelaine," Gloria's grandmother called from her bedroom, "what's going on out there?"

"Nothing, Mother."

Gloria watched as her mother, with quick, angry movements, knelt and grabbed up an armful of what she'd described as garbage—comic books, old school papers, scraps of balsa wood, a smashed model airplane, and a huge number of perfectly good pencils and crayons—and carried it from the corner of the room where she'd assembled it to another corner where she dumped it. "Mom, you're going berserk."

"You just shut up, May Queen, and do what you're told."

Gloria ran downstairs for the kitchen garbage can, but when she came back up, her mother had already moved on and was now in Gloria's room. "For crying out loud, Gloria, there's cartons you haven't even unpacked yet— Oh, God, Gloria, your *bathroom!*"

"Mom, get out of here."

"How can you *live* like this? How could you possibly *bear* it?" Her mother's voice was rising into a distraught wail. "Did I raise you to live like this?"

"It's *my* bathroom. You don't ever have to come in here. *Rolland* isn't going to come in here." Gloria heard her own voice rising into a wail to match her mother's. *"It's my damned bathroom!"*

"Well, do something about it then. And could you please finish up in the boys' rooms?"

"God forbid you should have to do any housework, Mom."

"What did you say? What did you just say to me? Don't you *dare* talk to me like that, Gloria Cotter!"

"Sorry."

Gloria walked past her mother, out into the hall and into Jimmy's room. In a moment, she heard her mother's sharp heels following her. "You're a great one to talk about housework, O lady of leisure."

"I said I was sorry, Mother."

"Don't you *dare* talk to me like that ever again, do you understand me?"

"Yes, mother."

"Oh, it's simply amazing how you can say, 'Yes, mother,' with your voice dripping with sarcasm."

"My voice wasn't dripping with sarcasm."

"The hell it wasn't. My God, Gloria, you make me sick. You've had every goddamned advantage— Well, every advantage except the ones you turned your nose up at. You know your father would have— He just doesn't come from the kind of background where you simply *fling* things at your children. Everything he's got in this life, he's had to work for, but you— What you spend on clothes would—I don't know—keep an ordinary family for a year. How many Mainbocher dresses do you own, for Christ's sake, how many Zuckerman suits? And French goddamned imported underwear— How many goddamned pairs of shoes do you own? How many pairs of *goddamned patent leather pumps* do you own? And has your father *ever* begrudged you anything? Has he ever said a word about it? No. Nothing's too good for his little girl. And what do you do around here? Not a damned thing. Does anybody even *ask* you to do anything? No, of course not. Don't disturb the princess, she's reading a book— No, don't disturb the princess, she's going off to *Columbia University* to get herself *a PhD*, good God! And then you have the absolute gall to lie to your father about where you've been, and when he catches you red-handed— 'I'm sorry, Daddy, I'm not going to tell you. It's none of your business.' Well, it damned well *is* his business, and you damned well better think about that, Gloria Cotter— Oh, my God, is your father ever *disappointed* in you!"

Gloria was so angry she had frozen into statuelike immobility. She could feel her temples throbbing. "Marcelaine!" her grandmother called from her bedroom, "I *said*: what *on earth* is going *on* out there?"

"Nothing, Mother. Really."

Gloria's mind felt like a kicked beehive; it was howling with a million stinging words, but her grandmother's voice had stopped her from saying any of them, and now the secret watcher told her: "Count to ten. The last thing you need right now is a big fight. Just get her calmed down."

Gloria took a deep breath. Her stomach was on fire. "I'm really sorry, Mom," she said, speaking slowly, pitching her voice barely above a whisper. "I really am. I feel really, really bad that Dad's disappointed in me. If I could have told him where I was without betraying a confidence, I would have."

Her mother was doing her lizard impersonation. "And I want everything to be nice too," Gloria said. "Of course I do. What do you want me to do?"

Her mother lit a cigarette. "Oh, honey," she said, "use your famous brains. You know what has to be done as well as I do."

Gloria hung the bed linen out on the line, tidied both boys' rooms, washed the floor and windows in Bobby's room, drove into Edgewood Lane and bought buns, hotdogs, hamburger, mustard, ketchup, relish, cheese, cold cuts, and beer, drove home and put it all away, took the linen down, ran it through the mangle, and made the boys' beds. At three forty-two, her mother said, "Come on, hon, we've got an appointment with Tony at four."

"Mom! I don't need to see Tony."

"Of course you do."

"Well, all right, but I've got to have a shower first."

"Have one when you get back. You'll get all sweaty anyway."

"I can't do that. Get my hair done and then have a shower? That's nuts."

"Guess what, princess? I hate to break the news to you, but it's possible to take a shower without getting your hair wet."

"Maybe, but it gets *steamed* —"

"Oh, for Christ's sake."

"My hair *does not hold a set*, Mom. Maybe your hair does, but—"

"All right, all right, have your damn shower. But *move it*."

Gloria was still in the shower, still shaving—she'd shaved that morning, but it wouldn't hurt to shave again, and the last thing she needed was to cut herself—when she heard her mother blowing the horn in the station wagon. I'll kill her, she thought. I swear, I'll strangle her with the clothes line.

Half wet, in shorts and a halter top and unlaced tennis shoes, Gloria jumped into the car, and, before she had the door shut, her mother pulled out and sent the car careening, tires screaming, down the narrow road toward town. "Mom! Try not to kill us, OK?"

"Tony does *not* like to be kept waiting."

"He'll wait for *us*."

Her mother didn't answer immediately, but, when she turned onto the National Road, she said, "You're right. He will."

Was that the offer of a truce? Gloria wondered. She looked over and saw that her mother was looking at her, giving her a tight, dry smile. Gloria smiled back. "Light me a cigarette, will you, hon?"

Gloria took the pack of cigarettes out of her mother's purse, lit one and handed it over. "Is there any particular reason why Rolland decided to come today?" her mother said.

Gloria deliberated a moment before she answered. "Well, you know, after the second dozen roses, I thought I'd better call him up and thank him. And we got to talking, and one thing led to another."

"Oh. So he *is* the one who sent them, hmm? I thought you didn't know for sure. Isn't that what you said?"

"Well, it did seem kind of mysterious, but— The second time he signed the card— And really, Mom, who else could it possibly have been?"

"So, ah— Are you still engaged?"

"I guess so. That's what we're going to talk about."

"Oh, I see."

"Mom? Are you still mad at me?"

"No, I'm not mad at you, sweetie."

Her mother parked down on Main, and they began walking up Twelfth toward Market. The sidewalks were blistering, and the humidity must have been close to a hundred, and Gloria was—her mother had been right, damn it— sweating fiercely. "Mom," she said, "yes, you are still mad at me. Hey, stop a minute and listen, OK?"

They were outside Tony's salon. Her mother, annoyed, turned and stared at her. "If I could tell Daddy where I was on Sunday, I would. I'd really really *really* love to tell him, but I made a promise to somebody, and I just can't, OK? I was *not* rolling around in the dirt with some boy—which is what he thinks I was doing—and I was *not* drunk. I didn't do a darned thing he'd be ashamed of. What happened was utterly absurd and ridiculous. I wish we could forget all about it."

She couldn't read her mother's expression. "OK," her mother said.

"*OK*? What's that mean?"

"I believe you, honey. But your father's another matter— Come on, we're good and late now."

Gloria told Tony she didn't need much of a trim but to give her a short, flippy, tight tight *tight* set in the hopes that it might actually stay in for longer than ten minutes, and she thought that while she was there, she might as well get her nails done to match the little-red-devil cocktail dress she'd bought in Philadelphia. She fell asleep under the hair dryer.

When they were walking back to the car, her mother kept stopping and fussing with Gloria's hair. "That dumb cluck—he's made you look like marzipan."

"Come on, Mom, stop it. In an hour, it'll be fine. If it doesn't loosen up, I'll brush it out, OK? Now *stop it*."

Instead of getting into the car, her mother lit a cigarette. Gloria read the thermometer on the side of the bank; it was eighty-six degrees. "You look nice, Mom," she said, hoping to divert her mother's attention away from herself.

"Thanks. Just between you and me, honey, it was a man, wasn't it?"

"What do you mean?"

"Don't be intentionally naive."

"Well—*entre nous*, Mom—I mean really *entre nous*—of course it was a man."

The late afternoon heat—reflecting off the buildings, rising off the sidewalks—felt thick, red, and poisonous. Unlike her father, Gloria's mother, when she was being serious, always looked directly at her; the light was so bright it hurt, but Gloria made herself look directly back. "You, ah, you did get out of it with your virtue intact?" her mother said.

"That goes without saying, Mother." Gloria hadn't meant to sound quite *that* prissy.

"And you're certainly not going to see him again, are you?"

"That goes without saying too."

"Listen, honey, men don't really understand things like that. Can't you think of something to tell your father? Something that'll put his mind at rest?"

"Oh, Mom, I've thought and thought and thought. I'm the world's worst liar."

Her mother took a deep drag on her cigarette and let the smoke seep slowly out of her nose. "Well, maybe I'll think of something."

11

Gloria was trying to do something with her hair when she heard what had to be Rolland's car pulling into their driveway. She made herself sit perfectly still. She heard the doorbell, voices, footsteps in the house. Then she heard Rolland's laugh, and her heart leapt. She couldn't resist a peek out her window. Yes, there he was, down by the pool with her mom and dad—in chinos and a pale blue shirt, just as deeply tanned as he always was in the summer. (How did he manage that when he was supposed to be working?) She couldn't see his face, but he was obviously keyed up—pacing and smoking. She sprang back so he wouldn't see her. "Make him wait another ten minutes," the secret watcher told her. She tried but she couldn't.

She was as nervous as if she were about to have a date with someone she hardly knew, but he was her pin-man, wasn't he?—just ordinary, utterly familiar, sappy old Rolland—so why was she so anxious? She should be planning the magic, persuasive words that would lead them gently to some mutually agreeable compromise, but her mind wouldn't cooperate, and it was taking all of her energy to fight off a growing panic.

She did manage to make something of an entrance—if one could call walking down to the pool an entrance. When he heard her heels, Rolland turned toward her and started to say something—probably one of those standard, smoothie lines that flowed out of him as easily as Reddi-wip out of the can—but the moment he saw her, all he could say—and that in an emotion-choked voice scarcely above a whisper—was "Gloria." She felt herself flush with pleasure.

Aware of her parents' eyes, she allowed herself to be chastely kissed and murmured, "Oh, honey, it's so nice to see you."

Gloria hated the smell of old sweat—that stale, nauseating smell of gymnasiums and unwashed sports uniforms—but he smelled of *fresh* sweat, and no, she didn't hate *that* smell at all. She tasted salt on his lips. She stepped back, looked into his eyes. Her nipples were burning.

"Oh, what a fabulous dress," her mother was saying. "Red's your color."

"Thanks, Mom."

Gloria risked a glance at her father; he was drinking his usual pre-dinner Scotch, and—wonder of wonders—he winked at her. Did that mean she was out of the doghouse, or only that he'd suspended hostilities for the interim? She smiled radiantly back: You see, Dad, everything's fine.

Her mind was blurring with sensations fluttering by too fast to catch. If she could only take Rolland away, be alone with him in some perfect, private garden— But, no; intruding were all these dreary commonplace tasks: she had to show him to his room, and he had to get his stuff from his car. He opened the trunk, and she saw his old, battered suitcase (why didn't he ever bother to buy a new one?) and his tennis racket in a press. "Wow, are you ever dressed up," he said. "Should I wear a tux tonight?"

"No, of course not, silly."

This time they exchanged a serious kiss, and she gave up trying to save her beautifully defined lip-line. She was sure if she could only find exactly the right words, everything would fall into place, make sense—make more than sense, make a magnificently conclusive statement the way refracted light makes a rainbow. "Oh, honey, I hope you can stay for the weekend. There's a big dance on Saturday."

"Sure, I can. I told Pop I wouldn't be back before Sunday."

They kissed again in Bobby's room, and she wondered if they could find some excuse to drive over to Waverley Park? No, there simply wasn't time. And she chased a fleeting wisp of memory—almost caught it—a shiver that went with the lights of New York as seen from a penthouse apartment where she'd been once with her stupid cousins—

"I got you a little present," he was saying: a small, blue jeweler's box. She opened it, found a charm for her bracelet—a plain, gold disk engraved with the words: "GLORIA COTTER, *Briarville University, Briarville, Pennsylvania, MAY QUEEN—1957.*"

"Oh, how lovely. How thoughtful." The idea was derivative; it was almost exactly like the charm her father had given her—but still, it really was sweet. She got the bracelet from her room, and Rolland—clever boy—had brought a tiny pair of pliers with him. He attached the charm, and she looked at her father's: "GLORIA COTTER, *Canden High School, Raysburg, West Virginia, PROM QUEEN—1953.*"

Rolland's charm wasn't merely *like* her father's, it was an exact match even to the typeface of the lettering. "I did a rubbing," he said.

"What?"

"You know, like you'd do with a grave stone. I put it under a piece of paper and rubbed it with a pencil."

"Oh. How very resourceful of you."

The next dreary thing she had to do was introduce him to her grandmother— who must have been expecting it: she'd put on a dressing gown and was seated in her chair by the window. "It's a pleasure to finally meet you, Mrs. Merriman. I've heard so much about you." Gloria was sure she'd never mentioned her grandmother to him. "I hope you enjoy your stay with us," her grandmother said just as though she were the chatelaine of the house. The low sun was pouring directly through the window; her grandmother's head divided the light into shafts of quivering dust motes, and Gloria, waiting, forced herself to stand perfectly still—the perfect lady—although she felt as vibrant and febrile as the light.

They walked downstairs hand in hand. "I can't take any more sun," Gloria said and led him into the living room. She sat down in one of her mother's fake Louis Quatorze chairs; he picked up another one, set it directly in front of her, sat down on it, and took both her hands. It was, she thought, an extraordinarily odd thing for him to have done.

"Look, Glo," he said, "we really have to talk— I want to apologize for—you know, for the way I was when I drove you home."

"Thanks. I appreciate it. You really hurt my feelings."

"I'm sorry. It was just— You know, you kind of sprang it on me. Out of nowhere."

"No, I didn't, honey. I never said absolutely, certainly, we'd get married this year. I know we talked about it as a possibility, but if you remember, I *never* said—"

"Gloria." He squeezed her hands. "That just isn't the way it was, OK?"

Her first impulse was to insist that, yes, indeed, that was exactly the way it was—but she couldn't bring herself to do it. Maybe I.A. Richards would have spotted the neat, tiny loophole she'd so carefully constructed, but she couldn't blame Rolland for not having noticed it. "OK," she said, "I guess I should apologize too— I *will* apologize. I didn't make it clear enough. I'm sorry, honey. I'll try to be really clear in the future."

He didn't respond. He took out a cigarette.

She got up and brought him an ashtray, but he didn't light the cigarette. "I just keep thinking, it should be, you know—simple," he said. "Love finds a way, and all that— You do love me, don't you?"

"Of course I do. You know I do."

Gloria heard her mother walking through the kitchen and into the dining room. What the devil could she be doing out there?

Rolland glanced quickly toward the dining room, then said, lowering his voice, "Is Columbia the only reason you won't marry me now?"

"Yes."

"Are you sure?"

"Yes."

Gloria's mother's voice came sailing in from the dining room like a bright banner: "Your roses are opening beautifully, Rolland."

Baffled, he turned toward the dining room, stared first at the roses in their crystal vase, then back at Gloria. "They're *yours!*" she whispered and gave him her most imploring look. It still took him another second to get it. "Yeah, they look great," he called out.

"Right," he hissed to Gloria under his breath, "just fabulous. So who's been sending you roses?"

"Just some jerk at the club."

"What jerk at the club?"

How *dare* he ask me that? she thought. "How's Heidi?" she said sweetly.

She saw the color mount to his face. With a sharp snap of his lighter, he lit his cigarette.

"Come on, honey," he said, "let's not do this, OK?"

Both Gloria and Rolland turned to look into the dining room. Gloria's mother was simply standing there, doing nothing whatsoever but looking at them. "Mom? Hadn't you better get dressed?"

Her mother gave her an embarrassed, apologetic smile. Gloria waited until she heard her mother walk all the way up the stairs before she said, her voice just above a whisper, "You were the one who said we could date other people."

"Stop it."

"It was your idea."

"*Stop it, Gloria.* Don't do this, OK? Whoever the guy is, I don't want to know anything about him, OK?"

"Hey, there isn't any other guy, OK? Some total, utter horse's ass at the club sent me those roses, OK? I already said that. Why don't you just *listen* to me for a change?"

"All right, all right."

He was staring at the carpet, and she knew, suddenly, that he was badly frightened. Why hadn't she seen it before? They both knew that this could be the honest-to-God end, and she was just as frightened as he was. "I don't want to break up," she said.

"Oh, honey, I don't either! Listen. Are you sure—absolutely, totally, one hundred percent sure—you want to go to Columbia?"

She hesitated, wondering whether or not to tell him the truth. She couldn't see any reason why not. "No," she said, "I'm mostly sure—but not *one hundred percent.*"

Looking into his face, she thought she'd made a mistake: she didn't want him to look quite *that* relieved. "OK, Rolly. Are you—? Just as you asked me—are you absolutely, totally, one hundred percent sure that if we got married right now, I *couldn't* go to Columbia?"

He wrapped his right hand around his face, and squeezed on his cheekbones. She'd never seen him do that before. "Oh, hell. No, I'm not *one hundred percent sure*—although—Jeez, Gloria, driving from Scranton to New York every damn weekend sure doesn't sound like a barrel of laughs, does it? Four years! Does it have to be four years?"

"Maybe not," she said although she knew that it pretty much had to be. "We'd have every summer together."

Oh, how she hated this! It was boring, it was tedious, it was infuriating, it was just plain stupid—and what she wanted was simply to leap over it in one miraculous bound. She wanted to make up so they could love each other again in the uncomplicated way they always had. She wanted to go to the club and show off her little-red-devil cocktail dress—and Rolland—to her friends. She wanted to have a wonderful time (didn't she deserve it?), but they were getting nowhere fast, and nothing she was saying was refracting into any darned rainbow—and then, with a dizzying rush of inspiration, she saw how she might be able to do it. "Oh, Rolly! Did you just hear what we said? We both compromised. We both gave in a little."

He gave her a blank look. "If we're both willing to compromise, we're going to find a way, aren't we?" she said. "Oh, I know we are."

"Yeah, that's right," he said slowly. "Sure we are."

"You said it yourself—love will find a way. Why can't we just be patient? You're going to be here for a few days. We have plenty of time. We'll work something out. Don't you think so, hon? If we're both willing to compromise—"

It was incredible, but he seemed to be buying it—or at least he was pretending to. Then, as though an invisible band had begun to play and they both wanted to dance, they simultaneously rose to their feet. He gave her what appeared to be a genuine smile. "You're right, Glo. We're sure to find a way, aren't we?" They kissed. Oh, wonderful, she thought; now I have four or five days to convince him.

While Rolland had a shower, Gloria walked down to the pool to see if she could do as well with her father as she'd just done with Rolland. Had her father's wink meant that he wasn't mad at her anymore? "Not a chance," the secret watcher told her. OK, but how mad was he? She couldn't simply ask him. She would have to say something innocuous, something slightly more significant than, "Wow, it's hot tonight," but not *much* more significant. "Boy," she said, "Rolland sure got here fast today."

"Oh, is that right?" Those were the first words her father had spoken to her since Sunday night.

He met her eyes briefly then looked away at the apple trees. She looked at them too. "You can really make time on a weekday," he said in a noncommittal voice. She waited until it was clear that he intended to say nothing more. Leaving him with a wistful smile, she walked back up to the house. No, the wink hadn't been a full pardon; it had said something like: "Don't worry, I won't embarrass you in front of your boyfriend." So she wasn't out of the doghouse yet, but at least the door was open and she could see daylight.

She found Rolland, his hair still wet, in dress pants and a sports jacket, sitting in the big overstuffed chair in the living room. "Hey, Glo," he said as though he'd just remembered a trivial but nonetheless fascinating fact, "did you know we have a university in Scranton?"

She felt herself bristle with annoyance. "Oh, really? What's it called?"

"What do you think? The University of Scranton."

The University of Scranton! The notion of it was so absurd, she almost laughed. "Come on, sweetheart," he said, "don't look like that. It's just something to think about, OK?"

He caught her by the waist. Reluctantly, she allowed herself to be drawn down onto his lap. "Hey, I thought we made up," he said.

"We did." To prove it, she kissed him.

She'd never liked sitting on a boy's lap; if she sat there long enough, she always began to feel like a great, big, mush-brained baby-doll—or at least that *persona* strongly suggested itself—and she didn't much enjoy feeling like that, although now she wondered if she could play it if she put her mind to it. Binkie was great at it; Binkie climbed onto boys' laps and actually cooed baby talk at them—which went somewhat further than Gloria was willing to go—but, glancing around to make sure her mother wasn't anywhere near, she cuddled into him, gave him another kiss—a coy, nibbling one—and undid the top two buttons of his shirt. She saw herself as clearly as if she'd just stepped out of her body: her freshly painted, schoolgirl-short, bright red nails fooling around in his curly, sunbleached chest hair. That picture should really get to him!

For some bizarre reason known only to the lower depths of her psyche, playing at being great, big, mush-brained baby-doll—however revolting it might be to her ordinary, conscious mind—was making her hot, and she didn't care now whether her mother saw them kissing because kissing had become an urgent need. Under the guise of straightening her skirt, she squirmed around on Rolland's lap in a manner designed to drive him nuts, and then thrust her tongue quickly into his ear.

She felt a small shock wave pass through his body. "Hey, no fair," he whispered.

"Come on, kids," Gloria's mother called out, "it's time to go."

Gloria leapt up, leaving Rolland to cope as best he could, ran straight up to her bedroom, and put on fresh underwear—nice, white, absorbent cotton.

At the club, Gloria's parents left them alone as soon as they walked through the door—Gloria knew it was a deliberate tactic on her mother's part—and she and Rolland strolled out onto the terrace. Wednesday was usually a pretty good night, but, so far, she hadn't seen any of her crowd.

They leaned on the balustrade and looked out over the golf course; it was going to be, she thought, a lovely, lovely evening—and she was flooded again with that elusive feeling, the one that went with the view from the penthouse in New York, with iced champagne and Lester Young on the Hi-Fi and her stupid cousins murmuring in their teensy deb voices, with Grace Kelly in *Rear Window* and Fred Astaire in anything, with patent leather opera pumps and evening gloves—yes, it was that delicious, perfect, nearly mystical conviction that she was about to have (and the clichéd phrase was entirely apt) an utterly *divine* evening. Being with Rolland often made her feel like that. Maybe, she thought, that in itself was reason enough to marry him.

"Why don't you sneak into my room at four in the morning?" she said in a little-red-devil voice, knowing he'd know that she didn't really mean it.

"It's a thought,' he said, squeezing her hand. "How squeaky's the floor?"

"Pretty squeaky."

"And where's your old man keep his shotgun?"

Her father didn't own a shotgun. "In the upstairs hall closet," she said. "It's always loaded."

"Yeah, that's what I was afraid of."

"Seriously," she said, "as soon as Dad gets his dinner in him, he's had it. He'll be in bed ten minutes after we get home. Then Mom will want to chat a bit, and then she'll go to bed—"

"Sounds good to me."

He looked at her, grinning, then bent and whispered: "Why don't you take your panties off?"

It wasn't the first time he'd asked her to do that; in fact, he'd mentioned it so many times it had become something of a joke. Always before she'd thought he was kidding, but tonight she wasn't so sure. She looked into his eyes and saw tiny imps dancing there. "What?" she said, "right here?"

"No, in the little girls'. Nobody'd know but you and me."

"Good golly, you sex maniac, you'd like that, wouldn't you?"

"Sure. And so would you." Somehow she doubted it. "I dare you," he said.

Oh, you *dare* me, huh? she thought—but said nothing and gave him the ole Mona Lisa.

He probably didn't remember, but she certainly remembered. It had been last summer, and she'd watched Rolland and Heidi Bronwyn Smith devastate several sets of opponents in mixed doubles. Gloria had been watching Rolland play tennis ever since she'd met him; he wasn't a stylish or graceful player, but he made up for it by sheer aggressiveness—with a game that was fierce, slashing, and murderous. Gloria had never before seen him teamed up with a girl; knowing him as she did, she would have expected him to be gallant, to come to his partner's aid, and he did do that, but, to Gloria's utter astonishment, he wasn't doing most of the work himself: he relied on Heidi and, when necessary, allowed *her* to help *him*. Rolland and Heidi played as people can play only if they've spent a million hours on the court together—as though connected by mental telepathy. When Gloria had first met her the Christmas before, Heidi Bronwyn Smith had been merely another pretentious country club girl—too blonde, too tall, in too-high heels—who had kissed Rolland too long under the mistletoe, but, watching her on the court with him, Gloria was so jealous she actually had to grit her teeth.

Later, when Gloria and Rolland were alone, she said something—now she couldn't remember exactly what—that gave her away, and Rolland, with his most ingenuous smile, said, "Hey, you're not jealous, are you?"

"Oh, no. I think Heidi's very sweet."

"You haven't got any reason to be jealous, hon. I've known her for years. We're like brother and sister."

Right, Gloria thought, Isis and Osiris. "We even fell out of a tree together," he said.

"You did *what*?"

"We fell out of a tree together. For real. Haven't I ever told you that story?"

She shook her head. "Yeah," he said, "I was about—oh, eleven or twelve, I guess, and Heidi— You wouldn't have believed it if you could of seen her as a kid, just this scrawny little beanpole. Nobody would have thought in a million years she'd grow up into such a beautiful girl, and she was just—well, the most unbelievable tomboy you ever saw. Her mom could never get a dress on her, and she wouldn't play with other girls, just wanted to hang around with us guys. So she was always following us around, and we tried everything we could think of to get rid of her—'Go home to your mommy, Heidi'—but nothing worked. So anyhow, it was spring, and somebody said, 'OK, Heidi, if you think you're so darned tough, let's see you climb that tree.' It was one of our regular climbing trees, and pretty soon we were all yelling at her, '*I dare you, I dare you, I dare you*—'

"So up she went just like a cat, and just like a cat, she got stuck. Way up in the top, and she couldn't get down, OK? So the last thing in the world we wanted to do was tell the grown-ups, because then we'd really catch it, so yours truly has got to be the hero, right? So I climb up after her, and I get up to her, and she's hanging onto the trunk with all her might, and she's so scared she's crying, and, ah—she's wet her pants—" and he gave Gloria that tense, little laugh he always produced when he'd said something that one shouldn't say in front of ladies but he *had* said, nonetheless, because they were, after all, *engaged*—

"And that made me feel—well, really superior. 'Come on, Heidi.' Big man, right? 'Hang onto me.' So that's exactly what she does. She wraps her legs and arms around me, and you couldn't of got her off me with a crowbar, and I'm trying to climb back down with all this dead weight attached to me. Real smart, huh?

"So I got us about halfway down and then the branch we're on just snaps right off, and ZING! down we go. We're snapping off branches and yelling and screaming, and I'm grabbing anything I can get ahold of, and everything I grab—well it snaps off or it just sort of bends and dumps us off, and then KAFOOM, SMASH, BANG! we've ripped off a bunch more branches, and we've run out of branches, and we're hitting the ground, and I land on my feet—well, sort of on my feet. Broke my left leg. Heidi hanging onto me for dear life, right? So I go right on over, WHAM, and go SPLAT and break my arm. And Heidi's still hanging onto me, right? And absolutely nothing happens to her. Some scratches, that's all. And I was in two damn casts for the whole rest of the summer. Can you believe it?"

And that, Gloria thought, is a story he told me *so I wouldn't be jealous?* Without saying a word, she turned and walked away. She was gone less than five minutes, and when she came back, she pressed her nice, fresh, cotton panties—she'd folded them into a tidy little package—into the palm of his hand. He winked, slipped them into his jacket pocket, and handed her a Coke.

They strolled out onto the terrace. She was wearing a nylon slip under her crinolines, and the only difference from what she'd normally be feeling was the extremely subtle sensation of the slip fluttering directly against her bare bottom, but, however subtle the sensation, it was enough to be a constant reminder—and here, walking directly over to them, was Lee Hockner, that jerk. "Hey, Spicer, you old load. What do you say."

Lee fancied himself a tennis player; each afternoon for a week last summer, Rolland had disabused him of that notion—which, in the strange ways of males, seemed to have made them good buddies. They pumped each other's hands and continued spewing automatic boy talk at each other. "So what brings you back to our fair city?"

"Just can't stay away. The scenery's too good."

"Oh, yeah, you bet." Grinning, they both looked at Gloria as though she were the view from the terrace. "Better keep a tight leash on that one," Lee said. What an image, she thought.

Rolland gathered her up by the waist and drew her into him. "Oh, yeah, I know all about you bird dogs." Boys are such jerks, she thought.

She led Rolland in a circuit of the club, stopped to chat with Binkie and her parents, and Judy and Nancy and their boyfriends, and even with Mike Clark and Jack Farrington. It was odd: if she'd forgotten her underwear by accident—although she couldn't imagine any situation in which she'd forget her underwear by accident, but let's say she did—well, she might even, after a while, forget all about it. But she shared the secret with Rolland, and he kept giving her amused, conspiratorial glances, and so, even though the *sensation* of not wearing under-wear was quite subtle, the *thought* of not wearing underwear was about as subtle as being clawed by a Bengal tiger.

Over dinner Rolland and Gloria's father began talking coal and steel. Gloria tuned them out. All she knew—and all she wanted to know—about Spicer Coal was that it produced, as Rolland always said as proudly as if he mined it him-self, the finest anthracite in the world.

"You really do look fabulous in that dress, sweetie," her mother said. "I wouldn't have thought you'd find something like that in Briarville."

"I didn't. I got it in Philadelphia."

"Oh? How did you get to Philadelphia?"

"Good heavens, Mom, Rolland and I popped over there all the time," Gloria lied. It had been she and *Susie* who had popped over there all the time. "I mean if you really want anything, you have to go to Philadelphia. There's simply *nothing* in Briarville, just— Well, the Campus Shop is wall-to-wall kick-pleats, and the Junior Deb is OK for some things. You can get dresses there, but you can't really get *a dress* there—" And that was beautifully put, you idiot, Gloria told herself, but her mother was laughing, and on the other side of the table, her father was saying something or other about the steel industry, and Rolland, who insisted upon calling her father "sir," was hanging upon every word.

Gloria had no appetite—which was surprising; usually by this time of night she was ready to eat anything in sight. She cut up her roast beef and moved it around her plate to give the illusion she was enjoying her dinner, and she did eat a potato and all of her Harvard beets. She was the only one who hadn't been drinking, but she felt as light-headed as if she had been.

Their waiter cleared the plates away, and her father produced an old enve-lope, and now Rolland was drawing something on it that looked to Gloria like a Rube Goldberg cartoon. It was, she figured out after a moment, a flow chart of Spicer Coal production. "Come on, hon," her mother said, "let's go powder our noses."

Walking with her mother across the dining room and down the hall to the ladies' room, Gloria was acutely aware with every step that she didn't have any underwear on. "So, honey," her mother was saying, "I take it you and Rolland have made up?"

"Well, yes and no. We like each other *so* much, and— Well, we just haven't quite gotten around to talking about what we're going to do next year." She shrugged, hoping that was enough.

Walking with her mother out of the ladies' room, up the hall, and back across the dining room, Gloria was acutely aware of being watched—by Rolland and her father, by Binkie and her parents, by Judy Staub, by Lee Hockner, by any-body who cared to look—and she was acutely aware with every step that she didn't have any underwear on. As they arrived at the table, her father was saying, "You see my point?" and Rolland was nodding like a goof.

"OK, Daddy," Gloria said, "enough man talk. It's my turn now."

Gloria led Rolland out onto the terrace just as though they were going for a breath of air, but, as soon as they were out of her parents' sight, she led him back inside and straight to the games room. There was an unwritten protocol among the younger members of the club that if the door was shut, you didn't come in— or, if you absolutely had to, you knocked first, and you knocked long and hard.

The door was partway open; Rolland stepped back for her, allowing her to walk in ahead of him. She was already well into the room—and Rolland's arm was around her waist, pressing her forward, cutting off any possibility of escape— when she saw Mr. Dougherty. He was alone in there. He was bent forward over the pool table, a cue poised in his big hands. He looked directly at Gloria. She froze. She couldn't begin to assimilate the nastiness of coming upon him so unexpectedly. With no expression at all, he was staring directly at her. Under the harsh yellow light above the pool table, his face looked old—tired and bruised. He didn't speak. He hesitated only a moment, and then, as though he'd never seen Gloria before in his life, dropped his gaze back to the green felt. Gloria had been so badly startled she hadn't reacted at all. She knew that her own face showed nothing. Turning slightly, she guided Rolland back through the door, and he stepped out of her way. Mr. Dougherty bent to the table, and, with a sharp snap, sank a red ball.

Gloria led Rolland outside and down the path toward the golf course. She was overflowing with relief—even with joy. She and Mr. Dougherty *did not know each other*—how wonderful! That was obviously the unspoken deal he'd struck with her in return for keeping her mouth shut, and so she'd never have to think about him again. She almost liked him now that he'd vanished from her life, and she offered him a thanks as heartfelt as the one he'd written onto the card that had accompanied the wretched roses. She could feel her luck changing: the great Renaissance wheel, *Fortuna*, was turning in her favor. Oh, everything was going to work out beautifully!

The sun was finally well below the tree tops; the light had shifted from ruddy raspberry to an iridescent blue-gray, but, in the last of that fading light, some dumb jerk grown-ups were still golfing. One of them—all Gloria could make out was a silhouette—was even trying to sink a putt. "How am I doing with your old man?" Rolland asked her.

"Oh, just great, honey. He really likes you, you know. He thinks you're very sensible."

Approaching the woods flanking the golf course, Gloria remembered— how could she have forgotten?—that she wasn't wearing underwear, and remembering was suddenly delicious. There were half a dozen trails in the woods—make-out heaven for the younger kids—and, in high school, Gloria had certainly wandered down every one of those trails with some boy or other, but they didn't have that much time left, and, stupid girl, she hadn't brought ballerinas with her, and one sharp twig or stone could put an end to her patents. She considered it nonetheless—maybe just a short stroll down to the little bridge over the creek. She turned to Rolland just as he turned to her, and they slipped into a long, dreamy kiss. She heard crickets and frogs and then, somewhere far, far away, a dog barking; she knew that she hadn't been so happy in a long time.

There was hardly any light left, so they were almost entirely safe, but, after a moment, she heard footsteps. She drew him quickly around behind the big oak and kissed him again, and a tiny white-hot needle sank into the side of her neck just below her ear; she bore with it as long as she could and then slapped hard. Looking at her fingers, she saw a black smear of what had been wings and a disgustingly vivid blotch of her own blood. "Oh, shoot," she said, "we're going to get eaten alive down here!" and, even as she said it, she felt another mosquito needling her calf.

Laughing, she walked him quickly back up the hill. As though reading her mind, he said, "Jeez, this is ridiculous. I feel like we're back in high school."

"Don't worry, honey, they won't stay up too long."

They made a circuit of the club with her parents, saying their good nights, then, getting into the back seat of her father's Buick, Gloria slipped in first, and, as Rolland settled next to her, allowed her hand—quite accidentally, of course—to rest on his thigh directly over the thickening shape of his penis. "What are you going to do with my panties?" she whispered. "Are you going to keep them for a souvenir?"

Her father started the car and pulled away. Rolland began to whisper something, but Gloria stopped him by slipping her tongue into his mouth. There were no lights from the club to her house, and her parents were chatting and—quite consciously, she thought—ignoring the occupants of the back seat, and so she began to stroke Rolland's trapped penis. She felt the shock of it pass through his body. Good, she thought. How do you think I've felt all night? Let's see how you like it. She stroked him steadily for the entire—but entirely too short—drive back to the house.

Gloria had observed over the years that boys, when they were really hot, lost the ability to speak. Rolland followed her mutely into the house and threw himself into the big overstuffed chair in the living room. Gloria's father was making drinks, and her mother was doing something or other in the kitchen, so Gloria settled herself demurely onto Rolland's lap. The back of the chair partially obscured her parents' view of what was going on in the chair—at least it did so long as they didn't walk all the way into the living room—and Rolland's right hand had already vanished under her skirt.

"*Don't you dare!*" she said to him in a fierce whisper and locked her thighs together. If he touched her *there*, she'd kill him, but he did nothing more than let his hand rest lightly on her unclad pubic area, cupping it. She was terrified that he was going to do exactly what he'd done plenty of times before—always when they'd been *alone*—moisten his index finger with her own juices, find her most sensitive spot, and rub it with a steady, gentle, circling motion, but he didn't do that. He didn't do anything. He simply allowed his hand to rest on her, unmoving. She kept imagining what he *could* do—so easily, with so very little effort— "Straight, water, or soda?" her father said, stepping partway into the living room.

"Water, please, sir," Rolland sang out in a cheerful, booming voice, "but just a splash."

Before now, Gloria would have hesitated to use the word "painful" to describe a blush, but this one was excruciating. Her face felt as though it had been scalded, and it must surely have been emitting a fiery, dark red radiance like a heat lamp. She didn't know where to look, and, if anyone were to say anything to her, she couldn't answer. She heard her father's firm footsteps, and Rolland withdrew his hand.

As her father approached with Rolland's Scotch, Gloria jumped up with a magnificent flourish of crinolines; it wasn't anything she'd planned to do. Her father gave her a curious look, and she fled into the kitchen where her mother was arranging pretzels and nuts and cheese slices on a tray. Good grief, she must think that Rolland required a constant supply of food like a shark. "You want anything, sweetie?"

"No, Mom, I'm OK."

Now that she was safe, Gloria felt absurdly, wildly giddy, and she knew that she could easily break into a fit of giggles at the slightest provocation. "Here, take this in," her mother said, handing her the tray. Gloria balanced it on one hand like a waitress and sashayed into the living room with an exaggerated swing to her hips. "You drop that and I'll kill you," her mother hissed behind her.

Gloria offered the tray to her father who waved it away. He was already yawning—paying hardly any attention to her—so, like the cigarette girl in an old movie, she flounced over to Rolland. Smiling significantly at her, he took a pretzel. "Why don't you keep me company?" Grinning, he gestured toward his lap.

She stuck out her tongue at him, walked away to one of the Louis Quatorze chairs, gathered her skirt under her, and sat on it. She crossed her ankles neatly and folded her hands in her lap.

Her mother, drink in hand, unwound herself onto the couch. "We're a lively crew, aren't we?"

"I don't know about you folks," her father said, "but no matter how pleasant the company, it's time for yours truly to turn in," and he downed the remainder of his Scotch like medicine.

"We should all probably turn in, don't you think, kids?" her mother said.

"You go on, Mom. Rolland and I just want a chance to talk a little bit."

"Oh, no, sweetie," her mother said, standing up, "I'm not going to let you do that to him after the long drive he's had. Don't be so selfish, Gloria. Tomorrow's another day."

The look on Rolland's face was almost funny.

Gloria locked herself in her bedroom, and, without taking off any of her clothes—not even her shoes—threw herself onto the bed. She took a moment to savor the fact that she was quite alone, that she could make it last just as long as she wanted— But she should have taken the dress off. The crinolines were in the way, were really annoying, as a matter of fact, and—finally allowing her exploring fingers to get right to the heart of the matter—boy, was she ever hot! Her slip was probably a mess, and she was making it even more of a mess, and she should stop and get undressed, but she didn't want to stop, and maybe she could slow down, but she couldn't do that either— A sudden, raw, jagged orgasm left her gasping for breath. All the electricity drained instantly out of her, and she was left, fully—cruelly—aware of herself lying splay-legged on her bed in a taffeta cocktail dress with the lights still on. How absurd.

What's the matter with me? she thought. Why couldn't I wait? She knew that if she lay there without moving, she'd eventually get depressed, so she forced herself to stand up, unzip her dress, step out of it, and hang it up. She put her slip in to soak in her bathroom sink. She stood under the shower until the hot water ran out. Then, in bed, she didn't feel the least bit sleepy. She kept reliving her favorite scenes from the evening, and she knew that she could, quite easily, do it to herself all over again. That wasn't normal, was it? But she had no intention of doing it all over again. She told herself to think about something else.

The last thing in the world she wanted to think about was Heidi Bronwyn Smith, but Heidi had just popped into her mind, and she wouldn't go away. The ironic thing was that, under different circumstances, Gloria might actually have liked her—and why does he want me, she wondered, when he could have Heidi just by snapping his fingers? His family adored Heidi, and Rolland and Heidi thought about the same things (if you could call it thought), and Heidi was pretty enough and dressed well (if you didn't mind a fairly heavy emphasis on sex appeal), and she certainly had a spectacular figure. Gloria could never have a figure like Heidi's; in order to have a figure like that, you had to be really, really athletic, and Gloria had never been the least bit athletic— Well, on second thought, that wasn't true; there were archery and swim-

ming, and archery was entirely useless, but swimming, on the other hand—
That's right, she could take it up again, seriously, and if she swam every day,
she'd get that lean, hard figure she'd had at the end of her Britomart summer,
and she could look damn near as good as Heidi, and she could wear skyscraper
heels and skin-tight capri pants and skimpy little sweaters with push-me-up
bras. So what if it was in bad taste? What's taste anyway? If you got right down
to it, *sex* was probably in bad taste. And she was a whole heck of a lot smarter
than Heidi—but that wasn't saying a lot; she was a whole heck of a lot smarter
than most girls, for all the good it did her. But whoever said that intelligence
was an advantage for a girl anyway? Oh, God, she prayed, please let me go to
sleep.

She fluffed her pillow up, turned onto her other side, and finally began to
drift off, but the sense of something lurking woke her again, and her mind
wouldn't stop chattering. If we get married, she thought, he's going to have to
find himself another tennis partner. I'll be damned if he's going to spend hours
on the court with Heidi. But, of course, Heidi would continue to be around; she
might even marry somebody in Scranton— Oh, help, was she going to have to
spend the entire rest of her life with Heidi Bronwyn Smith?

When Gloria woke up, it was already mid-morning and hot as blazes. She'd been
dreaming, could find hardly anything left of it, but, from the sensation between
her legs, it must have been a sexy dream indeed. She touched herself experimentally. Even though she'd given herself an orgasm the night before, she was
aroused all over again—and the feeling of her own fingertips suddenly brought
back the centerpiece of the dream: she'd been leaning on the kitchen table,
her elbows resting on the table top, and a man—an anonymous man with no
personality whatsoever—had stepped up behind her and embraced her. She
couldn't remember what she'd been wearing, but she clearly remembered the
sensation of his powerful body pressing hard against her bare bottom. She hardly
ever dreamed about sex, or at least about anything as clearly sexual as *that*, and
she was amazed at her own subconscious mind. From downstairs she heard—
had already been hearing for a while now—the clink of dishware and voices,
her mother's and Rolland's, and she remembered that her mother was going
shopping and it was Mrs. Warsinski's day off, so she and Rolland would have
some time alone together—wow!—that is, if she got up *right now*.

She leapt out of bed and into the shower. Drying herself, she heard her
mother's car drive away and felt as though someone had just clicked a stopwatch:
two hours at least, three if they were lucky. She cleaned her teeth, dabbed on
a bit of perfume, brushed her hair, did her makeup. Now she had to decide what
to wear, and decide pretty darned fast.

The obvious thing was a sundress, but—but what? But she knew how easy it would be to go all the way. She trusted Rolland, but he was *a boy*, after all; no matter how good their intentions, boys lose control, and a sundress would make things just too easy, so what other choice did she have? Pretend they were going out somewhere, put on nylons and girdle? In this heat, come on! (And besides, she didn't want to be quite that chaste.) Oh, how about a swimsuit? Right, perfect. You really have to *think about it* to take off a swimsuit, and her black maillot was certainly sexy. She pulled it on, snatched up the matching cap, ran downstairs, and arrived in the kitchen as breathless as a little kid.

Rolland, in navy blue trunks and a sparking white, beautifully starched and ironed, short-sleeved shirt—unbuttoned most of the way down his chest—was sitting backwards on a kitchen chair—straddling it—and reading the *Raysburg Times*. He looked up at her, met her eyes and didn't smile. One of his standard lines—something like, "Well, good morning, Miss Sexy. Get your beauty sleep in?"—was not forthcoming. Instead, he said, "Are you OK?"

"Sure, I'm OK. Are *you* OK?"

"Yeah," he said in a tone that suggested he might not be. Neither of them had moved since she'd arrived in front of him; she was looking into his eyes as searchingly as he was looking into hers.

"I just—" he started. He was having trouble finding words. "You know, after I went to bed, I started thinking about everything, and—I guess I got a little carried away last night, huh?"

You got carried away? she thought. Brother! But it certainly wasn't something she could say to him.

"Did we—go too far?"

Too far? What on earth was he talking about? They hadn't done much of anything— Oh, but he must think that talking your girlfriend out of her panties at the country club was really naughty—not to mention sliding your hand under her skirt right there in her parents' living room! Then she realized that his question was a test and either a simple "yes" or a simple "no" was an incorrect answer. She chose her words with the precision she would have used on one of Professor Bolton's pop quizzes: "I wouldn't do anything like that with anybody but *you*."

"I didn't think you would." Oh, sure, she thought, and then, reading the guilt in his shifty eyes, she knew he'd been playing around with Heidi. Well, that wasn't exactly news, was it? But still— She felt stupidly indignant, turned away and got herself a cereal bowl. "I love you, Gloria," he said to her back.

"I love you too," she said without looking at him and poured herself some cornflakes. The morning was not turning out the way she'd planned it, and she couldn't think of a thing to say to get it back on course without sounding too forward. It was, unfortunately, one of those classic situations in which the boy really did have to make the first move. After a spoonful of cereal, she knew she couldn't eat. She set the bowl in the sink and walked past him toward the door. "I think I'll have a swim."

"Hey, Glo, are you sure you're OK?"

"Sure, I'm sure."

"Really?"

"Yes, really."

She walked down the steps and out to the edge of the pool. We're just having a great time, she thought, just ducky, just peachy keen. But the day was magnificent, not too hot yet; the sun had just cleared the house, and, out on the lawn, the dew was still sparkling like scattered sequins. As she tucked her hair into her cap, a breeze stroked her skin into goose bumps. She heard Rolland walking up behind her. "Hey, that's a neat cap."

"Thanks. I got it in Philadelphia." Oh, what a dumb thing to say. "Why don't you come in with me?"

"No, thanks. I'll come in later. I just want to watch you."

Oh, you do, do you? she thought. She heard the hollow, metallic click of his Zippo, then smelled fresh tobacco. She dived into the pool.

After the shock of entry, the water was lovely, like velvet or silk or—no, there wasn't a metaphor that would do; the water felt like *water*, and it felt delicious. Aware of his eyes on her, she swam with her most relaxed stroke, breathing on both sides; it was, after all, the only athletic thing she could do. She told herself she'd keep swimming as long as it felt easy and was surprised when she swam ten laps with no effort whatsoever, but the twelfth lap began to feel like work, so she glided into the wall in the shallow end and stood up.

She climbed the ladder, and he was waiting for her on the other side of it. "You're just great in the water, Glo. Just beautiful." He kissed her.

"Wait, honey," she whispered, "my grandmother can see us." She pushed him gently away and walked toward the house. The lawn chair she'd dragged back out of sight of her grandmother's window was exactly where she'd left it, but she looked up nonetheless, checking to make sure. She saw him following her gaze. "We're OK," she said.

She folded down the back of the chair so she could lie in it, and then, so he'd get the point, kissed him. He tasted like Pepsodent and smoke. She reached for the strap on her bathing cap; he intercepted her fingers and guided her hand away. What? she thought, he wants me to leave my cap on? He thinks bathing caps are *sexy*? Oh, boys are just so unbelievably *weird*! But the secret watcher who was observing from approximately twelve feet away said, "Come on, Gloria, you know you look cute—all sleek and wet."

She stretched out on the lawn chair. The sky was so bright she had to close her eyes. Through her closed eyelids she saw a shadow fall across her, then felt his lips on hers. Swimming had relaxed her; flat on her back, she allowed her entire body to go limp. He nibbled at her lips; she opened her mouth, and his tongue slipped in.

She decided to pretend she wasn't too interested yet, so the only part of herself she allowed to move was her tongue. After a few minutes of soul-kissing, he slipped the straps of her suit down and freed her breasts. She was thoroughly enjoying the game—pretending that she was altogether indifferent, or, better yet, that she was Sleeping Beauty and the spell she was under was going to take a whole heck of a lot to break—and so she didn't respond, not even when he stroked her bare nipples. Then she felt his fingers slip inside the crotch of her suit. Holding still for *that* was going to be more of a challenge—was going to be damnably difficult—but if she really tried, maybe she could do it.

She continued to lie perfectly still, her arms at her sides, her mouth open, her eyes closed. What he was doing was simply wonderful; he was stroking her with that maddening, lovely circular motion, and eventually she wouldn't be able to help it—she'd start squirming and that would be the end of the game—but for the moment she could still stand it, although what she couldn't stand was her bathing cap: her ears were on fire. But she told herself to lie still. Come on, Gloria, lie perfectly perfectly still.

An eternity drifted by, and she was so close to having an orgasm she knew if she allowed her hips to move, she'd have one in nothing flat, but could she have one if she didn't move at all? Maybe, but when she did have one, she wanted to be *with him*—and, besides, continuing to lie there without responding was beginning to feel like an exquisitely refined torture designed by an evil Chinese empress. Without having planned to do it, she pushed him away and sat up.

She heard him inhale sharply, and the world was too bright—was fiercely brilliant with hard edges. He'd stepped back. The sky behind him was so vivid with light it made her eyes water and she couldn't see the expression on his face. She was afraid that her sudden movement had made him feel rejected, and that was the last thing she wanted him to feel, so she wrapped her arms around him, drew him down, and thrust her tongue between his lips. Against her leg, his penis was trying to poke its way though the front of his trunks. She squeezed it lightly. "Oh, Gloria," he murmured, "I love you so much."

"Oh, I love you too!"

She couldn't stand her cap another second, whipped it off and threw it down. The air on her bare ears felt exquisite. *She* felt exquisite; her entire body sang. What she was feeling was so clear and balanced she didn't want to speak. She kissed him again, then took his hand and led him into the house. She made a shhh gesture. Tiptoeing, she led him up the stairs.

It was the first time a boy had ever been inside her bedroom. She eased the door shut, stripped off her maillot, and threw herself onto her bed. He stood above her, staring. "Wow," he whispered, "you're just as beautiful as I knew you'd be," and she realized he'd never seen her entirely naked before.

If he hesitated any longer, the spell would be broken. She caught his trunks by the waist band and tugged; he pushed them down, stepped out of them, and his penis sprang instantly erect. She watched a small, glistening drop of dew form on the tip over the tiny wink of an opening.

She opened her arms for him, and he sank into them. Her naked skin rubbed against his naked skin, and she was tingling all over. She wanted to open her legs as wide as her arms—which she absolutely shouldn't do—but she'd already done it, and she could feel him down there brushing against her. She was sure he'd slip in easily no matter how big he was. She wanted him in her, but she didn't want to have to say it. "Come on, come on, come on," she told him by mental telepathy.

"Honey, you're killing me," he murmured. She felt something—it had to be the head of his penis—parting her, hovering just at her outer opening. She arched up and felt him draw back. She felt like screaming.

"Oh, honey, we can't," he whispered, "not *yet*."

The jerk, she thought, and her delicately poised mood was shattered.

It took her a moment to figure out what was going on; when she did, she sat up, confused and dizzy. What on earth had she been thinking? Oh, but she hadn't been thinking *at all*, and she felt a wave of horrible, sickly shame. Not only had she been practically begging him to take her hypothetical virginity, but there was another little matter that had never crossed her mind: birth control. Yikes, and she was right smack between her periods—and the secret watcher was yelling at her, "Get control of yourself, Gloria, you idiot."

The obvious thing she had to do was finish him off—poor boy. She fumbled for the hand lotion on her bed table. She'd done this for him lots of times; without ever saying a word, he'd taught her exactly how he liked it, but they'd never before done it in full daylight with all their clothes off. As she made the smooth, rhythmic motions she knew he liked, she stared, fascinated, at his penis. She felt it swelling up in her hand. She rose onto her knees, reached behind him with her free hand, and slipped her fingers into the crack of his bottom. It was exactly the way he teased her when he gave her an orgasm. He groaned, and she could feel a wonderful tightening in his muscles.

She speeded up her hand motion, felt his bottom tighten up even more, and knew he was going to have an orgasm; the moment she knew it, he was already having one. She held on until she was sure he was finished.

He was panting slightly, his mouth hanging open; his eyes were blurred and shining. It's not fair, something in her said; before she could figure out what that had meant, he bent and kissed her on the forehead. "You're a doll," he said.

He slid down toward the foot of the bed. She couldn't imagine what he was doing. He parted her legs, one big hand on the inside of each thigh. "Rolly?" she said.

He didn't answer, but it was obvious that he was going to return the favor she'd just given him — but in a way that had never crossed her mind — although, now that he was doing it, she couldn't understand why it had never crossed her mind: it felt natural, even inevitable. "Rolland, honey, don't do that," she said without much conviction.

She envisioned exactly what he was doing: he was down there pressing his mouth into the middle of all that awful black hair. His tongue had found her most sensitive place. "No," she said, "Rolly, come on now. Please, no. I mean it. No."

But she didn't mean it at all and wondered if she should bother to tell him. She allowed herself to sink back onto the bed — and *that* should tell him. His fingers had always felt wonderful, but his fingers, however clever, however gentle, could not match his tongue for warmth, for softness, for wetness, and for subtlety. She heard herself groan. She had just enough consciousness left to slide a pillow under her head.

Laney was leaning into the station wagon to pick up a bag of groceries when she heard a single, high-pitched, piercing, prolonged, cat-like yowl. The origin of such a sound was unmistakable — as Laney knew perfectly well, having heard, more than once, exactly that sound coming out of her own mouth. Well, well, well, she thought, Princess Priss just got nailed. She didn't know whether to laugh or be furious.

She straighted up with no groceries and looked toward the suddenly silent house. The little tramp! she thought. What makes her think she can get away with that *under my roof?* But, the longer Laney stood there, the more she realized she wasn't as angry as she had every right to be. It took her a moment to figure out why. Oh, she thought — the truth finally dawning on her — she wouldn't be sleeping with him if she wasn't going to marry him. And if she married him, that would take care of everything. Goody.

She was halfway up the steps with the first bag of groceries when Rolland came running out to meet her. "Here, Mrs. Cotter, let me help you with that."

"How sweet of you." He scooped the bag out of her arms and went running into the house ahead of her. She followed him into the kitchen and lit a cigarette, watched as he bounded back outside for the other bag, watched as he bounded back in with it and set it on the counter. He'd carried that bag — the one with all the cans — as though it had been light as a feather. Well, for a boy like that, it probably had been. "Thank you so much."

"Don't mention it, Mrs. Cotter." Grinning, he looked first at her, then out through the wall of windows into the shadowless blaze of noon. "Going to be another terrific day, huh?"

"Oh, it certainly is," and she allowed herself a smile. "Yes, it certainly is."

Well, well, well, she thought, there's nothing like getting his needs met to set a man up. He looked like a great, big, self-satisfied pussycat, and he must spend half his life outdoors to get that tan; why, even the hair on his chest was bleached out!

She hadn't fully realized before just how tall he was, or how muscular. Look at those calves, she thought; just standing there not doing anything, they were hard as rocks. He wasn't what she would have called handsome, but you couldn't ever really trust handsome men; there was always something sinister about handsome men. What you wanted was a good, solid, serviceable man who would wear well; that's right, and a man needed a bit of homeliness—like Rolland's big beak of a nose—to be truly attractive, to be truly masculine. Laney shouldn't have been so worried: of course Gloria was going to marry him. What girl in her right mind wouldn't?

Gloria wondered if what she was feeling wasn't merely some version of Saint Augustine's post-coital *tristitia*. But no, that wasn't right; she didn't feel the least bit sad. She felt clear and calm and fully in command of her usual intellectual faculties—which was something of a relief, considering that she hadn't been fully in command of them for a while—but she also felt thoughtful and puzzled. She'd had enough experience by now to know that all orgasms are not the same, and if she were to put a grade on the one she'd just had, it would rate a super double A plus. It had been painful but in an entirely delicious way, and she'd been reduced—or elevated, depending on how one looked at it—to the state of an ecstatic animal or angel. And then, in spite of the fact that she'd yelled her head off and her grandmother must surely have heard her (good grief, they'd probably heard her all the way over at the club!), in spite of the fact that her mother had come home and almost certainly knew—at least approximately—what they'd been doing, in spite of the fact that Rolland had gone rushing downstairs to try to brazen things out and she'd heard his voice and her mother's chattering away in the kitchen, in spite of *all that*, she'd fallen sound asleep for a few minutes—had just awakened in exactly the same position in which she'd achieved orgasm: flat on her back with her legs spread wide open. And now, her eyes still shut, not quite ready to greet the world and its nasty complications—oh, it's going to be so embarrassing!—she gingerly drew her legs back together until she felt the familiar normalcy of her knees touching. Something inside her felt sore and *used* exactly in that pleasant way her muscles felt used after a long swim. Her body's capacity for ecstasy, she thought, was truly astonishing. What was equally astonishing—and disconcerting—was her mind's capacity for sexual obsession. And Gloria decided that—so long as she was in this detached, cool, truth-telling mood—she might as well face yet another sordid truth: she didn't have, as she'd always thought, merely an abnormally high sex drive; it was worse than that: she had a sex drive *like a boy's*—just as hot and fast and hungry and single-minded as a boy's. Dear God, she asked—not for the first time—why have you done this to me?

From the middle of yesterday afternoon until only a few minutes ago—which added up to approximately twenty hours—Gloria had not been able to think about anything but sex. She and Rolland had teased each other half to death, and she'd given herself an orgasm, and she'd *still* gone to sleep thinking about sex; she'd dreamed about sex, and she'd awakened thinking about sex, and now the only reason she could think about anything other than sex was because she'd just *had* sex. But the cool clarity she was currently enjoying was likely to be a short-lived state indeed, because she knew herself well enough by now to know that having orgasms didn't simply leave her relieved—although they did do that sometimes, at least for a while—they also raised her level of desire. The orgasm she'd given herself the night before hadn't relieved much of anything; the one she'd just had—wonderful though it might have been—was unlikely to grant her much peace; within hours of having had such a wonderful orgasm, the only thing she would be capable of thinking about would be having another one.

Now she was becoming truly gloomy—even morbid—because she was thinking about Freud and Schopenhauer. "Biology is destiny," Freud said, and she was one of that "under-sized, narrow-shouldered, broad-hipped, short-legged race"—as Schopenhauer called women—and she was right smack in the midst of that time of her life when Nature (Schopenhauer capitalized it) intended a *striking effect*. She was, at twenty-one, as striking as she would ever be, and she had been taught —and had enthusiastically taught herself—every trick in the book to enhance that striking effect, and the purpose of that striking effect was to attract a man, to ensnare him, to make him marry her, to make her pregnant, to give her a baby, so human life could continue, on and on, pointlessly forever. But why hadn't she realized before how strongly, overwhelmingly, her own sex drive was cooperating in this divine—or demonic—drama of blind, mindless desire? And who was she to object to the grand design of the universe no matter how stupid it might seem when, having had a super double A plus orgasm, she was granted a moment of respite—of cool, dispassionate objectivity—that enabled her to think clearly about it? That's right, who was she to go against biology, against Nature herself?

But then, after another cycle of increasingly gloomy rumination, she decided that she'd overstated things—she had a nasty habit of doing that—and she couldn't really say that she had a sex drive like a boy's. She *was* capable of thinking about something other than sex; in fact, she could think about other things for really quite long stretches of time—look at her Britomart summer, for example—but she was convinced that boys couldn't go for very long without thinking about sex. So far as she could tell, boys thought about sex constantly—which was only normal, she supposed—and boys probably couldn't go for very long without *having* sex—at least, once they'd become accustomed to having it—or, to get specific, she was convinced that *Rolland* couldn't go for very long without having sex, so, if she wanted to marry him, she couldn't make him wait forever, or even for very much longer, because if she did, she knew exactly with whom he would be having sex—and so she really did have to decide: *did she want to marry him or not?*

"We're perfect for each other, you know that?" Rolland said.

Well, at least our bodies are perfect for each other, Gloria thought but didn't say. They were sitting by the pool eating ham and Swiss cheese sandwiches made by her mother. Gloria couldn't remember the last time her mother had made her a sandwich, so her mother couldn't be all *that* mad at her, and, therefore, must not have heard Gloria screaming her head off—or if she had, she wasn't letting on.

"I think we're perfect for each other too," Gloria said because she had to say something, "at least in a lot of ways we are."

"Tell me a way we're not."

She felt unaccountably annoyed. She would have liked to have told him about Freud and Schopenhauer; over the last three years there had been lots of things she would have liked to have told him about—and it wasn't that she hadn't tried, and it wasn't that he hadn't been interested— Well, that wasn't quite right; he was always interested in *her* but never in *her ideas.* If she were to talk about Freud and Schopenhauer, he would listen politely and even encourage her, but he wouldn't understand a word of it, and he wouldn't feel even slightly guilty that he didn't understand a word of it, because he believed that all that stuff was just so much meaningless intellectual crap. "Come on, Rolly," she said, "we don't think about the same things."

"Who ever said we were supposed to?" he said with a laugh. "That's why God made men and women."

Oh, right—and that was exactly what he thought. It was just fine for *girls* to be interested in meaningless intellectual crap, but you certainly couldn't expect *boys* to be interested in it any more than you could expect them to be interested in Paris fashions—and, moreover, that state of affairs was somehow decreed by God. "How very theological of you," she said and immediately regretted how sharp her tone had been.

"For crying out loud, Glo, do you have to take everything so seriously all the time? We love each other. Isn't that the only thing that matters?"

"Sure it is. Of course it is." Maybe he was right. Maybe she did take things too seriously. Maybe she needed to be married to somebody who didn't.

"What's the matter, honey?" Rolland said. "You don't, ah, feel bad about what we did, do you?"

Was that another test question? She'd been thinking about Freud and Schopenhauer, and it hadn't occurred to her to feel bad about what they'd done. What was it they'd done she *should* feel bad about? Well, obviously, having allowed herself to have a super double A plus orgasm while he'd had his mouth down there. So what did he think? That she should be embarrassed? Ashamed?

While they'd been doing it, everything had seemed—well, *Natural*—but now, sicklied o'er with the pale cast of thought, it was beginning to feel problematical—and she was beginning to feel like Eve after she'd eaten the apple. What if he thought it was something only a tramp would enjoy—or enjoy that much? What if he thought she had a sex drive like a tramp? That, of course, would change everything—would be utterly humiliating. Oh, she thought, and last night I was walking around the country club with no underwear on. Talk about blind, mindless desire—I must have been *really* out of my mind!

She was still trying to think of something to say when he said, "Glo, you're an angel. A living doll."

She couldn't read his expression beyond calling it "sympathetic," but she didn't understand why she should deserve his sympathy. The sun was making her eyes water; she shaded them with a hand and looked out over the pool.

"Remember a couple years ago," she heard him saying, "when you made me promise never to ask you to go all the way. Remember that?"

"Yes."

Oh, so that was it. Neither of them had to say another word because they both were supposed to understand what had happened: he'd had his chance, and he'd been a gentleman. What more could she ask for?

She looked directly at him; at the same moment, he'd turned to look directly at her. In the fierce light, his eyes were enormous bluish-gray pupils with tiny black dots at the center—and the sun was really too much. It hurt! She closed her eyes, saw fiery spots dancing in her field of vision. Oh, it was all too confusing.

It wasn't just that their bodies were perfect for each other; it was something bigger—something scary and dark, something (damn it anyway) driven by Nature's blind, mindless desire. When it came to sex, they'd never fumbled around; each had always known exactly what the other wanted, and today— Well, suppose he hadn't been a gentleman? Then she could very well be, at this very moment, as pregnant as pregnant could be, and she'd *have to marry him.*

But, if they were married, they could actually *do it* every day, and they would be perfect together. If, as Freud said, the conscious mind is just the tiny tip of the iceberg, then down in that enormous and inscrutable and ultimately triumphant region below the surface, their sexual energies were a perfect match—and *that,* she thought, is why he loves me and he doesn't love Heidi. It didn't have a thing to do with rational choice. Poor Heidi. Then, after a moment, she added: poor me.

He'd obviously been thinking his own thoughts while she'd been thinking hers. "Look, Glo—tell me what it is you want—that you can't do if we're married."

What popped instantly into her mind was, "Study with Lionel Trilling," but she knew he'd never understand that, and she wasn't entirely convinced that she did want to study with Lionel Trilling. "English Literature isn't a hobby with me, hon. It's really serious."

"But what are you going to do with it? You know, when you get the degree? Do you want to teach?"

"I don't know. We've talked about this, Rolly. Oh, we're just going to go around in circles again— OK, I want to be able to *decide*, you know? Maybe when I've got the degree, I'll want to teach. Or maybe not."

"It can't be for the money. We'd have plenty of money."

"Oh, no, it wouldn't be for the money. It would be for—" She didn't know what it would be for. Once again, she couldn't imagine herself in front of a university classroom lecturing on T.S. Eliot—or, rather, she could imagine the lecturing part. If she had to, she could lecture on T.S. Eliot right now. What she couldn't imagine was *who that person would be* standing up in front of the classroom and lecturing—certainly not any version of Gloria Cotter she'd ever met.

"You know, Gloria, about money—it makes things easy. There's nothing you couldn't do. You kind of turned your nose up at the University of Scranton, but it's a good school. I've talked to a lot of kids who've gone there, and— Well, it's a Catholic school, but they don't push religion. They've got a lot of Jesuits out there, and you know how intellectual the Jesuits are. And a degree's a degree. And the U. Penn and Penn State both have extensions in Scranton, did you know that?"

"Hey, what happened to *your* compromise? Why can't we get married and I go off to Columbia for a year at least, and then—well, let's see how everything goes after that?"

"I've been thinking about that, honey, and—well, if it was just up to me, then maybe we could do it, but it's—well, it's, you know, how it would look to everybody."

Oh, right, she thought. She'd almost forgotten about that horde of *everybody*: his parents, his grandparents, his sisters and their husbands, and everybody else who counted in Scranton. It wasn't fair, but whoever said life was fair? And if anybody could be relied upon to understand the importance of how things *would look*, it was Gloria. OK, so it really was an either-or decision. Well, if she married him, she could stop worrying about Lionel Trilling.

It was too hot in the sun, and she was just going around in her usual inconclusive circles and getting absolutely nowhere—but if blind, mindless Nature were so powerful as to have made her do the crazy, irrational things she'd done, then why fight it?

"OK, Rolland," she said, "maybe."

"Maybe what?"

"Maybe I'll marry you."

By late afternoon Gloria had come to regret her "maybe"; it had allowed Rolland to get the fine end of the wedge in, and, after that, he'd done nothing but hammer away at the wide part—well, maybe "hammer" was too strong a word; he was being, as always, a gentleman. They were wandering through the trails in Waverley Park. She was surprised that she didn't want to make out and, apparently, neither did he. They were strolling along in this (as she couldn't help calling it) *sylvan scene*, while he told her how great it would be if they were married.

Had he ever told her that his dad would buy them a house for a wedding present? It could be any kind of house Gloria wanted. If she liked new houses, they could build it from scratch, and she could work out the plans with the architect; if she liked old houses, they could buy a Queen Anne. She could furnish it any way she wanted; he was sure he'd like anything she liked. Did she want a pool? Well, then, they could certainly have one. Or anything else for that matter. How about a conservatory? Or better yet, a library? With all the books she had, they'd really need a library.

And they'd have to have several guest rooms, because he was sure she'd want to invite her friends. Morgan and James could come up for a weekend, or Susie and Don. Sure, Morgan could bring her baby; they could hire a nursemaid. Morgan could probably use a break, and, while they were on the subject, when the babies started coming along, they'd have to have a full-time nursemaid. And a housekeeper. No, *Mrs. Spicer* wouldn't ever have to do any more housework than she wanted to. Oh, and where would she like to go on their honeymoon? London? Paris? Rome? Maybe they could even take a couple months and see all of Europe. He'd always wanted to see Europe. And all of this was put in such a way—"*whenever* we get around to getting married," he said several times—that it would have been utterly churlish of her to feel as though he were trying to buy her.

By the time they got home, Gloria had a headache. Her mother stopped her on the way upstairs. "What's the matter, sweetie? Rolland said you weren't feeling well."

"I'm just tired, Mom. I just want to lie down a minute. Give him a beer, and he'll be happy as a clam."

"You didn't have a fight, did you?"

"Oh, no. Everything's fine— I told him maybe."

"Maybe what?"

"Maybe I'd marry him."

"Oh, honey, that's wonderful! When?"

"Mom, I said *maybe*."

Gloria drew her drapes, took off her sundress, and stretched out naked on her bed. It was absolutely bizarre, but the more Rolland was offering her in his sweet, gentlemanly way, the more she was filled with dread. How could she ever live up to *all that?* And, if you were offering *all that*, shouldn't you get somebody truly beautiful—somebody like Susie, for instance?—and not some dark, hairy, rat-faced, hopelessly neurotic, little intellectual snot. And maybe Gloria would meet a boy in grad school at Columbia who was both sexy and intellectual— That was all well and good, but what was she going to do with the boy she had at the moment, the one who was down by the pool drinking beer with her obviously delighted mother?

In order to stop thinking about whether or not to marry him, Gloria began to plan what she was going to wear out to dinner. She didn't know why—probably because she'd behaved like such a wanton little tramp the night before— but she wanted to look girlish and virginal, so she stripped off her red nail polish and gave herself a coat of clear. Then she climbed into the attic and slid things along the racks. Neither she nor her mother ever threw clothes away, and she found a sparkling white sailor dress from the summer after her junior year in high school and even the white baby-Jane shoes that went with it. It was amazing how fashions had changed; she remembered the shoes as charming and cute, but now they looked hopelessly dated and utterly infantile. But did she have to be a fashion plate all the time? Wasn't she allowed to be whimsical sometimes?

The dress had been loose on her when she'd been sweet sixteen, but now her breasts really filled it out, and it was actually quite fetching. She wasn't even remotely interested in making out, so she pulled on a no-nonsense, long-legged pantie girdle—which should, she thought, be more than enough to discourage anybody. She did a light makeup with wide wide eyes and wore no jewelry but her charm bracelet. As she passed her in the kitchen, her mother said, "What's the matter, honey, did you miss the school bus?"

"You just shut up, Mom," Gloria said, laughing.

"You didn't tell me about the University of Scranton."

Oh, screw the University of Scranton, Gloria thought. "Oh, didn't I?"

Her mother was giving her a narrow-eyed, inquisitive look. "Do you want a drink, sweetie?"

"No, thanks, Mom."

As Gloria and her mother approached the pool, Rolland—well-trained boy that he was—rose to his feet. "Don't get up, you silly thing," her mother said and handed him his beer. He was staring at Gloria, and, before he'd been able to do anything about it, his face had registered sheer bafflement. I don't look that outlandish, do I? Gloria thought. They all sat down, and, for the moment, there was no sound but the rhythmic splashing of Gloria's father doing his laps.

"Well," Gloria's mother said, "so how was Susie's wedding, by the way? You never told me."

"Just great," Rolland said, "terrific."

"Just lovely," Gloria said. "Her mother and her aunts made her wedding dress. By hand, can you believe that? It took them months, but wow, you should have seen her! She was just heart-stopping."

"What kind of a dress?"

"Just an old-fashioned, romantic wedding dress. Veil, crown, the whole works—"

"Would you want something like that?"

"Oh, Mom," Gloria said, giving Rolland a dirty look, "it isn't definite. I told you that. We're just talking."

Gloria's father climbed out of the pool and threw himself down on a lawn chair. "You look nice tonight, princess," he said.

She was glad *he* thought so. "Thanks, Dad." So now she was even farther out of the doghouse, but why? Did he want her to get married too?

Walking out to the car, Rolland said, "Gee, I feel like I'm robbing the cradle."

"Do you want me to change? There's probably time if I do it right now."

It took him a fraction of a second too long to answer: "Oh, no, you're fine, honey."

During the ride down to the club, he tried to hold her hand, but she pulled it away. She slid all the way to the other side of the seat and stared out the window. She felt sour and ill done by—although she didn't have anybody to blame but herself. What had she been thinking to wear this dumb outfit? It didn't make her look cute or fey or whatever she'd been stupidly thinking. These silly, kiddy shoes with a skirt this long, what a joke! So much for the famous Gloria Merriman Cotter and her unfailingly excellent taste. The darn girdle was already driving her nuts, but she was stuck in it for the rest of the night.

As soon as they stepped inside, the men, of course, headed for the bar. "Do you want anything, honey?" Rolland said.

"Oh, I don't know. A Coke maybe. Or a Seven-up— Oh, no, I don't really want anything."

"You sure?"

"I don't know, honey. No, I guess not."

Gloria followed her mother out onto the terrace. "I love this time of night," her mother said, "when it finally starts to cool off."

"Yes, it's nice," Gloria said, not finding it the least bit nice.

"So really, sweetie—what's with the schoolgirl outfit?"

"Oh, I don't know, Mom. I just felt like it. Don't you ever do that—just put on something to be whimsical?"

"After forty, you don't have a lot of room for whimsy."

Her mother lit a cigarette. "Are you—? Is your maybe—? Is it a maybe on the no side or a maybe on the yes side?"

"Oh, I don't know, Mom. I guess it's a maybe on the yes side."

"Well, if it is, then we'd better start talking about it."

"I suppose so."

"Gloria, do you have any idea how much time and energy goes into planning a wedding?"

"Probably not. *Vogue* did a big thing on weddings this month. Did you see it?"

"It kind of went right by me. Today's the first time I've heard you say a word about a wedding."

"It's all still pretty iffy, but— You're right; it doesn't hurt to talk about it. Anyhow, there was this dress in *Vogue* that was just super. Circles and circles of organdy and lace, you know, with a million crinolines—a big *big* skirt. It would move just beautifully."

"Oh, Gloria," her mother said, laughing, "you've always been so theatrical."

Rolland and her father appeared with drinks. Rolland had brought her a Coke. "I *said* I didn't want anything," she snapped at him. "Don't you ever *listen?*"

He made a gesture with his head, and she followed him to the other side of the terrace. "What the hell's the matter with you?" he hissed at her.

"Oh, I don't know, honey. I've still got that darned headache."

"Look, Glo—are you mad at me?"

"Oh, no, I'm not mad at you, sweetie. Why would I be mad at you?"

In the mood she was in—not to mention her stupid outfit—Gloria didn't feel like doing the mandatory circuit of the club, but she couldn't really avoid saying hi to Binkie. "Hey, I remember that dress," Binkie said, grinning. "I remember the shoes too— Don't you just love her, Rolland? She's got such a good sense of humor."

Oh, is that what it is? Gloria thought.

It was buffet tonight, and, as she watched Rolland heaping up his plate, Gloria felt sick. How could anybody eat anything hot on a night like this? All country clubs were pretty much the same—the Raysburg Country Club, the Briarville Country Club, the Scranton Country Club, the Whatever-it-was-called Country Club out on Long Island where her stupid cousins went—some were better and some were worse, but they all had a swimming pool and a games room and tennis courts and a golf course; when they had dances, they all had bands that played the same old swing tunes from the war; they all had spotlessly clean ladies' rooms with huge mirrors and fancy soaps and bottles of hand lotion and little boxes of Kleenex, and they all had *the same darned food*, and no, she did not want a nice slice of roast beef or—how could Rolland possibly eat that enormous mound of them?—scalloped potatoes. Her father was saying, "If I were you, I'd just put the whole works in bonds and blue chips and forget it for twenty years," and Rolland was grinning at her father like a simpleton, and Gloria had to eat something, didn't she? OK, green salad and a bit of potato salad. Then, because they were the only thing that appealed to her at all, she took six deviled eggs. I've got years of this ahead of me, she thought. Simply years and years and years.

When they were seated at their table, her mother said, "You know, honey, I was just thinking. There's not just the wedding, there's your trousseau. Even if I started tomorrow, we couldn't possibly do it before October."

"Mom, I said *maybe*."

"I understand that, but if you're thinking about it, we've got to talk about it."

Gloria heard her father say "trust fund," and her ears perked up. Her grandfather Merriman had left her some money; no one had ever told her how much, and she'd never asked, and she'd never thought about it because she wouldn't get a penny until she was thirty-five, but here they were talking about it—about *her dowry* just as though she were a girl in a Jane Austen novel. That's really what Rolland needs, she thought, more money.

"June weddings are so blah," her mother was saying, "not to mention the heat. But October's the only time this damned place actually looks pretty good. Who would you have for bridesmaids?"

"Binkie, of course. And then I'd have to have Judy Staub or her nose would be out of joint—and Susie and Morgan—"

"You can't have them. They're married."

"Well, I have to have them *somehow*—"

"Bridesmaids can't be married. That's why they're called brides*maids*—"

"I know. I know. But—"

"Pick one of them for your matron of honor."

"I can't pick one over the other. Can't you ever have two matrons?"

"Absolutely not."

"Oh, Mom, it's just—"

"If you don't believe me, ask *Mother*. She's a walking etiquette book."

"Oh, I believe you. So Susie then. She's my best friend. But Morgan was my big sister, and she had me as a bridesmaid for her wedding, and she hadn't even seen all that much of me, you know, after she graduated. Can't we—"

"Oh, Morgan will understand! She's had a baby, hasn't she?"

"What's that got to do with anything?"

"When you've had a baby, you've got more important things on your mind than being left out of somebody's damned wedding party."

After dinner, Gloria and her mother excused themselves to go to the ladies' room. As they stood side by side in front of the mirror, Gloria said, "I was just thinking about the bridesmaids—you know, if we actually did it. I'm not keen on the rainbow effect. I'd want them to be absolutely identical—in pink, maybe. Everybody can wear pink—"

"Come on, hon, pink's kind of—"

"Or even powder blue or lilac."

Their makeup refurbished, they wandered back through the dining room. Neither had mentioned going outside, but, just as though they'd planned it, they walked right past the table where the men were sitting and continued out onto the terrace. "Anything but yellow," Gloria was saying. "My dress would have a big big, *huge* bell skirt, and so the bridesmaids would echo the bell shape, only shorter—princess length. Satin heels dyed to match and pale pastel gloves. And then the matrons—"

"Matron."

"Oh, all right, *matron*—in a pastel suit—"

"You really want to mix a suit in with all that froth?"

"Why not?"

"Look, there'll be lots of women my age in suits. For your wedding party you should, you know—"

"OK, OK, you're right. Keep the same theme throughout. But then the matron would have to be a contrasting color— If it's Susie, then maybe the bridesmaids should be powder blue so Susie could be pink. Susie's *fantastic* in pink. She'd look just like a porcelain figurine—"

"You don't want her to upstage the bride."

"Oh, she won't do that, believe me. If it's planned right, she'd be *contrasting* so she'd really set me off—"

"And you'd want flower girls, of course."

"Oh, sure. Two of them. And a page—"

"Oh, Gloria! You really want a *show*, don't you?"

They were walking through the parking lot, halfway to the car, when Gloria said to Rolland, "Oh, shoot! I've left my purse back on the table. Will you get it for me, please, honey?"

He gave her such a sharp, annoyed look that she wouldn't have been at all surprised if he'd said, "Get it yourself, you spoiled little brat," but, without a word, he turned and walked back inside. Then, during the ride up the hill, he tried to give her a kiss, just an affectionate peck on the cheek, but she was feeling so irritable—just on the edge of blowing her top over nothing at all—she pushed him away. "*Don't*, sweetie. I'm too hot."

At home, Gloria left Rolland in the living room—he and her father seemed to be getting along great—and followed her mother into the kitchen. "Oh, Mom, you think *I* want a show, you should have seen Morgan's wedding. She's an Episcopalian, and the service was really elaborate. She had us in very simple dresses—baby pink, which is why I know it would work—although I'd like *my* pink pale pale *pale*— But you should have seen us: eyelet lace, very demure, and then Morgan was very traditional—just a dazzling, radiant white confection—"

"Did *she* have a page?"

"No. But that doesn't mean that *I* can't have a page."

"So what would you put on this wretched little boy?"

"Just what you'd expect, a little white satin suit."

"My God, Gloria, you're the last of the true romantics. These days, there's not a boy in the universe who'd put up with that—and you'd want it at the Edgewood?"

"Well, of course I would. That's our church."

"OK, but it only seats—what? A hundred and fifty? Two hundred at the most, and they'd be crammed in like olives."

"My gosh, Mom, how many people—?"

"Look, honey, you either do a very small ceremony—just immediate family—or you invite simply everybody. If you try to do anything in the middle, somebody's bound to be miffed. And so there's our friends here, and, you know, your father's connections, and then there's my family. My God, there's relatives I haven't thought of in years. I'll have to talk to Mother and get a complete list, and— Even if they don't all come, boy, will you ever get the presents! But we'll have to decide on your china and silver patterns fairly soon— And then there's all your sorority friends and their boyfriends. Before you know it, you're over three hundred."

"Mom? We're still just *talking*, right? This is all *hypothetical*, right?"

"Oh, of course, Gloria. But you can't blame me for— Oh, sweetie, I just want everything to be perfect for you!"

It was after midnight, but Gloria knew she didn't have a prayer of getting to sleep. Gee, she thought, this is getting to be familiar— "Just like your Britomart summer," the secret watcher told her, but Gloria didn't want it to be just like her Britomart summer. She sat at her bedroom window and stared down at the quiet swimming pool. I guess I'm going to marry him, she thought. Everybody wants me to.

What Professor Bolton had told her that day in his office was turning out to be true, so she just might as well grow up and face the facts: there really wasn't anything she could be except somebody's well-kept wife. She started making a list of wedding guests but gave up after she'd filled four pages with nothing but her high school friends and her sorority sisters. Her mother was right; it was going to be way too big for the Edgewood—but she was tired of thinking about it. What she needed was distraction.

She picked up and rejected in rapid succession *The Collected Poems of John Donne, To Catch a Thief* borrowed last week from her parents' bedroom, the *Vogue* with the wedding spread in it, Eliot's *Sacred Wood* dense with her own marginal notes, and the most recent *Saturday Evening Post*. Then she tried *The Pisan Cantos* again. This time she simply jumped right in, skipped the foreign languages she didn't know, caught what she could of the meaning as it went by, and let Pound's music wash over her—and this time something clicked. After an hour, she realized that it was the first time she'd read *The Pisan Cantos* not as an elaborate puzzle but as poetry.

She read Pound until she was yawning and her eyes were burning. It was nearly five. She switched off her light and stretched out under her sheet. Since she'd been a child, she'd been able to save herself by reading; at least she still had *that* and always would no matter what happened. She could hear the birds waking up—and that too was familiar. Just as she was falling asleep, she thought, I'll have to call Susie and tell her I'm getting married.

When Gloria woke, she knew she'd been dreaming, but the dream had largely vanished; all she could remember was standing in front of the mirror on her vanity table while she'd listened to her mother and Rolland downstairs in the kitchen, talking in low voices. She hadn't been able to make out what they were saying, but she'd known that they were talking about her—and now, listening, she *did* hear her mother and Rolland downstairs in the kitchen, talking in low voices, and she did know that they were talking about her. Gee, she thought, maybe it wasn't a dream at all— Then she remembered something about her hair falling out—the hair *on her head*—and she thought, hey, that's an interesting variant; usually it's on my legs and growing madly out of me—and another part was coming back, something about having to wear a wig. She could see it: a blonde, curly, Goldilocks wig, how bizarre!— And then there was something else about seeing a doctor. He'd been giving her a stern lecture about something or other, and he'd been wearing a slide rule in a case attached to his belt like the crude, boring engineering students at Briarville. She hadn't liked the doctor—there'd been something nasty and stupid about him—but she'd liked the nurse, could see her clearly now, a cute blonde who reminded her of Susie—maybe it was Susie—in a dazzling white uniform so starched it crackled when she moved.

Downstairs her mother laughed; it was one of her mother's richly resonant laughs, audible for a mile, that said, "oh, aren't we having fun!" and Gloria felt her skin prickle. For a minute or two she'd forgotten completely about her mother and Rolland. Maybe he was telling her about the University of Scranton. Then she thought: *I can't marry him.*

Wait a minute, when had she decided that? But it wasn't something she'd decided; it was just there, as though workmen had come in the night and deposited it in her mind like some massive, formidable object—a grand piano, or a chaise longue. Oh, dear, she thought. What was going on? She wanted the secret watcher to answer her, but the secret watcher must have gone on vacation. Gloria crept up to that massive object—that utter certainty—and examined it gingerly. She began to cry.

Oh, it was sad. She hated hurting people, but she was going to have to hurt him—and she did love him. Now that she knew she couldn't marry him, she knew just how much she did love him—although, as it was turning out, not quite enough—but oh, was she ever going to miss him!

Yes, it really was sad, and there wasn't any way she could make it less sad—and it wasn't the least bit fair. No, he didn't deserve it, but she couldn't marry him in October, and she couldn't marry him in four years, and she couldn't marry him *ever*. Of course he'd want to know why, and she'd have to pretend she'd been up all night wrestling with it like Jacob with the angel. That's right, that's what she'd say; that was the least she could do for him, and she'd have to come up with reasons—lots of them, and big, convincing, logical reasons—because now she had to tell him.

12

"The paper said the President was playing good golf—" Ted let his sentence hang, hoping the old bastard would pick up the hint and run with it.

"Oh, hell, yes," Carl said, "he was playing just dandy golf. Good feelings all around that day, I assure you. He likes us 'cause we're little, ha, ha, ha."

Ted and Carl were driving to Pittsburgh. Ted was doing the driving and trying not to feel like the chauffeur, and they were on their way to another of those top secret meetings Carl enjoyed and Ted didn't. It went without saying that not a word about those meetings should ever leak out, but Carl took things to extremes—he acted like he was in a spy movie, for Christ's sake—and since he'd come back from his golf game with Ike, the old bastard had been playing it even closer to his chest than usual. Tonight's meeting must surely have something to do with Carl's chat with the President, but Ted couldn't even be certain of that because Carl hadn't told him, and he resented being kept in the dark—for all the good it did him. "So you get along with Ike OK?" he asked.

"Oh, yeah. I've met him before, you know. We always get along. I told him some funny stories about the bad old days—got him laughing. Told him about my grandad out in the streets of Raysburg shooting it out man to man with his employees. Yeah, that's how you handled labor disputes in those days—with goddamn pistols! He liked that story. 'Well, sir,' I told him, 'I'm just an old-fashioned steel meister, and things nowadays are just too damn complicated. In the old days all you worried about was melting metal and making a buck,' ha, ha, ha."

Ted laughed too, and he wondered what the President had *really* made of Carl W. Eberhardt. Well, Carl was a cagey guy—Ted had to give him that—and tonight he'd get to see the old bastard in action again. If past performances were any indication, Carl would direct him to some quiet, not quite first-rate hotel, not quite in the center of Pittsburgh. Everything would have been arranged, and they'd sneak in a side door. They'd have an executive suite— maybe a whole floor—and the top brass from U.S. Steel and Bethlehem Steel and the other big steel companies in the east would show up, but nobody would act like it was a business meeting. Whiskey and Scotch would be drunk, and cigars would be smoked; then, after a few good laughs had gone around, the talk would get serious, and it would go on till midnight or one in the morning. After it was over, the meeting, by God, had never happened—because if the press ever got wind of the fact that these boys were meeting in secret, there'd be all hell to pay. Ted kept his mouth shut at these meetings, and his ears open; it was the only thing to do, really, and it pissed him off that he probably came across as Carl's yes-man.

"Ike will *never* interfere with the industry," Carl said. "He'll talk. He'll try and persuade. He'll try and get sweet reason involved. But he'll never just step in like that son-of-a-bitch Truman. He made that real clear to me— So as long as we've got him in the White House, we're in pretty good shape—but fifty-nine's going to be one hell of a year."

That was the year the industry was going to have to negotiate a new contract with the USW, but Ted wouldn't have to do anything but sit on his ass and watch; U.S. Steel would do the negotiating for the whole industry, the same as always— but, on second thought, maybe Ted could play a part in it. Carl would be out of the picture by then, and Ted might get a chance to say a few well-chosen words to the right people. "Is he thinking about fifty-nine already?" he said.

"Well, you better believe he is. He's going to do his best to convince the big boys that the days of pass-through pricing are over, and he's going to have some straight talk for the union too. But it could be a rough year, so you be careful—and then after that—well, Ted, you're a churchgoing man, aren't you?"

The question, Ted knew, was entirely rhetorical; the Cotters attended the same church the Eberhardts did, but nonetheless he said, "You bet."

"Well, every Sunday you better be praying for a Republican landslide in sixty, ha, ha, ha!"

OK—so was *that* what Carl was going to tell the big boys? Be careful in fifty-nine and pray in sixty? Oh, hell, no; there had to be more to it than that, but Ted supposed he was going to have to wait to hear it because Carl was fiddling around with the radio. "The crap that's on the air these days," Carl said, "if you ask me, it isn't even music," and he found a distant, staticky station playing an old swing tune, lit himself a smoke, and settled back in the seat.

The only good thing about this damn meeting, Ted thought, was getting out of the house. Since Gloria had sent that Spicer kid packing back to Scranton, being in the same house with his wife and daughter was about as relaxing as being stuffed into a feed bag with two cats. From living with Laney for all these years, Ted had learned that the female mind works in dark and mysterious ways, but the dark mysteries of his wife's mind had gradually become—well, he wouldn't have said *clear*, but, at any rate, he'd become used to her, and if she was irrational, it was an irrationality he'd seen before, and these days she hardly ever took him completely by surprise. Gloria was another matter. Except for right after he'd come back from the war, Gloria had never been any trouble at all, and he'd never worried about her, and that had been a mistake. For one thing, they never should have sent her to boarding school, and for another thing—but he didn't know what that other thing was. Up until a week ago he would have said he had a perfect daughter.

Laney had wormed it out of Gloria that she'd been out with some guy the night she'd missed dinner with the Connelys, so Billy's crazy story had turned out to be true—anyway, the main part of it must have been true—and Ted should have remembered that Billy was Irish and always had to make a story better, so, if Ted subtracted the colorful details Billy had obviously made up, what he was left with was that Gloria had been seeing somebody and keeping it a secret, and never in a million years would he have thought she'd do that. Gloria had told Laney she'd just met the guy casually and had no intention of ever seeing him again, and Laney believed her, but that still left the fact that Gloria had *lied* about it, and then that had all got pushed aside because, with no warning at all, there was the Spicer kid from Scranton and Gloria was talking about marrying him, and then, just as fast, he's gone again, and she's not going to marry him, and Laney's fit to be tied, and Gloria's in her room crying her eyes out.

Gloria and Laney were not speaking. It was amazing how two women not speaking could make so damn much noise. But Laney was certainly speaking to Ted, and he had to listen to her every night: "I'm going to kill her. I swear to God, Teddy, one of these days I'm simply going to kill her. He was perfect for her, just perfect. How could she be so *goddamn dumb!*" Ted, meanwhile, had not much wanted Gloria to marry that Spicer kid, and he'd been delighted when she'd decided not to, but it was an opinion he certainly could not express to his wife—and it never would have occurred to either Laney or Gloria to ask his opinion in the first place. As usual, whatever the girls decided, it was none of his business, and the only thing they needed him for was to pay for it.

"You know," Carl said, interrupting Ted's train of thought, "when I brought you in, there was some that was highly pissed off. 'He's not from the Valley,' they said, 'and even worse than that, he's one of these college-educated boys that don't know their ass from a tea kettle. Hell, he's never even set foot in a steel mill.' But there was something I could see even if they couldn't—and that was the handwriting on the wall. Shit, left up to them, we'd still be making cut nails, ha, ha, ha."

Ted laughed right along with him, but he was going crazy trying to figure out what was on Carl's mind. "I appreciate your confidence in me," he said.

"Oh, I know that. I certainly do— And by the way, just what were you thinking of doing down at Old Reliable? Last I heard, you were thinking of putting Al Connely in there."

So that's it, Ted thought. He chose his words carefully. "You know, Carl, I thought it was pretty simple, but I had Charlie Edmonds look into it, and— Well, you know how thorough he is? Well, it turned out to be nowhere near as simple as I thought. I don't suppose you had a chance to look at Charlie's report, did you? I sent it over to you yesterday."

"Hell, you know how I hate to read those damn things. Can't you just give me the gist of it?"

"Well, I could, but I'd prefer not to. If you don't mind. I'd really appreciate it if you'd have a look at that report. As a kind of—well, you know, as a favor to me, Carl—if you wouldn't mind."

"When you put it that way, Ted, of course, I wouldn't mind. I'll take a good, hard look at it," and, with that, Carl lit another cigarette, turned and stared out the window. He's really pissed off, Ted thought. To hell with him.

When Ted had been hired in 1950, his first impression of the overall operations of the Raysburg Steel Corporation—by then the ninth-largest producer of steel in the United States—was of a profound, almost willful, irrationality, and the most willfully backward and irrational piece of the whole crazy pattern was Old Reliable. No one could remember when the Indian Works had been nicknamed Old Reliable, but it had probably been during the Civil War when the mill had been humming along at top speed filling government contracts, and no one could remember exactly when the Indian Works had been established—sometime in the 1830s—but it had been the first iron mill owned by Carl's great-grandfather, the legendary founder of the whole shooting match, that broad-shouldered gnome in a tailcoat, Karl Eberhardt, whose furious, accusing eyes stared out of a dirty, old painting that hung in the main board room in the Eberhardt Building. Under the trademark of an Indian in a blanket and full headdress, Karl had built his first mill, set up his puddling furnaces, and, using pig iron shipped down the river from Pittsburgh, had gone into the cut nail and sheet iron business. Except for brief periods of labor unrest, Karl's Indian Works had been in continuous operation ever since.

During his first year on the job, Ted made it a point to visit, if even for only an hour or two, every mill operated by Raysburg Steel, but he spent the better part of a week at Old Reliable. Ted had learned at Penn that it didn't matter exactly what a business was doing—whether baking doughnuts or manufacturing steel—because *all* businesses could be managed efficiently by the rigorous methods of control accounting, and nothing he'd learned after he'd graduated had taught him anything different—until he'd come up against the Old Reliable Indian Works.

The godforsaken place emitted such a constant barrage of noise along the entire spectrum of audible sound—from profound quakelike growlings and thumpings through skull-splitting hammering and throaty roarings to tiny ear-piercing metallic shrieks—that you had to yell yourself hoarse to have even the most rudimentary of conversations. The lighting was appalling: the tiny windows had obviously not been cleaned in the last hundred years, and the only daylight that penetrated to the interior came through those that had been smashed out; dim yellow bulbs hung around on fraying black cords that would have failed a sane industrial code from the twenties. Walking anywhere was like traversing a minefield—the floor was strewn with nuts, bolts, coils of wire, scrap metal, God knows what all—and the grime-smeared men rushed around frantically, engaged in a fierce activity that appeared undirected, even random, as though somebody had told them, "OK, boys, I don't care what you do just so long as you do it in a hurry"—except when they weren't doing anything at all, which seemed to be quite often. Then they stood around in sullen clusters, smoked cigarettes or chewed tobacco and spat the juice on the floor, hunkered down and read paperback novels, or stretched out in dark corners and slept.

The general manager, old "Nip" Norton, wore suspenders and chain-smoked two-for-a-nickel Raysburg stogies; the first thing he did when Ted appeared was to offer him—with not a sign that he considered the offer even slightly improper—a shot of rye whiskey in a used paper cup. The calendar hanging over Nip's desk was open to July 1938, and Ted had the horrible suspicion that Nip might not have thought seriously about steel production since then. Ted requested a flow chart, and Nip looked at him with sad, watery eyes. "I'm not sure I follow you, Mr. Cotter."

"OK," Ted said patiently, "I just want a big, general picture of what goes on in here."

"Well, sir, I'm not real sure I can give you that."

"Oh? Why is that?"

"Well, you see, Mr. Cotter, you'd have to be working here a while to get that big, general picture you want. For one thing, every heat of steel's different, and for another thing—well, with the equipment breaking down all the time, lots of things are different, you know, day to day. We don't do the same thing the same way all the time, you know what I mean?"

No, Ted didn't know what he meant. Doing the same thing the same way all the time was the absolute rock-bottom minimal requirement for efficient, rational industrial production—and so, of course, were accurate figures, which Nip couldn't seem to supply either.

"Why," Ted asked, "do the men spend so much of their time not doing anything?"

"Well, either something's broken down or something hasn't caught up to them yet. You really can't expect them to do anything when there's nothing to do, can you?"

Safety standards at Old Reliable were not merely low, they were nonexistent; the men frequently lost fingers and toes and even whole limbs to various pieces of archaic equipment that should have been on display in an industrial museum, and the union currently had on file twenty-seven grievances related to on-the-job injuries. Merely walking around and looking, Ted was splashed with oil, singed by a furnace, bumped by a fork lift, and nearly decapitated by a crane that leapt at him suddenly out of the darkness; every day after he left, his ears rang for an hour. Pig iron from the Staubsville furnaces (well, usually from Staubsville) entered the mill on railway cars, and finished steel left on railway cars (except on those odd occasions when it left on trucks): that much was certain; what happened inside the mill remained mysterious. Ted wouldn't have been surprised to find, in some dim corner, men frantically rolling out sheet iron for Farragut's Navy, and he remembered the quiet, clean, gracefully appointed and thoroughly modern offices of the Xenon Corporation and the beautiful charts and graphs and columns of numbers that he loved and understood, and he wished to God he'd never left there.

Ted had never seen so much management in one place as they had at Old Reliable. Nip Norton was the general superintendent; under him was an assistant general superintendent and the division superintendents; under them were department superintendents, assistant department superintendents, and general foremen. At the bottom of the heap were turn foremen who had yet more guys working for them — usually at minimum wage — whose job seemed to be writing down on the proper forms what some guys in the union had already written down on random scraps of paper. "Why don't you eliminate that job?" Ted asked, "and just take the figures from the union guys?"

"Can't do that," a turn foreman told him, "keeping records is a management responsibility."

Ted talked to superintendents and foremen at various levels, and they all said the same thing. Everything wrong with Old Reliable was the union's fault. The Indian Works had been a sweet little operation back in the good old days, but since the union had got so much power, things had just gone nuts. Every job was clearly and narrowly defined, and no union man could cross job boundaries, so of course you had guys standing around doing nothing all over the place — and Christ, if we didn't keep our eyes on them every damn minute, they wouldn't even do the bare minimum.

Ted talked to the shop stewards who told him that everything wrong with Old Reliable was management's fault. How the hell could you expect any efficiency when everything's in the wrong goddamn place? Just count the number of times shit gets hauled back and forth across the mill before it gets finished — whose fault is that? And you want to see feather-bedding, just look at management. Those guys just come in here, sit on their asses, draw their pay, and go home. And while we're at it, Mr. Cotter, if the company gave a rat's ass about the men, they'd get some decent lighting, clean the place up, and put in a nice canteen the way they got up in the Staubsville Mill.

Ted found a huge machine. It was roughly the size of Nip Norton's office. It had gears, levers, and wheels, dials, switches, and an engine. It was covered with a thick layer of grime and was badly rusted. Ted couldn't find anyone at Old Reliable who knew what it was. "Damn thing was here when I came to work right after the first war," Nip said. "Nobody knew what it was even back then."

"Why the hell don't you get it out of here?" Ted said. "The cranes have to maneuver around it."

"Yeah, that's true — Well, you see, Mr. Cotter, when I made general superintendent back in forty-two, I sent a memo upstairs asking permission to dismantle that goddamn thing and haul it out. Waited six months, and then I got my answer. Better keep it, they said. You never know when it might come in handy." Good Christ, Ted thought, this place is worse than the navy.

It was considered unlucky for a woman to enter a steel mill, but the men made up for the lack of flesh-and-blood femininity by plastering every available surface with pictures of women; no one ever took a picture down, so underneath the Marilyn Monroes and men's magazine foldouts were Betty Grables and old calendar girls, and underneath those were even older pictures, yellowed and flaking, and Ted found Bond Drive girls from 1918, and a corset advertisement from God knows when, and even the bleached-out, barely visible image of Lily Langtry—and when he'd spent nearly an hour one afternoon doing nothing but looking at the pinups, he knew it was time for him to get the hell out of there.

Ted had accumulated a number of serious questions to ask Carl Eberhardt, not the least of which was how a man seventy-two years old could be expected to manage a steel mill. "Oh, well, old Nip's been there over forty years," Carl said. "If he doesn't know what's going on at Old Reliable, nobody does."

That's right, Ted thought, nobody does.

Raysburg Steel owned mills in West Virginia, Pennsylvania, and Ohio, and some of them were among the most up-to-date and efficient in America. Ted pointed out to Carl that Old Reliable accounted for less than eight percent of the total production of the Raysburg Steel Corporation. "We've either got to modernize it or shut it down," he said.

"Oh, well, Ted, that's been said lots of times before. Yeah, I expect we could round it out a bit, but as to throwing a ton of money in there—you know yourself we haven't got two cents to spare what with that goddamn socialist son-of-a-bitch in the White House. And as to shutting her down, well, the board would never approve of that. Hell, I wouldn't either. It was my great-granddad's first mill, you know. Might as well talk about tearing down the Statue of Liberty, ha, ha, ha."

Just after Christmas that year, who should turn up but William Parnell Dougherty. Billy was just passing through town on Route 40, he said (Ted couldn't remember now if he'd claimed to be going east or west), and he figured he'd stop in and just say hi—which was a pretty good stunt considering that the only way Billy could have located Ted would have been to call his parents back in Briarville—but Ted rolled out the red carpet nonetheless. "Be nice," he told Laney, "I owe that guy a lot."

Billy was driving an old flatbed pickup truck with everything he owned tied to the back—it looked like something out of an Okie caravan—and, since Ted had seen him last, he'd acquired a family: a pretty, little, feather-brained wife, barely out of her teens, with a whiny, snot-faced, two-year-old boy clinging to her leg. The poor, dumb girl was a good eight months gone with the next one, carrying that baby so big and low that Billy had to fasten the straps on her shoes for her. Just as Ted had known he was going to, Billy asked for a loan. Ted had never in his life loaned anybody money, and he wasn't about to make an exception for his old exec, but he looked at that big, ugly mug grinning at him and thought: he did a damn good job for me in the war. Yeah, he got things done when nobody else even knew where to start. "You still like to work?" he said. He offered Billy a salary so big his jaw dropped.

"What I want from you is real simple," Ted told him. "Try to get things more efficient. Send me some numbers I can believe in and show to the board. Keep production steady. But here's the most important thing: I never want to think about Old Reliable again, and the day I have to think about it, you're out of a job."

"Aye, aye, sir," Billy had said, springing to his feet with a sharp salute, and, for the past six years, Ted had not thought about Old Reliable. But he was thinking about it now. The mistake he'd made had not been hiring Billy; it had been bringing Billy into the country club where Carl Eberhardt had to see him.

One of the most valuable things about being in the war was that it really made you appreciate America; it wasn't something Ted had thought about while the war had been going on, but he'd sure thought about it since. Why, he'd had every kind of guy under his command: Jews, Italians, Portuguese, even a couple red Indians from North Dakota—and Negroes, hillbillies, Southern crackers, Polacks, Irish, Mexicans, you name it—yeah, just about everybody you could imagine, and they'd all been fine men and good Americans every last son-of-a-gun of them, and where else but in America could a poor boy from Briarville, Pennsylvania, whose old man hadn't been anything more than a glorified janitor, end up as a senior vice-president of a steel corporation? Oh, he knew that most of the time the notion of equality was honored in the breach more than in the practice, but at least there was that ideal to live up to, and if a guy wanted to make something of himself, where else would he stand any better chance than in America? And nothing pissed off Ted more than some son-of-a-bitch who thought that because he'd been born with a silver spoon in his mouth, he was better than somebody else, so when Billy had said, "Hey, skipper, do you suppose I could get into that goddamn country club?" Ted had thought, well, why the hell not?

Billy had never seen as much money in his life as he was making in one month at Raysburg Steel, and he'd bought himself a nice little house in Meadowland, and back in those days, he'd had his drinking under control, and he'd do pretty much anything Ted told him. When he'd just had a shave and was wearing the gray flannel suit Ted had picked out for him, Billy didn't look half bad, and Dottie had cleaned up beautifully. With her hair and nails done and a nice dress on her—Laney had taken her shopping—Dottie really was something to see, and, best of all, the little lamebrain knew when to keep her mouth shut. So, for the first few years, things had been just dandy, but Billy was one of these guys who seemed to come with his own disaster built right in. He hadn't been able to stay away from the track and all-night poker games and the chip-pies in South Raysburg, and Dottie hadn't liked that so she'd started running around on him, and he'd smacked her a few times, and one thing had led to another, and so here he was divorced and drinking like a fish and catting around town in that goddamn impractical Porsche he'd bought out of spite. But—and here was where things got tricky for Ted—it didn't seem to affect his work any.

On Wednesday Ted had got the final report from Charlie Edmonds, and he'd read it. He'd called Charlie into his office. "Look," he'd said, "this isn't what I asked you for. You're just telling me things I already know. Yeah, the place is a nightmare. It always has been. But production's been up a little bit every year since Dougherty's been in there, and so what? How the hell are things over there anyway?"

Charlie hemmed and hawed for a while until Ted told him, "Hey, I didn't call you in here to be a yes-man. Don't tell me what you think I want to hear, just tell me the truth as you see it."

He saw Charlie thinking about it, and he saw Charlie decide to stick his neck out. "Well, it is the craziest damn excuse for a steel mill I ever saw, but when it comes to making it work, Dougherty's close to a genius. He knows how to patch things up, make do, jerry-rig it, keep it going. He knows how to *improvise*. You'll never find him in his office. He's always out on the floor somewhere making sure things get done, and he's well liked. The rest of the management personnel, the guys on the floor, even the damn shop stewards like him. Somewhere else—say at the Staubsville operation, where everything's up to date and clicking right along—he might fall flat. But at Old Reliable, I'd say he's the right man in the right place.

"OK, so if you pull Dougherty out of there and put Al Connely in— Oh, I know Connely's a good man, and he's ambitious, but he just doesn't have a clue just how plain *nuts* Old Reliable is, and he's had no experience to prepare him for anything like that— Well, the first thing that happens with Connely is your production figures are going to drop right off, and he's going to have perfectly good reasons why. Then he's going to start shutting down one thing or another, and he's going to say, 'Come on, Ted, do you want to see some-body *killed?*' and you won't be able to argue with that. And then you're going to start getting four or five memos a day asking for things, and eventually— because he's a good man—he'll write you a report, and it's going to be such a hell of a good report, you'll have to take it to the board, and the board will say, 'Look, we just haven't got that kind of money,' and things will limp along for a while, and then in, oh, about two or three years, we'll be shutting Old Reli-able down. And maybe it should be shut down, but in the meantime, it's still making steel, and it's still making us money.

"OK, so you asked me, Ted—and if I were sitting in your chair, I wouldn't be thinking of canning Dougherty, I'd be thinking of giving him a bonus."

"That's pretty damn straight, Charlie. Thanks. But let me ask you one more thing. Does he ever drink on the job?"

"Well, of course he drinks on the job. He's an alcoholic, and everybody knows that. If he didn't drink on the job, he couldn't *do* the job. But nobody's ever seen him stinking drunk on the job, and he works ten, sometimes twelve hours a day, and he's in there lots of Saturdays and Sundays, and he hasn't missed a day's work in over two years. If we can find some more alcoholics like that, maybe we ought to hire them."

So Ted had told Charlie to write up that report again, to leave out the drinking part but to put in everything else and to back it all up with facts and figures. The new report had been just what Ted had wanted, and he'd sent it over to Carl Eberhardt's office, because, damn it, he was going to buck Carl on this one. He'd never bucked Carl on anything since the day he'd been hired, but he was going to buck him on this one, because, by God, it was a matter of principle. If Carl was tired of seeing Billy around, he could damn well have his club membership revoked—it'd be easy enough to do—but if Ted canned Billy, then who the hell was going to run Old Reliable? And if Carl was ever going to retire, Ted was going to have to make these decisions, so why shouldn't he start now?

And speaking of decisions, they were just coming into Pittsburgh, and Ted still didn't know what the damn meeting was about. "So, Carl," he said carefully, "what's on the old agenda tonight?"

"Gee, Ted, I thought you'd never ask."

Ted looked over and saw that Carl was giving him his biggest shit-eating grin. Then Carl started to laugh just as though he was telling the funniest joke in the world. "The Kefauver Committee," he said.

"Shit! No. You're kidding."

"Nope."

"When? Very soon?"

"Next month."

"Oh, shit."

"Yep, we're all of us going to be there in Washington testifying. And you know what those New Deal pinko bastards are going to want to know? They're going to want to know why we're all charging the same damn price for a ton of steel," and, laughing like an idiot, Carl reached over and slapped Ted on the knee. "Yeah, that's just great, isn't it? Yeah, Ted, like they say: only in America. So what's on the agenda tonight? Well, I'll tell you. We just want to be sure that when we're in Washington, we're all of us going to be singing the same damn song."

• • •

The night was unbearably hot and close, but Gloria was stuck in her bedroom because her mother was sitting down by the pool with a drink in her hand and showed no signs of moving. The big midsummer dance had started at the club, and Gloria could hear the band through her window, but she wasn't even faintly tempted to get dressed and go down there; she couldn't think of anything more painful than having to tell Binkie or Judy or anybody else that she and Rolland had broken up—definitively, irrevocably. She imagined herself weeping all over Binkie out on the terrace, and the thought of it was simply too ghastly to contemplate.

Maybe she'd cried enough. All she felt right now was numb, but she couldn't resist exploring her pain to see if, underneath the surface layer of emotional exhaustion, she still hurt quite all *that* much, so she opened her jewelry box and took out her Delta Lambda pin. When she saw the bit of cut chain still attached to it, her nose filled up and two dumb, hot tears trickled down her cheeks. Stop it, you idiot, she told herself. She cut off that last, sad bit of gold chain and dropped it into her wastebasket. He hadn't believed her until she'd cut the chain. She'd cut it with the kitchen shears—one fatal snip—and had handed him his pin back. He'd been gone within minutes.

Neither of them had remembered the Beta Theta Pi charm he'd given her so long ago. Determined to make a new beginning—to get on with her life no matter how miserable it might be at the moment—she cut the charm from her bracelet. But what was she supposed to do with it? She couldn't very well mail it back to him—that would be cruel—and she couldn't very well throw it away, could she? "Oh, yes, you can," the secret watcher told her.

After a moment's reflection, she realized that simply depositing the charm in her pink plastic wastebasket along with lipstick-smeared Kleenexes and clumps of hair picked out of her brush was a fairly tawdry gesture. She knelt and retrieved the charm and the fragment of chain and laid them on her vanity table. She needed a ritual. Throwing them into the ocean was the first thought that came to mind, but Raysburg was hundreds of miles from the ocean. OK, how about the river then? She could walk out into the middle of the Suspension Bridge, say a few carefully chosen words, and drop them in. Right, that would do it.

But could she still wear the gold disk Rolland had given her, the one that commemorated her winning May Queen? No, that would have to go too. She cut it off—and then she considered the charm bracelet itself. She wasn't sure she even liked it; whenever she wore it, the darned thing made a constant, teensy, tinkly tintinnabulation that drove her nuts, and, after a while, she began to feel like a harem girl. Maybe she'd like it better if she pruned it— Yes, that felt like a good thing to do: the beginning of a redefinition of herself.

Her mother had given her the bracelet with its first charm—a little gold teddy bear—when she'd shipped her off to Fairhaven, and, of all the things in her life that absolutely should not be commemorated, Fairhaven Hall was certainly at the top of the list, so she cut off the teddy bear—and then all of the other Fairhaven charms. There were a couple she wasn't sure about, but they could stay for the moment: Mrs. Warsinski's real mustard seed in a glass bead and her grandmother's golden violet meant to remind her of her roots in Rhode Island. And finally there were the ones she absolutely had to keep: her father's Prom Queen charm, her Delta Lambda charm, her Phi Beta Kappa key, and a gold disk embossed with Delta Lambda's stylized sun that had been given to all the members of the graduating executive. Susie and Gloria, in a vow of eternal sisterhood, had swapped theirs, so, instead of her own name and position, the sun disk on her bracelet bore the words: *Susan Jane Steibel, Treasurer*.

Oh, Susie! she thought. Susie was the only person in the world she wanted to see right now. Maybe she could call her—but, no, Susie and Don were staying with his parents until they got their own apartment, and Gloria didn't want to call Susie at her in-laws'. Besides, the last thing in the world Susie needed to hear right after her honeymoon was Gloria weeping on the telephone.

For the millionth time, she looked out her bedroom window, saw that her mother was no longer sitting by the side of the pool, so, without a second thought, ran straight downstairs and dived in. After the muggy, sticky heat of her bedroom, the water felt like heaven. She'd already swum forty laps that morning, but now she swam twenty more without any effort at all and ended them with her fastest stroke. Winded, she stood up in the shallow end and looked across to the apple trees where the last breath of daylight had discolored the sky into a fading, sickly radiance—muddy pomegranate tinged with an honest-to-God lime-green—and she almost hated to admit it, but she did feel a bit better.

Then she smelled cigarette smoke, turned and saw that her mother had returned to her deck chair. Oh, just great, Gloria thought; she's been watching me.

Gloria climbed slowly out of the pool. Her skin felt itchy with her mother's regard—if her mother was regarding her; her mother's face was shadowed, and Gloria couldn't see the expression on it—not that being able to see it would make any difference. Since Rolland had left, her mother had been giving her the silent treatment, but two could play that little game, so, without saying a word, she walked right past her.

"Gloria?"

She stopped and turned. She still couldn't see her mother's face. "Have you had anything to eat?"

"Yes," Gloria said, "I made some scrambled eggs."

"Good. I don't feel like cooking."

Was that an invitation to a conversation? Gloria didn't feel like a conversation—and she was just on the point of walking away when her mother said, "I hate it when your father has to go to one of his damned meetings."

Her mother inhaled deeply on her cigarette; a ruddy glow illuminated her eyes for a moment and made her look like something out of a horror movie. The night was so still that Gloria could hear the tobacco burning. She could hear the band at the club quite clearly. Her mother must have heard it too. "Aren't you going to the dance?"

"No."

"Whyever not?"

"Because I don't feel like it," Gloria said and walked away.

"Sweetie? Wait a minute."

Gloria bounded up the steps two at a time. She stopped in the kitchen. Her mouth had gone dry; she was breathing in short, panting breaths, and she didn't know what to do next—or even where to go. She couldn't understand why she was so angry—far more angry than anything justified by what was going on, but, justified or not, she was afraid that if she had to talk to her mother, she'd start screaming. Nobody had lit any lights, and the entire first floor was dark. It was bizarre what happened on those rare occasions when her father was out of town: life simply stopped until he came back. She saw the silhouetted form of her mother stepping through the French door. "Sweetie? Can we just start over?"

What? Gloria thought. She can give me the silent treatment and then decide to call it off when she feels like it? What if I don't feel like it? But she took several deep breaths and made herself say: "Sure, Mom."

Then, instead of saying anything, her mother walked through the kitchen and into the dining room—to the liquor cabinet to be exact. Gloria heard the sound of the Scotch being poured; she could even smell it. Somebody should turn a light on. It was ridiculous—the two of them wandering around the house in the dark like this.

She followed her mother into the dining room, but her mother had already moved into the living room—or at least that's where Gloria guessed she'd gone; the only light left was coming from the back of the house; looking toward the big picture window, Gloria could see nothing at all. Then, as she waited, the parts of her eyes designed for low light—she couldn't remember if they were the rods or the cones—must have opened up because, if she didn't look directly at her, she could make out the shape of her mother sitting on the couch. "God, it's close!" her mother said.

Gloria sat down on one of the Louis Quatorze chairs. She didn't know whether her mother could see her or not. "Mom? Why don't we turn some lights on?"

Her words seemed to have vanished into the darkness with no effect whatsoever, and, as Gloria waited for a response that was obviously not going to be coming, she began to feel an oppressive sense of—she wasn't sure what. It was as though she were imagining all of this, and, if she opened her eyes, she would find herself sitting on her bed with the reading light on and *The Pisan Cantos* open on her lap. "I'll bet you and Rolland have had fights before," her mother said.

She's incredible! Gloria thought. Her mother just went right on talking, but Gloria didn't want to listen, so, without making a sound, she stood up and crept out of the living room and back into the kitchen; as soon as she arrived there, she couldn't believe she'd done such a crazy thing. She heard her mother's voice murmuring, but she couldn't make out the words—which was just fine with her. The tone was coming through clearly, however; it was self-pitying, whiny—sad, uncertain—and a voice in Gloria's mind rattled on: "silken sad uncertain rustling of each purple curtain—" Then, rebelling against the crepuscular, Poe-like atmosphere into which her mother had dragged her, Gloria finally clued in: her mother was drunk—had been drunk for quite some time. A drunken man was bad enough, but a drunken woman turned Gloria's stomach; there was nothing more cheap and vulgar than a drunken woman. Only once had Gloria ever blackballed a rushee: a girl she'd seen stupidly, loudly drunk in the Blue Cellar.

"Sweetie? Where are you?"

Gloria snapped on the kitchen light, walked briskly through the dining room and snapped on the light there. Her mother peered blindly at her. "Mom? Don't you think you better eat something?"

"Oh, honey, it's too hot."

Gloria couldn't stand the whine in her mother's voice. "Come on, Mom. I'll make you some eggs."

With a wan smile, her mother shook her head. "Maybe later."

"Sure, but if you, um, keep on drinking Scotch on an empty stomach, you're going to get totally sloshed."

"Oh, don't worry about me. I've had years of practice. You know, sweetie, it's not unusual for young couples to have fights. It takes years to—I guess you could say, to have your sharp edges knocked off. Even your father and I. We had some real doozies"

I can't stand this, Gloria thought, but, reaching for a jocular, girls-in-it-together voice, she tried again: "Mom? You know, I really do think you've had enough to drink."

Her mother was so slowed down it took her a moment to react; Gloria saw her decide to be offended. "Good heavens, Princess Priss, I really don't see how that's any of your business."

The words were out of Gloria's mouth before she could stop them: "I'm not the princess around here."

"What did you just say to me?"

"Nothing, Mom. Forget it. I'm sorry. Don't you think you ought to eat something?"

"No, I will not forget it. What did you just say to me?"

Gloria sighed. "I said, 'I'm not the princess around here.'"

"What the hell's that supposed to mean?"

"Forget it, Mom. It was just something to say. But please don't call me Princess Priss. I hate it."

"You have no right—no right to say anything, Gloria Cotter—not a word—after what you did."

"What did I do? Break up with Rolland? Well, it's my life, Mom."

"You think you're so damned smart, don't you? Miss Smarty-pants. Miss Smart Answers. Miss Phi Beta Kappa—"

Gloria was breathing hard. "Get out of here," the secret watcher said, "or it's going to turn into something really ugly."

"Let's just forget it," she said and was already walking away.

"You get back down here right now!" her mother shrieked after her. Gloria slammed her bedroom door and wished—not for the first time—that it had a lock on it.

I'm not going to take any more from her, she thought—even if she is drunk. She's been picking at me ever since I got home. As far as she's concerned, I can't do anything right. Well, I've just had *enough*. After a moment she heard her mother slam-banging up the stairs. Gloria had always been amazed that a woman who couldn't have weighed more than a hundred and thirty pounds could make so darned much noise just walking. She'd better not come in here, Gloria thought. The door burst open.

"Get out of my room, Mom. Just let me alone."

"I wasn't going to say a word. I was just going to let it go by. But when you— When I see open defiance—"

Defiance? Gloria thought. How old am I supposed to be? "I don't want to talk right now. Please get out of my room."

"It's not your room. It's *my* house. You're under *my* roof."

"Dad's roof."

"What?"

"It's *Dad's* roof. You don't do a damned thing around here."

To Gloria's shock and horror, her mother started to cry. "I've tried with you, Gloria," she said. "God knows I have. I've tried and tried to get close to you, but all you do is push me away. You don't even talk to me—"

"Oh, Mom, come on." Her mother leaned against the doorjamb, hung her head, and wept. "Come on, Mom, let's get you to bed."

Gloria put her hand on her mother's shoulder, but her mother batted it away. "Don't you dare try that with me, Gloria Cotter!"

"This is ridiculous, Mom. You're drunk."

"Oh, am I? Well, if I'm drunk, I have my reasons. You just shut up, May Queen. I don't have to take that from you. I don't have to take *anything* from you, Miss High and Mighty. Just who the hell do you think you are?" She walked out.

She's not going to get the last word, Gloria thought. Not this time. "Why should I talk to you?" she yelled into the empty doorway. "You don't even like me."

Gloria stepped out into the hallway and saw her mother standing at the top of the stairs, frozen, looking back at her. Gloria had not yet lost the ability to assess what she was doing; if, in that moment, she'd decided to stop, she could have done it, but she hesitated—listening to the hammer of her heartbeat—and by then it was too late. She felt like a launched missile, and she didn't care. "You sent me away," she yelled.

Her mother might as well have turned into a statue. "Why the hell *should* I talk to you?" Gloria yelled at the statue. "I wrote you letter after letter, and you just left me there."

Gloria saw her mother start to cry again. Good, Gloria thought, good, good, good! But someone else inside her, someone far at the back of her mind, was weeping along with her mother. Gloria felt an ugly joy—a perverse pleasure in something precious breaking—and she was afraid now, but she *still* couldn't stop. "You never liked me after Bobby was born. You hated everything I did. You hated me for being a cheerleader. You hated me for—"

"That's crazy. I'm not going to listen to this—"

"Oh, yes, you are. You started it, so you're going to listen to it. You wanted to get rid of me when I was eight, and you want to get rid of me now. You just can't wait for me to get out—"

"You shut up. You just shut up. How can you say that to me? You selfish little—selfish and cruel—"

"Cruel? Oh, that's really funny. That's a real riot. You sent me to grade school in a chauffeured limousine. What the devil were you thinking about?"

"Oh, my God, Gloria—"

"You had that stupid Irish maid set my hair in sausage curls, and you put me in a pale pink—"

"For Christ's sake! That's years ago. My God, Gloria, all you ever think about is yourself. How can you—? Why don't you ever think about *me* for a change? The war had just started, and Bobby—"

"What? When I'm six years old? I'm supposed to think about *you* when I'm six years old? I'm supposed to—"

"You're not six years old now, for Christ's sake!"

"I don't give a damn what you were thinking about. Not a damn. You sure weren't thinking about *me*."

"Oh, my God, you selfish—selfish, self-centered, egotistical—"

"That's *you*, Mom. You're the one who's selfish and self-centered and—"

"Bitch. You bitch. You goddamned little bitch."

"That's enough!"

Both Gloria and her mother spun in the direction of the voice. Gloria's grandmother had just stepped through her bedroom door. She was wearing a long flannel nightgown, and her hair was down. She looked enormously old.

Gloria felt the image of her grandmother as a sharp strike at her breastbone. She saw her mother standing—wide-eyed and, once again, immobilized, one hand caught in mid-air, like a snapshot lit by a flash bulb.

"I'm ashamed of you." It seemed impossible that such a hard, cutting, angry voice could be coming out of that little, withered person.

"I'm ashamed *of both of you*. You both have Merriman and Whittock blood in your veins, and Merrimans and Whittocks do not shriek at each other like fishwives. Nor do they use the language I have just heard from you, Marcelaine. Now you girls get control of yourselves and *act like ladies*."

The part of Gloria's mind that hadn't been working kicked back in with a vengeance, and she thought: oh help, what have I been saying! She'll never forgive me. All I've done is guarantee myself a miserable summer—even more miserable than it has been already. Why couldn't I have kept my damned mouth shut?—and Gloria's mother was saying to *her* mother: "Oh, Mother, you shouldn't be out of bed!"

"Well, perhaps I shouldn't, but someone had to do something to put an end to that crude, vulgar, disgusting display. And you certainly can't accuse me of eavesdropping, Marcelaine. Just be thankful that you have no neighbors within a five-mile radius."

Gloria's mother sent her a look that said, "Help!" and Gloria was perfectly willing to help, but she didn't know what she was supposed to do. Following her mother's lead, she approached her grandmother cautiously; they edged up to her as though she were something dangerous that had escaped. "Oh, Mother, your heart!"

"My heart will give out when it's damn well ready and not a moment sooner."

"I'm sorry, Mother. I really am. You should try to sleep now."

"I'm not ready to go to sleep—thanks to you, Marcelaine. You girls have had your say. Now you're going to listen to *me*."

Gloria's grandmother looked directly at her with an expression that Gloria imagined an owl might wear when regarding a vole. "I'm sorry that you were not happier when you lived with me. My dear husband had just passed on, and I was little use to anyone—certainly of very little use to you and your mother. You must know that your mother's nerves have never been strong, and she had a difficult time of it after your brother was born, and she certainly made mistakes, as I did in my time. I'm sure she'd be quite happy to tell you all about *my* mistakes— But, believe me, Gloria, she did the very best she could for you, and that's all of us ever do, as you'll find out yourself when you have children of your own. I'm sorry if it embarrassed you to be sent to school in a chauffeured limousine. It was the only way to get you there.

"And you, Marcelaine, I can't imagine what— Well, at least Gloria has some excuse for losing her temper. She is still a young girl, and that hot Spanish blood of hers will out, but you, Marcelaine— I'm simply shocked and dismayed. You have both the blood and the breeding, and you're over forty years old, and if you haven't learned to comport yourself with a modicum of dignity by now— Why, good heavens, compared to the way you were as a girl, Gloria is no trouble whatsoever. I used to pray to the Lord—oh, yes, indeed, I prayed quite often when you were a girl, Marcelaine—I used to pray: please, dear Lord, just give her an ounce of common sense, just an ounce!"

"Oh, Mother, please— Let's get you back in bed!" Once again her mother sent Gloria a piteous, imploring look. She and her mother stepped forward, and her grandmother allowed them each to take one of her arms.

"You were vamping every man and boy in Providence by the time you were fourteen." The bright, hard energy was draining out of the old woman's voice, and she was beginning to sound querulous. "You should have seen her, Gloria, fourteen years old and—"

"Oh, Mother, that's ridiculous."

The old woman felt as delicate as a stick figure. They led her back to her bed. Gloria fluffed the pillows, and they settled her into them.

"You've heard of 'flaming youth,' haven't you, Gloria? Well, your mother was positively *ignited*. Riding around in motors with men old enough to be her father—"

"Oh, I did not."

"Yes, you did. I had eyes in my head, Marcelaine. And drinking bathtub gin— Oh, I knew you drank. You needn't think you were putting anything over on me. But you did have enough sense to make a perfectly sound marriage—"

"Oh, Mother! You certainly didn't think so at the time."

"No, I didn't. That is true enough. But I was wrong and you were right. And you're just as wrong about that Spicer boy. Believe me, Gloria in her own good time will marry just as well as you did, and you won't like the man she chooses any more than I liked Theodore when I first met him. Now, Gloria, you go downstairs and make me a martini."

Delighted with the chance to move, Gloria jumped up and ran. She was so keyed-up her entire body was shaking and even her teeth were chattering. How strange that her grandmother had suddenly appeared—an improbable ally— to rescue her from utter, irrevocable disaster—that is, if she hadn't already plunged to utter, irrevocable disaster. Now what on earth could she do to fix things? "Be nice, be good," some idiotic voice in her mind nattered at her. She cracked a tray of ice cubes into the picnic pitcher, emptied the gin bottle into it, and added a gurgle of vermouth. She set the pitcher, a jar of olives, a stack of napkins, and three martini glasses on a silver tray. Her heart was still going like crazy. She ran back upstairs.

The moment she walked into her grandmother's bedroom, she felt that the atmosphere had changed. She'd poured out three martinis before she'd found the words to describe the change she'd felt: the danger had been drained away. Her mother was sunk into the wingback chair, was sprawled there in a dishrag torpidity; she was saying nothing, was wearing the resigned look of someone who has resolved to go on saying nothing as long as it was required of her.

Her grandmother was talking steadily. Now that she was back in bed, half-reclining, she seemed to have regained something of her earlier vigor; she was talking like someone who is pacing herself, who has settled in for the long haul. "I was just telling your mother that the two of you are quite similar. You're both high-strung, thoroughbred girls, but you're high-strung in different ways. That china doll complexion you used to have, Marcelaine—before you started baking yourself in the sun like a damn fool—well, that's pure Whittock, and the Whittock girls—the ones with the pure Whittock strain—have always been high-strung. But you just take one look at Gloria and you can see the Spanish blood, and that's high-strung blood too, but it's different. It isn't— How can I put it? It isn't *nervous* like the Whittocks. It's *passionate.*"

"Thank you, my dear," her grandmother said, accepting the martini Gloria had offered her. "You see, I don't have the pure Whittock strain. I'm more like the Comptons. But I certainly passed on the pure Whittock blood to you, Marcelaine. Now when the Whittock blood breeds true, you get someone like your Aunt Mildred. You know how she's prone to nervous stomach and fainting fits and sick headaches? And what a Whittock girl needs is a man who'll pamper her and indulge her and cater to her every whim, do you see what I mean? But when that hot Spanish blood breeds true, then you get a girl who's like a very fine thoroughbred horse—a fine Arabian mare— And all you need to do is *look* at Gloria, and you can see the Spanish blood, and with a girl as fiery and passionate as all that—well, she's going to need a strong, forceful man who can keep her in check. A man with any weakness in him, she'll go straight for that weakness and exploit it and use it against him. And that Spicer boy— I'm not saying a word against him, you understand? He's a perfectly nice boy, but you could tell in five minutes he just wasn't man enough for Gloria. She'd just seize the bit between her teeth, and away she'd go, and then there'd be all hell to pay. No, Gloria needs a man of the world, someone much older and wiser in the ways of the world— Do you see what I'm saying to you, Marcelaine? So everything's worked out for the best."

Gloria didn't believe for a minute that her mother thought everything had worked out for the best, but she saw her mother nod wearily and sip at the martini Gloria had given her. Gloria sipped hers too. Was it possible that she was actually getting to like the darned things?

"Gloria, my dear, could you pass me my cigarettes?"

"Oh, Mother, you shouldn't be smoking."

"There are many things I shouldn't be doing, Marcelaine. Now what was I saying? Oh, yes. That Spanish blood is very powerful. When it gets going, it just washes all the other blood completely out. And it isn't just down one side. It crossed over. I think it crossed over twice, so you've got it coming down from both the Merrimans and the Whittocks."

"Crossed over?" Gloria said.

"Well, you see, Captain John Merriman married a Spanish girl. That's when it all started. And one of her daughters married a Whittock—I think it was one of her daughters. Maybe it was one of her granddaughters. So that was the first time the blood crossed over, and then, later on— Oh, I'd have to look it up to know exactly—"

"Do you know her name?" Gloria asked.

"Who?"

"The Spanish girl."

"Well, of course I know her name. Veronica Isobel Macias y Gomez."

"I thought it was Marquez or Martinez or something like that," Gloria's mother said.

"No, no, Marcelaine. Macias y Gomez. The 'y' means 'and' in Spanish. They keep track of both their families that way. That would have been in the seventeen-nineties when Captain John Merriman brought her over. Pure Castilian. It's in that big family tree over in the dresser if you want to look it up. Veronica Isobel Macias y Gomez."

"Are you sure it was Veronica? Nobody was named Veronica in the seventeen-nineties."

"Of course they were. In Spain. You don't know a thing about it, Marcelaine. And she was only twenty when he brought her back to Newport. And the Merrimans were not pleased that the young captain had taken a Spanish bride, but then they took one look at her and that was that. She was the most beautiful girl anyone had ever laid eyes on, and she was very, very Spanish. Arrogant, some said, and flirtatious, but it was all—well, *in the Spanish manner*. Very, very high bred Castilian, and you know the way those people are. The women are very passionate—fiery and passionate—and they're *always* flirting, but if a man so much as dares to lay a finger on them—well, that's another story altogether. Those girls caused duels and riots. All about *honor,* and blood flowed by the gallon over those girls, and they thought it was their just due. Why, if a man wasn't willing to bleed for you, he was no man at all."

"Oh, Mother, you've been reading too many ten-pound novels."

"Marcelaine, you really *don't* know a thing about it. Your father and I were in Spain *several* times—back in the twenties before the communists ruined it for everyone. She never converted. Did you know that? It was something of a scandal in the family because the Merrimans considered Papists to be kin to Satan, and none of her children were raised Catholic, but she stayed Catholic her whole life. Gloria, if you don't mind—"

Gloria refilled her grandmother's martini glass. To her surprise, Gloria seemed to have drunk her entire martini too—she didn't remember doing it— so she refilled her own glass. "You watch those things, sweetie," her mother said under her breath. "They've got a kick like a mule."

Good grief, Gloria thought, could it be that she's not all that mad at me? Maybe she didn't believe anything I said. Or maybe it was all just a big, mean-ingless storm—mere sound and fury—and now it's simply blown over. That would be wonderful if it were true.

"Aunt Isobel—you remember her, don't you, Marcelaine? You *should* remember her. She gave you your grandmother Whittock's wedding dress to get married in—against my express wishes. Well, you must know that Isobel was named for Veronica. Her name was Veronica *Isobel* —and Isobel—that's my Aunt Isobel, your great-aunt, Marcelaine, remembered that old Spanish lady clear as day. She said you would go to visit her in her rooms, and there would be crucifixes and statues of saints and all kinds of idols everywhere you looked. And candles. Candles by the yard, and— Oh, Marcelaine, I don't know why I said that about Mother's wedding dress. Looking back on it now, I'm glad you had it to be married in, although it quite astonishes me you could get it on, and looking back after all these years, I'm only sorry I wasn't there. Well, Marce-laine, you were right about Theodore, and your father and I were dead wrong, and you've made a splendid marriage. And when Gloria does marry, you may not approve of her husband any more than we did of yours, but if she follows her heart— Gloria, my dear, you can wear *my* wedding dress when you get mar-ried, if you'd enjoy that. It's in storage in Providence, and you make sure that you get it— Marcelaine, you see that she gets those trunks of clothes. She's the only one in the family who'd appreciate old, fine things like that— Oh, good heavens!" and she covered her mouth and yawned.

"You see, Marcelaine, a good martini's worth ten sleeping pills. Doctors! What do they know? But what was I saying? Oh. Yes, that dress was made by the House of Worth, and my father told me it cost more than a new carriage—

which was one of the few times he ever mentioned the cost of anything in my hearing. You'll never see craftsmanship like that today. Every seam is a work of art. But you mustn't have it altered. It's a sin to alter an old dress. You'll just have to wear stays under it. Marcelaine, do you still have Mother's dress?"

"Of course I still have it. Did you think I'd throw it away? It's upstairs in a trunk—along with my Schiaparelli glass slippers."

"Oh, good heavens, do you still have those silly things? Why didn't you give them to Gloria?"

"Oh, Mother, she'd never get them on. My feet were tiny."

"Hey, wait a minute," Gloria said, "my feet aren't exactly barges."

"Oh, but honey, I mean *tiny*. I was really vain about my feet."

"You were vain about more than that, Marcelaine. You should have seen your mother, Gloria. A pie couldn't have been any more *à la mode* than she was. Whatever they were wearing in Paris, she had to have it. I remember, it started when she was at Fairhaven. She'd come home in the summer, and she'd turn herself into flaming youth, and I couldn't do a thing with her. Her father indulged her utterly— Well, men can be such fools about their daughters, but you should have seen her! She bound her breasts and painted herself up like a Kewpie doll and slithered around like a snake. All the girls stopped wearing their stays. They used to take them off at the dances and leave them in the cloak room—can you imagine that! And her skirts up to her knees. You have no idea how shocking those skirts were when they first came in, and the girls looked like great, big, painted-up children, but they certainly didn't behave like children! Marcelaine, you have nothing to complain about with Gloria, nothing what-soever. You girls can leave me now. I believe I'm quite ready for sleep."

Gloria took the glass from her grandmother's fingers and set it on the tray. "Kiss me now, please, girls, and say good-night. And don't fight anymore, please. Life's too short."

Gloria kissed her grandmother's cheek. She watched as her mother bent and delivered her kiss. It felt like a ritual to Gloria, a touching scene beauti-fully concluded.

Gloria gently shut her grandmother's door. As though they'd planned to do it, Gloria and her mother walked away from the closed door and paused in the hallway to look at each other. Gloria could feel the alcohol in her blood; it was enough to make her gently, sweetly buoyant—that's right, it was *just* enough, and she certainly didn't want the second martini she was carrying—and then, in an unexpected, bittersweet inner turning, she realized that she was almost happy. She was sure that if she said exactly the right thing, she could repair any damage she might have done.

"Mom," she said, speaking just above a whisper, "I'm sorry—really sorry for what I said to you. I didn't really mean it. It's just— You've been picking at me ever since I came home, and— Oh, Mom, can't we just try to get along better? I do love you, you know."

Her mother was looking directly at her, but, as usual, Gloria couldn't tell what she was thinking. "Grandmother was right about Rolly," Gloria said. "I don't know how she knew it, but she did, and— Oh, I know you're disappointed. I know you were looking forward to a big wedding with all the trimmings, but—I'll have a big wedding someday. With the right man. But Rolland just wasn't— I mean, if he hadn't come to visit, maybe it would have taken me longer to see it, but this time I really did see it. Mom, he just wasn't the right man for me."

Her mother looked at her a moment longer. Then she said in a voice just as quiet as the one Gloria had been using: "Why'd you sleep with him then, you little tramp?"

13

Tears pouring down her face, Gloria slammed her bedroom door and leaned against it. She was so angry, everywhere she looked she saw a smeary red haze pulsing to her heartbeat, moving with her eyes, floating over the tops of all the ordinary objects in her room. "You bitch," she said to her mother half aloud, "damn you, damn you, damn you."

It hurt to be this angry—it was *unendurable* to be this angry—and already she was afraid of it; already the secret watcher had appeared to say, "Stop this right now, Gloria," but nothing she could imagine—throwing her books across the room, upending her vanity table, beating her fists against the wall—was fast enough, big enough, hard enough, savage or brutal or just downright *spectacular* enough to stop it. Oh, how wonderful it would be to give into it, fling herself to the floor—writhe, kick, howl, and spit—have a frenzied, stunning, terrifying temper tantrum just the way she'd seen other little kids doing but had never allowed herself to do, and the fact that she hadn't simply done it, was *thinking* about it, meant that she couldn't possibly do it, and she was already lecturing herself: "You're not a four-year-old, you idiot. Remember what your grandmother said. *Now you just get yourself back in control and act like a lady.*"

Breathe, she told herself, and she breathed. She was shaking all over. She was still holding her undrunk second martini in her hand, and she took a long drink of it. A poem had been set going in her mind—a jingly, jangly nursery rhyme kind of poem. As soon as she turned her attention to it, she recognized it as a bit of A.A. Milne: "Have you been a *good* girl? Have you been a *good* girl? Have you been a *good* girl?"

"Fuck you," Gloria said.

She'd never said that word out loud. It was cheap and vulgar for girls to say that word. She hated it when Susie said that word. She said it again: "*Fuck you.*" There was something very satisfying about saying it. She drank the rest of the martini.

Not giving a damn whether her mother heard her or not, she walked out of her room, down the hall, and up the narrow stairs to the attic. She lit the single bare bulb in the middle of the ceiling and stopped, disoriented, as though she'd never been there before. The dead air stank of hot unfinished wood and mothballs and old dust and old fabric; she was already sweating, and she felt dizzy, but she couldn't let herself think about feeling dizzy, because if she did, she'd just creep back down to her bedroom and cry herself to sleep.

She didn't know exactly what she was looking for, but she'd stopped in front of her formals, each of them neatly preserved in a dry-cleaner's bag: her Prom Queen dress and her May Queen dress—and dozens of times she'd dreamed a secret door up there in the attic; now the memory of that dream door felt so real that she half believed she could turn around and step through it into a corridor leading to enormous closets, each closet leading into another one like a maze—or maybe she could walk straight into Professor Bolton's living room— But she kept sliding the formals along the bar until she saw, right next to an enormous crinoline, the sexy black sheath she'd bought on her wild shopping spree at the end of her Britomart summer. When she'd worn it, she'd been as thin as she'd ever been in her adult life, and she wasn't sure she could still get it on, but she took it down and draped it over her arm.

She opened the cedar chest where accessories for formal wear were stored in layers of tissue paper and selected a firmly boned merry widow from high school and a pair of long, black evening gloves of her mother's. Then—and she didn't quite remember walking back down the stairs, didn't know whether she'd turned out the light in the attic or closed the door, and didn't care—she was back in her bedroom, looking at herself in the mirror.

She smoothed a thick layer of foundation over her face and carried it down onto her neck and chest and even over the tops of her breasts. Something strange had happened to her anger: it had been annealed; her hands had stopped shaking, and she knew she couldn't make a mistake. Instead of her usual needle-thin eyeliner, she drew catlike rings as thick and black as if she'd been going on stage; she carried the lines well beyond her eyes and swept them upward. She did her eyelids in ultramarine. She used brown rouge to give herself a model's glamorous, sucked-in cheeks and lots of vivid red above to highlight the bones. She curled her lashes, combed on three coats of mascara, curled them again, and separated them into discrete spikes. She drew a hard lip-line, painted on a big, blood-red mouth and shined it with gloss. She looked at the final creation and thought: good. There's the fiery, passionate Spanish girl from a velvet painting my grandmother thinks I am.

The merry widow was, just as she'd wanted it to be, a mile too small for her, and she fastened it on the tightest row of hooks. She was spilling right out of it; she tucked her breasts in and tightened the shoulder straps. She didn't often wear black stockings, but she was sure she had a pair, and she did.

She slipped the sheath over her head and knew immediately that it had been a stupid thing to do—it would be impossible to get it on that way—and, for a moment, she was tangled up in it, fighting with it. She shook it off, let it fall to the floor— And how could she have been so cold only a moment before? Wildly frustrated, she was raging again; the intensity of her anger terrified and immobilized her. She'd been holding her breath; as soon as she let it out, she began to cry; as soon as she felt herself crying, she was bent double with it—as though struck by fierce cramps. No, she thought, don't do this. You'll ruin everything.

She forced herself slowly upright—breathing, breathing—sniffed in her tears and swallowed them. Her mind seemed to have taken off on it's own— Why couldn't she simply have married Rolland and submerged her personality in his? Wasn't that what a girl was supposed to do? Wouldn't she have to do that with some man eventually? Wouldn't it be better than this—whatever *this* was, this pain and rage? Wouldn't it be *a relief?* Then she wouldn't have to worry about going crazy, or doing crazy things, because she'd know exactly who she was: *somebody's wife.* And, for a second or two, she thought that maybe it wasn't too late. She could use the kitchen phone. Her mother had shut herself into her bedroom; she wouldn't hear her.

"Change your mind again?" the secret watcher said. "Oh, that's just great, Gloria. That's really just what he'd love to hear. Forget it. Let him go. He deserves better than you. It's over."

She'd stopped crying. It felt as though her tears had been absorbed inside. She picked up the sheath. Did it need a slip? Yes, probably, if she wanted to be absolutely safe, but it was beautifully lined in black silk, and she could get away without one. OK, she thought, making a deal with herself, if you can't get it on, you stay home. Using a trick Susie had taught her, she fed the hook of a coat hanger through the little hole in the zipper latch; then she stepped into the sheath, squeezed her knees together, and worked it up gradually over her thighs. Holding the zipper together at the top with her left hand, she zipped herself up with the coat hanger. OK, all right, she thought, and now what shoes? The too-high heels from the May Queen candidates' party, of course. They were still in their box. She took them out and slipped them on.

She closed her eyes—breathing, breathing—and felt the moist, cloying, vegetative heat of the summer night pressing in on her; through her open window, she could hear the band playing at the country club—a sound that came and went, evanescent as a fairy orchestra—and she felt a strange knotting sensation she couldn't define, but, withdrawn into the soft darkness behind her eyelids, she was safe for the moment. With every breath, she felt the boning in her merry widow; it made her feel poised, balanced; the heels made her feel poised, balanced; she felt as though she were poised, balanced on the edge of an inner diving board. Hold it there, Gloria, she thought—carefully, carefully—

She opened her eyes and looked in the mirror. With her theatrical makeup and the lines of her figure simplified and exaggerated, she looked like a cartoon girl—and, for a moment, there were two of her: one was a cartoon looking at itself in a mirror, and the other was a girl looking at the cartoon looking at itself. She'd never created an image so artificial, so far removed from—her first thought had been so far removed from *herself*, but that wasn't right— OK, then, so far removed from any of the *personae* she ordinarily presented to the world. That she'd been able to accomplish this transformation gave her a dangerous rush of elation, and the secret watcher said: "Be careful, Gloria. Don't rejoice."

She worked her hands into her mother's black evening gloves; like everything else she was wearing, they were too small for her, and she was probably stretching them, but she didn't care. She drew them up tightly and snapped her pruned charm bracelet onto her left wrist. Then as an afterthought—something of a joke—she put on a string of pearls. She threw her cosmetic case into an evening bag and walked out.

The sheath was so tight she could easily have ripped it straight up the back, so she took short, fast, clipping steps, and her heels made a sharp staccato tapping on the hardwood floor. She couldn't find any way to walk that would stop that annoying sound, and then she knew that she didn't want to stop it. She wanted her mother to hear her walking out, wanted her mother to wonder where the hell she was going at eleven o'clock at night. *OK, Mom, you think I'm a little tramp? Well, here goes your little tramp.*

"Why," the secret watcher asked her after she'd come to rest by the side of her mother's station wagon, "are you wearing a dress so tight that you're standing here wondering if you can drive a car in it?" It was a perfectly reasonable question, and Gloria didn't have any good answer for it. She opened the door on the driver's side and saw that the keys were in the ignition just where she'd hoped they'd be.

She threw her bag in, pulled off her heels and threw them in. She slithered her skirt up high on her thighs, settled gingerly sideways onto the seat, gripped the steering wheel, and swung her legs in. Then, perched on the very edge of the seat, she started the engine. She revved it several times so her mother would be sure to hear it and pulled out, fast, spinning the tires.

In her mind the road to the country club had been impossibly long—a million or so miles—and she'd been planning to use the drive to collect herself, but she was already drifting the station wagon into the shadows at the far edge of the parking area. She opened the door. Holding her knees tightly together, she rotated in the seat, slipped her heels back on, set her feet down side by side on the asphalt, and stood up. So far so good. Her breasts felt dangerously close to popping out of the merry widow; she hooked her thumbs under the straps and pushed them forward—stay in there!—smoothed her skirt down until she'd recreated that sleek silhouette she'd seen in her bedroom mirror, picked up her bag, and closed the car door. Now there was nothing left to do but walk. She took a deep breath and walked. Inside the club, the old, wheezy band was doing its best to play rock 'n' roll.

If the drive had been instantaneous, the walk was interminable—across the lot, past the parked cars (it was crowded tonight), around to the entrance, and up the steps—and she had nothing to do but concentrate on walking, placing each short step directly in front of the other, feeling her knees brushing against each other, hearing the faint, insectlike hiss of her nylons and the sharp sound of her heels on the concrete—not quite a click, more like a brittle scratching. Without being able to see herself, she knew, nonetheless, exactly how she looked, and she was doing just fine. In these very heels Susie had demonstrated the way you were supposed to walk in a beauty pageant—not a chorus girl's sashay with an exaggerated crossover step and a big swing to the hips (to show her the difference, Susie had demonstrated that too), but something more subtle—a cute, girlishly sexy walk—and Gloria had done her best to walk that way at the May Queen candidates' party. This tight skirt made it feel almost easy, and she wished Susie were there to see how well she was doing.

As she always did when entering a public arena, Gloria paused just at the edge of the dance floor, looking. From her bedroom (where, she had somehow been, surely only a moment before, planning to be here, *thinking* about being here) the sound of the band had been as elusive as the perfume of someone who is long gone, but now it had achieved a massive solidity, and Gloria was suffering a disconcerting sensation—like a Rimbaudian derangement of the senses—as though the huge volume of sound had pinched off her ability to see clearly, or, if not precisely *to see*, at least her ability to make visual sense of anything: it was only with a decisive effort that she could impose the terms "couple" and "jitterbug" on these forms engaged in such aberrant, disjointed motions, and Gloria's disorientation was so extreme she had the good sense to be afraid of it. Oh, help, she thought, I should be at home in bed.

For dances like this one the tables were pushed back to create a small ballroom, and the old bald guy on the stage was someone she had seen many times before—was, in fact, the leader of the band—and what he was trying to play was called "yackety sax," and the good old mirror ball she'd seen a million times before had been hung from the ceiling, while a few hidden electric lights, shrewd and indirect, played against it to create a cascade of moving, shattered polka-dots of brilliantly confusing light the size of dimes. The flickering fires around the outer margins of the room were not part of a sorority ritual but only the ordinary candles on the ordinary tables, and the man dancing nearest to her was just a stupid guy she'd known for years—Jack Farrington, to be exact— and his partner, a cute little blonde spinning in a froth of crinolines, could not possibly be Susie because that *really* wouldn't make any sense.

The band brought the tune to what was supposed to be a rousing finale. Jack and the blonde—she was giggling and fanning herself with a bare hand— were walking off the dance floor, and Gloria followed them to their table. She saw Binkie and Judy and a younger girl she didn't know very well—although she was a country club kid and Gloria did know her name: Mary Anne some- thing-or-other. The girls were all wearing full skirts with masses of crinolines. She saw Mike Clark and Lee Hockner, both, like Jack, wearing ties, although they'd shed their jackets by now. Oh, she thought, it's just the same old crowd in the same old club—but what had she expected? This wasn't a formal dance, but it was a big deal—at least for kids her age; she didn't see too many of the older folks in the room. As she'd approached, the guys at the table had risen to their feet, and, oddly, so had Binkie, who emitted a small yelp. "Hi, Bink," Gloria said to her.

Binkie had caught Gloria's hand and was whispering: "Wow, are you ever dressed up! When you first walked in, I thought you were your mother."

Oh, just great! Gloria thought.

"Sit down, Gloria," somebody else was saying, and Mike pulled out a chair for her, but sitting down was simply not possible, and she wondered how she was going to manage the rest of the night without doing it. Would the boys ever sit down, or would they just go on standing interminably, like statues, waiting for her? She couldn't remember now why wearing the darned sheath had seemed so crucially important, and she envied the other girls their full skirts. Lee—of course it was Lee—was asking what she was drinking. "Martini, thank you," she said automatically. "You sweet boy," she added, just as automatically, but wasn't sure he'd heard her, and Binkie was saying, "Look who I found!"

Gloria looked, and she was being directed to look at the little blonde, and Gloria's mouth went dry because it really *was* Susie—which, of course, was impossible. But the little blonde was staring back at her, and then—horribly, like one of those maddening visual puzzles in the Psych 100 textbook in which you suddenly see that it's not a lamp on a table but a lady wearing a hat—*of course* it wasn't Susie, but someone else, someone she didn't know at all, and Gloria felt sick at heart. "Come on, Glo," Binkie said, prompting them, enjoying herself, "the senior prom—"

"Oh," the blonde said, squealing, "oh, my gosh, it's Gloria Cotter!"

As much as Gloria was longing to squeal back a name as effective as Rumplestiltskin's, she still couldn't do it.

"Come on, I haven't changed that much," the blonde said, "at least I don't think I have—but boy, have *you* ever. I didn't know you at all."

Gloria's face was burning, and she still didn't know this person who was saying, "Oh, this is silly! Come on, Gloria, I was your princess."

"Oh!" Gloria said, "Sandy Caldwell"—the same Sandy Caldwell she'd beaten by only a few votes for Prom Queen—but Sandy wasn't a country club girl. Gloria had never seen her in the country club. What the devil was she doing here? And the only thing left for Gloria now was to impersonate a normal girl, so, giggling, she reached out to take Sandy's hand, but Sandy stepped toward her unexpectedly, and they hugged each other a moment, awkwardly.

"I must be crazy," Gloria said. "You haven't changed at all."

Sandy was one of those damnably cute, baby-faced, pint-sized girls who'd looked fourteen when they'd been eighteen; like everyone else in their class, she was a year older than Gloria so now must be twenty-two, but she *still* looked fourteen—and was dressed like it: her hair up in a high ponytail, no more makeup than mascara and a neat splash of brilliant lipstick, so many crinolines under the skirt of her sprightly pink dress it looked like candy floss, and, on her tiny feet, flats, of course, and not any old flats but perfect white Capezios. Sandy Caldwell had been head majorette their senior year, and Gloria felt again what she'd felt in high school: awe and envy and a nasty—utterly unbecoming—sense of superiority. "Wow," she said, "it's great to see you. How have you been?"

Lee Hockner had arrived at her side; she felt his breath on her neck. She turned toward him, and he pressed a glass into her hand. So far as she could see, Gloria was wearing the only shoulder-length evening gloves in the club, and the only other sheaths were on grown-up ladies, and so, keenly aware of how *outré* she must look, she gave Lee the mysterious, Spanish smile that went with her costume and—just as though she drank the darned things all the time—gulped down half the martini. The band had launched into an old, slow, syrupy tune, and she could see that Lee was about to ask her to dance, but Jack Farrington beat him to it: "How about it, you sweet thing?" She smiled at Lee and stepped into Jack's arms. Neatly done, she thought: she'd just been extracted from the embarrassing situation with Sandy, and now she had a perfectly good reason to keep on standing up.

Dancing with him, she had to admit that she was a little bit afraid of Jack, but in these heels it was a relief to have someone to lean on. She liked his age, the feeling of being held not by some sappy boy but by a man, and she liked his size—it was a substantial, embraceable, comfortable size—and she liked the bay rum and pipe tobacco smell of him. "So, my little, dark beauty," he said, "who are you dressed up for tonight?"

"For nobody, Mister Wolf. Just 'cause I felt like it." Well done, Gloria, she thought. That had sounded exactly like something a normal girl would say if she were trying to be disgustingly cute.

Jack was dancing her out onto the terrace—a standard maneuver for a guy who wanted to make out—but she didn't care, and she couldn't stop thinking about Sandy Caldwell. It was bizarre; the last person in the world she would have expected to see—or would have wanted to see—was Sandy, and it was almost as though she'd magically made her appear by thinking about Susie, and that didn't make any sense at all, but she'd been convinced for a moment that Sandy *was* Susie—which, maybe, wasn't all that surprising: they were both cute, blonde majorettes, and their names both started with S—and, looking over Jack's shoulder, she saw Mr. Dougherty. Oh, just terrific, she thought. He was sitting alone, unmoving, his head tilted down toward his table. But, as she danced slowly past, he looked up and saw her; his expression didn't change, but he followed her with his eyes, then with his entire head, turning constantly in her direction like a mechanical device. She pretended she hadn't seen him.

So what was Sandy Caldwell doing at the country club? Gloria had just been flooded with memories—and their concomitant emotions—from high school, and she was trying to sort them out. Majorettes were never anyone—as her mother would have put it—of *our sort*; their fathers owned garages or used car lots or worked in mills or were farmers. Gloria didn't know Sandy well enough to know if her father had really been a farmer (Gloria had trouble imagining that *anybody* could be a farmer), but the other kids had teased Sandy about being a farm girl, and she'd lived so far out the pike, way out beyond Hayley's Rise somewhere, that she'd had to ride the school bus into Canden High every morning— and Jack had just allowed his hand to slide from the small of her back down to the tight seat of her sheath, but she didn't care. Susie was so much a better twirler than Sandy that there really wasn't any comparison, but, in high school, Sandy had certainly been the best majorette Gloria had ever seen.

And now they were out on the darkest part of the terrace—still dancing. The air was nice, a relief. "Hey, Gloria, you're really a sweet kid, you know that," Jack said. Just as she was supposed to, she turned to look at him, and he kissed her. She allowed him to bump into her closed lips for a while, but then, sighing—a sigh seemed to be exactly what was required to match the courtliness he was radiating—she opened her mouth, and they drifted into a long, soft, smoky soul kiss. His hips were pressed firmly into hers, and they were moving gently, like a boat rocked by ripples, and she replied by gently stroking his neck and ear with her gloved fingertips—she was sure he'd love the gloves—and she understood now what should have been obvious from the moment she'd decided to go to the club tonight: *this* was why she'd decided to go to the club tonight— if not Jack, then somebody else; any reasonably tall, reasonably good-looking guy would do.

"Hey," she said after a while, "we better go back in," and they both sighed. "Ah, so sweet," he murmured, "so very, very sweet."

You're pretty sweet yourself, you old faker, she thought—but he might be amusing for the rest of the summer. She allowed him to hold her hand until they were inside, and then, with what she hoped was a sufficiently sweet and promising smile, she used Binkie to detach herself. Now she and Binkie seemed to be holding hands—how odd—and Binkie bent to whisper in her ear: "Hey, Glo, you all right?"

"Oh. Sure. Don't I look all right?"

"You look kind of—I don't know. A million miles away."

Gloria couldn't find any reply to that. "You look just fabulous, by the way," Binkie said. "So what's the big occasion?"

Tell her something she'll understand, Gloria thought. "Oh, Bink, Rolland and I split up. I mean for good."

"Oh, you poor thing!"

"I really don't want to talk about it, Bink. If I do, I'll just start bawling."

"Oh, gee." Binkie squeezed Gloria's hand. "You want another drink?"

"Heavens, no. That's the last thing in the world I want."

Sandy Caldwell was jitterbugging with Mike Clark. Binkie was watching, and so Gloria watched too. Mike was a good, energetic dancer (not as good as Rolland, she thought with a pang), but Sandy was truly magnificent. Gloria watched her execute three tight, continuous turns as perfect as a ballerina's pirouettes; they sent her crinolines spinning beautifully, and some of the other dancers had stopped to watch; some were even applauding. Then Mike turned her again, and, as she was turned, she laughed as though she'd guessed what terrible thing was coming straight at her—for Mike caught her and thrust her into a brutally precipitous reverse turn—but easily, without even the faintest stutter of her tiny feet, she was already unwinding in that impossible other way. With a brisk snap, her skirt and crinolines stood straight out, allowing Gloria— and everyone else who was watching—the briefest, flickering glimpse of her stocking tops and white garters and adorable lace-trimmed panties. Gloria felt a raw emotion she couldn't quite identify; it was a *mental* response, surely, yet it felt *physical*, like something chafing at her. How utterly, revoltingly *cute!* she thought. The rest of her martini was waiting on the table; she drank it quickly so she wouldn't chicken out, and then she ate the olive.

"She's a great dancer, isn't she?" Binkie said.

"Oh, she certainly is. Although don't you think that outfit's a little—you know, just a little excessively *jeune fille* for somebody our age? What is she *doing* here?"

"Oh, I ran into her on Market Street and we went into Howe Ferris, and, well, you know, she doesn't live here anymore, just home visiting, and one thing led to another, and she said, 'Hey, I'd love to go to that dance tonight,' and I said, 'Well, good heavens, you come over to my house, and I'll take you.'"

And that, Gloria thought, was fairly gracious of Binkie considering the fact that when they'd been in high school, Binkie wouldn't have given Sandy Caldwell the time of day.

Lee was coming over, and Binkie bent again to whisper in Gloria's ear: "You better watch out for him. He's pissed, and he's on the make."

"That's news?" Gloria said, and they both laughed. Lee was offering Gloria another martini. "Well, thank you, kind sir," she said.

"Don't mention it, fair miss," and he gave her a deep, theatrical bow. She replied with as much of a curtsy as she could manage in the sheath. He was staring with frank appreciation at her cleavage. The jitterbug had ended and a waltz had begun, and Binkie, with a significant look at Gloria, wrapped one of her large, white arms around Lee's neck: "It's my turn now, you big goof." She thinks she's protecting me, Gloria thought, amused.

As she watched Lee and Binkie waltzing away in a stiff box step, Gloria saw that Sandy was walking off the dance floor, her face beautifully flushed, and Gloria said: "Hey, Sandy,"—still thinking about Susie, she was very careful to say *Sandy*—"you're just a great dancer."

"Oh, I should be." It was something Gloria was sure Sandy wouldn't have said if she hadn't been breathless and giddy from dancing—and then, looking directly at Gloria, she said, as though catching up with herself: "Holy cow, is it ever a hot night!"

Their eyes met, and, unexpectedly, Sandy's face changed; she gave Gloria a wry, quizzical look—it was an expression that revealed both intelligence and self-awareness—and Gloria knew that she liked Sandy Caldwell and always had. It had been her wretched, country club snobbery that had stopped her from being Sandy's friend.

"I'm sorry I never got to know you very well in high school," Gloria, surprised, heard herself saying. "I always admired you."

"Me?" Sandy said, obviously just as startled, and pressed her fingertips against her breastbone, indicating, Gloria supposed, the essence of me-ness.

Gloria's tongue seemed to have run away with her, and now it was all she could do to stop herself from saying: "And *you* should have been Prom Queen."

"Well, I always admired you too," Sandy said. Before Gloria could think of how to reply to that, she felt a sweaty hand on her shoulder, turned and saw Mike Clark giving her a big, gleaming smile—all teeth—and she had a snapshot memory of him as a scrawny little kid with braces. "So, Miss Cotter, do you still remember how to fox-trot?"

"Sure, Master Clark, but in this skirt don't expect me to be Ginger Rogers."

"Oh, no, we'll take it easy."

She'd known Mike since they'd been in dance class together; he was a year younger, and she still thought of him as a little boy—which was not hard to do; in these heels, she had to be a couple inches taller than he was—but, to her surprise, she liked holding his tense, compact little body, and he'd always been a good dancer. He was even shortening his steps for her. "Hey, gorgeous Gloria," he said, "you look great tonight—just like a picture in *Esquire*."

"Oh, you say the sweetest things."

"Yeah, I do, don't I? Hey, why don't you marry me?"

"Michael! I never knew you cared."

"Didn't you? Why, I've always been your number one fan, glorious Gloria." He was dancing her through the side door and out into the hallway.

"What are we doing out here, Michael?"

He pointed at the crack between her breasts. "I'm fighting off an uncontrollable urge to drop a penny down there."

Laughing, she realized how much of a relief it was to find something genuinely funny.

"How about a kiss for old time's sake?" he said with what she supposed was intended to be a leer.

She and Mike had kidded and teased each other for years, but she'd never kissed him; it would never have occurred to her that it was even possible to kiss him, but now she gave him a look that said: go ahead. He grabbed her, pushed her against the wall, and shoved his tongue into her mouth. It had been so sudden and rough she felt like slapping him, but after she'd recovered from the initial annoyance of it, she found his kiss quite engaging, even exhilarating: she liked his urgency—his open, boyish hunger—and she especially liked it that the kiss would have no consequences whatsoever. Jack would almost certainly call her up tomorrow, but Mike wouldn't.

She heard footsteps and pushed him away. A couple her parents' age walked by, pretending they hadn't seen anything. "What are you drinking?" he said.

"Martini."

As they were standing at the bar, Mike let his hand slide down from the small of her back to her derrière. Gloria was not exactly inexperienced with fraternity boys, and Mike was most emphatically a fraternity boy—was, in fact, a KA, as he bragged constantly—and, with fraternity boys like Mike, the only possible tactic was to get right to the point. "If you don't take your hand off my bottom, I'm going to throw this martini in your face," she said sweetly.

He laughed, removed his hand, toasted her with his double bourbon. "Come on, kitten," he said, "chug-a-lug."

"Meow," she said and tilted back her martini.

He jerked his head back in a mime of someone who's been punched in the mouth—"Yowee!"—and they clinked their empty glasses.

As he walked her back to their table, he said, "So Miss Pussycat, what are you doing later tonight?"

"Getting my beauty sleep."

"Want some company?"

"Well, of course. I'm sure my parents would just love that." She deliberately walked within a foot of Mr. Dougherty's table and didn't notice him at all.

As much as Gloria wanted to avoid Sandy Caldwell, there seemed to be no avoiding her—it was beginning to feel *weird*, fated—because they seemed to be walking off the dance floor together. Mike asked Sandy to dance, and she said, "The next one, OK? I need a breather."

The girls were left momentarily alone. "Love your dress, Gloria," Sandy said. "I'd never have the guts to wear something like that out in public."

"Oh," Gloria wanted to say, "where *would* you wear it?" but she didn't.

"It's funny," Sandy was saying, "it feels just like back in high school. We were always waiting to see what you'd be wearing. Wow, did you see what Gloria had on today! And you were always one-upping everybody. Yeah, you sure knew how to get the boys going— You still do."

That speech had been delivered in a breathy, girlish, perfectly friendly voice—punctuated with a self-deprecating giggle—but Gloria had heard the rancor in it, and she didn't know what to say.

"Hey, that sounded catty," Sandy said after a moment. "I didn't mean it that way."

"That's OK. I didn't take it that way." Looking closely at her, Gloria remembered the complicated—at the time, utterly confusing—emotion she'd felt watching Sandy in her cute, glittering, blatantly sexy uniform as she'd led the Canden High band across the football field, twirling her baton, marching with a perky, self-assured strut, the blonde embodiment of everything Gloria could never possibly be. She'd felt smugly superior to Sandy—and she'd had no right to feel like that—and she'd been jealous of her too. Now she knew that Sandy had been jealous *of her*. How very sad.

"You ever see Lisa?" Sandy was saying. That was Lisa Metzger, the other majorette Gloria had beaten for Prom Queen.

"No, I haven't seen her for a couple years—heard she was married," and then, responding to what she *knew* Sandy had to be thinking: "I was amazed when I beat both of you. I really was. I always thought you deserved it more than I did."

She looked straight into Sandy's pale-blue eyes and read her mind again. She doesn't believe me, Gloria thought, and she felt an enormous weariness. Words were so darned slippery; you had to use them so carefully, and sometimes even then they didn't work right.

"Well, you were the most popular girl in our class," Sandy said.

"Oh, no, I wasn't."

"Well, who was then? Couldn't have been me. Couldn't have been Lisa. We didn't get the votes."

"It was a close vote. Mr. Clements told me that."

"Yeah, he told me that too. But a vote's a vote. That's democracy."

"Oh, Sandy— Look, I think people just voted for me because I was the underdog. And anyhow, I never *felt* popular. It was all just a big act. The whole time in high school, I was just scared to death."

Sandy again gave her that clear, level, attentive look which Gloria had decided was one of her most distinctive features. "You too, huh? Hey, you want to get some air?"

"Sure." They began walking toward the terrace, but Lee Hockner and Mike Clark were heading them off. Like a vaudeville team, the boys were yelling alternating lines:

"Come on, ladies—"

"The night's young—"

"The shank of the night—"

"When the doings are right—"

"Got to get out—"

"On the ole dance floor!"

They must have decided ahead of time who got whom, because, without hesitation, Mike scooped Sandy and Lee wrapped Gloria up in his sweaty arms. Having just played dreamy-young-thing for Jack and naughty-sex-kitten for Mike, she wondered who Lee might want her to be. Then, feeling how tightly he was holding her, how firmly he was pressing his pelvis into hers, she knew that he didn't require a fully embodied *persona*: all he wanted was a compliant girl. He was dancing her off into the darkest part of the room, but she didn't care. "Having a good summer, Gloria?" he murmured wetly in her ear.

"Oh, yes," she said, "just dandy."

"Cool."

"How about you?"

"Oh, yeah, just dandy too." Now she could feel his penis down there poking at her like a big, irritating finger—but she didn't care. "Boy, do you ever look beautiful tonight," he said, and she knew he meant *sexy*—and she thought that there might be something to be said for alcohol after all because she'd just felt an enormous, soaring lift as though she'd just been shot into space, and her mind was moving at a million miles an hour. It had started with thinking of "beautiful" and Stevens' lines:

> Beauty is momentary in the mind—
> The fitful tracing of a portal;
> But in the flesh it is immortal.

And now she was thinking about that ancient dichotomy: the mind and the flesh, the body and the spirit—asking herself what it means to be immortal *in the flesh*, and remembering all the times she'd dreamed of being back in high school, and, therefore, dreamed of Sandy—there were often majorettes in her dreams—but then, of course, it wasn't Sandy *herself*, the real person, but that beauty she embodied *in the flesh*, and that beauty—however hard to define—of which she was emblematic, because, as Gloria had learned from her friendship with Susie, a majorette embodies the ideals of small-town, working-class America, and Gloria wondered if she herself had ever been emblematic in that way. Well, she'd never had the privilege of that ritualized, impersonal, numinous beauty that was attached to a majorette— although, on second thought, what else was a Prom Queen or a May Queen but a ritual object? And she wished she could have seen herself being May Queen, and she wished she could talk to Susie because she really missed her—and if she went slowly, step by step, patiently through all of this, Susie would understand exactly what she was talking about, and she didn't know anyone else who would—

Lee caught her under the chin and turned her face up toward his. She didn't know whether she wanted to kiss him or not, but she'd just kissed Jack and Mike, so why shouldn't she kiss him? It was true that he was a complete and utter jerk, but he was a good-looking jerk, and he was certainly tall enough, so she opened her mouth. His tongue shot immediately between her teeth just as she'd known it would.

Having led them away into a dark corner by now, Lee abandoned any pretense of dancing; he gripped her derrière firmly with one hand, the back of her neck with the other, and ground his groin into hers. He was, she decided after a few minutes, a pretty darned good kisser—which, of course, he should have been with all the practice he'd had—and, in fact, he was so good a kisser that her whole line of thought had come unwound like a dropped spool of thread, and she didn't want to think about anything much except enjoying the physical sensations of being kissed. He was very inventive, and, whatever he did, she did it back to him, and she began to feel that familiar melting sensation that told her she was getting hot, and she thought how odd it was to be getting hot with someone she neither knew very well nor liked even remotely—and then she wondered if she'd been getting hot before, with Jack and Mike. Of course she had.

The tune ended. "Hey," she said. He didn't want to let go of her. "Hey," she said again, "I've got to go to the little girls'."

"Yeah, right." He reluctantly allowed her to push him away, then looked at her as though deeply surprised at precisely whom she'd turned out to be. "Wow, Gloria, you're something else. Yeah, you really are."

That's right, she thought, I'm a real party doll, and bent close, as though to whisper something to him, caught his earlobe between her teeth, and bit it somewhat harder than she'd intended. She heard a gratifying gasp, and, before he could do anything at all, she walked away. Carrying the image of his unnerved and angry eyes, she felt disgustingly pleased with herself, and now she was in the hallway and her bag was still right where she'd left it—back on the table—so what was she supposed to do about that?

Not having found any satisfactory answer, she was already in the ladies' room. A dozen or so girls were primping in front of the wall of mirrors above the pink-tiled counter; many of them looked so young that this could easily have been their first country club dance, and they were emitting a constant high-pitched chirping like tweety birds—

"So cute, yes, really, wow!"

"You know, I had her all year in home ec—"

"You've got to be kidding!"

The place stank of perfume and sweat, and the girls were busy, busy, busy. They were wearing crinolines and flats. Their nail polish was either pink or bright red. They were putting on lipstick, powdering their noses, flicking their eyelashes, putting on rouge, taking off white shorty gloves, putting on white shorty gloves, checking a zillion tiny details. There was a constant rustle of crinolines—

"And then you know what he did? He kissed *my fingers!*"

"No, come on!"

"Had it made by the lady at Eberhardt's—

"But does he *really* like me? You know, *really* really?"

Gloria wondered vaguely if she had to go to the bathroom, but if she did, she just might as well go home—and, in a free bit of mirror, she saw a distant image of herself: standing just inside the door, standing stupidly, looking blankly at herself with bloody lipstick smeared ear to ear.

"Pittsburgh. You know, at Kaufmann's. For real. Nine-ninety-eight."

"And you know what he said to him? 'Take it easy, greasy—'"

"Oh, no, it's just stunning on you—"

"Of course he likes you, you silly, just look at the way he *looks* at you!"

Gloria had a strong sense of *déjà vu*—but no, that wasn't right; it wasn't as though she'd been here before, it was as though *before* had become *here*, whatever that might mean. I can't stand this, she thought. She turned and walked out.

The band wasn't playing at the moment, and Gloria heard her heels going click, click, click on the hardwood floor. Oh, but high heels were a strange invention! When they were this high, she hated wearing them for very long— although she loved the way she looked in them and was proud of herself for being able to put up with the discomfort, and now she wondered if it were possible to see herself walking in heels the way a boy would see her. Probably not. Maybe her appreciation of herself in heels wasn't sexual at all, but *aesthetic*— But then Freud said that *everything* was sexual even if you weren't consciously aware of it, so maybe it was like that wonderful title of Edna St. Vincent Millay's less than wonderful poem: "Euclid Alone Has Looked on Beauty Bare," and so, unless you were Euclid looking at a triangle, maybe everything *did* have a sexual element to it, even her experience of *poetry*— And then her mind, skittering off again, suggested that it might be fun to make a list of literary works whose titles were better than the works themselves. But the first one she thought of she didn't know whether it was better or worse because the title was so wonderful she'd always been afraid to read the book: "Everything That Rises Must Converge." And, in a distant, ineffectual way she was still worrying about the lipstick all over her face, and then she felt a thought enter her; she felt as detached from it as if it had literally been dropped into her skull from somewhere else: *none of this is real*—

She felt somebody's fingers on her arm. It wasn't a boy; it was Susie. "Gloria? Do you mind if I talk to you a minute?"

No, of course it wasn't Susie, it was *Sandy*, and Gloria's mind was scattered into a thousand useless pieces—it had been that way for a while—and all she could do was respond to the literal sense of what Sandy had said: "Oh, no. Why on earth would I mind that?"

"Well, you seem to be having such a good time, and I don't want to—you know, spoil it."

"It's not *that* good a time, believe me. Come on, let's go outside."

Passing their table, she snagged her evening bag. "This is really silly," Sandy was saying, "but— Look, I'm sorry for this, but— What you said really upset me. Did you think I held it against you because you beat me for Prom Queen?"

"I never thought about it at all," Gloria said—in the state she was in, she couldn't imagine saying anything but the absolute truth—"and even if you did hold it against me, it wouldn't matter."

"But I *never* held it against you. I really didn't."

"OK," Gloria said although she knew perfectly well that Sandy *still* held it against her.

Gloria found a table with a patch of light spilling onto it from a window. She put her bag down on the table. She opened it. She took out a compact and a little package of Kleenex and a toy-sized jar of cold cream. She looked at herself in the compact mirror. A smeared-mouthed, excessively made-up, dimwitted little idiot was gazing back at her with eyes as big, black, and vacant as a doll's—and how could she avoid getting cold cream smeared all over her mother's ungodly expensive, made-in-Paris, finest-quality-kid evening gloves? She could, of course, take them off, but then, of course, she'd have to put them back on again, because, if you've worn something that pretentious, you don't simply chicken out and leave them off. She felt as though she were confronting a task—or was it a series of tasks?—as mindless, maddening, finicky, and interminable as Psyche's. Coming to the club tonight was the dumbest thing she'd ever done in her life.

Sandy had been watching her. Without a word, Sandy opened the jar of cold cream, put a bit of it on a Kleenex, and cleaned Gloria's mouth. "Thank you so much," Gloria said, "you're really too kind," and from what old novel had that line come?

Gloria painted a bright red mouth onto herself again while Sandy, without speaking, continued to watch her, and, in that moment of being so purely scrutinized, she realized that she was drunk—well, maybe not wildly drunk, not as drunk as a fraternity boy would have put it—stinking, pissed, plastered, or bombed—but maybe just a teensy bit drunker than she'd ever been in her life.

Sandy walked over to the balustrade, and Gloria followed her. They turned and faced each other. I don't know why I keep thinking of her as pint-sized, Gloria thought. She's not any smaller than I am. It must be these heels. And she was still waiting to hear the real reason why Sandy had wanted to talk to her.

"Oh, gee, I never thought I'd be here," Sandy said in a bemused voice that was meant, Gloria knew, to imply that what she was saying had just popped into her mind. "This was always—you know, for the select few, the ultra, ultra. The cream of the crop. Yeah, the lovely, lovely, lovely country club girls. You and Binkie and Judy and all the rest of you."

Gloria knew that it wouldn't do any good to say, "Believe me, if you'd been coming here for years, you'd find it all just too boring for words," but she couldn't think of anything else—and then she knew that she'd been wrong before: she *was* just as drunk as any fraternity boy would have put it. She was, as a matter of fact, pissed out of her damned skull.

"I'm sorry," Sandy said. "I don't know what's got into me. I shouldn't have said that."

Gloria made an effort to pull herself together. "Don't be sorry. You can say anything you want. It's OK. I was jealous of you too. But that's a long time ago, so why don't we start over and be friends?"

After a moment, Sandy said, "How on earth could you have been jealous of me?"

You've got to simplify it, Gloria told herself. Unless you do, she won't understand a word you're saying. "Because you were so cute," she said. "Because you were head majorette."

"Oh, come on."

"No, I mean it. I would have loved to be a majorette—and you were just *so darned good*. And I always thought that being a majorette was something really special."

Gloria looked down toward the dark shadow of the golf course. It was a dark night. Where was the moon tonight? "Yeah?" Sandy said, "so what's so special about it?"

She thinks I'm patronizing her, Gloria thought, and the unfortunate thing, of course, was that she had been. So what could she say now? Could she tell her about beauty being embodied in the flesh, made immortal in the flesh— that elusive beauty of which Sandy had been emblematic in the Yeatsean sense? Oh, sure.

Please, Gloria thought, when do I get to go to sleep? Thinking of Susie more than of Sandy, she said, "It's an art."

"Art?" Sandy said in a quiet, deadly voice, "come on."

Gloria didn't dare look at Sandy. Her mother's evening gloves were suddenly so tight and hot she wanted to rip them off—and then she realized that she'd just broken out in a sweat. The secret watcher had not been around for a while, but now it said, "You didn't just beat her for Prom Queen, *you took her boyfriend*."

Oh, help! Gloria thought. She can't still be holding that against me five years later, can she?

"You bet she can," the secret watcher said.

Gloria felt sick. She hoped that if she stood there long enough without speaking, Sandy would simply walk away, but Sandy didn't walk away.

"Come on, ladies," Mike was calling to them across the terrace, "you can't hide out here!" Lee was with him, and he was bringing Gloria yet another damn martini.

Gloria turned toward Sandy, and one look at her eyes told her everything she needed to know. "Well, what do you think, guys?" Sandy sang out sweetly, "doesn't our Gloria look simply lovely tonight!"

"Oh, yeah," Lee said, "she sure does. Cool. Super cool."

With a slow, pitiless deliberation, Sandy looked Gloria over, from her heels to her face. She looked directly into Gloria's eyes. Never since she'd been at Fairhaven had Gloria seen anyone look at her with such undisguised loathing. "So sophisticated," Sandy cooed, and, smiling, she said to Mike, "Come on, sweetie, I hear them playing our song."

To hide her shame, Gloria drank the entire martini and felt her stomach contract violently. Sandy had left her alone with Lee, and he was drunk. His face showed exactly what he was thinking.

Her desire to dance with Lee Hockner—or with anybody for that matter—was nonexistent, and all she wanted to do was run home and cry. She knew exactly what was about to happen next, and she didn't want it to happen, but it felt, nonetheless, inevitable. She allowed Lee to guide her onto the dance floor.

In the same dark corner where Lee had put the make on her the last time, Gloria dutifully tilted her face up and opened her mouth. He tasted like whiskey and cigarettes; he'd tasted like that the last time around—all the boys tasted like some kind of alcohol and some kind of tobacco—but then it hadn't bothered her, and now it was making her sick, and this time she wasn't getting hot at all, or, if she was, it was an itchy, unpleasant sensation not too different from needing to pee. "You want to go in the games room?" he asked her in a husky voice.

"Sure," she said.

She wondered if he'd checked to make sure the games room was empty—or maybe he'd talked to the other guys and told them to stay clear—and, as soon as they were inside, he grabbed the back of her neck, shoved his tongue into her mouth, jammed her up against the pool table, and slammed his groin into her pelvis. Her sleek silhouette—however sexy it might be to look at—seemed to be presenting him with quite a challenge: he kept shifting his hips around, trying to find some angle in which all that driving, grinding, thrusting motion would feel better—or maybe even just feel reasonably *good*—and if she hadn't despised him, she would have felt sorry for him. It was, from her point of view as the passive recipient of it, an entirely meaningless activity, and the only pleasure she could find in it was in the contemplation of the thoroughly repellant notion that she was getting exactly what she deserved. She wanted to get it over with as quickly as possible, however, so she turned slightly to allow him to wrap his legs around the outside of her left thigh, and that seemed to have improved things because he began to hump more quickly.

The way he was kissing her was making her sick, and she wanted to speed things up even more, so she pried his face off hers and did intentionally what she'd been afraid of doing accidentally all night: arched her back, thrust her chest forward, and allowed her breasts to bob free. He made a sound halfway between a groan and a sob, pawed her breasts out of her scooped neckline, and began sucking and licking her exposed nipples—and the last scintilla of that rationality that, according to Aristotle, separates the human from the animal vanished: like Circe, Gloria had transformed him into a swine.

Gloria closed her eyes and prayed for it to be over. The sensation of his fingers, teeth, and tongue on her breasts was making her hot, and, even though she was trying to be a good sport about this, and even though she could very well be getting exactly what she deserved ("let the punishment fit the crime," her mind was stupidly singing), it was nasty, sticky, ugly, and profoundly annoying, and if he didn't get finished soon, she'd just have to push him off. She opened her eyes and, looking over Lee's shoulder, saw, standing in the partially opened doorway, staring directly at her, Mr. Dougherty.

Oh, just great, she thought. She closed her eyes to make him go away, and then, when she opened them again, she saw, to her amazement, that it had worked: he was gone.

Now Lee was making a sound like, "ugh, ugh, ugh," and with each "ugh," he slammed into her so hard she could feel the heavy pool table being driven backward inch by inch. Gloria was sure that if someone were to press a gun against Lee's forehead and say, "Stop or I'll blow your brains out," Lee would keep right on going. No matter what happened, Lee simply could *not* stop, because Lee was no longer that smug, self-assured, country club boy she'd detested for years; now he was a pathetic, witless hog, and some part of herself— a part she didn't like very much—was pleased to see him like that. He was slamming her harder and faster; he emitted several more, "ugh, ugh, ughs," and then with a final huge, groaning "ugh!" he finished.

He continued to clutch onto her for a few seconds longer. As she felt his entire body going slack, she began to disentangle him. She pushed his hands away, stepped away, bent over and tucked her breasts back in. She straightened up and saw that he was looking at her with a sorrowful, flaccid face. "Ah, Gloria," he said.

She smiled at him just the way Sandy had smiled at her, pointed at the big stain on the front of his pants, and walked out before he could get either of his reaching hands anywhere near her. In the hall she bumped into Mr. Dougherty—literally *bumped* —and rebounded from his chest. He didn't step aside for her but stood, barring her way, and made no sign that he intended to move.

"Good heavens, Mr. Dougherty, *excuse me*," she said.

He stared down at her without speaking. Then, grinning, he said, "What do you say there, princess? You want to take a little walk with your Uncle Billy?"

"No, not much."

She tried to get around him, but he stepped to the side so she couldn't do it. She was afflicted by an enormous weariness.

"Come on, princess, let's take us a little walk."

"Why on earth would I want to do that?"

"Oh, I just think you and me need to have us a little chat."

"I don't think so."

"Yeah? Well, suppose I just tell your old man exactly what I seen in the games room back there."

"What makes you think he'd believe you?"

"Oh, he'd believe me all right. Your old man and me go back a long ways."

"I know. You've told me."

"Come on, honey. I just got something I want to say to you. You won't even miss the next dance, swear to God. Come on, OK? And then I'll just forget everything I seen. How's that? We got a deal?"

Gloria leaned against the wall and closed her eyes; she was tired of wearing these shoes—as a matter of fact, they were killing her—and a circular, dark motion swirled under her as though she could fall right off her heels and go careening down a well a million miles deep. Oh, dear, she thought, am I going to pass out? I don't *want* to pass out.

She opened her eyes, and Mr. Dougherty was still there, still grinning. He offered his arm, and all she could find in herself was a numb, tired acquiescence. She took his arm and allowed him to lead her through the front entrance and down the steps.

A light breeze was drifting up from the golf course, and it felt delicious; she'd been in the club so long she'd forgotten how hot and close it was in there. Now she could see the moon; it was the newest of new moons—a crisp hair-line of silver—and a voice in her mind said: "In the moon barge—pale eyes as if without fire."

The sky was the color of charcoal, and it was pulsing with stars like a Van Gogh, and she thought: I'm not a part of this, not really. My life doesn't depend on this. I'm leaving in September, and after that, I'll never have to set foot in the Raysburg Country Club, never never never never. Thinking of that, she felt the possibility that she might actually be happy sometime again.

She allowed Mr. Dougherty to lead her down the walk toward the golf course. She listened to her heels going scritch, scritch, scritch on the concrete. "Nice night," he said.

"Splendiferous."

"You're one hell of a girl, princess. Smoke?"

She shook her head. He stopped. She let go of his arm, and he lit a cigarette for himself. "Listen, honey," he said in an earnest tone, "I got your best interests at heart, believe me. Now just answer me a couple questions, OK? What the hell you think you're doing, teasing the boys like that? What the hell you doing letting that little asshole do that to you? That little punk Hockner kid, Jesus. You like him getting his rocks off up against you like that? Your titties all hanging out? That your idea of a good time?"

"I don't think it's any of your business, Mr. Dougherty."

"Oh, snooty, snooty! Well, shit, I guess I'm just making it my business. Look, princess, all I'm trying to say to you is— Goddamn it, you're gonna pick the wrong guy sometime and end up in the old deep doo-doo without a paddle. You with me?"

She didn't want to talk about this; talking about this was making her really tired. "You haven't got any right to say a word, Mr. Dougherty. After what you did."

"Jesus, honey, what do you think I did?"

Why was she out here in the dark with this stupid idiot? Another unpleasant spinning sensation swirled under her, and she badly wanted to go home and go to sleep, but she heard her own voice proceeding doggedly onward: "You know damned well what you did, and I covered up for you. Oh, I can't believe I was that stupid. I actually lied to my father for you. And if he knew what you were doing, he'd— I don't know what he'd do."

"Honey, I'm sorry I got you home late. Is that it? I don't even remember much of that day. I was drunk as a skunk. Believe me, princess, I really *am* sorry."

He was looking at her with his big, cretinous grin—like Apeneck Sweeny's grin that turns into the moon. Wipe your hand across your mouth and laugh? Oh, you bet. He shook his head in puzzlement, and, for a moment, she wondered if he *had* been too drunk to remember—and then she knew that he was drunk right now, really drunk—plastered stupid drunk—and so was she, just two dumb, plastered stupid drunks standing around in the dark saying plastered stupid things to each other.

With an effort, she focused on him. "Good Christ," he was saying, "if your old man could of seen you tonight— Well, it'd just break his heart, that's all."

She hated him for hitting that particular organ note, and, at the same time, she felt she deserved it, so, without speaking, she allowed him to take her arm and lead her all the way down the side of the golf course to the big tree at the edge of the woods.

"Look, honey,"—and now he'd adopted a wheedling, pleading tone—"you don't know it, but I'm the best friend you got."

"Oh, really?" she heard herself saying in a bored, tired voice, "how very astonishing."

"Yeah, I am. And you damn well better believe it. You think I don't know what you think of me? Dumb as a mud fence, right? Stupid as they come, right? Well, that's just fine. That's just dandy. Yeah, lots of people got themselves in the deep doo-doo underestimating old Billy Dougherty, and that's just goddamn fine. But nobody puts anything over on old Billy Dougherty, and that's the honest to God's truth."

A perfect line from somebody or other had just appeared in her mind, and she couldn't resist it: "Oh? Even the potato has its own sly cunning?"

"What the hell you talking about?"

Oh, dear heaven, she was tired! She despised this man, and she no longer had the energy to pretend she didn't. "You, Uncle Billy. I'm talking about you."

He dropped her arm, turned, and thrust his index finger under her nose. "Hey," he said, his voice harsh and thick, "you just watch it, you spoiled little brat. You just watch what you say to me."

She wanted to brush him off like a fly. "Oh, you can just go to hell, Mr. Dougherty. You make me really tired. Please just let me alone, OK? I don't want to drive your silly old car. I don't even want to talk to you— And I don't want to see you watching me. I don't want any more darned roses. *You just let me alone*—or I swear I'm going to tell my father."

"Yeah? And just what the hell you think you're going to tell him? Huh? And just what makes you think he's gonna believe you? Yeah, you lied to him, *and he knows it.*"

For a moment she couldn't believe she'd heard him right, and then, instantly, that curious sense of unreality that had been oppressing her for the last hour was whipped away. She was so angry she could feel her entire body shaking, and she said to him what she'd wanted to say to someone all night: "Fuck you."

He stared at her. Terrified at what had just come out of her mouth, she watched him carefully. Now she understood that the face he ordinarily wore must be a consciously chosen mask—because *this* surely was his authentic face: it was darkly contracted and shrewd and cruel. "Hey," he said, "that's nice."

He was speaking quietly, measuring out his words. "Yeah, Gloria, that's real nice. Jesus, are you ever spoiled rotten. Yeah, Jesus, you're spoiled like a piece of meat that's been laying out in the goddamn sun all day. Jesus, if you was a kid of mine, I'd shove a big bar of soap right in that foul mouth of yours—and I'd goddamn well make you like it."

He stepped back and examined her as though she were a window display— and she'd become detached from her monstrous lassitude; it had been revealed as something self-imposed like a stupidly chosen ensemble (like the one she was wearing at the moment, for instance), something she could remove at will—something she *had* removed—for now she was intensely conscious of a multitude of sensations: the hot churning in her stomach and the sour, acidic taste at the back of her throat; the sweat between her thighs and in her armpits and along the full length of her arms under her mother's gloves; the mosquitoes humming around her face and the bite of the boning at her waist; the painful spasm that was winking on and off in her lower back; the poised tension of her thigh and calf muscles, of her arched feet; she could even feel the narrowness of her heels and the roughness of the concrete under the balls of her feet. She wished she hadn't drunk the martinis; the alcohol was a foreign presence, and it had muddled everything; it was spinning at her, tilting her; it threatened to tip her away.

"Jesus," this man was saying, his voice rising, "who the hell you think you are anyway? The queen of goddamn Sheba? Who give you the right, huh? Jesus, you think your shit don't stink? Walking around looking down your nose at— And just look at that goddamn tight dress and little chippy shoes. Listen. Jesus. Letting some little punk— Jesus, with your goddamn titties hanging out!"

His mouth had dropped open, and he was panting. "Why, you goddamn spoiled little brat," he yelled, "I ought to turn you over my knee right here and now and spank your stuck-up little ass for you."

Now the secret watcher said, clearly and urgently: *"Get out of here."*

Gloria turned immediately and walked back up toward the club. The last thing she needed at the moment was a beauty queen walk, but her costume didn't give her much choice. At least she could take the heels off, and she was bending, reaching for one, when Mr. Dougherty was suddenly right behind her. He grabbed her arm and spun her around. She heard a ripping sound from the darts in her skirt. Oh, great! she thought.

"You don't walk away from me, you little bitch!" he yelled. "You got that?" He squeezed her arm hard and shook her. She gasped, tried to twist away from him, and he laughed.

She was falling off her heels, but he was still clutching her arm, and she used him to steady herself. "Stop it!" she yelled back at him.

He didn't let go of her. "Shut up," he said, "you little cock teaser— I'm gonna tell you a thing or two, and you goddamn well better listen to me and listen real good. You're playing with fire, you know that? You ever had a good fuck? Have you? I mean a real, honest to God, good old-fashioned fuck?"

His fingers were digging into her arm, and he just kept on squeezing harder. "Don't just stand there," the secret watcher said. "Do something. Say something. Get yourself out of this."

"You're hurting me, Mr. Dougherty," she said.

"Hurting you, huh? Shit, you don't know nothing," and with no warning, he delivered a hard, stinging slap to her bottom. She yelped involuntarily, and her eyes flooded. This can't be happening, she thought, her face burning. She wanted to run away like a little kid, but running in this outfit was not even a remote possibility.

"Like that, huh?" he whispered into her ear. "Want more of it? Want your ass toasted real good? Jesus, princess, letting that little asshole get his rocks off on you, and you don't even know what a real man is."

"You bastard!" she said.

"Shut the fuck up, princess," he said. "Jesus, are you ever ripe for it! Good Christ, one of these days you're gonna be down on your knees, just begging for it. Good Christ, just like a goddamn hungry dog. First guy with a hard dick that comes along."

He suddenly let go of her, sprang back, and waved his arms in the air; slowly he began to rotate them in big circles; he swung them faster and faster, like a child pretending with all his heart to be an airplane. It was a movement so unexpected, so entirely outside the realm of anything a grown man—a man her father's age—could possibly do, that she stared at him, fascinated, unable to think.

Panting, he slowly let his arms fall. He paced back and forth pounding his right fist into the open palm of his left hand—smack, smack, smack! And he was yelling again: "Oh, shit, shit, shit, I swear to God, you better learn a thing or two—or someday some guy's just gonna pound you good."

He leapt straight at her with his fist raised. She cringed, and he laughed. Then, still laughing, he grabbed her behind the neck and pressed his fist into her mouth and nose. "See that, princess. Smell your master."

He let go of her and stepped back, laughing hard, doubling up with it like a bad actor told to laugh. She knew she should cry, and she was already crying, so she made herself cry even harder. She was hoping desperately that he would remember who *she* was and who *he* was and where they were, that he would feel sorry for her the way men are supposed to when a girl cries and stop whatever crazy thing it was he was doing, but he walked directly up to her, leaned down into her face, and stared into her eyes, grinning.

"Yeah, go on and cry, little girl," he said in a cheery, crooning voice. "Bawl your eyes out, little girl. You think you're so fucking goddamn smart, huh? Well, you don't know dickshit, believe me. Not goddamn dickshit."

She could feel the rage building in him again. "And these goddamn dumbass—little pissass, limp-dick boys around here—ain't gonna do it for ya. No, honey, believe me. You need a real man with a real cock, shoved up that tight little twat of yours. Uuuh, goddamn, you'd love it!" He grabbed the front of his pants and began kneading himself. Appalled, she looked away.

He seized her jaw with one hand, jerked her head around. "You look at me!" He swung his fist directly at her and stopped just a few inches short of her nose. "And don't you dare make a fucking sound."

She could think again. It had never occurred to her to yell until he'd told her not to, but back in the safety of the club the band had kicked into a loud swing tune, and even if she yelled her head off, nobody would hear her, and even if they did, they'd think it was just some kids fooling around. Shrieks and yells from down on the golf course were not all that uncommon at the Raysburg Country Club late on a Saturday night. Deliberately, Mr. Dougherty was undoing his belt, unzipping his fly, pushing down his trousers and boxer shorts.

But he couldn't possibly hit her. He was bluffing. He *had* to be bluffing. If he hit her, he'd be out of a job—or even worse. She couldn't imagine what her father would do to him, but if he hit her, her father would do something truly terrible to him—and that's what she should say: "Stop it. My father's going to kill you." But she couldn't get the words to come out.

A thick uncircumcised penis stood up between his legs. "See that!" he hissed at her. "That's what a man's got."

"Yes, he'd really hit you," the secret watcher said. "Keep your mouth shut, and don't move." And that was right: he couldn't stop now any more than Lee could have stopped; he couldn't stop even if what he was doing were to wreck his entire life, and Gloria knew with absolute certainty that if she tried to stop him, he would hit her, and once he hit her, he might very well go on hitting her, and it would take forever for anybody up in the club to do anything about it.

"You take a good look, princess," he said. "Here's what you need."

She closed her eyes. She felt his hand slap onto the back of her neck and squeeze. *"I said look at it."* He shook her head, then tilted it down.

Dizzy and nauseated, she kept her eyes focused on his penis. All on its own it was standing up like a thick, hard fist. He closed his big hand around it. "You like that?" he yelled. "Do you? Big, fucking, hard thing shoved up your twat? That what you want? Shoved up you real good? Real deep? Real hard?"

He began pulling rhythmically on his penis. "Jesus fuck. Gonna shove it in, shove it in—gonna pound you, pound you, pound you good." His other hand was still squeezing the back of her neck, bearing down, digging in. She tried to wince away, but his grip was a tightening vice. She heard a thin, involuntary line of pain unwinding from her throat.

"You slut, you cunt, you bitch, you whore," he hissed at her. "You bitch, you bitch, you bitch, you bitch, you bitch— Gonna pound you, pound you, pound you, pound you, pound you, pound you, pound you— *Jesus. Fucking. Shit.*" A thick, whitish fluid spurted out, and then—pulsing—several weaker spurts that diminished to a dribble. He held himself a moment, let go. His penis deflated and sank. She heard him sigh.

"You goddamn dumb little girl," he muttered in a throaty voice, pulled up his shorts, then his pants, zipped himself up, fastened his belt. She hadn't dared to look at anything but his penis; now she risked a glance up at his face. His mouth was hanging open. He was breathing hard. His small eyes looked sickened and terrified.

She didn't move a muscle and neither did he. She couldn't stand the sight of him, so she looked out over the golf course. She kept waiting for him to yell at her again, but he didn't. They stood unmoving while she listened to the band finish the swing tune to a big round of applause.

It was eerily quiet without the band playing. "Oh, damn my soul," he said under his breath. She turned back to look at him, and he couldn't meet her eyes. He pawed his cigarettes out of his shirt, offered her one. She shook her head. He lit one for himself, inhaled deeply on it. She still didn't dare move.

"Aw, shit," he said. "You know, kid, I always liked you. I was just trying to—you know, just trying to teach you a lesson, but— Aw, shit, I'm sorry, OK?"

What was she supposed to say to that?

"Oh, just get the fuck out of here," he said quietly and made a pushing motion. "Go home, sweetheart." He turned away from her and walked onto the golf course.

14

From the narrow wooden shelf where she was clinging precariously in her dream, Laney knew she didn't want to wake up, but some utter ass was fooling around with one of those silly gadgets they play in bands—a little box on a handle, and when you swing it around, it goes *arrrr, arrrr, arrrr*—and she was *already* awake—the sun and the pain, oh God. They said if you drank every day, you stopped having hangovers. That was a lie. If you drank every day, you always felt awful in the morning, but it was a matter of degree: there was mildly awful, and then there was *awful* awful. From bitter experience, she knew it was useless to try to get back to sleep, so she sat up and the entire room moved. Oh, yessiree, it was going to be one evil morning. On her bed table was a martini glass and an empty fifth of Scotch—Scotch and martinis *both*, Marcelaine, how charming of you—and even through the sheers, the sun was like— In some dumb historical novel, she'd read a description of somebody having his eyelids cut off, and had that been a full fifth of Scotch several days ago, or had that been a full fifth of Scotch *last night?*

Some people claimed they could tie on a good one and remember everything they'd said and done in vivid detail, and that was another lie. As usual, what was left in her mind was a jumble of disconnected fragments. When had she started drinking? Oh, dear, about two in the afternoon. It had been so damned hot, and she'd had one of Teddy's beers; it had tasted so good she'd had another, but beer was *food* wasn't it? And she remembered eating Swiss cheese and crackers with the second one, so she'd eaten *something*, but when had she started on the Scotch? As she'd been falling asleep (or passing out, to call a spade a spade), Princess Priss had been poking around in the attic, and then she'd driven away in the station wagon. Laney hadn't heard her come home. Had she *ever* come home?

Laney pulled the sheers back and managed to discern, in the excruciating dazzle, the shape of her car sitting at a crazy angle just at the foot of the steps, its front wheels on the lawn. You damned little jackass, she thought. Can't you even park right?

She fell back on the bed and pulled a pillow over her eyes. As much as she would have liked to blame her current state on someone else—her wretched daughter would have been a good start—she really couldn't blame anyone but herself. Oh, God, drinking. It was a wonder she hadn't gotten herself into even more trouble than she had over the years. The only time she'd stayed with another man since she'd been married, she could remember what they'd been drinking—whiskey sours—but not what she'd done with him, Gordon Something-or-other, an army Lieutenant about to go overseas, but they must've had themselves one hell of a good time. Her thighs had been as sore as if she'd spent the night doing the splits; she'd acquired bite marks on her neck and an itch between her legs, and her Lieutenant had acquired a spectacular pattern of claw marks on his back and even on his lean, hard ass. By dumb luck—certainly not by planning—it had been the wrong time of the month to get her pregnant, and when, a few days later, she'd gone to a strange doctor she'd picked at random out of the phone book, the itch had proven to be not the dire social disease she'd dreaded but a dumb, minor infection—"probably caused by friction," the doctor had said with a straight face. And it had always seemed to her cruel and unfair that, upon the one occasion when you've been unfaithful to your husband with what has obviously been wild abandon, you can't recall a single detail of it.

She heard the damnable sound again and suddenly remembered what that musical gadget was called—a ratchet—but this time it sounded like somebody having the dry heaves, and Laney's stomach contracted in sympathy. The little idiot, she thought, I warned her about the martinis—and another fragment of the night before popped into her mind: she and Mother and Princess Priss had been sitting around in Mother's bedroom drinking martinis. How the hell had *that* happened? Now she heard her daughter sobbing. Oh, lovely. She must have gone down to the club and gotten loaded, and so there's going to be both of us wandering around here hung over, and Teddy's in goddamn Pittsburgh!

Feeling every miserable joint in her miserable body, Laney slowly unfolded herself from bed. She should change into something, but what? It was too much bother, so, still in her sweat-soaked nightgown, she wandered out into the hall. Princess Priss was crying with the unrestrained, end-of-the-world, heartbroken wailing of a child, and Laney was both pleased and aghast. She wanted to walk into her daughter's bedroom, slap her face, and say, "Shut up, you little idiot. What do you think happens when you drink too much?" and she wanted to walk into her daughter's bedroom, take her into her arms, hold her and rock her and stroke her hair and say, "Shhh, sweetie, don't cry. You'll feel better after a while." But she didn't do either of those things. Clinging to the bannister, she crept downstairs. You're a terrible mother, Marcelaine.

Oh, God, Mother would want her breakfast soon, and it was Sunday, and Mrs. Warsinski wouldn't be here until two, and Princess Priss was obviously in no shape to do anything, and when Laney tore open a package of Bromo, her hands were shaking like an old lady's. She imagined herself as a pathetic, dried-out old drunk sitting in a rocking chair in a sanatorium somewhere—doing what? Knitting? In an exercise of willpower (it wasn't much, but what the hell), she forced herself to wait until the powder had dissolved entirely before she drank it down, but all the Bromo did was make it appallingly clear just how thirsty she was, so she opened a Coke and guzzled half the bottle. Now you're a true West Virginian, she thought: you're drinking Coke for breakfast.

She'd intended to go down by the pool—it was sweet and cool and airy there this time of the morning—but she didn't make it any farther than the kitchen table. She would drink the rest of the Coke slowly. That would give her something to do. She would smoke a cigarette—and she lit one. A Coke and a smoke, she thought; gee, I should be in advertising. And now she was remembering something about having a fight with Princess Priss—a real screaming match—oh, dear. She tried to remember how it had started or what they'd said, but she couldn't; all she could remember was the feeling of it: angry and ugly. And then she remembered that Mother and Gloria had ganged up on her. Oh, no wonder she'd been so angry—and, speaking of angels, here was the May Queen herself, with her arms full of bed linens.

Gloria stopped dead. She obviously hadn't expected to see anyone in the kitchen. Her eyes were red, and her face was shiny with sweat—it looked like it had been greased with Crisco—and she was as pale as she was ever going to get. "Rough night?" Laney said.

Gloria nodded. "Let me fix you a Bromo, sweetie," Laney said.

"I've got to get this stuff in the wash."

Even from six feet away, Laney could smell the vomit. "Put some bleach in with it."

When Gloria came back upstairs and took the Bromo, Laney noticed, with considerable satisfaction, that her daughter's hands were shaking nearly as badly as her own. "Oh, Mom, I'm so sorry."

She's sorry? Laney thought. It was a pretty good bet that they *both* should be sorry—even if Laney didn't remember what it was they should be sorry about. "Me too, honey. You'll feel better in a few hours. You always do."

Gloria sat down at the kitchen table and tears began to trickle down her cheeks. Go ahead and touch her, Laney told herself; she's your daughter—and she gingerly reached out and took Gloria's hand. It was ice-cold and wet. "Go back to bed, honey."

Gloria shook her head. "I really am sorry, Mom. Really really."

God, Laney thought. "Me too, sweetie."

"Oh, Mom, and I made such a fool of myself at the club last night."

"Don't worry about it. I'm sure you weren't the only one."

"No, but—I mean, I just—utterly disgraced myself."

Gloria looked at Laney with her sloe-berry eyes—her sad, bloodshot eyes spilling over with tears—and Laney was suddenly feeling something horribly complicated. She hadn't been able to put it out of her mind: catching Gloria and Rolland *in flagrante*, hearing that whore's yodel coming out of her daughter's mouth—and *she wasn't going to marry him.* Every time she thought about it— just how pigheaded and stupid and self-righteous Gloria was being about it— Laney was still so mad at her she could have cheerfully slapped her silly, but now she remembered the happy four-year-old in Mary Janes skipping along behind her and thought, oh, dear, how could everything have gone so wrong?

Even though Gloria was wearing sunglasses, the glare off the hood of her mother's car was truly hideous. Why was she being so nice to me? she wondered. Was it some kind of trick? But maybe her mother *was* sorry; Gloria was certainly sorry. It would have been inconceivable to Gloria that her mother didn't remember what had happened; Gloria remembered every disgusting detail.

Gloria was driving slowly and carefully down the hill. As bad as she felt, it was crazy to be going anywhere, but the strawberry milkshake she wanted felt like the Holy Grail, and then, as she turned onto Edgewood Lane, she was struck again—as she had been repeatedly since she'd first awakened at dawn, nauseated and cruelly sober—with wave after wave of sickening, intolerable shame. *She* had done it. No one else had. *She* was the one. *She* had put on that trashy outfit and gone down to the club in it. *She* had got stinking drunk. *She* had made out with Jack and Mike and Lee, one right after the other, like a one-girl assembly line. *She* had bared her breasts so Lee could get his rocks off faster. Oh, dear God, she prayed, I'm sorry! I'll shave my head. I'll let the hair grow out on my legs. I'll wear a burlap sack. I'll eat dirt.

Gloria parked on Edgewood Lane across the street from the drugstore. She looked at her nails. They were catching tiny globules of hideous light. They were starting to chip. That was probably OK because it was clear polish and the chips didn't show very much. She'd put it on the night she'd gone to the club in that sappy little-girl outfit with Rolland—oh, how sad, that seemed like a million years ago. "Why aren't you getting out of the car?" the secret watcher asked her.

She considered the word "glare." It meant a nasty brightness, as in "the glare off the hood," but it also meant a light that exposed secrets—laid them bare for all the world to see—as in "the glare of publicity," and then it also meant a hostile, threatening look, as in "he glared at me," and that could be used metaphorically, as in "the sun glared at Gloria—" Without words, there'd be no metaphors;

without words, maybe the sun would never have been anthropomorphized and it would just be a big, fat, stupid light. But what if you could perceive the sun, perceive its brilliance, perceive the fiercely painful light without sticking a word in front of it? Could the mind work without words? That's what that Robert Graves poem was about—if you didn't have words, you'd go crazy—and she must have been crazy to leave the house. Wouldn't it be nice if somebody invented a nail polish that didn't chip.

She didn't want to be wearing shorts and a halter top; she wanted to be covered up from top to toe—which was ridiculous, because it must be ninety-some degrees, and if she *were* covered up from top to toe, then people would do more than look at her; they'd stare at her, and they'd think she was crazy—if not crazy, then at least not normal, so why had she brought a patent leather purse with her? Would a normal girl be carrying a patent leather purse when she was wearing shorts and a halter top and it was ninety-some degrees? Probably not. A normal girl would probably have put her money in the pocket of her shorts. It was strange: she was so used to seeing red polish on her nails that, without it, her hands looked naked. "Get out of the car," the secret watcher said. She could always take the money out of her purse and put it in her shorts.

Of course, maybe she *was* crazy, and what if something happened to her mind so that she couldn't stretch out and relax in it? The moment she thought that, it had already happened: her mind was no longer safe or secure but filled with terrible things—not big, hideous things like concentration camps or nuclear bombs, but little, stupid, dumb things like purses and nail polish and the word "glare"—

She'd watched him walk away onto the golf course. Oh, thank God, she'd thought, it's over, and I'm free. Taking the short, clipping steps required by her skirt and heels, she'd begun to walk back up to the club. None of this is real, she'd thought, or if it is, I'll worry about it later. Then, with no warning at all, she'd bent forward—the motion had been exactly the one she would have used if she'd been told to bow—and thrown up. The revolting mess had poured down the front of her dress, and over her legs, and over her shoes. She would never in her life—not ever, ever, ever again—drink a martini.

"Stop this right now," the secret watcher told her, "before it goes any further," but her heart was already hammering in her throat, and her mouth had gone dry, and there was a roaring in her ears, and her mind wasn't working right, and she'd never be able to stretch out and relax in it—not ever, ever, ever again. She had to get home. Then she could look up "glare" in the OED. She was genuinely terrified of getting out of the car. Oh, help, she thought.

"You've made it through these things before," the secret watcher told her. "Take a deep breath. That's right. Now pick up your purse. No, don't think about it. Now get out of the car. Now close the door. Good girl. Now look both ways. Now walk across the street. That's fine, Gloria. You're doing just fine."

One six is six, she chanted in her mind, two sixes are twelve, three sixes are eighteen, four sixes— No, this is ridiculous— Recite something. What? Something you know really well.

To be or not to be, that is the question—whether 'tis nobler in the mind to suffer the slings and arrows— She was in the drugstore. She put her patent leather purse down on the counter. Normalcy probably allowed sufficient individual variation so that she could get away with the patent leather purse.

Now she was sitting on a stool. Some grown-up ladies were in the back buying things. Nobody was glaring at her. Everything was perfectly ordinary. She'd been in this drugstore a million times before. Her church was only a block up the street.

"Hi, Gloria, what can I do for you?"

It was only the old guy who owned the drugstore. She'd chatted with him a million times, so why hadn't she ever learned his name? Oh, she thought, what a self-centered little bitch I am.

"OK, now say, 'Can I have a strawberry milkshake, please?'" the secret watcher told her.

"Can I have a strawberry milkshake, please?"

"Sure thing. Coming right up."

The slings and arrows of outrageous fortune, or to take arms against a sea of troubles, and by opposing end them? To die—to sleep—no more, and by a sleep to say we end the heartache—

"Say something normal," the secret watcher told her. "Say, 'Sure is a hot one.'"

"Sure is a hot one."

"You can say that again, Gloria. So you're out of school for the summer, huh?"

What was she supposed to say to that? Was there a standard response? Was a smile good enough? No, probably not. What would a normal girl say?

"Say, 'Yep. Out of school for the summer,'" the secret watcher told her.

"Yep. Out of school for the summer."

'Tis a consummation devoutly to be wished. To die, to sleep—to sleep, perchance to dream—ay, there's the rub—

Gloria sipped her strawberry milkshake. It tasted like heaven. "Excuse me," she said, "do you have a phone book?"

What dreams may come when we have shuffled off this mortal coil, must give us pause—us pause—us pause— What next? Oh, right. There's the something-or-other that makes calamity of so long life, for who would bear the whips and scorns of time—

"OK, that's enough," the secret watcher said, "you're all right now. Breathe!"

She looked in the phone book for Caldwell. "Where's Bethel Grove?" she said before she'd thought about it. Had that sounded all right? Would a normal girl have said, "Where's Bethel Grove?" Wasn't that too abrupt? Maybe it had sounded arrogant. Wouldn't a normal girl have said "please tell me" or "excuse me"? But she'd already said "excuse me." She couldn't very well say "excuse me" before every sentence.

She planned her words carefully as though she were translating into a foreign language. "I mean. I know where it is. Roughly. But how do you get there? Exactly?"

He leaned on the counter directly in front of her; he was a nice old man, but all she wanted to do was back away from him—he was too close—so she forced herself to sit utterly motionless and smile. Boy, his teeth were white. They were probably false.

"Well, you go out the National Road, you know, and out beyond Halley's Rise—?" He smelled stale, like old bread.

"You know where the road forks? Well, you just follow the sign and you can't miss it."

They were absolutely clear directions, Gloria thought, except for a geographical idiot, and she didn't know why she wanted to see Sandy anyway. What was she going to say to her? Hi, I know you hate my guts, but I thought I'd drop in without bothering to call you first. I just wanted to say I'm sorry—can you please forgive me? I'm sorry I beat you for Prom Queen and stole your boyfriend. I'm sorry I never invited you home with me—or to the country club where you were obviously dying to go. I'm sorry I never said more than ten words to you in the three years we went to high school together. Can we forget it all and be friends? Oh, just great! she thought.

Maybe she didn't want anything from Sandy. Maybe she was just going for a drive—to clear her mind. Like that bastard: "take the silver bullet out and clear my mind." Except she didn't like driving all that much and never had— So what if he'd done it to himself and made her watch? That hadn't hurt her, had it? Right, it wasn't as though she'd never seen one before or didn't know what they did when they got hard. What was she, some sensitive little Victorian maiden? She was perfectly fine— But, no, she wasn't perfectly fine.

I'll tell, she thought. I'll get him fired. He deserves it. But the only way she could tell was if she told *everything*—the whole miserable, sordid, tawdry tale—and she felt hopelessly compromised. If she told what *he'd* done, she'd have to tell what *she'd* done; if she didn't, she'd be an utter hypocrite, and besides, it was only her word against his, and who on earth would believe that anybody could possibly do what he'd done?

She was out beyond Halley's Rise, and she'd found the fork in the road, and the sign had said "Bethel Grove," and she was following it. Could it really be that simple? The fierce July sun had burnt the grass by the road to straw; everything looked dun-colored and parched—the undiscovered country from whose bourn no traveler returns—and what if death were utter nothingness? But no, don't think about that. It was too bad it was Sunday; if it were Monday, the stores in town would be open—although she didn't know what she might want to buy in any of them. Well, at least she could've had a manicure.

It really was that simple: a hand-painted sign above the letter box said CALD-WELL. It was a wood-frame house that badly needed a coat of paint. The little patch of lawn in the front was grown high with dandelions gone to puff, and Sandy's father was certainly no farmer: nothing was cultivated anywhere that Gloria could see. In fact, there was nothing to cultivate; this was just one of a dozen similar houses strung out along a ridge. The front porch was sagging. There was a glider on it, and Gloria imagined Sandy sitting there swinging with a boyfriend on a hot summer's night. She knocked on the screen door, and a dog inside exploded into frenzied, rapid, high-pitched yapping.

"Fritzie, now Fritzie," a woman's voice called out. "That's enough now, Fritzie."

The woman had hair the color of weathered aluminum. She was wearing a blue floral housedress and carrying a tea towel. The closer she got to the screen door, the more the dog yapped. Gloria could see it now—no bigger than a cat and grotesquely fat. With a pointed snout at one end and a stub tail at the other, it looked like a partially deflated football on tiny, clicking feet.

The woman didn't seem at all surprised to see Gloria. "Just a minute, dear. I've got to give her her little treat or she'll never shut up. Ooo wants her widdle tweat? Does ooo? Go get it, Fritz!" The woman threw a small, brown pellet, and the dog scrambled after it, skidding on the linoleum. Waiting, Gloria felt like Philip Marlowe. This was exactly like one of those sordid places he had to go and ask questions that no one wanted to answer—but, if she were a detective, just what was it she was supposed to be detecting?

"Can I help you?" the woman said.

"Excuse me. Does Sandy Caldwell live here?"

"She used to. She lives in Columbus now. I'm Sandy's mother."

"Hi. I'm glad to meet you. I'm Gloria Cotter. I ran into Sandy last night at the country club—"

"Oh, good heavens, I should have known. Sandy told me she saw you. You're even prettier than your picture. Come in, Gloria. She'll be so sorry she missed you— No, you really *do* have to come in. After driving all this way. Let me get you something. Lord preserve us, it's hot! A soda pop? You just missed Sandy by a matter of minutes, and she'll simply die when she hears about it. You were just in the paper, weren't you? A few weeks ago? That's right, I remember now, you won another beauty contest. Isn't that so?"

She led Gloria into the parlor. There were crocheted doilies and anti-macassars on every chair and a fine layer of dust on every wooden surface. The top of the piano appeared to be a shrine dedicated to Sandy; there were half a dozen framed pictures of her ranging from the plump, dimpled child in sausage curls to the sexy, Canden High majorette showing off her legs. The blinds were drawn against the sun, and the papered walls throbbed with a flat, disagreeable brilliance. The house stank of fried meat and another smell Gloria couldn't identify—something like old galoshes. She knew, absolutely, that she had no legitimate business there; it felt shameful, even indecent, that she should be seeing this room without Sandy in it. The dog had followed her and was sniffing at her ankle. Its eyes were clouded over with cataracts the color of skimmed milk.

When she'd been writing a paper on later Eliot, Professor Bolton had suggested she look at *The Book of Common Prayer* to see, not only where Eliot had got some of his free verse cadences, but also some of his sentiments, and now she thought of the general confession: "We have left undone those things which we ought to have done, and we have done those things which we ought not to have done, *and there is no health in us.*" And there is no health in me, Gloria thought.

Sandy's mother was offering Gloria a glass of orange Crush, and Gloria took it. "I've heard so much about you, I feel I know you. It's a crying shame you missed Sandy. So tell me, Gloria, are you going to enter any more beauty contests?"

"I don't think so."

"Oh, I bet you are. I bet you just can't wait for the next one. Tell the truth, now, Gloria. I bet one of these days I'll open up the paper and there'll you'll be—Miss West Virginia."

Try as she would, Gloria couldn't find a thing to say. She couldn't conceive of what Sandy's life had been, waking up in this house, smelling these smells, riding into Canden High every day on the school bus, being a majorette, going to school with girls like Binkie Eberhardt and Gloria Cotter. Ashamed, she smiled and smiled and smiled. Sandy's mother winked at her.

Panic was sniffing at the back of Gloria's neck. "Breathe," the secret watcher said. "That's right. Now say, 'Thank you so much for the drink, Mrs. Caldwell. I'm so sorry I missed Sandy. You give her my best. And I really should be going now.'" But she couldn't say any of it. She felt her lip quivering.

Slam-bang: car door. Footsteps outside. A man's voice: "Jesus Kee-rist!" Footsteps on the steps, and the dog barking hysterically. "Fritzie. Now Fritzie, stop that."

"Who the hell owns that damn Estate Wagon?"

"Fritzie. Fritzie!"

The little brown pellets were chocolates from an old, heart-shaped valentine's box. Mrs. Caldwell threw one; the dog scrambled and gobbled. The screen door banged; a man strode into the parlor. He was wearing shiny black pants and a white dress shirt, open at the neck. He looked angry enough to hit someone. "*She* own that Estate Wagon?"

"Why, of course she does, dear. This is Gloria Cotter. She just missed Sandy by a matter of minutes."

Gloria couldn't believe how quickly the man's anger was deflected; he stared at her a moment, then looked away, shifty-eyed. When he spoke again, his voice was querulous: "Pleased to meet ya. Look, honey, you're parked right smack in the middle of my driveway. Why didn't you pick one side or the other?"

Gloria was suddenly granted the gift of speech. "Oh, I'm so very sorry. How silly of me. I'll move it right now. I really do have to be going anyway," and, continuing to prattle away in a bright, breathy voice she hoped sounded as though it were emanating from someone who regularly entered beauty contests, she deftly deposited the orange Crush on the top of the piano and bounded for the door. Mr. and Mrs. Caldwell followed her outside. "What do these things sell for these days?" he said, gesturing toward her mother's car.

"Oh, I'm sorry, but I don't have any idea."

"What is it? A fifty-five or a fifty-six?"

"Oh, how silly of me. I don't know that either."

"A fifty-six. Yeah, that's right. How's your gas mileage?"

"Pardon?"

"Gas-guzzler, is it?"

Gloria emitted a jagged giggle. "It's really my mother's car."

He opened the door for her, and Gloria got in behind the wheel. The dog had followed them outside and was yapping. Mr. Caldwell leaned into the car window. "One of these days," he said out of the side of his mouth, "I'm going to boot that blind thing right off this ridge."

Gloria giggled. He stepped back, and she pulled out. She smiled and waved. "Give Sandy all my best!"

"We sure will," Mrs. Caldwell called back.

Gloria drove back to Halley's Rise. She was surprised she'd made it that far. She pulled over, leapt out of the car, and vomited the few mouthfuls of orange Crush and the entire strawberry milkshake into the ditch.

As often happened after she'd cried for hours, Gloria fell asleep. She woke when she heard her father come home, tried to make herself get up but couldn't do it. When she woke again, it was twilight. She didn't hear any movement, so her parents must have gone down to the club, and she found herself in that detached—nearly depersonalized—state that came over her sometimes when she'd slept deeply in the daytime. She'd been dreaming, but she couldn't remember any of it. She was, the best she could tell, feeling not much of any-thing, and her lack of emotion was a relief; it left her mind free to sniff around like a raccoon in the garbage.

She'd utterly disgraced herself at the club, so obviously she could never set foot there again. She wasn't at all certain she could go *anywhere* in Raysburg. But in six weeks she'd be in New York, and what was six weeks? Nothing really. So maybe it wouldn't matter if she couldn't go anywhere. She had food and a bed and a swimming pool and books to read and her grandmother to play bridge with; what more did she need? And, speaking of food, she'd thrown up every-thing she'd swallowed for the last twenty-four hours, but now the aching, bruised sensation in her stomach was beginning to feel more like hunger than nausea, so she should probably eat something. Right, how about a nice bowl of dirt?

She liked the flat, gray twilight and the hushed, suspended feeling that accompanied it so she didn't light any lights in the kitchen, and— Why hadn't she thought of it before? She hadn't needed to go out; there had been strawberry ice cream in the freezer the whole time. She scooped out a bowl of it, cut it into small pieces, broke an egg into it, added milk, and beat it up with an egg-beater. The first sip told her it was exactly what she needed. She was so empty she felt it sinking icily all the way down to the bottom of her stomach. She'd never before been drunk enough to have a genuine hangover; the times when she'd thought she'd had one, she'd only been fooling herself.

The phone began to ring, but she didn't want to answer it in case it was Binkie—or even worse, Jack or Lee—so she walked away from it and carried her milkshake down to the pool. She liked the twilight outside even better than she'd liked it in the kitchen; the fireflies had just come out, were still low to the ground, and she thought that there must be, just as people said, some-thing in the human spirit that was irrepressible, because she felt OK—at least for the moment she did. But maybe it didn't have a darned thing to do with the human spirit; maybe all it meant was that she'd slept off her hangover.

She drank her milkshake. Then she walked around the house to the garbage cans. She braced herself and opened the one with her clothes in it. She stepped back from the stench of vomit, her stomach contracting, but she really did have to do it, so, holding her breath, she fished out her charm bracelet, her pearls, her mother's evening gloves, and her heels. But where was her evening bag? Oh, she'd left it at the club, on the table out on the terrace. But so what? All it had in it was makeup.

Back in the kitchen, she washed the jewelry, wiped off the shoes and gloves. It seemed impossible that only a couple days ago she'd been crying over Rolland. She had a lot more to cry about now. But if you've spent years worrying about doing something to disgrace yourself utterly, and then you've done it—then you don't have to worry about it any more, do you? And she thought of Wyatt:

Fortune doth frown:
  What remedy?
I am down
  By destiny.

But what on earth had she thought she'd been doing, driving out to Sandy Caldwell's? Atoning for her sins, probably. Trying to do something good—not namby-pamby, Sunday school, have-you-been-a-good-girl good, but genuinely, courageously good, like something Britomart, or Susie, might have done. She still didn't know what she could possibly have said to Sandy if she'd been home, and then, as her mind continued to chatter away to itself, another part of her was driving again down the parched, dun-colored road to Bethel Grove—

She sat on a kitchen chair looking out the back windows as the last of the twilight gradually faded away. She would have preferred to be outside, but she was afraid of disturbing something fragile that felt like a dream she'd forgotten—and was almost ready to remember. The closest she could come to it was by metaphor: it was like the momentary pattern of ripple created by breath on clear water. Why, she thought, if we are nothing more than highly evolved apes, have we been given consciousness so far in excess of anything required for propagation and food gathering? "To praise God," was the answer she'd learned in Sunday school, but what kind of God would want His people to sit around all day, singing "praise, praise, praise"? A God like that would have to be as egomaniacal as an Eastern potentate. But what if praise meant something else?

But this was getting her nowhere. She still felt—what? An expectation—a predicted, implied, annunciation—but she couldn't catch it. She waited until it was entirely dark, until whatever had been hovering had been dissolved. Her chance had passed, and sitting around in the dark regretting it was, she was sure, an unhealthy thing to do, so she turned the light on.

Even though she should have been expecting it, the light was too sudden, and she recoiled, blinking; then, and only for a moment, she saw all the objects in the room as strange and wonderful—clearly drawn and perfectly themselves—and that was precisely when the memory came back: driving with Susie down the bleak, dun-colored road between Cloverton and Jordanstown— Thanksgiving weekend, their junior year—coming back so vividly she could almost smell the snow in the air. Without a moment's hesitation, she jumped up, found her address book, shut herself into the kitchen, and called Susie's in-laws in Merion.

She got Don's mother: "Gloria, what a coincidence! The kids were just talking about you at dinner."

"Oh? What were they saying?"

"They were just remembering how they met. You know how newlyweds are."

Gloria didn't have a clue how newlyweds were, but she produced what she hoped would sound like an appropriately complicitous giggle. "Are they there?"

No, they weren't there. They'd found a charming little apartment near the university. They hadn't planned to move till the first of August, but it had been standing vacant, and it was absolutely perfect for them, so they thought they'd better take it before somebody else came along and snapped it up, and they were working like dogs—painting and papering, you know how it is. Again, Gloria didn't know, but she wished she did. "They'll be so sorry they missed you."

It was ridiculous, but Gloria was so disappointed her eyes were stinging with tears. Now what? She found her grandmother playing solitaire and watching the TV. "Come in, my dear."

Gloria sat down gingerly in the wingback chair by the bed. "Shall we play some bridge?" her grandmother asked her.

"I'd rather not. I'm tired tonight. Can we just watch the TV?"

"Certainly, my dear. I'm somewhat tired myself."

There was some dumb murder mystery on, but Gloria didn't mind. In fact, she rather liked it for demanding so little of her. In spite of having slept for most of the afternoon, she was sleepy again, and, the moment she'd walked into the room, she'd felt that peacefulness she'd come to associate with her grandmother. It wasn't as good as talking to Susie would have been, but it would have to do—and she liked sprawling in the wingback chair, hearing the click of her grandmother's cards, liked the uncanny sense of looking out into the world—or at least some minor, black and white version of it—through the window of the TV set.

So Don and Susie had been talking about her at dinner, had they? Don, who was a true Romantic (he'd written his honors thesis on Wordsworth) had always called Gloria his guardian angel because she was the one who'd brought him and Susie together—how odd—and she had to admit that she was envious of Don and Susie, although she didn't know whether she envied Susie for being happily married or Don for being with Susie. It would be so much fun to fix up an apartment with Susie. They were probably having a ball.

Like Gloria, Don had been in honors English, so she'd known him since her sophomore year, but she'd never paid much attention to him. He was an easy boy to overlook. He was reasonably tall but not as tall as Rolland; he wore his hair neither excessively long nor short; he dressed much like every other fraternity boy at Briarville and never affected anything "cool"—would never be seen, for instance, like a jaunty Sigma Chi, strolling across campus with his tie flung over one shoulder. He was a good student, articulate enough when he talked, but he didn't talk too much, and Gloria had never heard him express an opinion she hadn't already read somewhere. The only reason Gloria had ever paid the least bit of attention to him was that he'd begun to pay too much attention to her.

They had two classes in common, and, more often than not, he sat next to her. He often seemed to want to chat after class, and, a couple times, those chats had continued on to Sneaky's. At first she hadn't thought much about it—they'd never discussed anything but literature—but the first week back after Thanksgiving break, it finally dawned on her that he was just a little bit too glad to see her. Shades of Ken Henderson, she thought; she'd better nip it in the bud. She wasn't surprised when, after Professor Bolton's Thursday night bull session, Don asked her if he could walk her back to the house. "You know, Don," she said, smiling in a friendly but distant way, "I'm pinned." She'd automatically pointed at the linked pins on her sweater.

"No, I didn't mean that." He started to say something more but couldn't manage to finish it. He drew a clean, neatly folded handkerchief out of his slacks, took off his black-framed glasses, polished them, put them back on. Feeling a mixture of sympathy and the detached curiosity of someone peering at a paramecium through a microscope, she watched as a ghastly rhubarb flushed his face. "Gosh, I know you're pinned, Gloria. I just want to talk to you about Susan."

It took Gloria a moment to translate Susan into Susie. "You mean my roommate?"

"Yes."

"What about her?"

"Is she going with anybody?"

"No, not really."

"I thought she was going with Chuck Bartweiler."

Chuck Bartweiler was a fullback and so stereotypically a football player that he'd always reminded Gloria of Moose in the *Archie* comics. "She's gone out with him a couple times, but she's certainly not *going* with him."

"She seems to go out with a lot of football players—?"

"Well, of course she does. She's a majorette." She looked at him closely. The poor guy was obviously suffering. "Come on," she said, "you can walk me back to the house."

The night was crispy clear with a lovely, fragile, iced-over feeling to it; as they crossed the quad, their footsteps squeaked in the new snow, and Gloria was delighted by the sound. After the Thanksgiving weekend in Cloverton with Susie, Gloria knew that she would never think about snow the same way again. She'd learned that she was—and there was no getting around it—a city girl; she liked winter well enough if she could walk through it, for perhaps a brisk fifteen minutes at a time, on the perfectly flat, perfectly defined, snow-sifted greens of the campus, preferably while wearing, as she was at the moment, deft little ankle boots lined with lamb's wool and a romantic, royal red winter coat with a big, swirling skirt and a Russian princess hood. She felt just splendid—in fact so splendid she had good feelings to spare for Don Taylor—and later she would think about how amazing it was that the entire course of Don and Susie's life could have depended upon the kind of night it had been—and upon her mood—because, under a different set of circumstances, she could easily have brushed him off. Maybe she *was* his guardian angel. "OK," she said to him, "spill the beans."

"Oh, it's just—I don't know, kind of silly."

He stopped walking, and so did she. "She sure looks great on the football field," Gloria said.

"You're telling me!"

He gave her a long, dark, sorrowful look. "I feel like such a jerk. I might as well have a crush on Janet Leigh."

"How long has this been going on?" she said, putting a wry inflection into her voice.

He rewarded her with a grim laugh. "Only since the first game of our freshman year."

"Oh? You must not be the impulsive type."

"I guess not. I mean it just seemed so— And lately the guys in the house have been saying, 'Hey, why don't you ask her out? The worst that can happen is she says no.'"

"That's true enough."

She glanced over at him. He was actually good-looking when you got around to noticing him. He had a clear, deep, masculine voice, and he was certainly tall enough for Susie who never wore heels unless she had to. And Susie would like it that he didn't smoke; cigarette smoke bothered her so much she was always opening the windows even when it was ten below zero outside. But was there anything about him that Susie would find attractive? Gloria didn't have a clue. She knew what Susie didn't like in boys but not what she did like.

"Look," he said, "can I ask you some things about her?"

"I guess so. It depends on what they are."

"Is she a nice girl?"

Gloria had to laugh at that. "They don't come any nicer."

"What's she like?"

What *was* she like? If Gloria didn't know Susie, nobody did, but still she couldn't find any easy way to summarize her. "She's— I guess you could say a bit deceptive because she seems so— well, like the perfect majorette. All bouncy and friendly and bright. But she's a serious girl underneath. She's very religious."

She saw him blanch at that. "Religious? How religious?"

"She's an old-fashioned Christian. She reads the Bible and tries to do what it says. I take it you're not very religious?"

"Oh, you know, Christmas and Easter— So what else?"

"I don't know what else. She isn't an easy person to get to know. At first anyway."

"Do you like her?"

"Oh, gosh, Don, what an odd question. Yes, of course I like her. Do you think I'd have a roommate I didn't like?"

"What do you like about her?"

"Good grief! She's loyal and kind. The perfect sorority sister. She's very funny. She's—" She was what? And then, with one of its surprising jumps, Gloria's mind presented her with an image of Susie as Britomart: dressed in shining silver armor like an illustration for a children's book on the Knights of the Round Table, an expression of fierce determination on her face, riding at full gallop through the smoky flames surrounding the dreadful house of Busyrane, her blonde ponytail flying behind her. But, even though Don must surely have read Spenser, she couldn't very well say, "She's like Britomart." Then she'd have to explain it, and she wasn't sure she could. "There's something clean and admirable about her," she said.

Don sighed. "I almost wish you'd told me she was shallow and superficial."

Gloria laughed. "Even if she was, do you think I'd say so?"

"But she's not?"

"No, of course not. She's the farthest thing from it."

"Is she serious about anybody?"

Gloria almost said, "Heavens, no," but, after a moment's reflection, amended it to a simple, "No."

"Would she go out with me?"

"I don't know. Do you want me to ask her?"

When she was alone with Susie in their room that night, she wasn't sure how to put it. "There's a guy in one of my English classes who's got a terrible crush on you," she said.

"Oh, great," Susie said, "another guy who wants to make out with a majorette."

"I don't think he's like that."

"Oh, yeah. What's his name?"

"Don Taylor."

"I never heard of him. What's he like? Is he nice?"

"He asked me the same thing about you— He seems nice enough. He's a Phi Delt. An English major. Serious. On the Dean's List. He's going to go on and get his PhD. He's just the kind of guy who's sure to end up as an English professor somewhere."

"Gee, he sounds like your type. Why don't *you* go out with him?"

"I'm pinned, remember."

"I was kidding."

"I know you were kidding."

"What do you think, Glo? Should I go out with him?"

"Oh, I don't know, Suse. He might be a nice change from all those football players you keep telling me how much you don't like."

She saw Susie thinking about it. "OK, tell him to call me."

For their first date, Don asked Susie out to the Italian restaurant on Washington Street. "What should I wear?" Susie asked Gloria.

"I'd look like Betty Coed if I were you. Sweater and saddle shoes."

"Oh, that's what he likes, huh?"

"I don't have a clue what he likes. I'm just guessing."

"OK. Can I wear your baby pink cashmere? I just hope he doesn't expect me to talk about poetry."

Gloria was dying of curiosity and stayed up to hear what Susie would have to say, but Susie seemed reluctant to talk about it. "It was OK."

"Well, at least tell me we picked the right outfit."

"Oh, yeah, I guess we did. He told me about a million times how cute I looked."

"Did you get along with him?"

"I suppose so. It was kind of strange, not at all what I expected. It was like— I don't know how to— Well, he's sure easy to talk to. After a few minutes I wasn't nervous at all. We talked about everything under the sun. The time just shot by, and I was sorry it was over."

"You like him?"

"Well, sure I like him, but—I don't know, Glo. We're really different. I mean really really *really* different. I can't imagine what a boy like that would see in somebody like me."

It was, indeed, an unlikely match, and, as Don and Susie had become increasingly serious about each other, Gloria had worried about it. She wanted Susie to be happy, and she didn't entirely trust Don's feelings no matter how intense they might be. "She's like a dream come true!" he told Gloria with stars in his eyes, and she felt uneasy, wondering if he were in love with the idealized image of the majorette and not the real Susie.

He was from a little town just outside Philly; his father was a doctor, and not just a GP but a specialist—a very successful man—and Gloria could hear the awe in Don's voice when he talked about him. Don was an only child; he'd been a National Merit Scholar and the valedictorian of his high school class; he'd wanted to go to Penn, but Briarville had offered him a full scholarship. He'd started out in pre-med but had switched over to English the end of his sophomore year. He'd found, he said, what he really wanted to do with his life, and Gloria had no doubt he'd be good at it, but would Susie be happy married to an English professor?

Well, now Susie *was* married to him, so Gloria might as well quit worrying. As the old chestnut had it: only time would tell. They did seem to love each other, and maybe that was enough—and she wished, once again, that she'd loved Rolland enough. Oh, she thought, if you were married, how simple it must make everything!

Gloria went to bed early—even before her parents came back from the club—and fell asleep immediately. When she woke, she felt fully rested, ready to start her day, and she couldn't understand why it was still dark. She looked at the clock on her bed table, saw that it was three-thirty in the morning. Oh, just great, she thought. Just peachy-keen.

She tried to go back to sleep, but, as her mind was drifting, she saw—just as she'd been seeing all day—the road she'd driven down to Bethel Grove that morning and then, as though superimposed over it, the roads Susie had driven—from Briarville to Cloverton, from Cloverton to Jordanstown. Again it was that maddening sense of something elusive in her mind; this time she thought of it as a Russian Easter egg of memories. So what would she find if she uncovered the innermost egg? She could almost smell the snow, hear it going *shush, shush* as she and Susie and Susie's brother crossed the blank, white pasture to the shelter of the lone apple tree.

Now she remembered the car Susie had been driving. Susie's father sold used cars and lent Susie whatever was handy; that weekend it had been a black Buick. Susie was a good driver and knew a lot about cars; she'd called the Buick a "straight-eight." It had a long, grinning snout, was as shiny as patent leather, and had belonged to the undertaker in Jordanstown. "Dad knew you were coming, and he wanted you to have a nice ride," she'd said, and then, with her little fox grin, "Well, at least it's not a hearse."

Gloria lit her light, got up, pulled the diary from her junior year off the shelf, and took it back to bed with her. She flipped through it until she came to the heading: "At Susie's for Thanksgiving," and read what she'd written—a fairly detailed account that covered four pages—but it was largely devoted to the events of Thanksgiving Day when nothing much had happened, and the listing of Susie's multitude of relatives and the description of the food that had been cooked and eaten made fairly tedious reading. She'd always felt hesitant to write about that weekend—as though trying to put it into words would drain away the mystery of it—but she saw now that she hadn't attempted even the barest sketch.

She remembered worrying about the same thing she always worried about: would she look all right? (How boring.) "Just bring a nice dress for Thanksgiving dinner," Susie had told her, "you know, something simple. And something nice for church. Not a suit. Maybe a tartan jumper."

"Heels?"

"If you want, but I wouldn't bother. It feels like it's going to snow— And most of the time you just wear jeans." Then, reacting to the expression on Gloria's face, she'd laughed. "You do own a pair of jeans, don't you? No? Not even *a single pair*? Oh, I don't believe it, Glo, you really are a princess from a fairy tale! OK, here's my chance to lend *you* something."

Susie drove like a boy—her right hand on the wheel and her left arm draped on the open window—and the icy air whipping into the car made Gloria glad to be wearing Susie's jeans. They'd left Briarville just before nightfall when the sky at the edge of the western horizon had been a shivering sooty smear under a flapping black banner. Gloria had watched as the last of the light had transformed itself into something dull and unreflective like zinc and then had extinguished itself; now there was nothing whatsoever to be seen through the windshield except what the headlights saw. When Susie was nervous, she talked either nonstop or not at all; she hadn't said a word for the last ten minutes. Gloria would have liked Susie to roll up the window, but she didn't think she had the right to ask her to do that, so, to distract herself from how cold she was growing (tiddely pom), she concentrated on the round, cheery faces on the dashboard, on the tiny red light that came on whenever Susie stepped on the bright switch.

"A princess from a fairy tale" was still resonating in Gloria's mind, and the last thing in the world she wanted to do was play the princess who felt the pea under all the mattresses, but if she got any colder, her teeth were going to start chattering. The countryside was now so dark it was nearly featureless except for occasional yellow lights twinkling in an immense distance, and, just to have something to say, she said, "What do you suppose it would be like to live out there in the middle of nothing?"

"Oh, that's not the middle of nothing. That's the middle of a farm. Besides, we're just a couple miles out of Jordanstown."

"That's where you had dance classes with Miss Laverne?"

"Hey, you've got a good memory."

Gloria waited for Susie to say something more, but she didn't. "What was it like?" Gloria said.

"What?"

"Taking dance with Miss Laverne."

"Oh. You really want to know?"

"Sure."

"She was a real character," Susie said in a distant, preoccupied tone that Gloria could easily have read as: "I don't feel like talking."

They had just entered a tiny community—presumably Jordanstown—and Susie turned off the main road, drove into what looked like the town center—

there was a war statue in a tiny park—and stopped in front of an old, three-story, red brick building. "It was right there in the Odd Fellows Hall," Susie said, pointing. "They've got a little old theater in there where she'd put on her recitals every spring, and her studio was upstairs in the back— Gee, it's cold, isn't it?" She wound her window up, reached out and flicked on the heater.

"I started coming in here when I was four, and I thought it was just the most wonderful thing in the world. I loved the cute outfits I got to wear, and I got to be alone with Mom, and— It was, you know, just something for us girls. I did a ballet class, and then right after it a tap class, and then we'd have lunch at the five-and-dime. I'd always have a hot turkey sandwich with stuffing and gravy."

Susie put the car in gear and drove back to the main road. "Must sound like hicksville to you, huh?" she said.

"Oh, no, Susie. You don't ever think I think that, do you?"

Susie laughed. "I wouldn't blame you. *I* think that sometimes."

Jordanstown was already gone, and they were out in the black nothingness again. "You know, Glo, as much as I knock it—Cloverton, and growing up in the boondocks and all that—I wouldn't trade it for anything. I was a happy little kid. I thought life really *was* a bowl of cherries."

The heater in the car was throwing off a nice, warm blast, and Gloria was leaning toward it, warming her hands. She'd been listening carefully to what Susie was saying and hearing under it something else, but Susie had stopped talking, and Gloria couldn't find any useful, ordinary words in her mind. She felt unaccountably awkward, even shy, and tiny flickers of snow had begun to appear in the headlights.

Susie turned on the windshield wipers. "You know, Miss Laverne?" she said. "I never could figure out why she was *Miss* Laverne. She was married. To a little bald guy. He was a bus driver, I think. And was she ever something! When I was little, I couldn't imagine anybody as glamorous as Miss Laverne. She wore the highest heels you ever saw, and a stole with the real fox head right on it. And she'd take it and just *fling* it around her neck, like she was saying, 'Screw you guys.' And she wore perfume that would knock your socks off at forty feet— 'fly spray' Mom called it—and boy, could she tap! She wasn't any spring chicken, but she could still tap up a storm. She was, I guess, an old-time chorus girl—a 'hoofer' she used to say. She danced in vaudeville, on Broadway—

"She said to me once, 'Susan, you could go through life on that smile of yours. If you ever make a mistake on the stage, you just smile at the audience, and they'll think you're an angel from heaven.' And you know, it's true. You can do the dumbest things, and if you keep on smiling, nobody'll notice— Well, here we are, home sweet home."

Gloria didn't see anything that looked like home, sweet or otherwise; Susie had just turned off the road, and they were passing between the dark forms of massive trees that looked like the illustration for a children's book—the scary part where the children get lost in the woods. Then she saw that they were on a long, winding driveway with a house at the end of it. Two pickup trucks and a station wagon were parked near the porch; Susie pulled in next to them and leapt out of the car. Gloria had just begun to get warm; she stepped out gingerly, braced against an impending cold, but she was surprised by a night that felt mild and sparkling fresh. It was snowing, but not hard. It didn't seem to be sticking.

"Oh, I love the smell of wood smoke, don't you?" Susie said. She gave Gloria her angel-from-heaven smile, and Gloria thought, yes, she could very well go through life on it.

Susie took the suitcases out of the trunk and seemed prepared to carry both of them inside until Gloria reached for hers. "Thanks for coming home with me, Glo. I'm really glad you're here."

"Oh yes, me too," she said automatically although the butterflies in her stomach had turned into a genuine, wrenching pain. Why did anything new scare her to death?—and she followed Susie around the back of the house and up the steps to what she expected to be the kitchen but turned out to be a pantry loaded with zillions of Mason jars of preserves. She heard a woman's voice calling, "Oh, here are the girls," and then saw someone who should have been Susie's mom but who looked too young to be. "Susan Jane, what took you so long! You had us real worried. The man on the radio says we're going to get lots of snow. Oh, and you must be Gloria. How nice to meet you finally. I'm Susan's mother. Come in by the fire, you must be frozen."

Susie and her mother were both talking at once. "—wanted to leave right after our last class, but you know how it is, one thing after another—" "—at Granny Steibel's this year. Steve and Debbie are driving in from Philly. Oh, I hope the roads stay clear—"

Mrs. Steibel was a good head taller than Susie; she was wearing a nice house-dress and low-heeled pumps, had a figure like a lean, tall girl's—that's why she'd seemed so young before—but the light in the living room revealed an intricate pattern of weathering cut into her pale, nearly white, skin; she was a smiling woman, and the lines around her mouth kept on smiling even when she stopped.

"Oh, Mom, the roads aren't that bad. It isn't sticking at all—Hi, Daddy."

"Hi, kitten." Mr. Steibel had such a rumbly, deep voice, and looked, at first glance, like such a powerfully built man, that Gloria expected him to be as big as a mountain, but when he stood up, he was shorter than his wife. "I'm pleased to meet you, Gloria. Come in by the fire, get warm."

"And this is my brother Rick."

Perhaps because he was so tall and so improbably good-looking, and perhaps because he seemed to have posed himself against the mantel above the fireplace

in an attitude she could easily have described as "brooding," Gloria felt an immediate dislike for brother Rick. Who did he think he was playing? Mr. Darcy? Heath-
cliffe? Then he stepped forward to take her hand, and she saw that he had his
sister's brilliant blue eyes and lovely smile—and, with that smile, his gloomy
pose vanished so quickly she was left wondering if she hadn't imagined it. He held
her hand a moment too long—what was she supposed to do with it, shake it?—
and she felt herself blushing. His voice, like his father's, was pitched low, but his
had a youthful, singing resonance: "Susan sure thinks the world of you." Oh, she
thought, instantly reversing her first impression, what an attractive man.

"Well, do you kids want to eat? We've been waiting dinner on you."

Sitting down at the dining room table, Gloria felt agonizingly self-conscious.
They were all so blonde that she might as well be from a different species—
and was her cashmere sweater too dressy? Too prissy? Would anyone care?

"Let us ask God's blessing on this meal," Susie's dad said. They bowed their
heads, and it became immediately apparent that this was not going to be a per-
functory grace. Mr. Steibel asked God's blessing not only on the meal, but on
himself and his wife, on the town of Cloverton, on his friends and neighbors
who were ill or suffering hardship. Gloria had never before heard anyone
addressing God the way he did: "Now you know, Lord, my boy Stephen's on the
road tonight, and you know he likes to drive fast. Well, please make him
remember that he's got his babies in the car with him, and it's snowing tonight,
and he should slow down. And keep him in your care, Lord, and bring him
safe home to us.

"And bless my other two boys, Lord—Franklin and Peter. They're far away
from home on this holiday, so you watch over them. And bless my boy Rick
who's right here with us. And you know, Lord, Susan's got her best friend from
college here with her, so you watch over them too. Bless this house, Lord, and
everyone in it. We ask the Holy Ghost to descend on us, Lord, to show us the
truth and the way. We ask this in the name of your only son, Jesus Christ, who
freely gave his life to save us miserable sinners from Satan and death. Amen."

They all said "amen." Susie and her mother sprang up and began bringing
serving dishes. Gloria was startled to see a full water tumbler full of milk appear
in front of her, and soon there was so much food on the table she thought it
could feed twenty people—fried chicken and pork chops, gravy, mashed potatoes, stewed tomatoes, creamed corn, string beans, and a whole loaf of what
appeared to be Wonder Bread.

After the long, serious prayer, Gloria had expected the dinner to be a quiet
affair, but it turned out to be not the least like that; everyone was talking at once,
and it was hard for her to follow the multiple conversations. Rick and his father
seemed to be talking about the garage—Gloria heard something about ordering
parts in—and Mrs. Steibel was still worrying about Susie's other brother out on

the road in the snow, and Susie was talking about the state band championships. On the wall directly in front of Gloria was an old, framed sampler. The letters were in elaborate Gothic script, and she'd been staring at it without comprehending it—she'd taken it to be a message in German—but now, suddenly, the lettering transformed itself into something she could read:

WINE
IS A
MOCKER
STRONG
DRINK IS
RAGING
AND
WHOSOEVER
IS DECEIVED
THEREBY
IS NOT
WISE

"Susan tells me you've got family from around here," Mr. Steibel was saying to Gloria.

"That's right. My dad's from Briarville. My grandparents still live there."

"So this part of Pennsylvania must feel kind of like home to you?"

"Oh, yes," Gloria answered automatically, although it wasn't true. How strange, she thought. The Steibels couldn't be all that different from Grammy and Gramps Cotter, so why did she feel as alien here as if she were dining with Mongols in a yurt? And where was *home* anyway?

"So, Susie-Q," Rick said, "we going to do some hunting?"

"You want to go hunting, Glo?" Susie said.

Gloria thought they were kidding, so she said, "I'd love to."

"Oh, Rickie, you're not really going to take these poor girls hunting, are you?" Mrs. Steibel said.

"It's the tradition, Mom. You know that. The Steibels always go hunting over Thanksgiving." Rick was sitting directly across from Gloria. He winked at her. She looked down at her plate and felt like a twelve-year-old. So much, she thought, for the sophisticated, big-city girl.

"Susan tells me you plan to go on with your studies so you can teach in college," Mrs. Steibel was saying. Gloria turned toward her and attempted her best Prom Queen smile. It was nice how they kept trying to include her in the conversation—even though she would have felt more comfortable if they'd hadn't. "That's right," she said, "I'm going on to graduate school."

"More power to you. That's a long, hard row for a girl. Poor Susan Jane was never much of a student. She could never sit still long enough."

"So how'd the old Blue Bulldogs finish up their season?" Rick was asking his sister.

"They won as many as they lost. For Briarville, that's a great season. We've got the best twirlers though—"

"Yeah, we know that, all right. And who's going to be head majorette next year?"

"Well, who do you think?"

"Good going, Susan Jane."

"I didn't do it. God did it."

"Amen," her father said.

"We try to get over whenever they're playing at home so we can see Susan," Mrs. Steibel told Gloria.

That's interesting, Gloria thought. So why hadn't she met them before?

"They put the game with Penn State on the radio," Mr. Steibel said in his rumbly voice, "and I listened to it." Gloria was startled to see, momentarily, the prototype for Susie's wicked fox grin on her father's broad, weathered face. "Thirty-five to nothin'," he said, shaking his head. "They ought to of put you girls in."

"Well, Daddy," Susie said, matching her father's deadpan delivery, "I did talk to the coach about it, and he said if the majorettes started playing football, the boys would just quit."

Everyone laughed at that, and Mrs. Steibel said to Gloria, "They been doing that for years. Whatever he says, she'll do him one better."

After dinner, Susie and her mother brought in deep-dish apple pie and tea. "That looks just great, Mom," Rick said, "so you be sure to save me a piece. If you'll excuse me, folks, I've got to duck out for a bit."

"Oh, Rickie," his mother said, "the roads are going to be terrible!"

"It's not sticking," he said, grabbed his coat from the front hall, gave his family a wave—and a big smile to Gloria—and was gone through the kitchen and out the back door, leaving behind a momentary pocket of silence. "He couldn't stay home a night," his mother said, "if the very salvation of his soul depended on it."

When Gloria was alone with Susie in her bedroom, she said, "I really like your family," and then she couldn't help adding, "Wow, is your brother ever cute!"

"There's only about a thousand girls ahead of you who've thought that— he's off to see one of them right now. Either that or he's going into Jordanstown to drink some beer— Yeah, drinking's a sin in our church, but he doesn't think it's a sin."

Gloria had set her suitcase down and stopped just inside the door as she always did when entering another girl's bedroom, hesitating with what she considered the proper respect. Susie had opened her suitcase and begun to unpack; she looked back at Gloria, puzzled, and then, misinterpreting her hesitancy, said, "I'm sorry you're stuck with me tonight, Glo. But it's only one night—while Steve and his family's here."

"Oh, that's all right. I was just—" Just what? "Just looking around," she said, and then, having said it, she felt impelled to do it. She'd imagined Susie in a feminine, girlish environment, but she hadn't been ready for anything quite so dramatic. "Holy smoke," she said, "is this ever *pink!*" The drapes, the wallpaper, the woodwork, the little throw rug, the desk, the dresser, and the shelves were baby pink. Even the little Philco radio on the pink bed table had been painted pink.

"That's Mom. She painted every inch of everything. I didn't have any choice in the matter. I was the only girl, so pink was it. You should of seen how she dressed me—"

"It couldn't have been pink, could it?"

"How'd you ever guess?"

Gloria had been drawn to the bookcase in the corner. Except for what appeared to be photo albums, it didn't have a single book in it but was jammed full of trophies and framed pictures. "Mom did that too," Susie said. "It's everything I ever won. She was going to turn me into the next Shirley Temple or die in the attempt. It's kind of embarrassing."

Gloria stepped closer to examine one of the big photographs. Five girls in evening gowns were smiling ecstatically at the camera; the one in the center was wearing a crown; Susie was standing directly to her right. "What's this?"

"Oh, that? That's when I was runner-up for Miss Pennsylvania."

"You never told me that. I knew you were a runner-up for *something*, but—"

"It's not a big deal. It would have been a big deal if I'd won it."

Gloria couldn't imagine how anyone could *not* think it was a big deal, and what was in her mind must have shown on her face. "It's not like horseshoes," Susie said, "getting *close* doesn't count—and beauty pageants are a pain anyway. Twirling competitions are a lot more fun. Here's the trophy I got when I won the Nationals. Isn't that something?" Indeed it was: an elaborate, bronze, coliseum-like structure with the stylized figure of a majorette perched on top. "And here's my first baton," Susie said.

"The one you slept with like a doll."

"Hey, you really do have a good memory. Yeah, that's it."

"And you've kept *all* your dolls."

"That's Mom too. I keep trying to throw them away, but she fishes them out of the garbage. I think she'd like to keep me a little girl forever."

"That's just the opposite of my mom. The first year I went off to Briarville, I came home and she'd thrown them all away."

"Yeah? What a creepy thing to do— And the funny thing is, I didn't even like dolls all that much."

"Really? I didn't either."

"I didn't want to dress *dolls* up, I wanted to dress *me* up. And besides, there weren't any other girls around, and the boys sure weren't going to play dolls."

"I had a teddy I really loved, but dolls aren't very cuddly."

"That's right. They just sit around and stare at you when you're trying to go to sleep."

One might imagine, Gloria thought, that having roomed with someone for nine months of the previous year and nearly three of this one, one might have become used to her—might even have begun to grow bored with her—but that hadn't happened; she'd always been fascinated by Susie, and she was still fascinated by her, and she realized now that there was nowhere else she would rather be, nothing else she would rather be doing, than talking to Susie—sitting on the floor and looking through her photo albums.

The earliest pictures were small, glossy, brown-tinged rectangles—family groupings posed outdoors. Bending close, Gloria had no trouble recognizing Susie in the smiling, alert baby or the solemn two-year-old; she knew her by her heart-shaped face and clear, direct gaze. "Boy, were you ever a skinny kid."

"Yeah, that's what everybody said. Mom got sick of hearing it— 'Don't you ever feed that girl?' She did her best. But I've never been able to put on weight."

Turning through the pages, Gloria found a studio photographer's portrait that perfectly corresponded to how she'd imagined Susie at five or six: party shoes, frothy frock, and an enormous bow in her hair—an image of little girlness so conventional it could have been on the cover of the *Woman's Home Companion*. "Did you like wearing sausage curls?"

"Yeah, sure. Everybody always said how cute I looked. But I hated getting them put in."

"Oh, me too! My grandmother had a really dumb maid, and she put them in with a curling iron. I really really *really* hated it. She burned me a couple times. My hair's straight as a poker, and the darned things wouldn't stay in for longer than an hour."

"Oh, mine stayed in pretty good. Mom'd put them in with rags the night before. If I was careful, they'd stay in all the next day—of course I wasn't *ever* careful. I drove Mom absolutely nuts. She'd get me all dressed up, and then I'd run off somewhere and come back looking like I'd been in a hog wallow. We're stuck out here in the woods, three miles into town, and there just weren't any girls around for me to play with. So if the boys got into something, I had to get into it too. It's a wonder I've got any kneecaps left! Finally Mom wised up and let me wear pants for playing in— Here—this is how I was most of the time."

In another small, brownish rectangle, Susie, her hair in pigtails, in jean overalls and a Huck Finn straw hat, smiled shyly at the camera. She was standing next to a cow. "I've always had to wear hats in the summer. I can get a sunburn from a flashlight."

The cow had not been, as Gloria had guessed, on some neighboring farm; she'd belonged to the Steibels. "You would've thought with all us kids around, we would of named her, but we didn't. We just called her 'the cow.' We had pigs and chickens too, and a big vegetable garden. I loved watching the plants come up—their little shoots poking out of the ground."

Gloria was amazed to hear that they hadn't had electricity. "Yeah, they didn't run the lines out here until I was in grade school. Mom cooked on a wood-burning stove, and we had oil lamps. They gave a real nice light—soft, yellow, kind of mysterious. It's a lot prettier than light bulbs. I still dream about it sometimes."

Gloria couldn't imagine a childhood any more different from hers than Susie's, yet she began to feel an uncanny sense of familiarity. "Gee, your two younger brothers look a lot alike."

"Well, they should. They're identical twins. Didn't I ever tell you that?It's funny, I can't remember what I told you and what I didn't. Yeah, Pete and Frank are twins. When they were little, they were like a single person. You'd ask one of them a question, and they'd both answer—and usually they'd say the same thing! It was a real riot. And they always said 'we'—you know, 'We don't feel very good,' 'We don't like broccoli.' And then, when they got older, they sort of— I guess they wanted to go their separate ways. Which was hard for them. Because they're so much alike. And so finally they decided to go into the service, and to, you know, split up just so they could be on their own for a while. So they flipped a coin to see who'd go into the army and who'd go into the navy.

"I was really jealous. I would of given anything to be a twin. Imagine being born with your best friend—how lucky can you get? When me and Tommie Jean were twirling together, we used to pretend we were twins."

For each year there were two studio portraits of Susie in costume, one for Miss Laverne's spring recital and one for the Jaycees' talent contest. "Mom made all my costumes. It just took her forever, you can't imagine. She's kept them all too. They're in the cedar chest in her bedroom."

Susie turned the page in the album, and Gloria was startled by the next picture. It had been torn into four pieces and then stuck back together with Scotch tape. "What on earth happened?" she said.

"Oh, Mom tore it up. That's Tommie Jean. You probably knew that, didn't you? That's her graduation picture. Mom was so mad at her she was going to rip up every single picture I had, but I wouldn't let her. We had a big fight about it. I still can't put any pictures of her out in my room."

As long as Gloria had lived with Susie, she'd lived with the image of Tommie Jean on Susie's bed table, but Susie had never talked very much about her cousin, and Gloria had always been curious about her. "Why on earth was your mom so mad at her?"

"Oh—" Susie hesitated. "Well, she got in trouble. Right after she graduated. She had to move to Philly. Nobody even talks about her now. I just hate it."

As Susie turned the pages of the album, something told Gloria to keep her mouth shut. There were dozens of pictures of Susie with her cousin, and there was a strong family resemblance between them. They had the same coloring and were nearly the same height. They were often dressed in identical majorette uniforms, and they even wore their hair the same way. But they were far from looking like twins. Tommie Jean was pretty enough, but she didn't have Susie's eerie, alabaster beauty—which wasn't surprising; hardly anyone had that— and Tommie Jean had a woman's figure. Posed next to her, Susie looked like a child.

Susie sighed. "Poor Tommie Jean. It always makes me sad to look at these pictures. When we were little, she wouldn't have much to do with me because she was, you know, two years older—but then, later on, I taught her to twirl. She really took to it right away. The girls around here couldn't twirl for beans, and nobody'd ever seen anything like us. We went to county fairs all over this part of the state."

Susie paused, looking away, her eyes narrowing, and Gloria knew there was more to the story, but all Susie said was, "Yeah, she got to be a real good twirler," and closed the photo album.

Susie stood up and yawned. "We should get to sleep, Glo. Big day tomorrow."

Gloria hadn't thought about it until now, but she'd never slept in the same bed with anyone else, and she wasn't sure she could do it. She had a horrible premonition she was going to lie awake all night, staring at the ceiling. "I'll take the inside," Susie said. "It's colder by the wall."

Susie shed her clothes and pulled on striped pajamas. Feeling absurdly self-conscious—although she didn't know why; Susie certainly knew what she slept in—Gloria changed into baby-dolls. Susie turned out the lights and got into bed. Gloria slipped in under the covers and stretched out next to her. Just as she'd guessed they'd be, the sheets were freshly ironed and smelled like sunshine.

Gloria didn't realize she was holding her entire body rigid until Susie said, "You can move around, you know. When I'm going to sleep, nothing bothers me."

Gloria wondered if there were a special etiquette for sleeping in the same bed with someone else. Were you supposed not to touch them? In a bed this narrow that was going to be somewhat difficult. "You sleepy?" Susie said.

"No, not yet."

"You want to talk about something?"

"Sure."

"What do you want to talk about?"

Gloria laughed. "Oh, I don't know— Tell me again how you decided you wanted to be a majorette."

"I've told you that."

"Yes, I know. But this time, tell me everything. Tell me every single thing you can remember."

"Gee whiz, Glo! OK, let's see— Rickie and his girlfriend took me to the county fair. I forget which girlfriend it was— No, I don't. It was Rae Anne Hackenheimer. How's that for a name? Isn't that just a dandy name? And some of his girlfriends minded me hanging around with them, but she didn't. She was real sweet to me. She went off to nursing school— You really want to hear all this?"

"Yes. Anything you remember. Anything you want to tell me."

"OK. So it was the summer after—let's see—after the third grade, so I must of been nine. Dad was away in the war, and— You'd think with Rickie being so much older than me, he wouldn't of wanted anything to do with me, but he always liked me. I kind of attached myself to him and he didn't seem to mind. It's funny, most guys wouldn't of let their kid sisters hang around with them the way he did.

"So anyhow, Rae Anne and Rickie and I were at the fair, and they had a parade. It wasn't much of a parade, but I hadn't seen a lot of parades, and I thought it was just something wonderful. And there was a—well, just a crackerjack marching band. I don't even know now where they were from. They could of been a college band. They could of even been from Briarville—wouldn't that be *ironic?*" Gloria smiled because Susie had learned to say "ironic" from her, but she still said it as though it were a word in a foreign language.

"And they were led by a drum majorette," Susie went on, "and I might of seen drum majorettes before—I don't know—but that time it was like the scales dropped from my eyes and I really *saw* her, you know what I mean? And she wasn't doing anything fancy, but it seemed like magic to me. And what really got to me was here was this *girl*, and she was leading this whole band *all by herself*. And her uniform was like—well, just about the cutest thing I ever saw in my life. I just loved her white boots with the tassels on them. And I thought, oh, that's what I want to be. Whatever she is, that's what I want to be, and I want it more than anything in the world!

"And when the parade was over, I followed her all around. But I was too shy to talk to her. So finally I begged and begged, and Rickie went up to her and said, 'Will you talk to my little sister? She's just dying to talk to you.' And she was real sweet to me. I wish I knew her name. And she let me hold her baton, and she told me, 'This is the shaft, and this is the tip, and this is the ball, and you hold it right smack in the middle.' And she showed me a pinwheel—you know, real slow. When somebody's twirling fast, you can't see what they're doing, but I watched her doing it slow, and I thought, gee, that's not so hard. I can do that."

And I was living with my grandmother the summer I was nine, Gloria thought. They sent me to Fairhaven that fall.

"Oh, heavens, I forgot to pray! Sorry, Glo— No, you don't have to get out." Susie pulled the covers down and, in a quick, somewhat startling movement, vaulted over Gloria's legs. She knelt by the side of the bed and pressed her hands together.

It was hard for Gloria not to envy Susie. How wonderful to be able to decide at nine what you wanted to do, and then do it. Gloria was nearly twenty and still didn't know what she wanted to do—other than being what she'd always been: a good student.

Susie climbed back into bed. "I'm a terrible cover stealer," she said. "That's what I've been told anyway. If I do that to you, you just yank 'em back, and I won't even wake up."

"OK."

"Good night, Glo."

"Good night, Suse."

In what must have been less than five minutes, Gloria heard the soft, deep breathing that told her Susie was asleep. How could she just stretch out and fall asleep like that, so quickly and simply? Gloria turned over onto her left side, pulled the covers up to the back of her neck. She didn't hear any change at all in Susie's breathing. Then, as she was still worrying about falling asleep, she fell asleep.

15

Gloria kept expecting to exhaust her memory, but the more she wrote in her diary, the more she remembered, and she was determined to keep at it until something told her she'd done enough. "We kept waiting for it to snow," she wrote. "Even on Friday, when it was clear and sunny, we could feel the snow in the air."

"What do you want to do?" Susie asked her.

"Oh, just see where you grew up. Meet your friends."

They were drinking tea in Susie's room after breakfast—an oddly ladylike thing to be doing, she thought now; the Steibels usually drank coffee—and she remembered Susie saying, "After Tommie Jean left, I really didn't have any friends."

She couldn't quite hear Susie's voice, but she could see her: wearing a baby-blue sweater and blue jeans, sitting with one leg extended, the other on the seat of the chair, her arms wrapped around her bent leg, her chin on her knee, a pensive expression on her face. If Gloria had tried to sit like that, she would have felt like a contortionist, but Susie managed to look graceful and relaxed. "Gee, that sounds worse than it was," Susie had said—or something like it—and, without stopping to think, Gloria wrote the rest: "I got along with every-body. If you asked the girls around here, a whole bunch of them would probably say they were friends of mine, but there was just nobody like Tommie Jean."

Gloria paused, looked over at her bedroom window where the light of dawn was beginning to filter in. She allowed herself to feel the full heat of the summer morning, the sweat on her neck under her hair. Winter and snow seemed so impossibly far away, yet that's what she had to imagine. She closed her eyes. Instead of seeing snow, she saw Susie's white cowgirl boots.

She remembered sitting cross-legged on the floor, examining them. Why had she been doing that? Could they have been talking about something that had prompted Susie to get them out to show her? She remembered Susie saying, "I got those in St. Louis when I was fifteen. I thought I was a real cowgirl," and she remembered running her fingers over the smooth, white leather.

When she'd been little, Gloria had thought that "our sort," meant the same thing as "ladies and gentlemen." It had taken her years to figure out that it didn't. "What Mom means by it," she wrote in her diary, "obviously depends upon the context. If one is referring to the society of Raysburg, West Virginia, then all of the men who work for Dad are our sort, but, if one is referring to society in a larger sense, then none of them are. For another instance: our sort of young ladies do not ask other young ladies where they bought their clothes and cer-tainly not how much they paid for them, yet Binkie, who is from the most pres-tigious family in Raysburg, talks about hardly anything else. When considering Raysburg, our sort belong to the country club and the Edgewood Presbyterian Church; when considering the universe, however, mere membership in any-thing is insufficient, and, to be genuinely our sort, one must have been born that way. My stupid cousins and my relatives in Providence are genuinely our sort, and so are a few girls in our chapter, and Rolland, and maybe two or three of his Beta Theta Pi brothers. I'm supposed to be our sort, yet Mom conveniently forgets that half of me is from Dad, and, although she'd never ever say so, Dad's not really our sort at all.

"The rules applying to our sort of ladies are more stringent than those applying to mere ladies. Ladies, for instance, do not wear ankle bracelets, high heels with blue jeans, gloves with big bows on them, or anything made of fake leopard skin; our sort obey all of those rules and add a few more. I can't think of them all right now, but our sort certainly do not wear rhinestones or imitation pearls. Our sort rise to our feet when an older lady walks into the room, and, all through high school, I embarrassed myself over and over again by being the only girl to stand up for other kids' moms. Our sort are not cheerleaders— which I didn't understand when I decided to be one. Our sort do not chew gum, drink anything straight from the bottle, eat on the street, tape pictures of movie stars to their walls, listen to polka music or country music, learn to twirl batons, or wear white cowgirl boots. In fact, white cowgirl boots are just about as *not* our sort as you can possibly get."

"Can I wear them?" Gloria said.

"Oh, sure," Susie said—and then with her wicked grin, "You want to be *me*, huh? OK. You've got to wear sweat socks with them," and she threw a pair— neatly tucked into a ball—across the room. She'd aimed them so perfectly that Gloria had already caught them before she'd had a chance to remind herself she could never catch anything.

"OK, and now I'll be you," Susie said. "You got any real Gloria shoes with you?"

"What are real *Gloria* shoes?" Gloria said, laughing.

"You know, prissy as all get-out, and one look, you know they cost a mint." Had Susie really used the word "prissy"? Gloria couldn't remember, but that's certainly what she'd meant.

"How about my patent oxfords?" They'd been hand-made for her in New York, and she wasn't sure they were quite as prissy as what Susie wanted, but they certainly *had* cost a mint.

"Yeah," Susie said, "perfect."

"Susie and I both love clothes," Gloria wrote into her diary. "At the drop of a hat, we can turn into two little girls playing dress-up."

"Do you want to do the whole look?" Gloria said.

"What's the whole look?"

"Forest green knee socks and a tartan skirt."

"Oh, right. And a beret. And I could do those cats eyes on myself the way you do—"

"Cat's eyes? Oh, you mean the eyeliner?"

"Yeah— And if *you* want *the whole look*"—Susie was a natural mimic, and she'd imitated Gloria's pronunciation perfectly—"you wear jeans so tight you've got to lay on the bed to get 'em zipped up. And a real tight sweater with half a box of Kleenex shoved in your bra. And just as much cherry-red lipstick as you can get plastered on yourself."

"Oh, no! Did you actually do that?"

"You bet. That's how me and Tommie Jean went around for a while—until Mom caught me. Then I couldn't leave the house for a month. OK, do you want to do it?"

But then, looking at Gloria's face, she said, "Aw, come on, Glo. I'm just teasing you." She pulled on thin white socks, slipped her feet into Gloria's oxfords and laced them up. Gloria would never have thought of wearing them with jeans, but they did look cute. On Susie almost anything would look cute.

But no, that wasn't exactly what had happened. Gloria was forgetting Tommie Jean: that odd moment when Susie had said that her mother had always thought Tommie Jean was a bad influence, and then Susie had added under her breath like a Shakespearean aside: "Well, and maybe she was." That couldn't have happened later when they were in the car; it must have been when they were still in Susie's bedroom, giggling and talking about trading identities, because Gloria remembered the feeling of Tommie Jean casting a pall over things, and she remembered resenting Tommie Jean—that girl she'd never met—and feeling irrationally jealous of her.

Susie still had the use of the shiny black Buick, and they drove in to what Susie, laughing, called "downtown Cloverton"—the first Gloria had seen of it—and it was, just as Susie had always described it, "a bend in the road with a gas station, and the gas station's my dad's." He was working on a car and, when they pulled in, crawled out from under it, wiping his hands on a rag. At least a dozen cars and trucks were parked along the road with prices written on their windows. "I never planned to be in the used car business," he told Gloria, "but the good Lord kind of pushed me into it."

"Where's Rick?" Susie asked her dad.

"He said he had some personal business to attend to."

"Personal. Right."

Gloria heard something embarrassed and apologetic in his voice: "Oh, well, it's kind of a slow day, Susan Jane."

Gloria couldn't remember now what they'd chatted about. Susie must have told him they were going into Jordanstown because he said, "If it starts to snow, you head straight back." People were always saying that to them the entire weekend.

"I will, Daddy."

"God be with you girls."

"And with you too, Daddy."

Now, writing, Gloria could hear Susie's voice clearly, as though she'd managed to tune in an elusive radio station. They were at Jefferson Elementary, the small, brick school building where Susie had gone for the first eight grades.

"It was real hard for me when I was a little kid," Susie said, "I couldn't sit still. Oh, you can laugh all you want, but it's no joke! School was just *torture* for me. I'd sit and watch the clock, counting the minutes off to recess or— We had to sit real still or we'd get our hands slapped with the ruler. Oh, it was just awful!

"The minute that bell rang, zing! I'd be out the door—just take off at a dead run. Sometimes I'd run in circles around the school I was so glad to be outside. And at lunchtime, I couldn't be bothered to eat my lunch. It wasn't that I wasn't hungry, and it wasn't that I didn't like what Mom made for me, but, you know, in order to eat something you have to *sit still* long enough to eat it. It was even hard at dinner to sit there long enough. Mom would say, 'You're not leaving this table, Susan Jane, until you take three more bites.' And I'd sort of stand there jumping up and down and take my three more bites."

"Grade school was torture for me too," Gloria wrote, "and I told Susie that. But I liked the school part and dreaded lunch and recess. It's amazing how different we were."

"I thought I'd never learn how to read," Susie said. "Everybody else could read but me. I was so ashamed, I just can't tell you. And then, when we started the third grade, all of a sudden I could. Bang, just like that. I thought it was a miracle from God. But doing school work—just forget it. In order to do school work, you have to sit still. And I'd keep putting it off and putting it off until I went to bed, and then I'd try to read, and I'd read about three sentences, and I'd fall sound asleep. Oh, it's a wonder they passed me along from grade to grade!

"I didn't read much of anything until I was eleven or twelve and started reading the Bible. And you know how I did that? I'd walk around in circles in the back yard— You're going to think I made this up, but I didn't. You can ask Mom or Rickie. I wore a circle in the grass—"

"Oh, no!"

"Oh, yes, I did. Boy, was I ever a strange kid! I was always in trouble at school."

There was nothing about grade schools that Gloria liked, and she didn't like walking around Susie's; she was more than ready to leave, but she could see that Susie wasn't. Susie had led her into the playground and stood now, looking back toward the building, frowning. "I was always real glad I wasn't a boy," she said. "The boys around here fight a lot, and I just hated that— Did you play this?" She pointed at the hopscotch pattern chalked onto the concrete.

"Oh, sure, but I wasn't very good at it."

One moment Susie was standing still; the next moment, having given not the slightest sign that she was about to do anything at all, she was already hop-ping deftly through the chalked squares. To be able to move so instantly from a state of repose to a state of motion, as Susie often did, had always seemed wonderful to Gloria; by the time she could overcome her own surprise enough to see clearly what Susie was doing, Susie had already done it, leaving behind in memory the complex pattern traced by Gloria's patent oxfords, twinkling in the thin winter sunlight like an afterimage. "Did you skip rope?" Susie asked her.

"Oh, sure. All the girls skipped. I wasn't very good at *that* either."

"I was a skipping fool. I skipped for hours and hours. I could skip all day."

They began walking back to the car, but again Susie turned back to look at the mute brick building. "The hardest thing about being a Christian," she said, "is turning the other cheek. I had four brothers telling me, 'If you don't fight back, you'll get picked on every day of your life,' and then you go to Sunday School and they tell you, 'Turn the other cheek.' I sure couldn't do it when I was a kid. Anybody dared lay a hand on me— Did you get in fights?"

"No. I was one of the ones who never fought back. I was one of those wretched little kids who got picked on every day— It never even occurred to me I could fight back."

"Well, it more than *occurred* to me. I never could understand what they meant by a fair fight. I figured there isn't anything fair about a fight to start with, so why even talk about fair, and once it got going, I'd just—you know, I wouldn't stop at *anything*. There was a girl—let's see—I was in the sixth grade, and she was one year ahead of me. Her name was Cindy Schultz. She called me a name, and I called her a name back, and she kicked me in the shins, and so I kicked her back, and she tried to hit me so I just whaled the tar out of her!"

For years, Gloria had deliberately not thought about grade school, and her memories—except for the nasty clarity of specific incidents like the peanut butter and jelly sandwich rubbed into her face—were little more than a hazy impression of misery. Girls weren't supposed to fight—everybody knew that—but some of the girls in her class had got into fights. It seemed sad to her that she couldn't remember the names of any of the kids she'd gone to grade school with.

"I had her down," Susie said, "thrashing her good, and a couple of the teachers had to pull me off. I was so mad and scared I bit one of them, and— Well, it's the only time in my life anybody ever spanked me. Dad did it. The worst thing was he cried the whole time. As soon as I saw him start to cry, my heart just broke. He could of beat me bloody, I wouldn't of cared. And I had to get all dressed up and go apologize to Cindy and her parents, and to the teacher I bit, and that was really awful! Cindy and me got to be pretty good friends after that. She used to help me with my homework. It's funny how things turn out sometimes, isn't it?"

"It's not that funny," Gloria said. "Of course she made friends with you and helped you with your homework. She was scared to death of you."

"Oh, no. It was *me* that got in trouble." But then, after a moment, Susie said, "Maybe she *was* scared of me. I never thought of it that way."

Writing in her diary, Gloria confirmed what she'd always known: that she was profoundly uninterested in landscape, that she paid attention to it only when it was forced upon her. She could recall next to nothing about the road from Cloverton to Jordanstown, only a vague, undetailed impression of the sullen wintriness of the hills. Susie had drifted away into one of her silences, and Gloria had said, without stopping to think about it, the first thing that had popped into her mind: "Tell me about Miss Pennsylvania."

"Oh, right. I should of known you'd just be dying to hear about Miss Pennsylvania."

"I'm not *dying* to hear about it," Gloria said, irritated, "but I am, you know—curious."

"Oh, yeah? You're just like all the other girls in the house. You think it's a big deal."

"No, I don't. Come on, Suse."

"OK, OK— You want to hear about it, huh? It was— Well, I kept wishing I could get out of it. I was too young, for one thing. I should of waited till I'd filled out a little more—although, come to think of it, if I'd done that, I'd still be waiting. But I never would of thought of entering the darn thing except I'd won Miss Mountain Laurel and everybody expected me to.

"There's tricks to beauty pageants. It's like—well, the race isn't always to the swift. It's funny, but twirlers are real nice. You go to a twirling competition, and you always make new friends, but girls at a beauty contest are like a bunch of cats with one sardine."

"What an image!"

"Well, they are— Oh, maybe not *all* of them. Some of them were real nice down-to-earth girls. I met a real nice girl from Slippery Rock. We still write to each other sometimes. But anyhow, you've got to think of *everything*. The women judges are worse than the men. They watch you like a hawk—even your hands. I used to sleep with gloves on. Can you imagine *me* doing that? And you're always smearing stuff all over yourself—and staring in the mirror, praying, oh, please, Lord, don't give me a pimple, not *now*. So— I don't know what else to tell you. What do you want to know?"

"What tricks?"

"Well, OK, for weeks before the contest you wear heels every day so they'll feel like second nature on the stage. And you practice walking in them so— It's a hard walk to get exactly right. It's not an ordinary walk, but you can't carry it too far either or you'll look like a showgirl, and the judges don't like that. And then there's— Yeah, there's even tricks to how you put on a swimsuit. It gets so you're not thinking about *anything* except what you look like. That's no way to spend your life."

"So what did it feel like?"

"What did *what* feel like?"

"Being on stage—being judged on what you look like."

"It didn't feel like *anything*. I've been on stage my whole life, being judged on something or other. I did a twirling routine—you know, for the talent part of it—and that was the only fun I had. I won the talent part, and that's how I scored as high as I did. But then you've got swimsuit and evening gown, and, in some ways that's easier because you don't have to do much. But in other ways it's harder—kind of nerve-racking—just because you *don't* have to do much. I get too nervous just to walk around and smile.

"Anyhow, I got killed in swimsuit. You know what my figure's like. So you put a padded bra on me, and a real tight waist cincher, and you put me in an evening gown, I can look like a doll, and I did OK in that. But you put me in a swimsuit and you've got this skinny little kid, and I finished way down. The judges like to see girls with something up front. And they've got these ladies to check and make sure you're not cheating.

"I was relieved when I didn't win it. After I got over the disappointment. Because if I'd won it, I would of had to go on to the Miss America Pageant, and it would of been fun I guess, but— Well, I asked myself what God had meant me to learn from it, and I decided I'd gone just as far as I could with beauty contests—and there was another road God had sent me down. If I'd won Miss Pennsylvania, it would of just been a detour."

Gloria knew she should say something, ask what road God had sent Susie down, but she was thinking—or feeling—something fairly complicated, and she didn't want to lose it.

"You ought to enter a beauty contest sometime, Glo," Susie said. "Then you'd know what it's like."

"Oh, sure!"

Gloria had always known that she was smart, but she'd never believed she was beautiful—although she never got tired of being *told* she was beautiful (which was one of the things she'd always liked about Rolland), and it *would* be kind of fun, she thought, not to have to worry about anything except what you looked like. In some strange way, it would almost be a relief. "The horrible thing is," she said, "I'd probably like it."

"Oh, yeah? Tell you what. You spend next summer with me, and we'll enter you in a bunch of contests. The County Fair, Miss Mountain Laurel. If you do OK, Miss Pennsylvania—"

"Oh, right," Gloria said, laughing, "and my mother would strangle me with her bare hands."

"Hey, Glo, I'm not kidding," Susie said with a wry inflection in her voice telling Gloria that of course she was kidding.

"Oh, come on," Gloria said—it was fun to play along—"I couldn't win a beauty contest."

"Sure you could. I know every trick in the book. As smart as you are, you'd learn everything real fast."

Kidding around or not, Gloria was getting annoyed at herself for liking the idea and getting annoyed at Susie for *knowing* that she liked it.

"You *still* think I'm kidding, don't you?" Susie said. "I'm not. What else you have to do next summer?"

Gloria couldn't think of anything to say that wouldn't sound as though she were protesting too much.

"Suppose you won Miss Pennsylvania," Susie said. "How about that? Then maybe Miss America? Even if you didn't win it, just think what the girls in the house would say. I bet Rolland would like it. Who wouldn't like it? 'My girl-friend was in the Miss America Pageant.' And then, what if you *did* win it?"

"Stop it, Susie. You're starting to sound like the voice of the serpent."

"Who, me? Oh, no, not me— Come on, Glo, just think about it. The judges sometimes go for exotic-looking girls like you. Remember Bess Myerson?"

Susie turned in the driver's seat to give Gloria a hint of a smile. "And you've got a perfect figure. Yeah, you do. Nice big breasts, tiny little waist, long legs— You'd kill everybody in swimsuit."

Gloria was getting genuinely embarrassed; she heard herself giggle. Susie, of course, didn't really understand about social distinctions. If Gloria entered a beauty pageant, Rolland would hate it. He might not even want to marry her if she did something like that— But, wait a minute! It was crazy even to be thinking about it. She wasn't about to enter a beauty pageant. Not on a bet.

"For the talent part, you could do a recitation," Susie said, "something from Shakespeare. The judges like that highbrow stuff. They'd think it was real neat you were going to grad school."

From everything Gloria had heard about the beauty pageants, Susie was absolutely right. "You're thinking about it, aren't you?" Susie said. "You're thinking, does Susie really mean it or is she only kidding me? Fess up. That's exactly what you're thinking, isn't it?"

"You're really wicked!"

"I'm not kidding you. I told you that. If you want to do it, all you have to do is say so."

"Oh, Susie, I couldn't. You know that. I just couldn't."

"Yeah, I knew you'd say that, but you were really *tempted*, weren't you? There for a minute, I really had you going, didn't I?"

• • •

Near Jordanstown, Susie pulled into a drive-in restaurant. "You wanted to see all the sights, huh? OK, this is a really big deal. You drive through to see who's here, and maybe you have a hamburger, and then you drive around for a while, and then you come back and you drive through to see who's here, and then you drive around for a while, and then you come back and drive through—"

"Oh, I get it," Gloria said.

"Yeah, I thought you would."

A pretty carhop in a bright blue uniform appeared at Susie's window. "Hey, Susan Jane. Neato. How you doing anyway?"

"Well, hi there, Janet. Nice to see you. I'm doing just fine. How about you? How's your dad?"

"Oh, I'm OK. Dad's doing as well as can be expected. No, can't really complain— So, you home for Thanksgiving, huh?"

"Yep. This is my roommate, Gloria," and Gloria heard herself saying normal, stupid things to the carhop.

Susie ordered a cheeseburger and a strawberry milkshake, so Gloria ordered the same thing. "I bet this all seems like hicksville to you," Susie said. "I bet you're bored silly."

"Oh, no. This is fun."

Gloria couldn't understand why she was suddenly feeling so irritable, so oddly tired. She'd felt fine that morning. Maybe her period was coming early—that would explain it—and she was stuck here until Sunday; oh, how was she ever going to survive the rest of the day and two more whole days after that? The only thing she wanted to do was crawl into bed with a book. Could she tell Susie she had cramps?

"You know Janet?" Susie said.

"Who? The carhop?"

"Yeah. *Janet*," and then she added under her breath, "She's got a name, you know."

Gloria felt the skin on her arms prickle. Great, she thought, now she's mad at me for some reason. "Oh. Right. Janet. What about her?"

"She's married."

"Oh, really? She seems so young."

"Yeah? Well, she's my age. Lots of the girls in my class are married."

That wasn't surprising, Gloria thought. Small-town girls probably did get married young. What else did they have to do?

Susie paid for the cheeseburgers before Gloria could even think about it. She wanted to offer to pay her half, but she knew how proud Susie was.

"Well," Susie said, starting the car, "I guess you're going to have to see the great—the one and only—the magnificent—downtown Jordanstown."

Susie drove slowly through the quiet streets. Gloria recognized the little park with the war memorial. On Wednesday night it had looked poignantly beautiful to her—nearly enchanted—but now, in the pale, ineffective sunlight, it had a seedy, ungroomed, apologetic air to it like an old veteran who's fallen on hard times.

"Oh, *hell*," Susie said. Since joining Delta Lambda, Susie had made an effort to stop swearing, so Gloria was startled not only by the word but by the vehemence with which Susie had said it; she'd made it sound like a truly *bad* word.

"There's Rickie's truck— See. Right there in front of the tavern. Come on, let's give him a hard time." Susie pulled over and jumped out of the car, slamming the door behind her. There was nothing for Gloria to do but get out and follow her.

Gloria was already inside the tavern—the bar, the dive, the saloon, the beer joint, whatever it was—before she had a chance to stop and think that she'd never been in a place like that in her life. (The Blue Cellar didn't count; it was a student hangout.) The first thing she would notice, of course, was that there were no women—and certainly no girls—anywhere to be seen. At a table just inside the door, four old men were playing cards; the bartender—she supposed that's what he was: after all, he was behind the bar—appeared to be doing nothing whatsoever, and he and the old men stared at her, and at Susie, followed them first with their eyes, then turned their heads to follow them, not bothering to disguise their creepy interest. Susie didn't pay them the least bit of attention, so Gloria didn't either, but their regard made her skin crawl. The cigarette smoke was piled up like something solid, layer upon layer, just like the cliché: blue with smoke. But the Blue Cellar had never felt as bad as this; already her eyes were starting to water.

"Hey, Susie-Q!" "Hey, Miss Cloverton!" Neither of the guys who were yelling and whistling and catcalling were Rick Steibel; he was sitting in between them, however, at the table by the jukebox, grinning, and Gloria felt the heat in her face.

"These clowns are Phil and Eddie," Susie said to Gloria. "This is my roommate, Gloria Cotter."

"On your feet, animals," Rick said, and he stood up with a lazy grace that made Gloria think of a movie actor—she wasn't sure which one, maybe Gary Cooper—and gave her a smile that shot straight through her. Oh, come on, Gloria, she told herself—but, oh boy, was he ever cute!

"Pleased to meet ya," the one called Phil said. He was short, built like a football player gone to pot, and so fair he was almost an albino; his wore his white-blond hair in a buzz cut.

"Likewise, I'm sure," the other one, Eddie, said. He had long, black hair, greasy with brilliantine, and sideburns. He was wearing glasses held together with electrical tape; the left lens had a crack right down the center.

"What are you up to, girls?" Rick said.

"Just seeing the sights," Susie said. "What are *you* up to, Rickie Steibel? I thought I'd find you at the garage."

"Slow day."

"Yeah. Right," she said. "Real slow. Lots of days are real slow now, huh, Rickie?"

They held each other's eyes a moment; then he shrugged, reached into his jeans, pulled out a quarter, and flipped it in Susie's general direction. She took a step back and snagged it out of the air as neatly as a frog eats a fly. "Play us some music," he said.

"Who was your servant this time last week?"

"Play 'Jambalaya,'" he said.

"Naw," Eddie said, "I'm sick of that song. Play Merle Haggard."

"Play some rock 'n roll," Phil said.

"I'll play what I want," Susie said and turned to the jukebox.

"Nice boots, Gloria," Rick said.

"They're Susie's." She felt herself blushing again—and again reacted in the same humiliating way she had a dozen times before: she dropped her gaze to the floor. This is getting ridiculous, she thought, and forced herself to look up. He winked at her. He knew perfectly well the boots were Susie's. He'd pulled out a chair for her; she sat in it and hid her feet under the table.

The jukebox began to play "How Much Is That Doggy in the Window?" and the three guys hissed. Susie, with a smug smile, grabbed a chair, turned it around, and sat on it backwards, straddling it like a boy. "Why don't you get your glasses fixed, Eddie?" she said.

"Just haven't got around to it."

"What a useless bunch of boys," she said to Gloria. "They haven't got enough ambition between them to cross the street."

"Will you have a beer, girls?" Phil said.

"Her?" Eddie said, "Saint Susie? Strong spirits have never crossed her lips."

"Well, that's not quite right," her brother said.

"He got me drunk one night," Susie said to Gloria.

"Yeah, that's right. *I* did it. I held your nose and poured it down your throat."

"I just wanted to see what all the fuss was about," Susie said.

"You know what she ended up doing?" Rick said, laughing, "Singing hymns with tears pouring down her face."

"It's true," Susie said, "and that was my first and last— Oh, yuck, did I ever feel awful the next day."

"Pea green," Rick said. "Literally. She was the color of a tree frog."

"I was filled with deep remorse," Susie said in a deadpan voice.

"I take it that's a no?" Phil said.

"Buy me a Coke," Susie said.

"How about you, Gloria?"

"Miss Cotter, to you, slob," Rick said.

"A Coke, please," Gloria said.

Phil brought the girls Cokes and the guys another round of beer. Nobody had been bothering to clear away the glasses, and there were at least a dozen empty ones on the table—and a single, large ashtray overflowing with butts. A pack of Camels and a pack of matches were lying in the center; Eddie picked up the pack and offered it around. The three guys tapped their cigarettes vigorously on the table top—it looked like a ritual to Gloria—and then lit up. She didn't know how much longer she could stand to be in there; the smoke was making her sick, not to mention the smell of stale beer. She hadn't seen Rick smoke before. Maybe it was something he only did outside his parents' house.

"Jambalaya" came on the jukebox and Rick said, "Thanks," to his sister—then, jerking his thumb toward her: "So this here's next year's head majorette over at Briarville. What do you think of that, guys? Pretty good, huh?"

"Hey, way to go, Susie-Q," Phil said.

"Give us some reason to haul our sorry selves over to Briarville next year," Eddie said.

"Yep, see the ole Blue Bulldogs get creamed," Phil said.

"The team's going to do better next year," Susie said.

"I'll believe that when I see it. Whew, what a bunch of losers."

"This one here should of played college ball," Eddie said to Gloria, pointing at Rick.

"You should of seen him in high school," Susie said. "He was the best thing they'd ever seen around here."

"Those days are long gone," Rick said with his lovely smile. "So you ready to go hunting?" he asked Gloria.

"You aren't taking these girls hunting, are you?" Phil said.

"You bet."

"You're a braver man than I am, I can tell you that."

"Oh, yeah, the buckshot's gonna be flying around out there in the woods, boy."

"Yep, you better watch yourself, Steibel, or you'll have bodies piled up out there like firewood."

"Aw, no," Rick said. "Got a couple college girls here. Real smart girls. They're gonna do just fine. Aren't you, girls?"

"I don't know. I think you're taking your life in your hands, boy. That's what I think."

"Aw, no. Susie-Q's real good with a gun," Rick said. "I taught her myself."

"Yeah," Susie said—and then, in one of her sudden, unannounced movements, dismounted her chair and stood up. Gloria knew they were leaving.

"Yeah, Rickie taught me everything I know," Susie told Gloria in a voice that included everyone at the table. "That's why I'm so ignorant."

Susie strode out of the tavern so fast that Gloria had to run to catch up. "Always leave 'em laughing," Susie said. Her face was flushed, and Gloria could see how angry she was. "Sometimes I really hate this place!"

Gloria didn't know what to say. After a moment Susie asked her, "Do you want to walk up to the high school?"

"Sure."

Even though the sun was out, it was distant and watery—not warm at all— and Gloria was shivering. "My boots look nice on you," Susie said. "You look like a real country girl."

"They feel great. I could walk for miles in them."

"Yeah, they've got enough of a heel for you."

How observant of her, Gloria thought, to notice that I'm not comfortable in flats. And she finally had to admit to herself that she'd been annoyed at Susie; she could admit it because she wasn't annoyed any longer. Then, as though her mind were running along the same track as Gloria's, Susie said, "You're not having a good time, are you?"

"I didn't like being in that bar."

"Yeah? Me neither."

Susie's face had changed; she'd been transformed into that expressionless doll Gloria had seen so many times before—and now Gloria understood it. When Susie was upset, she closed her face so that nothing showed; that's what gave her that blank, shop-window mannequin look. "What's the matter?" Gloria said.

"It's just—" Susie shrugged. "I don't know. Maybe we shouldn't of gone in there. Tommie Jean used to cut school and meet her boyfriend in there. She got in real trouble doing that— And seeing Rickie in there— I don't know what's happened to him. He's my favorite brother, you can probably tell. He used to be so— Lots of girls around here would marry him in a flash, but he just won't get serious with any of them. He's always got a new girl, and— He used to be real ambitious, but now all he wants to do is work in Daddy's garage—when he *bothers* to work—and live at home, and— I don't know what he thinks he's going to get out of life that way."

Susie sighed, then looked directly into Gloria's eyes. Her face had come alive again, and she wasn't happy. "This isn't turning out the way I wanted it to— Oh, I don't want to go up to the high school. What's there to see at the darn high school? Do you want to go up there?"

"Not unless you do."

"No, but— Oh, I just wish we were having more fun."

"It's just fun being here with you. You don't have to *entertain* me."

Susie looked at her without speaking. "Come on, Suse," Gloria said. "You were going to show me everything. You haven't shown me *everything*, have you?"

"What do you want to see?"

Riding her intuition, Gloria said, "Why don't you show me where your dance school was?"

As soon as they were inside the Odd Fellows Hall, walking across the empty lobby with the sound of their heels echoing back from the walls, Susie gave her a shy flicker of the smile, and Gloria knew that everything was going to be OK again. She smelled something sweet and waxy—furniture polish?—that set off a complex bundle of associations in her mind: she liked that smell—and the ancient brass handles on the doors and the filtered yellow light from the high windows. As she followed Susie up the deeply worn wood of the broad stairs, she thought that there was something about walking into old public buildings—especially when they were deserted—that was poignant and timeless and profoundly American, like opening a dusty first edition of a Theodore Dreiser novel.

Susie stopped outside a dentist's office. "This used to be— Well, when I was a kid, old Doc— Gee, I can't remember his name. He had a beard. Yeah, he really did. I always thought he looked like one of the Smith brothers on the cough drops box." As they stood looking at the closed door, they heard a stealthy movement inside. Gloria had been sure that they were alone in the building; she found it creepy that they weren't. It had sounded as though a large person had shifted in a chair.

"He wasn't an ordinary doctor," Susie said, dropping her voice to just above a whisper, "Old Doc Whats-his-name. He was— I forget the word for it. Mom swore by him. He'd give you hundreds of teeny-tiny little-bitty pills to take." She gestured with her head: come on. Gloria followed her up another flight of stairs.

The pink sign on the wall said that Roberta Anne Carson taught toe, tap, and baton. "This was Miss Laverne's studio. I don't know this Roberta Anne character. See, everybody thinks they can teach twirling now. Most of them don't know beans about it. Somebody told me she's a pretty good ballet teacher though."

Susie bent close to look through the window in the door, so Gloria looked too. She could see, distorted by the pebbled glass, a small reception area and, beyond, a large hall with mirrors and a bar. "I didn't like ballet all that much," Susie said, still speaking *sotto voce*. "It's so— Well, I was going to say it's hard, but it's not that. It's so *picky*. Although— Oh, boy, did I love my first pair of toe shoes! I'll never forget it. The first day I had them, I wore them to dinner, and afterward, when I started clearing the table, I did everything on toe. You know, here I am carrying an armload of dishes, and I'm on toe. Mom was doing her best to be mad at me, but she couldn't because she was laughing too hard.

"There's something about going on toe that feels—I don't know. It's hard to do right. Get everything pulled up. But when you get it, it feels— It just feels *neat*—"

She gave Gloria a puzzled, exasperated look. "*Neat?* Great, huh? Oh, I envy you so much, Glo, the way you're never at a loss for words. I hear what's coming out of my mouth sometimes, and I want to shoot myself! Hey, let's see if we can get into the theater. I bet we can. They never lock the back way."

Gloria followed Susie to the end of the hall to a door marked: FIRE EXIT— KEEP CLOSED AT ALL TIMES. Susie opened it and held it for her. Narrow steps led downward. Their feet made a terrible racket on the hard wood, and Gloria felt a growing alarm. But what was she afraid of? That they'd be pursued by the fat dentist? Four flights down, they were met by another door: ABSOLUTELY NO ADMISSION. Susie opened it without hesitation. "See, I told you."

Gloria followed Susie down a long hallway that appeared to be leading them into total darkness. "Hey, Suse, wait a minute. Do you really think we ought to be in here?"

"Oh, don't be such a cherry!"

"Wait! I can't see anything." Gloria reached out to steady herself against the wall. "I don't know where I'm going."

"It's just straight ahead— OK, just stay there till I get the light."

Waiting in the dark, Gloria tried to identify the smell that was all around her; it was highly evocative—reminded her of Gramps Cotter—and then, suddenly, a single, bare, low-watt bulb went on, and she could see what she'd been smelling, laughed because it was so simple: old, unpainted wood. Susie was a slim silhouette at the end of a narrow passageway. "You OK?" Susie called back to her.

"Sure, but—" Gloria hurried to catch up. Susie was opening a metal box on the wall. "What on earth are you *doing?*"

"I'm lighting the house lights, silly," Susie said, pulling switches.

"You shouldn't do that. What if we get *caught* in here?"

"Come on, who's going to catch us?"

Again Gloria followed. Now she could see that they were backstage—in the wings to be exact—and then, before she had a chance to think about it, she'd followed Susie right out onto the stage itself. She turned, startled, and was momentarily dazzled by the footlights. She saw that they were facing rows and rows of empty seats. "Wow," Susie said, looking out at the nonexistent audience, "this really brings back memories."

The little theater was in that style of decor which Gloria's mother called "Southern bordello": dark red upholstery and gilt. It must have dated back to the turn of the century, or even earlier, and could not have been refurbished in years—had, by now, taken on a distinctly tawdry character. Two enormous caryatids—Amazonian ladies swathed in drapery, their paint fading and their legs chipped—held up the boxes on either side; the soot-stained ceiling was ornamented with a dizzying pattern of leaves and Victorian curlicues carved in plaster; grotesquely convoluted chandeliers with half of their bulbs out depended dangerously from vast medallions. "Wow," Susie said, "the number of times I danced on this stage— The first time I was four, and the last time I was eighteen. Tommie Jean and I did twirl routines here too— Yeah, I guess I must of done every kind of dance routine you could imagine."

Gloria walked cautiously to Susie's side and stood next to her, looking out. "It's funny when I think about it," Susie said, "the costumes I wore. I always figured if Pastor Harris had— He sure never would of thought I was a model Christian girl if he'd ever seen me on this stage! I used to have nightmares of looking out in the audience and seeing him sitting there. But he never came to see me, not once, and I was always grateful for that. He must of known I was dancing. Everybody in Cloverton knows everything about everybody—but I never heard him preach on the subject. The poor Baptist girls had it really rough. They couldn't even go to the school dances."

The few times Gloria had been on a stage, she'd been scared to death, and she tried to imagine what Susie's life must have been like, growing up with the stage so much a part of it. There was something about the idea of voluntarily putting oneself in a position in which an entire theater full of people could stare at you to their heart's content that Gloria found both appalling and seductive.

Susie shook her head and laughed. "What?" Gloria said.

"I was just remembering one year. I was too hot for the Jaycees. I can laugh now, but at the time I just bawled my eyes out. I was—let's see—eleven. And for my solo that year, I was making fun of a burly-Q. Of course I'd never even *seen* a burly-Q so I didn't know what I was making fun of, but I just did what Miss Laverne taught me, and I was doing bumps and grinds, the whole bit— I thought I was pretty good, but I didn't even get an honorable mention. And then the Jaycees started getting calls from all these mad moms saying, 'How dare you put on a spectacle like that? This is a *Christian* town.' They, you know, didn't think it was funny. I mean, I even did pratfalls, how could they not think it was funny? But they didn't. Oh, there's nothing worse than doing something funny and nobody laughs. Nothing! You just die right there on the stage.

"'The people around here are as dumb as the Gaderene swine,' Miss Laverne said. And the next year she put me in this little pinafore, you know, with petticoats, and I had lace ankle socks and lace gloves and a pink parasol for a prop, and I did just the sweetest little tap routine you ever saw, and I won first prize." Susie broke into what might have been the concluding steps of her tap routine—Gloria's hard-soled oxfords were perfect for it—and, lifting an imaginary skirt, concluded with a deep, sugary curtsy and a simpering, utterly revolting smile.

Gloria was laughing so hard she was bent double with it, squeezing her sides. "See, *you've* got a sense of humor," Susie said. "*You* think I'm funny. Maybe I *am* funny."

Gloria couldn't stop laughing. "Stop it, Susie. You're killing me!"

"Maybe I missed my calling. Maybe I ought to be one of these comic performers—you know, like Fanny Brice."

Gloria followed Susie back the way they had come. "I always figured if I hadn't been a twirler, I would have been a tap dancer," Susie said. "I was *good*. Maybe I'll take it up again."

After being in the theater, even the thin, lemony sunlight was too bright. The real world looked curiously flat, two-dimensional, and it was too cold. It had begun to snow just enough to be noticeable: tiny, stinging sparkles punctuating the sky.

"Showing you around's kind of— Well, it's making me think about things, remember things. I don't know. I feel kind of—funny."

Susie stopped walking, so Gloria stopped too. She looked at Susie, saw that Susie was already looking at her. "It really hurt me," Susie said, "when those moms were saying, 'This is a Christian town.' What did that make me?"

That night they talked for hours. Trying to reconstruct their conversation two and a half years later, Gloria remembered how fidgety Susie had been, and she wrote in her diary: "She really *is* like a high-strung horse that needs to be galloped. Just pacing around her bedroom, she must have walked five miles."

Much of what they'd talked about was gone from her mind, but Gloria was surprised at how much she did remember. They'd talked about how easily they might never have met. Gloria might have gone to Vassar or to one of the big state universities; if Susie hadn't won the National Teenage Majorette Championships, she never would have gone to college at all.

"After I got my trophy," Susie said, "this man came up and introduced himself— Mr. Allen, the band master from Briarville College. And he congratulated me and all that, and he said he wanted to talk to me and my mom and dad, so he took us out for lunch. He asked me how my grades were. I was so shy, I couldn't say a word, so Mom answered for me, 'Poor Susan Jane's never been much of a student,' and he said, 'Susan, I really want good twirlers at Briarville, and you're just about the best twirler I've ever seen in my life. OK, so if you can get your grades up for the next two years— if you can get all Cs and maybe even throw some Bs in, I think I can get you a full scholarship. Would you like that?'

"It'd never even crossed my mind I could go to college, but the minute he said it, I knew that's why God had let me win the Nationals—because He wanted me to make something of myself so I could serve Him better, but I was still so shy I couldn't say a word, so I just looked at Daddy, and he said, 'Susan Jane, there's never been anybody in the family been able to go on with their education. We'd sure be proud of you,' so I said I'd try my best. And it was hard for me, but I did what Mr. Allen asked me—got all Cs with some Bs thrown in, and that's how I got to Briarville.

"You know 'Amazing Grace'? I always cry when I sing that hymn. Because it's *true*. If it wasn't for the Grace of God, I'd—I don't know, just be stuck here in Cloverton doing nothing, or—you know, going nowhere, getting in trouble—" Susie hadn't said "like Tommie Jean," but Gloria had heard it anyway.

"Hey, we really should go to bed or we won't want to get up in the morning," Susie said.

"Maybe your brother won't want to go," Gloria said. Rick hadn't come home for dinner, and he was still out.

"Oh, no. You don't know Rickie and hunting. It doesn't matter when he gets in."

"Oh, that's too bad." They both laughed.

"Yeah, he's off seeing some girl. Don't know which one. I can't keep track of them anymore. He'll come sneaking in at two in the morning— Yeah, we really do have to go to bed."

But they didn't go to bed.

"I was so scared when I went off to Briarville," Susie said. "College girls are *fast*—you know, everybody says that. And then the Lambs rushed me, and the Lambs seemed— I thought, wow, I bet some of those girls are *really* fast." Susie gave Gloria a wry, puzzled look. "Glo?" she said, "how far have you gone?"

Faced with such a simple, direct question, all Gloria could say was, "Pretty far."

"All the way?"

"No." It didn't feel like a lie to Gloria. What had happened with Ken had been, she was sure, something so outside Susie's experience as to be utterly incomprehensible to her—and it hadn't really been *all the way*.

"Rolland and I have an agreement," Gloria said. "We're not going to go all the way unless we're married. But we've done—well, we've had some really heavy make-out sessions."

"What's that mean? What's *heavy* mean? You mean more than taking your bra off?"

Gloria nodded and felt herself blushing—embarrassed more for Susie than for herself.

"Oh, I feel like such a little dope sometimes! You know, I never even kissed a boy with my mouth open until last year. You probably think that's real dumb, don't you? It's— Well, it's not just, you know, being religious. I guess what happened to Tommie Jean really scared me, and I didn't want boys touching me. And whenever they'd try anything, I'd say, 'What do you think Jesus thinks of what you're doing?' It'd just stop them dead."

"Oh, I bet it did!"

"Everybody knew I wouldn't pet. Around here, things go around like—you know, a fishbowl. The boys called me 'Saint Susie,' but they asked me out anyway. And even George Davis—his dad owns the bank in Jordanstown—he even took me out. He took me to the Prom both our junior and senior years. I heard his parents gave him a real hard time about it, but he did it anyway."

Gloria had been sure that Susie was going to say something more, but she didn't. She'd been sitting cross-legged on the floor; now she sprang up and began to pace again.

Gloria wanted to encourage Susie to keep on talking, but she didn't know quite how to do it, so, to break the silence, she said, "Wow, is it ever cold in here."

"Yeah, Daddy's let the furnace die— You know, Mom never told me about *anything*. All she'd ever say was, 'Susan Jane, you just keep yourself pure, and everything you need to know, your husband will tell you,' and so I stopped asking her. And then— Oh, Gloria, I can say *anything* to you, can't I?"

"Yes, of course you can."

"Well, Tommie Jean started sleeping with this guy and I just couldn't believe it. I've never told this to anybody, you know. I said, 'Doesn't it *hurt?*' And she said, 'It hurts at first when you're a virgin, and then after that it doesn't hurt so much, and then it gets so it feels really good.' And I said, 'It feels *good?*' And she said, 'Yeah, it feels like heaven,' and I said, 'But Tommie Jean, *it's a sin,*' and she said, 'I love him and he loves me, and we're married in the eyes of God, so it's OK,' and I believed it.

"That's how dumb I was! Tommie Jean said it, so it must be true! I'd always thought, you know, that if something was wrong, Jesus would tell me and I'd *feel it*. And what Tommie Jean told me didn't feel wrong. And I thought, oh, so that's the way it is. If you love a boy and he loves you, and you're going to get married, then you're already married in the eyes of God, and you can go all the way, and it's OK. Really dumb, huh?

"And then Tommie Jean got in trouble. And she had to leave town— I heard she kept her baby. I don't know for sure, but that's what I heard—but anyhow, I never saw her again."

"Oh, that's really sad."

"Yeah. It really is— And I knew it wasn't OK, all that stuff she'd been saying— and I felt so ashamed. I can't begin to tell you how ashamed I felt."

Susie walked over to the radiator and pressed her hands against it. "Cold as a stone," she said. "Daddy's way of saying, 'Go to bed, girls.'" She paced from one side of the room to the other, blowing on her hands. "We might as well be outdoors." She grabbed the blanket from the foot of her bed and threw it onto Gloria's lap. "Here. You must be half frozen."

"No, I'm all right."

She gave Gloria a long, somber look. "I used to wonder why God lets bad things happen. I still do. Pastor Harris says it's to test our faith, but— Well, that just seems cruel to me, and God's not cruel. Oh, I don't know what I'm saying. Come on, Glo, we really do have to go to bed."

Gloria was sleeping in the guest room. They tiptoed across the hall. Gloria could hear someone snoring. Susie shut the door behind them, began pacing up and down in the guest room, and Gloria didn't know what else to do but put on the pair of pajamas Susie had lent her and get into bed. It was odd, but she wasn't all *that* cold; Susie seemed to be the one who was half frozen. She was shivering. Even her teeth were chattering. "Now *you* go to bed, dopey," Gloria told her.

"Yeah, I will in a minute—I just want to— You know that part of the Lord's Prayer, 'deliver us from evil'? When I was little, I didn't really know what that meant. I didn't think anything was really *evil*—you know, bad maybe, but not *evil*."

"Do kids ever really believe in evil?" Gloria said. She found it an interesting question. After a moment she realized that *she* had certainly believed in evil.

"I don't know about other kids," Susie said, "but evil was something in the Bible. I wasn't scared of Satan at all. I was a good girl. There was nothing he could do to *me*. That just goes to show you how dumb I was, huh?"

"Come on, Suse, stop saying how dumb you were. You weren't dumb, you were just a kid. That's probably the way most kids are."

Susie shrugged. "Yeah, I guess— Oh, we really stayed up way too late. We're gonna feel awful in the morning."

"Well, *go to bed*, silly!"

Susie looked far too restless to go to sleep, but she said, "Yeah. Sleep well, Glo. God bless you," and, with a shy smile, slipped out of the room and shut the door.

Gloria lay between the sweet-smelling sheets, hugging herself, waiting to get warm, and she couldn't stop thinking about all of the things she should have said. "Hey, you think *you* were dumb?" she should have said, "Remember Ken Henderson?" and she should have told Susie the whole dreadful, absurd story. Isn't that what best girlfriends were supposed to do—share secrets?

Well, she consoled herself, at least I'm a good listener—and, yawning, feeling her toes finally beginning to thaw out, she felt bad that Susie had been so open with her, had told her everything about herself, but she hadn't been open with Susie—and now she wished she'd told her not only about Ken but also about what had happened to her at Fairhaven, about her desperate need to be liked, about the way she'd never felt authentic. She didn't have her watch on so she'd lost track of the time, but she knew it was late, late, late, and she didn't feel the least bit sleepy. It was nice being in bed though—finally getting warm all over—and then, as happened to her every night during that weekend in Cloverton, as she was worrying about falling asleep, she fell asleep.

Someone was shaking her. "Come on, Glo, we've really got to get rolling."

For a moment, Gloria was afraid she was missing classes, and then she remembered where she was. She smelled meat frying. "What time is it?"

"Six-thirty," Susie said.

An ineffectual, dirty light was spilling around the drawn window blinds, and Gloria felt a hushed presence that could have been a leftover bit of dream. Susie was already dressed, wearing corduroy pants and a thick flannel shirt. "Come down by the fire," she said.

Snug under the eiderdown, Gloria could sense the malevolence of the cold waiting in the room. Oh, help, she thought, we're supposed *to go hunting*. She couldn't move. "Come on, sugar." Susie reached under the covers, found Gloria's hand, took it and pulled.

"OK, OK," Gloria said. She needed more time. Her mind wasn't working yet. "You look like a cold snake," Susie said, laughing.

"I feel like a cold snake." Under her bare feet, the wood floor felt like a sheet of ice. She allowed Susie to lead her down the steps and into the living room where someone had built a good, crackling fire.

"You ever see a cold snake?" Susie asked her.

"No."

"They're funny. They can't move or do anything much. You can pick them up and wind them all around, and they can't do a darn thing about it." She handed Gloria a mug of coffee. The living room windows were frosted. She heard Mrs. Steibel's voice from the kitchen: "It's cruel what you're doing to these poor girls."

"Aw, Mom," Rick said, "it's nice to get up in the morning—"

Then, to Gloria's amazement, mother and son sang the next line together: "But—it's nicer to stay in bed!"

Glad to be wearing Susie's pajamas instead of her own ridiculous baby-dolls, Gloria cupped herself around the ball of warmth swelling out from the fire; she sipped her coffee. Susie had remembered the way she took it: the smallest splash of cream, no sugar. Had Susie really called her "sugar"? How odd.

"You can dress in here," Susie was saying. "Don't worry, I'll keep Rickie out." She had brought Gloria her bra and underwear—and a boy's T-shirt, a flannel shirt, wool pants, and heavy socks.

"What time did we go to bed?" Gloria said.

"Must have been after two. Have some breakfast. You'll feel better."

Dressed, Gloria sat shyly at the kitchen table, saw Rick looking at her, saw the small indentations at either side of his mouth when he smiled—much like the small indentations at either side of Susie's mouth. It was uncanny how much he looked like his sister, and, at the same time, how masculine he was.

"This really is cruel of you, Rickie," Mrs. Steibel said.

"You don't understand the principle of the thing, Mom. Hunting's kind of like going to church. If you're not suffering, you're not really enjoying yourself."

Breakfast was more coffee, and toast and eggs, and—Gloria couldn't believe it—fried pork chops. She wasn't sure she could eat anything, but Susie said, "Force yourself. If you don't eat, you'll be real sorry later."

"Did you bring any boots?" Susie asked her.

"Yes, of course. The little—" She looked over and met Susie's eyes.

"Oh, right. Those cute little things that fold down at the ankle. Gloria, you're such a dope."

"I'm sorry. I wasn't thinking. Why don't I wear your cowgirl boots?"

"Not to go hunting in." Now Susie sounded genuinely annoyed. She was wearing yellow leather boots done up with rawhide laces. She whipped them off and tossed them over. "Don't worry. I'll wear Mom's."

Susie's rustic boots were perfectly flat; wearing them, Gloria felt unbalanced—tipped backward—and splay-footed. Susie and her brother were in the hall, handling guns. Gloria could *smell* the guns: metallic and oily. "Sure you don't want the twelve-gauge?" he was saying.

"Naw," Susie said, "it kicks too hard. You take it."

Rick was offering Gloria a gun. Instinctively, she stepped back.

"She doesn't want to carry a gun, Rickie."

"Not much damage she can do with this."

Gloria was afraid she was going to panic, but Susie said, "Come on, Rickie. She really doesn't want to. She doesn't like guns."

Why can't I talk? Gloria asked herself to no good effect.

Mrs. Steibel was forcing a huge, silver thermos on her son. "Give me something heavy to carry, why don't you?" he said.

"I don't want these poor girls catching pneumonia. And Rickie? If you get any game, you clean it yourself."

"Sure, Mom."

"It starts to snow hard, you come right back."

"You bet, Mom."

They rode in the pickup truck. Like Susie, Rick drove with his right hand on the wheel and his left arm draped on the open window. Susie had probably learned it from him. Gloria thought that it must be nice to have older brothers you actually liked instead of younger ones you detested.

Rick parked by the side of the road. They got out, and, without speaking, walked in single file along a dirt path up a hill. They seemed to be on a farm. Cultivated acres strewn with a beige stubble Gloria couldn't identify stretched away to their right; a fence several hundred yards to their left must, she thought, mark off somebody's property line: the hill beyond was heavily wooded. If Joyce could call the Liffey "snot-green," Gloria thought, then she supposed she could call this sky "snot-colored"—and yes, that was exactly the color it was. Although it wasn't snowing yet, she could feel how much it wanted to.

Susie and her brother walked easily, the barrels of the guns riding casually in the crooks of their left arms, but Gloria was hard pressed to keep up with them. Somewhere, far away, a dog was barking. It was a lonely sound—a bleak, crude, melancholy sound—or, Gloria thought, maybe it was her own state that made her hear it that way: the raw ache of her muscles forced into movement with not enough sleep and the chill of wind on the back of her neck. She should have brought a scarf.

They reached the top of the hill and then, without pausing, started down the other side. They were walking away from farmland. Gloria could see several hills in the distance. The trees had been stripped for winter and stuck up in dark, angular patterns as crude as if a child had slashed them onto the sky with a black crayon; all around them, fallen leaves had piled and drifted. She didn't know much about trees—"bare ruin'd choirs," she thought. They were probably oak or elm. Maybe poplar. She considered asking, but she didn't have the energy—and besides, she didn't really care. Restless birds seemed to be following them. They might be crows—yes, of course they were crows; nothing else made that scraped, ugly noise. Oh, she thought, what a barren landscape. Everything she could see that wasn't black was a dirty gray or a dirty brown, and she felt as though she were walking into a Brueghel painting.

Rick, who was leading, turned back to see how far they were behind him. "You watch where you're pointing that thing, little sister," he said.

"I can handle a gun as well as you can, Rickie Steibel."

"That'll be the day."

They reached the bottom of the hill and started up another one. Is that what they were going to do all morning? Just walk steadily into these awful hills? Then, as though she were reading Gloria's mind, Susie said, "Hey, Rickie, slow down for her. She's not used to it."

"I just wanted to get us off old man Hunsicker's property."

They climbed another hill, more slowly this time, and paused at the top. "Feels good to be out this early and moving around, doesn't it?" he said.

"Yeah," Susie said. "I like this time of year. It's so bare and—I don't know."

"Bleak," Gloria said.

"Yeah, that's right. It makes you feel—" Susie's brow furrowed; this happened to her a lot: she would have an idea—or a feeling or a thought or a *something*— but not the words to go with it. Sometimes Gloria could give her the words and sometimes she couldn't; this time she didn't have the faintest idea what Susie wanted to say, and she was curious how Susie would end her sentence— but, as Gloria waited, she realized that Susie had given it up.

Trying to see what Susie was seeing, Gloria felt a shift in her perception. The landscape was not a Brueghel—not a picture at all—and she was not separate from it, not a detached observer. She was walking through it; she was, therefore, a part of it, and it was nothing she could have imagined beforehand. The real was a constant surprise—or at least it should be—but sometimes she was so preoccupied with herself she didn't notice.

They were walking at a more leisurely pace now, and Gloria had no trouble keeping up. She found herself mulling over everything she and Susie had talked about the night before. Yes, it had taken a whole series of odd events working out exactly right for them to meet at all—let alone become friends.

"Usually hundreds out here. Just not today," Rick said.

"Yeah, they heard we were coming."

Gloria didn't even know what animal they were hunting.

"A real cold snap," Susie said to Gloria. "It shouldn't be this cold for November."

"Aw, you girls don't know what cold is," Rick said.

"Now he's going to tell us how cold it was in Korea."

"No, I'm not."

"Come on, Rickie. Tell us how cold it was in Korea."

"Nope. You're not interested. You made that plain enough."

"Sure, we're interested. Aren't we, Gloria? Come on, was it cold in Korea?"

Gloria thought he wasn't going to answer, but then, with a sly smile, he said, "I've never been so cold in my life. I didn't think cold came that cold. It was a cold like death. It was so cold I forgot there was ever anything warm. The wind came howling down on us—cut like whipcord. The fuel lines froze in the night. The tubes you—you know, where you're supposed to do your business—they froze. The tears in your eyes froze. And the snow came down on us and just buried us alive. I can't begin to tell you—"

"Well, you just told us pretty good," Susie said.

Gloria must have begun to feel better; she could actually laugh with them.

"Stop telling us how cold it was," Susie said. "That's the last thing we need to be hearing today. Tell us how hot it was in Korea."

"Yep, it was hot in the summer." He stopped walking, took some tobacco and papers out of his pocket, and began to roll a cigarette. Gloria and Susie had come to rest on either side of him. They'd made it to the top of yet another bleak hill. Talk, Gloria told herself; make conversation like a normal person. "When were you in Korea?" she asked him.

"Oh, let's see. I got there early in fifty-one. Right smack in the middle of the winter—"

"What she means is, were you in the war?"

He looked startled. "Well, yeah, I saw some action. That's something I don't like to dwell on. By the time I left, things had got pretty much quieted down."

He'd finished rolling his cigarette. He licked it shut and lit it. "A police action, they called it. That's funny, isn't it? Yeah, it seems like a lot of bloodshed to accomplish as little as we did."

"He got a medal," Susie said, "for bravery."

"You keep your mouth shut about that medal, Susan," he said in a hard, angry voice Gloria hadn't heard from him before. "It's not something I feel that good about."

Then, after a moment, he added: "Anyhow—bravery had nothing to do with it," and smiled at Gloria.

"It's funny," he said. "I hated Korea. I counted the minutes till I could get out of there—and I also got kind of fond of the damn place. The Koreans are OK."

"He means he liked the girls," Susie said.

He shook his head and grinned, took a deep drag on his cigarette. "They've got a pickle dish called kimchi," he said, "you take a little bit and it blows the back of your head right off. I got so I really liked it. The guys couldn't believe it. Look at that crazy Rick Steibel gobble up the kimchi. But if you eat too much of it, you're doing the Pusan two-step— And another thing they've got, called bull-gogie. Man, was that good! It's strips of steak. They cook it up right in front of you. Sort of like barbecue. I could eat just plates and plates of that stuff— And yeah, the girls were sweet, I've got to admit it."

"The girls are sweet everywhere you go, Rickie."

"Yeah, that's true enough— The thing about girls is if you're sweet to them, they're usually sweet right back. Now isn't that true, girls?"

"You bet, pretty boy," his sister said.

Laughing, he snapped his cigarette down, ground it out under his heel, and walked away. They followed him.

Susie had lent Gloria a checked wool coat, but the Steibels were wearing sleeveless vests, and she hadn't been able to understand why they weren't freezing to death. Now—amazingly—she was actually getting too warm, and she thought that they were the ones who were sensibly dressed. She took off her gloves and put them in her pocket, undid the top two buttons on her coat. She was getting used to walking. It almost felt good.

Rick stopped under a tree, leaned his gun against it, shed his pack, took out the thermos his mother had given him, and poured coffee into metal cups. "I started taking Susie hunting when she couldn't of been much more than eight or nine," he told Gloria.

"Yeah," Susie said, "I trailed around after him like a little puppy dog."

"I couldn't ever leave her home," he said, "she got too sad— That sure was a hard time for us. Dad was off in the war, and Mom with five kids. Yeah, we ate a lot of rabbit in those days. We hunted them in season and out, we didn't give a damn."

Oh, Gloria thought, they're hunting rabbits. How Lawrencian.

Rick extracted a pint bottle from his pack and poured a modest shot into his cup. "Rickie Steibel," Susie said—and sounded genuinely shocked—"it's not even nine o'clock."

"Isn't it Paul who says, 'Take a little wine for thy stomach's sake'?"

"Yeah, but that's not wine."

"No. You're right. It's good blended rye whiskey. You want a snort, Gloria? It'll cut the cold."

She shook her head. "Here I am," he said, "out hunting with a couple temperance girls."

He looked directly into Gloria's eyes and smiled. If another boy had smiled at her like that, she would have been sure he was flirting with her. "You got any Indian blood in you, Gloria?"

"Oh, Rickie, what a thing to say," his sister said.

"I didn't mean anything by it. It's just— I've been trying to figure out who she reminds me of, and it just hit me. Johnny Corngiver. Indian guy I served in the army with. Real good-looking fellow. It's funny. He didn't have to shave. His face was smooth as a girl's."

"She's Castilian," Susie said.

"Spanish," Gloria said.

"Oh, yeah? Spanish, huh? 'Spanish is the loving tongue—' You know that song? Yeah, I can see it now. You're like a rare, beautiful flower, Gloria. You know, like a perfect, dark orchid."

"Oh, Rickie, come on," Susie said, "we're going to get plenty of snow without you adding to it."

"I'm not snowing her. I'm just telling the truth. Isn't she a beautiful girl, Suse?"

"Well, sure she's a beautiful girl. And she's a *pinned* beautiful girl—"

"Hey, I'm just trying to give her a compliment. I didn't mean any offence—"

"No offence taken," Gloria said. Of course he'd been flirting with her—why was that so surprising?—and, for the first time since she'd arrived in Cloverton, she understood how to play with him; she didn't know where that knowledge

had come from, but she slipped into it gratefully, as though putting on a fortu-
itously discovered mask. "And maybe I am like an orchid—they don't last more
then a few seconds out of doors."

She was rewarded by his deep laugh, and she felt a thrill of pleasure so intense
it was a physical sensation, a warmth in her stomach. "Oh, you're doing great,
Gloria," he said.

"Yeah," Susie said, "she's a real sport, isn't she?"

He put the thermos away, shouldered his pack. The walking had begun to
feel natural—almost easy—and Gloria thought that maybe this was what it
was like to be a girl in a Jane Austen novel: you went out every day and took
enormously long walks all over the countryside, and you flirted—in the most
discreet possible way. "So, you enjoying yourself in Cloverton?" Rick asked
her.

"Oh, yes. I'm having a wonderful time."

He gestured with his head, then swung his gun, indicating a rising slope
leading into what Gloria supposed might be called a meadow—although it
was hard to think of anything in this austere, wintery landscape as a meadow—
grown high with brown weeds. He was walking quite slowly now with Susie
following a few feet back from him, and both of them were looking up toward
the horizon where the dirty sky was piling up and thickening. For the first time,
Gloria saw them as *hunting*—that is, looking for something to shoot with the
guns they were carrying. A few snowflakes had begun to shake down on them.

"Thanksgiving a big deal in your family?" Rick asked Gloria. As he'd spoken,
he'd turned back toward her—seeking her out with his eyes—and now he
stopped walking and waited for her. She hurried, caught up with him. "Not that
big a deal," she said. "My family's scattered all over the place, and we hardly
ever get together for anything."

They continued on up into the meadow. Rick and Gloria were leading now.
It had become beautifully simple for her to chat with him, and it didn't matter
at all what they were saying. After a moment, she realized that she'd lost track
of Susie and looked to see where she'd gone. She was off to their right and was
walking with the air of someone very much alone.

"Granny Steibel can't do all that much anymore," Rick was saying, "so Mom
spends days and days getting ready, and then everybody descends on her like a
plague of locusts, and they eat up everything in sight as fast as they can, and then
it's all over. Yeah, but it's nice to get the whole family together."

"I just wish it *was* the whole family," Susie said, veering toward them.

"That's right. You've got to come back sometime when the twins are here,"
he said to Gloria. "You get all the Steibel boys together, and it's some show."

"And it'd be nice to see Tommie Jean in our home again too," Susie said.

He looked at Susie, then away. A quick motion—a tightening—had passed over his face, but Gloria hadn't been able to tell if it had been annoyance or merely surprise. She was somewhat annoyed too; she was beginning to get sick of hearing about Tommie Jean.

They walked on in silence for a while, and then he said, "So, Gloria, I guess Susie must of told you about the black sheep in our family."

Gloria tried the most neutral thing she could find: "She said something about it."

"You're not one of the ones who doesn't ever want to mention her name, are you?" Susie asked her brother.

"Oh, come on. You know me better than that."

"It's really weird. There's Aunt Ruth eating Thanksgiving dinner with us, and I can't say, 'Hey, how's Tommie Jean doing?'"

"If you did that, honey, all you'd do is make her feel bad."

"Yeah, I suppose so."

"You got some skeletons in your family closet, Gloria?" Rick asked her.

"Doesn't everybody?"

He laughed, and she was glad. "I suppose," he said. "But everybody doesn't necessarily want to talk about them."

"Why shouldn't we talk about her?" Susie said.

"No reason at all, Suse. No reason at all."

"It just feels hypocritical, you know, Rick? If she was dead, we could at least talk about her. But we're not even allowed to mention her name—even though everybody in town knows about it. Pastor Harris even preached a sermon against her—"

"What do you mean?" Gloria said. "With her right there in the church?"

"No, she'd left town by then. But Aunt Ruth was there. I couldn't help looking at her. Everybody was looking at her. She went white as a sheet—"

"Well, I gather that he wasn't so much preaching against Tommie Jean directly as talking about—you know, things in general."

"You weren't there, Rickie. You were in Korea."

"That's what Mom told me anyway."

"Well, what do you think she'd say? No, he didn't mention Tommie Jean by name, but it was as clear as a bell who he meant— Going on about fornication and bearing children out of wedlock— Gee, I wish you'd heard him, Rickie. He must of mentioned every scarlet woman in the whole Bible. Jezebel and the Whore of Babylon were just for starters—"

"Oh, yeah, I can imagine," Rick said, laughing again.

"And I've never felt right about the church since then. It's like— It's hard to describe. It's like everything's going on just the same, but there's a—I don't know—like a little spark that's gone out. For me. And without that spark, it doesn't mean anything. Or it doesn't mean what it should. Do you know what I mean?" she asked Gloria.

"Oh, yes!"

They'd arrived at a row of tree stumps—who on earth could have cut them down way out here?—and Rick sat down on one of them. He leaned his gun against one side of the stump, and Gloria was suddenly aware of just how *careful* he and Susie were with their guns. She hoped they wouldn't find anything to shoot.

"Isn't that what a preacher's supposed to do?" he said. "Preach against sin?"

Susie had come to rest standing directly in front of her brother. "Against *sin*, sure, but—oh, Rickie, I can never tell when you're kidding."

"I'm only about half kidding. So what was he supposed to do? By your lights?"

"You know Luke Fifteen, Four? 'What man of you, having an hundred sheep, if he lose one of them, doth not leave the ninety and nine in the wilderness, and go after that which is lost, until he find it?' Well, OK, instead of preaching a sermon against her, he should of found her— and brought her home and called her friends and neighbors together and said, 'Rejoice for we've found our lost sheep.'"

"Dream on, Susan Jane."

"It's what Jesus would of done."

He shook his head. "Honey, there's a lot of things that Jesus would of done that don't get done around here—as you should know pretty well by now."

Susie looked at her brother a moment then walked around behind him, took the thermos and the tin cups out of his pack. She poured coffee into a cup and handed it to Gloria. "Give me a snort, will you, hon?" Rick said.

"You can pour your own damn whiskey, Richard."

"Well, hand me the bottle then."

Susie handed him the bottle. "You know the thing that really gets to me?" she said. "I went off and won the Nationals, and she stayed home and got in trouble."

"What's that supposed to mean, Susan?"

"If she'd gone to Milwaukee with me, it wouldn't of happened to her. She was supposed to go. We had a routine worked out and everything. I knew something was up. She was just nuts about that jerk. She was sure he was going to marry her—"

"Oh, sure! And the sun sets in the east. The thing about Tommie Jean is that she didn't have the brains of a flea."

"Come on, that's not fair."

"It might not be fair, but it's the truth."

He poured himself a shot of whiskey. It was beginning to snow seriously now. He looked up at the sky, then at his sister.

"You know," Susie said, "I wrote her three times and she never wrote back."

"Yeah? Well, maybe your little lost lamb doesn't want to be found."

"Well, maybe she doesn't."

He set his cup down on the ground, took out his tobacco and papers and began to roll a cigarette. "I know what she's thinking," Susie said. "She thinks I'm a model Christian girl. Oh, I wish Pastor Harris had never called me that! She thinks I must of judged her too."

"Come on, Susan Jane, just let it go."

Susie looked at him, then at Gloria. Her pale face was flushed with cold and had no expression on it that Gloria could read.

"Oh, I know you looked up to her and admired her," Rick said to his sister, "but it was bound to happen. Her father was killed in the war," he told Gloria, "and Aunt Ruth just spoiled her to death, and she'd been running wild for years."

"She wasn't that wild."

"Tell me another."

Gloria saw anger like a sudden blue flash in Susie's eyes. Susie started to say something but then stopped herself. Gloria saw Susie and her brother exchange a long, searching look.

Susie sighed, said, "I'm sorry, you guys. I know I'm being a drip, but I just can't get her out of my mind. I don't know why." She looked at Gloria. "Maybe it's because you're here, I don't know."

"Aw, honey, just let it go," Rick said. He stood up, wiped snow from his hair. "Hey, it's getting serious," he said. "You want to go back?"

"Not yet," Susie said.

"OK, little sister, you call it."

Susie put the thermos, cups, and bottle back in his pack. He ground out his cigarette. He and Susie picked up their guns in the respectful, careful way they handled them—since she'd first noticed it, Gloria couldn't *stop* noticing it—and began to climb the hill.

Gloria trudged along behind. If this landscape wasn't a picture, then neither was it the setting for any pretty story she might have wanted to tell herself. They were miles from the truck, and now it was snowing hard. She could feel the temperature dropping, and it frightened her.

As Rick approached the crest of the hill, he stopped suddenly, swung his gun up to his shoulder, and fired. Then, almost immediately, he fired again. The voice of the gun had been bigger, deeper, than Gloria could possibly have imagined. She'd actually seen flame and shot coming out of the barrel; she could smell the gunpowder. Instinctively, she'd slapped her hands hard against her mouth; now she slowly lowered them. What had she been doing? Stopping herself from screaming? Nothing had been in her mind. She hadn't seen anything move. He couldn't have been shooting at nothing, could he? "I think you got him," Susie yelled.

"No, I didn't. I know I didn't." Rick did something that made his gun open up—made it fold in the middle—and jerked out what Gloria guessed must be spent shells; he thrust in new ones and shut the gun.

Rick and Susie jogged up toward the crest of the hill, and Gloria felt as though her nice Jane Austen novel had been transformed into something dumb by Ernest Hemingway—but, even though she couldn't share it, she could feel the intensity of their exhilaration. They were leaving her behind, moving away quickly into a strange, hard, demanding world—one that she could comprehend only at a distance, as though it were a grotesque conceit.

"He's long gone. He's off telling his pals: 'Get your ass out of here, boys. There's a dumbass Dutchman out there with a shotgun.'"

"Yeah, and his dumbass sister— You know where I think he's gone? Over there."

"Yeah. You're probably right."

"I got dibsies on him next time."

"Sure you do—if you see him first. Let's cut around and come in from that way. Sneak up on him."

"Gee, Rickie, if I didn't know better, I'd think you knew what you were doing."

Gloria was jogging, trying to keep up, and she wondered if she shouldn't simply let them go—and then she stopped wondering and allowed herself to shuffle to a standstill. She had a stitch in her side. To quell it, she wrapped her arms around herself and squeezed. Frightened and cold, she watched them moving fast through the knee-high stubble, moving in a big semi-circle as though they were homing in on something. The snow was coming down wet and thick, and it was sticking. The dull brown ground all around her was blurring with white.

She saw them stop. She ran to catch up. "Long gone," Rick told her just as though she would care.

"You must think we're nuts," Susie said.

"Oh, no," Gloria said, "this is great fun."

Susie and Rick were simply standing there, looking out from the hilltop, so Gloria looked too. The snow was falling so fast that the distant hills were gradually fading away as though someone were lowering gauze over them. "Great, huh?" Rick said, turned and started to walk back the way they had come; Gloria followed him, but Susie didn't move. "Suse?" he said.

"I don't know," she said, "maybe I didn't need to tell anybody—"

"What *the hell* are you talking about?"

"I'm sorry, I just can't get her out of my mind. A lot of people knew they were sleeping together, and—I just keep wondering if I should of *said something*. I promised her I wouldn't, but— You remember what you said to me? When you came back from Korea? You said, 'It's a fact of life, honey. When a girl starts putting out, the guys come around.'"

In the same hard, angry voice he'd used to tell his sister to keep her mouth shut about his medal, he said: "You don't give a damn what you say in front of her, do you?"

"No, I don't give a damn. Gloria's my sister. We don't have any secrets from each other."

Gloria watched them. They were glaring at each other, so angry they had been frozen into immobility like terriers with their hackles up. "She knows I've got a foul mouth," Susie said.

"Yeah?"

"I got it from you, Rickie Steibel," Susie said with a faint smile.

"Come on, honey, don't blame that one on me."

Gloria didn't have any idea why they should be so mad at each other. Maybe she could figure it out later. "Hey," he said, "you think you can give Tommie Jean a rest?"

Susie didn't answer. After a moment, he said, "We've got to get back. This is getting ridiculous."

They both turned and looked at Gloria. "You OK, Glo?" Susie said.

"Oh, yes, I'm fine."

"Let's not give up just yet," Susie said. "If I was a rabbit, I'd be right along that fence up there. Hiding in the weeds."

Rick looked at her a moment, frowning. "You would, would you? OK, go get him."

Susie took off. Her brother followed. "Glo, you stay behind us, OK?" Susie yelled, "I mean, you know, *way* back."

Gloria let them go on ahead, but then, as they circled around and jogged down toward the fence—approaching from the uphill side—Gloria knew that she couldn't simply wait; she didn't have time to figure it out, but it had something to do with her fear of being left alone. She began to jog toward them.

This time Gloria actually saw the rabbit—saw it as an unexpected motion in the weeds like a bouncing ball. Susie already had her gun up and was turning in the direction the rabbit had gone. "Lead him, lead him!" Rick was yelling at her. Gloria saw that bouncing movement again, and Susie fired—a brighter, smaller sound than her brother's gun had made. In the instant the gun had spoken, another voice had answered it: a high-pitched keening like the anguished cry of a hurt child.

Later, Gloria would not be able to remember why she had run toward the

rabbit, but Rick and Susie were running, and she ran too—flinging herself head-
long into the motion. It was, she would write in her diary, as though they had all
been running toward a shrieking tea kettle, but that metaphor would not begin
to express the pain and panic of it—as though all the suffering of the world had
been sounding in that pitiful cry.

Rick ran past his sister and got there first. Winded, Gloria slid to a stop, bent
forward, hands on her knees, panting. Rick was already grabbing the rabbit up
by its hind legs. He thrust his gun at Susie, and she took it. Holding the rabbit's
feet with one hand, he seized its head with the other, wrapped his fingers around
its neck. He stretched the rabbit out—Gloria imagined someone pulling taffy—
and then, with a sharp motion, jerked its head upward and stopped its voice.

"Oh, dear Jesus," Susie said, her voice quivering, "I hate it when they cry like
that."

Rick took his gun back from Susie and handed her the rabbit. "Good
shooting, Susan Jane."

She held it a moment, then smoothed her fingertips over its fur as though
stroking a cat. "Poor fuzzy little thing." She looked up, blinking tears.

"Aw, you're too tenderhearted, honey. It's not like it's the first one you ever
killed."

"I'm not crying about the rabbit."

"Oh, for God's sake, Suse. It's not worth crying about. It's just the same old
story."

"Yeah? The same old story. Right. So how do *you* know what the story is?"

"I don't get you."

"What I mean is, how do you know what happened?"

"What the hell are you talking about, Susan? *You* told me what happened.
The guys told me. It was common knowledge."

"Oh, yeah? So what did they say?"

"What do you mean, what did they say? You know what they said."

"No, I don't. I'm not a guy. Tell me what they said."

"Oh, for God's sake. They said it was common knowledge—"

"*Common knowledge.* Oh, that's just great. And that's just what you said to
me. 'All the guys in town knew she was putting out.' That's what you said."

"So what? I don't get you, Susan Jane. Why shouldn't I have said that? That's
what they told me."

"Well, maybe it *was* common knowledge. But you know what really happened? I'll tell you what really happened. The guy she'd been going with and
some of his buddies, they went and got good and stinking drunk. And they picked
her up and drove out back of Ripley's, and they got *her* drunk. And the guy she
was going with said to one of his buddies, 'Hey, why don't you try her out.
She's a good fuck.' And she said her heart just broke on the spot and she didn't

care whether she lived or died. And they hauled her out of the car and threw her down on the ground. And she never knew which one of the four guys was the father."

Rick took a step back from her. "You never told me that."

"She made me promise I wouldn't tell anybody. She was ashamed."

Hearing the story, Gloria had felt a lurching motion inside herself, precipitous and violent, as if she'd been seized bodily and thrown down the hill, and now her mind was falling away just as violently, was rapidly losing its ability to hold onto anything.

"Give me your damn knife," Susie said to her brother.

"I'll do it."

"No. Give me your knife."

He unsnapped the strap holding the knife, drew it out of the sheath on his belt, and offered it to his sister, handle first. She took it, sank into a squat, laid the rabbit out on its back, and, without a moment's hesitation, cut straight down the rabbit's belly. She stuck the knife into the snowy ground, and then, with a motion like beginning to turn a sweater inside out, she pulled the rabbit open and shook it. Intestines—vividly colored—fell out, steaming.

Gloria didn't want to watch anymore. The fat snowflakes had looked white against the ground, but now, against the sky, they looked gray. "You want to know their names?" Susie said. "Those guys. I know their names."

Rick didn't answer. Gloria looked back, saw Susie wipe the blade between her bare fingers. Susie stood, flipped the knife around, and gave it back to her brother. She picked up the gutted rabbit by its ears. Snow was falling on the pile of entrails she'd left behind. "So nobody told you what really happened, huh?" she said.

"No, they didn't."

"I swore I'd never tell, but why shouldn't I? Jimmy Styles was the guy she was going with. And the other guys were Skipper Pearson, Mat Hostetler, and Terry Schmidt. And what happened to those guys? Nothing. Did they get a sermon preached against them? No. Did they have to leave town? Hell, no."

Rick looked at his sister. She seemed to be waiting for him to say something, but he didn't. Carrying the rabbit, she turned and walked away. They followed her. Gloria heard cawing. She looked back, saw crows landing by the rabbit entrails. Her teeth were chattering.

"Let's cut right through Hunsicker's," Susie said. "He'll never see us."

"Yeah," Rick said, "he'll be in by his fire."

Susie stopped and turned back toward them. "Rickie," she said, "you know that passage in John? It's in John Eight. 'And the scribes and Pharisees brought unto him a woman taken in adultery, and when they had set her in the midst, they said unto him, Master, this woman was taken in adultery, in the very act—' I must of read that passage a million times. 'Now Moses in the law commanded us, that such should be stoned, but what sayest thou?— But Jesus stooped down, and with his finger wrote on the ground, as though he heard them not— and he said unto them: He that is without sin among you, let him first cast a stone at her.'

"And the people in Cloverton started casting stones just as hard and fast as they could cast them. And you know who cast the biggest stone of all? Pastor Harris. And you know who the biggest hypocrite of all was? Me. Because I didn't stick up for her." She looked straight into Gloria's eyes. "And that's the worst thing I ever did in my life, may God forgive me."

"Amen," her brother said.

That must have been how Susie had answered the first question in the Trial of the Three Questions; Susie's single, direct look had said as much. They were walking quickly, and Gloria knew it was good to walk. She'd seldom endured such states as this, in which suffering was so purely physical, but it had stopped mattering to her. It wasn't as though she were feeling any of it less intensely; it was more that she might have reliquished the right to ask that she not feel it.

"Susan Jane," Rick said, "you listen to me. I said 'Amen' to your prayer even though you're way too hard on yourself. How old were you then? You were just a kid. And what do you think you should of done? Stood up in church and said, 'You're all a bunch of hypocrites'?"

"I was sixteen."

"Yeah. Right. Sixteen. Yeah, you should of taken on the whole church. That's right. That's just what a sixteen-year-old girl ought to be doing."

"I should stand up in church *now* and say, 'You're all a bunch of hypocrites.'"

"Yeah. Right. That's a great idea. You warn me ahead of time when you're going to do that so I can be out of town."

They had reached a fence. Gloria watched them climb it; then she allowed them to help her over. She'd been sure they were lost—or, in this terrible snow, that if they weren't lost yet, they soon would be. Now she realized that Susie and her brother had always known, and would always know—here in this country where they had grown up—exactly where they were.

"So what are we going to do with her?" Rick asked Gloria. "She's going to make herself miserable and everybody else around her."

"No, I'm not," Susie said. "I just had to get it off my chest, that's all."

It was astonishing how everything was turning white, and it was just as astonishing how quiet that whiteness was. Their feet in the snow made muted *shush, shush* sounds. They crossed a pasture that was already a piece of blank paper. Rick led them to a lone apple tree that looked like a painting on a Christmas card; its branches were piling up with snow, and, beneath it, a perfect oval of brown stubble had been left untouched. It was noticeably warmer under the branches.

Rick propped his gun against the tree, shed his pack, took out the thermos. Susie had stopped just inside the sheltered circle and turned, looking out, her back toward her brother. "There's a little bit of this left," Rick said, pouring out coffee. "You girls drink it."

Susie didn't move. "Susan Jane," he said, "I've had just about enough out of you." She spun around to face him.

"Now you're going to— What? Just brood the whole damn rest of the day?" he said. "That's great hospitality, isn't it? How do you think your friend feels? And you think you've been— You think God's sent you to sit in judgment over Cloverton, Pennsylvania? It was a terrible, terrible thing that happened to Tommie Jean, but are you really thinking about her? Or are you thinking about *yourself*? How good and righteous you are compared to all the rest of us miserable sinners?"

Susie looked at him, her face expressionless. Then she propped her gun against the tree and laid the rabbit down next to it. "Hey, you guys go on ahead, OK? I'll catch up to you in a minute."

"We'll wait for you," Rick said.

"No, go on. Oh, poor Glo, you must be frozen."

"I *said* we'd wait for you," her brother told her.

Susie looked at him a moment longer, then walked away into the snow. Soon she had become invisible. "She's the *sweetest* girl," Rick said, "but she's stubborn as a mule."

Gloria took the cup from him and sipped. The coffee was still warm. Nothing imaginable could have been as good as that warm coffee. "You know what she's doing, don't you?" he said. "She's praying."

Oh, Gloria thought, of course that's what she's doing.

"You a religious girl, Gloria?"

She couldn't very well not answer a direct question like that. "I suppose so," she heard herself saying, "in my way."

"Yeah, that's exactly what I'd say. *In my way.* I go in there to Pastor Harris' little church just often enough so people won't start saying, 'That Rick Steibel's a son of Satan.' Well, they may say it anyway, but who cares?"

"Is she OK?"

"Sure, she's OK. I'll go get her in a minute if she doesn't come back. Drink that coffee. Yeah, go on, drink all of it."

It wasn't that Gloria hadn't been able to think but rather that the way she normally thought—turning events over and over endlessly in her mind, turning them into words she could turn over and over endlessly in her mind— had been stripped from her, and she hadn't been capable of even knowing about that loss until now when she could feel her normal mind returning. She heard some lines from Yeats: "A stricken rabbit is crying out. And its cry distracts my thought," and then, as she began to make words again—and to turn them—she saw how she and Susie and Rick must have walked out of the ordinary world sometime ago, and into another one—a strangely lit world in which every event carried within it the possibility of redemption.

"Well, maybe we better go get her," Rick said, "seems like God's giving her a pretty rough time today."

Gloria didn't try to disguise the anger in her voice. "*You* gave her a rough time. You were wrong to say what you did."

She met his eyes and held his gaze. He was the first to look away. "Yeah," he said, "I was. I'll tell her that." Gloria wished she'd followed Susie into the snow to pray with her. She should have done it even if she couldn't believe what Susie believed. "Forgive me," she prayed silently.

Rick must have heard the soft *shush, shush* the moment Gloria did; they were both turning to look, and, as they saw Susie coming back, gradually coalescing into a bright, slender shape emerging from the snow, Gloria knew that even though she might not believe in the God that Susie believed in, she believed in Susie.

16

Gloria woke to the sound of voices. She didn't know where she was or even what day it was, but something told her she'd better figure it out pretty darned fast—and she knew then that she was lying prone on the grass in the full sunlight where she'd thrown herself when she'd climbed out of the pool and it was Wednesday. She heard someone walking down the steps, pushed her head up to look, and saw—oh, help!—Binkie. It wasn't fair. Gloria wasn't even remotely ready, but now she was going to have to face the music.

She sprang to her feet. It had seemed important that Binkie not know she'd been sound asleep, but now she felt as giddy as if she were balancing on a teeter-totter, and already stupid, unplanned words were pouring out of her mouth: "Oh, Bink— Oh. I'm so sorry I haven't called you back—I really am—I've just been—"

Mrs. Warsinski must have given Binkie a Coke. "Can I have a sip, please?" Gloria said, but once she started to drink, she guzzled most of the glass. Oh, dear, she thought.

"Are you OK?" Binkie asked, looking at her closely.

"Yes. Of course."

Binkie was wearing one of her crisp tennis dresses and looked cool and tidy. "Here. I thought you might need this." She handed Gloria the bag she'd left on the table Saturday night. "I've called you about a million times."

"I know. It's just—" Just what? As much as Gloria wanted to impersonate a normal girl, she couldn't find even a dumb, hackneyed remark. "Boy, it sure is hot today," obviously wouldn't do—or maybe it would, so she tried it.

"Well, it's July, isn't it? What do you expect? Come on, Glo, wise up. What have you been doing? Brooding? Come on, *tell me*. It's really over this time, huh?"

What was over? Gloria's reputation? Her life? Civilization as we have known it? "Pardon?"

"With Rolland."

"Oh!" Gloria hadn't really forgotten Rolland, had she? No, of course not. Only the most shallow, unfeeling little bitch could have forgotten him so quickly. "Yes, it really is," she said, allowing her voice to quiver.

"Not just another—?"

"No. Really over. Really, really, really. I gave him his pin back."

"Oh, you poor thing. Well, you just can't lay around here anymore, OK? I won't have it."

Speak, Gloria told herself, but nothing came out.

Binkie sighed. "So, was it your idea or his?"

"I guess it was mine. It's hard to— I guess I'm just not ready to get married, and he made it into a now-or-never."

"And he wouldn't wait for you, huh?"

Gloria could tell by the way Binkie was framing her questions that she was making up her own version of the story. OK, she thought, let her do that; it's a lot easier than trying to tell her what really happened. "No, he wouldn't wait. And I thought if a boy won't wait, then he's not the boy I want to marry"—which isn't what she'd thought at all, but she was sure it would fit right into the dopey Reader's Digest condensed novel Binkie was writing in her mind.

"Is there someone else?"

Oh, perfect! Gloria thought. "Well, I— Yes, I guess so. A girl he grew up with—his childhood sweetheart," and she couldn't resist adding the clinching detail: "She's an ace tennis player. They play mixed doubles together."

Binkie's mouth pressed itself into a firm line. "You're better off without him."

"Yes, I probably am." Since it seemed to be going over, Gloria thought (to mix metaphors) that she might as well squeeze another few drops out of it. "But it's just—you know," and sighed.

"Well, of course you feel bad, you poor thing. Who wouldn't? You'll meet lots of cute boys in the fall."

"I keep telling myself that."

"And you've got to stop brooding. Oh, I just *knew* that's what you'd been doing. I bet you've been reading poetry too. OK, enough's enough. We're going to have dinner tonight, just the two of us. I reserved the table on the terrace."

"Oh, Bink, I can't go to the club!"

"Why not?"

"Because. Oh, I made such a—*spectacle* of myself."

Now it was Binkie's turn for the blank look.

"I was just so sloshed, good grief. I'd had a couple drinks before I got there, and then Mike and Lee kept shoving martinis at me, and—I ended up making out with both of them on the dance floor. I was even making out with Jack Farrington, can you believe that? Oh, Bink, I just made such a—"

"Oh, come on, Glo. So what if you were making out with those guys? Everybody was drunk. Everybody was making out with somebody."

Gloria wanted to be sure that Binkie understood, and, if she shocked her in the process, that was just too darned bad. "I let Lee Hockner take me into the games room," she said, "and—you know—finish himself off. I just stood there and let him push me up against the pool table—"

Binkie didn't look the least bit shocked. "Billiards," she said.

"Pardon?"

"It's a billiards table. They don't play pool at the country club."

Their eyes met, and they both laughed. "OK," Gloria said, "the billiards table."

"What did you expect? Lee Hockner? I warned you, didn't I?"

"Yes, you did, but— Oh, I can just imagine what all the guys were saying: 'Hey, did you get a load of Gloria? Wow, is she ever hot to trot!'"

"So what? If they were gentlemen, they wouldn't have taken advantage of you."

"Binkie, come on. Stop trying to defend me. I was just awful. The horrible truth is I *was* hot to trot. Anything with pants on could have taken me in the games room."

"So what's the big deal? Everybody knows what kind of guy Lee Hockner is. Don't look at me like that, you silly thing. You're making a mountain out of a molehill—I'll come by around seven. Really dress up, OK? I've got a little number in silver and smoke I'm just dying to wear."

"What kind of little number?"

"You know, just a cocktail dress. Princess length. Pouffy."

"I don't know, Bink."

"Come on, we'll eat Crab Louis and drink champagne. We'll— What is it you used to say? 'Let's pretend we're spoiled rotten rich girls.'"

•   •   •

I don't deserve friends as loyal as that, Gloria thought. She set her hair in pin-curls and sat by the pool with the sun hot on it—and why was she so afraid to go back to the club? Not just because of Lee or Mike or Jack—although what she'd done with them had been bad enough—but had anyone seen her walking down to the golf course with that son-of-a-bitch? Maybe so, maybe not, but she had to pretend it had never happened—and, indeed, how *could* it have happened, something as impossible as that? He was always at the club in the evenings. She'd almost certainly see him. When she did, she'd look right through him. That's right, she'd cut him dead. It wasn't much, but it was all she had.

She wished she could go to sleep again and knock an hour or so off the mas-sive tedium of the interminable afternoon, but Mrs. Warsinski's nephew appeared and began riding the big lawn mower around the lawn; even when it was as far away as the apple trees, the darned thing made a constant, roaring din and filled the air with the dirty blue stink of oil. She fled inside. The roar and the stench were penetrating her bedroom window, but if she shut it, she'd seethe in her own sweat—and her tummy was burning, oh, great! What if I simply broke down? she thought. What if I just lay here and never got up again?

The nasty pulsing of the lawn mower seemed to have prompted a sympathetic throbbing in her temples; she felt the telltale icy perspiration trickling down her neck. Oh, please, she thought, I don't want to do this. She stood up, dizzy, guided herself with fingertips extended to the wall, plodded into the bath-room, knelt, and dumped the entire contents of her stomach into the toilet.

She rinsed her mouth out with water. It was a shame; she'd been doing so well too. Except for Saturday night and its aftermath—which had been the result of all those damned martinis and so didn't count—she hadn't thrown up once since the night of the May Queen Candidates' party. Then, only twenty min-utes before she'd been scheduled to make her entrance, she'd lost her dinner. Susie, who'd been standing in the bathroom with her—the only person in her entire life she'd ever allowed to watch while she did it—had said, "If you get it on your dress, I'll kill you," but Gloria, who'd had lots of practice throwing up in formal attire, hadn't got it on her dress. She'd gargled with Listerine, cleaned her teeth, freshened her makeup, dabbed on a hint more of Miss Dior, and then had gone out and charmed everyone—but could she charm everyone tonight? Or was that even what she wanted to do? She couldn't imagine anyone at the Raysburg Country Club worth charming.

She lay on her bed in a tight fetal position with a pillow pressed into her stomach. I'm not even remotely normal, she thought. How have I managed to fool everyone for so long? It's a minor miracle I'm not locked up in an institu-tion somewhere. It was her old litany—boring, stupid, repetitive—but she couldn't stop it. When had her life gone wrong? Sometimes she thought it had been at Fairhaven, but, no, Fairhaven had only been a confirmation of what she'd known already—that she was a sick, strange, abnormal girl.

What if she'd committed some terrible sin she couldn't quite remember, something as primeval as Eve's chomp of the apple—had been born deep in sin, just as the Puritans thought? This really was utterly, utterly pointless—but when had she started having panic attacks? When she'd been little, she hadn't called it "panic," of course; she'd called it "feeling bad," but she still had to do all those things she'd learned at six: breathe slowly and recite the multiplication tables, plan every action, plan every word— *Oh, stop it, Gloria!* All right, "pouffy," Binkie had said, so she could wear the *other* cocktail dress—understated and virginal white—she'd bought at the same time as the little-red-devil one, bought for some enchanted evening with Rolland. Oh, just great, just dandy. Had she ever really loved him? Could she ever really love anybody?

When Binkie arrived in her dad's car, Gloria was already standing out by the front driveway with her gloves on. For one thing, she never would have kept a girlfriend waiting as she might have a boy, and for another she'd run out of things to do. Her hair was perfect, her makeup was perfect, her ensemble was perfect, but, no matter how many times she'd gargled and cleaned her teeth, she couldn't get rid of that give-away, sickly sweet, yeasty smell—although, really, nothing could be left of it by now but a fiendish illusion. Her stomach was killing her again, and there wasn't a thing she could do about it.

Binkie watched her walk over to the car. "Nobody's got a figure like you, Glo."

Gloria slid into the passenger's seat. "Say, 'Thanks, Bink,'" the secret watcher told her, so she said, "Thanks, Bink," and then, to have something more to say, added, "Well, I always wanted to be a blonde."

"Yeah? Why don't you buy a blonde wig?"

"No, not just blonde hair. Blonde all over. Like you."

"The grass is always greener, huh?"

When her stomach was like this, something tight around it actually felt good, so she was wearing her severest waspie done up on its tightest row of hooks, and it *was* helping—both the compression and the heat of it were helping—but eating much of anything was out of the question. If she had an enviable figure, she paid a high price for it—much more, she suspected, than Binkie would have been willing to pay. And, walking across the parking lot, she had a nasty sense of *déjà vu*—and her mind was blurring, buzzing, turning yellow— "What are you so nervous about?" Binkie asked her.

"Oh, I'm not nervous."

Binkie, in her smoke and silver, looked fabulous; the secret watcher told Gloria to say so, and she did. Binkie glanced at her, obviously pleased. Gloria was glad, for once, that Binkie had outdressed her, and then, just inside the doors of the club, before she was even remotely prepared for it, she nearly bumped into Mr. Dougherty.

Something went squish inside her ribcage, and the back of her neck felt as though it had been licked by an enormous, rough, fiery tongue. She'd stopped in mid-stride. He'd recoiled from her. So they hadn't *quite* bumped—had avoided it by mere inches. It was all happening lickety-split, and, in that fraction of a second when they'd looked directly at each other, she'd seen shock pass across his ugly eyes and then a sneaky, furtive shifting away. Now, aiming his gaze into the far distance, he simply kept on walking. Oh, she thought, he wants it to be *easy*, does he? And, before she could consider whether it was a good idea or not, she heard herself singing out, "Good evening, Mr. Dougherty."

He looked at her quickly, then away, his mouth hanging open. "Oh. Hi, there, princess." There was nowhere else he could have been going except the bar, and she saw him arrive there.

Binkie was giving her a curious look, so she said, under her breath, "Jerk."

"You bet."

At their reserved table on the terrace, the waiter held their chairs for them just as though they were grown-ups. Gloria sat down, murmured, "Thank you," and, smiling, looked out over the golf course. The players seemed to her as artificially arranged and implausibly colored as if they were in a Technicolor movie. When she took her gloves off, she saw how badly she was trembling. Well, she thought, *that's* over—but it didn't feel over. Her mouth was dry. Their waiter was drawing a bottle out of an ice bucket.

The last thing in the world Gloria wanted was champagne, but she raised her glass in a toast: "Cheers, Bink. Thanks."

"Don't mention it. And if you ever don't take my calls again, I swear I'll strangle you. I mean it literally."

What Gloria really wanted was a glass of water, but she sipped enough of the champagne to rinse out her mouth. Binkie caught Gloria's hands in hers and bent forward to whisper, "Here come the guys."

Gloria hadn't been thinking about Lee and Mike. She didn't care about Lee and Mike. "Could you use some company, ladies?"

"Not tonight, Lee," Binkie said. "Girls' night out."

"Oh, right—" and directly to Gloria: "Well, maybe I'll catch you later for a dance, huh?"

"Say, 'I'm not dancing tonight, Lee,'" the secret watcher told her, "and give him a distant, icy smile."

"I'm not dancing tonight, Lee," Gloria said and gave him a distant, icy smile.

For a moment he didn't know what to do or say. Watching from her enormous distance, Gloria felt sorry for him; there wasn't, however, much she could do about it—not without destroying the effect she'd just worked so hard to create—and then he did manage a few dumb remarks, and Binkie tossed a few back at him while Gloria and Mike inquired of each other how they were doing and learned that they were both doing fine. "See you around, huh?" Lee said, and Mike gave Gloria a wink. Oddly enough, if she had to pick someone to play around with, it could very well be Mike; Jack and Lee had called her after Saturday night, but, just as she'd predicted, Mike hadn't.

"Good going," Binkie said after they left, and Judy Staub was waving from the far side of the terrace. Binkie gave her a big come-on-over gesture.

"Oh, Gloria, how *are* you?" Judy said in a funereal voice. She, like Binkie—like everyone—must have thought that Gloria had been devastated by splitting up with Rolland. Well, she had been, hadn't she? "Thanks, Jude. I'm feeling much better."

"You with anybody?" Binkie asked Judy. "Come on, join us."

Gloria tried her best to make small talk but eventually gave up; Binkie and Judy seemed to be doing just fine without her, and she should be allowed to be quiet, shouldn't she—recovering from grief as she was? But then she couldn't stop thinking about that son-of-a-bitch. He'd called her a spoiled little brat; he'd called her a cock teaser. She had never been, and was not now, a spoiled little brat—although, if she made the effort of standing back from herself, she could see how someone might see her that way. Ken had certainly seen her that way, and probably lots of other boys saw her that way too. But to what extent was she responsible for how other people saw her? What was she supposed to do, wear sackcloth and ashes?

And a cock teaser? Well, she'd teased Jack and Lee and Mike, that was true enough, but, at least with Lee, she'd delivered the goods—oh, yuck—and if you delivered the goods, you weren't really a tease, were you? And she would have bet that none of the boys had minded anything she'd done on Saturday night. So when he'd called her a cock teaser, he'd meant that *he'd* felt teased, and he had no right to feel like that. None. He was as old as her father, for one thing, and, for another, it had never occurred to her, even remotely, that she might be *teasing* him. She'd only thought she was being *nice* to him.

She'd asked herself a million times if she'd done anything—even the slightest little thing—to deserve what he'd done, and, the best she could tell, the only mistake she'd made had been talking to him *at all*— But no. There'd been one crucial moment: when he'd asked her to go for a ride in his wretched car, she should have said, "Sounds like fun. I'll have to ask my dad." But she hadn't said that, and everything else had followed from that one little slip—and this was getting her nowhere. Every time she thought about it, she felt, all over again, mad enough to kill him, and there was obviously not a damned thing she could do about it.

But, oh yes, there was. "Excuse me a minute," she said. Binkie looked at her curiously but let her go without a word.

To disguise her purpose, Gloria went first to the ladies'. She didn't need any more lipstick, but she put some on anyway, and then, not sure why she was doing it, pulled her gloves back on. It seemed important that she should have her gloves on. The pain in her stomach was like—well, the easiest of similes was perfectly accurate: like a twisting knife.

If Binkie and Judy looked, they would see her doing what any polite young lady ought to be doing at some time during the evening: making her obligatory circuit of the dining room. She chatted for what seemed an eternity with Judy's parents, stopped at a table of younger girls to exchange a few fatuous remarks with Mary Anne Whatever-her-name-was, even found something to say to Jack Farrington, and then walked to the bar where she would, she knew, be well out of Binkie and Judy's view. He was standing at the end of the bar alone, hunched forward over his drink. She arrived next to him; in the mirror, she saw him look up. Strangely enough, he didn't seem the least bit surprised to see her. "A large ginger ale, please," she said to the bartender, "no ice."

As the bartender moved away, Mr. Dougherty dropped his gaze back to his drink and began talking immediately, under his breath, quickly, as though he'd rehearsed every word: "Hey, look, princess, I'm really sorry, OK? I just can't tell you how sorry I am. I was drunk as a skunk. I woke up in the morning, and I thought, jeez, Dougherty, you've really torn it this time—"

"You just shut up," she said just above a whisper. "Don't you *ever* say a word to me again. Do you understand me? Don't you even *look* at me. Or you're out of a job."

He looked up, and their eyes met in the mirror. "Do you understand me?" she said.

"Yeah, I understand you." She couldn't imagine how anyone could have poured hatred into his eyes any more clearly than that; her own face, she saw, had no expression at all. Like Susie could be, she was, in that moment, nothing but a pretty mannequin.

"Thank you," she said to the bartender and walked away with her ginger ale. It wasn't until hours later, back at home, as she was getting ready for bed, thinking about how sour and tedious the evening had been, that Gloria admitted to herself that something might have gone terribly, terribly wrong.

Gloria didn't know she'd been asleep until the sound of her father's car woke her. She was indignant, furious, because she badly wanted to dream, and, almost immediately, dreaming was again a possibility—it felt like grass springing back after it has been stepped on—and she knew she was late for the May Queen candidates' party. Then she was already deep inside the dream, was already wearing the taffeta dress Susie had chosen for her and the too-high heels that went with it. She wasn't quite sure where the party was being held this year, so she hurried down the hall in the English Department looking for someone to tell her where to go.

Professor Bolton's door was locked. She peeped into the main office where the secretary should be, and everything was covered with a fine layer of dust. She knew she should be quiet, but it was impossible to be quiet in taffeta and heels. She had to pee, badly, and she couldn't find the ladies' room, only the men's. Even though she was pretty sure no one was inside, she didn't have the courage to go in there.

She remembered that the party was in the auditorium. She expected to find a crowd milling around outside, but the lobby was deserted. She pushed open one of the big swinging doors and wasn't surprised to see the little theater where Susie had danced for all those years. The stage was empty, the curtains drawn, but every single seat in the house was taken.

There were no girls, only boys. In a tense, deathly quiet they were writing an exam while invigilators—grown men carrying baseball bats—paced the aisles and glowered at them. The boys must have heard Gloria come in; their faces had been tilted down toward their blue-books, but now, simultaneously, they lifted their heads and turned to stare at her. They were expressionless. As she backed toward the door, they followed her, in perfect unison, with their eyes. There were hundreds and hundreds of turning heads following her, and, as they continued to turn in her direction like mechanical devices, Gloria knew that they were tracking her with radar. It was something they'd learned how to do in the Second World War.

Her face burning with shame, she backed out and closed the door quietly behind her. She saw that her name had been posted on the door in large scarlet letters: *GLORIA MERRIMAN COTTER: F.* Oh, how terrible, she thought, I've failed. What am I going to do now?

She was walking around outside the football stadium on a muggy, overcast afternoon and saw no one. She was pretty sure she had a date with Rolland, but she seemed to have forgotten all about it right up until that moment, and she was afraid she was late. She still had to pee, and she began searching desperately for the ladies' room—and finally did find it on the other side of the stadium. Just as she was about to open the door, a little blonde girl stepped out and stood right in her way.

"Excuse me," Gloria said, "I have to go in there."

"I'm sorry, but you're not allowed," the little girl said in a tiny, metallic voice and quickly shut the door. Gloria heard the lock click firmly into place.

Gloria sensed more than saw the silver limousine that was drifting up next to her left shoulder. She risked a glance at it. The driver was wearing a slouch hat so his face couldn't be seen. The little girl opened the door to the limousine, and Gloria remembered that she had to go back to Fairhaven for seven more years. Oh, how terrible, she thought. It'll be a lot worse now that I've grown up. She felt utterly humiliated, but she had to ask, so she said, "Please let me go to the bathroom first."

"Of course not," the little blonde girl said firmly. "It's your own fault, and you deserve to be punished."

Gloria knew that it was her own fault and she did deserve to be punished, so she got into the limousine. The little girl quickly pushed the door shut, and Gloria heard the lock click firmly into place. There were no door handles on the inside, and, when she saw that, Gloria felt a hideous, mind-numbing panic. She tried to take a deep breath, but all she could do was pant like a dog, and then, with no transition from dreaming to waking, she was sitting bolt upright in bed, panting like a dog. She jumped up and ran into the bathroom. Just as in the dream, she had to pee, badly, but she had to do something else first.

She'd learned long ago that it only made it worse if she fought it, but now she fought it. "No, no, no—*please*," she prayed and tried to breathe, to force it back down, but each spasm was worse than the last. If she fought any longer, she was going to tear her stomach apart from the inside, choke on her own agony—and then fire was pouring out of her throat; she heard the disgusting splash into the toilet bowl. Why hadn't the Crab Louis been digested? Why was it still in recognizable pieces like that?

She lay in bed wrapped in a sheet, her arms wrapped around her tummy, and waited for the chills to go away. Her entire body was slicked with a cold, foul perspiration, so she would take a shower later and wash her sheets and pretend it had never happened, but this was the second time in less than a day, and what if she had to do it every day now? "Don't be ridiculous," the secret watcher told her.

Why had she thought she could eat crab and drink champagne? OK, so she'd just take it easy. In a while she'd try to drink water; if that stayed down, she'd try milk toast. Maybe she'd take a dose of paregoric. Everything was going to be all right—but, of course, nothing was all right. Why wouldn't her subconscious mind let her alone? Ever since she'd left Fairhaven, she'd dreamed she had to go back there.

The waiting had been terrible. After they'd left the rubber rat in her bed, they'd made her wait for weeks. The rat had been one of those things with a metal squeaker in it you could buy for your dog at a pet shop. She'd stuffed it into the garbage can at the back of the kitchen, but then she'd worried that maybe she should have kept it on her desk to show them that she was truly repentant.

They were careful, never left any evidence behind—nothing like a note that could have been used to identify them—but every few days, just when she'd begun to hope they'd forgotten about her or maybe even had forgiven her (fat chance), an older girl passing in the hall would whisper, "Hey, Worm, you're really going to get it." Sometimes she tried to talk to them—any of them but the really scary one, the one the big girls called "Sal"—but they'd just laugh, or sometimes look right through her as though she wasn't there.

She was throwing up every day and sick with worry that the teachers were going to find out about it. She tried to stop eating so there wouldn't be anything to throw up, and she kept getting thinner. In bed at night, she ran her fingers over the sharp edges of her ribs and hip bones, and she wondered how much longer she could go on like that. Wouldn't she eventually just starve to death? She wrote to her mother and told her that she really had to bring her home this time, that this time she wasn't kidding, that she really really *really* had to come home, but her mother didn't answer her letter. She went to sleep every night sick with fear, and woke up every morning sick with fear, and when they did finally come to get her, she didn't try to run away. She didn't scream or fight back. She didn't make any fuss at all. She simply stood up and walked with them over into the deserted east wing. When they'd told her she was really going to get it, they hadn't been kidding.

She could have got them all expelled—it would have been easy enough— and the one called Sal actually did get expelled later in the year, Gloria had never known exactly why. Fairhaven had been the third private girls' school to expel her, and, looking back on it, Gloria knew that there had been something seriously wrong with Sal, that she shouldn't have been in a girls' school at all but maybe locked up in an institution.

After Sal was expelled, nothing at Fairhaven was ever again as bad—or even close to it—as what they'd done to her in the big girls' room in the east wing while all the teachers, and all the other girls, had been out playing in, or watching, the field hockey game. But what Gloria had learned was that something as bad as that was *possible*, and she'd spent the next four years worrying that it could happen again.

After they'd let her go, she'd simply walked back to her own room where she was supposed to be lying down—she'd been excused from the field hockey game because she was sick—and she'd crawled into bed and lain on her stomach with her arms wrapped around herself. She'd known it was over, that they'd let her alone now, because Sal had not only scared Gloria, she'd scared the other girls, and they'd all been yelling at Sal to stop, and the secret watcher had appeared and told Gloria that some of the girls were getting *really* scared— and ashamed of themselves—and so it would be over soon, and that's exactly what had happened.

Then, as she lay in her bed, shivering and hugging herself, the secret watcher appeared again and told her that she didn't have to throw up any more, that she could eat again—and that made her feel a little bit better. But she couldn't stop thinking about how she'd said everything they'd told her to say and done everything they'd told her to do and cried just as much as they'd wanted her to cry. She swore to herself that she'd never rat again, that she'd never do *any-thing* to make the older girls mad at her, and the only way she could think to get even with them was to promise herself that no one at Fairhaven would ever ever ever again get to see her cry.

For the next few days Gloria was so restless—so irritable and jumpy—she knew she wasn't fit company for anybody, but she didn't want to be alone, so, in the daytime, she attached herself to Binkie and Judy. Her psychic radar system for detecting anything unusual at the club—in furtively exchanged glances, in conversations that stopped for a fraction of a second too long when she walked into a room, or became suddenly too vivacious—was picking up nothing at all, so it really did seem to be true: nobody gave a damn about what she'd done. What on earth would I have to do, she wondered, if I *really* wanted to disgrace myself?

She spent the evenings with her grandmother. They played two-handed bridge or watched the television, and sometimes Gloria paced up and down until her grandmother snapped at her: "For heaven's sake, stop that! You look like a caged animal."

After her grandmother retired—usually by midnight—Gloria was faced with four or five hours to kill. If she tried to go to sleep before she was utterly exhausted, something like a voice whispering in her ear woke her up. Sometimes she sat up violently, her heart pounding, listening, almost convinced she'd heard a real voice. Then she'd turn the light on and her radio on and try to think of anything to make the time pass. She collected all of her mother's murder mysteries, stacked them up on her bed table, and began reading them in the same grimly purposeful way she would have tackled a tiresome school assignment.

She couldn't stop thinking about Fairhaven. All children get hurt, she told herself. It's just an ordinary part of growing up, just something you have to get over, and why did she think she was so darned special anyway? Compared to something really terrible—what had happened to Tommie Jean, for instance—it had been all quite trivial. But no, that wasn't true. Worse things might have happened to people, but what they'd done to her at Fairhaven had been far from *trivial*.

It was strange how violently she'd reacted to hearing about Tommie Jean; it had been, she thought, one of the few times in her life when she'd experienced genuine empathy, and she remembered Susie saying, "But you know what really happened? I'll tell you what really happened." Given the Biblical mood of that day, it was inevitable to think of "the truth shall set you free," and that's what Susie had done—told the truth. "You want to know their names?" Susie had said. "Those guys. I know their names." Much to her surprise, Gloria found that she remembered the names of all the big girls who'd done those terrible things to her, so she wrote a list of their names into her diary. She was gritting her teeth; her hands were shaking; she had to get out of her room.

She walked around in circles in the backyard. The worst thing Miss Devon ever did to kids at Fairhaven—short of expelling them—was making them stand up in assembly in front of the whole school and tell everyone exactly what they'd done and how sorry they were about it, but had she made any of those girls do that? No. Had she expelled any of them? Hell, no. Sal *had* got expelled but not for what she'd done to Gloria, and nothing bad ever happened to any of the rest of them—and, walking fast, so angry she couldn't see anything beyond the pictures in her mind, Gloria designed a special prison for those rotten girls, one where they'd really get it every day for the rest of their wretched, meaningless lives. Forgive your enemies? That was a joke. She'd never forgive them, never ever ever.

Every night now, as Gloria sat in her grandmother's room, chatting or playing bridge, she saw her grandmother take one of her little pills and place it under her tongue. She didn't know whether she should comment on it or not, and finally said, "Are you in a lot of pain, Grandmother?"

"Oh, it's not that bad."

But her grandmother no longer demanded martinis or Turkish cigarettes. Gloria had stopped being afraid of her grandmother some time ago, so now she had the courage to say, "Don't you think you'd better see Doctor Clark?"

"Do you know what would happen if I called that man? He would put me in the hospital just the way they did the last time—and believe you me, my dear, the hospital is not a particularly pleasant place to while away what remains of one's days upon this earth."

After a while, trying to find something else to talk about, Gloria asked, "Do I really look like Veronica Isobel?"

"Of course you do, my dear. I've told you that."

"I'm glad I look like somebody in the family. I grew up thinking I didn't look like anybody."

"Well, you should see the painting then. Your Uncle Edgar has it, I think. In Providence. You will, I'm sure, be quite astonished at how much you resemble her."

"Do you think she might have had some Gypsy blood?" Gloria heard herself asking before she had a chance to think about what a sappy question it was.

She expected her grandmother to deny it vehemently but was surprised to hear: "You know, my dear, that's not entirely out of the question."

"It's not?"

"Well, she was as dark as a Gypsy; that's what everyone said. She was certainly painted as dark as a Gypsy. You must go see for yourself sometime. Her family was very high-bred Castilian—that's what everyone said, but what else could they say? The Providence Merrimans back in those days? As snobby as they were? It was bad enough that the captain had married a Spanish girl at all—and with the Spaniards, of course, anything is possible."

Gloria sat on the edge of her bed as her grandmother traced the blood lines down the family tree—neatly inscribed in India ink by Gloria's long-dead great-great-aunt Issy—and Gloria saw that Veronica Isobel's line had, just as her grandmother had said, "crossed over twice." Her grandmother's theories about blood, of course, were utterly loony—one doesn't simply inherit a full set of characteristics across a span of a hundred and fifty years—but there had to be some reason why Gloria was so dark. Had there been enough of that Spanish girl's genetic stock available to produce another dark, hairy, black-eyed girl in 1936? Only God knew for certain, but Gloria liked *the idea* of Veronica Isobel—liked it as a metaphor—and she thought: what if it's true? Maybe that's why I've always been different. Maybe I can blame everything on Veronica Isobel.

She would always remember that the night it happened she was halfway through the mystery that had been made into a movie with Grace Kelly in it. She heard what, at first, she took to be the voice from her dreams. Then, when the sound was repeated, she wondered if it might actually be real. She'd been—well, if not fully asleep, then certainly drowsing. She sat up, turned off her radio, looked at her clock. It was after five—and she heard it again, distinctly: a faint, groaning noise. Oh, no, she thought, sprang out of bed, ran into her grandmother's room, and switched on the overhead light.

Her first thought—later she would realize how stupid it had been—was that her grandmother couldn't possibly be comfortable lying at that strange angle, partially off her pillows, dangerously close to falling out of bed. Then she saw that her grandmother's right hand was gripping the side of her neck. The pill bottle was open, had spilled; there were pills on the bed table and the floor. Gloria heard that terrible groaning again—yes, it was coming out of her grandmother, out of her partially open mouth, a line of spittle running down from one side. Gloria saw a flutter in her grandmother's free hand—the beginning of a gesture, an attempt to communicate. She was looking at Gloria from under half-closed eyelids, and Gloria saw an instant of fierce, fully alert consciousness. "What?" and she felt the answer as a sudden, unmistakable certainty, seized a pill and offered it; her grandmother's mouth opened—Gloria thought, absurdly, of a baby robin—and Gloria thrust the pill under her tongue. Help, help, help, she thought—or prayed—and ran downstairs. "Dr. Clark," she yelled at the operator. "I don't know his number— He's on Edgewood."

Gloria and her mother were not allowed to see her grandmother until late in the afternoon. Gloria had been afraid they'd find a pathetic, inert, semi-conscious figure in the hospital room, but, the moment they walked in, she saw the old lady's hands gesticulating frantically on the other side of the plastic window of an oxygen tent. The nurse unzipped the tent; Gloria and her mother bent down to peer inside. Gloria's grandmother stared out at them with ferocious, red-rimmed eyes. "Get me out of this damned thing."

"Now, Mrs. Merriman," the nurse said, "we're not supposed to get excited now, are we?"

"I am *not* excited. How am I supposed to carry on a conversation with this idiotic thing roaring in my ears? I'm at death's door, and I want to have a conversation with my daughter and granddaughter. Is that so difficult to comprehend?"

"I'm sorry," the nurse said, and, turning to Gloria and her mother, "You see how she is. I can't let you stay very long. Don't say anything to upset her."

Gloria and her mother pulled their chairs close to the bed. Gloria's grandmother tugged at the unzipped slit in the side of the tent; Gloria grasped it and held it open. "Well, what do you think of this, Marcelaine?"

"Oh, Mother, you heard what the nurse said. Don't get upset."

"I am *not* upset, but this is—well, simply the most ridiculous position in which I've ever found myself, bar none. This morning, just before that damned nurse came in— I don't know how one is supposed to rest when they're always poking at you. Oh, before I forget, I wanted to ask you about that minister. Your father was very generous to the church, and so was I, after he passed on, but— Oh, I won't say it doesn't mean *anything*. But I've often thought that one act of human kindness means more than all one's money— I've never been much of a religious person. Going to church and being religious are not necessarily the same thing, as I'm sure you know, Marcelaine. You're much like me in that regard. What was I saying? I keep losing my train of thought. It's difficult after a lifetime— Most of my life I worried about what other people would think, and, looking back on it, it seems— Oh, I know what I started to tell you. This morning I dreamed about a little fur muff I had when I was twelve, and why should I dream of something as frivolous as that? Will you please do something for me, Marcelaine? Will you get that minister from your church to come in and see me?"

"I didn't think you liked him."

"Well, I don't, but that's neither here nor there, now is it? He seems a sincere man. Oh, heavens, you should have seen what they tried to feed me. If you have time, Marcelaine, could you bring me a peach?"

That evening they returned with a bag of peaches and the Reverend Acker. "I believe that Mrs. Merriman has found peace within her soul," he announced after his meeting with her.

"I'm glad to hear that," Gloria's mother said dryly.

"She's worried about several matters. I assured her I would discuss them with you. She's afraid that she might be buried in Raysburg—"

"Oh, for crying out loud! *I* don't even want to be buried in Raysburg. Of course she won't be. She'll be buried right next to her husband in Providence. That was all arranged years ago; what on earth could she be thinking about?"

"If you would reassure her— And she feels that she should have been more generous with Gloria. All of the grandchildren are mentioned in her will, but she wanted Gloria specifically— And it seems it's too late to change anything now?"

"Oh. Well, whatever she leaves me, I'll take a portion of it and put it in trust for Gloria. I'll tell her that."

"Very good. And one other matter—a spiritual concern— She regrets— Oh, she did not go into detail with me, Marcelaine, I must assure you of that— But she regrets certain things. To put it in a nutshell, she wishes she had been a better mother to you. Oh, I'm sure she was a good mother. I'm sure you would be the first to say so, but, at the end, one often—I've seen this often—one dwells upon the smallest of faults. Yes, and only our Lord knows how our lives have been lived, and we are all of us sinners. Mrs. Merriman has asked pardon of her Savior, and He, I'm sure, has already granted it— But if you could speak to her about this, Marcelaine, assure her that you too have forgiven her—"

"Yes, yes, yes. Yes, of course I forgive her. I'll tell her that."

Afterwards, back at the house, Gloria's mother was so angry she couldn't sit still. "How typical of her. How very, very typical. She can't say any of that to *me*, but she can tell all of it to that damned mealy mouthed minister with no trouble at all—a perfect stranger! Good God, I'm supposed to tell her I forgive her? I can just see it now. If I tried to say anything like that, she'd take my damned head off. That man simply doesn't understand—well, how could he? With Mother, there are some things one simply does not discuss."

Gloria's grandmother didn't die. "She's not out of the woods yet," Dr. Clark told them, "but she seems to be making a reasonably good recovery. She's a tough, old gal, and she might have a few good years left in her." The next day she was allowed out of the oxygen tent, and the day after that, she was feeling strong enough to sit up and play three-handed bridge with Gloria and her mother. If she continued to rally, Dr. Clark said, there was no reason why she couldn't go home the following week.

Gloria felt as though she'd been deeply entrenched in some distant, dark corner of herself and that her grandmother's heart attack had blown her right out of it. Ready or not, she was back in the real world. Is that what was required, she asked herself, somebody almost *dying?* Gloria and her mother took turns visiting the hospital. Gloria bought a honeymoon bridge set; it made the games with her grandmother much more interesting.

When Gloria came home on Wednesday night, she saw that her mother had written on the pad by the phone: "Mrs. Susan Taylor called you - That's exactly what she said! Here's her new number."

Oh, Susie! Gloria thought. Her parents were still at the club, so she called from their bedroom. She couldn't have predicted the intensity of her reaction to hearing Susie's voice: she started to cry quietly, and she couldn't stop. She covered the mouthpiece so Susie wouldn't hear her.

"Oh, Glo, wow, is this ever great! I'm sorry I didn't call you back before, but we wanted to have *our own phone*, you know, in *our own apartment*. Guess what? I got a job! Can you believe it? It was the first school I applied to. It's right near the university, and I start in September— Except I already started. The band teacher just gave me the majorettes, and I called them all up and we had a meeting— I'm not getting paid yet, but I don't care— Anyhow, I said, 'OK, girls, I know it's only July, but we've got to get down to business, because you guys are going to be the best darned twirlers in the whole state of Pennsylvania!' I've got a whole bunch of gym classes, and I've got to teach Eighth Grade Socials! Don says he'll help me with it— But I'm so happy, Glo. I'm a school teacher, can you believe it? Now I can start paying Daddy and Rickie back— Hey, are you crying?"

"Yes. How did you know that?"

"I could—I don't know, kind of feel it. What's the matter?"

"Oh, Susie, it's just so great to hear your voice."

"Oh, yeah, it's great to hear yours too. It hasn't been that long, but it feels like a million years."

Now that she was actually talking to her, Gloria knew that the only way she could tell Susie *everything* was in person—sometime when they were alone and had hours and hours—but she told her about her grandmother's heart attack and about splitting up with Rolland. "I feel bad for you," Susie said, "but I never thought he was the right guy for you. He's—well, he's the nicest guy in the world, but he's not serious. And you're just about the most serious person I ever met in my life. I just couldn't see the two of you married."

"Why didn't you ever say that before?"

"It's just—well, you know, the last thing you want to do is knock your best friend's boyfriend."

Gloria had stopped crying. She stretched out on her parents' bed, closed her eyes, and tried to imagine Susie in her new apartment. She would have cheerfully gone on talking for hours, but Susie kept saying, "This must be costing you a fortune!"

"Don't worry about it. So, do you have a pink bedroom?"

"Are you kidding? I've had enough pink to last my whole lifetime. Besides, Don's in there too. We did it sort of browny greeny— Hey, you don't sound very happy, Glo. Why don't you come over and visit? We've got a spare couch. Oh, it'd be so great to see you."

"Come on, Suse, you haven't even been married six weeks."

"What's that got to do with anything? Wait a minute."

Gloria heard Susie and Don talking, but she couldn't make out the words, and then Don came on the line: "That's from me too, Gloria. You're always welcome. Any time. We'd love to see you. And I'm not just saying it, Gloria. You're our guardian angel."

Some angel, Gloria thought. Then Susie came back and began speaking quickly, her voice lowered: "Don just went in the other room. He's respecting my *privacy*, you know? He's real thoughtful that way. We're getting along great. We've only had one fight, and it only lasted about an hour, and I can't even remember what it was about. Something stupid— You know what? He does the dishes sometimes, and he even cooks! I thought boys never cooked. I mean, he really cooks, you know, he roasted a chicken! With stuffing in it. Oh, Glo, I never got a chance to tell you—I mean, really tell you, thanks so much. You know how we went to sleep for a little while? Well, the minute I woke up, I knew God had forgiven me. Oh, gee, was I ever impossible! Thanks for being, so—just so wonderful. There's a nice Baptist church not too far from us, and I've been going there, and once we went to the Episcopal— Don keeps saying, 'It's not the *Episcopalian* church, Susie, it's Episcopal!' By the time he's done with me, I'll be saying everything right. Maybe. Anyhow, we went there once. He's not religious the way we are, but he does believe in God and all that— You know what's really strange about being married? Making love. You spend your whole life thinking it's a sin, and then you're married, and it isn't a sin anymore but part of God's plan for you, but it still feels, you know, kind of funny. I don't know if I should be talking about this, but—oh, I've always been able to say anything to you. It feels really—I don't know how to say it— When Don's— You're so *close!* You know, actually *inside—* I'm blushing, can you feel it on the phone? I can't begin to tell you. I cry sometimes about how beautiful it is—that God made us male and female. We were meant to be married. I mean you too, but with the right guy. Somebody serious. Somebody who really understands you and knows how to cherish you. Oh, Gloria, you really do have to come see us. I feel like everything's working out for us. I mean all of us—Don and me and you too. I just know I'm going to find Tommie Jean now that I'm living here—in God's own good time. I'm just dying to see you. I've been missing you so much. At the reception when— Oh, it felt so sad when we had to say goodbye. Oh, Gloria, I pray for you every night. You know, God means us to be together even when we're apart."

After she hung up, Gloria went back into her own room, threw herself onto her bed, and cried. Even as she was doing it, she thought it was a peculiar kind of crying. She didn't feel the least bit sad; if anything, she felt happy; it was as though her body, in some deep, reflexive, cellular way, had badly needed to cry. Her grandmother wasn't right down the hall, and her parents were still at the club, so she didn't even have to be quiet. She cried for over an hour and then, after she stopped, fell asleep.

For the first time in weeks, Gloria woke feeling fully rested. Her mother was at the hospital, and Mrs. Warsinski had the day off; Gloria liked being alone in the house; she carried her bowl of corn flakes into—of all unlikely places—the living room. She felt calm and hopeful in a way she hadn't since before the night when she'd disgraced herself. She sat down on the couch facing the French doors and saw how the sunlight was bringing out the colors in the carpet—the incandescent richness of the reds and greens and earth tones woven on somebody's loom in far-off Persia—and she felt an intricate, luminous perfection to the morning; it was, in fact, the perfect morning for the ritual she'd planned.

She considered wearing her initiation dress—it was packed away in the attic—but no, she'd *already* been initiated. She did have to undergo a purification ritual, so she stripped off her nail polish, showered and shaved, washed her last set out of her hair, and scrubbed off every trace of makeup. She put on white flats, a plain white linen dress, and no more jewelry than her charm bracelet. Her mother came home at noon, exactly when Gloria had expected her. The last thing Gloria needed was for her mother to see her like that— she'd be bound to make some sarcastic remark—so she waited until her mother was settled onto a lawn chair by the pool and called to her through the French doors, "I'm taking the car, OK?"

Gloria drove into town and parked down by the wharf. As much as she wanted to be thinking serious, meaningful thoughts, her mind wouldn't cooperate, and she was worrying about running into anyone she knew who might see her looking like a skinned rat—how shallow and superficial could you get! Then, as she walked up to Main Street, she thought how odd it was that Raysburg should seem both so familiar and unfamiliar. She'd lived there since she'd been fourteen, yet she'd never called it home; she knew she could leave it forever without a backward glance.

As she approached the Suspension Bridge, she realized that she'd never walked over it. She'd ridden over it dozens of times—with boys, just driving around—but she'd never had any reason to walk over to the Island. She walked past the theater where they had the Jamboree, past the door that led up to the dance hall where they had the Friday Night Hop. She'd never been to the Jamboree or the Friday Night Hop because *our sort* don't go to places like that. No boy had ever taken her to drink a beer in South Raysburg or had bought her a Polish sausage sandwich. She could do the rumba and the cha-cha, but she couldn't do the polka. Everything she owned had been paid for by the Raysburg Steel Corporation, but she'd never met, let alone talked to, a steelworker. She'd always thought of Raysburg as a "dumb little town." Maybe it was an interesting little town, but how would she know?

The bridge was high enough above the river to give her more than a hint of vertigo, but that was OK: a ritual should be scary, shouldn't it? She walked to what appeared to be the exact center of the bridge and opened the little silver box holding her rejected charms and the bit of cut chain that had bound her pin to Rolland's. Now she should say some suitable words—or she should pray—but she didn't know what to say. The painfully bright sky above the river was smeared white with air pollution.

She wanted to pray as fervently as Susie prayed, but, unfortunately, she didn't believe in Jesus the way Susie did: as a real person standing by her side. She'd always been glad that Susie had never tried to convert her, and it wasn't that Gloria hadn't told her what she believed—she'd told her repeatedly and in depth—but niceties of doctrine didn't appear to concern Susie overly much; her religion was quite practical: if you were worried about something, you prayed, and Jesus spoke to you and told you what was right. Sometimes Gloria wondered if Susie's Jesus weren't simply Susie's secret watcher—but, no, there was more to it than that.

Gloria felt again that uncanny and entirely irrational conviction from the day they'd gone hunting: if God really existed, if it were possible to talk to Him directly, then Susie had been talking to Him alone in that terrible snow. "I'm sorry I didn't have the courage to follow you, to pray with you," she said to Susie in her mind.

"That's OK, Glo," she imagined Susie answering. "You can pray with me now."

"Oh, Susie, I'm not sure I believe in anything like what you do— or even if I believe in anything very much."

"That's OK too, Glo. Pray anyhow. With God, all things are possible."

Gloria closed her eyes and tried to imagine *her* God—an incomprehensible, impersonal, sexless force—the God of coincidences, of her dreams and mental floodings, of the strange leaps her mind made when she knew something absolutely without knowing how she knew it; the God of love, certainly, and of the created world when it had been given to her to see it with heart-stopping crystal clarity; the God of poetry, she realized with a sudden inner leap—*true* poetry, she amended it—the God who inspired the words when they were *true words*—and her mind, taking off on its own, found the breath in the root of the word "inspire." *Oh*, she thought—and she was praying just as fervently as she'd wished: "Thank you for sending Susie to me. And help all of us—my Mom and Dad and my brothers, and the girls in Delta Lambda, and everyone everywhere who needs your help. Give Grandmother a few more years, and give Susie a happy marriage. And let her find Tommie Jean— And please let this ritual mean something. Let me become an entirely different person. Let me know who I really am."

She opened her eyes to the flat, white brightness of the light. She opened her hand and watched the tiny speckles of gold that no longer defined her—if they ever had—fall more quickly than she would have imagined and vanish without a splash in the dirty, brown water. She'd expected to feel a pang of loss but she didn't. Then she knew that there were still too many charms on her bracelet, although she also knew that she wasn't required to throw any more of them away.

She walked quickly back to her mother's car, sat in the passenger's seat, and, with a nail file, began removing charms and dropping them into her purse. She didn't stop to think but trusted herself entirely to her first reaction to each one—whether or not it felt like an image that would carry her into the future, toward that unknown person she was about to become. When she was finished, only three were left: her Delta Lambda charm, her Phi Beta Kappa key, and the gold disk that said, *Susan Jane Steibel*.

After Gloria had been to Susie's home, she'd really had no choice but to invite her to hers, but she'd always been—for the most miserable of reasons—reluctant to do it: she'd been worried sick about what Susie might think of the well-to-do Cotters and all the money they had to throw around. Susie arrived on the Greyhound bus two days after Christmas; when Gloria turned her mother's station wagon into the driveway and they could see her house emerging from the trees—that enormous house plunked on top of the highest hill anywhere around there—it didn't help that Susie said, "Wow, Glo, you really *are* a princess!"

As Gloria showed her around, Susie's face closed into that pretty, blank mask Gloria had seen so often, and Gloria felt her stomach knot up. "I can't believe it," Susie said, "you have five bathrooms," and then, with her wicked, little smile, "but I bet we've got more cars than you do." Gloria couldn't stop laughing.

They exchanged belated Christmas presents in the privacy of Gloria's bedroom. Susie had said once that she'd always wanted a pair of red dress gloves but couldn't imagine anything more frivolous or impractical, so that's what Gloria had chosen for her—in the brilliant, little-girl's-raincoat red she was sure Susie wanted—and Susie seemed genuinely touched. "I better watch what I say around you. You never forget anything—and they're *French* too." Gloria didn't bother to point out that all good dress gloves were French.

Susie began to apologize for her present even before Gloria opened it: "Not much of anything, you know, kind of silly, but— Well, it's real hard with you, Glo. I kept trying to think of something you didn't already have."

Gloria was utterly delighted and tried to say all the right things so Susie would know it. Susie had given her the cowgirl boots she'd worn in Cloverton. She'd had new soles and heels put on them and had polished them the way she did her majorette boots—until they looked too perfect to wear, like art objects made of white porcelain. "That's so you can be a country girl any time you want," Susie said. Gloria couldn't imagine where she could wear them—except maybe to a Halloween party—but they were, nonetheless, one of her most prized possessions.

That spring Susie had talked Gloria into going to Philadelphia with her. Susie hadn't mentioned Tommie Jean until they were wandering around Fish Town, so, for all Gloria had known until then, Susie had intended the trip to be nothing more than a lark. It had taken Susie days to convince her that it was even possible. "Two single girls do not simply take off and drive from Briarville to Philadelphia."

"Come on, Glo, don't be such a cherry. Dad wouldn't lend me a car that wasn't in A-1 running order. What could possibly happen?"

"We could have a flat tire."

"Do you think I don't know how to change a flat tire?"

"We could get lost."

"It's like Dad always told me: 'Susan Jane, as long as you've got a mouth, you're never lost.'"

"Oh, Suse, it's just out of the question. We'd never get permission."

"Well, I guess we'd better sign out for Cloverton then, hadn't we?"

Once they were in Philadelphia, Susie drove straight to a sordid, run-down boarding house, stinking of cooked cabbage—Tommy Jean's last address— where the landlady, who seemed to Gloria like a spiteful, slatternly caricature out of a Dickens novel, told them: "Oh, yeah, I remember her. She hasn't lived here for years. How the devil should I know where she went?"

Afterward, Susie said, "Well, I guess she didn't keep her baby after all. Somebody like *that* would of never let her live there with a baby."

It never seemed to occur to Susie—maybe because she'd been raised with four older brothers—that there were some things girls simply did not do. "Why not?" she'd say, and Gloria never had a convincing answer; in the various cars Susie brought back from Cloverton—even once in a pickup truck—they drove to Philadelphia a dozen times or more. Gloria never got over the feeling that they were being daring and naughty, violating some fundamental and obvious rule that she understood even if Susie didn't, but she followed wherever Susie led.

They always went to Fish Town because Susie was convinced that eventually, in His own good time, God would bring her and Tommie Jean together again. Susie was always hungry, so, in a little waterfront café with sawdust on the floor, they ate huge slabs of nameless fried fish laid between slices of white bread smeared with hot mustard, and, afterward, wandered through seedy streets with lovely names—Amber, Almond, Emerald, Coral—while Gloria recited in her mind: "I wander thro' each charter'd street, near where the charter'd Thames does flow—" although it wasn't the Thames at all but the Delaware or the Schuylkill or some darned river, and sometimes guys in windbreakers would try to pick them up. "Buzz off, fellahs," Susie would tell them in a good-humored voice that usually made them buzz off.

They never stayed in Fish Town for long—Tommie Jean, after all, could be anywhere in Philadelphia—and Gloria was overjoyed to find not only Bonwit Teller and Wanamaker's but Blum's shoe store and lovely little shops like Sophie Kurzon's and Nan Duskin's where the prices actually made Susie break out in a sweat: "We shouldn't be in here, Glo. They're going to charge us for *breathing!*" Then it was Gloria's turn to be the cool, collected one, and she bought a copy of a Chanel suit they could both wear. After Susie began to go steady with Don, sometimes, when he'd gone home for the weekend, he'd drive in to meet them in the university district. Meeting a boy in Philadelphia, of course, was really against the rules, but Gloria had become the president of their chapter by then, and she wasn't about to discipline herself for it.

As apprehensive as she always was—she never got over her nervousness—Gloria loved these secretive excursions to Philadelphia. The possibility that they might find Tommie Jean at any moment, imbued even the most commonplace events with an exotic, almost mythic quality—as though they might turn a corner and end up in Faerie Lond—and the search for Tommie Jean began to feel like a quest, with Gloria and Susie taking turns playing Britomart.

"I don't *want* to be May Queen," Gloria said early in their senior year. It was the same thing she'd said about being the president of their chapter when Susie had nominated her the year before.

"Sure you do."

"Come on, Suse, we should nominate *you*. You'd be a shoo-in."

"Oh, forget that. I was Valentine's Queen, OK? How many queens do I have to be? Besides, if I had a choice between riding around in a limousine and leading the band, which one do you think I'd want to do?"

"That's the same thing you said about Homecoming Queen—"

"Yeah, and I *still* mean it. Come on, Glo, how about you? I just know you've been dying to enter a beauty contest, and May Queen's the closest thing you're ever going to get."

"Lay off me, Susie! I haven't got time. I've got my darned Wyatt paper to finish—"

"Hey, stop trying to weasel out of it. You know it's your duty to Delta Lambda."

Thus began the most frantic semester of Gloria's academic life. The year before, she'd suggested to Professor Bolton that she write her honors thesis on Spenser; she'd thought that all she might have to do would be expand what she'd written over her Britomart summer. "Oh, no, no, no, no, no," he'd said. "You could vanish into Spenser and never come out again. Put him aside for the moment, my dear. To complete what you have begun with Spenser, you should devote, oh, no less than ten years. It could make your reputation, hmmm? But later, my dear. For the moment let us consider the good Sir Thomas the Elder— Oh, and Miss Cotter? You will discover, when you try to find it, that I have withdrawn my modest monograph from circulation."

Grinning, he'd waved it at her; she had already, in the Briarville catalogue, located the intriguing reference—*On the Poetry of Sir Thomas Wyatt* by Trevor Algernon Bolton—and had been disappointed to find the book itself vanished from the stacks. "Oh, I will allow you to read it eventually, my dear, but, given your oft demonstrated ability to quote me back to myself in brilliant para-phrases—not quite yet."

By that spring Gloria had read every line of poetry attributed to Wyatt and had considered the difficulties of attributing them. She'd considered the Egerton, Devonshire, and other manuscripts, and, of course, Tottel's *Miscellany*, and had compared variants—and that section of her paper had already been passed: "Very thorough, my dear. Even if I were judging it as graduate work, I would call it thorough. I would imagine that you're simply dying to get into the British Museum now, hmmmm?"

Gloria was still having some difficulties finding a properly objective stance to take with the historical background. Wyatt and Anne Boleyn had certainly known each other; Wyatt had certainly written poems to her and about her. But, with no more evidence than the feelings evoked in her by Wyatt's poetry, Gloria was convinced that he and Anne had been madly, passionately in love; she doubted that she could convince Professor Bolton, however, so restrained herself in her thesis and saved her wilder conjectures for her diary where she could allow herself to be as fanciful as she pleased—where she called Anne and her confreres "sixteenth-century country club girls."

She was fascinated with the idea of poems and riddles being passed back and forth clandestinely among courtly lovers, of secret trysts in dark hallways at a time when the "daunger" Wyatt wrote about was not the least bit the conventional metaphor it would become later but the literal truth: if a girl at the Tudor court flirted with the wrong guy, she could be banished, or imprisoned in the tower—or lose her head. Gloria didn't know whether to believe the shadowy Spanish Chronicler who told of Wyatt sneaking into Anne's chamber at night; "For Christ's sake, Wyatt," Anne is supposed to have said, "what are you doing in my bedroom?" True or not, it was a darned good story, and you couldn't argue with evidence written into the manuscripts: Wyatt's riddle: "What wourde is that that chaungesth not, though it be tourned and made in twain?" that is answered by "Anna," and the cryptic entry in the Devonshire Manuscript that ends with "I ama youwrs an." Although she was certain of it, Gloria merely suggested—after listing the evidence on both sides—that Wyatt's brunette, and "Lux" his fair falcon, and the fire that has burnt him out when he flees from Dover to Calais against his mind, and, of course, the hind who wears the don't-touch-me collar all could very well have been Anne. When Wyatt wrote that the bell tower showed him "such a sight that in my head sticks day and night," that, surely had been the sight of poor Anne's execution. "Country club girls in those days," Gloria wrote in her diary, "played for far higher stakes than we do."

Susie came back from Christmas vacation pinned to Don. She'd been to visit him and his family in Merion, and she could hardly wait to tell Gloria about going to church with them. "I walked in there, and I was afraid I was going to faint. Everywhere you looked there were graven images, and I kept thinking, what am I doing here? This is the temple of Satan! Because— Well, Pastor Harris always told us that the Episcopalian Church was founded on sin. It started when King What's-his-name wanted to commit adultery—"

It was weird, Gloria thought, how everything in her life seemed to be fitting in with everything else. "Henry the Eighth," she said patiently.

"That's right. And he wanted to commit adultery and the Pope wouldn't let him do it, so he made up a church that would let him do it, and anything founded on sin can't bring forth anything but more sin, and I— Well, people kneel in that church, you know. They've got these things you kneel on, and I knelt down when everybody else did, and I prayed, 'Oh, please, Jesus, forgive me for being here,' and then—

"You know, they've got everything all written out, and you follow it along in a book. I guess it must be like what the Catholics do. And most of the hymns they sing are different from ours, but they did one that we do—'In Christ There Is No East Nor West'—and I felt good singing that, because—well, in Christ there *is* no east nor west, and— You know, everybody goes up to the front to take communion. And they give you this little cracker with a cross on it, and you get a drink of *real wine*.

"I've prayed for guidance on this, Gloria, and I haven't got the answer yet, but you know what I thought afterwards? Well, the way I was always taught, if you want to know the truth, you read the Bible. Like the way Christ was baptized. He didn't have a little dab of water put on his forehead when he was a baby. He was a full grown man, and John the Baptist took him and *immersed* him in the River Jordan. OK? Well, at the Last Supper, Christ wasn't passing around Welch's grape juice."

That was the last thing Gloria had expected Susie to say, and she had to laugh. Susie laughed too, and, for a moment, they were both hysterical.

"And so you came back pinned to this heathen, huh?" Gloria said.

Susie took the question far more seriously than Gloria had intended it. "We love each other, Glo, and— You know, Don's mom and dad just knocked themselves out for me. You couldn't ask for anybody any nicer to me than they were. And I don't think Jesus wants me to say to Don, 'The place where you worship God is the temple of Satan.'"

Gloria and Susie shot off to Philadelphia to find the right dress for the crucial May Queen Candidates' Party and went to Gloria's favorite little shops, but nothing she tried on in any of them pleased Susie. Then, when they were wandering around Wanamaker's, Susie said, "Hey, how about this?" Gloria's first impulse was to reject the dress out of hand, but something about it was oddly intriguing—maybe that it was so unlike anything she would have considered on her own—so she followed Susie into the change room and slipped it on.

Plum was a color Gloria didn't ordinarily wear; looking at herself in the mirror, she made a mental note to add it to her list—but the dress itself? Never in a million years would she have picked something straight off the rack in a department store, let alone something with such a pretentiously enormous bow at the throat. "Oh, no, Suse," she said, "it's just not me."

"Well, yeah. But stop thinking about what's *you*, and think about what's gonna go over. Imagine you're one of those young professors they stick on the May Queen Committee, OK? Now isn't that a girl you'd want to represent Briarville?"

"Well, maybe."

"I know you don't think it's very sophisticated—and it's *not* very sophisticated—but you don't want those guys looking at you and thinking, wow, she must of spent a million bucks on that dress! What you want is for them to look at you and think, wow, what a cute, sweet, pretty, *nice* girl, right? Just exactly the kind of girl we want in the Briarville catalogue."

"I guess so."

"Sure. And with real high heels so you're a teeny bit naughty— believe me, Glo, they'll eat you up with a spoon."

"I don't know, Suse."

"Well, I do—and besides, nothing *sounds* as yummy as taffeta."

So, against her better judgment, Gloria bought the plum taffeta and then, to go with them, a pair of too-high heels in which—as she'd begun to insist even as she'd first tried them on—she simply could not walk, no, not even two steps.

"Sure you can," Susie said, "I'll show you," and, back in Briarville, in the rec room, with half a dozen other Lambs watching, she demonstrated the perfect Miss America walk—and then made Gloria try it. Susie told her to imagine each tiny heel falling onto a straight line stretching out before her. "Smile," Susie kept saying. "Relax your shoulders. Keep your knees together. Don't look at your feet," and Gloria wondered what Margaret of Austria had made Anne do before she was shipped back to England and presented to the Tudor Court. They didn't have skyscraper heels in those days—at least Gloria didn't think they did—but she was sure that Anne had been required to practice something equally irritating.

Susie came back from spring break engaged and planning to be married in June; what else could Gloria do but suggest to Julie and Marnie and Susie's other good friends that they help her plan her wedding? Gloria had always needed less sleep than other girls her age, but now she wasn't getting even the bare minimum, and she kept wondering why Professor Bolton was doing this to her. In the reading room in the English Department were bound copies of all the previous honors' theses, and Gloria had skimmed through enough of them to know that what she was being asked to do far exceeded anything that was ordinarily demanded of undergraduates; what she was doing was beginning to resemble a master's thesis.

By now she was trying to summarize several hundred years worth of the critical opinion of Wyatt, and she agreed with hardly any of it. Wyatt's poetry had lost none of its luster for her, and when the critics called him harsh and rough, she thought that they were wrong and Wyatt was right—although she knew she'd never risk saying so in print. But, near the end of April, she blew up in Professor Bolton's office. "I simply don't agree with Dr. Johnson," she said.

"You will find, my dear," he said in a bland voice, "that the good Dr. Johnson is often wrong."

"Well, he's *really* wrong about Wyatt. And so's Saintsbury."

"Ah. Indeed?"

"Some of the things they think are rough are just because they don't understand how words were pronounced in Wyatt's time."

"Yes, you're absolutely right—spot on."

"And— Well, Wyatt's just all 'round better than they think he is. *Nobody's* better than Wyatt until you get to Shakespeare."

What a terribly reckless thing to say, she thought; she shouldn't have dared to say anything at all like that until she'd read every word written by everyone of any note between Wyatt and Shakespeare—but Professor Bolton didn't seem to be annoyed; he was giving her his best pussycat grin. "That's a fairly extreme position, my dear," he said. "What about your beloved Spenser?"

"OK, forget I said that—but why do people keep thinking he was trying to write blank verse and couldn't quite figure out how to do it?"

"An excellent question. Yes, indeed, why do they think that? Go on, my dear."

"I don't think he was trying to write blank verse at all. He was writing his own verse, and he had his own rules for it."

"Yes, yes, yes?"

"Look at 'They Flee From Me,' for instance. Who cares if some lines have five feet and some four—or even if some lines can be read as having either five or four feet depending on how you pronounce them. Read it out loud, and it works fine. The music's simply lovely. I don't think Wyatt was counting feet. He was counting something, but not feet—well, at least not in the way Surrey counted them."

Professor Bolton's grin couldn't have grown any wider if he'd been transformed into a jack-o'-lantern. "Now, my dear," he said, "you may read my modest monograph."

Gloria read the little book at one sitting, stayed up all night, cited Professor Bolton seventeen times for conclusions similar to those she'd already reached on her own, handed in her thesis, and received an A plus on it. "Forgive me for being so hard on you, my dear," he said, "but now you have the core of your doctoral thesis. Oh, my, won't Lionel be impressed!"

When Gloria walked—in tiny, perfected steps—into the May Queen Candidates' Party, the secret watcher told her, "Be careful. With one quick turn, the wheel of Fortune could dump you straight down into the deepest pit," but the great wheel didn't dump her; it carried her to the top. The ensemble Susie had chosen for her obviously affected the young profs on the May Queen Committee just as Susie had said it would.

On May Day, Susie was in charge of the team of Lambs who assembled— yes, that was the proper word—Gloria for her crowning and the parade afterward. Susie put stage makeup on her—pancake applied with a sponge—and smoothed it not only on her face, but on her ears, her neck, her shoulders, and even down over the tops of her breasts as Gloria sat patiently (and eventually not so patiently), and wondered what on earth they were doing to her. (Had Anne ever been this impatient as her maids prepared her for a court appearance?) Susie drew enormous doe eyes on her, glued on great sweeps of false lashes. With a sable brush, Susie painted in the lip line she'd drawn. "Don't eat anything or drink anything until it's all over. Don't even *touch* your mouth."

Then the girls took the pin-curls out of her hair, brushed her out and sprayed her, worked her arms into her grandmother's evening gloves and did up the buttons (this time Gloria had remembered a button hook), fastened on a single strand of pearls, and attached pearl earrings. Only then was she allowed to look in the mirror. "Good grief," Gloria said, "I don't look real!"

"You're going to photograph beautifully," Susie said.

Gloria had always been proud of her small waistline, but, having not slept much since spring break, having lost most of her interest in food, and, having been hooked into the deadly serious French corselet she'd bought for the occasion, she was, she was sure, the smallest she'd been since childhood—and that tiny waist rose, stemlike, above the largest skirt she'd ever worn in her life; it was supported by hoops and a zillion crinolines. If her May Queen costume didn't incapacitate her entirely, it came close to it. She moved in it as slowly, carefully, and ponderously as any float in the parade. Like the queen she was about to become, she didn't walk, she made a progress.

Later, Gloria would not remember much of the festivities at the fairgrounds. May Day had always been an event shared by the college and the town, so she was crowned by the University President and presented with a bouquet by the Mayor of Briarville. Attended by her four princesses, she listened to the speeches and presided over the May Pole dancing; then her team of Lambs helped her to ascend her float and arranged her upon it. Oddly enough, what she would remember vividly—and was sure that she would remember just as vividly for the rest of her life—was the ten minutes or so she waited for the parade to begin. The Blue Bulldogs Marching Band, which was to follow directly behind her, was already in place. Susie, who was to lead them, walked forward to call up to Gloria atop her float: "Hey, sugar, you look like a dream."

"So do you."

"No, I don't. I just look like myself."

That's interesting, Gloria thought: to Susie, a majorette's uniform must represent her authentic self.

As it became apparent that the parade was still not about to get underway, Susie began clowning around for Gloria's benefit. She did a number of highly unlikely twirls and then, as though disgusted with the whole procedure, flung up her baton and walked away from it. She sent Gloria a single, baffled look as though she didn't know what to do next; at the last possible moment, she stepped back and snagged the baton casually out of the air.

"Don't make me laugh," Gloria said, "I'll run my mascara."

In her majorette's uniform, Susie looked as slender as a boy; in fact, with her tasseled boots and military jacket and tiny skirt, she could have been the modern version of a page boy from an old court pageant—and Gloria again had the sense, this time quite strongly, that she and Susie had entered into Faerie Lond; if they had, there was no doubt what roles they'd assumed: Susie had become Britomart, the chaste warrior maiden, whilst she—the mystical May Queen immobilized and displayed on her flower-bedecked throne—had become Amoret, trained up in true femininity to be the example of true love alone and Lodestar of all chaste affection to all fair Ladies.

Susie blew her whistle to call the band and the majorettes to attention, took her position at the head of them, and, blowing her whistle again, spun her baton into the signal that said: forward march. The joyous blare—the brilliance of the brass and the snarl of the snare drums—lifted Gloria's heart, and, when she smiled and waved at the crowd on the sidewalks, she wasn't faking her pleasure a bit. This might not be, Gloria thought, the pageantry of Anne Boleyn's court, or of her daughter Elizabeth's, but it was better than nothing. As they approached the bandstand, Gloria saw Professor Bolton standing at the edge of the curb. When her float drew abreast of him, he doffed his hat, extended one foot, and executed an absurd, flourishing bow so deep his forehead almost touched his toes; May Queen or not, Gloria couldn't help laughing.

In the afternoon Gloria took a long, hot bath and tried, unsuccessfully, to sleep. That night she was reassembled all over again so she could preside over the May Day Dance. Rolland had driven in for it; he and Gloria led the promenade and danced the first dance. For the big campus events, the house had a two o'clock curfew; as President, Gloria had to obey it, but she had no intention of disciplining the girls she heard sneaking through the kitchen window after it—one of whom was Susie. "You still awake, Glo? I thought you'd be dead to the world."

"No, I'm too wound up."

"Yeah, me too. Wow, what a day!"

They went to bed, and they intended to go to sleep, but they talked all night. They went over all the events of the day and then the most memorable events of the year—and the past years; they talked about how uncomfortable they'd been with each other that day when they'd met for a Coke at Sneaky's, and they laughed about it. Susie talked about Don; Gloria talked about Rolland. Later Gloria wouldn't be able to remember quite how they'd arrived at the topic, but they talked about what each of their minds looked like from the inside.

Gloria was surprised to hear that Susie often didn't have words in her mind— she had pictures or feelings—and she didn't know whether to believe her; she couldn't imagine anyone who did not have words in her mind all the time, who wasn't, constantly drowning in words—as Gloria was. And she said to Susie what she'd often thought: "I wish you'd stop telling me, 'Gloria, you think too much.' You think about things plenty."

"Oh, I never meant that you shouldn't *think*. It's just— OK, let me see if I can find a way to say it— Well, look, you're real smart. And usually you get something real fast. But then you think about it. And you think and you think and you think about it—just like a dog chasing its tail. And after you've been doing that for a while, you forget what it was you thought in the first place."

Gloria was astonished. That was the most astute assessment of her she'd ever heard from anyone.

When the first light began to appear at their window, Susie said, "Come on, let's go somewhere and watch the sun come up."

Susie drove to the highest point above the campus. Gloria's tiredness had gone far beyond mere exhaustion; her senses felt raw, and the light of the rising sun shining on the little creek, on the distant campus, seemed painfully beautiful. "The world is charged with the grandeur of God," she said.

Not recognizing it as a quotation, Susie said, "Oh, it sure is, isn't it? Oh, isn't God's creation so beautiful? You know that passage in John? 'For God sent not his son into the world to condemn the world'?" She looked at Gloria, smiling, and then looked away again, taking it all in. As she often did, she began to sing a hymn. It usually startled Gloria, and sometimes annoyed her, when Susie spontaneously broke into song like that, but now she was pleased. She loved hearing Susie's singing voice that morning; it wasn't a strong voice, sounded much like a child's—thin and breathy—but she was always in tune. "'Through many dangers, toils, and snares I have already come; 'Tis Grace that brought me safe thus far, and Grace will lead me home—' Oh, Gloria, I'm so happy!"

"Me too."

"I want to—I don't know how to say it. I guess I just want to say thanks for everything you've done for me."

Gloria couldn't imagine what Susie thought she'd done for her; she'd lent her clothes, but that wasn't much of anything. "You've done a lot more for me, Suse," she said.

"Oh, come on. Like what?"

Susie had become so important to Gloria that she couldn't imagine her life without Susie in it, but she couldn't find any way to say it that wouldn't have embarrassed her—and Susie—so she said, "Well, you made me into the May Queen."

"No, I didn't. I just gave you a little push. But I guess what I'm trying to say is, I always wanted a sister, and— Well, you're not just my sorority sister, and you're not just like a sister. You really are my sister. Forever and ever."

Gloria was so full of emotion she was tempted to make a joke to brings things back to normal, but she stopped herself. Nothing felt normal at the moment. "Me too," she said. "I mean, I feel the same way," and she wanted to say, "I love you," but she couldn't bring herself to say it. "I've never felt closer to anybody in my life," she said instead.

"Yeah, me neither."

"Hey," Gloria said, inspired, "you want to do a ritual? Sisters forever. You know the gold disks we just got? You want to trade?"

"Oh, sure. That would be real nice—" Gloria heard one of Susie's dangling sentences, and she waited. What was she thinking? Was there something wrong with the idea of trading disks? Did Susie think Gloria's suggestion had belittled what she'd been feeling?

"Gloria? I want to tell you something I've never told anybody in my life."

"OK. Are you sure you want to?"

"Yeah, I'm sure. I don't know why I never told anybody. It just felt—I don't know—sacred, I guess. You know, about winning the Nationals?"

"You've told me about that."

"No, I haven't. Not the important part, anyway. Can I tell you?"

"Sure."

"OK. Well, I thought I'd come back with a trophy, but I didn't think I'd win anything big—and then I won the strut. You know what that is? You carry your baton, but you're not allowed to twirl it. So it's like a dance routine for majorettes, and I'd been dancing my whole life, and I'd been working on my routine every day since school was out, so I did some pretty fancy stuff, and I won it. And I was as shocked as anybody. And I thought, oh my gosh, now if I could win the solo twirl, I could win the whole Nationals!

"So, anyhow, thinking I could win made me so nervous I couldn't believe it, and the closer it came to the time for my routine, the more nervous I got— You ever get so nervous you can't *see*?"

"Oh, yes!"

"Well, you know what I'm talking about then. Everything was just a kind of blur. And my mouth was all dry, and I was shaking, and my hands— You always carry around corn starch to put on your hands, because when you're twirling, the last thing in the world you want is your hands sweaty. So I kept mine in a little bag, and I kept putting it on, but it didn't do any good. My hands were like— It was just like I'd rubbed them with lard, that's how bad it was. And cold? Oh, I can't tell you. It was a hot day, but my hands and feet were like ice, and I kept dropping things. Everything I touched just sort of shot away from me, and I kept thinking, oh, I'm not going to be able to twirl at all. I'm just going to drop the baton over and over again.

"So I had to pray. I didn't want to make a big deal of it just, you know, drop down on my knees in front of everybody, but I didn't want people to think I was ashamed of my faith either, so I went off to one side where—well, if the other girls were looking in my direction, they'd see me, but they didn't have to see me. And I knelt down. And I don't think I ever prayed so hard in my life.

"I'd thought I was going to pray for God to help me to win, but the minute

I was kneeling there, I knew I couldn't do that. And then I thought I'd ask God to help me stop being so nervous and to do my very best, but I couldn't do that either. So finally I said, 'Lord, you've given me this gift, and it's not mine, it's yours. You know how hard I've worked, Lord, how many hours I spent practicing and all that, but I just can't do it without you. I'm yours, Lord, so you do with me whatever you want—not my will, but thine be done, Amen.'

"And—well, the minute I said that—I mean, right that very minute, the Grace of God came and filled me up. It was like pouring water into a glass, and— No, it wasn't. It was more like tea or cocoa or something because it was *warm*. And it filled me up right through my whole body, and I stopped sweating— *bang*—just like that, and I could see everything clear as a bell. And I stood up, and I didn't need any corn starch on my hands.

"I've thought about this a lot. You know the story where Peter walks on water? And he loses his faith and starts to sink? Can't you just see it? I mean, there he is, and he's walking along on the water and everything's fine, but he thinks, wow, I'm walking on water—that's impossible! So naturally he starts to sink—and I've often wondered why that didn't happen to me. There were three girls ahead of me, so I had all of this time I had to stand there. And if just once I would of doubted, I would've sunk—but I didn't. I waited my turn, and then—

"Well, I'd planned just to go out, stand there at parade rest, waiting for my music to start—real relaxed, you know—but God told me to do something else, so I went into the majorette pose. You know what that is, don't you? I know you've seen it a million times. You do a relevé on your right leg, and you bend your left leg up, toe to knee. It's a lot harder than it looks. If you don't pull up for all you're worth, you'll fall right off it, and it was a dangerous thing to do because sometimes it takes forever for them to get your music going, but I just held it like I was nailed there. And my music started, and I held my pose right through the drum roll, and then I stepped out and started to twirl.

"Military bands march at eighty, you know, like this," and Susie snapped her fingers so Gloria could hear the tempo. "But a majorette wants to hear a nice, bright, snappy cadence, like this—about a hundred and twenty, right? Then you can really strut. And I'd picked a good, snappy march. And you've got two and a half minutes, and when they say two and a half, that's exactly what they mean. And so for my first minute I'd planned a routine that had all the basic twirls in it, so the judges could see I knew them all. I'll never forget it. Starting with the right hand—cartwheel, pinwheel, around the body, around the body reverse, flats, side to side flats, then cartwheel right hand to left, and so on—and everything was perfect. And I remember I was twirling so fast that if I'd just once thought about how fast I was twirling, I would've stopped dead.

"Well, that first part was supposed to end with a throw, and I'd do a pirouette under it. So I did the throw. It was a good, high throw, but I didn't do one pirouette. God made me do two of them, just hard and tight and fast—*bang, bang*—and I put out my hand and the baton was right there. If somebody had asked me if I could of done that, I would of said, no, I couldn't. But with God, all things are possible, and I wasn't even surprised.

"I finished the first part of the routine just the way I was supposed to, with a salute in lunge position. And I was supposed to hold my pose for two bars so people could applaud, but God said I should only hold it for one bar, so just when people were starting to applaud, I came out of it. I did a little dance step that turned my right side to the audience, and a reverse cartwheel with another little dance step that turned me the other way, and then a forward cartwheel. I hadn't planned to do any of that, and so I knew my plans had just gone out the window and I had to put my whole trust in God. I don't even remember exactly what I did after that. I did a lot of twirling with my left hand. I even did catches with my left hand—and I did kicks and wraps and finger twirls and thumb twirls and some really fancy twirls I'd been afraid to try, and I did twirls I'd seen other girls do but I'd never tried, and they all worked just fine—and I did twirls I'd never even thought of before.

"I remember doing a catch in arabesque. I remember doing a palm twirl that I thought would just go on forever—and I did 'spank the baby', and it came down and kept right on twirling like it had a life of its own. I did a full back bend, and it just seemed easy. I did hurdle jumps, all kinds of jumps. Everything just seemed easy. One of the judges afterward said to me, 'Susie, I've never seen a twirler as fluid as you—the way everything flowed together. You must of practiced that routine a million times.' But I hadn't. The second part I hadn't. *I* didn't do anything, except— God did it, and I was just the— I don't know—"

"The vessel."

"That's right. That's exactly right. And I finished with a salute into the splits and held it. And there was this dead silence. You could of heard a pin drop. And then people just went nuts. They were all just screaming their heads off. And I thought, they're not cheering for me, they're cheering for the Grace of God, they just don't know it. And the minute I thought that, I started to cry. I came out of my pose, and they were still cheering. They'd all jumped up. They were all standing up. So I made a little curtsy to thank them, and I ran off— because I was crying so hard. And I ran straight into the ladies' room and knelt down and just bawled. All I could say was, 'Thank you, Lord. Thank you, thank you, thank you.' I knew I'd never twirled better in my life, but I didn't care about that. I'd felt the Grace of God moving through me, and that's the only thing that mattered."

Gloria didn't know what to say. She looked at Susie and saw that Susie was looking at her. "So that's how I won the Teenage Majorette Championship at the Nationals," Susie said, "and—I don't know. I just wanted to tell you that because— I just wanted you to know that God's with us all the time, and— well, sometimes I don't think you believe it. I'm not talking about going to church. You know that, don't you? But— I just wanted you to know."

Oh, Gloria thought, she's just given me the most precious gift she owns, and, when she understood that, she began to cry. She was embarrassed, but she couldn't stop herself. She was actually sobbing. Susie was crying too, but quietly, with no signs of it but the tears on her face. "I'm sorry," Gloria said, "I'm really tired."

Susie pressed her fingertips against Gloria's mouth. "Shhh," she said.

They stood silently on the hilltop for another few minutes and then, silently, drove back down to the campus. As soon as they were in their room, Gloria gave her disk to Susie and Susie gave hers to Gloria. For once in her life, Gloria knew better than to try to find something to say.

She didn't know whether Susie had slept that morning or not, but she had, deeply, for nearly two hours, until the noises in the house woke her up. Now, wherever she was, if Susie was wearing her charm bracelet, there would be a gold Delta Lambda disk on it that said, *Gloria Merriman Cotter*.

On Sunday afternoon, Gloria finally broached the subject of going to Philadelphia. "Good God, sweetie," her mother said, "they're just married. Why don't you just let them alone for a while?"

Gloria had just finished her swim. Her parents were sprawled in lawn chairs by the side of the pool; as always on Sunday afternoon, they were drinking Scotch. "It would only be for a few days," she said.

"I don't see any reason why she can't go," her father said. "She's probably bored silly here."

"That's right," her mother said, "Mother nearly died, and she's still in the hospital, and the boys will be home next week, and *the princess* has to go to Philly."

"I wouldn't go until Grandmother comes home."

"Well, thank heaven for small favors."

"Look, cookie, if you need a practical nurse for your mother, we'll get one, OK? This whole thing's been hard on Gloria too. I bet she could use a bit of a vacation."

Gloria's mother directed a slit-eyed, lizardy look her way, and Gloria guessed that she must be thinking: "What about *me*? Don't *I* get a vacation?" but she said, "Oh, all right."

Goody, Gloria thought, and, to mollify her mother, said, "Why don't you and Dad go on down to the club? I'll drive in and see Grandmother tonight."

Later, Gloria wouldn't be able to remember much about her visit. She and her grandmother played bridge. Gloria would remember that her grandmother asked her, "What is it like outside?" She'd sensed that her grandmother really wanted to know.

"It's a little bit overcast. It's kind of muggy—one of those nights when you wish it would rain but you know it's not going to."

She wouldn't remember what her grandmother had said after that, but she would remember kissing her on the cheek. "Good night, Gloria," her grandmother must have said, and she would remember saying, "I'll see you tomorrow." All that she would remember about the rest of the night was that she'd read for several hours—a Philip Marlowe novel—and that she'd felt calm and entirely at peace.

Gloria heard the cheeping of a million birds, so she knew it must be dawn, and she told herself to go back to sleep, but then she heard the telephone ringing. She couldn't tell whether it was ringing in the real world or only in her dream, but it stopped, so she allowed herself to drift downward until she heard a voice that seemed to be saying something, but she couldn't quite catch it, and— Oh, what a dumbo she was. She'd forgotten that she was getting married in the morning.

Why had she put everything off to the last minute? She still hadn't found the right wedding dress. She jumped out of bed and climbed the narrow stairs to the attic and pushed through the secret door that opened into the secret closets, each one leading into the next like a maze. She found her Prom Queen dress and her May Queen dress, and she wondered if either of them would do, but getting married was far more important than being Prom Queen or May Queen, and she wanted to look exactly right on her wedding day.

She found her mother's watered silk wedding dress, the one that had belonged to her great-grandmother, and it was quite beautiful in an antique, otherworldly way, but she certainly didn't want to wear the same dress her mother had been married in. Then she saw her mother's glass slippers. She hadn't expected them to be real glass, but that's exactly what they were—lead crystal—and her mother had been right: they were far too small for Gloria.

Looking down the rack, she saw other old dresses from many years ago, and she knew that they were her grandmother's. For a moment, she considered going back to her grandmother's time. It was just a matter of following her grandmother through the secret door where she'd gone. That's what happened to people when they were completed: they went through a secret door and got folded back into their own time, but you could always visit them. Then she remembered that she wasn't planning a visit, but a marriage, and she had the rest of her life to visit other times.

This is all very interesting, she thought, but it's not getting me anywhere, and she slid the dresses out of her way so she could get to the archway—no, it was a pergola with ivy and morning glory growing on it—and she walked through it and found herself outdoors in the courtyard behind the Admin building. There was a fair going on, and booths had been set up for vendors to display their wares. This is perfect, she thought. I'm sure to find something here.

She wandered from booth to booth, but none of them were selling wedding dresses, and then she saw one that didn't seem to be selling anything; it had an iron door that led into a little house. The sign above the door was written in six-teenth-century script and said: TWYNNES. Gloria had always wanted to be a twin, so she opened the door and walked in without knocking. There was nothing inside but a full-length mirror, and she knew she'd been tricked. She was about to turn and storm out—boy, was she going to complain to the administration about this one!—when she saw that it wasn't a mirror at all but an empty wooden frame. The person she'd thought was her reflection was Susie.

Gloria remembered that she and Susie were identical twins—the product of a very rare kind of twinning in which one twin came out dark and the other light—and she said, "Oh, Susie, I'm sorry I forgot we were twins."

"For somebody as smart as you are, you can be such a dope sometimes," Susie said. "Come on," and she led Gloria over to a display of wedding dresses.

On a mannequin in the center of the booth was the most beautiful wedding dress Gloria had ever seen. It was fitted at the bodice and had an enormous skirt trimmed with circle after circle of lace; she knew it would move wonderfully and she'd look absolutely fabulous in it. But then she remembered breaking up with Rolland. Oh, how sad, she thought, I can't get married after all!

Suddenly, in an unexpected rush of inspiration, she knew how she could fix everything. It was so simple, she couldn't understand why she hadn't thought of it before. "We're twins," she said to Susie, "so you can get married and wear that wonderful dress. That way we'll all of us get exactly what we want." But the minute she said it, she realized that *she* wasn't getting what she wanted. She had taken plenty of time, but she still didn't know what she wanted.

With a radiant smile, Susie turned Gloria around to see what had been directly behind her, and there, on display, was a majorette's uniform in dazzling white. The jacket was trimmed with scarlet braid; the white boots had scarlet tassels. "We're twins," Susie told her, "and we've traded places. Now you're going to be head majorette."

This can't be right, Gloria thought. Unlike the formals she'd worn as Prom Queen and May Queen, a majorette's uniform was not merely ornamental but structural—that is, she couldn't simply look right; she would have to perform. "I can't be head majorette," Gloria said. "I never learned how to twirl a baton."

"Come on, Glo, don't be such a dope. You've been practicing your whole life."

The moment Susie said it, Gloria knew it was true. She had been practicing her whole life. How could she have forgotten something as important as that? And she knew then that what had been chosen for her was her own heart's true and secret desire. She woke filled with immaculate happiness.

Gloria lay in bed, her eyes still closed, and balanced her joy carefully like a cup filled to the brim. She didn't understand what the dream could possibly have meant. How, even as metaphor, was she supposed to be Head Majorette? But she knew she had to be. It was as though an utterly unexpected path had opened up for her—one that would alter the entire course of her life.

Then—reluctantly, gradually—she allowed herself to know that something wasn't right in the house. She was hearing her parents' voices—a dim murmuring. It was time for her father to be going to work, and her mother should still be in bed. For a moment she thought that they were in their bedroom, but then she heard that they were down in the kitchen. What on earth was going on? What could they be talking about? But she knew already. Oh, no! she thought. It's not fair, not when I'm so happy—and she hated herself for having such a mean, selfish thought.

She jumped up and ran straight downstairs. Her mother had made coffee; she and Gloria's father were drinking it in the breakfast nook. They looked up when she rushed in, but neither of them said a word, so Gloria simply sat down with them. Without speaking, her father poured her a cup of coffee.

"Mother passed away last night," Gloria's mother said. "She wasn't in any pain. She passed away quietly in her sleep."

PART THREE

17

If viewed from the west, from a vantage point just above the topmost branches of the apple trees, Ted Cotter's house would have appeared as a dark, rectangular shape with the corona of the rising sun flaring around its edges, and Ted Cotter himself, as he stood by the side of his pool, as a small, featureless, humanoid figure in a gray, unidentifiable costume. He was staring out across his lawn at the hole that had been dug near the apple trees. The rectangular shape of the hole echoed that of the house, and the hole lay along a north-south axis exactly parallel to the house. Until the sun rose high enough to illuminate the bottom of the hole, even someone looking directly into it would not have been able to tell how deep it was. From Ted's point of view, the hole was little more than an ugly black stripe at the far side of the lawn, but he knew that each day it would get deeper until it exceeded, by a good twenty feet, the specifications suggested by the civilian defense authorities.

To one side of the hole and some ten yards to the east of it, a bulldozer was parked; at either end of the hole, dirt was piled up into enormous mounds. Ted hated the way the raw earth made his backyard smell like a cemetery, and he hated the way the bulldozer and dump trucks and other heavy equipment were ruining his lawn, and, when you got right down to it, he hated the hole itself, but he was stuck with it. He wanted the job done right, and so they probably wouldn't get it finished much before Christmas, or, at the rate the dumb clucks were going, maybe not till next spring, but then, after the landscapers did their work, nobody would ever know, unless he chose to tell them, that he had— yep, right out there in his own backyard—one of the damn finest private bomb shelters in the whole damn country.

He hadn't wanted to go to the funeral, but it was a good thing he had because it'd given him a chance to think things through. Laney had been so exhausted— poor girl—she'd fallen sound asleep on the plane coming back, but Ted hated flying, and he'd sat there with every muscle in his body as tensed up as if he'd been spring-loaded, drinking Scotch and smoking cigarettes and staring out the window at the big, fat, whipped cream clouds that looked solid enough for somebody to take a nap on them—which was a perfect example of how your mind could play tricks on you—he'd thought about the fact that the only thing separating him from death was a few inches of steel, and he'd thought about the Merriman estate. It would be in probate for at least a year, but nobody was going to contest anything, and, when it was all sorted out, Laney might well stand to inherit something on the order of a cool million, and he, Theodore R. Cotter, wasn't exactly a piker either, and he imagined himself sitting at his desk—or, maybe by that time, it would be *Carl's* desk—and he'd hear the air raid siren go off, and he'd think: oh, my God, we've got a couple hours at the most before the bombs start to fall, and Laney and the boys don't have anywhere to go because *I wouldn't spend the money.*

Well, he was spending it now. By the time he got done with it, the shelter was going to cost him more than a brand new house, and there were still hundreds of details he had to work out—the exact design of the steel-reinforced concrete walls for one thing, and the ventilation and air filtration system for another, not to mention planning for three months' supply of food and water, and he was going to have to make every single decision on every single detail, and, what with the shitload of stuff Carl wanted from him, when was he going to have time for that?

Ted butted out the last of his smoke, bounded up the steps, hurried through the house where the rest of his family was asleep—gee, it sure must be nice—scurried into the garage, jumped into his car, and fired up the engine. Usually he liked driving to work, but not these days, and he had to remind himself that there weren't a hell of a lot of men in America making the kind of money he was. But money wasn't everything, and he wished he could take some time off. Most of the guys on the board took off the whole month of August, but he couldn't take off even a single day because Carl was getting ready to testify before Senator Estes Kefauver and those other New Deal pinkos, and Ted had to prepare everything Carl might need—all the arguments, all the facts and figures—and he was going to have to be there in Washington, sitting right next to Carl, prompting him, making sure he had lots of ammunition, always saying the right thing.

Carl was going to have to say that even though the Raysburg Steel Corporation charged the same price for steel—right down to the penny—as every other steel producer in the United States, Raysburg Steel's pricing policies really *were* competitive—and no, there certainly had been no collusion involved in arriving at those prices. And Carl would have to insist that Raysburg Steel's profits were not excessively high, that Raysburg Steel needed every dollar it made in order to modernize, that if it didn't modernize, then it didn't stand a sorry hope in hell of remaining competitive. And Carl would have to argue vehemently and cogently that the steel industry had never been and was not now contributing in any way whatsoever to the nasty inflationary spiral that was currently bedeviling the economy. And there was, of course, a grain of truth in all of that—Raysburg Steel *did* need every spare dollar if it wanted to stay in the game—but the rest of it was lies, and Carl would have to tell those lies with a straight face just as though he believed them—which, God knows, maybe he did. But Ted wished that Carl could do the impossible and tell them the plain truth: "Don't you fools understand *anything?* If steel goes down the drain, then the whole rest of the country's going down the drain right along with us!"

Since she'd come back from her mother's funeral, Laney had been spending the greater part of every day in bed. She'd called Patsy; carefully pitching her voice into the tone of someone struggling bravely against a nearly over-whelming burden, she'd said she didn't want to see people for a while—could Patsy please call everyone and tell them?—and so, for the moment, she had nowhere to go and nothing to do, and that's exactly how she wanted it. She'd told Teddy that she simply couldn't *bear* the club, and she'd told Mrs. Warsinski to make *masses* of cold food—chicken and ham and potato salad—so there'd always be something ready at hand in the refrigerator.

She knew that her friends and family would assume she was too torn up to do much of anything, and that's exactly what she wanted them to think. She hadn't told even Teddy what she was really feeling—which was pretty much nothing. Oh, she hated the hole and all the noise that went with it—damn Teddy, anyhow, why hadn't he at least *discussed* it with her before he'd just gone ahead and done it? And, like everyone else, she hated August, but something else was bothering her, something big, and her mother's death might be a good enough excuse for everyone else, but she knew that wasn't really it. She told her-self that when it rained again and cleared the air, she'd get on with her life, but, in the meantime, it was perfectly fine to float along day to day and not do much of anything.

For years, for every possible occasion, Teddy had given her a negligee. When a man buys a negligee, the last thing in the world he's thinking about is whether his wife will enjoy *sleeping* in it, so Laney owned dozens of the insubstantial, lacy, scratchy little things, many of which she'd never worn, but now she seemed to be wearing a new one every night. When she'd wake up around noon, she'd always be feeling fairly rocky, and she'd find herself yet again dressed like some-body's frivolous valentine. Gloria and Mrs. Warsinski knew the routine by now, so Gloria would bring up a tray with a Bromo, a tonic water on ice, and a piece of toast with marmalade. After Laney got the liquids down, she would begin to feel well enough to nibble the toast and smoke a cigarette, and then she'd try to figure out what was bothering her. Once again, she wouldn't be able to put her finger on it.

She'd float off into a strange, dreamy state, and she'd remember the damnedest things: a turquoise green Schiaparelli she'd worn to a dance at Princeton on a night when she'd probably looked the best she'd ever looked in her life—it was a shame Teddy hadn't known her then—and she'd remember other things she'd worn at Vassar, or at Fairhaven, or even when she'd been a child. One thing she had to say about Mother was that she'd always dressed her beautifully.

When she thought about Paris before the war, she couldn't remember much more than the interminable fittings—oh, it seemed a lifetime ago, another world, when even her lingerie had been handmade—and it might be fun to go to Paris again, fat chance of that the way Teddy was about his work, and she couldn't imagine going with Princess Priss, and, besides, she'd never been the kind of woman who enjoyed going places without a man— And she remembered riding around with someone— It had been before the Crash; she couldn't have turned fifteen yet— Oh, what was his name? It was a very prominent name. Not a boy but a real *man*, somebody's brother; he'd been in the first war—and he'd petted her and petted her. Oh, dear God, it's a wonder she hadn't been raped, some of the things she'd done. It had never crossed her mind that a man could be too old for her.

Eventually Laney would get bored with lying in bed floating along with these strange, dreamy, not very nice thoughts, so she'd change into her swimsuit, wander downstairs and try to eat something—some Swiss cheese or a slice of ham—and then it would be time for a drink. There was no point in drinking beer; it just made you bloated. So she'd have a teensy Scotch, but she had to be careful; if Teddy ever knew she was drinking in the daytime, she'd just die. At the last possible moment—about a quarter to six—she'd run upstairs, clean her teeth, gargle with mouthwash, take a shower, throw on something pretty, do her makeup, and arrive downstairs just before he walked through the door, and then they could have a drink *together*. He'd grumble about not going to the club, and she'd sigh and say how hot it was and leave him to think that she was still prostrate with grief.

For the first time in her adult life— Well, it wasn't that she'd lost her interest in sex; it was more that she didn't care one way or the other, but, after all, a man has to have his needs satisfied, so she left it up to him. He was always sound asleep by ten-thirty or eleven, and then she'd creep out of bed. As hot as it was, no part of the house was *cool*, but the recreation room in the basement was the closest thing to it she was likely to get. She'd had Mother's TV put down there, and she'd lie on the couch in the conversation pit and watch anything at all. She hadn't gone through a full case of Johnny Walker yet, but when she did, there was another full case waiting right behind it.

Gloria and Mrs. Warsinski were running the house. Gloria did the shopping, and Mrs. Warsinski did the cooking, and, without discussing it, they shared the housework. Gloria was never able to sleep for much longer than an hour or two in her bed; she always woke knowing she'd had bad dreams but not able to remember them. She slept naked but wrapped up in a cotton sheet like a mummy because, in spite of the screens, several mosquitos always found their way into her room every night.

The deep snarling of the bulldozer, the yelling of the workmen, and the clattering of the fans was all simply too much to bear this morning, and now, to top it off, the brats, down by the pool, seemed to have dedicated themselves to driving her crazy. Gloria could hear them clearly through her window. "Candy ass," Jimmy was intoning. "Candy ass. You're a candy ass—"

"Don't call me that." Bobby was attempting an aggrieved but patient tone that said, "*I* am the older brother; *I* am infinitely more mature than dumb, stupid, infantile you." Gloria knew, even if Bobby didn't, that it was precisely such a tone that was guaranteed to keep Jimmy going forever. "Candy, candy, you're a candy," Jimmy chanted gleefully. "Candy ass. Candy! Candy!"

"Shut up, you little creep!"

"Candy ass. Candy ass. You're nothing but a candy ass. Candy, candy, candy—" Then, from the loud *smack*, Gloria knew that Bobby must have landed Jimmy a good one. One could usually estimate how badly Jimmy had been hurt by how long it took him to start screaming; this morning's prolonged inhalation predicted a howl as fierce as an air raid siren—and, yes, there it was.

"Gloria! Do something, for God's sake!"—and that shrieking, disembodied, off-stage voice was, of course, Gloria's mother flat on her back in bed. I can't stand this, Gloria thought.

She sprang up from her desk, ran downstairs, through the kitchen and down to the pool. Bobby had Jimmy pinned down and was twisting his arm. Now they were both screaming.

"Stop it!" Gloria heard herself shrieking in a shrewish tone exactly like her mother's. "Grow up, for heavens sake!"

The boys instantly shut up, released their grasp on each other, and looked at her with quiet death in their eyes. The moment she'd appeared, she had, as always, become the enemy. "How old are you guys anyway? You're behaving like infants. Knock it off. I mean it. Show a little common courtesy. Mom doesn't feel good. You know that."

"Screw you, bitch," Bobby said, so quietly that his mother wouldn't hear him.

"Go to your room, Robert," Gloria said.

"Who's going to make me?"

I can't stand this, Gloria thought, but she said to him exactly what she'd heard her mother say, and she used exactly the same tone of voice her mother would have used—slow, deliberate, and venomous: "When your father gets home, do you want me to tell him how you've been behaving? Do you want me to tell him *what you just said to me?*"

To her surprise, it worked for Gloria just the way it always did for her mother. Bobby gave her a long, flat stare of concentrated loathing and muttered, "All right, all right, all right, all right—" He stomped off into the house—insofar as one could stomp barefoot—and chanted his way through the kitchen and up the stairs, getting louder as he went: "All right, all right, all right, all right, all right—" Gloria heard her mother shriek "Robert!" He slammed his door so hard the windows rattled. Was he really fifteen?

"Great!" Jimmy hissed at her. "Thanks a whole bunch, Glo. Now who am I supposed to play with? Jeez!"

"Go play with yourself!" Gloria hissed back at him, fully aware that she was employing one of the simpler of Empson's seven types of ambiguity.

For days it had been too hot to eat. Gloria drank a glass of orange juice. She and Mrs. Warsinski exchanged a single, richly communicative glance, and, in that moment, Mrs. Warsinski managed to achieve a remarkable resemblance to one of those Catholic statues—sentimentalized and far too lifelike—of a saint caught in the midst of some messy martyrdom. She'd already begun the tray for Gloria's mother; Gloria finished it, poured the Bromo into a crystal glass, added water from the refrigerator. When she delivered the tray, her mother said not a word—certainly not "thank you." Before she could stop herself, Gloria said what she'd been thinking for days: "You know, Mom, when I go to Columbia, you're going to have to get out of bed, so why don't you start now?"

Her mother gave her a look of utter betrayal and drank her entire Bromo down without pausing for breath. She was wearing a black negligee trimmed in red lace; under the shadowy nylon, her nipples looked as big as demitasse cups and dark as bruises; with an inward shudder, Gloria wondered if she'd get to be that big when she was her mother's age. "Oh, Mom, you know it doesn't do any good just to lie there and think about it."

"I'm not thinking about it." Her mother made a feeble gesture in the direction of the bed table. Gloria handed her the pack of Tareytons and the lighter.

"I'm going downtown," Gloria said, having just decided to do it, "Do you want anything?"

"No."

I can't stand this, Gloria thought. She changed into shorts and a halter top; within minutes, the sides of her halter were soaked with perspiration. She stepped into the hallway and stopped there, oddly reluctant to proceed. The doorway to what used to be her grandmother's bedroom was standing open. Her mother had stripped the room the day of her grandmother's death, had told Mrs. Warsinski's nephew she wanted it painted and papered by the time they got back from Providence, and, for once, he'd done exactly what he'd been told. The room was now what it used to be—a guest room—but Gloria never passed the open door without feeling a dark tide of grief. She hadn't cried since she'd been in Providence; she still wanted to cry, but, as Ken Henderson would have said (why was she thinking about *him?*), given how *rat's-assed horrible* everything was, tears seemed beside the point. She stood listening to the fans. There was one in her bedroom, one in her parent's bedroom, and one at the end of the hall. Downstairs Mrs. Warsinski had every drape closed against the sun.

"HEAT WAVE CONTINUES WITH NO END IN SIGHT," the wretched *Raysburg Times* had proclaimed that morning; the temperature never fell below ninety, the humidity hovered near the saturation point, and the air stubbornly refused to move. As far out as the country club, the sky was a milky haze; downtown, closer to the satanic mills, it was like a thin, white porcelain cup pressing down over the valley, and the only way Gloria could locate the sun was by turning toward the most intensely painful area of the glassy sky, the one into which she could not look directly. The streets shone with an evil, flat, unnatural brilliance, and she couldn't tell whether it was the light or the air that was making her eyes burn. "Hey, Mom," she called out, "maybe I won't go downtown."

Gloria was sure that she wouldn't make a very good existentialist: when she thought of death as the extinction of the human personality, she couldn't hold the idea in her mind for longer than a few seconds. She was still trying to absorb her grandmother's death — absorb the simple fact, known to every conscious person in the world, that someone could, one day, trump your trick with a triumphant flourish and say, "I told you, Gloria, never lead away from an ace!" and the next day could have ceased to exist. If she wanted to think about *her own* death even less than she wanted to think about her grandmother's, she certainly didn't want to think about her own death arriving unannounced, literally falling out of the sky, while thousands of other people died right along with her — yet that's what the hole in her backyard was inviting her to think about.

The first time Gloria had thought about it had been during her first year at Canden High when Mr. Clements had organized the entire school into a civil defense team. During the weekly air raid drills, they'd been taught to duck and cover; they'd been issued metal tags stamped with their names, addresses, and phone numbers to wear on chains around their necks — her father had said they looked exactly like dog tags from the war — and Gloria's had been stamped P for Protestant. She'd worn her tag for several days before the full significance of it had struck her: this is so they can identify *my body*.

The second time she'd thought about it — and had come to the conclusion that it didn't do any good whatsoever to think about it — had been during the spring of her freshman year at Briarville. Hell Week had been over; she and her fellow pledges had been initiated into full membership so the sorority house was *theirs*; they could use the living room or the beau parlour or the rec room — or watch the television. She didn't remember where she'd heard it, but the buzz had been going around the campus: "They're showing the H bomb on the TV.

They're going to show it again." So many girls packed in to see it, some had to stand up in the back of the room. Gloria remembered a lot of giggling, a festive air as though they were about to watch a variety show.

The centerpiece of the government film had been the fireball that had entirely destroyed a Pacific atoll, had dug out a crater extending several hundred feet below sea level. On the TV screen, the fireball flashed into existence, swelled, and swelled further, rose up and lit the night sky like—the simile was inevitable—*noon*. The fireball grew, continued to swell; it seemed to be going on forever. Then, just before the mushroom cloud began to appear, the film froze on the image of the fireball; suddenly superimposed upon it, in a miniature silhouette, was the New York skyline. A voice sounded from the television: "The fireball alone would engulf about one-quarter of the Island of Manhattan." Not a girl in the room spoke or made any sound at all.

After the show was over, the Lambs drifted away in small groups, whispering. Gloria would always remember that no one had dared to talk in a loud voice. She and Susie had walked all the way over to campus and back without speaking. When Susie had finally said, "Oh, Gloria, I wanted to be able to grow up and have children!" it hadn't sounded the least bit melodramatic. Gloria did not think of her father as a stupid man, but she couldn't imagine anything more stupid than building a bomb shelter in the backyard.

Gloria felt incapable of engaging in a genuine conversation and was surprised how easy it was to live at home and at the club without ever engaging in a genuine conversation. She kept her hair up in a high ponytail, wore nothing but bathing suits and no more makeup than lipstick. The pool at the club was always crowded, so she swam at home, once in the morning and once in the afternoon, just as she had during her Britomart summer. She drank gallons of liquid—ice water, iced tea, tonic water, ginger ale, and Coke—but wasn't interested in food; a few mouthfuls of whatever was in the refrigerator seemed to be enough. Her misery was, of course, doing wonders for her figure, and she supposed she should at least be glad about that, but she couldn't make herself care.

All she wanted to do was stop thinking about her grandmother and death and the hole and nuclear war and, most of all, *herself*. She was—she had to keep repeating it—*not going to go crazy*. The appalling voice that woke her by whispering in her ear would, she was sure, go away after she got to Columbia—but, for the moment, she seemed to be stuck with it, so she gave up even trying to sleep at any regular time and let sleep catch her whenever it could.

"Like a dream" had always been one of her favorite similes; in her early diaries it recurred dozens of times. In recent years, she'd been trying to break herself of it—how hackneyed, how clichéd, how downright stupid could you get!—and now she always crossed it out as soon as she'd written it. But, unfortunately, the trip to Providence to bury her grandmother *had* been like a dream; in fact, some of her dreams—the long, detailed, movielike ones—clung to her memory more tenaciously than all but a few of the events during those four dreadful days.

She'd dressed all in black for the funeral—had even worn black stockings and black gloves and a black hat with a veil. She'd bought the ensemble in a shop so expensive that nothing had a price tag on it. She couldn't remember how she'd got to the shop; one of her stupid cousins, probably Lizzy, must have taken her—and she really should stop thinking of them as "my stupid cousins" because they'd been so kind to her they'd made her cry.

Her mother had taken one look at the all-black ensemble and said, "Gloria, you're overdoing it," and she'd said, "Grandmother would have wanted me to look like a lady." The day had been overcast and muggy; she'd suffered agonies in her high-collared, black wool dress and thought it only just. She didn't remember much of the service. She did remember that she hadn't been able to get a line from cummings out of her mind: "gone into what?— like all them kings you read about—"

She probably should have stayed for the reading of the will at her Uncle Edgar's house (it was, after all, part of the ritual), but she'd been getting claustrophobic, or panicked, or *something*—had been using all of her mental energy to talk herself out of the growing conviction that she was about to do something mad and unforgivable like throwing herself onto the floor and howling like a dog, and she'd murmured, "Excuse me. I'm not feeling well. Please don't wait for me," and had drifted—or at least done her best not to look as though she were *fleeing*—out of the room, and out of the house, and once around the lawn, and back into the house through a different door, and down a long hallway, and into the library where she'd come upon the painting of Veronica Isobel and had promptly burst into tears.

Until she'd been confronted by the actual painting, she hadn't realized that she'd been imagining it in a wildly dubious way: her Spanish ancestress wearing a mantilla and a comb in her hair—and what else? Doing the flamenco? She'd also imagined Veronica Isobel corseted to within an inch of her life, but Gloria hadn't gone far enough back in time: she saw a girl near her own age dressed in a thin, loose, flowing, semi-transparent costume that resembled nothing so much as a nylon peignoir; she was wearing with it—of all bizarre things—elbow-length leather gloves. The painting wasn't crude enough to call primitive, but it had something of the naive charm of a primitive. At first glance, it appeared to make a simple enough visual statement—a pretty girl sitting for her portrait—but, the longer Gloria looked at it, the less simple, the more strangely ambiguous, it seemed.

Veronica Isobel appeared to be out of doors; that is, there was a vague impression of greenish-blue foliage behind her—trees or bushes—and a watery stripe that could have been either the sea or a badly painted road, but she was sitting on something resembling a couch or a divan over which folds of thick, murky cloth had been draped, covering it completely except for an exposed curve of—well, plastic hadn't been invented yet, so it was either painted wood or carved marble extending outward at an implausible angle to provide her with a support for one of her slender arms. Her hair was parted in the middle and had been set (how did they set hair in those days?) into perfect ringlets nearly as big around as her wrists. Her filmy gown, gathered with a ribbon just under her obviously unsupported bosom, was rose-petal pink; her gloves were an ashen brown. The painter had put so little detail into the background as to leave it nearly undefined, yet had worked so diligently at rendering Veronica Isobel's gloves that Gloria could make out the outline of several of her fingernails inside them.

Standing next to the divan was a large, hairy, fanciful animal that must have been intended to be a dog, perhaps an Afghan; his ears were perked up, and he was staring intently out of the left side of the frame; the painter had managed to imbue him with a quivering tension as though he were just about to bolt off and vanish into the mysterious shrubbery. Veronica Isobel, however, wore an air of studied calm and was looking directly at the viewer; her hair and eyes had been done in pure lamp black—there was no distinction between pupil and iris—and made to gleam with ivory highlights. She had a pleasantly ovoid face, a long straight nose, eyelids as huge and sensuous as Scheherazade's, and full, slightly parted lips that seemed to have been coated with a deep burgundy lipstick. Gloria's grandmother had said that Veronica Isobel had been painted as dark as a Gypsy; indeed, she had—and, in that cold, olivish brunette, Gloria recognized the tone of her own difficult skin so improbable that it required the most improbable of colors to bring it to life: deep burgundy and rose-petal pink and ashen brown.

In no other way than her coloring did Gloria think she resembled Veronica Isobel; yet that was enough. It was impossible, but it was true; whatever *she* was, Gloria thought, that's what *I* am. When she rejoined the others an hour later, she learned that she'd inherited yet more money she wouldn't be able to spend until her thirty-fifth birthday.

On Friday Gloria felt something change in the atmosphere. She didn't know how else to describe it except by the overwrought metaphor of the very air around her being pinched gradually toward anguish. "Do be an angel, Gloria," her mother had said—still, of course, from flat on her back in her bed—"and pick up all that junk the boys left around in the yard. You know, that's one thing *she* won't do."

How had the wretched creeps actually managed to scatter clothing all over the place? Gloria was picking up jeans, tennis shoes, even underwear—and comic books, pop bottles, partially eaten sandwiches, plates and glasses, knives and forks. She picked up Bobby's bow and leaned it up against the archery butt, collected a dozen arrows and put them back into the quiver, picked up tennis rackets and badminton rackets and baseball bats—and balls, of course; boys and balls went together like— Oh, forget it! She was moving slowly and deliberately. Her bathing suit was as wet as if she'd been in the pool, but she hadn't been in the pool. She had to keep wiping perspiration out of her eyes.

She stopped, looked out at what should simply be a nice view of the apple trees but was now a setting for *the hole*. The bulldozer wasn't doing anything at the moment. The workmen had stripped off their shirts; their bare chests were wet and shiny, and they were moving as slowly as Gloria had been moving. Ordinarily she would have admired a few of them as excellent specimens of the other half of the human species, but it was too hot to admire anything. Then, as Gloria was carrying the brats' soiled clothes through the kitchen, Mrs. Warsinski told her: "The man on the radio says it's going to rain." Oh, so that's what that ominous feeling was? How wonderful.

But, by evening, it still wasn't raining, and the tension in the air was even worse. Gloria was laid out on her bed and had been laid out there for at least an hour. She could hear her parents' voices; they were sitting by the pool. She could hear the ice cubes tinkling in their glasses. Her brothers were down at the club along with all the other country club brats. She should probably eat something, but she couldn't imagine eating anything. It was simply ghastly waiting for rain that might never come, but she couldn't imagine doing anything else.

She woke and didn't remember falling asleep; when she'd last had a thought in her mind, it had been daylight, and now it was dark. She was sure she'd just heard a whispering voice, but, listening, all she could find were the dim locusts: za-ZIZZ, za-ZIZZ, za-ZIZZ, za-ZIZZ, za-ZIZZ. She walked down to the pool.

Looking toward the west, she saw a distant flash bulb go off in the sky. She waited for the thunder—and waited and waited. There was no thunder. Oh, no, she thought, heat lightning. It's never going to rain! She turned back toward the house and saw, through the basement windows, the flickering light of the television set in the rec room. Her mother was watching the late show and drinking. Without bothering to look for her cap, Gloria dived into the pool. She'd only swum two laps when she heard her mother's voice: "Gloria!" She stopped in the shallow end. "Gloria, how inconsiderate can you get! You'll wake your father."

"OK, Mom. Sorry, Mom." I can't stand this, Gloria thought.

Back in her room, she stripped off her bathing suit and, without bothering to dry herself, stretched out on her rug with the fan playing directly on her. Because she wasn't trying to fall asleep—because it never would have occurred to her that she could fall asleep lying on the floor—she fell asleep.

She woke to the ear-splitting sound of the sky cracking apart. Oh, dear God, she thought, the war just started!

The thunder was still reverberating, echoing off the hills; furies were assaulting the house. She heard slamming, crashing, banging from every direction. The rain was driving so hard against her window she was afraid the screen was going to be blown right out of its frame. The papers on her desk were flying away. She rolled to a crouch, leapt up, was struck full in the face by a hissing blast of ice water. She grabbed her window and slammed it down. Someone in the house was running. Her window went sheet-white, and, immediately, thunder pummeled the rooftop, unfolded, and tumbled down the walls. She snatched a dressing gown from her closet and ran out into the hall, stopped, amazed, wondering where to go next, and then shot down the stairs. The thunder was repeating itself at a distance: a-BOOM, a-BOOM, a-BOOM—

Someone was running through the living room. Another bolt of lightning—so close she could have sworn she heard it sizzle—lit the entire first floor, and she saw a brilliant snapshot of her father in the living room attacked by the thickly billowing drapes. He yelled at her, but thunder drowned him out. He tried again, and she heard him: "Get the kitchen!"

The Venetian blinds were waving frantically at her, beating themselves to death. She slammed the windows down, one after the other—*bang, bang, bang*—and saw something blowing across the backyard; it was careening end over end like a runaway Ferris wheel; she didn't have a clue what it was. "I think that's all of them," her father yelled. The house shook and rattled but nothing more seemed to be banging or crashing down. Laughing, he said, "Really something, huh?" and then added, she wasn't sure why, "Your Mom's out like a light." He gave her a wave and trotted up the stairs.

It was crazy, but Gloria had to get outside. She was afraid to try the French doors, so she went out through the basement door, and heard herself yelp as the rain slapped her silly. Her breath caught at the top of her chest and stuck there. She had the terrifying sensation of being *drowned* by rain—this can't be real!—but she covered her face with her hands, panting, and edged forward toward the pool. She didn't know why she was doing it, only that she had to, but it was nothing like what she'd imagined—standing under a cold shower; it was more like facing a battery of fire hoses. The howling deafened her. She was afraid she might actually be blown over. Lightning forked, persisted so long she could see it branch out like the roots of a terrible plant. Thunder exploded directly on the top of her head. Branches ripped from the apple trees went whipping by.

She'd hoped for a ritual of celebration—the heat wave broken, the joy of release—but the rain was hurting her; she felt beaten by it. Terrified, she tried to find something to hold onto. All the lawn furniture had been blown back against the wall of the house. She couldn't breathe right. She panted in tiny gasps. She was freezing to death. She thought she might be crying. "That's enough, Gloria," the secret watcher told her, "now get back into the house!"

She had to lean on the basement door to shut it. She locked it. Water was streaming from her. Her teeth were chattering. Yes, she was crying. It didn't matter. No one could hear her. In the basement shower room, she peeled off her dressing gown, wrung it out, hung it on a hook. She wrapped a towel around her body and another around her hair. She was cold to the bone; her very blood felt cold; how was that possible? And she was enormously tired. She fled back to her bedroom, piled three blankets on her bed, crawled under them and immediately fell asleep.

Gloria woke to a sharp clarity of mind she hadn't known for days. She guessed that she'd been asleep for not much longer than an hour. She got up and opened her window. It was still raining steadily, but the storm had passed. She could hear distant thunder. The temperature must have fallen thirty degrees; her room was cold and clammy. I've got to get out of here, she thought.

She knew if she hesitated for even a moment, she'd talk herself out of it. She opened two suitcases. Into one she threw everything she might need at Susie's: shorts and halter tops, dresses, stockings, underwear, her jewelry box and her cosmetics bag, her tennis shoes and sandals and her favorite patent opera pumps. Would she need a cocktail dress? Probably not, but it wouldn't hurt to have one just in case, so, into another suitcase she squished her midnight blue Traina-Norell and a set of crinolines. Then she put on plain cotton underwear, bobby socks, her charm bracelet, and an old white shirt of her dad's.

After her first visit to Cloverton, she'd bought herself a pair of jeans; she'd thought a modern girl should at least *own* a pair, but she'd worn them maybe twice. She found them on the back of her closet shelf and put them on. She took the shoe trees out of Susie's white cowgirl boots and slipped her feet into them. They were just as comfortable as she remembered.

She checked her purse, and she had seventeen dollars. She helped herself to twenty more out of the cash left for Mrs. Warsinski in the cookie jar in the kitchen. She left a note on the pad by the phone that said: "I've taken the Buick and gone to see Susie for a few days. Don't worry about me. I'll be careful. I'll call you when I get there. Love, Gloria."

She didn't catch up to the full enormity of what she'd done—was doing—until she was driving through the first of the tunnels on the Pennsylvania Turnpike. Girls do not take off, alone, in the middle of the night and drive from Raysburg to Philadelphia, and no explanation—no matter how ingenious, or remorseful, or charged with pathos—would save her. She didn't know what her father would do to her when she got home, but it would certainly be dire, and so she was speeding rapidly toward her own ruin. She could, of course, turn around; if she did it right now, she'd be back by the time he got up to go to work. But she didn't do that. She drove through the tunnel and kept on going.

She could hear the dim mumbling of thunder, see occasional flashes on the horizon, but all she had to face was a hard, methodical rain. There appeared to be no cars on the turnpike, only huge trucks; they passed her in the left-hand lane—monstrous blocks streaming water. They frightened her. She couldn't imagine how anyone could drive as fast as they were going. Whenever they came abreast of her, she eased off on the accelerator, and then, for several ghastly seconds, so much water poured over her that the windshield wipers couldn't clear it; she'd hold her breath, and hold the wheel steady, and trust the wipers to flap the road into view again—and they did, and she would see the truck moving into her lane, watch its red tail lights pulling away, and then, to her surprise, she would still be on the road, still going in a straight line.

She tried to maintain a true sense of herself as a soft, vulnerable animal directing the mechanisms of a steel box down an unknown road—but she couldn't do it. She'd turned on the heater, and she was warm. She'd turned on the radio, and she felt, as she often did in her bed in the middle of the night, that impersonal, mysterious, and genial connection to other people who were awake in the middle of the night. She might as well be at home, listening to the rain and the radio. It was an illusion—dangerously, falsely comforting—but she couldn't shake it: she was driving her bedroom.

What she was doing was crazy, crazy, but it was exhilarating too. Perhaps she was driving into Faerie Lond, and this time her quest had Susie at the end of it. "I'm not as much of a cherry as you thought I was," she said to Susie. "I'll be there in time for breakfast."

They'd never had a chance to talk about what had happened the night before Susie's wedding. It had been truly dreadful, at least much of it had been, but maybe Susie had achieved some distance from it by now—or maybe not. If the roles had been reversed, Gloria would never have wanted to mention it again, but Susie wasn't like that. What had she said on the phone? "I was impossible," she'd said. "I never got a chance to tell you—I mean, really tell you, thanks so much," she'd said, so Gloria must have done at least something right.

When Gloria had gone to Cloverton to help with the final preparations, Susie had been quiet and withdrawn, but Gloria hadn't paid much attention—when you're getting married, you've obviously got a lot on your mind—and, by the time she'd begun to suspect that Susie might be experiencing something far worse than a normal case of jitters, it was the night before the wedding. Susie's brother Steve and his family were sleeping in the guest room, so Gloria and Susie were in Susie's bed. Gloria had come to rely upon her roommate's ability to fall asleep within minutes; she couldn't go to sleep until Susie had gone to sleep, and Susie, most emphatically, was *not* going to sleep; Gloria could sense her wakefulness like a dark, rigid, angular shape in bed with her. "Hey, what's the matter?" she said eventually (it must have been well after midnight by then), "are you nervous?"

"I don't know."

"What are you thinking about?"

"Oh, I don't know— Well, I guess now I'll never be Miss America."

Gloria thought it was a joke, so she laughed, but Susie didn't. "Hey, you're not serious, are you?"

"I don't know. I guess I'm not. I'm still too skinny. Yeah, I probably couldn't even— You know, if I tried again, I probably *still* couldn't win Miss Pennsylvania. But after you're married, you can't— Oh, it's really dumb, huh?"

"You bet. Really dumb. Come on, kid, you're getting married in the morning. Go to sleep."

"OK, OK, but—" and then Susie had to go over a thousand details: the ceremony, the reception in Cloverton, the reception in Briarville. Somebody other than Susie was in charge of everything she was worrying about, and Gloria told her as much.

"Oh, Glo," she said, "I don't know what the heck I'm doing! Why'd I ever let Mom and Dad talk me into being married at Pastor Harris's dumb little church. I feel like such a hypocrite. I haven't set foot in that dumb little church in months. I should of been married in the Baptist church in Briarville. That's my church now."

"You're doing it for your parents—your family. That's what you said."

"Yeah, that's right."

"It's going to be a lovely wedding. Just stop worrying. You've really got to get some sleep."

"A lovely, wedding. Yeah, sure. I ought to get married in my majorette uniform. That's the only reason he likes me."

"Oh, come on. That's crazy."

"You think I'm kidding? Don got himself a majorette. Every boy's dream. Wowee. Big deal. But how long's that going to last? And when the rose-colored glasses drop off, oh, is he ever going to be disappointed in me! He's going to think, why'd I ever marry that dumb, little blonde? And now I'm stuck with her."

"Susie, what are you talking about? He really loves you. I never saw a boy so in love."

"Well, he loves me *right now*."

"Do you love him?"

"Oh, sure. You know I do."

"Then it's all going to work out. Really, it is."

"Yeah, I guess so."

"Are you going to go to sleep? Please."

"OK, OK."

Susie turned over onto her side, pulled a bit of the blanket around her, but then, after a few minutes, said, in an alert, cheery, conversational voice: "You know, Rickie doesn't believe in hell. Did I ever tell you that?"

"Oh, for crying out loud!"

"I'm sorry. I just can't stop thinking about it. Rickie really doesn't believe in hell. He told me he saw hell over there in Korea. And he said if Jesus saw what they were doing in Korea, he wouldn't of been thinking about who he was going to damn to hell, he would of just stood there and cried, the way, you know, he did when he heard Lazarus was dead. So Rickie says we've got all the hell we need right here on earth. Gloria? What do *you* believe?"

Gloria had almost been asleep. She was so tired it was making her sick to her stomach, but she resigned herself to talking about hell—she hoped for not longer than a few more minutes. "I guess I believe something like what your brother believes."

"Yeah, I thought you'd say that— Oh, Gloria, sometimes I wish I'd never gone to college!"

Without warning, Susie threw off the covers, scrambled out of bed, and lit the overhead light. The sudden brightness seemed to have startled her, or maybe it was the pinkness of the room. (At least that's what would have startled Gloria; she forgot, from time to time, how pink it was.) Susie was caught, stopped, with her hand still on the light switch. Gloria couldn't read her expression, but, in another context, it might have been called "surprised." Susie slowly let her hand drop away, crossed the room and sat down in the only chair. Now she had no expression on her face at all. Gloria sighed and sat up in bed. Even the blankets were pink.

"I'm sorry," Susie said. "I just can't go to sleep. What time is it anyway? I just keep thinking about what Pastor Harris told us about hell. I can't help thinking, what if I'm going to be damned to hell for all eternity? And I keep thinking about what he told us—about what it feels like to burn your finger or something—and in hell it's *all of you*, all of your muscles and even down in your bones, just sizzling away like a pork chop, burning up forever and ever and ever and you can't get even a single little drop of water."

"Do you really believe that?"

"It's in the Bible."

"Well, maybe what's in the Bible is a metaphor."

"That's what you *always* say. I *have* thought about it, Glo. If you start saying, *this* is a metaphor, and *that's* a metaphor, then where do you stop? Pretty soon you don't know what's true anymore, and then where are you?"

"Well, I guess you might as well be a Presbyterian."

Susie didn't laugh. She didn't respond at all. She'd drawn one leg up onto the chair and had wrapped her arms around it; she sat, her chin on her knee. She'd turned away from Gloria and was staring in the direction of the book-case where her trophies were displayed.

"Suse, come on. What's the matter with you?"

"I don't know."

"Sure you do."

"It's hard for me to talk."

That was strange. Now what was Gloria supposed to say? She was still searching her mind when Susie said, "One of the psalms— I don't know if— 'Thou hast laid me in the lowest pit, in darkness, in the deeps.' You remember that psalm? I never knew what that meant before."

Susie had turned to look directly at Gloria. Again, she seemed to have sur-prised herself. Now she blinked several times, sprang to her feet, walked across the room, turned and walked back. She draped one foot over the back of a chair, bent forward, stretching. She stretched the other leg. Then she fell back into the chair and sat in it as though she'd never moved at all.

"What do you mean 'in the lowest pit?' What's the matter with you?"

"Oh, I don't know."

Gloria was getting exasperated. "Come on! You've got to know something."

Susie must have heard the anger in Gloria's voice because her own voice was just as angry: "All that poetry stuff you and Don talk about—I don't understand any of it. He tries to talk to me about it, and— Someday he's gonna wake up and say, 'Oh, what did I do? I married a dumbass little baton twirler without a brain in her head—just 'cause she's pretty. What a big mistake. I guess I better try it again with somebody else.' But divorce is a sin. It's right there in the Bible clear as any-thing. It's so clear I don't see how anybody can even argue with it. And if he divorces me, it'll be my fault, and I'll be the one who led him into sin."

"That's the most ridiculous thing I ever heard of."

"Oh, yeah? Why's it ridiculous?"

"Because it just is! You're not responsible for Don's decisions."

"Yeah, right. I'm not my brother's keeper—or my husband's either. Yeah, right. Saint Susie, the model Christian girl. Boy, is that ever a joke!"

Gloria was so angry all she could imagine doing was leaping out of bed, grab-bing Susie, and shaking her. She waited until she was sure she could control her voice and said, "What on earth are you talking about?"

"Oh, I don't know."

"If you say that again, I swear I'm going to kill you."

Gloria waited. Susie said nothing. Gloria desperately wanted to be a good friend and a good sister; she wanted to be able to say the right things so Susie would feel better and go to sleep and get up tomorrow and get married the way she was supposed to. Susie had invited every girl in the house, and at least half of them were coming: twenty-some Lambs driving over from Briarville. And all Susie's relatives would be there and at least a dozen people from Don's family. And everything would be just fine—except, possibly, the bride. And if the bride wasn't fine, it would be Gloria's fault.

"Hey, you jerk," she said, "listen to me. You're not a dumbass little baton twirler without a brain in your head. You're the farthest thing from it. You're one of the most complex and interesting people I've ever met. Don's not going to be disappointed in you. For the whole rest of his life he's going to be amazed that he's married to somebody as wonderful as you."

Susie said nothing. Oh, help, Gloria thought. "Just wait," the secret watcher told her, "she'll say something eventually," so Gloria sat on Susie's bed and watched Susie sitting on a chair. After a while she decided to try a different approach. "Susie, this is ridiculous. You're being really self-indulgent. There are all these people depending on you."

"You think I don't know that?"

"I'm just trying to help."

"I know you are. I'm sorry." Susie squeezed her arms tight around her bent leg, pressed her mouth against her knee; her shoulders began to shake.

"What *is* it?" Gloria said.

Susie looked up. She was sobbing so hard her words came out in short gasps. "Rickie was right! I did think I was better than Tommie Jean— *I* didn't get in trouble. *I* was a good girl— *I* was going to find her and bring her back to the fold— Oh, I'm such a hypocrite! I'm ten times worse than she ever was. Jesus was right there with her when those boys were doing those things to her—and then the whole world was against her, and nobody'd stand up for her, and *I* wouldn't stand up for her—but Jesus never left her side—and who was I to think I was better than she was? And now I'm getting punished for my sin."

"Sin? For what sin? For your pride? Come on, it's not—"

"No, no, not just for the sin of pride."

Susie stopped crying as abruptly as she'd begun. She took a deep breath. "Don and I went all the way."

Something in Gloria wanted to laugh, but the anguished expression on Susie's face made that impossible. "I'm sorry, Gloria. Oh, you must be so disappointed in me."

"No, I'm not. Listen, Susie, it isn't—"

"We only did it once. I could of stopped him. I knew it was a sin. But I didn't stop him. I let him do it. You know what? When he saw me with all my clothes off? He cried. Yeah, he really did. Because I was so beautiful. That's what he said. And so I let him do it."

Oh, Gloria thought, so that's it—something as simple as that. She should have guessed it would be something as simple as that. From her point of view, it wasn't a sin at all—wasn't even close to being a sin—but her point of view didn't count. She had to say something that would make sense to Susie. "Honey, listen to me." Gloria felt as though she were speaking to a child. "God will forgive you. You *know* God will forgive you. What's that scripture you quoted to me? God didn't come into the world to condemn the world—"

"Yeah," Susie said in the same flat, dead voice, "John three, seventeen: 'For God sent not his Son into the world to condemn the world; but that the world through him might be saved.' But in order to be saved, you have to repent. *And I'm not sorry.*"

"Oh, come on. Sure you are. I never saw anybody so sorry."

"Yeah? I guess I am. But I don't know. I don't know if I'm sorry *enough*. Oh, Gloria, I never felt so lost. I've got to go into that dumb little church in my white dress— Oh, everybody's being so nice to me! If they only knew. My Mom and Aunt Ruth made that dress by hand, every stitch of it. And I've got to go in there and— Oh, I'm gonna feel like such a hypocrite. I'm a million times worse than Tommie Jean ever was. When she started sleeping with that guy, she didn't know she was committing a sin, but I knew it. I lay there and I thought, if I let him do it, I'm committing a sin, and then I let him do it. And I've got to go in there in that white dress and pretend I'm something I'm not—and everybody's going to think I'm a nice girl, but I'm not a nice girl—*a model Christian girl*. Oh, I feel so awful! And— I don't know, I just don't know how I can walk in there tomorrow and get married. I just keep thinking that nothing can come from sin but more sin."

Now Gloria felt like a hypocrite. Why hadn't she ever told Susie about Ken? She considered telling her now but then thought better of it; the last thing Susie needed to hear at the moment was Gloria's confession. She was having enough trouble making her own confession. "Susie," Gloria said, "listen to me. You've got to rely on your faith, OK? If you pray to God, He'll forgive you. You know He will."

Susie closed her eyes. Tears began to stream out from under the closed lids. "I can't. I can't pray. I've tried and tried and tried. Ever since I did it, I've tried to pray, but I just can't. Oh, Gloria, I'm afraid. I guess I must of committed the sin against the Holy Ghost—the one you can't get forgiven for."

For the first time since she'd known her, Gloria thought that there was something in Susie's religion that was stupid, and pig-headed, and even downright destructive.

"I'm afraid," Susie said again. She'd stopped crying, and she spoke in a low, dead voice. "I never thought this would happen to me. I've always been able to pray, but now— I just can't find God anymore."

Gloria approached Susie carefully, slowly, knelt next to the chair and took her hands. They were cold and wet. "Oh, sweetheart," she said.

"I don't know what to do. I'm so lost. Please help me."

Gloria felt lost too. She realized that she'd come to rely on more than Susie's ability to fall asleep the instant she hit the bed; she'd always relied on Susie's faith — that's what it was, she supposed, that made Susie's presence in the world seem so much more substantial, so less problematical, than her own — and she'd felt toward her something of what she'd felt, when she'd been nine, toward Patty, her beloved camp counselor: a complex emotion akin to hero worship. But what was she supposed to do, now that Susie wasn't Britomart and neither was she? "I'll do anything for you," she said. "You know that. What do you want me to do?"

Susie opened her eyes and looked into Gloria's eyes. "Pray for me."

"Of course I'll pray for you," Gloria said automatically. Then it struck her that Susie didn't mean *sometime*, she meant *right now*. And she didn't mean for Gloria to go off in the privacy of her mind and have some nice thoughts about her; she wanted Gloria to do what they did in Susie's church: get down on her knees and *pray* for her — out loud and for real.

How could she possibly do that when she didn't believe in the God that Susie did? But she was already kneeling. All she had to do was find some words to say. What words? Words she believed in.

It's not fair to do this to me, she thought; this is worse than the Trial of the Three Questions. Her heart was hammering in her throat, and her mouth had gone dry, and she could feel herself trembling. Surely Susie, who was holding her hands, must feel it too. But, unfair or not, she had to try. She closed her eyes and prayed silently to her obscure God: "Help me. Tell me what to say."

Then, as though her prayer had been answered the moment she'd asked it, she knew what to say. It was an utterly crazy idea, but it felt right too. Susie was so immersed in the King James, she might be able to follow the Tudor English, and it certainly had all the right sentiments; as with many of Wyatt's poems, Gloria had memorized it, could have written it out, complete with the archaic spelling, but could she recite it with conviction? She'd have to change Wyatt's first person to third for Susie. She'd have to say it slowly, with modern pronunciation, so Susie could understand it. She'd have to believe in every word of it.

She released Susie's hands. She clasped her hands and bowed her head. She waited until Susie knelt down next to her. "Dear Lord," she said, "I am praying to you on behalf of your servant, Susan Jane Steibel."

Gloria was shaking so hard she expected her teeth to start chattering at any moment. She risked a glance, saw that Susie's eyes were firmly shut, that her interlinked fingers were clenched so tightly their tips were turning red around the nails, and that image flooded Gloria with such love and pity it was all she could do not to burst into tears. She took a deep breath, and then another one, sure that what she was about to emit would be a piteous squawk, but, to her surprise, her voice rang out firmly:

> "O Lord, since in her mouth thy mighty name
>   Suffereth itself her Lord to name and call,
>   Here hath her heart hope taken by the same,
>
> "That the repentance which she has, and shall,
>   May at thy hand seek mercy as the thing,
>   Only comfort of wretched sinners all."

Gloria felt a growing sense of rightness—and it was getting easier as she went along, as she sank into the language and allowed it to carry her. But then, darting ahead in her mind, she realized that the transformation of the first person pronouns would soon kill the end rhyme. But that was OK. In fact, she didn't have to recite the entire psalm—for she'd found, suddenly, the perfect place to end it. What she was doing required all of her mental energy—it was like an excruciatingly complex juggling act—yet, at the same time, she felt the full, measured impact of every word:

> "O Lord, she dreads, and that she did not dread
>   She her repents, and evermore desires
>
> "Thee, thee to dread. She opens here and spreads
>   Her fault to thee; but thou, for thy goodness,
>   Measure it not in largeness nor in breadth,
>
> "Punish it not as asketh the greatness
>   Of thy furor, provoked by her offence.
>   Temper, O Lord, the harm of her excess
>
> "With mending will that she for recompense
>   Prepares again, and rather pity her
>   For she is weak and clean without defence."

Gloria finished with the standard formula, "I ask this in the name of the Father, and of the Son, and of the Holy Ghost. Amen."

"Amen," Susie said.

And Gloria added silently, praying to her own God: "Please help Susie, and please forgive me if I've done anything wrong in saying Wyatt's psalm for her—

and in praying to the Christian Trinity in which I'm not sure I believe. Amen."

When Gloria looked at Susie, she saw that Susie was already looking at her with huge, grave eyes. Susie stood up, turned off the overhead light. Gloria was so exhausted, she couldn't make herself stand up. Susie held out a hand to her; Gloria took it and allowed Susie to lead her to bed. Susie slipped under the covers and held them up; Gloria lay down beside her. Within minutes Susie was asleep.

Susie's mom hauled them out of bed when the first carload of Lambs arrived. Gloria kept waiting to get a chance to be alone with Susie—even a minute or two would have been enough—but there was simply too much going on. While Gloria was sponging the translucent ivory foundation onto Susie's translucent ivory face, Susie looked directly into her eyes and said, "I'm OK," and Gloria had to content herself with that. Susie indeed did seem to be OK, although she wasn't talking at all.

One could always depend upon sorority girls to know how to organize things; the Lambs had struck committees to handle every detail of the wedding. The bridesmaids were wearing pale pastels, princess length, to set off Susie's classic white wedding dress; Gloria had suggested that they have matching gloves, but only she and Marnie McIver had bothered, and all the rest wore white shorties. Gloria had bought her gloves first and then the dress to match; it hadn't been easy to find the finest quality French kid in exactly the right style and the right pale pale *pale* blue in a 6, and she was so pleased with her baby-blue gloves, she wore them most of the day.

Susie's wedding was perfection itself—everybody said so. Susie had never looked more beautiful, and Gloria wasn't the only one in the church who cried. Nobody could have asked for a nicer day; it was clear but not too hot. At one point, Gloria saw that Susie's mom had walked away to admire things from afar, so Gloria joined her to survey the food-laden picnic tables, the guests in their finery milling about in the lovely June sunshine, the little country church in the background. At that distance, Susie and Don looked exactly like the small figures on the top of their own wedding cake. "Oh," Mrs. Steibel said, "it's as pretty as a picture," and Gloria had to agree.

The toasts to the bride and groom had, of course, been postponed until later in the day when the wedding party reconvened at the Briarville Country Club for what Rick Steibel was calling "the heathens' reception." Gloria dutifully drank champagne after each toast and quickly realized that she shouldn't have done it. She was running on far too little sleep, and she hadn't eaten much of anything; the champagne was only making her feel worse. All she wanted to do was get back to the Delta Lambda house and crawl into bed. Susie had danced with Don, and then with her dad, and then with Don's dad, but she was not dancing at the moment, and, as Gloria began to walk toward her, she saw Susie glance in her direction and detach herself from the crowd around her. She caught Gloria's hands and led her away into a corner.

"I haven't had a chance to— I just wanted to— Oh, I'm going to cry—"

"Me too." They stood, holding onto each other's hands, neither of them, for a moment, able to speak.

"Let's not cry, OK?" Susie said.

"OK." Gloria looked away. If you have to, she told herself, you can always recite the multiplication tables.

"Where'd you learn that old prayer you prayed for me?" she heard Susie asking her.

"It's Wyatt. You know, the guy I wrote my honors thesis on. It's one of his psalms."

"Will you write it out for me sometime?"

"Sure."

"When Don and I get our own place— You'll have to— Oh, I really am going to cry."

"Take a deep breath."

Susie took a deep breath. "Are you OK?" Gloria said. "I mean really really?"

"Oh, yeah. I'm wonderful. Really really. I'm so happy. Oh, Gloria, God bless you and keep you always."

Gloria's eyes flooded.

"You OK, sugar?" Susie said.

Gloria laughed. "Sugar—" she said, but, whatever it was she'd thought she was going to say after that, she couldn't manage. Susie squeezed her hands. She squeezed back. They smiled. Susie turned and walked back toward the dance floor, and Gloria walked toward the doors that led to the terrace.

Gloria wanted to escape, to be alone for a moment, but there were people everywhere. She was passing Rick Steibel and his current girlfriend; Gloria had been introduced to the girl but hadn't made any effort to remember her name, had dismissed her as of no consequence—just a cute country girl, probably just out of high school, who thinks getting dressed up for a wedding requires super-high heels—and, exhausted, still working hard at stopping herself from crying, Gloria thought, I can't go on like this. A truly gracious person would have remembered the girl's name.

She gave Rick and the girl her warmest smile. They smiled back, and, thank heaven, didn't seem to want to chat, so she kept on walking. Now she was outside where she'd wanted to be, and the late afternoon light pouring down over the golf course was so exquisite—so full and rich and pink and golden—she wasn't sure she could bear it. "Breathe," the secret watcher told her, and she breathed.

The band was playing, and people were laughing and talking. One of the voices behind her was Rolland's. Give me a minute, please, she thought; can't I, please, just be alone for a minute? She was trying to imagine her life without Susie in it, and she couldn't—but she didn't have any choice. She should have seen it coming; maybe she *had* seen it coming, but, as she so often did, hadn't paid any attention. She should be happy for Susie. Every girl wants to get married; it's every girl's dream; everybody knows that. And everybody knows—or should know—that when your best girlfriend gets married, she vanishes out of your life. Even if she doesn't vanish entirely, nothing will ever be the same as it was before, and *everybody knows that*, so why was she feeling so terrible?

Without looking to see, she was aware that Rolland had come to rest next to her. He was leaning on the balustrade next to her. It was fitting, she supposed, that she should spend her last night in Briarville with Rolland at the Briarville Country Club where they'd spent so many other nights. "Hey, what a terrific wedding," he said. "Wasn't it beautiful?"

"It sure was," she said. He'd brought her another glass of champagne she didn't want. She took it. "Thank you, you sweet boy."

He lit a cigarette. She should, she thought, take her gloves off. Leaving them on any longer would be pretentious, but she was sick of worrying about what was or wasn't pretentious, and, besides, anyone who cared about such things would have to be just as snotty and bitchy as she herself was, and anybody like that could simply go to hell, so she left them on. She *really* didn't want the champagne, but she drank some of it.

She supposed she would have to say something. It didn't much matter what it was. "Oh, yes," she said, "it was a beautiful wedding, all right. A beautiful, beautiful wedding."

"Ours is going to be just as beautiful, honey."

The automatic response would have been "of course it is" or something like that, but she couldn't make the words come out. If she drank any more on an empty stomach, she was probably going to throw up.

"Are you still thinking about September?" he said.

Oh, had she *ever* been thinking about September? "We can't get married this year, honey," she said quietly before she had a chance to stop herself.

The silence lasted so long she was beginning to wonder if he'd heard her. Then she glanced over at him and saw that, yes, he certainly had heard her. "What did you just say to me?" he asked, his voice hardly louder than a whisper.

Now was the time to backtrack, to equivocate, to say something sweet and flirtatious—some dumb, girlish remark that would save everything—but, oh, she was tired. "I'm sorry, honey. We can't get married this year."

He'd never yelled at her before, not once in all the time they'd been going together, but he yelled at her now: "When the hell'd you decide *that*! Jesus,

Gloria, it's just not fair, you know? It's just not. How the hell long you expect me to wait for you anyhow?"

Gloria drove steadily eastward over the Pennsylvania Turnpike because there wasn't much of anything else she could do. The rain had stopped; she was driving into the rising sun, and the glare off the wet highway was dreadful. She had sunglasses in her purse—or at least she was pretty sure she did—but, in order to put them on, she'd have to pull over, and she was terrified of stopping on the turnpike. There were even more of the gigantic trucks on the road now; they continued to pass her every few minutes. She had a fierce headache. She was sick with hunger. The back of her neck was knotting up. There was no getting around it: she felt like hell. She could sleep now—oh, joyfully, easily!—but she was stuck on the turnpike. Afraid of falling asleep at the wheel, she turned the radio up loud, rolled down her window, and drove the way Susie did—with one arm draped over the door and the wind hitting her in the face.

It didn't make the least bit of sense to get off the turnpike and make a long meandering detour over miles of two-lane country roads just so she could pass through Briarville. So what if she'd never gone to Philly except from Briarville? What was she, a laboratory rat? All she'd have to do was stay on the turnpike and eventually signs would appear. They'd surely have big signs that would say "Philadelphia"—so everything would be simple, but then, when she saw the familiar turn-off to Briarville, she took it without a moment's hesitation and felt an enormous sense of relief.

Once she was off the turnpike, she was delighted to see, just as she'd known she would, acres and acres of cows. She pulled over, turned off the engine, and got out of the car. The sun hadn't yet burned off the rain, and the fields looked freshly washed. She took a dozen deep breaths. For the last few weeks, the Ohio Valley had smelled like the inside of a rusty DDT can, but now she smelled hay and earth and cows and last night's rain—how wonderful! She'd just added several hours to her trip, but she didn't care. She had, without planning it, even dressed for the occasion. Enjoying Susie's boots, both the look and the feel of them, she strode up and down by the car—to work the kinks out, as her father would have said. She thought about how strange it was: she was the furthest thing from a country girl, yet she was absurdly happy to be back in the country.

Her moment of euphoria didn't last longer than a few minutes. By the time she got to the Delta Lambda house, fatigue had reduced her mind to a jumble of disconnected fragments. There were, luckily (and strangely), no cars on the street, so she parked at the foot of the front steps. She bounded up to the door, tried it, found it locked, couldn't believe it, pushed on it, rattled the handle, struck the door once with her fist, hurt herself and burst into tears. Stupid girl, she thought; stupid *stupid* girl. The house, as she knew perfectly well, was closed for the summer. Mrs. Donner was visiting her daughter in Cincinnati. Gloria felt as though she'd just walked into one of her own nightmares; it was eight o'clock in the morning, and she was utterly alone in an abandoned world.

There was, now, nowhere else to go, so she went there. Grammy Cotter was shocked to see her: "Good Lord, almighty, I simply don't believe it. Jimmy! Look who's here. It's Gloria come to visit us— Is your father with you?" And so Gloria had to explain that, no, her father wasn't with her, and she made an attempt to be a little bit on the vague side about how she'd got to Briarville, but her mother's station wagon with its West Virginia plates wasn't exactly unobtrusive, parked as it was right outside the living room window. She heard herself chattering away and was so exhausted she couldn't keep track of anything she was saying.

Was she hungry? "Well, Grammy, it sure is nice of you to ask, and, yes, now that you mention it—" so two slices of bread were slapped into the old-fashioned toaster, and the big cast iron skillet came down from its hook, and a couple of eggs went sizzling into it. The food hit Gloria like a knock-out punch. "Would you mind if I slept awhile?" she asked in a bright, chirrupy voice and saw her grandparents exchange a dark look. "I'll have to put some clean sheets on," Grammy said.

"Oh, no, you don't have to do that."

"Don't be silly, honey, of course I do."

The moment Grammy left her alone in her old bedroom, Gloria stripped herself naked and slipped between the stiff sheets. The Briarville pennant had been taken down, and the old, blonde doll with her cretinous blue eyes was no longer staring at her from a shelf, but the pink woodwork and the Victorian valentine wallpaper were still the same, and Gloria remembered her freshman year before she'd pledged Lamb—remembered lying there, staring up at the apex where the sloping walls met, listening to the rain slamming the storm windows, thinking: this is *my father's* bed; I wonder if he was anywhere near as miserable as I am. She closed her eyes to shut it all out, and, for a moment, she was back on the Pennsylvania Turnpike, but she shut that out too and, gratefully, allowed herself to be blotted out.

Gloria woke, fully alert, and knew at once exactly where she was and how she'd got there. She also knew that an unfamiliar sound had just awakened her, but she didn't know what it might have been; all she could hear were the pigeons in the eaves. It was early in the afternoon. She didn't feel rested, but she was certainly in better shape than if she hadn't slept at all, and then she thought: *I've got to get out of here.* It was more than merely wanting to get back on the road to Philly. Her need to get out of her grandparents' house was so intense it was close to panic.

She found Grammy and Gramps sitting at the kitchen table drinking iced tea. The newspaper was spread out between them, but they weren't reading it. They wore the look of long-suffering folk who have nothing to do but wait. "You're to call your father the minute you get up," Grammy said. "He wanted me to wake you, but I wouldn't. I said, 'That poor girl needs her rest.' I said, 'You should have seen her, Teddy. Dead on her feet.' But the minute you wake up, he said you were to call him. The very minute. There's the phone."

"Oh," Gloria said, "you called him."

"Of course I called him, Gloria. I wasn't born yesterday."

Oh, great, Gloria thought. She picked up the phone and told the operator she was calling collect. Her father's voice sounded like the machine gun fire in a World War Two movie: "*I told you* you could go to Philly. All you had to do was ask. You could have flown. You could have taken the train. What the hell's the matter with you?"

It was actually a good thing he was yelling at her; it meant that he was really angry but not as angry as if he were talking in the slow, quiet, deliberate, utterly reasonable voice that always made her blood run cold. She waited, knowing that he'd eventually calm down and give her a chance to say something back. She heard: "crazy, irresponsible, selfish." She heard: "spoiled rotten." He was going to fly to Briarville, he said, and drive her home.

"Oh, come on, Daddy. You don't need to do that. You'd waste the whole day—"

She was—she gathered from the next rapid burst of fire—in no position even to have an opinion; when he got her home, he was going to lock her in her room and throw away the key. In the next pause, she said what she knew she had to say if she wanted to get anywhere at all with him: "Oh, Daddy, I'm *so* sorry. I can't begin to tell you how sorry I am," and she spun a sad tale of a scary thunderstorm and an awful nightmare and crazy, thoughtless impulses. She couldn't very well refer to herself as a silly, irrational girl, but she gave him lots of hints so he could see her that way and, therefore, forgive her—just the way men are supposed to forgive girls when they've been outrageously, inscrutably feminine.

She could hear that he was calming down, but he was still saying he was going to fly over. "There's no airport in Briarville," she said, "or anywhere near Briarville. You know that, Daddy."

"I'll fly to Philly and take a cab over—" And that, of course, was so absurd that even *he* knew it was absurd—she could hear it in his voice. "Oh, Daddy, for heaven's sake, I got here on my own, I can get back on my own."

Throughout all of this, a demonic plan had been solidifying in her mind: she was *still* going to Philadelphia. "Look, Dad, I'm really tired. Even if I left right now, I wouldn't be home till way *after dark*. I just *hate* being on the turnpike *in the dark*. And seeing as I'm already here— There's some girls here I'd like to see. I'll stay at the sorority house tonight. I'll be perfectly safe. Come on, we've driven it together a million times. I'll stop at the Ho-Jo's where we always stop. I'll take my time—"

It would have been utterly churlish of Gloria not to stay for at least a few minutes longer to chat with Grammy and Gramps, so she'd done that, but now she was driving away. She still couldn't quite believe it: she was on her way to Philly, *free!* She had an inkling of what Ken Henderson must have felt when he'd jumped into his pickup truck and driven to Washington to see Ezra Pound; she could go anywhere, do anything, and nobody could tell her not to, and she was elated, euphoric, exhilarated— Wow, how many more words could she find that started with E? OK, how about ebullient, ecstatic, enchanted, excited, exuberant— "Stop it, Gloria," the secret watcher said.

Because she was a geographical idiot, she was driving back to the Delta Lambda house; she was sure that if she started from there, just as she and Susie had always done, she would remember the route Susie had always taken. She was feeling daring and naughty, just as she used to, but the times before when she'd lied—signed out for Cloverton and then had gone to Philadelphia—she'd been with Susie. Now she was alone.

After a moment's reflection, she decided that, this time, she was just about as alone as she could get, because no one—not a soul in the entire universe—knew where she really was. It was fun and exciting but also somewhat frightening.

Oh, but she could go anywhere—walk into a diner, for instance, and there would be *no one with her,* and so she wouldn't have to act in any particular way. And none of the other customers, and none of the people who worked in the diner, would know her. They wouldn't look at her and think: there's Ted and Laney Cotter's daughter Gloria. They wouldn't think: there's Gloria, the president of Delta Lambda, or there's Gloria who's always on the Dean's List, or there's Gloria, the May Queen. They'd see a dark girl in a white shirt, and jeans, and cowgirl boots, and they'd probably think: I bet she's from around here somewhere. She imagined the waitress—a nice girl from around here somewhere— stopping to chat and asking, "You from around here?" and she imagined answering, "Oh, yeah, I'm from Cloverton. It's just a bend in the road with a gas station—and my dad owns the gas station." And she imagined the waitress saying, "Hi, I'm Linda," and she could say, "Hi, I'm Susan Jane." But why stop there? She could say, "Hi, I'm Veronica Isobel—" Or, for that matter, she could say she was *anybody.*

She drove past the Delta Lambda house and down to the end of Sorority Row. Where Susie always turned left, she turned left, and then, as she proceeded along Main toward Washington, she discovered that the very thing she'd been trying to avoid had slithered—mysteriously and nastily—into her mind: the

thought that this time she'd gone too far, had allowed herself no way back—
and, whoops, here were the same old symptoms: her mouth was going dry, her
heartbeat was speeding up—

"Come on, Gloria," the secret watcher told her, "you don't have to do this.
Nothing bad is happening to you. Take a deep breath. That's right. No, don't
think about it. You don't have to go fast. Just drive straight ahead until you're
off campus."

She drove slowly down Washington Street. One eight is eight, she chanted in
her mind, two eights are sixteen, three eights are twenty-four, four eights— No,
this is ridiculous— She pulled over, turned off the engine, and buried her face
in her hands. She was shaking so hard her teeth were chattering. She'd get into
Philly around four-thirty or five, and then how was she going to find her way to
the University district? And, wait a minute—shouldn't she have stopped somewhere and bought gas? And shouldn't she have called Susie? What if, for some
reason, Susie and Don were back at his parents' place? Maybe they'd been invited
there for dinner. She couldn't possibly find Merion. But what if she did find Susie?
They'd probably stay up half the night yacking, and then, with hardly any sleep,
she'd have to drive all the way back from Philadelphia to Raysburg.

"OK," the secret watcher said, "it's not the end of the world if you can't
drive to Philadelphia. Just go back to your grandparents' and say that you'd forgotten that the Delta Lambda house was closed for the summer." How utterly
ignominious, she thought. But the moment she'd decided that she wasn't necessarily going to Philadelphia, she began to feel better. She turned off Washington onto College and drove toward the center of campus; she'd never been
there in August, and she was amazed at how deserted it was.

She stopped at the gas station on Main—and a darned good thing too; she'd
been running on empty—and then turned and drove west toward the creek. Her
moment of panic had fallen away; now she wasn't feeling much of anything,
and that was a relief. She would, she supposed, end up back at her grandparents' house, but she was in no particular hurry to get there. Following the
creek, she took the little road that led off into the woods.

It didn't occur to her that she could call on Professor Bolton until she saw
his house. Oh, but he was probably out of town, visiting some famous poet or
scholar; maybe he was in New York or over in England. Every September he'd
always come back with wonderful stories of the people he'd seen over the
summer. "As I was remarking to Lionel—" he'd say, or "when I was having lunch
with Wystan—" Then she saw his little Nash Rambler, and her reaction took
her entirely by surprise: she was so glad to see that dumb, little blue car that
her eyes stung. She parked next to it.

She never would have thought of Professor Bolton as a gardener, but there
were the obvious proofs that he was one: flowers her mother had always called

"common"—marigolds, nasturtiums, petunias, daisies, foxgloves—and a thorny, unkempt profusion of rose bushes, many of them in bloom. The slanting after-noon sunlight was stretched out through the hoary trees by the creek into long golden strands. No one, apparently, picked the roses; many had gone big and blowsy, were shedding their petals; the sun struck them at precisely the right angle to melt their pinks and reds and yellows into incandescence against the deep green moss and ivy spread out everywhere beneath them. She could hear the creek running and the hum of bees and, from the house, faint music. As though afraid of breaking something delicate, she approached cautiously, nearly on tiptoe.

She mounted the steps that led to the front door which opened—as she remem-bered clearly from the only time she'd been there—into a hall leading into the dim, fusty parlour. The music proved to be an old, scratchy record of a fox trot—mechanically stiff and maniacally cheerful—that sounded as though it might have been recorded in 1910. Gloria hesitated. Maybe he wouldn't want to be disturbed. She could always sneak back down the stairs and drive away—but why would she want to do that? She knocked tentatively, and then, after a minute or two, slightly louder.

The door swung suddenly inward. It seemed to be her destiny to surprise people today; Professor Bolton looked just as startled as Grammy had been. "Ah, Miss Cotter," he said.

He was wearing old carpet slippers, a striped blue dress shirt, and grotesquely wrinkled Bermuda shorts in a shrieking red plaid. His bare shins—she'd never seen them before—were shiny and milk white and outlined with random scrag-gles of insistent black hair. He was carrying a book, had closed it over one finger; he emitted a small, embarrassed giggle.

"I'm sorry if I've disturbed you, Professor Bolton," she said, trying to hit the right note—formal but friendly—that was supposed to convey the message that she certainly enjoyed seeing him, but she could leave instantly if he wanted her to. "I imagine it *is* a surprise," she said.

"Yes, yes, yes— Well— In the general scheme of things, one's students *grad-uate*, and then, having graduated, they *go away*—and one gets a new crop. And so it is a bit of a—shall we say, somewhat disconcerting—not to say that I'm not delighted to see you, my dear."

Oh, he *did* want her to leave—and, absurdly, ridiculously, stupidly, she began to cry. "My dear Miss Cotter," he said in a dismal voice.

"I'm sorry. I really am sorry—to just—you know—turn up like this. I know I should have called first. I mean, how inconsiderate can you get, but— Oh, but I've had such a horrible summer. I split up with Rolland and I disgraced myself at the country club and my grandmother died and— Oh, I sound just utterly ridiculous! *Oh, I'm just so miserable.*"

Through her tears, she saw him give her a long, deliberate, assessing look. "Well, then, my dear," he said, "you must come in and tell Auntie all about it."

18

"Isn't this a beauty?" Professor Bolton said. "You can feel the sun in it." Gloria accepted the huge beefsteak tomato he was offering her and cupped it in the palms of her hands. First she felt the fine grit of soil on the surface and then, beneath, a living warmth—nearly a pulsing—and, for one brief, spooky moment, thought: yes, it's sucked up the sun—but that, of course, was ridiculous; surely what she was feeling was her own living heat.

She'd cried herself empty in his shadowy living room; here in the fat heat of the August afternoon a zillion housewives were doing their shopping, and Gloria felt dazzled by the light, stupefied by the cheery pandemonium; she felt silly and golden, giddy as a June bug. "Oh, jolly good tomatoes," Professor Bolton sang out in exactly the same voice she'd heard him use, at football games, to encourage the Briarville team, and the farm wife standing at the back of the stall, under the roof, out of the glare, grinned back at him.

He'd been so obviously—to use his own word—disconcerted when Gloria had appeared at his door that she'd been afraid she'd committed a ghastly breach of etiquette, but now she guessed that he'd simply been embarrassed at having been caught *en déshabille*; at the first possible moment, he'd darted off to return freshly shaven, his hair brushed and brilliantined, wearing a crisply ironed shirt, khaki walking shorts, gray knee-socks, and sturdy walking shoes—as though he'd gone out of his way to turn himself into a caricature of the Englishman who goes out in the sun with the mad dogs, a role he clearly enjoyed playing for the amusement of the good folk at the Briarville Farmers' Market. Everywhere he went, people broke into laughter the minute they heard his accent—which he seemed to be exaggerating for their benefit. He swept an arm into an expansive gesture toward the stalls piled high with the blazing colors of fruits and vegetables: "Such plenty, such abundance, such largess. It's a living cornucopia!"

He was carrying a shopping basket much like the one Little Red Riding Hood carried to Grandmother's house, its handle suspended over one of his hairy forearms. He'd invited Gloria to stay for dinner; they were shopping for it. "Ah, green beans," he said, picking one up and snapping it, "left on the vine to *precisely* the right moment."

She still wasn't entirely comfortable. Oh, he must think her the wettest, weepiest girl in the world; how many times had she bawled in front of him? He'd said little more than variations on, "There, there, my dear," and she couldn't remember much of what she'd said, but she supposed it had been little more than variations on, "Oh, I've had such a miserable summer." She hoped he didn't feel stuck with her.

Gratefully, she followed him between two stalls and into the cool darkness of the market itself. The color of the tomato she was still holding was so close to that of her nail polish she could have chosen it to complete her ensemble, and she imagined herself the subject of a splashy painting in primary colors: "Gypsy Girl with Tomato," perhaps by Matisse. She slipped the tomato into his basket.

"I feel really funny," she said. "You know, just barging in on you out of nowhere."

"No, no, no, you must not feel the least—" He suddenly stopped walking, and so, therefore, did she. "*Tibi, non ante verso lene merum cado,*" he said with his mad grin, "*iamdudum apud me est; eripe te morae.*"

"Hey, that's familiar. Say it again."

He said it again. "It's Horace," she said.

"Good girl."

"It's from one of the Odes—one of the ones with the '*carpe diem*' theme. I've translated it."

"Oh, doubly good girl."

"Wow, it gave me a heck of a time. Let's see if I can still— Oh, I remember! '*Verso*' isn't what you'd think it would be; it isn't a verse. '*Non ante verso cado*' is an unopened cask or a jar. That drove me nuts. I had to look in the trot or I never would have got it. And '*apud me*' is 'with me,' but it has more weight than that. It's more like 'at my home'—"

"Right you are."

She knew she was showing off, but she didn't care; she felt as pleased with herself as a little girl in a dance recital who has every step down to perfection. They'd stopped just inside the market, and people were walking around them, giving them curious glances; what they were talking about must surely sound quite odd, but she didn't care about that either. "And *eripio* is 'snatch away' or 'rescue,'" she said. "I kind of liked 'snatch away delay,' but it's probably better as simply 'don't delay'— So it's something like: 'For you, I've had at my home a long time now an unopened jar of gentle wine. Don't delay.'"

Then the obvious dawned on her: more than merely an exercise, it had been a message for her. "Well, thank you," she heard herself saying in a voice as prim as Alice's.

"Don't mention it," he said and gave her a light, deft pat on the shoulder.

He bought cheese in the delicatessen, murmuring, "Ah, Danish blue—as close as we're going to get to a Stilton. But then, you've probably never tasted a Stilton, have you my dear? A good Stilton simply does not travel— Pickle?"

"No, thank you." With the tongs, he fished an enormous dill out of the brine and bit into it; she heard the crisp, wet snap, and her back teeth ached in sympathy. She followed him into the bakery.

"You Americans understand many of the finer things," he said, "pies, for instance— My friend here, Mabel, bakes exquisite pies. She does a pie with small, sour, green, Dutch apples and very little sugar that is— Words fail me; you must taste and see for yourself. Ah, that's almost Biblical, isn't it? Have you one of those pies today, Mabel?"

"Sure do, Professor."

Under his breath, he said to Gloria, "But you Americans do *not* understand bread. Alas. There is nothing here even faintly resembling the humble baguette. No, no, we must not be tempted by the German rye. When confronted with Coq au Vin, it could well precipitate the Franco-Prussian War all over again upon the tender fields of our palates."

Striding through the door of the poultry shop, he called out in a rotund, Dickensian voice: "Have you a fat, young hen for me, Andy?"

"Saved one specially for you, Doc."

"Fresh is it?"

"Running around the yard this morning."

"A well fed, happy hen, was she?"

"Well fed, I can attest to. She got lots of kitchen scraps. But happy? Say, Doc, you ever spend much time around chickens? Didn't think you did. Well, I guess if you can call a hen happy, she was a happy enough hen. If she weren't, she didn't let on."

"You're a man of rare wit, Andy."

"You're no slouch yourself, Doc. See you next week."

Professor Bolton's basket was crammed. Gloria was carrying the pie. "I do believe that's—yes, nearly everything. Oh. Let us see if my friend Danny has some of his fine peeled shrimp," but Danny said, "No, not today, Professor. Well, anyhow, I haven't got any shrimp *you'd* want. But how about a nice trout? Couldn't get any fresher unless you caught it yourself."

"Do we want a trout?" Professor Bolton said to Gloria. "*Do we want a trout? Oh, by all that's sacred, of course we want a trout!*"

By the time they were putting things away in Professor Bolton's kitchen, Gloria could feel that the underarms of her father's shirt were soaked through. Then Professor Bolton was thrusting into her hands a tankard—yes, it really *was* a tankard; it appeared to be pewter—of foaming beer. Gratefully, she took a long drink. It was darker, had more of a bite than the Miller's High Life she usually drank. "I must apologize for the chaos," he was saying. The sink and both counters on either side of it were stacked high with dirty dishes.

She sat down at the little kitchen table and tried to look as though she were not about to die of heat prostration. He took a long drink from his own tankard, flung soap into the sink, and turned on the hot tap. "Have I ever told you about my somewhat unusual color scheme?" He gestured toward the screaming yellow walls with their gruesome lime-green woodwork.

"No? Well, shortly after I bought my little house, several dear friends motored down from New York to see how I was getting on, and they were in a Russian mood—precisely why, I can't recall."

He began tossing dishes into the sink so vigorously she was sure he would break some of them. "Let me help you," she said, not really meaning it.

"Oh, no, no, no. I wouldn't think of it— Well, my friends had brought with them vast quantities of the finest caviar, and exquisite pickled herring, and lovely clotted sour cream and excellent black rye bread— Oh, my dear, you must think I have food on the brain today— And they brought Russian phonograph records to play and Russian poetry to read—although none of us could read a word of Russian. Now the most peculiar thing about my friends feeling so very, very Russian is that there was not a snowflake in sight. It was, as a matter of fact, a hot summer's day, much like this one. But Russian they felt, and Russian we were, and Russian we were to remain the entire weekend, and they had brought with them half a dozen bottles of Russian vodka of a potency that defies description, and it was a requirement of this beverage, so they assured me, that it must be placed in the freezer compartment of my refrigerator until it achieved the requisite temperature and viscosity—and then drunk from tiny glasses no bigger than thimbles. They had, as you might imagine, brought just such glasses with them.

"Perhaps you, my dear, have had the experience of drinking Russian vodka— oh, for perhaps three or four hours? No? There is a certain charm to it— However— And then a happy idea overtook my friend James. 'Oh, Trev,' he said, 'we simply *must* do something to alleviate the *dreadful* oppression of this *dreary* kitchen,' and so, before you could say Dostoyevsky, we were staggering back from the paint store with the subtle hues you see before you. It is astonishing how quickly four English gentlemen transmogrified into Cossacks can paint a kitchen. I wouldn't have thought these colors were particularly Russian, would you? And the next morning. Oh, my dear Gloria, *the next morning*—"

The sink was overflowing with soapsuds. "Professor Bolton—" she said.

"Please. My dear. You have been graduated. We are colleagues. You really must learn to call me Trevor."

"Trevor? Do you suppose I could change my clothes?"

"Well, of course, of course. You should have mentioned it before. Enchanting as you are in your Dale Evans outfit, you must be simply liquefied. By all means— Yes, and, if you will forgive my asking a personal question, where were you planning to spend the night? Not that it's any of my business, as the actress said to the bishop."

"At my grandparents?"

"Ah. And they expect you?"

"Not really, but I could always call them."

"Or perhaps you were planning to drive to Philadelphia after all?"

"No. I don't think so. It's way too late in the day."

"Oh, and by the by, your parents do know where you are, now don't they?"

"I talked to my dad this morning. I told him I was going to the Delta Lambda house. It's closed for the summer."

"Oh, my dear, you *are* out on a limb—or perhaps we should say, out on a lamb—"

She groaned, then, looking up, met his sympathetic, chocolate-brown eyes. "You must stay with me," he said. "Really, you must. Oh, I'm aware that the suggestion is unconventional, but you're quite the unconventional girl, now aren't you?"

Me? Gloria thought. *Unconventional?* How could anyone possibly think that? "That's really kind of you."

"Nonsense. It's purely practical."

"It's very nice, but— Look, um, Trevor, I don't want to cause you any trouble. You know, any trouble *at all*."

"And how would you do that?"

She wasn't sure how frank she was expected to be. Before she could find a reply, he said, "Come, come. You, my dear, are no longer my student, so the university has—or should have—no interest in the matter. I would, I must admit, find it somewhat disagreeable if your father, in the charming American fashion, were to appear waving a pistol in my face. I assume that I would have no occasion to worry on that score."

"Of course not. But look, if it's at all—"

"Gloria," he said, "I would be delighted to have you." Again their eyes met. She felt utterly, stupidly tongue-tied. In a moment, she was going to start blushing.

"Well, I'd be delighted too." She wanted to add something deliciously light and airy and sophisticated—a few well chosen words that would tell him that she'd understood the message he seemed to have been going out of his way to convey to her since she'd shown up on his doorstep: that he really was exactly what everyone on campus had always thought he was—and it was OK with her. But there was nothing in her mind but an embarrassed blur.

"Good. It's settled then. No, no, you musn't say another word. Let's fetch your bags."

Not sure why she was doing it, she allowed him to carry the suitcase with her crinolines and cocktail dress while she carried the one with everything else. The guest room was on the north side of the house, and her first impression of it was of wonderful coolness and quiet after the loud, Fauvish blaze of the kitchen. The walls had been papered in a deep forest green; a framed reproduction from a page of the Book of Kells hung on one wall. Most of the space was taken up by an enormous four-poster bed with a generous, white and green coverlet. There was a genuine—and, she guessed, quite good—Oriental on the floor. Her mother had trained her to know antiques, and she ran her fingers lightly over the wood of the dresser, not quite believing it could be as old as it looked. "Yes," he said, "it's Georgian—from my mother's family."

"Holy smoke!" she said, and thought: well put, Gloria, you idiot. "And now, my dear, if I am reading your mind properly, I would guess that you might enjoy a bath?"

"Oh, Trevor, that would be heaven."

Did she want her *shampooing avec balsam?* she wondered. He'd told her to use anything she wished, and she'd found baskets full of scented soaps, and a dozen jars of various potions with labels entirely in French. Where on earth did he get the stuff? She sniffed a bottle of what appeared to be cologne, or perhaps shaving lotion, and discovered the source of his distinctive lilac scent. The bathtub, which was filling, was enormous, had a wooden rim, and rested on brass claw feet. Everything she saw delighted her—but, oh, how odd it was to be there. She slowly lowered herself into the water, then lay back, not caring if she got her hair wet; yes, she might as well wash it—and she suddenly realized that she was happy for the first time since her grandmother had died.

When, barefoot, in shorts and a halter top, she returned to the kitchen, she saw that he had managed to get at least half of his dishes washed. "Ah, there you are," he said. She'd had five classes with him; he'd been her thesis advisor, yet she felt shy and tongue-tied. She sat down at the kitchen table and hoped her smile would do for the moment.

"We must have our trout," he said—and cut a bit of butter into a cast iron frying pan, banged it onto the stove. "I see, my dear, that you varnish your toenails. How very American of you. Have I ever told you about my first year here at this great Athens of the new world?"

The frying pan began to sizzle; he lifted it up and swung it about, spreading the melting butter, lowered it again to the flame, and tossed in the fish. "We were but Briarville College then," he said, "and I was but a lowly assistant professor, and I had been given, God help me, two sections of freshman English. In one of these I found, to my horror, that an entire wing of the women's dorm had enrolled en masse. Twenty-some splendid specimens of *the American girl*—a phenomenon of which I had never so much as dreamed—"

He threw a few crystals into a small mortar that looked like something from a high school chemistry lab, took up a pestle and reduced the crystals to a white dust, deposited a pinch of it into the palm of his hand, and offered it to her. She was taken aback; what was she supposed to do, lick it up like a pony? He made a sniffing gesture. She sniffed. "It smells like the sea!"

"Indeed. And that is what salt *should* smell like—because it comes from the sea, as we should remind ourselves daily. Both the Greeks and Roman offered up salt on their altars, and the trade routes— Ah, but you do recall the origin of our word 'salary' in *salarium*?"

"The Roman soldiers paid in salt?" Gloria said, not knowing until she'd said it that she'd known it.

"Good girl— And so a man could be said to be worth his salt, as we know from Petronius—and, as I was saying, the trade routes— Ah, but I recall a departmental dinner party. Again, during my first year. I remarked that if one wishes to understand silver Latin literature, one should begin with salt—true enough, but also, as many remarks at a dinner party so often are, offered *cum grano salis*, hmmm?"

Gloria had to giggle at that, and he rewarded her with a curiously cheerful facial tic that, she decided, must have been intended as a wink. "But my eminent colleague, the learned Doctor Stupor—in those days we could still manage a bare minimum of civil discourse betwixt us— Yes, the good doctor said, 'Bolton, you're talking like a Marxist.' I was flabbergasted. A Marxist! Great and triumphant Christ, the poor fellow did not have the wit to see a rock-ribbed, hidebound, public school, C of E Tory when it was twitching there before him."

He had underlined what he was saying by chopping a lemon, first in half, then in quarters. "One becomes interested in *anything*—salt, let us say—and, if one follows up every line of inquiry that leads away from salt, then one will eventually know *everything*— Unfortunately, death will intervene before one reaches the end, but the journey, partial though it be, is enough to justify a lifetime, hmmm?"

He twisted a corkscrew into a bottle waiting ready at hand, yanked the cork with a satisfying pop, poured out a pale, golden wine into crystal glasses. "Ah," he said, "a gentle Riesling—*after* having been pulled."

Her half tankard of undrunk beer still stood in front of her; he must have seen her involuntary, embarrassed glance at it; he seized it at once and dumped the contents into the sink. He toasted her with his wine glass. "*Nostrovia, prost, l'chaim, salud, salute, bas in Erin*, to the Queen, to the Dean, to you, to me, to what have you— It is simply lovely to have you—here, my dear."

"It's lovely to be here." She'd never tasted a white wine as delicate, and immediately her half of the trout—magically sans head, tail, and bones—appeared before her, steaming, accompanied by a pinch of freshly ground salt. The cobalt blue ground of the plate brought vividly to life the colors of fish, lemon, and watercress; she tasted, said, "Oh, wonderful," thought how difficult it was to describe flavors; "shadowy" she might have called it, which would have taken her not very far. He was seated on the other side of the table grinning madly; the late afternoon sunlight seemed to be melting down the yellow walls like Little Black Sambo's tigers. "But what about the American girls?"

"Ah, yes, I did lose the thread of that, didn't I? Yes, those girls in my eight o'clock class— They all had extraordinarily long legs, commodious bosoms displayed in close-fitting sweaters, brilliantly gleaming blood-red lips, alarming white and perfect teeth—" He gnashed his own teeth, which were yellow and crooked; she giggled again and thought: oh, help, I'm behaving exactly like one of the girls he's talking about.

"Now you must understand that I was not then terribly well acquainted with your fair sex, but as for the *American* girl—*the* American girl—nothing could have prepared me. What quite unnerved me was how they functioned as a single organism. They dressed as one, they spoke as one, they moved as one—as one sees flocks of birds suddenly turn and wheel about and knows not whence cometh the motion, yes—a common mind, yes?—and if I offered up the slightest word of criticism to any one of them, the entirety upon the instant turned upon me— 'Scuse me, Professor, 'scuse me, Professor— Oh, oh."

She had to put her fork down she was laughing so hard. "Gloria, I cannot begin to tell you how I dreaded that hour, that glittering phalanx awaiting me—their sweaters, their teeth, their sharp pens poised above their virginal notebooks. Oh, how I longed for the year to end. Yes, yes, my dears, *all of you* have Cs, now please, please," and here he made a shooing motion with his fingertips, "*just go away.*"

Even though she was still laughing, she was thinking: just as he kept trying to get *me* to go away—and then, as though he'd read her mind, he said, "I must admit, dear Gloria, that you did fool me for a while. But the truth of the matter is that you have *never* been one of those girls—no matter how well you have learned to disguise yourself as one of them."

Something at the center of Gloria had gone still as stone, and she experienced the familiar yet disquieting sensation of being disembodied, of observing herself from a distance. They were finishing their trout; they were drinking the gentle wine. He was telling her another amusing anecdote, and she was smiling or laughing in the proper places. He scraped their plates and slipped them into the sink's soapy water. He gave her a knife, a cutting board, and several cloves of garlic. She'd never minced garlic in her life. "Never? *Never?* I find that nearly impossible to believe. You don't cook with garlic?"

"Garlic powder."

"Oh, my dear, how utterly barbaric." He showed her how to squash the cloves with the flat of the knife blade so the papery shells would pull free, then how to hold the French knife correctly, one hand on the handle, the other on the blunt top edge of the blade, to chop the garlic fine.

He browned salt pork in butter, added onions, shallots, carrots, and the garlic, and left it to simmer. He browned the chicken in an iron pot. She followed him into the garden where he clipped thyme and parsley, followed him back into the kitchen where he washed and sliced mushrooms. Glad to have something to do, she snapped the green beans.

They hadn't finished the Riesling, but he corked the bottle and opened another: a good claret, he said, a red Bordeaux. Gloria knew nothing about wine. "No," he said, "most Americans don't. You're either guzzling soda pop or that weak, watery beer you brew to the consistency of soda pop—or else you're knocking yourselves silly with your lethal highballs."

He added the vegetables and a good splash of wine to the chicken and covered the pot. "We've earned ourselves a moment of respite," he said, topped up their glasses and led her into the living room.

As Gloria settled into one of the big overstuffed chairs, she felt a subtle form coalescing in her mind. Although she'd been in this room only once before, she felt, perhaps because she'd dreamed of it, as though it had a particular significance for her. But she'd always dreamed of it at night, and she'd actually seen it as she was seeing it now: bathed in the ruddy-golden light of late afternoon. The big doors were standing open; looking through them, she could see the hills back of Briarville, the stand of ancient trees by the creek, and his garden in a last bloom of the season—the impressionistic blur of his floppy roses, their fallen petals like drops of melted crayons on the ivy. She heard crickets and birds and the plash of the creek. "This is lovely," she said.

She sipped her wine and heard herself stupidly asking, "Do you have a lot of mosquitoes?"

"Indeed. They come out in droves. But not until twilight."

A well-fed gray squirrel suddenly appeared to stare in at them across the threshold, his thick shoe buffer of a tail thrust up behind him. "The cheeky things," Professor Bolton said. "I looked up from my reading the other day and actually found one of them regarding me from atop an end table."

He stuffed his pipe and lit it. The sun was shining in on the mahogany furniture and wainscoting, on the walls of books, the lacework of the doilies and antimacassars, on the brandy-gold leather of the camel saddle, on the stuffed owl (sacred to Athena? she wondered), on the mandolin (did he play it? probably not; it was too dusty), on the clocks and bell jars, the statues and gewgaws and—well, she didn't have a clue what some of those other objects could possibly be. "Is that a real human skull?"

"Oh, no, it's a cast—a gift from a student. Splendid fellow. He sent it to me from medical school."

"As a *memento mori?*"

"Indeed— O spare me a little before I go hence and be seen no more."

She felt as though she'd just awakened, for the inner stillness that had been oppressing her for the better part of an hour was gone—but, no, it hadn't been a stillness; it had been more like being frozen.

"You're safe here," the secret watcher told her, and she could feel now, as she hadn't before, that outer stillness all around her—as an enfolding, or a pause, or an inhalation.

"I've dreamed of this room," she thought of saying—or, "I dreamed that you told me to read Spenser," or "in my dreams I go into the attic and push through a secret door, and sometimes it leads directly into this room." No, the unfamiliar doesn't necessarily have to mean frightening—or dangerous. "How did you know I was disguising myself?" she said.

"Oh, my dear, how does the American idiom put it? It takes one to know one?"

"So what are you disguised as?"

"I should have thought that was obvious. I am disguised as an eccentric British professor. Knows his subject well enough, but a bit of a fool. Amusing—at times quite daft—but essentially harmless."

A few minutes before, she would have laughed at this, but now she didn't. "Sometimes I can't tell the disguise from me," she said.

"Ah?" His pipe must have gone out; he struck another kitchen match and held it to the bowl.

"Ever since I got to high school," she said, "all I've wanted to do is fit in. I fit in so well I was Prom Queen. I fit in here so well I was the president of my sorority and May Queen. I almost got married because I wanted to fit in—but I just couldn't make myself do it. I don't know exactly how to say this. I don't know who I am, I guess, deep inside. Sometimes I feel like I'm nobody—that there's nobody home." Could it be, she wondered, that she'd driven several hundred miles just to be able to say that?

"My quandaries were somewhat different from yours." He exhaled a final mouthful of smoke, laid his pipe aside in a Wedgewood bowl on the coffee table. "I never fit in—didn't give a hang about such things, so I was always finding myself in some dreadful, farcical scrape or other—until I came to this great Athens of the new world and said to myself, 'Bolton, it is high time that you became respectable'—and so I have.

"But, my dear, when I was only a few years older than you are now, I was— Well, I could read Latin and Greek as easily as I could read Chaucer's English. I could make my way though Dante's Italian and Goethe's German and Racine's French. I could discourse wittily on Longinus, Magnus Aurelius Cassiodorus, Sir Thomas Browne, Guillaume de Machaut, Lord Thomas Vaux, or Sir John Davies. I had just begun to write my modest monograph on Wyatt, which I had undertaken from the shabbiest of motives—to show off my vast erudition to a lovely boy with whom I was hopelessly enamored and to annoy the good Miss Foxwell. I was stuffed full of opinions and information like a force-fed goose. In short, I was a complete and utter twit. If I had looked, as you say, deep inside myself, I dare say I wouldn't have found much of anything worth mentioning, but it would never have occurred to me to bother looking—so much the worse for me."

She was laughing again—how could she not be?—but she wasn't sure he'd understood her. "You must trust, my dear, that all will be revealed in the fullness of time," he said. "Shall we dress for dinner?"

The notion was so odd, it took her a moment to get it. "Oh, you mean *really* dress."

Gloria liked the cool, shadowless north light in the guest room so much she was reluctant to dispel it. The only mirror was a tilting, full-length one; she wondered if she were the first girl who'd ever looked into it. She wished she had a formal— wearing a formal would have been *really* witty—but she didn't, so her midnight-blue Traina-Norell would have to do. She'd drunk enough wine to feel a pleasant fizz in her brain. Maybe she could write off her strange mood to a few alcohol molecules.

She tilted the mirror back to favor her face; even with no more light than the soft, flat glow from the window, she could, if she bent close, do her makeup perfectly well. For the two-person masquerade in which she was about to assume a starring role, she wanted to be genuinely *masked*, so she sponged on a thick layer of foundation, then painted onto that primed, empty canvas the image of a sophisticated grown-up lady from a *Vogue* cover, stopping just short of parody. She hooked herself into her waspie, put on her underwear and hose—and paused, aware of something going on in a dim, far corner of her mind.

She looked around for a clue as to what she might be feeling, was drawn to the reproduction from the Book of Kells. The caption told her that it was the opening words of St. John's gospel, but she couldn't find anything that looked as though it might say what it was supposed to say: "*In principio erat verbum—*" The ground was parchment yellow; the elaborate Celtic curlicues had been worked in lovely blues and oranges—or at least that's what remained after centuries of fading. Perched on the top near the left was a bearded man with huge, sad eyes—presumably the saint himself—wearing what looked like a purple bathrobe and holding on his lap a rectangle that was probably meant to be a book and not a tea tray. A smaller man to his right appeared to be inhaling from a funnel. (Clearing his sinuses with the mediaeval equivalent of Vicks Vaporub?) "*Biderat*," was all she could read. What on earth could that possibly mean? The soft ticking in her mind had, as it so often did, turned out to be a poem, lines from Graves: "—the greatness, rareness, muchness, fewness of this precious only endless world—"

She stepped back. She should finish getting dressed—it would be impolite to keep him waiting too long—but she still didn't want to leave the guest room. She had a strong sense of—well, not exactly of *déjà vu*; it was more like the illusion she could sometimes create at night: that she'd rotated, that her head was now at the foot of her bed and all the objects in her room were in a reversed position. With similar conviction, she felt that the door of this room could open into the upstairs hallway at home; if she stepped through it, she could walk either into her own room or her grandmother's—would find her grandmother propped up on pillows, watching the television—

Then she was aware, suddenly, of herself in this *particular* room, and aware with such an intensity it made her feel as though she must spend the greater part of her waking life sleepwalking: the way the light fell *right now*—the muted, green-tinted colors it created—and the calling of a bird, the sound of soft footsteps in the house, a hint of a breeze through the screened window tickling the hair on her arms; and the weight of her body flowing down through her hips into her legs and feet, the immediacy of the sensation of the thick nap of the rug felt through the slipperiness of her nylons— The fear of death struck her. Oh, she thought, how could this elaborate, intricate, wonderful web of interconnections ever be extinguished?

She turned on the light on the dresser, the one by the bed table, and the overhead light. If there had been a radio in the room, she would have turned that on too. She didn't have to think about death for another fifty or sixty years at least. It didn't do the least bit of good to think about it—

She stepped into her nylon half-slip and her crinolines. She put on her Traina-Norell and zipped it up. Oh, her wretched straight hair; she needed some big, bold earrings to take the attention away from it. She looked in her jewelry box, selected pearl dangles and clipped them on. She stepped into her opera pumps, pulled on her gloves, added a diamond bracelet to her left wrist. She straightened the mirror, studied herself, and was pleased: she looked every bit as wittily artificial as she'd wished. She drew herself up until she found that crucial inner edge she always needed before she made an entrance.

As she stepped into the hallway, the magnificent smell of the cooking chicken reminded her she was hungry again. Placing each foot carefully onto an imaginary line stretching before her, she walked into the living room. Professor Bolton

was sitting in one of the big chairs, reading—wearing a tuxedo and, of all wonderfully ridiculous things, patent dancing pumps. He looked up, smiling, and
watched her cross the room to the sound of her rustling crinolines.

He rose to his feet and took her arm. She allowed herself to be escorted into
the dining room. He held a chair for her. She couldn't contain herself any longer
and began to giggle. So did he. "Gloria," he said, "you are simply marvelous."

"I love playing dress up," she said. "I always have."

Gloria had never tasted anything to compare with the chicken. The artificial
lights had been turned off; half a dozen white tapers lit the table. Her white
kid evening gloves were folded neatly and laid aside; seeing them made her
feel like a girl in an Edith Wharton novel. They were dining upon what were
obviously heirloom plates, eating with ancient silver—which appeared not to
have been polished for thirty years, but she couldn't expect everything to be perfect, now could she?

She'd lost all sense of observing herself from a distance, and even her ordinary
shyness had melted away. She'd just realized that she didn't need to, as she would
have for most people, plan everything she was about to say and simplify her language and her thoughts, and she could tell that he liked her as a person—above
and beyond whatever he might have thought of her as a student—that she amused
and interested him. It was exhilarating. This, she thought, is what a genuine conversation should be like.

They were talking about Eliot. "I got so fascinated by some of the examples
he uses," she said, "I kept forgetting the points he was trying to make. Do you
remember when he quotes from Baudelaire? Of course, I had to go look up
the poem and read it, and read a whole bunch more Baudelaire— I suppose
that's what Eliot wanted me to do. But it really got me—those lines: '*Pour
l'enfant, amoureux de cartes et d'estampes—*'"

"Yes, yes?" He reached across the white linen to fill her wine glass again.

"But you see," she said, "Eliot talks so much about not taking it personally,
and I took it personally. It just plunged me right back into that childhood
feeling. I never collected stamps, but I remember looking at maps, thinking,
'I'll go there someday.' I remember that feeling—'*L'univers est égal à son vaste
appétit*'—although a little kid wouldn't think of it that way— But I wanted to
jump right out of childhood into adulthood. I wanted to know *everything*. I can
remember that feeling so *clearly*—" and, with that, she felt an enormous,
soaring lift. She couldn't get the words to come out fast enough.

She could see herself—no, more than that; she was *inside* herself, a little
girl sitting on the Oriental rug in the living room in their dear apartment before
the war—and she was clipping out pictures from magazines and pasting them
into her scrapbook. She heard herself trying to describe it, the feeling of it,

how magical it was, and she thought: just as *this, right now*, is magical. "They were always pictures of what I would be—when I was big, when I was grownup like Mommy. Oh, I wonder whatever happened to that scrapbook?"

She could see—as she told him—the way the lights fell, made pools of yellow brilliance on the floor—"*à la clarité des lampes.*" She could see her mom's feet and her dad's feet. They were listening to the radio. It was one of those huge, old cabinet radios with the push buttons for the stations and the small, yellow dial gleaming at the top.

"I was, I guess, five or six. Mom put really short skirts on me—so I can remember the feeling of the rug on my bare legs, and I clipped the pictures of ladies in long gowns because that was the essence of grownupness. But when Baudelaire says, 'how small in the eyes of memory,' I didn't agree at all. It's *not* small. It's *big, big*— But you see how personally I take everything?"

"But *you* must see, my dear, that Tom is quite wrong actually."

"He is?" She couldn't imagine anyone knowing enough to say that T.S. Eliot was wrong.

"Poor old Tom is telling us how he *wishes* things to be. *He* would like to be impersonal. *He* would like to be the catalyst unchanged by the chemical reaction, eh? But how can we not be changed by what we learn, by what we write? Of course we are. And there's the crucial distinction between Eliot and Pound. Tom offers up Baudelaire as an example—calls him a psychologist, an explorer of the soul. But what does the adult Baudelaire make of that childhood memory? He makes it *small*—and that is precisely what appeals to Tom, that distance, that reduction— Just as Baudelaire tells us that paradise is artificial—"

"Oh! And Pound says—"

"Yes. Paradise is *not* artificial. Do you see?"

Gloria was dazzled. Wow, she'd thought *her* mind moved quickly. She looked across the table and saw, shining through that middle-aged man's face, a bright little boy enormously pleased with himself.

"You've met Eliot, haven't you?" she asked, knowing, of course, that he had.

"Met him? Good heavens, I've known Tom Eliot for years. I knew him when he was a clerk who wrote book reviews— Oh, heavens, what a catty thing to say! Govern your tongue, Trevor, you nasty boy— Yes, and I knew his first wife too. Sad, difficult woman. One can hear her voice in *The Waste Land* quite clearly. I used to entertain the notion that Tom might be a gentleman of my persuasion—hyacinth girl, indeed!—but he does appear to be quite happy with his second wife, hmmm? I could perhaps arrange for you to meet him—or perhaps not. He has become quite inaccessible of late."

Gloria was stunned. He might as well have suggested that she could meet God face to face. He had, earlier, poured a second bottle of wine into a decanter so it would, as he'd said, breathe; now he was offering some to her. "Don't even consider it if you've had enough— Oh, just a drop? Yes, yes. The connoisseurs tell us there is a correct order for drinking wine, but it has always seemed to me that one should drink it in the order one *likes it*, hmmm? How pleasant to have you here, my dear." He toasted her. Automatically, she toasted him back and drank.

"Now Pound is another matter," he said. "I will write you a letter. Remind me. He will simply adore you. He'll talk your ear off, believe me—and do more than that if you're not careful. He's always been quite taken with the ladies. Ah, yes, you really must know him—and Dorothy and Olga too, and his daughter, the princess—a lovely girl. They're all quite approachable. I'll arrange it."

Good grief, Gloria thought, he means it! "Thank you," she said—and heard the voice a little girl might use when she's been given a bonbon—"that would be lovely."

Annoyed at herself, she said the first thing that popped into her mind: "Trevor—how on earth did you ever end up at Briarville?"

"Ah, now there's a tale. Are you certain you want me to—? Very well, then, but consider yourself warned. It's likely to be somewhat circuitous. Where to begin? Let's see— I was born on a bleak and rainy Wednesday. No, no, that's a little *too* far back, wouldn't you say?"

He winked at her. "Yes, let us begin with the war years," he said. "That does seem as good a place as any. Ah, yes—and so I passed the war pleasantly with a number of frightfully clever chaps playing with cyphers under conditions of the most outlandish secrecy—*in cubiculum cubiculorum*, as it were. We were quite good at it, by the way. Dear Adolf couldn't flush the loo without our knowing about it. And when I was off duty, I amused myself by— How shall I put this?— Well, let us say that I often enjoyed impulsive and exceedingly brief adventures of an highly intimate nature with splendid young men of the enlisted ranks.

"One develops a sixth sense about such things, but, upon occasion, one's sixth sense can prove to be disastrously wrong, and so one day I found myself in the infirmary suffering from a concussion, a broken nose, and several cracked ribs, whilst being regarded by the sorrowful eyes of the poor sod whose unhappy lot it was to be in command of me, Major Godfrey Theoben Sparshatt—and a grand old queen he was, too—who asked me a question the contemplation of which proved to be the beginning of wisdom. 'Bolton,' he said, 'what are we to do with you?'

"Time passed. The war came to an end, and I found myself teaching— although that word may be too strong—at a dreary little institution in the Midlands. I had, for several years, been involved in a liaison that was beginning to grow tedious—oh, the midnight storms; oh, the broken crockery!—and, from time to time, I asked myself again the good Major's profound question. Then I heard upon the grapevine that several American colleges were seeking to purchase British scholars at bargain prices. Ah, I thought, how pleasant it would be to journey to a brave new world in which one might be known as the author of a modest monograph upon Sir Thomas Wyatt instead of—as I was still remembered at Oxford—'that frightful Bolton boy.' So I dispatched a number of letters saying, 'Sir, if a truly *cheap* British scholar is your desire, then I am for you.'"

She was laughing so hard she had to cover her mouth with her napkin. He waited for her to regain control of herself and then said in the most bland and unctuous of voices: "And so, my dear, shall we take our coffee in the living room?"

At night, it was much the way Gloria had dreamed it: the illumination low and golden, constrained into discreet circles; the corners and the intervals between lamps obscured by deep umber shadows; mile-high walls of books creating a floating backdrop to everything. She wasn't surprised that it looked the way she'd dreamed it, but she *was* surprised that she wasn't surprised. "When I woke up," she was saying, "it was just *there* in my mind—and I knew I couldn't marry Rolland. It was sad, really."

They were drinking brandy from crystal snifters and real Turkish coffee from tiny demitasse cups decorated with violets; she'd never drunk either before, and she liked their heat. "But of course you couldn't marry him," he said.

"Oh, that's easy enough for you to say," she said just as she would have to someone her own age—she was feeling quite comfortable with him by now—"but it didn't feel that way to me."

She was sitting in exactly the same chair in which she'd sat that afternoon two years before when she'd wept about what had happened with Ken Henderson; resting her feet on the camel saddle was reminding her of the milky gleam of the white sandals she'd worn then—and tonight she was wearing her favorite patent opera pumps; lying at the edge of the small pool of light falling from the tall bronze lamp, they shone like black glass, and she found their image deeply pleasing—but then most things were pleasing her. "My roommate Susie says I think about things so much I'm like a dog chasing its tail," she said, "but, in the end, it never seems to matter what I think. Things get decided in me down deep somewhere. I'm scared to death of going to Columbia, but I guess I have to—"

"Once you're there, my dear, you will forget to be afraid."

"Will I?"

"Yes. Absolutely. You will be a swan amongst swans, and you will swim exquisitely."

She should, she supposed, reply, if only to keep the conversation going, but silence between them had become perfectly comfortable, and, besides, she didn't need to chatter away like a magpie. She was—well, not drunk, but certainly, as Rolland would have put it, *buzzed*—but in an entirely pleasant and manageable way. Oh, what was she thinking? The colors in the room seemed extraordinarily vivid. She particularly liked the Tiffany lamp.

"I wonder what happened to Ken Henderson," she said.

"Ah, I was thinking of him, too— Has the subject, perhaps, become less painful for you?"

Had it? Yes, she supposed that it had. "I feel sorry for him now. I sure didn't at the time."

"No. Indeed not. The flaming little idiot had no right to involve you in his personal melodrama—although such things are entirely predictable. One must be absolutely *certain*, hmmm? And so some innocent, unsuspecting maiden is drawn into the plot. I thank God I never succumbed to that particular temptation. But some of the lads do have a terrible time of it. Poor Ken certainly had a terrible time—and he led you into an utterly squalid little adventure, eh?"

"Yes, he did. But I took your advice."

"Oh? My, my. And what advice did I give you?"

"You said—" She probably shouldn't be doing it, but she couldn't help it; she imitated both his accent and his orotund delivery: "'Consider, my dear, that virginity is not so much a state of the body as a state of the mind—' And I did consider it, and I decided you were right."

He was laughing. "One is glad to have been of some use. One so often is not."

He offered her more brandy. She shook her head. "Oh, there was one lad," he said, "come to think of it. I daresay I actually did him some good. A big, sturdy fellow. We were sitting right here, as a matter of fact, on either end of the couch, and the beer had been flowing copiously for quite some time, and he took it into his head that he must *confess*. It was, I'm sure, no accident that he should choose *me* as his confessor. And he launched into the tale of the various unnatural acts that he and another lad had once committed upon each other in, I believe, a hotel room in Schenectady—both of them, as he kept insisting, pissed to the gills."

She smiled back to encourage him. "Proust," he said, "could not have recalled the incident any more vividly than that poor fellow did. To relieve his conscience, he felt impelled to give me a detailed account—and I do mean *detailed*—and it was clearly costing him enormously. He sighed, he groaned, he squirmed in his chair. 'And do you know what he did then?' he asked me. He must have asked me that a dozen times.

"'No,' I would say, wide-eyed, leaning closer, hanging upon every syllable— and he would tell me. As he neared the end of his tale, the poor lad's voice receded into a choked and fearful whisper. 'And do you know what he did *then*?'

he said. 'No,' I said, whispering back. 'What?' And he told me of the final, ghastly, delicious, unnatural act that had been performed upon him. 'Oh, did he *really?*' I said. I paused significantly. I looked him straight in the eye. Then I said, 'And it was bloody *marvelous*, wasn't it?'

"Have you ever seen a bull pole-axed? Well, actually, I haven't either. But the shock on that poor boy's face. There ensued a moment of prolonged silence. And then he started to laugh. And I started to laugh. Oh, my dear, we howled, we chortled, we screamed with laughter. We slapped each other on the back. We laughed until we were sick. We had another beer. He left here, I do believe, a changed man. And that, my dear, is my one and only successful venture into social work."

She was laughing too. "How did you decide to be—?" she said, not sure how to put it. "You know, decide that you were, um—"

"Decide? It isn't something one *decides*. It's something one *is*. Did you decide to have brown eyes?"

Oh, she thought, I've offended him, and I was trying so hard not to—but then, as though regretting the anger he'd allowed to sound in his voice, he said quietly, "I was lucky. For me, there was simply never any doubt."

She looked at him carefully; he appeared to have gone off into his own thoughts. "Maybe I *will* have another drop," she said.

"Oh, yes, yes." He carried the bottle over to her and poured an inch into her glass.

"Just so long as you don't mind me getting a bit silly," she said.

"Ah, my dear, let us both get a bit silly."

"What are you thinking?"

He met her eyes. "Ah— I was thinking how pleasant it is to be an object of desire—as you must have found yourself so often, my dear."

"Oh, I guess I have. Well, of course I have. Yes, it *is* pleasant—if it's the right guy who's doing the desiring, although— Well, something in me always says, 'Gloria, you shouldn't be enjoying it all *that* much.'"

"Indeed. But for lads, the time is so—oh, so bloody brief. They have a moment of beauty, delicate and shimmery and altogether exquisite, but it lasts only a few months, a year at the most, and then it's gone, leaving behind— well, your commonplace adolescent wretch stumbling into the furniture. Come, my dear, let me show you something."

He held out his arm for her; she rose and took it. He escorted her into the parlor and lit the lights. "Forgive me, my dear, for subjecting you to the reliquarium." From one of the ancient tables, he selected a framed photograph and handed it to her.

At first she thought she was looking at a teenage girl in stage makeup and tights—but no, that wouldn't make any sense after what he'd been saying. Her second thought was that it must be an altogether exquisite boy he'd once loved—but then she recognized the wicked gleam in the dark, intelligent eyes. "Good grief," she said, "it's you!"

"Indeed. In my first Shakespearean role."

She couldn't quite believe it. "Wow, you really were a doll."

"I like to think that I was," he said with an embarrassed titter, "and thank you for saying so. It was, I must admit, a triumph. I played Viola as though I'd been born to it—and received for my pains a standing ovation."

"How old were you?"

"Fourteen. The youngest in my school ever to be given a major role—"

Gloria was expecting to hear more of the story—another amusing anecdote wittily told—but, as she waited, she realized that she must have heard everything he intended to tell her. They were standing close together, hemmed in by the tables, surrounded by yet more framed pictures, by old glass, by punch bowls and figurines and vases stuffed with peacock feathers and dusty dried flowers. She glanced at him and sensed his discomfort, guessed that he might welcome a delicate way to abandon that particular line of conversation, so, setting down the photograph, she said, gesturing toward the dozens of other framed photographs, "Who are all these people?"

"Ah. Boltons and their relations quick and dead. I won't bore you with an account of the lot of them, but here is my marvelous sister, the Duchess, caught in the act of becoming a Duchess, and this troubled fellow is my dear papa, may God rest his soul, and here—yes, she is still very much with us—is my venerable mother with whom I maintain entirely amiable and cordial relations so long as she remains firmly upon her side of the Atlantic and I upon mine. Would you care to dance?"

"Pardon?"

They had to wind up the ancient Victrola between tunes. The sound came out of a small, round speaker riding directly above the needle, and it was nearly as loud as any 45 player in somebody's rec room. The records were from the teens and twenties, and Gloria was amazed at how crisp and bright they sounded. "Every bit as high as one requires one's fi to be," he said. They danced, dodging the occasional end table, in a wide circle around the outer margins of the living room; he was easy to follow. "You're a terrific dancer, Trevor," she said.

"And you, my dear, are as easy to lead as thistledown."

"Well, thank you. I think I was born for formal dances the way you were born to play Viola. You should have danced with me at the White and Gold."

"Yes, I daresay I should have. We would have flabbergasted everyone."

She almost had the hang of the funny little hesitation step he did. "Were the old foxtrots always this fast?"

"Oh, yes—as done by the Castles long, long ago, in quite another age, before the First War. This way of dancing was already old-fashioned when my sister taught it to me, and no one remembers now. Can you do the tango?"

"I don't know. Try me."

She thought she knew what a tango was, but the record he put on sounded nothing like "Hernando's Hideaway." He clasped her into a tight, lilac-scented embrace and swept her off in an odd, slithering motion unlike any dance she'd ever seen. She felt her feet tangling up beneath her. "Oh, dear," she said.

"Perhaps not," he said, releasing her. "You see why I don't dance in public. No one could follow me."

"I thought I was doing OK."

"Oh, you were indeed. It's not your fault that my brain is a terpsichorean museum."

He knelt in front of the Vic and searched through the cardboard sleeves that held the records. "Ah—and here's a splendid example from my days at Oxford." He lifted the needle from the strange tango and put on a new record that was unmistakably a Charleston. He surely couldn't expect her to do that, could he?

He fixed her with an especially maniacal grin and suddenly launched into a preposterous solo performance. His eyes glittering, he jerked about to the music in the most improbable frenzy, twitching and kicking; he bent forward, swinging his hands like an ape, snapping his knees together and apart like a nutcracker; he blew her a kiss; he threw one arm into the air and drew a mad circle with his index finger. She was so startled she didn't know how to react; then, watching his tiny feet in their absurd patent pumps twinkling to the ragtime beat, she could do nothing but laugh.

He stopped as abruptly as he'd begun—as abruptly if he were a marionette and someone had cut his strings. "One is— oh," he said, gasping for breath, "somewhat— long in the tooth—"

"Hey," she said, "we could jitterbug to this."

"Oh. Dear. I doubt—"

"Come on, Trevor," she said, feeling wicked as a cat.

"Ah—will the Lindy Hop do?"

"Sure." Managing a feeble smile, he took her gloved fingertips, drew her into a closed position, then spun her away. That's what these dresses were made to do, she thought as she felt her crinolines swinging. Although what he was doing wasn't exactly a jitterbug, she could certainly follow him. She was having a marvelous time, but she could see that he was working hard. It was cruel, she thought, to do this to him. She was glad when the record ended.

"Merciful God," he said, bending double.

He brought them each a glass of water. He mopped his forehead with his handkerchief. She was sure that must be the end of the dancing, but he said, "Ah, but we haven't waltzed."

The tune was ten times faster than any waltz she'd ever done in her life, and she suspected he'd chosen it to get even with her. "Didn't you guys do anything *slow* back in the olden days?"

He didn't answer but spun her around and around. She saw the lights whipping by in spirals, and all she could do was hang on and allow herself to be spun. As the record ended, he swept her gracefully to a conclusion and bowed deeply. She curtsied like a belle.

A bizarre, falsetto, repetitive hiccuping was coming out of him. He was— good grief—giggling! And that set *her* off into a giggling fit. He led her to the couch. They both sank down on it. She covered her mouth with her hand, but she couldn't stop. Neither could he. "Oh, help," she said, "we're hysterical!"

"Oh, yes, yes, yes. Oh, my dear." Still emitting occasional bursts of laughter, he rose to his feet, strode energetically around, searching for something that turned out to be his pipe. He lit it, said between puffs, "What a jolly evening this has been. Yes, yes, yes. Indeed. I was just remembering— Yes, my second theatrical triumph, which occurred several months after my first one, eh? I attended a dinner party wearing an ice-blue gown of my sister's—"

"You didn't!"

"I did. Some chaps who were friends of my sister's had been reading Cellini— Do you know Cellini?"

"I'm afraid I don't. I'll put him on my list though."

"Well, he tells a lovely story about dressing up a young lad *il travesti*, taking him to a party, and fooling everyone. I said, 'I could do that.' My sister cast upon me one of her famous long, level, lazy looks and said, 'Trev, I dare say you could.' 'No, he couldn't,' someone else said. 'Someone would twig.' 'You're on for a bob,' my sister said. Well, the following night they were all going to a frightfully posh dinner party, and so my sister called around and inquired if she could bring her distant cousin who had just appeared unexpectedly from Yorkshire—"

"Trevor," she said, "are you sure you're not making this up?"

"I swear to you on the collected works of the sanctified Doctor Leavis, every word of it's true. Well, my sister took me in hand. A debutante about to be presented at court could not have been groomed any more carefully than was I, and I loved every minute of it—terrible little tart that I was. 'You give the game away,' my sister said, 'and I'll break your bloody neck.'

"I will not claim that I made a beautiful girl, but I made an entirely plausible one. I bore, actually, a strong resemblance to certain horsey young ladies of the royal family. But, oh, how I was tempted to overplay the role! Restraint is something I had to learn late in life, and how I resisted temptation, I'll never know, but restrain myself I did, and my sister won her wager, and— well, the upshot was that when my unfortunate papa heard all about it—as, indeed, it was inevitable that he should—he was insufficiently amused, and I was dispatched upon the instant to my uncle, the vicar, who said everything one might imagine a vicar would say."

She laughed as she was supposed to, but she was still trying to imagine what it must have been like for him pretending to be a girl. "How did you feel?" she said.

"Eh?"

"At the frightfully posh dinner party?"

"Oh, heavens—I'm not at all certain I remember how I felt. Exhilarated, certainly. Apprehensive. I remember thinking that it was surprisingly easy— just so long as I kept my bloody mouth shut. I didn't enjoy it quite as much as I had thought I would."

"Why is that?"

An unfamiliar expression spread itself across his face. "Odd as it might seem, my dear, I don't really know."

"Gee, I never thought I'd hear you say that—that there was something you didn't know."

She still couldn't guess what he might be thinking. "You know, Trevor," she said, "I've been at parties where I was pretending to be a girl—and I already *was* one."

She thought she'd just made a terribly witty remark, but he stopped smiling. He gave her a long, somber, assessing look. "Indeed," he said. "Ah, I do know what you mean, my dear. Indeed I do. Perhaps we should have our pie."

As much fun as it had been playing dress-up, it was a relief, Gloria thought, to stop playing it. "What should I change into?" she'd asked him, and he'd said, "Whatever you would be wearing at home," and she'd decided to take him at his word, had put on a cotton nightgown and a dressing gown over it. Now she was standing just inside the closed door, worrying, like Prufrock, that maybe that's not what he'd meant at all. The forest green room with its lovely, big bed looked so inviting she would have preferred to stay there, curled up with a book, or perhaps simply sleeping—she'd just stifled a yawn—but she should say good-night at least.

After the music—she still had one of the old foxtrots jingling in her mind— the house seemed impossibly quiet; even her bare feet squeaking on the floor boards felt like an intrusion. Many of the lights had been turned out, and she couldn't see where he might have gone, but she followed the smell of his pipe. He was standing just inside his closed screen doors, puffing away and looking out into the night.

"Ah, there you are," he said and didn't seem the least bit startled by her appearance. Then she saw that he was wearing a dressing gown over striped pajamas, on his feet the same old carpet slippers he'd been wearing when she'd appeared at his door that morning. She came to rest next to him, looked out, saw the dark shapes of the trees and a sprinkle of moonlight in the creek. She heard crickets and frogs.

"I do love this," he said and turned to smile at her. "When I first arrived in this great Athens of the new world, I feared that I had condemned myself to an exile worse than Publius Naso's— Oh, the cows; oh, the students— But I cannot now imagine a life that would suit me better. I am quite content here. Yes. I would recommend it to you, my dear. Find yourself a little college far from the center of the empire, work diligently, become tenured. Then you may think and write as you please."

"Sounds wonderful. But I've got to get the degree first."

"Yes, yes—and we must eat our pie first."

He offered his arm, escorted her into the kitchen. How odd we must look, she thought, both of us dressed for bed. The overhead lights were out and two tapers were burning on the table; the pie was awaiting them on a platter surrounded by grapes and wedges of cheese. He poured her a glass of, as he described it, "a most light and delicate dessert wine." She hadn't planned to eat anything more, but the pie was exquisite—and so, for that matter, was the wine.

"Trevor," she said, "I'm scared to death of Columbia. Are they going to give me a hard time because I'm a girl?"

"Oh, Lionel would never do that. But some of the others—yes, they might indeed."

"Thanks for being so reassuring," she said, laughing. "What if Trilling doesn't like me?"

"How could he not?"

"What if he thinks I'm shallow?"

"Whyever would he think that?"

"Oh, I don't know— I'm just so— I'm afraid people will think I'm a rich country club girl— some sort of flighty dilettante."

"Well, then, you must take some pains not to appear like that, hmmm?"

"What on earth do I wear? Black dance tights and a beret? Oh, I just don't know what to— How on earth am I supposed to turn myself into a professor? I've never even had a lady professor. Never. Not once. The only one I know is the Dean of Women, and I sure don't want to be like her."

"I should think not," he said, smiling.

"Maybe they'll want me to be a TA. Then I'll actually have to stand up in a classroom and teach. I'm not worried about what I'm going to *say*. I'm worried about—you know, who I'm supposed to *pretend to be*."

"Oh, I'm beginning to understand your quandary. Yes, yes. Do you want me to tell you how to do it?"

"Yes. Please."

"I would suggest suits. Modest. Conservative— Your sense of style is impeccable, my dear. You will know what to wear— And in the classroom, never bluff. If you don't know something, say so. You are not required to know everything. And you must allow your students an opportunity to laugh with you—even, at times, *at* you—but you must never, never, never flirt with them. Early on in the year, I would say within the first week or two of classes, present them with a formidable pop quiz—yes, demonstrate to the little buggers just how monstrously ignorant they are."

Even as she was laughing, Gloria realized that this was the first time it had seemed to her that she might actually be able to do it. "Do you want me to go on?" he said.

"Oh, yes. Please do."

"You must never make love with your professors."

"Good grief, why would I even—?"

"You must not think for a moment I'm referring to Lionel. You will find him the perfect gentleman always. But some of the others will most certainly do their best to take you to bed. Believe me, they will consider it a part of their manly duty. You must resist."

"OK."

"Unfortunately, my dear, your path will be strewn with *many* pitfalls, not the least of which will be the next charming young man who will want to marry you. You must never, under any circumstances, marry a fellow graduate student."

"Oh. Why not?"

"Because you will write his thesis for him, and he will get his degree and you won't. You must not consider marrying until you are tenured—which you certainly should be well before thirty. When you do marry, you must not marry a fellow academic. Choose—oh, I don't know—a tradesman, perhaps. A plumber. A builder. A lad who is not interested in the least in what you do—a lad who goes off every day and *goes to work*. When you begin your family, you must follow the tried and true British tradition—engage a nanny."

"Hey, you've got my whole life planned for me!"

"Well, you did ask, did you not?"

"Oh, indeed I did. This is great, actually. OK, is there anything else?"

"Yes. How shall I put this? Concerning the lads—just because you make love to them, my dear, does not mean that you have to marry them."

"I don't believe it. Are you telling me to have affairs?"

"Come, come, Gloria, don't pretend to be naive. One must be discreet.

One must choose one's friends carefully. But there is no reason to live one's life like a nun, now is there, hmmm?"

All she could do was look into his amused eyes. It was too much to take in, and she was too tired. She'd think about it tomorrow.

When they finished their pie, they carried their glasses into the living room and sat together on the couch looking out at the night through the screen doors. Dutiful girl, she was wearing, as she'd been told, what she would have at home, and, curiously enough, she felt more at home than if she were at home. He was talking about something, but she wasn't quite listening to it. He seemed, somehow, to have got onto Henry James; she heard: "Wicked, old Europe— innocent, young America—" She was yawning. She covered her mouth. She hoped that he didn't think he was boring her; it was just that she was melting into the couch—

It never in a million years would have occurred to her that a professor could sleep with a student. Oh, she knew that some of them must *think* about it— creepy Dr. Stauffer, for instance—but as to actually *doing it?* Well, maybe some of them did. That just went to show how naive she really must be.

"Yes, my dear," he was saying. "We are strangers here, and sojourners, as all of our fathers were—" What on earth could he be talking about now?

Could she have an affair? What a thought! But if she wasn't allowed to go out with grad students, then— Oh, but maybe somebody in her cousins' circle, an older guy who knew how to keep his mouth shut— Come on, Gloria, don't even *think* about it. It's really wicked. But it was too bad Rick Steibel didn't live closer to New York—

He was putting fire to his pipe and puffing at it. He seemed to spend more time lighting it and letting it go out than he did actually smoking it. She sipped a bit more wine. She couldn't help it, but she just had to close her eyes for a moment. He was still talking, but she couldn't any longer even begin to make sense of the words.

She must have fallen asleep; the first she knew of it was when she felt the glass being lifted gently from her fingers. "Come, my dear, I've kept you up far too late."

He took her by the hand just as though she were a child and led her to the guest room. She felt as though she were walking through sleep like a bug through molasses. "Trevor," she murmured, "this has been lovely, lovely."

"Indeed it has, my dear. I can't recall when I've had a more pleasant evening."

He turned the covers down for her and obviously expected her to get under them, so she did. She wondered if he were going to tuck her in like a four-year-old, but, no, he only stood there a moment, his grin floating above her like the Cheshire Cat's. He stepped to the door, turned out the light. "Goodnight, Trevor," she said. "Thank you."

"Ah. Gloria," he said. "Yes. May God defend you from all the perils and dangers of the night and grant you the gift of sleep."

Throughout the night, Gloria heard the creek running. She'd wake for a moment, listen to it, and think, "How lovely. Oh, it's so wonderful to sleep—just wonderful," and she'd snuggle again into the soft warmth of the bed.

She dreamed she was at the Delta Lambda house; it was exactly where she wanted to be. She woke briefly and guessed that it must be nearly dawn. A faint blue light was spilling in the window under the blind, and she could hear the birds. That's right, she thought, I'm not at the house, I'm at Professor Bolton's—and that was just fine too. She turned over and went back to sleep.

Again she dreamed she was at the Delta Lambda house. She and Susie were getting dressed for a formal dance. She woke and saw that the brightness at the edges of the window now looked like full daylight. She had to go to the bathroom, so she got up, pulled on her dressing gown, and crept out into the hall. She couldn't hear any sounds of movement and worried that maybe she shouldn't flush the toilet, but she did anyway. Closing the door to the guest room quietly behind her, she considered getting dressed, but the bed just looked too darned pleasant so she climbed back into it. Maybe for just a few more minutes, she thought, and fell asleep at once.

When she began to dream again, she picked up her last dream just where she'd left off. She had loaned Susie her grandmother's diamond choker and long kid gloves, and Susie had loaned her a pair of sky-blue dancing pumps she'd once worn in a recital. It's wonderful, Gloria thought, how we're as close as twins.

The next time she woke, she knew that she'd been asleep for a long time, and she told herself that she really should get up, but, while she was thinking about it, she fell asleep. She dreamed that she and Susie were walking through the Delta Lambda house. Beautiful white tapers were burning everywhere, and Gloria knew that they must be for a ritual. When she woke, the first thing she saw was how green the room was—like a bower.

She felt terrific—except that she was now so hot she was perspiring. She threw back the covers, sprang out of bed, and looked at her watch. It was nearly two in the afternoon. Oh, my gosh, she thought, and I told Daddy I'd be on the road bright and early! She pulled on her dressing down, went rushing out to find sunlight blazing in the kitchen and Professor Bolton washing the dishes. "Ah, my dear," he said, "you must be hungry." She'd been asleep for close to fourteen hours.

She wanted to leave as soon as possible, but he talked her into eating toast and eggs, and she talked herself into having a quick bath. She put on clean shorts and a halter top, packed her suitcases. The night before, it had been easy enough to call him Trevor, but now, in the middle of a sunny afternoon, it felt strange to her. "Trevor, I can't begin to tell you how wonderful this has been for me." She wished she'd been able to find something better than a polite formula. She could have said something like that to nearly anyone.

"Ah, yes," he said, "and it was quite wonderful for me, too. Yes, how delightful it has been." He beamed at her, and she smiled shyly back. What was the matter with her? She hadn't felt shy with him last night. Oh, she really did have to get going; her father was going to kill her!

"My dear Gloria," he said. "We must keep in touch. Yes, yes. I must tell you— I've never had a student in your league, my dear, nor one even remotely close to it. That is why I've pushed you so hard—in the hope that you might go on, do great things. It's not merely that you're bright, or that you work hard, or that you're so dead keen. It's the *quality* of your mind."

For a moment, all she could do was stare at him. Then, as she felt herself blushing, she dropped her gaze. She sat down again at the kitchen table. He was looking at her curiously.

"Mom told me when I was little," she said, "that a lady knows how to take a compliment. It's one of a million things a lady's supposed to know how to do. And most of the time, when somebody says something nice to me, I know what to say, but this time I don't. I really, *really* don't— If you've liked having me as a student, I'm glad. I've sure liked having you as a teacher. Thank you for being so sweet to me."

"You are not in the least a person difficult to be sweet to."

"Trevor? Do you get to New York very often?"

"Not as often as I used to when Wystan was there—but quite often actually."

"Will you—call on me? Good grief, I sound like a girl in an old novel."

"I would be delighted to call upon you, my dear."

"Do you like the ballet? I could get tickets."

"I adore the ballet. I'll be there with bells on."

"We've got a date then— You know where to write to me, don't you? The grad dorm. Tell me when you're coming— Oh, I really do have to go."

As she stood up, he said, "I am certain, my dear, that one day when you look deeply inside yourself, you will find—why, nothing less than an old friend—richly complex and utterly sound. You must allow yourself to be happy, Gloria. Indeed you must."

19

Ted, preparing to tee off on the eighteenth hole at the country club shortly before noon on Sunday morning, thought that if every summer day in Raysburg, West Virginia, looked like this one, you might get fooled into thinking that this dumb, dirty, bush-league town was paradise. He and Carl were playing a full round; the old bastard liked to get an early start, and they'd been at it since seven-thirty. Ted's game had been no worse than usual, but Carl had been really burning up the course, and, even with his handicap, Ted was several strokes back. "You're not slicing as bad as usual today," Carl said, looking down the fairway with a dreamy smile.

Thanks for mentioning it, Ted thought. "Yeah," he said, "not too bad today."

It felt so fresh and clean out on the links that Ted was almost enjoying himself. The big storm on Friday night had broken the heat wave and cleared the air, and, so far, the air had stayed clear; God willing, the air might even stay clear for another few days—and, meanwhile, his damn fool daughter was driving alone three-quarters of the way across Pennsylvania. If he'd stayed home, he'd just be sitting around worrying about her, so golf was a good distraction. And, anyway, he might as well enjoy it because he didn't have any choice in the matter: Carl had invited him, and you don't say no to Carl W. Eberhardt. Instead of the usual foursome, there were only the two of them, and that ordinarily would have meant that Carl had something important, something *confidential*, to tell him, but, if he did, Ted had yet to hear it.

Carl extended a hand, and his caddy put a driver in it. Carl didn't like talking to caddies, and they all knew it. He stepped up to the tee, took a couple gentle practice strokes, and then, without further ado, drove—CRACK!—and drilled her straight down the fairway clean as a whistle, a good 250 yards, easy. He held his follow-through and watched the flight of the ball.

"Terrific, Carl," Ted said, "picture perfect."

"Oh, my," Carl said, "now isn't this the life? You know, Ted, we got us one of the prettiest little courses in the country right here in our own backyard, wouldn't you say that?"

"Yeah, I sure would."

Carl stepped away from the tee, grinning his biggest, sunniest grin, and said, "I'll bet you've been thinking— For the last year or two, I just *bet* you've been thinking: is that old fart ever going to climb out of the saddle and let me climb on? Ha, ha, ha."

Ted laughed too. It was the only thing to do.

"Oh, yeah, I'd be thinking the same thing in your place, believe you me. Well, I'm not going to keep you in suspense any longer, Ted. Seems to me the time's *now*."

Oh, my God, Ted thought. "Is that right?" he said in a noncommittal voice, and, to collect himself, turned to his caddy—who already had his driver out.

Ted's heart was pounding, and his mouth had gone dry, and he was afraid that if he hesitated even a moment, his knees might start to shake, so he stepped right up to the tee—Goddamn it, control yourself!—and, without giving it a second thought, smacked the son-of-a-bitch good. He felt the face of the club meet the ball beautifully. The sound of it was music to his ears. He'd put it right where he'd wanted it, and it was moving like a streak. Yeah, rocketing away like a little white bullet. Oh, my God, it was curving—describing a nasty parabola— It was the worst damn slice of the day. Down it went—WHAM— dead in the rough. "Shit," he said under his breath.

"Tsk, tsk, tsk," Carl said, "looks like you're buying the beer."

They began strolling down the fairway with their caddies trailing at a respectful distance behind them. Ted wouldn't mind buying the beer, and now that the news was sinking in, he didn't even mind his rotten slice. What he felt like doing was jumping for joy. Carl was retiring, but when? After all these years, he could wait a few more months—but, good Christ, wouldn't it be sweet to know the end was in sight?

"You ought to do something about that slice of yours," Carl was saying. "You ever get her straightened out, it'd knock four or five points off your handicap."

"Well, you can't say I haven't tried."

"At least you get lots of practice with a chipping iron, ha, ha, ha— So anyhow, I've been thinking about throwing in the towel. Yeah, I'm not kidding you. Before the month's out. My health's not what it could be. Blood pressure's up, having a little bit of prostate problems. Nothing serious, but it makes you think."

"I'm sorry to hear that, Carl."

"Oh, well, the doctor says I better start taking it easy. Yeah, well, and it's about time too. Why should I go to Washington and talk to that bunch of New Deal pinkos when *you* can do it, ha, ha, ha!"

Ted tried to laugh right along with him, but this time he wasn't having much luck. Although they were walking downhill, he was breathing hard. He chose his words carefully. "I don't know, Carl. There's nobody understands steel any better than you do."

"It's nice of you to say that, Ted. But things have got too damned compli- cated for me. My own dad hung on too long, and— It's only natural, I guess, but— Well, he made a few mistakes, and I had to go to the board and have a little tussle with him. It's kind of rough, you know, when it's your own father. And I vowed I'd never do what he did. Always said I'd get out when I was still thinking straight— Yeah, and with a good, solid, reliable fellow like yourself ready to step in, well, I've got nothing to worry about, and— You know, Ted, we've got *lots* of excellent men. Thanks to you. And even if *you* were gone—God forbid—I wouldn't have a thing to worry about."

Ted kept right on walking just as though everything was still hunky-dory. "Now you take Charlie Edmonds," he heard Carl saying. "I'm real glad you brought him in. Yep, that was a real smart move on your part. A man like that is sure hard to find. Smart, reliable, good family man, grew up in the steel industry, knows it inside out, works like a dog, and *young*, you know what I mean? Got lots of years left in him. Shit, what is he? Thirty-six? Thirty-eight? Couldn't be much older than that. Why, if something was to happen and you couldn't step in, why, I bet Charlie could take over and do a terrific job. Nowhere near as good as you'd do, of course. I know that. You're the best we've got."

Ted had once served briefly on a small, ugly oiler called the *Betsy Ross* but known to everyone but the Captain as the *Betsy Rust*. Before the war, the captain had served for seventeen years in the Coast Guard, and he hated nothing worse than ninety-day wonders with college degrees, and all the officers assigned to the *Betsy Rust* were ninety-day wonders with college degrees. Most of the men had joined up after Pearl and were green as grass, so the captain didn't much care for them either. The captain, in fact, hated everybody on board, and, for reasons Ted could never figure out—although, God knows, he'd tried—the captain hated Ted most of all. The only place Ted could go where he was assured of being left alone for a few minutes was the officer's head, and, on one particularly hot and boring day in a dead calm sea out in the middle of nowhere—certainly nowhere near the enemy—Ted was peacefully settled down on the can. He had thoroughly evacuated his bowels; he had, in fact, just taken the most pleasantly satisfying dump he'd had in days, and he was drifting away into a pleasantly dreamy state that was far, far from the *Betsy Rust* and the whole damn, stinking war when a demented kamikaze, having badly miscalculated his approach to the DE steaming off the *Betsy's* starboard bow, decided to take a shot at the *Betsy* herself and scored a direct hit on the pilot house, killing the captain and every other officer who outranked Lieutenant Theodore R. Cotter and thus leaving Ted, with his pants down around his ankles and a Perry Mason novel open on his lap, in command of the ship.

Even though what he'd done in the next several hours had earned Ted a decoration and a promotion, it had been living hell—nothing else to say about it—and, throughout every minute of that living hell Ted had been forced to listen to Ensign Marcovy, badly in shock, who'd stuck to Ted like his shadow, muttering over and over: "*Jeez, we didn't even see him coming.*" Now Ted felt exactly like Ensign Marcovy.

Carl slapped Ted on the shoulder. "Hey, there's no need to get alarmed at anything I'm saying, Ted. I'm just thinking out loud, you know what I mean?"

Ted's ball was in the deep grass. "A seven iron?" he said to his caddy.

"Yes, sir, that's what I'd use."

Ted took the club. Bear down, he told himself. Now's not the time to blow apart. And he chopped her good—a terrific shot that sent a divot up like a flushed grouse—and laid his ball right up to the edge of the green. "Good going," Carl said.

"Thanks."

They waited for Ted's caddy to fetch the divot and pat it back into the turf. Then they strolled over to Carl's ball. "You know," Carl said, "when I get a report as good and thorough as that one you sent over— Yeah, I finally got around to reading Charlie's report on Old Reliable. Yeah, I know it took me long enough, but I'm sure glad I got around to it, because it really made me think. Boy, there's a son-of-a-gun who knows the steel business. Yeah, does Charlie ever know what's going on at Old Reliable, you bet your ass! Painted a real clear picture. All the facts and figures. I can't recall when I've *ever* seen anything presented as clear."

Grinning, Carl eyeballed his shot. "Eight iron," he said to his caddy, took it, and, with a neat little snap, shot it straight to the pin.

With all the time in the world, Ted walked over to his ball. "Nine iron?" he said to his caddy.

"Yes, sir."

"Pitch it nice and easy?"

"Yes, sir, a nice, easy shot."

Oh, nice and easy, you bet, Ted thought. He was so angry, he knew he had to hold back. He looked away at the sky a moment. Gently, gently, he told himself. He addressed the ball. He thought about it, planning his stroke. He pitched it right up to the hole. "Now that's some good golfing," Carl said.

"Thanks, Carl."

"So I bet you must of made up your mind by now, huh, Ted? Isn't that right? So just what *is it* you're planning to do down at Old Reliable?"

You fucking bastard, Ted thought. "Well, sir," he said, "the reason I sent you that report— I know how you hate to read those damn things— But it was such a damn good report, like you said— And the reason I sent it to you was I'd really value your opinion."

"You know, Ted, it crossed my mind that's what you might be thinking."

Carl's caddy pulled the flag out. "Yeah," Carl went on in the same gentle, conversational voice he'd been using all along, "I said to myself, I bet Ted wants to be sure I know what's what—that I can see the big picture like you young guys say—because he wants to sway me to his way of thinking. Kind of like showing me the handwriting on the wall," and, almost as an afterthought, he sank his putt.

"Nice," Ted said.

"Thanks. I just can't remember when I've had as good a day out on the links. Must be the weather—and the company. You know, Ted, I've been thinking about what you told me all the way back when we first hired you, and I thought, well, goddamn it, it's taken all these years, but— Well, you know, I believe you're right. Between you and Charlie Edmonds, you've brought me around to your point of view. We've got to modernize the Indian Works or shut her down. Isn't that the picture you wanted me to get?"

"Well, pretty much. But, ah— There's a number of ways to look at it, Carl, and I didn't want to proceed until I'd talked to you about it."

"I really appreciate that. I sure do. OK, so here's my thinking on the matter. It's been a hell of a good year. Our profits are way up, and Ike's in the White House, but he won't be there forever. If we want to stay in the game, we've got to start plowing some of it back in. Wouldn't you say that? And Old Reliable's long overdue. So if we got us a good, efficient, young general super, let's say Al Connely, for instance— Didn't *you* suggest him? And if we turned him loose, not a blank check, mind you, but with reasonable dollar—and if we decided to narrow down, don't you suppose we could have us the sweetest, most up-to-date little rolling mill you ever saw? Yeah, I bet we could—with a man like Al Connely. I bet he could do it in six months."

"That's a terrific idea, Carl. And Connely's exactly the right man for that kind of restructuring. Right up his alley."

"I'm just delighted to hear you say that, Ted. You know, since the day you came down here, we haven't had us a serious disagreement about anything. Do you realize that? Sometimes you swayed me to your way of thinking, and sometimes I swayed you to mine, but a serious disagreement? Between us, that's just not possible, ha, ha, ha. You shouldn't have any trouble with that putt, now should you?"

Ted had been standing there like a fool not even thinking about his putt. He turned angrily toward his caddy; the boy must have sensed that something was up: he gave Ted a small, hesitant, encouraging smile along with his putting iron.

Ted stroked the ball—a nice, easy tap—and it went in. "What are you now?" Carl asked, "with your handicap? Four back?"

"That's about right, Carl. Five, I think."

They began to walk back to the clubhouse. "You boys go on ahead," Carl told the caddies.

Ted trudged along at Carl's side. Then Carl stopped walking, and so did

Ted. "I thank my lucky stars we were smart enough to grab you away from Xenon. Now that Ted Cotter, I always thought—that Ted Cotter's a man who'd never let his *personal feelings* cloud his judgment. Yep, that's why he'd make an excellent president. He'd always put the good of Raysburg Steel first, no matter what."

"I appreciate your confidence in me, Carl."

"Oh, I know you do, Ted. I know that. And you know what? You've taught me a thing or two since you've been here, and I'd be the first to admit it. When you came down here and started talking about the kind of guys we needed— you know, the high standards we should set for our boys—why, I thought maybe you were carrying these modern management practices a little too far. But hell, I've come around to your way of thinking on that. It's just like you've always said, we need good family men, guys our children can look up to and respect."

Carl took out his cigarettes, offered Ted one. Ted took it automatically. Carl lit Ted's smoke and then his own. Carl wasn't smiling any longer. Carl spent so much time smiling, it was a bit of a shock to see him when he wasn't. Ted looked closely at Carl's face and saw that the old bastard was mad enough to kill.

"You know," Carl said, "when I start hearing certain stories, I get kind of upset. When it gets so far that my very own daughter is complaining about somebody who gets tight at the club night after night right there in front of God and everybody—I mean, falling down dead drunk—somebody who gets so stinko the colored boys have to drive him home— When I start hearing stories about somebody catting around down in South Raysburg— When I'm hearing those stories from every damn quarter so I know they're kind of what you'd call common knowledge— Getting right down to it, Ted, when everybody in town's talking about a certain son-of-a-bitch— Well, you know, it bothers me. It truly does. Because that kind of behavior reflects badly on all of us, don't you think so, Ted? It reflects badly on me, and on you, and on our wives, and on *our daughters*. Wouldn't you say so?"

"That's right, Carl. I couldn't agree with you more."

"And you know, Ted, this isn't a recent development. This has been going on for quite some time."

"I'm truly sorry about that, sir. I assume full responsibility. My personal feelings must have clouded my judgment on this matter, and I really appreciate your pointing that out to me. But let me assure you, sir, you don't have anything further to worry about."

Carl stared at Ted a moment longer with his murderer's ice-cold eyes, but then, slowly, his usual big, broad, shit-eating grin spread across his face. "I'm just delighted to hear that, Ted, ha, ha, ha. But hell, I wasn't really worried. I've always known I could count on you."

• • •

The bastard, Ted thought. The goddamn, sanctimonious, evil, old son-of-a-bitch. Ted had been barely able to hold himself together; he'd been counting the seconds until he could get that evil old prick out of his sight, but then he hadn't been able to stand the thought of seeing anybody — not even Laney and the boys — so he'd driven over to Waverley Park, and now he was pacing around on the top of a hill smoking cigarettes. That's right, he, Theodore R. Cotter, the most senior vice-president of the Raysburg Steel Corporation was pacing around alone on the top of a hill in Waverley Park on a hot Sunday afternoon smoking cigarettes because he couldn't think of anything else to do. Now wasn't that just marvelous?

Seven goddamn years he'd put into that goddamn crazy outfit. He'd worked his ass off — fifty, sixty, sometimes seventy hours a week — and he'd never taken much of a vacation, not more than a few days at a time, and it was all going to be worth it because he was going to be *number one*: what a laugh that was! So Carl was having prostate problems, was he? May the good Lord grant him bigger and better ones. May his whole damn asshole drop out.

Jesus, and Charlie Edmonds — what a piss-off — and Ted had been the one to bring him in, snatched him right out from under their noses at Bethlehem Steel, and Ted had been glad to get him — oh, wasn't that another big laugh? Oh, yeah, the world was just full of big laughs. And the crux of the matter wasn't firing William Parnell Dougherty; when it came right down to it, he'd just as leave see Billy gone as not, but the thing that galled the hell out of him was Carl holding a gun to his head — the old bastard had actually threatened him! — and he needed Carl. Ted had enemies all through the corporation — from the VPs down to the foremen — and, without Carl, Ted was nothing but an asshole from out of town.

After ten minutes or so, Ted began to calm down. What he needed now was a drink — a good, cold beer like the one he'd passed up back at the club — so he should go home, but he still wasn't ready to face his wife, and it struck him, looking down over the postcard-perfect, rolling hills, that not too long ago the whole damn park used to belong to the Eberhardts, so what did Carl know about growing up poor? Carl's old man had been *building* during the Depression — as Ted ought to know; he was living in the house Carl's dad had built — and you'd better believe that back in the thirties Carl had never eaten a ketchup sandwich or boiled beans. Carl had sure as hell never had to spread all his change out on his desk — most of it in pennies — to see if he could afford to blow five cents on a glass of beer.

At some time in your life — right about now, for instance — shouldn't you ask yourself if you haven't got enough money? Over the last few years Ted had been socking it away good, sticking it in bonds and blue chips, and when the Merriman estate was settled, he'd really be sitting pretty, so he didn't have to work, but the thing is, he *liked* working. OK, so all he had to do was pick up the phone tomorrow morning and he could have another job within the hour—he was pretty damn sure of that—and Laney had always hated Raysburg, but would she like Pittsburgh any better? No, probably not, and neither would he for that matter—Pittsburgh or anywhere up the Mon Valley. Jesus, the air pollution up there made Raysburg look like Atlantic City.

Then there was the bomb shelter, but hell, they hadn't even poured the concrete yet, and besides, he could build a bomb shelter anywhere. And there were the boys to worry about. They both adored the Academy—but if they liked that tin soldier outfit so much, they could damn well board there. So, yes, he could get out of the sorry valley, and— Hey, how about Texas? There was an idea. The Texans were getting into steel in a big way, and maybe that's what he needed at this point in his life: a big change, a new start. But, of course, wherever he went, he wouldn't be anywhere near the top. VP was the best he could ask for. Even if he played it cagey, got a hell of a lot more money—and he was pretty sure he could do that—he'd just be another dumbass VP working with a bunch of other dumbass VPs, and somebody else would still be number one.

Well, he could always go into work tomorrow morning and fire Billy Dougherty. It wasn't like Billy hadn't been warned, and he could always give him a halfway decent kiss-off—and then what? Would Carl really retire? But even if he did, what assurance did Ted have that he wouldn't be passed over for Charlie? And one thing he knew for certain was that he, Theodore R. Cotter, was not going to work for Charles T. Edmonds—not even for ten minutes. So, even if he canned Billy, he should hedge his bets, make those calls, but it was hard to be rational about this, because what he wanted to do—what he would have just *loved* to do—was drive straight over to Carl's house and grab the old bastard by the shoulders and stare him straight in the eyes and give him a big horse laugh and say, "Carl, now it's your turn to listen to *me*, you evil old prick. *I quit.*"

Laney was worried sick about Ted, and she was mad enough at Princess Priss to murder her in cold blood—if the spoiled little bitch ever came home. The sun was already beginning to sink behind the apple trees, and there was still no sign of her. "Where the hell *is* she?"

"Oh, don't worry, cookie," he said. "If she's in any trouble, she'll call."

That's probably what the poor guy had to keep telling himself. He was a real sap about Gloria; she'd always been his favorite—which was kind of funny; you'd think a man would favor one of his sons—but Laney was also dead certain by now that he had more on his mind than Gloria. Whatever it was, she just wished he'd come right out and tell her instead of making her sit there and guess.

He'd come back late from his golf game; he'd jumped right into the pool;

he'd thrashed up and down like a madman. Then he'd spent the afternoon in the bedroom with the *New York Times*. He hadn't wanted to go down to the club for dinner and he'd wanted the boys out of the house—they'd obviously been driving him nuts—so she'd called in some favors and arranged for both of them to go and stay with classmates for the night. Mrs. Warsinski had made him a nice chicken salad, but he'd hardly touched it. All he seemed to want to do was sit by the side of the pool and stare at the huge, ugly hole out by the apple trees and drink—now he was working on his *fifth* Scotch—and the moment Laney had figured out that he intended to get loaded, she'd quit. She'd only had two Scotches the entire damned day; it had been a couple of hours since the last one, and she was getting really jumpy.

"You know, cookie," he said, "when I was a kid, I used to caddy at the Briarville country club. We didn't have two cents to rub together, and I really needed every cent I made, and—God, I hated those rich bastards. They weren't that rich, I guess, but they sure looked rich to me. And now I've turned into one of them."

What could that possibly mean? "Oh, Teddy, no. Don't say that."

She waited for him to go on with his train of thought, but he lit another cigarette and sat there like a stone. All day long she'd been afraid he was going to say: "You know, cookie, you've turned into a real lush lately. Why don't you do something about it?" but then she'd be able to say, "Oh, I'm way ahead of you there, hon. It's really been worrying me too, so I've decided to cut down. I've only had two drinks today." But maybe he'd say, "You know, cookie, there's not much left of our marriage. Why don't we think about getting a divorce?" and if he said that, she didn't know what she'd do. Her heart would break. But, of course, that was ridiculous. Why would he say *that?*

She heard the sound of the station wagon turning into the driveway and glanced quickly over at her husband to see how he was reacting. He gave her a little smile, but she wasn't sure what it meant, and she thought, he's going to kill her, and if he does, she's got it coming. She heard the French doors slide open. "Mom? Dad? You out there?" Of course we're out here, you little idiot; take two steps and you'll see us.

Laney watched Princess Priss, in sun glasses and shorts, her hair up in a ponytail, walking down the steps to the pool. God, she had a terrific figure. Well, at her age, it was easy enough to do. "Here she is," Laney said, "home bright and early just the way she promised."

"I'm sorry, Mom. I slept in. I got a late start." Gloria picked up a lawn chair, set it next to her father, and sat on it. "Are you all right?" he asked her.

"I'm fine, Dad. I'm tired."

"Any trouble?"

"No. Everything's fine."

"Did you get gas?"

"Well, of course I did."

"OK, so what the hell took you so long?"

"I just told you. I didn't leave until afternoon. I slept in really late, and then I got talking to some of the girls— You'd be surprised at the number of girls who were around for summer school—"

"Thanks for the call."

"Oh, Dad, I told you I was exhausted. I thought you'd want me to get a good night's sleep."

"I don't give a damn about that. I just wanted to know what you were doing, OK? One damn phone call, OK?"

"I'm sorry, Dad."

Laney was waiting for him to take the top of his daughter's head off, and Gloria must have been expecting it too; her eyes were invisible behind her sunglasses, but her face was turned toward his. He wasn't wearing sunglasses, but his face was just as impossible to read as Gloria's. "Are you hungry?" he asked her.

"I guess so. Sort of."

"There's some cold chicken and potato salad," Laney said.

"Gloria," Ted said, "that was just about the most stupid, selfish thing you've ever done in your life. What the hell were you thinking?"

"I told you on the phone, Dad, I *wasn't* thinking. I'm really sorry. I won't do anything like that again."

"You're goddamn right, you won't. You're confined to quarters until further notice."

Gloria didn't say anything. "Do you think I'm kidding?" he asked her.

"No, I don't think you're kidding."

Gloria stood up abruptly, and, without another word, walked away. Laney watched her walk up the steps and into the kitchen. Laney saw the light in the kitchen go on, heard the refrigerator door open and close. After a while, she saw the light in Gloria's room go on. How could the little bitch do that to him— just walk away from him like that? She owes him a hell of a lot more than that. Oh, Teddy, she wanted to tell him, you've still got *me*.

"Cookie?" he said, "if you were getting up?" and he offered her his empty glass.

In the kitchen, Laney poured her husband another one on the rocks, and then— Well, then, she simply stood there, holding the damned bottle of Johnny Walker in her hands, thinking how cruel it was. She'd been good, hadn't she? She'd had only two drinks the entire day, and compared to— Don't kid yourself, Marcelaine— But, come on, a little one wouldn't— Stop it!— But she was getting the shakes, and Teddy was bound to notice, and she was doing a hell of a lot better than— Her hands were shaking like an old lady's, and she was sweating out of every pore—too hot and too cold, honest to God chills, like a fever. Her very bones ached. I can't do this, she thought, I really can't—oh, dear God—and quickly poured out somewhat more than a double and downed it in two long, exquisite gulps.

She closed her eyes and felt it burning down her throat and into her stomach. The elixir of the Gods. That's really funny. She felt tears start under her closed eyelids. Oh, she thought, how I loathe myself.

After a while she began to feel better. She sighed, opened her eyes, and wiped her face on the tea-towel. The light had changed, although she couldn't say exactly how; she couldn't really say it had become brighter or clearer. What was she thinking? That something had gone wrong over the years; it had been when Teddy had moved them to this dumb, dirty town, and everything had gone sliding downhill from there, so he couldn't really blame her, but—and there was something else. She couldn't quite put her finger on it— Oh, but there was that lovely time when they'd still lived in New York and they'd still been so very, very happy. Jimmy had just begun to sleep through the night, and so she'd been able to sleep through the night too, and getting enough sleep for a change had been pure bliss. Yes, that's how simple it had been—just getting enough sleep. Gloria had been at Fairhaven, and Bobby, when you finally got him tucked in, always went out like a light, and so, all of a sudden, she and Teddy had been alone every night, and it had been like a second honeymoon. So she was forty-three; what was that? Just a number. So maybe, just maybe, if she tried really hard—and, pouring herself another quick one, she smiled at how simple it really was after all. Oh, yes, tomorrow was Monday—a bright, sparkling new day—and tomorrow was the day when she'd quit for good.

Ted was glad that Gloria was home safe, and that should have made him feel better, but it hadn't made him feel much better at all. He hadn't planned on doing it, but he was drunk as a skunk. The sun was setting blood-red back there behind the apple trees, and now, suddenly, he knew what that light reminded him of. It was clear as the nose on your face, and he didn't know why it had never occurred to him before. He probably should have talked it out years ago—got it off his chest, like they say—because he still thought about it. Not all the time, but it stayed in his mind, and sometimes even now he could still see it. Sometimes when he was going to sleep, he could see it.

Laney was back, offering him a fresh drink. He smiled to say thanks, and she smiled a lovely smile back.

"Teddy? Sweetheart?" Sometimes his wife could look at him with a gaze that was straight and clean as a girl's. "Why don't you make that your last?"

He knew she was expecting him to be annoyed, but he wasn't annoyed. He wished she'd said it sooner. It had been years since he'd had this much to drink, and, even if he stopped now, he was going to feel like a wagonload of shit in the morning. "Sure," he said.

But he did want this one. He wanted every damn drop of it. He lit a smoke to go with it. Sometimes drinking helped you think—or anyhow, that's what you told yourself—but he didn't know whether it was helping him think right now or not. He looked out at the goddamned sun setting in the apple trees. It'd been near the end of the war. The Japs had pretty well been whipped, but they'd just kept on fighting. What the hell did they think they were going to gain from it at that point? They must have known they were whipped. And Ted hadn't known for sure that the war was damn near over, but he could feel it in the air. Hell, everybody could.

Before he'd seen a lot of explosions, he used to think they're all of them instantaneous, but sometimes they're not. Sometimes they're almost in slow motion, and other times they've got stages to them—so anyhow, there was a kind of a bloom to that one. A bloom of fire, sort of ball-shaped like a rose, coming out of that goddamn thing—Ted thinks it's in his tail, but he couldn't really see it—and then a kind of THWUP noise, and then what he'd call the real explosion: CA-BOOM! And then it's like somebody took a big hammer about the size of a skyscraper and hit the ship with it. Ted's flat on his back, sliding across the deck, and there's a rain of metal coming down all over the place, pieces of the bastard coming down all over the ship. Lieutenant Holcomb, who'd been standing not more than three feet away, has caught the number that Ted had been sure had been coming for him. The bottom half of Lieutenant Holcomb is sliding across the deck next to Ted, but the top half is not exactly salvageable. Never even found his dog tags.

They hopped up those little bastards on something before they sent them out. That particular little bastard had been coming in so low he hadn't shown on the radar, and if Billy hadn't reacted the way he had, as quick as he did, they would have lost *The Minnewaukan* and Ted wouldn't have been sitting around years later, drunk, thinking about it. He'd recommended Billy for a promotion. He'd recommended him a few times before that. Billy really should have had command of his own ship, but no, he'd pissed off too much brass. The story of his life, the sorry son-of-a-bitch.

Yeah, that's the way it goes. Ted had always figured the only reason he'd made Lieutenant Commander was because he'd been so good at kissing ass.

"A penny," Laney said.

"Huh?"

"A penny for your thoughts, sweetheart."

"Oh. I was just thinking that the rank never did me any good. You know, Lieutenant Commander. It was just a farewell present."

"You're not sitting there brooding about the war, are you, hon?"

"Oh, hell no. Not really. But your mind goes back sometimes. Aw, hell, cookie, it's so damn long ago."

"Yeah, it sure is. Come on, Teddy, the war's over. OK? I'm going to go up and get ready for bed, and— Hey, sailor, don't make me wait too long, OK?"

There was no misunderstanding *that* one, and he laughed out loud. "Just let me finish this," he said and winked at her. She winked back.

He watched her as she walked away. If he lived to be a hundred, he'd never get over how beautifully a woman is built—the curve of her ass, the way the weight of her is carried there, and in her thighs, that *female* shape. Oh, God, he'd missed her during the war. He didn't know what he'd do without her.

He'd been in the sack. He'd had a touch of something—the trots, running a fever, just plain beat—and Doc had said, "You got to get some sack time in, skipper," so Ted had been sound asleep—a million miles deep—and all of a sudden the ship's heeling over and the General Alarm's going off—*bing, bing, bing*—and Ted's first thought is: what's that clown doing? Because Dougherty's OOD. And Ted jumps straight up—he's sleeping with his clothes on—and he can hear the twenties open up, and he thinks: Jesus! And he takes off like a shot, still half asleep and not thinking clearly, and he goes running straight up onto the bridge. When the captain arrives on the bridge, the OOD's supposed to brief him, but Dougherty doesn't brief him because there's *no time*, and, besides, Ted's got eyes. He'd never tried to tell anybody what it looked like.

It's coming out of the sun. They liked to do that, the little bastards, wait till the sun's hanging right on the horizon, blinding you, and then they'd come at you right out of the sun. So there's the sun on the sea, big and blood-red—it looked just like that stinking flag they've got—and it's coming right out of it. And the sun's making a blood-red path on the sea so bright you can't look at it, and it's following right along that path, just as low to the sea as it can get, right there hanging in the sun. And then it starts to pull up out of the sea, and Ted could swear it's coming straight at him.

To this very day, he could close his eyes and see it. Hanging there. Getting closer by the second. Like a kind of black shape, like a big goddamn black bug, or— More geometrical than that. A machine shape, black at the center but smeared at the edges in the hot, red light. A one-engine Hemp. Impossible to really see it in the sun. And Dougherty's brought the ship around to give the gunners their best shot, and the forties have opened up, and the twenties are laying tracers into it, and then the forties are hammering it good, but nothing fazes it. Getting bigger and bigger—and Ted's just frozen like a statue, just standing there like a jerk, and it looks like it's coming right down his throat. He's not thinking about the ship. He's not even thinking about Gloria or little Bobby or even about Laney. All he's thinking is: Oh, my God, I'm dead.

• • •

Closed away in her hot, stuffy bedroom, Gloria was pacing up and down, seething with anger. She'd actually been happy when she'd walked into the house; she'd actually felt calm and at peace. But then, within minutes, she'd been transformed into a sullen, resentful little girl, and all it had taken had been hearing her father's Lieutenant Commander voice saying: "You're confined to quarters until further notice."

She had a B.A. Honors degree and a Phi Beta Kappa key. She'd been president of her chapter of Delta Lambda. She could vote, for heavens sake! She'd spent the day before with the most erudite man she'd ever met in her life—a witty and mature and sophisticated man—and not only had he enjoyed her company, *he'd taken her seriously*. She'd driven, safely and uneventfully, back to Raysburg, and the moment she'd arrived, she'd been confined to quarters until further notice.

Come on, she told herself, what did you expect? But nothing she was telling herself seemed to help. It just wasn't fair, that's all—and then she heard her parents stumbling upstairs. Her mother was laughing—no, *giggling*, actually. Drunk again. Well, that was no surprise; her mother was always drunk these days. At least they'd left the pool, so maybe she could have a quick swim—or maybe not. Did "confined to quarters" mean she couldn't use the pool? Oh, just peachy keen!

That terrible night when she'd been trying to cover up for Mr. Dougherty— she really should have her head examined—her dad had sent her to her room just as though she'd been fifteen, and it had been humiliating enough even when she'd *been* fifteen. "I'm paying the bills around here so I'm calling the tune," he'd said, or words to that effect, and she supposed he had the right to say it, but it still made her furious every time she thought about it, and— Good grief, what were her parents *doing* in there? Why didn't they just go to sleep?

But this, she thought, is what it all comes down to: I can go around pretending to be grown-up—mature, intelligent, fully in charge of my own destiny—but only so long as I'm a *good girl*. The moment I step out of line—wham!—I'm not grown-up at all, and I'm confined to quarters until further notice.

"Be reasonable, Gloria," the secret watcher said, "you knew he was going to have to punish you somehow or other," but she didn't feel like being reasonable—and why on earth were they making all that noise?

He could keep his damned money. Look at Susie; she'd always worked, even if it had only been giving twirling lessons to little girls. Look how happy it had made her to get her first real job. OK, Gloria told herself, *I* can do that too. When I get to New York, *I'll* get a job. I'll be a cocktail waitress or some darned thing— But, no, she didn't need to do that. She had a scholarship, and she'd apply for a teaching assistantship, and Columbia University would *pay her* to stand up in front of a classroom. Trevor had made her see how she might actually be able to do it—even enjoy it—so she'd get her PhD, and some college or university would go on paying her to stand up in front of a classroom. No matter what her stupid cousins said, she didn't need her own apartment in Manhattan. She didn't need Traina-Norrell dresses. She didn't need French underwear or fifty pairs of dress pumps. She'd live in the graduate dorm and teach Freshman English in one of the Zuckerman suits she already owned, and her father could keep every cent of his precious money! And, by now, it was fairly obvious what her parents were doing in there.

Gloria knew that her parents had to have sex sometime—if they didn't, after all, neither she nor the brats could have entered the world—and she'd certainly seen them hugging and smooching, but it had always been difficult for her to imagine them actually *doing it*. There'd been times before when she'd heard bangs and thumps and other furtive noises in the night and suspected that's what they'd been doing, but now it didn't take any imagination at all; it was, in fact, downright embarrassing. Come on, you guys, she thought, you shouldn't subject your daughter to *this*. Then she heard the small, whimpering gasps getting louder, heard them rise in pitch and volume, crescendo into a series of rhythmic, high-pitched squeals, finally transform into a prolonged, wildly keening wail. Good grief, Mom! she thought, exercise a little restraint, can't you?

But that seemed to have been it. All she could hear now was a resounding silence. Whewee, she thought, that was really something! And, as she sat and listened to the silence that was *too silent*, she felt her anger draining away and she wasn't sure what she was feeling. Hearing her parents making love had really upset her, and she didn't know why.

Well, for one thing, it just wasn't seemly. ("Yeah, you really *are* a priss, aren't you?" the secret watcher said.) And, for another thing, it reminded her that she didn't have a boyfriend. Maybe, she thought, that's what's so seductive about the idea of getting married: you could do it to your heart's content, even yell your darned head off, and it would be perfectly fine because it was—or at least most people thought it was—just as Susie had said on the phone, part of God's plan for you. And getting married also meant you didn't have to do all those hard, scary things like learning to be a TA or supporting yourself, and sometimes—like right now, for instance—she still missed Rolland so much she felt like weeping. Oh, help. Could she really have an affair? That was a terrifying thought. And, as she tried to sort everything out, she heard her father get up and go downstairs. She heard him settling onto one of the lawn chairs by the pool.

She looked out her window. There he was, sitting hunched forward with a drink in his hand. Oh, she thought, he must be worried sick about me—and why was she cursed with the ability, always, to be able to see things from somebody else's point of view?

• • •

Gloria was barefoot and didn't want to startle him, so, as soon as she reached the bottom of the steps, she called out, "Want some company?"

"Oh, sure."

She pulled up a lawn chair. "Anything the matter, Dad?"

"Oh, no. Just having a little trouble getting to sleep, that's all."

He picked up his Chesterfields and, just as she'd seen him do it a million times, tapped the pack sharply once with just enough force so that several cigarettes jumped partway out; without looking in her direction, he offered her one of them. "Daddy! Did you think I started smoking?"

Startled, he turned and looked at her; then he threw back his head and laughed. "Oh, hell. I don't know what I'm thinking about. I'm so used to sitting here with your mother."

Oh, she thought, he's had *way* too much to drink. She'd guessed it from the offered cigarette, confirmed it from the blur in his voice, the unfocused way he was looking at her. She'd seen her mother drunk but never her father, and she wondered if she shouldn't simply excuse herself and slip away. But, no, that would surely seem impolite— Well, as long as they were both sitting there, she might as well go right to the heart of the matter. "Dad? Are you worried about me? Are you still mad at me?"

He looked at her a moment before answering. "No, princess, I'm not mad at you anymore. I probably should be, but I'm not."

She wasn't sure she believed him. "Something's come up at work," he said, "and I can't figure out what to do about it. Just trying to get enough Scotch in me to get some sleep, that's all."

If he'd been anyone other than her father, she would have said, "Do you want to talk about it?" but she simply couldn't say that to him.

After a moment, he said, "The thing that really got me is I'd already told you you could go to Philadelphia—"

Oh, did they have to go around it again? Well, she supposed they did. "And I've already *told you*, Daddy, I'm really sorry. I really goofed. It was really dumb." After a moment she added, "I guess I just wanted to see if I could do it."

"Do what?"

"Drive somewhere on my own."

He seemed to be mulling it over. Then he didn't say what she would have expected any normal person to say: "Girls don't do that." He said, "Yeah, that makes sense."

It does? she thought.

"But don't expect me to condone it." He was suddenly either quite angry or trying his best to sound that way. "Never pull a stunt like that again. Do you understand me?"

"Yes, I understand you. I won't do anything like that again. I've already said that—about a dozen times. We've already talked about it, Daddy."

"Yeah, yeah, yeah, I know. I just want to be sure everything's clear, that's all, and— I bet you're probably still pretty upset about your grandmother passing on."

He glanced over at her and seemed to read agreement in her lack of response. "Yeah, I figured you were. You've always been a sensitive girl, and you got real close to her at the end, and— So I figured I'd give you the benefit of the doubt." Good grief, she thought, that's certainly a charitable interpretation. I wonder if there's any truth to it.

She didn't have a watch on, but she knew that her time sense wasn't working right. The fireflies were quite high by now, so it must be really late, but it didn't feel late. She'd slept so long at Trevor's she probably wouldn't get any sleep at all tonight, and so she didn't mind sitting up with her dad, but she began to worry that maybe he wanted to be alone.

She was about to say goodnight when he said, "You know, honey, what's the most important thing to me? My family— My family's always been the most important thing to me."

What an odd thing for him to say—a man as remote and uncommunicative as he was. What could he be thinking about? But then he startled her again: "What happened that Sunday when you missed the dinner with the Connelys? You want to tell me now?"

No, she didn't want to tell him any more than she ever had—but then something turned over in her mind and she saw how easy it was. "There was a guy I met in town," she said. "I kept running into him, and he seemed a nice enough guy. We'd go into Howe-Ferris and have a Coke and just talk, and— Well, finally, he asked me to go for a ride with him, and I thought, well, why not? So he picked me up, and everything seemed to be OK, but then he started drinking—" And even as she was telling this perfectly plausible story, she asked herself why she was doing it.

"Anyhow," she said, "I asked him to take me home, but he wouldn't, and he just kept on driving— all the way out into Pennsylvania somewhere. He parked the car, and I tried to get the bottle away from him. That's how it got all over me. Then he got so drunk he passed out. So I started walking to a farmhouse to call you, but he—kind of pulled himself together and followed me. He drove me back. He made me promise not to say anything, and I said I wouldn't. He works for Raysburg Steel. He was afraid you'd get him fired."

"Oh, yeah? Who the hell is this guy anyway?"

"I promised I wouldn't say, and I won't. Look, Daddy, I haven't seen him since, and I won't ever see him again. He hasn't even called me up. I'm really sorry. Can we just forget it?"

He turned and looked at her for a long time. "OK. All right," he said. "Let's just forget it. You should have told me, you know."

"Yes, I know."

"Hell, if he's a union guy, I couldn't get him fired. We can't touch the guys in the damn union."

"Well, he did say that, but he was just afraid—I don't know—that you'd make things rough for him."

"Yeah," he said with a small, humorless laugh, "I would have too— I should have known you'd have good common sense. That's something you've always had."

She felt bad about taking advantage of the opening he'd just revealed, and, not only that, it was humilating to *have* to take advantage of it, but she knew she did: "So am I still confined to quarters?"

"Oh, hell no. Forget that."

He'd brought a bottle of Scotch down to the pool with him, and he poured another inch into his glass. "You know, princess, I'm glad we've had a chance to talk like this. There's something I've been meaning to tell you— When you're thinking about getting married again—pick a boy who's had his mettle tested, you know what I mean? With a boy— Well, if it's been handed to him on a platter his whole life, you never know how he's going to react when the chips are down."

"You didn't want me to marry Rolland?"

He looked at her a moment. "No, I guess I didn't."

"Gee, nobody wanted me to marry him—except Mom."

"Well, you know how your mother is. But— just don't be in a hurry, OK? I guess that's a funny thing to say. Every girl wants to get married, huh?"

"Oh, sure. Someday. With the right guy. But I understand what you're saying, Dad."

"So what *is it* you want to do? You want to teach in college?"

"I don't know. Everybody keeps asking me that— I guess so. I love learning things."

"Yeah, you always did, didn't you?"

He lit another cigarette, took a puff on it, then put it out. "You know, honey," he said, "I always know what your brothers are thinking. It's like I can read their minds. But—well, I never know what you're thinking. I couldn't even figure you out when you were little."

She was shocked. In her entire life she'd never heard anything from him as personal as that. "Well, I haven't exactly known what *you* were thinking either, Dad."

"Oh, yeah? You probably wouldn't want to know. It's pretty boring stuff—you know, stuff at work."

"Well, what I think about's pretty boring stuff too—clothes and poetry."

He laughed just as she'd wanted him to. "You've got a good sense of humor, honey. That's something that's going to stand you in good stead all the rest of your life. You know, Gloria, I don't suppose I ever told you this in so many words, but I'm really glad you turned out to be well-rounded. Not just— Well, you know what I mean. All the things you've done—a well-rounded girl."

"Well, thank you," she said, and thought, oh, Daddy, you don't know how much work it's been, but she was touched—and now she felt like the worst of hypocrites for lying to him, although she couldn't very well tell him the truth, could she? No, not any more than she could say, "Oh, and by the way, Dad, I didn't really stay at the Delta Lambda house. I spent the night with my thesis advisor, but that's OK; he's a homosexual."

So here she was *still* lying to her father. So when did the lying stop? How old did she have to be? Or maybe it never stopped. Eventually she'd get married, and then she could lie to her husband the way her mom did.

"Come on, honey, we should both be in bed. I've got a hell of a day in front of me tomorrow." He stood up and, in a gesture she found both horrifying and wildly funny, tossed the remainder of his drink into the swimming pool.

They began walking back to the house, but he stopped at the foot of the steps. "Gloria, honey," he said, "I just want to tell you something, OK? Just get the hell out of Raysburg, OK? And don't ever come back here. There's a big, wide wonderful world out there, and you should see something of it before you settle down, and— Well, your mother would shoot me if she heard me saying this, but don't marry some nice rich boy just because it's easy. You want that PhD? Then go after it. Make something of yourself. Yeah, when you see something you want, get up and go after it. For a girl like you, the sky's the limit."

20

The events of the last few days had been so extraordinary—so charged with meaning—that Gloria wanted to record them while they were still fresh in her mind, so she stayed up until four writing in her diary; then she went to sleep easily, with no sense of nightmares lurking by the side of her bed, and she didn't wake up until the men arrived to work on the hole. She'd been having a long, complicated dream, but all she could remember of it was that she'd visited the national headquarters of Delta Lambda and had been shown a secret room lit with hundreds of white candles. The dream had left her with a quietly hopeful feeling, but when she delivered her mother's breakfast tray, she discovered that her mother was barely speaking to her. Oh, boy, were they going to have *so* much fun for the rest of the month!

She tried to work on her diary all morning, but the noise from the hole kept distracting her, and she couldn't even swim because she hated how the workmen stared at her whenever she appeared in a swimsuit. She walked down to the club and had lunch with Binkie. Afterward, as she watched Binkie and Lee play mixed doubles with Judy and Mike, she fell sound asleep. By the time she came home in the afternoon, the brats had returned from wherever they'd been the night before and her mother wanted them out of her hair, so Gloria drove back down to the club. It was too crowded in the club pool to swim laps, so she went home and helped Mrs. Warsinski with the ironing. As soon as the workmen left at five, she swam forty laps. When her father came home, he looked physically sick—drawn and pale and exhausted—but he smiled at her nicely and asked if she wanted to join them for dinner.

"Sure," she said automatically and went up to her room to change, but, instead of changing, threw herself onto her bed and lay there still wearing her damp swimsuit. She wanted to please her dad, but she wasn't at all sure she wanted to go out for dinner.

If the most important thing to her father was his family, why was it so darned hard for him to have a personal conversation with his only daughter—so hard that when he'd actually managed to do it, it had seemed like a minor miracle? But if she went to the club tonight, everything would be back to normal, and not only would she not have a conversation worth recalling with her dad, she would not have a conversation worth recalling with *anybody*. If you never stepped into the same stream twice, why did it feel as though you did? More than that, why did it feel as though you never got out of the same stream even once? Oh, she was in such a sour, scratchy, unpleasant mood, and that morning she'd actually felt pretty darned good, and the secret watcher told her, "Just go through the motions, Gloria. Pretty soon it'll all be over."

She took a quick shower, toweled herself as dry as possible considering the fact that the humidity was close to one hundred percent, put on a girdle and hose, stood in front of her mirror, not even fully dressed but already perspiring, and thought how absurd it all was. Why did she and the girls in her crowd have to dress to the nines just to go the dumb old club in the evening? And that was a stupid question, for the answer, as always, was that if one wished to be viewed as a normal girl, one must be as circumspect as Caesar's wife—constantly careful, constantly watchful—but then, surprised at herself, she stripped and started all over again with plain cotton underwear. OK, she thought, we can have a compromise, can't we? What's both pretty and cool? She picked a breezy, pink shirtwaist dress and white, low-heeled sandals. She hadn't appeared at the club after five without nylons since she'd been—oh, probably fifteen—but why shouldn't she? Wasn't it about time that people began to realize she was something of an unconventional girl?

But her mother said, "You're not going dressed like that, are you?"

"Why not?"

"Because if you are, you're not going with us."

"OK," Gloria said, "I'm not going with you," and banged her bedroom door shut just the way she'd done when she'd been fifteen, threw herself onto her bed and thought, oh, here we go again! After her anger died down, she began to berate herself for being childish. She'd just about convinced herself to change into a cocktail dress when she heard her father's car driving away. Well, she thought, that settles it.

Grimly pleased to be alone, she took her diary down to the kitchen, opened it on the counter, turned on the radio, changed the station to one that played pop tunes, opened a Coke, chopped some lettuce into a bowl and poured French dressing on it, scooped herself a mound of Mrs. Warsinski's chicken salad, and settled down to enjoy herself. She kicked off her sandals, ate slowly, and became engrossed in her writing. She wanted to get down as much as she could remember of her day with Professor Bolton, was just beginning to describe his lovely, green guest room when she heard a car pulling into the driveway. Why were they coming home so soon? It wasn't even eight. And then she recognized the sound of the engine. Oh, darn, she thought, sprang up and ran straight to the front door. She locked it just as the doorbell rang. She looked through the front window and saw—yes, the Porsche. What an idiot, she thought. What on earth does he think he's doing here?

Oh, but she had to get the back door—and, even as she was running, she thought how stupidly melodramatic it was. She slammed the kitchen door and locked it, turned, heard herself emit a small, involuntary, choked-off yelp—oh, how embarrassing!—and felt blood rising into her face. He was standing just inside the wide open French doors, grinning at her like the big, dumb, ape-jawed jerk that he was. "You can't come in here, Mr. Dougherty."

"How the hell can you say that, princess? I'm already in."

Her skin prickling, she did nothing but look at him. His hair must have started out combed—was shiny with hair oil—but now it was wind-whipped into a rat's nest. He was wearing a white dress shirt, most of it pulled free from his trousers and most of it unbuttoned, revealing not only his thickly haired chest but also the heavy, meaty balloon of his belly. He stood, leaning against the door-jamb just as though he had all night to lean there. "Sorry if I give you a little start," he said and chuckled. He was, of course, drunk. Everybody seemed to be drunk these days.

"Get out of here," she said. She wondered if she could shoo him away like a big dog. "Go on. Go home." Still grinning, he shook his head. How profoundly annoying, she thought. Without a moment's hesitation, she walked over to the counter and grabbed up the phone to call her father at the club.

She wouldn't have thought he could have moved that fast: across the kitchen in two big steps. He slammed his hand down on the telephone. She stepped back, away from him. He wasn't touching her, but his solid, sweaty, excessively real presence was pinning her to the wall. He stepped forward, using up the space that remained between them. He leaned down, close to her, shoved his sweaty face into hers. As usual, he needed a shave. He reeked of b.o. and whiskey and some foul minty smell. "Huh uh," he said, "you ain't calling nobody."

"What on earth do you think you're *doing?*" She tried to move his hand away from the phone. She might as well have been trying to move the wall. He laughed. She stepped around him. She was so angry she could feel it like banked fire at the back of her eyes, but she wanted to maintain her dignity, so she forced herself to walk away from him in a calm, deliberate, unhurried way. She was headed straight for the phone in her parents' bedroom. She felt his hands close on her waist; then—incredibly—he picked her bodily off the ground, turned, and deposited her back into the center of the kitchen.

For the ghastly moment when she'd been suspended in the air, she'd felt exactly like a kicking cat someone has grabbed up by the scruff of its neck. Bitterly offended, she heard herself shrieking at him: "You son-of-a-bitch, you keep your hands off me."

"Yeah, sure," he said, still grinning. He made a fist with his right hand and showed it to her. "And you just shut the fuck up, OK?"

She felt a chill on the back of her neck. "Yes," the secret watcher told her, "shut up, Gloria." She swallowed the next burst of furious words and looked at him.

He moved slowly toward her, backed her into the corner at the end of the counter. He pressed the fist gently against her mouth and pushed. He kept on pushing until her head was pressed against the wall. "Don't you give me any shit, princess, because I'm not in the mood for it. Not tonight, I'm not." He withdrew his fist slightly. "You understand what I'm saying to you? Hey, I asked you a question."

"Yes, I understand what you're saying to me."

"Good. Now you be a good girl, and we're gonna get along just fine. I was figuring we could have us a nice, friendly, little visit. Just a few things I want to get off my chest, and then I'll be gone, OK? But I've had me a hell of a day, and the last damn thing I need is you getting hysterical on me, OK? So you just calm down, OK?"

He withdrew his fist and stepped back. She felt like a coiled spring, but she forced herself to move slowly, stepping around him. She was so frightened she was close to losing control, and that was the last thing she wanted to do. "If my father ever finds out about this," she said, "he'll kill you."

"Oooo, scary, I'm shaking in my boots— Just get me a drink, OK? I really need a drink."

She tried to make her voice as frosty as her mother's. "Mr. Dougherty, I don't know what you think you're doing here—or what you think you're going to accomplish—but, believe me, the best thing for you to do is get out of here right now. If you get out of here right now—"

With no warning, he leapt at her, hunched down until his face was level with hers, and stared directly into her eyes. "Hey," he yelled—and she winced—"I said *shut up.*" Oh, help, she thought, he's not rational.

He straightened up. He was smiling again. He dropped his voice back into an easygoing, conversational tone: "Just calm down, huh? Relax. I ain't gonna hurt you. What the hell you think I'm going to do? Smash in that pretty little face of yours? Come on, Gloria, wise up."

"Stay calm, Gloria," the secret watcher said; she looked at him closely, trying to assess how drunk he was, what kind of state he was in.

He met her gaze a moment, then pressed his hand over his eyes and squeezed as though he were trying to wring out his face like a sponge. "You know what, princess?" he said in a blurred, throaty voice, "I sure as hell was gonna catch up to you *some* night, you know what I mean? 'Cause we got to talk. Just my luck it turned out to be tonight. But it's better sooner than later, huh? Oh, boy, do I need a drink. Make that a Scotch, huh?" He lowered his hand and looked at her. She couldn't read him at all. "Come on," he said, "move it, honey. Straight will be fine."

She walked slowly into the dining room. She opened the liquor cabinet. She knew he was watching her. She could feel his eyes on the back of her neck. She picked up the first glass she saw, a whiskey sour glass. She didn't want him any drunker than he already was, so she poured only a half inch of her father's best Scotch into it. She turned and offered it to him. He knocked it back. "Jesus," he shouted at her, "I said a drink, for fuck's sake. Jesus, Gloria, you know, a fucking *drink!*" Without the slightest hesitation, he pitched the glass into the living room. She heard it land with a thud and roll on the carpet. She froze and, again, simply looked at him. "Jesus," he said, "the hospitality around here sucks shit, if you'll excuse my French."

He walked past her, picked up the bottle of Scotch, uncapped it, and took a long drink. "Now you're a smart girl, princess, so you listen to your uncle Billy, and you listen real careful, because if there's one thing I hate, it's having to repeat myself. OK, so if things around here get kinda rough— Well, then you must of let some rough son-of-a-bitch in here. Yeah, that big, dumb Polack boyfriend of yours—the one I seen you with and told your old man about. You know what I mean?"

He seemed to want her to answer that reflexive, rhetorical question, but she couldn't speak. She nodded. "Breathe, Gloria," the secret watcher said, and she breathed. Not only had he told her father about some nonexistent big, dumb boyfriend, but she'd told her father about that same phantom. Oh, God, she thought, I'm fortune's fool.

He held the Scotch bottle up and grinned at it as though he were admiring its shape and weight. He took another long drink. "Now I bet you don't know there's a ridge road a couple miles over from the good old country club," he said, "and something else I bet you don't know. If you're sitting up there on that ridge road and you got yourself a pair of fine, Navy-issue binoculars, you can get yourself a pretty damn good view of what's going on over at the good old club. Yeah, you can see the golf course and the pool and the terrace. And guess what I seen? Right out there on the terrace—yeah, right there at that lovely table for two they got out there—yeah, big as life and twice as ugly, there was the great—the magnificent—the one and only—Theodore R. Cotter. Yep, and his lovely wife in a lovely dress. And, by Jesus, did they ever look lovely."

He laughed, drank again. She was astonished at how quickly the Scotch was affecting him; his color was changing right before her eyes. He'd been, she realized, pale, nearly gray-faced; now the pink was flooding back into his cheeks.

"And they was having themselves a little drinkie-poo before dinner, you know what I mean?" he said, chuckling. "Yeah, they hadn't even got around to tucking into the lovely prime rib yet. And the great Theodore's two lovely little boys? Well, they was still in the lovely pool, just having themselves a lovely time. You follow me? So the best I figure, you got a good two or three hours to entertain your Uncle Billy."

"Why would I want to do that?" she said carefully.

"Why? Well, maybe because you owe me, that's why."

Gloria—motionless—felt an unearthly, icy quiet fall over her and then, with no plan—with no intention of doing anything but getting away—she was running. She shot up the stairs. There was a lock on her parents' bedroom door; there was a phone in there. She heard him as a huge, dark, shambling noise behind her. "You don't run," he yelled.

She felt him grabbing at her left ankle. Then he got a solid hold on it. She fell, scrambled on her hands and knees and elbows, her face grazing her mother's nice stair runner. He was pawing at her legs. He got his arm wrapped around her waist. "You don't run," he yelled right into her ear and hauled her back down the steps. Horribly, he picked her up again, hoisted her onto his shoulder. She tried to kick him. She hammered his thick back with her fists. She didn't seem to have any effect at all. He dumped her onto the couch. When she tried to jump up, he pushed her back down. "You don't run," he yelled. "Goddamn you, you don't *ever* run."

She was sobbing and hated herself for it. "Shut up," he yelled. "Goddamn you. Shut the fuck up."

She forced herself to look at him. He was panting; sweat was pouring down his face. He was shaking all over. His face was red and shiny. "If you run, I got to chase you, and it's too fucking hot for that shit. You know what I mean?

"Oh, please don't do this!"

"Hey, shut up."

"Oh, please don't do this. Please, please, please—"

He leaned down and screamed into her face: "Just shut the fuck up."

She shut up. He pawed his cigarettes out of his shirt and lit one. "Jesus, Gloria, am I ever getting sick of the sound of your voice. Goddamn women, they just go yap, yap, yap, yap, yap. You tell 'em nice, and they don't listen to you. Jesus, I don't know—"

"Stop crying," the secret watcher told her. "Come on, Gloria, come on, come on, come on—"

"OK," he said, "let me put it to you this way. You're in the service now, OK? And I'm your commanding officer, OK? And you know the only thing your commanding officer wants to hear? *Yes, sir.* That's the only damn thing he wants to hear. You understand me?"

"Yes, I understand you."

"No, you dumb broad. Jesus, you still ain't got it. I was trying to make it real simple for you. OK, let's try it again. *Yes, sir.* That's all I want to hear. Nothing else. You got me?"

"Yes, sir."

"OK. Good. Now hear this—anything funny goes on around here, couldn't of been me that done it, right? Because there's five guys sitting in the back room down at Joe's ready to swear on a stack of Bibles that Billy Dougherty was playing pinochle with them the whole damn night. You with me, princess?"

"Yes, sir."

He's planned it, she thought. Whatever he's going to do, he's planned it, he's planned it— He stared down at her a moment, then turned, walked to the liquor cabinet and picked up the bottle of Scotch. He had turned his back on her. She leapt up and ran for the open French doors.

She heard him yell, "Shit!" and a crash. She felt him slam into her side, felt her stomach bang into his encircling arm. He spun her around and flung her backwards. The breath had been knocked right out of her. Wailing, blind, she tried to get by him. He caught her, flung her back. With short thrusts, open handed, he pushed her back into the living room.

She was stopped. He grabbed her under the chin and tilted her face up. "I said, don't run. Now didn't I say that?"

She couldn't answer. She heard a pitiful, pathetic wailing pouring out of herself.

"Now didn't I say that?" His thumb was under one side of her jaw, his fingers the other. He squeezed and lifted. He hauled her up onto tiptoe. "Now didn't I say that?"

"Please, please, please—"

"Hey! Didn't I say not to run?"

"Yes."

"Yes, what?"

"Yes, sir."

"Hey, great. We're getting somewhere. And you ran, didn't you?"

"Yes, sir."

"So you got it coming, huh? Hey, bitch, I'm talking to you. *You got it coming? Right?*"

"Yes, sir." The moment the words were out of her mouth, he struck her.

"Don't move yet," the secret watcher said. "Be very, very, very careful." Gloria was lying on the carpet where she'd fallen, sprawled on her right side. Her face was blazing where he'd slapped her. It was strange that she wasn't crying now, but the crying had stopped completely. She wasn't making a sound. She could think again, as she hadn't been able to before. Not thinking had been a big mistake. She wouldn't move for a while. She wanted him to believe she was really hurt. In the kitchen, the radio was still playing—Pat Boone singing about love letters in the sand. She could smell something burning. "Gloria, honey, are you OK?"

No, she thought, I'm not OK. I don't want you to think I'm OK. I don't want you to think I'm even close to OK. She could hear him pacing around. She heard him kneel down next to her. She felt his hand on her shoulder. "Come on, honey, sit up." She didn't move.

He put his hands under her arms. She couldn't stand the feeling of his hands on her, so she pulled away, rolled onto her knees. "Jesus, am I ever sorry," he said. "Jesus Christ, Gloria, I can't begin to tell you how sorry I am. Oh, fuck, this is terrible!" His mouth hanging partway open, he was staring at her with his small, red-rimmed eyes. Thank God, she thought, it's snapped him out of it.

"Come on, honey." She allowed him to help her up, to lead her over to the big chair in the corner of the dining room. "You just relax, honey— Oh, shit, your lip's cut."

She hadn't been able to separate the burning on her cheek from the burning in her lower lip. Now she licked and tasted salt. She ran her fingers over her lip and saw a smear of blood. "Here, let me see," he said, kneeling in front of her. "Aw, shit, it's not bad, honey. A day or two, you won't even know it happened."

He looked around the room, puzzled, as though he'd never seen it before. "Shit," he said and stood up. The cigarette he'd thrown down—probably when she'd bolted for the French doors—was burning a hole in the rug. Instead of picking it up, he stepped on it. Oh, just great, she thought; Mom's going to have a bird. He'd dropped the Scotch bottle too. He picked it up and looked at it. The rest of the Scotch must have spilled out; he set the bottle carefully onto the liquor cabinet.

"Hey," he said as though he'd just been struck by a brilliant idea, "let's get a little ice on that."

He walked past her toward the kitchen, then paused to give her a long, sorrowful look. "You ain't thinking of running again, are you?"

She shook her head. Through the open door to the kitchen, she saw him fumble around behind the radio, locate its cord, and yank it out of the wall. He opened the refrigerator, took out an ice tray and jerked the handle on it. He came back with an ice cube and handed it to her. "Thank you," she said automatically, took the ice and pressed it against her lip.

From where she was sitting she could look directly through the open French doors. The sun must be sinking behind the apple trees. She could see the long, black shadows on the lawn, and she wasn't feeling much of anything. It was as though she'd gone away, removed herself to a fantastic, nearly impossible distance. The wall clock in the kitchen said it wasn't quite seven-thirty, and the earliest she could expect her parents to come home was nine-thirty, so, until she could get him out of there—however long it took—she had to be very careful not to make him mad enough to hit her again.

He was wandering around through the dining room and living room. He kept looking at things—the pictures on the walls, the Wedgewood on the mantel, the plates displayed on the top of her mother's antique china cabinet. He lit a cigarette. "Aw, shit," he said.

"Mr. Dougherty—"

"Hey, shhh."

He walked over to her, knelt in front of her, looked into her eyes. "Come on, honey." He sounded as though he was pleading with her. "Now I *told you*, didn't I?" It was incredible—utterly bizarre—but tears were running down his face and he didn't seem to be aware of them. "What is it you say to me?"

"Yes, sir?"

He sighed, rose to his feet. "Good," he said. "That's real good. Yeah, that's what you say."

He stood up, walked to the liquor cabinet, picked up the empty bottle of Scotch, raised it to his mouth, and tilted it up. After a moment, he set it back down again, shaking his head. To get himself a new bottle, all he'd have to do was open up the liquor cabinet. Maybe she should tell him that. But, no, she wasn't allowed to say anything. He walked back to where she was sitting and looked down at her. Then, finally, he must have noticed that his eyes were wet; he wiped them with his fingers, again made that odd gesture of squeezing his face.

He lowered his hand and stared at her. His eyes looked bleak to her—sorrowful, even desolate—beyond that, she still couldn't read him. "OK, princess," he said, "now I'm gonna tell you a little story. Early this morning I'm out in the mill, doing my job, you know, the same as always, and guess what? One of the boys says, 'Hey, Billy, you better get back up to your office. Charlie Edmonds wants to see you.' Well, you know who Charlie Edmonds is, don't you, princess? He's one of them smart boys your old man keeps around to kiss his ass every hour or two—whenever he's in the mood for a good ass kissing. And so I go trotting back to my office, and guess what? Good old Charlie is real sorry to inform me that the great Raysburg Steel Corporation no longer requires my services—"

Oh, God, no, she thought. "Wait. Stop. Mr. Dougherty—I didn't do it. I swear I didn't. I didn't say a word—"

"Shut up! Shut up! I told you, bitch—just shut the fuck up. I told you all I want to hear out of you. You got that?"

"Yes, sir."

"That's better."

"But I didn't—"

"Hey! You're playing with fire. Jesus fucking Christ, are you ever dumb!"

He threw the cigarette away. She saw it land on the carpet. He waved both arms in the air. He grabbed up one of her mother's fake Louis Quatorze chairs. He used it to hammer her mother's china cabinet. The glass exploded. He smashed the cabinet again and again, breaking china and glass, splintering wood. He threw the chair away. It was ruined. Hand over hand, as though hauling in rope, he grabbed at china, and threw it all behind him. Each handful smashed.

"You goddamn dumb little girl," he yelled at her. Then, howling, he seized the top of the china cabinet, tilted it forward. It crashed down, flew apart. He kicked at the fragments of china, at the splintered wood. He kicked the top shelf away from the wreckage, chased it across the room, kicking it like a football. "Jesus, Jesus, Jesus," he yelled, "goddamn you, see what you made me do."

Panting, he paced up and down in front of her, waving his arms. Sweat was streaming down his face. "Boy, did you ever come close. Boy, did you almost get it that time. Jesus, I just don't believe it. Don't you understand *anything*? Jesus, didn't I tell you plain enough?"

He stopped in front of her. She hadn't dared to move a muscle. "OK, OK," he said. "Let's just get calmed down, right? Let me just tell you again. You must not of been paying attention the last time, so please, please, please, for God's sake, listen real hard, OK? The last thing we want around here is an accident, OK? So unless I tell you different, there's only one thing you say, right?"

"Yes, sir."

"Good, good. OK, things might work out after all— Shit, was touch and go there for a minute— Wheww, that Polack boyfriend of yours sure is one crazy son-of-a-bitch."

He walked all the way to the picture window and back again, puffing and waving his arms. "Hey," he said, "here's the sorry truth of the matter. When you got a pretty girl, and some crazy son-of-a-bitch punches her face in—just, you know, loses it and beats the absolute living crap out of her—well, she's never pretty again. Are you sure you're getting what I'm saying to you?"

"Yes, sir."

"Hoo-boy, am I ever glad to hear you say that. Boy, is that ever a relief."

Sighing, he sank back down on the other end of the couch and looked at her. He lit another cigarette. The one he'd thrown away was burning another hole in the carpet.

Watching from her enormous distance, Gloria thought it hadn't been real. Maybe the first furious outburst had been real, but after that, it had been a per-formance. He'd wanted her to think he could do that to *her*. Well, maybe he could. He'd slapped her with his open hand—her mind had retained a clear movie of him doing it—and, with a relaxed, fluid motion like a well-practised tennis stroke, he'd knocked her off her feet and cut her lip. She could still feel the heat of that slap on the side of her face. If he ever were to hit her even once with his fist—with his full force—he'd put her in the hospital. If he ever started hitting her and kept on hitting her— but, no, she'd have to make sure that he didn't do that.

"OK, now where was I?" he said. "Oh, yeah, I bet you was wondering if your Uncle Billy got a good kiss-off? Well, I'll tell you. Your Uncle Billy got kissed off real good. Yeah, I looked at all the numbers on that goddamn check, and I about dropped dead. And you know what that tells me? That tells me that the great Theodore R. feels real bad.

"Yeah, the poor, sorry son-of-a-bitch. Probably bawling his eyes out when he wrote that check. But did he have the balls to tell me to my fucking face? After six goddamn years? Huh-uh. And when I call him up to thank him—nicely and politely, thank him for the size of that check, guess what happens? His little dick-licking, chippy secretary says, 'I'm sorry, Mr. Dougherty, but Mr. Cotter is unavailable.' I just love them green apples, don't you, princess?"

"Yes, sir."

"So don't you say a fucking thing about what your old man's gonna do to me, because he's already done it. You with me?"

"Yes, sir."

"So, anyhow, princess, here's the upshot of the whole works—the long and the short and the sideways. I'm real sorry to inform you of this, sweetheart, but you're pretty much in the old deep doo-doo. Yeah, honey, you owe me big. Wouldn't you say you owe me big?"

"Yes, sir."

"I'm glad to hear that. But it's OK. Yeah, everything's really OK, and I'm not kidding you. You want to know why? Because when I walk out of here, we're gonna be squared away. Even Steven. You know what I mean? You're gonna make it all up to your Uncle Billy. Ain't that right?"

"Yes, sir."

"And you know what's funny about all this? I always liked you. And what's even funnier is I still like you. But there's one thing you never should of done— Nobody threatens Billy Dougherty. You got that? You goddamn spoiled rotten little country club slut? You understand what I'm saying to you?"

"Yes, sir." He gave her a long, bleak stare, jumped up from the couch, and began to pace up and down in front of her.

Oh, God, she was trapped in her own lies. After lying to her father all summer, she couldn't possibly convince him that his old pal from the Navy had come in and slapped her and smashed the china cabinet—especially when that old pal had gone out of his way to create an alibi for himself—and there didn't seem to be any way out, so she had to get through it the best she could—just as she had at Fairhaven. It probably helped that she'd been through it before. She knew what to do. She shouldn't try to talk to him. Whatever he told her to do, she should just do it.

He was pacing up and down more quickly now. "Shit, shit, shit," he said. He stopped in front of the coffee table and stared at it. She couldn't imagine what he could be looking at. "Aw, fuckin' A," he said. He threw his cigarette down, ground it into the rug with his heel, turned and yelled at her, "Come here!"

Without a moment's hesitation, she stood up and walked over to him. "Good fucking Christ," he yelled into her face, "you think I need this shit?"

Whatever was going to happen was going to happen, and all she could do was watch it happening. But no, that couldn't be right. She should do *something*, shouldn't she?

His eyes were darting around. What could he be looking for? He strode into the dining room, grabbed the empty Scotch bottle, and, once again, tried to get a drink from it. He threw it into the living room. She watched it bounce on the rug, roll all the way to the fireplace, and then stop there, unbroken. Waving his arms, he strode back, stopped just in front of her. He stared at her, his mouth twisting. With an explosive movement, he stepped forward and batted the ice cube from her fingers. She heard herself inhaling, felt the breath stuck deep in her chest. Her eyes filled. "Give me your bra," he said.

She couldn't believe it. He was holding out his hand just as though he expected her to do it. All she could do was stare at him. He bent down to shout into her face. "Come on. Hurry up. Do it. Do it. Do it."

This can't be happening, she thought, but she was trying to unbutton her dress. She turned away from him. "Huh-uh," he said. She turned back. He was staring at her chest. She couldn't get her fingers to work right. "Breathe," the secret watcher said. She counted the buttons: one, two, three, four. He was making an impatient gesture with his extended hand.

All she could do was to keep on going through the familiar motions just as though she were alone. She slipped her arms out of her sleeves, undid her bra in the back, shrugged forward, tugged it off, and handed it to him. Quickly, she pulled up the top of her dress, pushed her arms back through the sleeves, and began to button herself up.

He looked at her bra a moment, smiling. "Cute," he said. Then he walked into the dining room and hung it on the chandelier over the dining room table. "Funny sense of humor your Polack boyfriend's got. Yeah, he's a real clown, that guy."

He walked back, leaned down to grin into her face. "OK, now make your titties stick out the way you had 'em for that Hockner kid." She felt a sickening lurch in her stomach. Until now it hadn't been worse than Fairhaven, but it really was going to be worse. She quickly undid the top four buttons again, pulled her dress open, bent forward, and allowed her breasts to spill out. She felt heat blazing in her face—and that, of course, was exactly what he would want to see. Swallowing tears, she bit into the cut on her lip.

"Real nice set of jugs you got, sweetheart."

She was afraid he was going to reach out and touch her breasts, but he didn't; he only stared at them. He began to massage the front of his pants. "Ohh, yeah. No doubt about it. One hell of a fine set. Oooh, oooh, oooh, real nice." Humiliating her was making him hot. How awful.

"OK, now give me your panties."

Oh, God, no. "Don't think, just do it," the secret watcher told her. She reached under her skirt, slipped her panties down, stepped out of them, and handed them to him. "Gee," he said, chuckling, "I woulda thought you'd wear something fancier than that. Yeah, had you figured for a lace panties girl."

He held her panties up to his nose and took a deep, theatrical sniff; then he said, "Ooooh, de cologne!" and bent double laughing. He slapped his thigh. The laughter, she saw, was a performance—and not a very good one. "Aw, shit, honey," he said—still laughing—"you know that one? It's as old as the hills."

He stopped laughing. He glared at her. Staring straight into her eyes, he curled the fingers of both hands through the leg holes of her panties, clenched his hands into fists, pulled down and apart, and ripped them in half. He threw the pieces behind him. He leaned over and swept everything—ash tray, magazines, candy dish—off the coffee table. "Get your fucking ass up there."

She didn't know what he wanted her to do. "Stand on it, bitch."

She stepped gingerly onto the coffee table. "OK, now spread your legs apart— Aw, come on, you can do better than that."

She stepped out with her left foot, and the table tilted to the left. She heard herself cry out, and he laughed. "Spread 'em, bitch." Starting over, she stood in the exact center of the table and walked her feet out slowly, carefully. She could feel the table wobbling. She was sweating so hard it was burning her eyes. "Yeah, that's better," he said. "OK, now lift up your skirt and show me your twat."

The moment she raised her skirt, she couldn't any longer stifle her sobbing. She knew he was enjoying it. "Higher."

She lifted her skirt to her waist. Now she'd done it, hadn't she? That surely was enough, wasn't it? She began to lower her skirt, but he yelled, "No! Hold it up there. Yeah, don't move. You just stand there and let Uncle Billy get a good look. *Do you understand me?*"

"Yes, sir."

"Hey. Great. You learn real quick." He smiled into her face, then let his eyes drop to her crotch and stared at it, licking his lips.

"Remember," the secret watcher told her, "all this has happened before, so you know what to do. He wants to degrade you and humiliate you. You have to show him you're degraded and humiliated. Just say whatever he wants you to say and cry as much as he wants you to cry and do whatever he tells you to do, and eventually he'll be satisfied and let you go."

He turned suddenly and wandered away, left her standing, holding her skirt up. "Hey, let's get a little light on the subject," he said, chuckling. He lit the nearest of the standing lamps, lifted the shade from it, flung the shade across the room. He kicked a hassock over to the coffee table, lay the lamp on the hassock, angled it so the light shone up between her legs.

He stepped close and looked where the light was shining. "Pretty little black bush you got, princess. Nice. You shave in real close. I bet the boys like that, huh? Well, maybe not. That bunch of limp-dicked boys you hang out with, they wouldn't know a twat from a rose bush."

Oh, God, she prayed, please don't let him touch me there. Please, please, please don't let him touch me there.

"Hey, honey," he said, "open your eyes."

She opened her eyes. He was massaging himself steadily. "You enjoying yourself?"

"Yes, sir."

"Good. That's real good."

He pushed her father's easy chair over until it was directly in front of the light—and in front of her. He sank down into it, tilted it back, and lit a cigarette. "Good, good. Spread your legs *real* wide now—wide, wide, wide."

Terrified of unbalancing the coffee table, she shifted her weight from side to side, slithering her bare feet, inch by inch, across the smooth wood until she felt the edges with her toes. "Hey," he said, "there you go. That's great. OK, shove your twat out—*way* out."

Her legs were shaking. The only way she could continue to hold that grotesque position was by pressing her fists—clenched tightly on the fabric of her skirt—down hard onto the tops of her thighs. "Hey," he yelled, "when I'm talking to you, you look at me. Goddamn you, bitch, I said, *look at me!* Yeah, that's better. And don't move a fucking muscle, right?"

"Yes, sir."

She watched him watching her. He was steadily, methodically squeezing and pulling on the bulge in his pants—almost as though he'd forgotten he was doing it. "Well, I'll tell you something, princess. I bet you think you're far, far above the rest of us poor slobs. Yeah? Well, I'm sorry to have to break it to you, honey, but you're not. You're just a cunt. Same as any other cunt. And the sooner you learn that, the better off you're going to be. Wouldn't you say I got a point there?"

"Yes, sir."

He was tugging at himself so violently he had to be hurting himself. It was awful to have to watch it. "Hey." His voice was low and thick in his throat. "I bet you love showing off your twat like that. I bet it's making you real hot, huh?"

"Yes, sir." Her legs were shaking so badly she knew if she had to stand there much longer she was going to fall off the table.

"I bet you want it real bad, huh?"

"Yes, sir."

"Don't worry, sweetheart, you're gonna get it."

He stood up, and, with slow, deliberate movements, unzipped his pants. "OK, now turn around," he said.

She edged her feet in toward the center of the table and turned around. It was a relief not to have to look at him. "Now bend over. Come on, come on, I said, *bend over.* That's right. Now pull your skirt up and show me your ass. Come on, honey, stick it out good. Yeah, that's right. Now don't you move, OK?"

She wished she could see what he was doing. The waiting was terrible. She wished he'd do whatever he was going to do instead of making her wait any longer. "You know what happens to spoiled rotten, smartass rich girls?" he said in a wet, throaty voice. "They get their smart asses whipped good and proper, right? And then they get a good, big, hot cock shoved up there— *Do you understand me?*"

"Yes, sir."

Gloria had lost all of her distance: she wasn't anywhere else, anywhere safe, watching—she was stuck in her own body. She was stuck standing on a coffee table with her legs apart, bending over, holding her skirt up, showing him her bare bottom. "You want it?" he whispered.

Oh, God, no, she thought, but she said, "Yes, sir."

She heard him laugh. "You got it coming, don't you?"

"Yes, sir."

She'd stopped crying. It was too horrible to cry. She was still sweating, but she felt icy cold. She listened to her own heartbeat. Her mind wouldn't work. She heard him sitting down in her father's chair—at least that's what it sounded like. She heard a rhythmic, squeaking noise. Then it stopped. Oh, please, God, she prayed. Oh, Susie, Susie, Susie, she prayed, help me.

"OK, sweetheart," he said, "get down off there."

She edged her feet closer together, then stepped forward onto the floor. She stumbled and almost fell. She didn't know if she was supposed to keep on holding her skirt up, but she didn't want to take any chances, so she did. She turned around. He was lying back in her father's chair, holding his penis. He pulled on it several times. "Get your ass over here."

She couldn't stop her legs from shaking. She walked over to the chair. "Look at it, baby," he said. She looked at it. It was thick and red. "You listen to me," he said. "I'm gonna take you upstairs—up to that bed where the great Theodore R. fucks his lovely wife—and I'm gonna fuck the living shit out of you. Do you understand me?"

"Yes, sir."

"I got to warn you about something. Don't think for a minute you can get off with half measures. Cooperation ain't good enough. I'm looking for wild enthusiasm. You with me?"

"Yes, sir."

"Come here, princess." She stepped forward the last foot that separated her from the chair. "Kneel down."

She sank to her knees. "Keep your eyes right on it, OK? Hey, answer me."

"Yes, sir."

His penis was only inches from her face. She didn't dare look away from it. He tugged on it. "You keep thinking about where this cock's gonna go, right?"

"Yes, sir." She knew he wanted to see her cry, so she made herself cry.

"Jesus," he said, "it sure took us long enough, but I think maybe you and me understand each other now. Wouldn't you say that?"

"Yes, sir."

"Yeah, I think we do. OK, you piece of shit, now get up and get me a drink."

• • •

She stood up. Exaggerating her sobbing, she walked slowly toward the liquor cabinet. She was afraid he'd yell at her to hurry up, but he didn't. The distance between the chair where he was sitting and the liquor cabinet was a good twenty feet, but was it enough? And run where? Even if she could get it locked in time, he was strong enough to break down the door to her parents' bedroom. Maybe she could get outside, across the lawn and into the woods. She risked a glance at the open French doors. It was twilight, nowhere near dark enough. Now she was at the liquor cabinet. She could feel his eyes on her.

She opened the cabinet and took out a new bottle of Scotch. In a few minutes she would simply walk with him upstairs and into her parents' bedroom and let him do anything to her he wanted. It didn't seem right or fair that she was going to have to go through it all over again, but she supposed she did. At least this time she wasn't nine years old, so it wouldn't be as much of a shock as it had been then, but the sexual part of it was going to make it far worse, and she wasn't sure she could stand it. But she didn't have any choice, so she was going to have to stand it. Maybe she could find the way to go far, far away again just as she had when they'd started to do really bad things to her at Fairhaven. "Yes," the secret watcher said, "you can do that. I'll help you do that."

But Susie would never simply walk with him upstairs and into her parents' bedroom and let him do whatever he wanted. "Oh, no?" the secret watcher said, "so what would she do?"

With a rush of insight, Gloria understood that he'd made a mistake when he'd asked for a drink. He'd wanted to wallow in his power over her, and it had been a mistake. He should have taken her down from the coffee table and straight upstairs while she'd still been in that numb, mindless, hopeless state, and then she would have done anything he wanted—but now her mind was moving as quickly as in any of her mental floodings. Susie, she thought, help me, and the Susie in her mind said, "Don't pray *to me*, Glo. Pray to God." Gloria prayed to God. Help me.

A beer stein. No, that would give it away. Just a big glass. A highball glass. She took one out and began pouring Scotch into it. God help me, she prayed again. At least her hands weren't shaking. Her legs didn't seem to be shaking either. She poured the Scotch in slowly—not to the brim. She picked up the glass. OK, she thought, here you go. It's like swatting a mosquito, if you hesitate even slightly, you'll give yourself away. God help me.

She turned away from the liquor cabinet. Of course, he'd been watching her the whole time. His hand was still tugging away on his penis. Good. She didn't want him to be able to stop, didn't want him to be able to think. She began walking slowly toward him, crossing that enormous expanse of rug. So she'd look utterly obedient, she kept her eyes glued to his penis. If it doesn't work, she thought, I might be dead, but she knew she shouldn't think about that. God help me, she prayed. Her legs felt really quite steady. She was almost there. He was pulling at himself. That's exactly what she wanted him to be doing.

She looked into his face and smiled. She had no idea what kind of smile it was, but it would have to do. She saw the dawn of a fiery triumph that froze him for one crucial, ruinous moment. With a sharp, whipping motion, she threw the Scotch straight into his eyes.

She flung herself to the left, running. She'd guessed he'd pounce straight ahead, and that's what he'd done. She ran in a curve through the living room. She heard him howling. She risked a glance behind her, saw him stumbling forward, blind, waving his arms, his deflated penis flopping in front of him. She caught the top of the dining room table with both hands and turned it over. She ran through the French doors, slammed them behind her. She flung herself down the steps, miraculously arrived on the patio still on her feet. She grabbed lawn chairs as she passed and threw them behind her. She heard the crash as he hit the dining room table, then the slide and the bang of the French doors. "I'm gonna fucking kill you," he yelled.

She was running past the pool. She was on the grass. She hardly noticed a sharp stab of pain in her left foot. She heard him run into a lawn chair— "Jesus!"—and heard the lawn chair thrown across the patio. She was running for the apple trees, for the trail through the woods—God, she wished she had shoes on—and then thought, oh, no, *the hole!* OK, then, she'd have to go around the side. But she didn't have time.

"You fucking cunt," he yelled. Stupid as he was, she'd never fool him again. She didn't dare to look back. Help me, help me, help me, she prayed. She saw the archery butt. It was right in front of her.

Leave it strung, she prayed, I can't possibly string it—and of course Bobby had left it strung, the little jerk. It was leaning against the butt. She seized it, snatched an arrow from the quiver, and swung around to see where he was. He'd stopped, was mopping his eyes with a handkerchief. Then he ran straight at her. Dear God, he was getting so close. She already had the arrow nocked, and the bow was rising. Her lungs sucked air. With no effort, she'd drawn it. Remember the cast, something in her mind told her—and get it down. She kissed the string, and she was out of time.

The bow spoke. She'd meant the arrow to scare him, to pass harmlessly by several feet to the right of his head. But, sickened, she saw that it was going to come terribly close. He swung his arm up to bat it out of the air. He was too slow; the top of his rising arm intercepted the falling arc of the arrow. It raked along the length of his arm, hesitated at his shoulder, then went wobbling away. "Jesus! Jesus fuck! Jesus!"

He stopped running. She snatched up another arrow, nocked it, drew it.

She felt the string pressed against her nose, her lips. "You shot me with a fucking arrow, you dumb cunt!" he screamed.

She'd thought he was running away, but, no, he was looking for the arrow. He ran straight to it, grabbed it up and broke it over his knee. "Goddamn you." He mopped his left shoulder with his fingers, held them up, waving them at her. "Hey. I'm fucking bleeding." Good, she thought, blood for blood.

The sun was long gone behind the apple trees, but there was still plenty of light. To get the arrow, he'd run quite far away. Now he was standing, looking in her direction. She eased the tension off the bow. Again he mopped his eyes with his handkerchief. "I don't fucking believe this," he said.

He stared at her a moment longer and then began running at her. She drew the bow. He wasn't bothering to weave from side to side. He was simply running straight at her. The closer he got, the easier it was going to be. This time she wouldn't misjudge the cast. She sighted directly into the center of his chest. There was not a doubt in her mind that she was going to shoot him.

He suddenly slid to a stop about ten feet away. At that distance she couldn't possibly miss. "Hey," he said, "Jesus fucking Christ, Gloria, that thing's not a toy."

She wasn't going to do it unless she had to. He probably knew that. "Hey," he said, "those goddamn things are deer arrows. Don't you know that? You could fucking well kill somebody. Put that fucking thing down, OK?"

Eventually she would run out of strength. Then she would lose control of the bow. Before she lost control, she would have to do it.

"Hey," he said. "You didn't really think I was gonna hurt you, did you? Shit, I was just—you know, just trying to throw a good scare into you, that's all."

If he took one more step toward her, she'd do it. He was hunched forward, uneasily balanced, as though someone had drawn a line directly in front of his feet and told him not to step over it—but he badly wanted to step over it. At that distance, she could put the arrow anywhere she wanted. She didn't want to shoot him through the chest. God, that would be horrible.

She let the bow drift down, sighted on his left thigh, halfway between his hip and his knee. The arrow would penetrate the big muscle in the front of his leg. She used to know the name of that muscle—and probably still did. She might hit the bone in his leg. If she did, the arrow would crack the bone. After that, he wouldn't be going anywhere. She'd walk into the house and call an ambulance.

His eyes had followed when she'd shifted the bow. He must know exactly where she was going to shoot him. Now he looked into her eyes. She held his eyes with her eyes. She drew the string back even harder, making the string hurt her nose, her lips. She could only hold it another second or two. She saw something change in his face.

Spreading his hands out, palms open, he backed up. "Hey," he said, "stop pointing that fucking thing at me, OK? I'm going, OK?"

Slowly, he continued to back up. How could anyone enjoy the ugly feeling that comes from making someone else afraid? But he'd enjoyed it, and so had Sal and the big girls at Fairhaven, and so had the kids in grade school. The dreadful thing was that she could enjoy it too. Maybe it was only natural and human to enjoy it.

When he was far enough away, she slowly eased the tension off the string. Her arms and chest were aching. She didn't know if she had the strength to draw the bow again, but she stood ready with the arrow still nocked. She gestured with her head: get out of here.

"Yeah, yeah," he said, "I'm going. But, Jeez, princess, I just want— Shit, you didn't really think I was— You damn near blinded me, you know that? And you shot me with a fucking arrow."

She gestured again: go on. He backed up a few more steps. "Hey, why don't we just have a little talk, OK? You put that fucking thing down, OK?"

She raised the bow, prepared to draw it. "Look, princess, I'm gonna tell you the honest to God's truth now, OK? I can just talk to you a minute, can't I? Ain't nothing wrong with that, huh? Come on, what do you say?"

She wanted to say, "Just get out of here. Just leave me alone," but she knew that saying anything would be a mistake.

He backed up again, spread his hands in the air again. "Well, shit," he said. He took out his cigarettes, then he pawed around in his shirt pocket. "Oh, fuck," he said, "you made me lose my goddamn lighter." He continued to back up slowly, watching her.

He was nearly at the pool when he stopped. He was still holding his cigarettes in his hand. Then put them back into his shirt pocket. He stood there, his head bowed. Why didn't he just leave?

He was so far away now that she would have lots of time if he started running toward her again. Careful never to take her eyes off him, she picked up the quiver and slipped the arrow she was holding into it. Bobby had obviously not touched anything since she'd picked up his stuff for him. She'd shot one arrow, so now there were eleven in the quiver.

"Hey, princess," he called to her across the distance of the lawn, "you gotta listen to me now, OK? I wasn't gonna hurt you. I just wanted to scare you— You know what I mean?" He hadn't moved. He continued to stand with his head hanging down, looking at his feet.

Even as she was doing it, she thought she was probably taking far too big a risk, but she found the wrist guard in the quiver and put it on. Her one shot had left a burning welt on her left wrist. Then she slipped the strap from the quiver over her shoulder, felt the familiar weight of it settle onto the left side of her back. And he still hadn't moved, so she buttoned up her dress.

"Jesus, what kind of guy you think I am, huh?" he called to her. "Hey, I wasn't going to *hurt* you. Why, shit, I never laid a hand on you, did I?"

He seemed to be looking at her now, but he was so far away, and the light was getting so dim, she couldn't see the expression on his face. "Well, I did slap you, I gotta admit that. But I really pulled that one, you know? You didn't think I'd really hit you, did you?— Gloria, honey?"

Every instinct in her body was telling her to run. The longer she stood there, and he stood there, the less chance she had. A furious burst of energy had carried her out of the house, had made her mindless and intelligent the way an animal is mindless and intelligent. Everything she'd done had happened quickly, had required no thought whatsoever. But that furious burst of energy was over. Her legs were shaking; her arms were shaking. She was so terrified she was breathing in shallow gasps. She'd done her best, and he was still there. But he was so far away she could run around the side of the hole and into the woods before he got to her.

Then something made her think it through. She'd get into the woods, and she'd be barefoot. He'd have shoes on. In the woods, she wouldn't be able to get a clear shot at him. They'd play a cat and mouse game. He'd find her eventually. No, running was a stupid idea. The only way to get him to leave was to move *toward* him—to threaten him again—but, oh, dear God, she couldn't do that. Susie would have been able to do that, but she couldn't.

"Gloria, honey?" he called to her. "Are you listening to me? OK, here's the honest to God truth now, swear to God. Soon as I drank that drink you was bringing me, I was gonna stand up, and have a big laugh, and say, 'OK, honey, now we're square.' And then I was gonna be gone, right? Leaving you with a few things to think about and a little explaining to do, right? And that was gonna be it. You didn't really think I was gonna *do* anything to you, did you?"

She didn't have any choice. She was going to have to threaten him again. God, she prayed, just for a little while longer, please—let me be like Susie for just a little while longer. She drew an arrow out of the quiver, nocked it, and began walking toward him, slowly, pace by careful pace. She must have cut her left foot on something; it hurt like hell.

It was getting really dark now, and she hoped he wouldn't be able to see how badly she was shaking—but she could see the shape of him clearly enough to put an arrow into it. Susie wouldn't have been thinking how scared she was, she'd be thinking about what she had to do next. That's right—when you released an arrow correctly, it left cleanly, with no wobble. At Fairhaven she'd practiced for hours. She'd done it so many times she'd dreamed of doing it for years after she'd stopped doing it.

"Hey, Gloria," he called, "what do you say? Come on, fair's fair, huh? You went and threatened me—right there in the goddamn country club. And then you went and got me fucking well fired. What the hell you think I was gonna do, take that lying down? Come on, honey, talk to me. I gotta know what you're thinking."

When she was close enough to put the arrow where she wanted it, she stopped and raised the bow. "Jesus, honey," he said, "I must of really scared you, huh? Is that what happened? You thought I meant it, huh? Jesus, you must of been scared shitless, you poor kid."

Susie would have just kept on walking—slowly, deliberately—so that's what Gloria did. He spread his hands, open, in the air and backed up. Keeping his eyes on her, he began to back around the side of the pool. She moved with him, maintaining the same distance between them. She saw him flick a quick glance behind him to locate his car in the driveway; then he looked back at her. He stopped.

She took a step forward. He didn't move. Oh, no, she thought, it's not working.

"OK, OK," he said, "I guess I must of gone a little too far, huh? Well, I'm sorry, OK? Yeah, that's what happens sometimes. Things get kinda out of hand, you know what I mean? Hey, you hear me? I said I was sorry."

She wanted him to keep on moving back to the low, silver, gleaming scarab shape of the Porsche. She wanted him to get into it and drive away. But she'd taken yet another step toward him, and he was still holding his ground. "Gloria? I'm just gonna forget you shot me with a fucking arrow, OK? I'd say we're squared away, wouldn't you? Even Steven, OK? Come on, princess, put that damn thing down, and I'll go in and help you clean up the mess in there, OK?"

She could almost believe him—and it really was absurd to be threatening somebody with a bow and arrow. How could she have ever thought she could get away with it?

"Hey, honey," he said. "You gotta listen to me. I got even with you. So it's finished, right? Yeah, it's fucking well over. Hey, this is fucking ridiculous. Come on, honey."

She still didn't trust him. When she threw the bow down, she was going to have to run like crazy.

"Shit, Gloria, I need a drink. You understand me? Jesus, I need a fucking smoke— Help me find my goddamn lighter, OK? It's out in the grass here somewhere. Come on, honey, you're not gonna shoot me with that fucking thing. You don't want to do that. I know you don't."

He was right. She couldn't possibly shoot him. If she ran, though, it might make him mad. Maybe she should just lay the bow down gently in front of her and step back from it.

Then she understood what must have happened to Tommie Jean. She thought she'd understood it before, but she hadn't, not completely. In a single movement, breathing with it, Gloria drew the bow. When she felt the string against her lips, she knew it had been the right thing to do. He stared at her a moment. He turned and ran.

She released the arrow. At the sound of the bow, he threw himself face down onto the lawn. The arrow went where she'd willed it—high over his head—struck something with an enormous, metallic *whang*. He scrambled to his knees, and, crouching, ran toward his car.

Suddenly he sprang to his feet, turned back toward her, waving his arms in the air. "You bitch!"

She drew and nocked another arrow and continued pacing slowly toward him. It might be natural and human to enjoy making people afraid of you—even to enjoy hurting them—but, if so, then she didn't want to be natural and human. All she wanted him to do was leave. She didn't know how much longer she could go on. Please, God, she prayed, make him believe I could do it. Maybe if she said something to him— But he was yelling: "Jesus fucking Christ, now look what you've done!" Her arrow was sticking out of the side of the Porsche. It was so funny she almost laughed.

"Oh, my God," he said, groaning, "my poor car." He stumbled several steps toward her and stopped. He stood, his head hanging down. "Aw, fuck," he said. "Aw, fuck, fuck, fuck." He was making big, absurd, wracking boo-hoo sounds. She couldn't believe it. He was actually crying.

"What the fuck am I gonna do now?" he yelled at her. "You want to tell me that? Do you? You goddamn smartass rich bitch— You know it all, huh? So tell me. What the fuck am I gonna do now?"

He stared at her just as though he expected her to tell him. Then he made an explosive gesture as though throwing something away. "Aw, shit, you don't know nothing. Not a goddamn thing."

Waving his arms, he paced up and down in front of his car. "Oh, Jesus! Oh, Christ! My little boys. My *sons*. Jesus, that goddamn, fucking cunt, how could she do that to me? I got nothing left."

He made the sign of the cross. "Oh, sweet Mary, Mother of God," he yelled at the sky, "what the fuck am I gonna do now?"

He wheeled around and screamed at Gloria, "Listen, you goddamn cunt. You wanna know how old I was when I run away from home? Huh? Do you? Fourteen fucking years old. You wouldn't believe the fucking shit— Christ, I can't even believe it myself half the time, and— Jesus, it's just not fucking fair! You got me fired, you goddamn bitch! I lost my best friend in the whole goddamn world because of you— And you know what I am without that goddamn job? Just another fucking drunk. Just some fucking skid-row bum. And you did it to me, you bitch."

He stepped toward her, waving an accusing finger at her. She couldn't move. If he kept right on walking straight at her and ripped the bow from her hands, she still wouldn't be able to move.

"Who give you the goddamn right?" he yelled. "You want to tell me that? You walk around the fucking world like you own the goddamn place. You goddamn smartass rich bitch. Who give you the fucking right? You fucking well owe me, goddamn you!"

"Mr. Dougherty—" she almost said, but she couldn't get the words to come out.

"Oh, Jesus, Gloria, I loved you. Don't you understand that, you dumb cunt?" He hung his head and wept.

She knew she had to do something to get herself out of this awful, sickened, frozen state. What was she supposed to say? Surely she had to say something. "For Christ's sake," he wailed at her, "put that fucking thing down. You gotta help me. Please, Gloria, help me." He held out his hand to her.

He was right. It wasn't fair. She hadn't done anything to him; life had done it, but it still wasn't fair. So what was she supposed to do? Maybe she could talk her father into hiring him again. Maybe she could talk him into joining AA or something like that. She had to make him understand that she hadn't done any-thing to him. Had he really loved her? It didn't seem possible, but maybe— And maybe if she explained her point of view— She was just about to lay the bow down when something made her look at him carefully.

She studied him the way she imagined Susie would have, and she thought, if I lay this bow down, he's going to beat me up and rape me.

She drew the bow and aimed her arrow at his leg. Without a moment's hes-itation, he turned away from her, jerked open the door to the Porsche, jumped in and started the engine. It was as though that's what he'd been expecting to do all along.

"Listen, bitch," he said in a cold, flat voice, "if you don't put that fucking thing down, you know what I'm gonna do? I'm gonna get you someday. Might be next week or it might be years from now, but I'll find you, and when I do, I'm gonna fucking kill you."

The words were coming out with a hard, mechanical sound as though from a machine. "You understand what I'm saying to you? I'll do it slow. So you got lots of time to think about it. You understand what I'm saying to you?"

I almost believed him, she thought. I almost put the bow down. I came *that* close. He's really evil. He's not even human. He'll say anything or do anything to get what he wants. He really might come around and kill me. Oh, God, do I want to spend the rest of my life worrying about that?

She listened to that hard, fast, mechanical, inhuman voice going on and on, cataloguing all the things he was going to do to her, and it simply couldn't be happening. It was a nightmare or a bad joke or something, but none of it was real. *I could do it,* she thought. Nobody would blame me. Dad's one of the most important men in the valley. Nothing would happen to me. People would even feel sorry for me. If I did it, he'd be gone, and I wouldn't have to think about him ever again—

She didn't know how she knew it, but she knew that Susie wouldn't do it. Then she understood why Susie wouldn't do it—because it was wrong. She shot her arrow into the door directly below his face. She saw him wince. The air was still reverberating with the sound of the arrow penetrating metal. The arrow had sunk in deeply. She wondered if it were sticking into his arm. "Bitch," he said. She knew what he was going to do before he did it.

She ran toward the house, then leapt to one side. The Porsche roared by her. He was trying to turn it around. She ran again, made it to the steps. She heard metal smashing on the steps. "Shit," he yelled. She ran to the top of the steps, whipped out an arrow, nocked it and drew it.

He had the Porsche in reverse, but it seemed to be caught on something. The engine was going *rrrr, rrrr, rrrr.* She was looking down into the open Porsche. She'd never understood before the utter perfection of the cliché "like a sitting duck." She shot her arrow into the passenger's seat. It went in all the way to the fletching. "Jesus," he yelled. She drew another arrow and aimed it directly at him. "No," he screamed at her, "for Christ's sake!"

Suddenly the Porsche broke free and shot backwards. She hadn't wanted to revenge herself on him, but she had no qualms about revenging herself on his car. She shot an arrow into the passenger's side. The sound it made was like that of an enormous can opener ripping into an enormous can of tomato juice. He got the Porsche turned around, and she shot the next arrow into the trunk. He was roaring down the drive, and she tried a third shot, watched it arc and catch the Porsche in the left rear fender—and then all of her emotion—her anger and fear—struck her, and she started to cry, or maybe she was laughing.

He was still there. She couldn't see him, but she could hear the sound of the Porsche idling. It had to be down at the end of the driveway on the other side of the hedge. Why wasn't he leaving? She'd been standing there at the top of the steps listening for ten minutes—or at least it had seemed like ten minutes. She didn't know how long it had been, not really.

She was shaking all over. Her teeth were chattering. She couldn't stop crying. The last three arrows she'd shot into the Porsche had been a mistake—a self-indulgence—and now she was paying for them. She doubted if she still had enough strength left to draw the bow—let alone control it. She had nothing left—no strength, no courage, no conviction.

What he'd done to her in the house had been familiar—she'd lived through it before — but everything that had happened since she'd run from the house had been impossible. From where she was standing, everything she could see had a flat, stupid, tinny quality to it. The driveway and the trees and the hedge and the night sky didn't look real. She didn't know if God had been helping her, but something had, and nothing was helping her now. She'd never felt more alone, and she couldn't stop thinking that it was all somehow her own fault — as though she'd committed some monstrous crime she couldn't remember, and now she had to pay for it.

If she'd known he was going to stay there for so long, on the other side of the hedge with the engine running for so long, she would have locked herself in the house and called her father, but she hadn't known that. Each minute had dragged by slowly after the last minute until, soon, there wasn't going to be anything left of her. She had to keep wiping the tears out of her eyes so she could see whatever might begin to happen to her. She didn't know what she should do now, so she asked herself again what Susie would do, and she knew that Susie would simply wait as long as she had to.

But I can't go on any longer, she thought. There was nothing left — nothing to hold onto, nothing to believe in. "Susie, help me," she said half aloud, and the Susie in her mind said again, "Don't pray to *me*, Glo."

She couldn't do it. There was nothing left but herself, alone, exhausted and terrified, waiting, and that madman down below in his car, waiting for what? Until he knew for certain that nothing was left of her? "Oh, God," she prayed, and then she found, deep in herself, all the way back in her childhood, one of the first prayers she'd ever learned. "Our Father who art in heaven," she said, "hallowed be thy name —"

She heard the Porsche move from idle into low gear. She saw it emerge from the side of the hedge and begin to drift back up the driveway toward her. "Thy will be done," she prayed, "on earth as it is in heaven —" She nocked another arrow and waited, tears running down her face. The Porsche slowly turned off the driveway and approached the house. "Forgive us our trespasses as we forgive those who trespass against us —"

He stopped just at the foot of the steps. She heard him pull on the emergency brake. Then he stood up in the driver's seat. He was expressionless. It was as though he were presenting himself as a target — and she guessed that must be exactly what he was doing. He must have decided she was bluffing, so he was calling her bluff. He was going to force her to shoot him. "Deliver us from evil," she prayed.

Simply to hit him would not be hard. To put the arrow precisely where she wanted it would be another matter. Where she wanted it was in his shoulder high on the right side, well away from his heart. She knew she had to draw the bow in one continuous motion, without hesitation, or she'd never make it. She took a deep breath and pulled—felt pain searing across the muscles at the top of her chest. Oh, God, she thought, I've torn something. But she was kissing the string.

"I forgive you," she whispered. "Please forgive me." She sighted on his shoulder, but she couldn't hold it. The bow was wobbling badly. He stood there, staring at her with the same blank face. He hadn't moved while she'd sighted on him.

Then he whipped his right arm up and gave her a snappy salute. She was barely hanging onto her arrow.

He sank down into the driver's seat, put the car in reverse, and began backing away. She eased the tension off the bow. She knew she couldn't draw it again— not fully. She watched him turn the Porsche around. Without looking back, he drove down to the road. She listened until she couldn't hear the engine anymore. "For thine is the kingdom and the power and the glory," she said, "for ever and ever, amen."

She continued to stand at the top of the front steps for a long time—until it was fully dark and the mosquitoes were biting her badly—but she couldn't seem to do anything but continue to stand there. She still held the bow in her left hand. She was still looking down the driveway where the Porsche had vanished. Did she expect him to come back yet again? Was she waiting for her family to come home? She didn't know. I'm Britomart, she thought.

Her mind wasn't working properly. It was filled with broken pieces of thoughts—broken china, broken wood, broken crystal, broken thoughts, objective correlative, oh, stop it, Gloria— She was sure she'd torn muscles in her chest; she could feel them burning. She heard herself breathing strangely—a rapid, shallow panting—but she couldn't seem to make herself breathe any other way. Go into the house, she told herself firmly, so she went into the house.

She locked all the doors. She picked up the torn pieces of her panties and took her bra down from the chandelier. She should, she thought, clean up the mess, but she couldn't make herself do it. She started to make an odd noise, a little whimpering sound in the back of her throat. She didn't seem to have any control over it. So she wouldn't have to see the mess, she turned off all the lights—and that didn't make any sense. She climbed the stairs to the second floor. Walking took an enormous effort. The place on her left foot where she'd cut herself really hurt a lot. Maybe she'd have to get a tetanus shot.

She threw her bra and the pieces of her panties in the waste basket. She laid the bow and the quiver down by the side of her bed. She tried to take off her pretty pink dress. She couldn't make her fingers work on the buttons, so she ripped it open, heard the buttons fly loose and go clicking to the floor. She dropped the dress into her waste basket. She went into her bathroom and threw up some partially digested chicken salad. She flushed the toilet. She looked at herself in the mirror. Her hair was as wet as if she'd been swimming, her face wet and shiny, her eyes startling, unfamiliar.

She was sweating buckets, and she was freezing to death. Her teeth were chattering. She got an eiderdown out of the hall closet. She was still making that odd noise. It was like, "oh, oh, oh," over and over again. She wrapped the eiderdown around herself and lay down on her bed, but she still couldn't get warm. Then that little sound in her throat turned into a hoarse wailing. It was a sound, she thought, a dumb animal would make. What a cruel way to have to cry, she thought.

She wished her bedroom door had a lock on it, but she knew he wouldn't come back. If he'd said he wasn't coming back, she wouldn't have believed him, but she believed the salute. It had said: "That's all. It's over. We're square," or something like that. Maybe it had even said, "OK, you win." But she didn't care what it had said. All she cared about was that he was gone and he wasn't coming back. Without trying to, she stopped crying.

Her teeth weren't chattering any more, but she still didn't feel warm, and she still couldn't think straight. Fragments kept flickering through her mind, disconnected. Her mind was disconnected. Susie, she thought. Susie, Susie, Susie. She wondered if she shouldn't get some blankets too, but, now that she was in bed, she couldn't make herself get up again. "Gee," she and the secret watcher said in her mind, "maybe you're in shock." That was really weird: for a moment she and the secret watcher had been the same person. Well, maybe they always had been.

She had every right to feel sorry for herself, but she didn't feel sorry for herself. All she'd have to do was lie there in her own bed until she got warm, until she could breathe again in a normal way, until her mind worked again in a normal way. But she felt really sorry for the girl at Fairhaven who'd needed the secret watcher to comfort her and tell her what to do. She started crying again, quietly now, for that girl who'd been only nine years old, and then she knew that she was also crying for Tommie Jean, that girl she'd never met and probably wouldn't have liked if she had.

She was finally warm enough; she began to get drowsy, and then she was too hot. She threw the eiderdown onto the floor, and she heard her father's car coming up the driveway. They'll see the mess in the living room, she thought, and Mom will start screaming, and it'll be horrible. But, strangely enough, they didn't go into the living room. She heard them banging upstairs, the boys laughing and yelling, and her father going: "Shhh." She listened to the boys popping in and out of their rooms—and water running, toilets flushing, doors opening and closing. Her mother yelled, "OK, kids, that's really enough. Go to sleep." Everything sounded so normal.

She waited until things quieted down. She was thinking clearly again. She got up and pulled on a dressing gown. There was light under her parents' closed bedroom door, so she knocked. "Oh, go to bed, for heaven's sake," her father called out.

"It's me," she said. No one said anything, so, after a moment, she said, "Can I come in?"

"OK," her father said. She thought she heard her mother sigh.

She opened the door. They were sitting in bed, smoking and having a nightcap. Her father had on striped pajamas and her mother a pale rose peignoir. They were both looking at her—annoyed, puzzled. They seemed so cozy in bed together, so soft and vulnerable. "Mom? Dad?" she said, "I have to talk to you."

21

Near the end of August, Raysburg was blessed by a cool spell that felt like fall, but everyone knew it was deceptive. When it cooled off like that in August, they said, then the muggy, miserable dog days always came back again like a bad joke, and sometimes a long, hot Indian summer would settle over the valley and hang on well into October. But, in the meantime, everyone was grateful for the respite. The afternoons were clear and blue and breezy; the smoke from the mills hardly bothered anybody; at night you had to sleep with a blanket.

Unfortunately, Theodore R. Cotter wasn't in any position to enjoy the weather on that perfect Sunday afternoon; he was alone on the top floor of the Raysburg Steel Building. He'd been working the whole damn weekend, and he was satisfied with all he'd accomplished, but, God knows, he was weary to the bone, so he poured himself a Scotch and walked over to the broad expanse of windows. He lit a smoke and looked down across the rooftops of Market Street and Main Street to the Ohio River. Yep, he thought, the President of the Raysburg Steel Corporation sure has one hell of a view.

Of course he'd noticed the view on those occasions when he'd been in Carl's office, but he'd never been in a position to savor it; now that the office was his, he could take all the time in the world. He could see the Suspension Bridge and Raysburg Island and the Steel Bridge. He could see all the way to Ohio where, pretty soon, the sun would be setting. It might not be Manhattan, might not be much of anything—this dirty, dumb-ass, sorry excuse for a town— but still, the view was pretty damn sweet. Then he turned and looked at his office. It was pretty damn sweet too.

He had a mahogany desk not quite as big as a roller rink. The same colored boy who came in every night to vacuum the carpets and empty the ashtrays and clean the windows, also, of course, polished the top of the desk, and Ted made sure that his secretaries never left any paper on it. And he had three (count them, three!) secretaries: an older lady who took his important calls, scheduled his appointments, and who would, Carl had assured him, write all those damn reports for the board; a younger lady who took his routine calls, knew where everything was filed, and typed a hundred words a minute; and, finally, a girl who came to work in four-inch heels and who, the best he'd been able to tell, must have been hired for no other reason than to give the boys on the top floor a thrill. In the name of efficiency, he probably should have canned her, but, what the hell, she only cost the corporation forty bucks a week and she did make a good cup of coffee.

Carl and Patsy had flown away to a fancy resort somewhere up in Canada, and Carl had said they were going to stay right there as long as the beer was cold and the golfing was hot—maybe even to Labor Day. "But you're not getting rid of me yet," he'd said. "When I get back, I'll be sitting on the board, keeping you honest, ha, ha, ha. But don't get me wrong, Ted. It doesn't make any sense to put a new guy in charge and then cramp his style—so you just get right down to it— Oh, and I bet you've been dying to do some housecleaning, huh? Well, let me tell you something—where I'm going, they've got no telephone." Then, with a wink, he'd added, "Or anyhow, I'm not giving out the number."

The first round of firing had been easy. It wasn't as though Ted had kept a written list or anything like that, but he'd always known who his enemies were, and they'd been gone by close of business on that first Monday. When he'd walked in on Tuesday, he'd felt resentment—even anger—crackling in the air like static, and that had told him he still had lots more work to do.

The second round of firing had taken some serious thought. He'd wanted to clean out any little pockets of resistance that might fester and cause problems later—wanted to be sure to get not only the guys who'd always been out to get him, but their friends and sympathizers as well—so he'd called in Charlie and Al, and they'd gone over the personnel files with a fine-toothed comb. His rule of thumb had been simple: when in doubt, they go—and their secretaries right along with them because your average girl is far more loyal to the guy she works for than to the organization that's paying her salary.

When he'd walked in after the second round, he might as well have been walking into a funeral parlor, and everywhere he'd looked, all he'd been able to see were people so busy working their asses off they couldn't even glance up from their desks. Great, he'd thought. Now I'm getting somewhere.

He'd hit the upper ranks the hardest—half the VPs were gone—but he hadn't spared any level of management all the way down to the foremen, and the third round of firing was going to be the crucial one because it was based purely upon efficiency. To hell with the short-term solutions and the half measures he'd had to live with for seven years; he was, by God, restructuring the entire corporation. He'd been working out his new game plan the entire weekend, and he'd pretty much wrapped it up. The last of the pink slips would go out first thing the next morning. Of course he was going to have to bring some new blood on board; he'd already called two guys at U.S. Steel and one at Bethlehem and made them damn good offers. And he'd already made some key promotions—Charlie and Al for starters—and he'd have to give everybody the raise they'd need to keep them happy when it dawned on them they were going to have to work a hell of a lot harder, and a hell of a lot more hours, just to make up for the personnel that had been lost. And all the money he was saving was going straight into expansion because, by God, he was going after the big boys. By the time he retired, Raysburg Steel was going to be number four—hell, maybe even number three in the nation.

But it wasn't all peaches and cream. There were, he had to admit, a few things that were bothering him. The biggest one would be over soon enough: next week he was going to have to fly to Washington and appear before Senator Estes Kefauver and the other pinkos on the Senate Antitrust and Monopoly Subcommittee and do his best to lie to them with a straight face. And he hadn't been home much in the last few weeks; hell, he hadn't even had much of a chance to get into the pool, but you always had to make some sacrifices in this life, and, by sometime in the fall—well, at least by Christmas—everything might be getting back to normal. And then there had been that whole crazy business with good old Billy, and Ted still didn't know quite what to make of that.

It was, at least partially, his own damn fault; he'd known what the son-of-a-bitch was like when he'd hired him, but never in a million years would he have thought the man capable of doing what he'd done—good God, telling a pack of lies about Gloria, and then coming right into Ted's own home and wrecking the furniture, and breaking some of Laney's precious heirlooms, and pulling one of his sick little jokes on Gloria, scaring her so badly she'd had to shoot his Porsche full of arrows to get rid of him. She should have shot one right up his butt while she was at it.

Of course the first thing Ted had done was call up Al Connely and tell him to get some of his boys looking for Billy, but Billy had been long gone. And the next thing he'd done had been to stop payment on the check the stupid bastard hadn't had the sense to cash. A couple days after that, Ted had got a call from Dottie. He'd almost forgotten about her. Billy had called her up, collect of course, from somewhere or other—Ted hadn't been able to pry out of her from exactly where—and told her he was a little bit down on his luck. So how was she supposed to raise two little boys, she'd asked Ted, crying, without her alimony payments? Ted had mulled that one over. The funds for Billy's kiss-off had already been allocated and paid out of Central Accounting, and even the president of the corporation couldn't very well put them back without some kind of explanation, and, on this particular matter, Ted had no desire to explain anything to anybody. And besides, it wasn't those little boys' fault that their father was a prick. So, in a moment of happy inspiration, Ted had told Dottie, "You know, sometimes, in special circumstances, Raysburg Steel sets up trust funds for the children of former employees, and I think that's exactly what we're going to do now." She'd been pathetically grateful.

On Friday Ted had received a special delivery letter from Tacoma, Washington. He probably should have thrown it away, but he hadn't. It was, at this very moment, lying under some papers in one of his many desk drawers. He'd read the damn thing over maybe a hundred times, and every time he read it, it pissed him off all over again—and that was putting it mildly. If Billy had been anywhere within reach, Ted would have happily murdered him with his bare hands. The damn letter had no date on it and was written with a pencil on a piece of lined paper like a grade school kid would use for an assignment. Now— God knows why—Ted spread it out on his desk and read it all over again:

> Hi skipper hows it hanging— I herd from Dotty what you did for my boys & I just wanted to write & say I apresiate it— I dont know what else to say you know me when Im drinking the devil gets in me & Im real sorry for the way things turned out but theres another way to look at it— I didnt do half bad there for a while— you & me are two of the biggest assholes going the only difference is everybody knows Im an asshole but only a few guys know your one & if anybody knows your an asshole its me but Im not going to tell ha ha— after what happened I figured I better get out of town pretty dam quick & I drove straight thru to the coast without stopping but for gas & all the way guys would say hay what did you do buddy run into a tribe of Indians— I bet you dont think thats funny but I think its funny— when I herd what you did for my boys I figured you & me are squared away so nether you nor yours wont never see me again & I figure thats the dam best present I could give you ha ha— seriously I do apresiate it about my boys— Your pal forever William P. Dougherty

The sun was just beginning to sink behind the apple trees, and, in that hard, slanting light, the lines in the lawn where the turf had been replaced looked as if they'd been drawn with India ink along ruler edges. The hole had been filled in far more quickly than it had been dug; "Cotter's Folly" Laney thought of it but hadn't dared to try that little joke on her husband; he had more on his mind these days than building a bomb shelter—as he'd told her somewhat snappishly—and Laney supposed that he did indeed.

She watched her daughter arrive at the wall, bob up, turn, kick off, and glide. The crazy girl had been swimming for damned near forty minutes, but it didn't annoy her as it would have earlier in the summer. The low sun was striking the water at just the right angle to turn the flung droplets into molten gold, and Laney had to admit that the scene before her was as pretty as anything out of an Esther Williams movie. Whenever Laney thought about the antiques and china and crystal, she felt like screaming and crying all over again, but whenever she thought about what could have happened to her daughter, her blood ran cold. Now she watched Gloria complete her last lap and stand up in the shallow end, watched her bend forward, resting her hands on her knees, panting. "How many that time?" Laney asked out of politeness.

"Eighty."

Gloria climbed out of the pool, pulled off her cute black and red cap, and threw herself into a lawn chair next to Laney's. "You watch it, sweetie, or you'll get shoulders on you like a stevedore."

"No, I won't. I haven't got the figure for it."

"Oh, heavens, the kind of figure you've got has nothing to do with it."

"I didn't mean figure—I meant body build. You know, Mom. I'm not a meso-morph, so I won't put on muscle."

Well, of course Princess Priss would have all the answers, but Laney decided to let it drop. It was late enough in the day now that it was actually chilly—a faint breeze had sprung up—so Laney wrapped a beach towel around her shoulders. She looked out at the long, inky shadows that signaled the steady advance of the evening, and she decided that it was certainly late enough for her to have another drink. She'd been really cutting down, and now she was drinking at least half—well, if she were being honest with herself, maybe even a quarter—of what she had earlier in the summer, and she'd promised herself that if she ever got to the point where she wasn't fighting every day not to exceed her limit, she was going to cut down even more. She'd also been avoiding the heavy starch at the club, so she'd lost two pounds, and she was grudgingly pleased with herself.

She looked at her daughter looking out across the lawn; for a moment Gloria had an expression on her face exactly like Teddy's, and Laney felt a sharp, twisting emotion she couldn't quite identify. Gloria seemed to have taken it all in stride, but you could never tell what was going on in that crazy girl's mind.

"Why don't you come down to the club with us tonight, sweetie?" she said.

"OK," Gloria said.

"OK? Just like that?"

"Sure, why not?"

Gloria hadn't been to the club for dinner since before the big storm, and she wasn't sure why she'd agreed to go there tonight. Now she was asking herself if she were going to spend the rest of her life staring into closets wondering what to wear—which is what she'd been doing for the last ten minutes—and answered: yes, probably. Most of her clothes had been packed and shipped, so maybe she was going to have to look in the attic.

But, no, there was the plum taffeta Susie had talked her into buying for the May Queen candidates' party. It was a spring dress and could double as a fall dress; at the moment, the evenings certainly felt like fall. If the ensembles she always wore to the club could be called, as Heidi Bronwyn Smith would have put it, top drawer, then the plum taffeta was, if not *bottom* drawer, then pretty far down on the dresser. (And she wondered, without feeling more than a mild pang, if Rolland had proposed to Heidi yet.) She didn't know why, but the plum taffeta felt exactly right.

Her lip had healed, the strained muscles in her chest had healed, the cut on her foot had healed, but she didn't know if her mind had healed. Sometimes she felt so devastated that all she wanted to do was sit on her bed, propped up on pillows, and stare out the window. Other times she felt hardly more affected than if she'd read a disturbing scene in a good novel. She *had* been having some dandy nightmares. Most of them whisked out of her mind as she was waking up, leaving her with only a dark sense of lurking, sorrowful oppression, and the vivid images she could remember appeared to have little direct relationship to what had happened to her. She'd been expecting to dream of menacing, masculine figures, but she hadn't; as she had for years, she'd dreamed of wandering through deserted landscapes and empty buildings. Mr. Dougherty had appeared only once, and he hadn't been the least bit menacing but rather utterly ridiculous. She'd dreamed that she was driving her mother's station wagon and saw him standing by the side of the road trying to wave her down. When she drove right by him without stopping, it made him so mad that he began to squawk frantically, whipped off the slouch hat he'd been wearing, threw it to the ground, and jumped up and down on it. Writing it down, she'd realized that the image had come straight from a Donald Duck cartoon.

Tonight she decided, for the first time in weeks, to do a full evening makeup. She hadn't set her hair recently, so there was nothing she could do with it but put it up in a ponytail. Then, telling herself what she'd often heard Susie say— "may's well be hanged for a sheep as a lamb"—she slipped on the too-high heels that went with the dress. She and her mother arrived in the hall at the same time. Her mother must have been feeling autumnal too: she was wearing deep forest green.

"Where'd you get *that* dress?" her mother said.

Gloria didn't feel like getting into a fight about it, so she laughed. "Don't you like it, Mom?"

She saw her mother look her over from ponytail to the too-high heels. "Well, you do look a bit like a waitress on her big night out."

"Oh, come on, it's not that bad. If it's good enough to get me elected May Queen, it's good enough for the country club."

"Who on earth was doing the electing—the State Farm Society?" Gloria found that genuinely funny.

They walked out to the station wagon and got into it. Her mother turned the rear-view mirror to check her makeup. Gloria thought it an odd thing to do; surely her mother must have just checked her makeup in her own bathroom mirror. Then her mother twisted the mirror back into place, drove down the driveway and out onto the road. Without looking at Gloria, she said, "Did that pig actually *do* anything to you?"

Gloria wasn't sure what to say. She had, of course, told her parents a version— thoroughly expurgated—of what he'd done, but she hadn't told anyone the full account, and she didn't plan to tell anyone except Susie. "Well, not exactly," she said.

"What's that mean? Sweetie, sometimes you're so—well, so darn elusive."

Gloria thought about what to say. What she needed was a neutral, brief, reasonably accurate, but unemphatic summary. "Well, OK," she said. "He slapped me. Other than that, he didn't touch me. But he called me some really slimy things— He, um—made me show him my private parts."

Her mother drove in silence—on down to the club and into the parking lot. I shouldn't have said that, Gloria thought; now I've shocked her. "At a party once," her mother said in a slow, deliberate voice, "in one of the back bedrooms at the Eberhardts, as a matter of fact—the son-of-a-bitch talked me into taking my bra off. And then he finished himself off right in front of me."

"Mom!"

Her mother laughed with no humor in it. "God knows how he talked me into it. He isn't exactly subtle."

"Oh, you're sure right about that! Why on earth did you do it?"

"I haven't the faintest idea." And that, obviously, was the end of the conversation—well, maybe not so obviously: her mother was making no move to get out of the car. Gloria knew she should probably wait to see if anything more were forthcoming, but she couldn't. "Did he threaten you?"

"No, he didn't threaten me— I guess— This is all in hindsight— I guess I was really mad at your father for moving us to Raysburg. And I also was drunk as a skunk. And if you ever dare to breathe so much as a word of this to your father, I'll call you a liar to your face."

"Mom. Come on. I wouldn't say anything to Dad. You know that."

Her mother was still not getting out of the car. "Are you all right?" she said. "I mean *really*."

"I think so— Yes, I guess I am."

"Sweetie?— If a girl's pretty—well, then, she's bound to get herself in a pickle every once in a while, but— Oh, just be careful, OK?"

In the dining room of the Raysburg Country Club, Ted Cotter, his wife at his side, was sitting at the big, round table always reserved for him, the one that commanded a full view of the dining room and the terrace beyond it. Facing Ted were his right-hand man, Charlie Edmonds, and Charlie's wife; sitting next to their mothers were Ted's daughter and Charlie's daughter. It had always annoyed Ted that even though Charlie had been in town for damn near two years, he'd never joined the club, so Ted had given him—or rather, Raysburg Steel had given him—a full membership; it was, Ted had told him, part of his well-earned bonus, but he'd wanted Charlie to know that, as the senior VP at Raysburg Steel, he was expected to settle down in Raysburg and *live there*— and the simple fact that Charlie had appeared tonight with his family had told Ted that his message had been received loud and clear.

Ted had a good meal under his belt. The plates had been cleared away, and the waiter had just brought the brandies. Ted lit a smoke for himself and his wife, and Charlie did the same thing. The conversation had been quite animated there for a while, but all of a sudden, nobody was talking; it was, he thought, one of those funny moments when somebody says, "Hey, an angel must have flown over." The band kicked into an old, familiar tune, and Ted thought, that's right: it *is* the shank of the night. Then he thought, as he often had lately, well, Theodore R. Cotter, you've got everything you ever wanted, haven't you?

"The roasts always this good?" Charlie asked him.

"Most of the time," Ted said. "You can get a stinker every once in a while."

"You'd think," Laney said, "if they could get them rare enough some of the time, they could get them rare enough all of the time."

The breeze blowing in through the doors to the terrace was positively chilly, but there were still some kids splashing around in the pool; Ted could hear them yelling, and he liked the sound of it. His boys were probably munching their cheeseburgers by now; they both had enough sense to tell the waiter when they were hungry. Next year Bobby would be sixteen, so, whether he liked it or not, he was going to get hauled up here to eat his dinner with his parents. It was funny, but Gloria had never liked being told to stay out of their hair and take care of herself—yeah, "banished" she'd called it—but she was a girl, and girls are different, and— What the devil was he thinking about?— Well, it was nice to see that Charlie's daughter was a nice, quiet little kid, but it would be even nicer if she was down in the pool, and he'd have to say something to Charlie about that—and then, glancing over at his own daughter, it hit him like a ton of bricks: Gloria wasn't just the kid she'd always been; she was a grown woman, and she'd been a grown woman for a long time now if he'd only let himself notice.

He'd always looked forward to her coming home in the summer, but now he had the funny feeling that she wouldn't be around much anymore. Don't get sentimental, he told himself—but hell, it *was* sad.

Good Christ almighty, a man who'd make a pass at a friend's daughter was just about the lowest form of scum imaginable, and, again, Ted wished that bastard had stayed in town just long enough for Al's boys to catch up to him. But, even more than that, he wished that Gloria was all right. He was pretty sure she was, but, with women, you never knew anything for certain—and she'd just noticed that he'd been looking at her, so he toasted her with his brandy glass.

Gloria wasn't drinking brandy, but she toasted her father with her coffee cup— and smiled, trying to send back the message she knew neither of them could ever say out loud. That gesture of his had almost justified her coming to the club—almost, but not quite. It had certainly been a tedious evening.

Because Raysburg Steel's VPs usually took their vacations in August, most of the kids from Gloria's crowd were out of town, and her only friend there tonight was Binkie who was at a corner table dining with—wonder of wonders— Jack Farrington, but Gloria hadn't had a chance to talk to her yet. And the same old band was wheezing away, playing the same old tunes from the war, and the food—rare roast or not—was the same as it had always been, and the only thing that was any different was the presence of Mr. and Mrs. Edmonds and their darling daughter. If Gloria had known they were going to be there, she would have stayed home.

The daughter was really annoying her. When she'd first seen her, Gloria had taken her to be a tall ten-year-old, but, trying unsuccessfully to draw her out, she'd discovered that the miserable little thing was going into the eighth grade at Edgewood. The girl had a taffy-blonde pageboy and huge, startled, blue eyes. She'd answered Gloria's questions in monosyllables uttered in a tiny, breathy voice. Throughout dinner, she'd sat with her head bent in a sullen, hangdog way as though trying to hide behind her bangs. There was a quality about her—Gloria couldn't find a name for it—that was really irritating. Why on earth hadn't they left the little priss at home?

"You're a great one to be talking about little prisses," the secret watcher told her. Well, maybe, Gloria thought, but I was never *that* prissy. And she must surely by now have done her duty to her parents and their guests. "Excuse me," she said, "I'm going to go say hi to Bink."

Gloria was unsure quite what manner to take with Binkie when she was paired with Jack—were they actually out on a date, or was this merely a dinner of convenience?—and she looked to Binkie for a clue. Jack, of course, had risen to his feet. "Gloria. How nice. Will you join us?"

But Binkie stood up too, abruptly, and caught Gloria's hand. "You can join us in a minute," she said, and then to Jack: "I'll be right back, honey."

Honey? And what a gauche thing to leave him standing there with an astonished look on his face—but Binkie, being Binkie, could get away with anything. Now she led Gloria across the empty dance floor to a table for two in the corner—the setting for a private *tête-à-tête*—and Gloria's sixth sense told her that Binkie was mad at her.

Why? Gloria hadn't been avoiding Binkie; they'd had dinner together out at the Pines on Friday night—and Gloria had been horrified to learn that simply everybody had been talking about what had transpired between herself and Mr. Dougherty. The best she'd been able to tell, people were saying that he'd turned up at her house disgustingly drunk and had made a pass at her, that she'd had to use extreme measures to get rid of him. She'd found out later that even her little brother Bobby had heard about it. (In a gesture of rare graciousness, he'd asked Gloria if she wanted to take his bow to Columbia with her.) So she was, she supposed, destined to be remembered in Raysburg legend as the girl who'd shot a Porsche full of arrows. Binkie had thought it was funny, and Gloria had let her go on thinking it. But now what?

"Judy's at home bawling her eyes out," Binkie announced.

Gloria didn't have the remotest idea what Binkie was talking about. "She is?"

"Haven't you heard?"

"No. What?"

"Her dad got fired."

"Her dad—" And then Gloria got it: *her* dad had fired *Judy's* dad. "Oh, that's terrible," she said.

"You're telling me. It's a crying shame, that's all. Her dad's worked for Raysburg Steel his whole life, and now— The Staubs are an old family in the valley, you know that. Judy's great-grandfather—or maybe her great-great-grandfather— was a senator back when we were still a part of Virginia. What's going on?"

"You think I know?"

Ignoring her question, Binkie said, "Judy's dad— Well, he's just crushed. She says she can't bear to see him. He just sits in the den all day and stares out the window. He can't understand what he did wrong. She says his heart's just broken. It doesn't seem fair."

"Well, it's not fair, Bink." She looked into Binkie's angry, accusatory eyes. Did Binkie actually think she could do something about it? "My dad never talks about work," she said. "Never. I don't know what he's thinking about—I don't know why he would have done it."

"Could you talk to him?"

The idea was so preposterous that Gloria couldn't answer for a moment; what did Binkie think this was, the Tudor court? "Well, could *you* talk to *your* dad about something like that?"

Binkie held her gaze. Gloria saw something change in Binkie's eyes; then she looked away. "No, of course I couldn't—but my dad would never have fired Judy's dad. Oh, Glo, I know it's not your fault. I guess there isn't anything we can do about it, huh? It just makes me mad, that's all."

It made Gloria mad too, and she didn't know why. She supposed she should be defending her father, but she didn't feel like it—and besides, to defend him, she'd have to understand at least a little about what was going on, and she didn't. All she understood was her own complicated web of loyalties—what she owed Binkie, for instance. "Oh, Bink," she said, "I'm really sorry. Will you tell Judy how sorry I am?"

"Why don't *you* tell her? Oh, maybe not. That might make her feel— Oh, this is a tough one. I just don't know." Binkie stood up, and so did Gloria.

"So where you going to stay up at Columbia?" Binkie asked her. "Do they have a—you know, for grad students—a dorm or something?"

Gratefully, Gloria told Binkie that yes, they did have a dorm for grad students, and that's where she'd be living, at least to begin with, but her cousins had told her she simply had to get her own apartment, so maybe she would do that eventually—they'd said they'd help her find one—and she invited Binkie to come up and visit, and Binkie said she'd really like that, and, wow, it'd be great to go shopping in New York, and, with that, they slipped into talking about clothes, and Binkie asked Gloria where on earth she'd got that dress—"It's amazing, Glo, how you can make *anything* look good." And so Gloria had to tell Binkie the whole story about winning May Queen in it, how it had been the perfect thing—naughty but nice—for the horny young profs on the May Queen Committee, especially with these heels, and Binkie said that was a riot, and if she tried to walk in heels as high as that, she'd end up in the hospital, and she invited Gloria to come over to their table for dessert. "Oh, I think I'm going home now," Gloria said, having just decided to do it. "I've got a bit of a headache. Why don't we have lunch tomorrow?"

"Can't. I'm flying up to Canada—you know, that darned resort where Mom and Dad go every summer. And I want to do that about as much as I want to dive off the Suspension Bridge, but, oh, what the heck."

"I guess this is goodbye then."

"I guess it is. Don't do anything I wouldn't do."

"Not on your life, Bink." They hugged. "Hey, what's with you and Jack?"

"Oh, he's not so bad."

By the time the brandies had arrived, Laney had suffered Mrs. Charles T. Edmonds long enough. The woman's laugh was too loud, her voice too shrill, her nails too long, her lipstick too bright, and, whoever the peasant was who'd dyed her hair, she might as well have been using liquid shoe polish. On top of all that, the woman told long and pointless stories and could *not* be interrupted, and—here was the clincher, and Laney winced inwardly as she thought of it—she simply drank too much. So, shortly after Princess Priss made her exit, Laney murmured something about powdering her nose and was gone before that dreadful creature had a chance to even consider joining her.

Laney made her mandatory visit to the ladies', refreshed her lipstick, and then, instead of returning to their table, made a wide circuit of the dining room, staying well out of sight, and ended up on the terrace. She was alone there, and it was dark already. The days were getting shorter again—and yes, indeed, she *was* in a very odd mood.

Charlie was Teddy's right-hand man; she understood that and everything it meant. So she was stuck again with someone she didn't like, and she supposed that one of these days, fairly soon, she was going to have to take that boring, loud-mouthed woman to lunch. Oh, there was simply no end in sight, and it was a terrible, traitorous thought to be having, but she wished that Teddy hadn't been made president. As the wife of the president of Raysburg Steel, Laney would really have to watch her Ps and Qs. Well, she'd stopped herself from floating away, hadn't she?

Now she heard the clicking of heels, turned, and was surprised at how glad she was to see that Princess Priss was joining her. She had to smile at her daughter's cheap outfit; it actually, in a curious way, did look cute on her. Well, Marcelaine, she told herself, the height of good taste was not always at the forefront of your mind when you were twenty-one—nor, for that matter, were you a model of maidenly deportment. So Gloria had been sleeping with Rolland, so what? She couldn't very well stay a virgin forever, could she?

Laney's odd mood, she discovered, must have had an element of *in vino veritas* to it, because she heard herself saying, "You know, sweetie, I'm sure you think I'm a bitch, but that terrible woman is really a bitch."

Gloria laughed and laughed. "And the daughter—good grief, Mom, did you get a load of her?"

"What about her? Quiet little thing. I wasn't paying much attention."

"Oh, it's a crime. The poor girl's going into the eighth grade, so she's got to be thirteen. And she's got a figure. And did you see what her mom's got on her?"

"No, I told you, I wasn't paying a lot of—"

"Her skirt about a foot above her knees. White ankle socks and little kid's party shoes—I mean, *Buster Browns*. It's cruel to do that to a girl who's already got a figure. Her mother should be shot dead."

Laney thought it was a strange thing for Gloria to get so worked up about. Why should she care what Charlie Edmonds' wife put on their daughter? "Well, some mothers are overly protective."

"I guess so." Gloria leaned forward with her elbows on the balustrade—probably, Laney thought, to rest her feet—and then, looking up, said, "Boy, is it ever clear tonight."

"Lovely, isn't it? Although I should have brought my wrap."

Gloria seemed to have nothing more to say, and, strangely enough, Laney was content for the moment simply to stand there and share the night with her daughter. Yes, Laney thought, I certainly *am* feeling odd. Actually she didn't know what she was feeling. She'd thought she'd been putting something over on everyone by pretending that Mother's death had knocked the pins out from under her; now she knew that the main person she'd been kidding had been herself because Mother's death *had* knocked the pins out from under her— and she'd continued to float away right up until the moment when she'd been stumbling around her living room crying—absolutely howling with grief and rage—picking up bits of broken china and smashed furniture and throwing them down again, when something had stopped her as suddenly as if someone had dumped a champagne bucket over her head and she'd said to herself: "My God, Marcelaine, what ever are you doing?"

She'd been holding a fragment of an old, blue Whittock plate with a seascape on it; she'd let it fall, had walked across the room, thrown her arms around her daughter, and said, "Oh, sweetie, are you all right?" Since then, she'd mulled it over interminably. If she hadn't been such a rotten mother, it needn't have happened at all. If Gloria could have talked to her, she would have told her what was what in no time flat.

"Hey, it's a harvest moon," Gloria said.

"Yes. Isn't it lovely."

"And look, there's Orion."

Laney wouldn't have known Orion if it had fallen on her, but she said, "Yes. Lovely."

"So what are you doing out here, Mom," Gloria said, "hiding out?"

"Oh, I suppose I am."

"Overly protective— Not like you, huh, Mom?"

"I don't know what you mean," Laney said cautiously.

"Well, you remember when I left Fairhaven? When I was fourteen? And you came and picked me up? You got my hair cut and my nails painted, and you bought me a whole bunch of grown-up clothes—and a girdle and high heels and cherry red lipstick."

"Oh, did I?"

"Don't you remember?"

"Well, yes, of course I remember."

"I don't think I ever told you in so many words, Mom, but thanks. That really helped me fit in—really helped me a lot."

At first, Laney couldn't imagine that Gloria could possibly have meant it, but then, glancing over at her, she saw that she had. "Oh, sweetie, it was— I don't know— I'm just glad you appreciated it. Thanks for telling me."

Usually Laney knew when she was going to cry; this time she didn't, but she'd be damned if she was going to give in to it—ridiculous to get all choked up just because Princess Priss had said something nice to her for a change—so she lit a cigarette. "The cold nights must be killing the mosquitoes," she said. "Thank God for that." But maybe Gloria wasn't the only thing she was choked up about. She'd spent her whole life resenting Mother, and now Mother was gone, and what good had all those years of resentment done her?

"I could have been nicer to you this summer, sweetie," Laney said, "and I'm sorry I wasn't. Oh, I so wanted you to marry Rolland."

"I know you did, Mom, but I just couldn't. But I am going to get married someday. I know I am. And when I do, we'll have a wedding so big, you won't believe it."

"Well, it doesn't have to be that big."

Inside the band began to play. It did feel like October, and Laney was actually shivering. But she didn't want to go back. She inhaled the smoke deeply just as though it might make her warm. "Mom," Gloria said, "would you mind if I took off now—you know, just walked home?"

"Lucky you. Go ahead, sweetie. I'm stuck."

After Gloria left, Laney didn't have any reason to continue standing alone on the terrace—not only was she freezing, but it was getting to be downright impolite—but she couldn't force herself to move. The little smarty-pants, she thought; she should have let me pull some strings and get her presented in New York when it was still possible. But Princess Priss might do all right after all—and Laney thought that tomorrow she should call up her brother Alf's little nobody wife on Long Island and have a long, friendly chat. It certainly couldn't hurt. All Gloria needed, really, was our sort of boys to choose from.

Gloria stepped through the big front doors of the club and felt her spirits lift. She loved the sky the way it was tonight—brilliant with stars—and she loved the breeze and the chill in the air. She had no business to be feeling as good as she did, but— "Oh, why not?" the secret watcher asked her, and she didn't have a good answer.

Taking the tiny, poised steps required by the too-high heels, she walked down the drive past the parking lot and saw the fat, pink harvest moon still riding low in the sky over the golf course. Back inside, the band was playing a waltz; in all the trees for miles around, the locusts were telling her in their dreary, painfully evocative voices that summer was over. Hearing the locusts used to mean that football season was only a few weeks away. Would she care about football season at Columbia?

As soon as she was on the other side of the big hedge, out of sight of anyone in the club, she pulled off her heels and slipped her ballerinas on. "Goodbye, country club," she said, half aloud, and then turned and walked briskly up the hill. She listened to the steady rustle of her skirt and crinolines. She didn't know if she would have used Susie's word for the sound of taffeta—yummy—but it certainly was loud. Near the top, at the point where she'd first heard the Porsche following her, she turned to look behind her. There was, of course, no one on the road.

She remembered clearly the sound of the Porsche—its expensive, throaty purring. Now she was at the spot where she'd seen the low-slung, gleaming silver nose emerge directly below her left shoulder. She felt her skin goosebump, but she was alone. Then, just as she had on that night in June, she took the shortcut through the woods. This time she walked slowly, protecting her dress. Oh, she thought, finally understanding what she was doing, this is a ritual.

She followed the trail through the apple trees to the back lawn, crossed the fresh sod where the hole had been filled in, and walked around the side of the swimming pool. She didn't go up the back way but continued on around the house, climbed the front steps to the top and stood at the spot where she'd known she was Britomart. She looked down the driveway toward the road. She didn't feel the least bit smug or self-satisfied; to feel like that would have been, as the Greeks would quite properly have judged it, *hubris*.

Inside, the house felt both familiar and strange. How's that for ambivalence? she thought. Well, for one thing it was too quiet. The door to what used to be her grandmother's room was ajar, so she went in and lit the light. Everything in the room was different, but she hoped to feel her grandmother's presence nonetheless. She gathered her crinolines under her and sat in the chair next to the bed. "You're home early, Gloria," she imagined her grandmother saying. "Didn't you have a good time?"

"Oh, it was OK," she imagined answering. "Mom's not mad at me any more, so that's good. Are you all right, Grandmother?"

"I'm having some pain, but it's fairly mild tonight. Are you all right, Gloria?"

"I'm kind of sad, actually." She liked to think of her grandmother as she had in that wonderful dream—as completed, folded back into her own time—but if she sat there any longer, she was going to start bawling, and she'd already cried enough this summer to last her a lifetime.

She hung up her dress and crinolines, put her underwear and stockings to soak in her bathroom sink, and took a shower. She didn't want to close her windows, but it was getting pretty darned cold, and all of her winter dressing gowns had been packed and shipped. She found an old flannel nightgown in the top of the hall linen closet, put it on, climbed into bed, and turned on the radio. The first station she found was playing whiny country music; it made her think of Susie, so she left it on.

She heard her parents and the brats come home, waited until everyone was settled, then went in and said good night to her mom and dad. She felt restless, miles away from sleep. She'd snitched her mom's newest murder mystery to read on the plane; now she thought she'd give it a try, but she couldn't work up any interest in the silly plot and soon laid it aside. It was after midnight. She'd been in the pool twice that day—had swum herself half to death, actually—was feeling an irksome mixture of mental alertness and physical exhaustion, and none of her usual devices to while away the night seemed the least bit attractive. She thought she should at least *try* to sleep, so she turned out the light and snuggled into her pillow.

She kept drifting in and out of that creepy, elusive state halfway between waking and sleeping, and she knew that she should get up, drink a glass of milk, or read, or do *something*, but she kept putting it off. On Wednesday morning she and her dad were riding up to Pittsburgh together in a chauffeured limousine provided by Raysburg Steel; he was flying to Washington, and she was flying to Philadelphia. She was going to have four whole days with Susie before the fall term began at Columbia, and she couldn't stop thinking about her trip; in fact, it was getting really wearying, thinking about her trip—and then, gradually, thinking about it was transformed into going on it, and she was already riding in the chauffeured limousine. She thought for a minute it was Susie in the back seat with her, but it turned out to be the Edmonds' wretched daughter. Gloria kept trying to get her to talk, but the sullen little thing wouldn't say a word—sat hunched over with her hair hanging in her face, staring at the toes of her party shoes. Gloria wanted to slap her.

Then Gloria realized that she was dreaming. She didn't know how to wake up. A voice whispered in her ear, "Gloria."

"Stop it. Go away. Let me alone," she said, still partway inside the dream. She sat up and lit the light.

Her heart was slamming in her throat, her mouth was dry, she was covered with a cold film of perspiration, and she was afraid she was going to have to throw up. That didn't make any sense; she hadn't eaten all that much at the club—

and certainly not anything suspicious, seafood or anything like that. Maybe she was getting the flu. Oh, great, the perfect time for it.

She pressed a pillow into her stomach and curled herself around it. She was so tired she was yawning, her eyes watering, and sleep felt like a warm, beloved, childhood blanket she couldn't quite reach. If only her mind would let go of all the wearying things it seemed to be chasing, and she heard Susie's voice singing—a hymn, surely, but she couldn't tell which one—and it was a relief that Susie was driving so she didn't have to, and then, with a start, she woke up and saw that she was driving down the Pennsylvania Turnpike. She'd almost fallen asleep at the wheel.

That's right: Susie wasn't driving; *she* was driving. There was no one in the car with her. If she fell asleep, she'd run off the road and kill herself. A voice whispered in her ear, "Gloria."

"Stop it, stop it, stop it," she said. She was sitting up in bed, and she couldn't remember if she'd said it out loud or not.

What a terrible night it was turning out to be—the worst she could remember in a long time. She got up, crept down to the kitchen, and drank a glass of milk. She unlocked the French doors and stepped outside. It was quite cold, and she rather liked it.

Shivering, she paced back and forth at the edge of the pool. The full moon had lost its pinkish warmth, was now icy white and high in the sky—so bright it cast shadows. Surely, she thought, a seasoned insomniac such as herself must have been awake in the middle of the night to see a moon like that, but she couldn't remember having ever seen one quite that intense: so brilliant that if she were writing about it in her diary, she would have called the cold blaze *furious*—and so silent. She thought of Diana in her moon barge—a dawn goddess, seen in the first rosy light that made her eyes seem pale, as if without fire, but what would she be now? Terrible Diana, powerful Diana. You'd have to be Ezra Pound, Gloria thought, steeped in Greek and Latin up to your eyeballs, before you could write prayers to Diana without sounding forced or pretentious.

She walked out onto the lawn. What was she doing outside barefoot? Her feet were freezing. And, oh, the moonlight was strange—but then she thought how strange the world was *at any time* if one were able to see it truly. Something quite definite was frightening her, but she couldn't quite identify it. She felt tiny, tiny—a minuscule wisp of consciousness—and she wanted to pray. How odd, and at the same time how natural, that *The Lord's Prayer* had helped her. Perhaps God had helped her. Who are you? she asked—and felt nothing reply.

Oh, she thought, I feel *alone*—that's what's so deeply frightening. Whoever you are, she prayed, thank you. But she wondered if she weren't simply walking around in the backyard talking to herself.

The moonlight blazed up from the still surface of the pool, and now her mind seemed to be presenting her with formulaic prayers; one of them went: "The grace of the Lord Jesus Christ, and the love of God, and the communion of the Holy Ghost, be with you all." But she wasn't sure she believed in the Lord Jesus Christ, or in the Holy Ghost, or even in Christianity, and she'd feel hypocritical trying to pray that prayer. But then, what did she believe in?

"Pull down thy vanity," Pound told her, "it is not *man* made courage, or made order, or made grace." Yes, that was right.

She felt a blurring in herself, a faint but unmistakable softening as though the hard nugget of her conscious mind had just begun to melt in a double-boiler. Oh, wonderful, she thought. She crept back through the silent house. She curled up under the familiar covers on her own familiar bed, hugging herself, and soon she felt sleep rippling under her as though she were floating on it. *Thank God*, she thought.

For a long time Gloria moved softly through sleep, her thoughts like the lights below she'd seen only once—when she'd flown into New York at night—and sleep like the dark land between them, and then Susie parked the truck by the side of the road and got out, so Gloria got out too. She didn't know where they were going, but she would always follow where Susie led. They were climbing a hill.

Susie began to sing. At first it sounded like a hymn in a foreign language, but, listening carefully, Gloria realized that it wasn't foreign at all. "Tis Grace that brought me safe thus far," Susie sang, "and Grace will lead me home."

Gloria hadn't noticed before, but Susie was wearing a knife in a sheath on her belt just the way her brother did. Now she drew out the sharp hunting knife and offered it to Gloria handle first. Gloria knew she was supposed to take it. She reached for it. Then, as deftly as if she were twirling a baton, Susie flipped the knife over so that the blade was aimed at Gloria. She touched the point of the blade to Gloria's stomach just below her breast bone.

"Gloria," a voice whispered in her ear.

She sat straight up in bed, hugging herself and weeping. "No," she said out loud. "Go away. Please go away. Please, please, please, just go away and let me alone."

Her bedroom now, moonlit, didn't look ordinary, or comforting, or even familiar. If this keeps up, Gloria thought, I'm going to go crazy. Maybe I'm crazy already.

She knew every object in the room: her vanity table with her makeup on it, her full-length mirror, her desk, her books, the shelves where the many volumes of her diary were arranged—still not packed because she would never trust them to be shipped. She turned and looked through the partially open door of her closet, knew that the spectral shape floating there was just one of the many sets of the crinolines she owned, saw glints of light from several pairs of shoes on the floor—

But all the objects in her room were only the trappings of a girl living in this particular place at this particular time. If she were a girl in *another* time, she would be seeing a different set of objects. If she were *a boy*, she would be seeing a different set of objects yet. Her very body—her dark skin and black hair and the cells of her brain—were only another set of arbitrary objects. The thoughts she was thinking were the result of chemical operations in her brain. If her heart—she could feel it beating—were to stop, even for a few minutes, all of this would be gone. The very thoughts she was thinking would be gone—

Her terror was so intense she couldn't bear it. She sprang out of bed, raised the blind, and stared out into the backyard, hoping to find anything that was familiar and comforting, but, brilliantly lit by the moon, every object outside was just as strange and arbitrary as every object inside. She listened to a blurry buzzing inside of her, felt an aching inside her, like a bruising. She wondered if anyone had ever committed suicide because of the fear of being alive.

Oh, help, she prayed. Then, just as she'd seen Susie doing every night they'd lived together, she knelt by the side of her bed, folded her hands, and tried again to pray. She had wanted to say, simply, "Oh, please let me go to sleep," but she kept hearing the dim buzzing, or mumbling, in her mind. She was losing control over her mind—and heard it saying, "the grace of The Lord, the love of God, the Holy Ghost—" *Please, please help me*, she tried to pray, but now her mind was giving her Pound: "Pull down thy vanity, it is not man made courage, or made order, or made grace—"

To save a wretch like me, she thought. Oh, God, I really am a wretch. I can't stand this. 'Tis grace that brought me safe thus far, and grace— It is not *man* made grace. What thou lovest well is thy true heritage. Grace will lead thee—safe thus far, a wretch like me, not *man* made grace— And then, amazingly, as she knelt there, she felt herself beginning to fall asleep. "Oh, thank you, thank you, thank you," she said. She crawled into bed and pulled the covers over her.

She fell at once into a deep, dreamless sleep. It was as though she'd been wrung dry, and sleep was flowing into her now, moistening her and filling her up. She slept on and on, too far down even to feel grateful. Then, as she was sleeping, someone knelt by the side of her bed. She thought at first it must be Susie. The girl bent and kissed her on the cheek. The spot was tingling on her cheek where the girl had kissed her.

"Oh, my beautiful, blonde twin," Gloria said, "I've missed you so much."

For the fourth time, the voice whispered in her ear, "Gloria."

She knew from what was left of the dream that her twin was her death, but she sat up and said, "I'm right here. What do you want?"

The voice said, "I gutter in this wind. Extinguish me."

• • •

Gloria was sitting up in bed, listening. All she could hear were familiar, unobtrusive, middle-of-the-night sounds—clocks ticking, the settling of wood, the fuzzy murmuring of the locusts—telling her that everything was perfectly ordinary. But nothing *felt* perfectly ordinary. The hair had prickled on her arms and the back of her neck; she was holding her entire body as tensely poised as if she were standing at the edge of a high diving board. Later, when she would be able to think about this experience, she'd realize how odd it had been that she'd forgotten to be afraid.

She was certain that what she'd just heard had been a line from a poem. She often heard lines from poems, of course, so there was nothing strange about that, but she usually had *some* sense of where they'd come from even if it took her a while to figure it out. This one she hadn't recognized at all, and she still couldn't begin to identify it. Who was it a quotation from?

Oh, but it wasn't a quotation from *anybody*, and she felt a fiercely driven energy—as vivid, physical, and appalling as an electrical shock. She leapt out of bed, ran to her desk, grabbed her fountain pen, and wrote the line quickly, as though she was afraid of losing it—wrote it onto the first paper at hand, a pad of good vellum she kept for letters. She didn't want to light her desk lamp, and it didn't matter anyway; there was plenty of light in her room.

Was there more? She closed her eyes and heard that terrifying buzzing—or humming or mumbling—she'd heard so often before as she'd tried to go to sleep, but now, instead of trying to push it away, she tried to hear it more clearly. She heard whole skeins of words unwinding up from a blurry, rhythmic chaos.

"The way the mind casts nets to capture meaning," she heard—and wrote—and immediately heard Wyatt's line, "since in a net I seek to hold the wind," so she wrote that too, and Wyatt must have given her the image of the hind in the courtly love tradition: she heard, "the deer, beloved, turns and hunts the hunted—then something, something—burning ribbons—the Gypsy girl, my wild sister—and I'm afraid sometimes I made you up—"

This wasn't like any of her previous mental floodings; she was hearing what seemed to be an endless stream of unlineated verse: "How could she not see those images of hell, those tiny silhouetted forms of men struggling amidst sparks and fire, as something from a fairy tale, herself as Cinderella? About to become an entirely different person, childhood gone—"

"Wait a minute, wait a minute," she said, half aloud, "I can't keep up." But it wasn't going to wait a minute. She was writing as fast as she could, but she was still missing lots of it.

"As she sees this river road for the first time ever," she wrote, "in the ambiguous darkness of her mother's car—catches fire on tips of newly polished nails—how could she not think that grown-up means that red, that shine, that barely perceptible extra weight riding on her finger tips, or hear the clanging, metal on metal, as made by the dwarfish men who labor in the earth somewhere off at the edge of the story—as something, something— How could she not see all of this as magic, this dreamy, inward girl, alone too much—that dreamy, inward girl was me—"

She felt the sting of tears. Of course that dreamy, inward girl was me, she thought, and it seemed to have paused; in that moment of stillness—like walking into an empty, high-ceilinged room—she wondered if she hadn't always been afraid of being cut open like Susie's rabbit. Now that she had been, this torrent was pouring out of her. Was there more?

Yes, there was more. It hadn't really paused; she'd merely stepped back from the edge. Moving closer, she heard it running at full flood just below the dumb, ordinary place where her mind usually sat and protected itself by chattering away about dumb, ordinary things. "I've sickened in my tower," she heard, and wrote, "weaving tapestries I called my life— I'm sick of looking in a mirror—to try to see the passing world—but I don't want to die and float away—so that some passing knight can say, 'She hath a pretty face'—and having said all that—something, something— Oh, everything I have to say feels tentative, as though—"

As though what? But it was already gone, and she was writing so fast she was losing half the letters in her words; she could only hope she'd be able to read them later. "Dreaming girls in tiny towns recreate themselves," she wrote. "Your syntax is your motion through the world—"

As she filled up each page of vellum, she ripped it off and flung it onto the floor. She wrote furiously until her hand began to cramp and she had to stop every few minutes to massage it. She was dimly aware that a multitude of birds outside her window had begun to cheep like crazy, that the sun must be coming up, but those were insignificant events happening in another land a million miles away.

Gradually she began to understand that she was no longer required to take dictation from that maddening torrent. Now she had to assemble some of the words it had given her. She had to write something and finish it; she would only know what it was when she found it. She sprang out of her chair, heard it fall behind her and didn't care. She threw herself onto the floor, scrambled around on her hands and knees gathering up sheets of paper. She felt as harried as if something were pursuing her—but no, she was the one doing the pursuing. Whatever it was, it seemed to be staying one jump ahead of her.

Many of her scrawled notes seemed to be about riding down the river road from Pittsburgh with her mother when she'd been fourteen—just as one of the lines said, "so newly coiffed and waxed and painted"—when she'd known that she'd never have to go back to Fairhaven again, when she'd been about to become an entirely different person. She sorted through the paper, drew circles around the lines that seemed to fit, and began to tell the story all over again:

> They're driving down the river road at night.
> She sees whole cities made of sparks and fire
> And hears them pounding like metallic giants
> Exploding out of thickly moving shadows

No, she thought. That's not right.

Her original scrawled words had been "as she sees this river road for the first time ever," and that had a wonderful energy, but it also had two anapestic feet. So how strict was she supposed to be? She didn't know. She started over, this time sticking more closely to what she'd originally written:

> So what is real? Perhaps the way that this
> Barely perceptible weight riding on
> Her fingertips reflects the fiery light,
> So will

OK, she thought, so will *what*? She felt trapped by her own simile. Something had to reflect something. How about a mirror? But it couldn't simple reflect *herself*—and then she thought of Britomart and wrote, "So will her mirror manifest a knight." That seemed to have given her a rhyme scheme.

But she had one more line than she had rhymes. OK, so what if she picked *anything* that would fit for the last rhyme? It would be perfect, actually, because then she'd have seven lines, and, if she could get everything else crammed into another stanza, that would make fourteen lines, and it was about being *fourteen*, wasn't it? She wrote the last line with a flourish and read it over:

> So will her mirror manifest a knight
> To follow where her childhood has gone,
> And consummate her longing with a kiss.
> She's missed the point. Those flames are making steel.

She stood up, paced twice around her room, threw herself back onto the floor. She knew at a glance that what she'd written was wrong. As much as she liked the last line—a typically Gloria smarty-pants remark, she thought of it—she'd been imposing something that didn't belong. The knight didn't belong. He'd come riding in to rhyme with "light" and complete the simile. This is really hard, she thought. This is going to take a really long time.

She went back to her original scrawlings, saw at once another possible pattern and wrote:

She's sure she's finally found real life, but how
Could she not see this road unwinding now
As anything but fairy tale? Whole towns
Of fire blaze against the dark with sounds
Of furious giants banging metal. Light
Is flickering from her fingertips, and night

And *night?* Night *what?* She still had the same problem she'd had before: six lines when she wanted seven and no rhyme—and then she saw how her line was an echo of Lowell's: "The sea was still breaking violently and night—"

This wasn't merely *hard;* it was *demonically* hard. How were you ever supposed to sort out what was yours from what was somebody else's? Especially when you had a million miles of other people's poetry stuck in your mind?

What she had to do was a lot more complicated than she'd first thought. Here she was, seven years later, looking back on herself at fourteen, but she'd just found another position: herself writing, looking at herself looking back at herself—

Seven years, she thought, two sevens are fourteen, and I was fourteen years old, and now I'm three times seven—and she finally got it—*fourteen* lines, Gloria, you dope—and wrote "sonnet sequence" on the top sheet, and, beneath it, "layers of consciousness like a Russian Easter egg."

Could she do it? It would probably take her days to get it right—hours and hours of patient tinkering—but, in the meantime, there was still that elusive whatever-it-was she was supposed to be writing *right now.*

She looked at her last attempt. She felt an electrical tingle when she read: "how could she not see this road unwinding now as anything but fairy tale?" There was, indeed, a fairy tale implied in her notes: the story of a princess who has locked herself in a tower. Again she sorted through the pages, marking the lines she needed. Not paying much attention to what they might mean, she selected a dozen or so lines strictly for their sound. She smoothed them out, rearranged them, cut a bit, tried to make sense of what was left, cut some more, and quickly had a stanza:

Although she wore her mask of porcelain
And heels of polished black obsidian,
The music at the fairy summer balls
Was never quite the way it should have been—
Or so she thought—so beautiful because
Impossible, so sweet because so false.
She's haunted by the sound of dry applause.

Yes, she thought, reading it over, that's what I'm supposed to be writing.

She simply adored the princess. She could see her with intricate eyelashes like a stylized cat's painted onto her porcelain mask, taking tiny, ringing steps on a hard parquet floor that looked like a chess board. Everything about her, everything around her, would be hard, polished, shiny, utterly artificial. There'd be mirrors everywhere, and, later in the poem, she'd "lift her mask and find there's no one there." Writing about her was going to be so much fun! Would she ever get out of her tower, or would she be stuck there forever? Maybe, like Britomart, she'd have to defeat an evil enchanter.

Then she read her stanza again and asked herself what it was saying. The princess seemed to think that only what was impossible could be beautiful, that only what was false could be sweet. Or did she? Wait a minute; wasn't that what was wrong with the fairy ball? Maybe the princess was longing for something beautiful that was *possible*; maybe that's why she'd locked herself in her tower—maybe she's done it out of despair, sure that she could never find it— And then Gloria asked herself if *she* hadn't always believed that beauty was impossible—or at least impossible for her. But Stevens said that beauty in the flesh was immortal—

She closed her eyes and saw the way the light fell in Professor Bolton's green guest room, remembered the sudden, overwhelming sense of being alive—of being fully aware of herself alive—in that particular room, that particular time and place. She remembered the reproduction from the Book of Kells hanging on the wall, remembered staring at it, trying to find where it could have said, "*in principio est verbum.*" She wrote at the top of her stanza, "The Word was made flesh," and then, after a moment, added, "Paradise is *not* artificial (Pound)." Something else had coalesced in her mind, and she was resisting it. Don't ask why, she told herself, just write it, so she did: "I came not into the world to condemn the world, but that, through me, the world might be saved."

As soon as the words were on the page, she was struck with a deep, visceral sobbing that felt entirely beyond her conscious control. What she'd just written had evoked Susie so strongly she could feel her presence in the room.

She marked all the notes that seemed to be about Susie. She had to keep wiping her tears away. Almost everything she needed was written already; it was simply a matter of putting things in their proper places. The poem came together quickly, almost as though it were writing itself:

> What can I say to you, my lovely twin?
> That I'm afraid I might have made you up
> Because I needed you so much? I couldn't
> Love myself until I'd loved you first?
> My every word feels tentative— perhaps

Because I'm trying out a brand new voice
That's not Sir Thomas Wyatt's but my own.

Love's always the particular, this now:
The way your hair takes fire from the sun,
The way your voice is breathy as a child's.
You sing that old, familiar hymn that says
That grace will lead you home. It's led us both.
You were my mirror. Then you stepped aside
To let me see the sunlight face to face.

She read what she'd written. That's right, she thought. It's finished. She stood and stretched. Her back ached; her right hand ached.

While she'd been gone, her room had filled up with daylight. Only a few hours ago, everything had looked flat and cold and dead, but now the colors were vivid and warm, the shapes exquisitely precise, and it wasn't merely that the sun had come up. Her dreadful feeling of being tiny and alone was gone. Every commonplace, familiar object glowed with an inner life. The floor was covered with dozens of pieces of paper scrawled with her frantic writing, and even the paper glowed with an inner life. Everything she could see or imagine was alive, and her own joy glowed as brilliantly as the living light. Oh, she thought, it's not just going to take me days or even weeks. It's going to take me the rest of my life.

ACKNOWLEDGMENTS
AND NOTES

Gloria is the third in a series of novels I have written in a style inspired by, and similar to, a style current at the time when the book is set. In preparing to write this book, I read or skimmed a huge number of novels, both popular and literary, written from the late nineteen-forties to the late nineteen-fifties; I was looking not only for fictional strategies but for the attitudes, ideas, and preoccupations of the period. There is no single style typical of the fifties, so *Gloria* exhibits many features common to the fiction of that time, but it is imitative of no single work or of the works of no single author.

Although I was alive during the period when this book is set (I am the same age as Gloria's younger brother Bobby), my personal memories were inadequate to the task, and I was required to do as much research as if I had set the book a hundred years ago; although I do not feel impelled to cite all my sources, I want to cite at least the most important of them. I am, of course, responsible for *Gloria*, and anything wrong with it is my fault alone, but I could not have written it without the kind help I received from others, so I also want to thank some of the people who assisted me with various aspects of the book.

I found W. Tasker Witham's *The Adolescent in the American Novel: 1920–1960* (Frederick Ungar, New York, 1964) extremely helpful, and I read many of the novels from the fifties cited in that work. The magazines I consulted were *McCall's*, *Woman's Home Companion*, and—particularly for girls' and womens' fashions—*Vogue* and *Seventeen*. Especially revealing of the pressures on young women were "advice to girls" books and high school home economics texts. I also, of course, read social histories, memoirs, biographies, and autobiographies.

I could not find much written about sorority life in the fifties except for several accounts in fiction; the most interesting of these was Peggy Goodin's gently satirical *Take Care of My Little Girl* (E. P. Dutton, 1950), which provided me with a number of useful details like the beau parlour in Gloria's sorority house and slang terms like "pin-man." Far more important than any written material, however, was the guidance and advice I received from Stacey Torman. She not only provided me with masses of information about sorority life but also patiently read over several drafts of the first half of this novel, pointing out where I had got things wrong and suggesting how I might get them right. I owe Stacey a particular debt of gratitude. Delta Lambda, Gloria's sorority, is fictitious and is not meant to represent any real Greek letter society. I should also note that neither Stacey, nor any of the other women who shared their sorority experiences with me, revealed any of their sorority's secret rituals. The ritual that appears in Chapter 5 is my creation.

Scholars have yet to turn their attention to the role of the majorette in North American popular culture, and, even after an exhaustive search, I could not find a single serious article on the topic. I did read some half-dozen how-to books of varying degrees of usefulness. The nomenclature of twirling was not standardized in the fifties and varied from region to region; I have, by and large, employed terminology from Constance Atwater's *Baton Twirling: The Fundamentals of an Art and a Skill* (Charles E. Tuttle, 1964).

I had a number of extremely helpful conversations with twirlers and former majorettes. Margaret Smith, who, with her husband Merl, was a pioneer in the art of twirling, shared memories with me that went back all the way to the nineteen-thirties. Twirling teacher Maureen Johnson gave me a vivid account of twirling in the fifties; her student, Elan Paluck, also a twirling teacher, graciously talked to me for several hours and demonstrated twirls as they would have been done in the fifties.

The majorette contest that Susie wins, although it resembles real contests held in the fifties, is fictitious. Similarly, the beauty pageants in which she participates, even when they have real names (i.e., Miss Pennsylvania), are fictional creations. Some of Susie's comments on the tricks of winning beauty contests — especially her advice to Gloria on how to do a beauty-pageant walk in high heels — were suggested by *How to Win a Beauty Contest* (Curran Publishing, 1960) written by former Miss America, Jacque Mercer.

The development of iron and steel manufacturing in the Ohio Valley is far more complicated than I have painted it in this or any other of my novels, and the Raysburg Steel Corporation that appears here is my fictional creation and is not meant to represent any real steel company. For an overview of the American steel industry, I relied upon Paul A. Tiffany's excellent *The Decline of American Steel: How Management, Labor, and Government Went Wrong*; Oxford University Press, New York, 1988. Also very useful (in particular, the section of Chapter 12 entitled "'Working' in the Mill, ca. 1950") was John P. Hoerr's *And the Wolf Finally Came: The Decline of the American Steel Industry*; University of Pittsburgh Press, 1988. Although the big eastern American steel companies in the fifties certainly behaved as though their executives met together in secret, I have no evidence that they actually did, and the meeting in Pittsburgh described in Chapter 12 is purely fictitious.

Of the articles and books I read to help me imagine Ted's experiences in the navy in the Second World War, the most useful were Douglas Edward Leach's *Now Hear This: The Memoir of a Junior Naval Officer in the Great Pacific War* (The Kent State University Press, 1987) and, with its vivid descriptions of kamikaze attacks, Commander Edward P. Stafford's *Little Ship, Big War* (William Morrow and Company, 1984). For an account of the *Operation IVY* film (with its nuclear bomb blast) shown on American television on April 2, 1954 (Gloria and Susie watch it in Chapter 17), see Spencer R. Weart's *Nuclear Fear: A History of Images* (Harvard University Press, 1988).

The edition of the *New York Times* Ted is reading in Chapter 1 is that of June 30, 1957. The edition he's reading in Chapter 9 is that of July 7, 1957; in the story reporting President Eisenhower's happiness over his golf score, among his golfing companions was not, of course, my fictional character, Carl Eberhardt, but rather W. Alton Jones, a New York oil company executive.

As an aid to the reader, I have modernized the spelling of Spenser's and Wyatt's poetry. Gloria's ideas about Britomart in Spenser's *Faerie Queene* are based upon those in a paper written by my wife (Mary Skinner, as she was then) when she was a graduate student at Simon Fraser University, and I have adopted her work with her blessing. The approach to Wyatt taken by Gloria and confirmed by Professor Bolton was suggested by Raymond Southall's *The Courtly Maker: An Essay on the Poetry of Wyatt and His Contemporaries* (Barnes & Noble; New York, 1964). Also useful was A. K. Foxwell's earlier (1911) work, *A Study of Sir Thomas Wyatt's Poems* (reissued in 1964 by Russell & Russell, New York).

I would once again like to thank Ed Carson who, when he was still at Harper-Collins, encouraged me to write this book and kept me on track. Marie Campbell and Nicole Langlois at HarperCollins gave me invaluable editorial assistance. John Adames helped me with Latin. As he always does, Will Hadsell astonished me with his encyclopedic knowledge of automobiles. Dr. Hal Mueller reminisced with me over fifties medical practices and provided me with essential information about Porsches. Kathryn Knowell helped me sharpen my perception of the social distinctions implicit in my story and provided me with many lovely period details. Pat Temple shared her memories of teaching high school in the fifties, and Marjorie T. Tompkins provided me with a vivid picture of Philadelphia in the fifties. Violet and John Zaytsoff helped me get my golf scenes right.

My colleague Lynne Bowen should receive a medal for service above and beyond the call of duty; she read an earlier, and much longer, version of this book and offered detailed criticism so perceptive that I used much of it as the basis for later drafts. And, finally, I must thank my wife, Mary Maillard, who read every word of every version of *Gloria* as it was emerging over an eight-year period. Without Mary's encouragement, keen critical intelligence, and woman's perspective on my women characters, I would have found this book difficult, if not impossible, to write.

Although it strongly resembles my home town, Raysburg is a fictional creation. Jordanstown, Cloverton, Briarville University, and Susie's church in Cloverton are all fictional creations. Gloria and her family and friends are based upon no real people; all the characters in this book (with the exception of well-known historical figures like politicians, poets, and scholars) are fictitious, and any similarity between the people, names, and events in this book and any real people, names, and events is purely coincidental.

Keith Maillard
Vancouver, B.C., Canada
January 18, 1999

SOURCES OF
MODERN POETRY

CHAPTER 3

p. 80. "with the veil of faint cloud before her . . . pale eyes as if without fire": from "Canto LXXX," *The Cantos of Ezra Pound*.

p. 88. "Wipe your hand across your mouth, and laugh": "Preludes" by T.S. Eliot.

CHAPTER 5

p. 150. "This shaking keeps me steady. I should know—"; "The lowly worm climbs up a winding stair"; "what falls away is always, and is near—": "The Waking", copyright 1953 by Theodore Roethke. From *The Collected Poems of Theodore Roethke*. Used by permission of Doubleday, a division of Random House, Inc.

"the foul rag and bone shop of the heart": "The Circus Animals' Desertion" by W. B. Yeats.

"the nightingales singing near the Convent of the Sacred Heart—": "Sweeney Among the Nightingales" by T. S. Eliot.

"wordless as the flight of birds—": "Ars Poetica" by Archibald MacLeish.

"nothing left of the sea but its sound—": "Ballad of the Long-legged Bait" by Dylan Thomas.

"the word outleaps the world, and light—": "IV. The Vigil" from "Four for Sir John Davies" by Theodore Roethke.

p. 151. "in the words Richard Wilbur had given her: 'Please give me—yet another sun to do the shapely thing I have not done!'" Gloria is paraphrasing Richard Wilbur: ". . . yet another sun / To do the shapely thing they had not done." Excerpt from "Year's End" from *Ceremony and Other Poems*, copyright 1949 and renewed 1977 by Richard Wilbur, reprinted by permission of Harcourt Brace & Company.

CHAPTER 6

p. 161. "What am I now that I was then / Which I shall suffer and act again—
": "Calmly We Walk Through This April's Day" by Delmore Schwartz, from
Selected Poems: Summer Knowledge. Copyright ©1959 by Delmore Schwartz.
Reprinted by permission of New Directions Publishing Corp.

p. 190. "A poem should not mean, but be"; "'palpable and mute' and
'dumb'and 'silent' and 'motionless'": "Ars Poetica" by Archibald MacLeish.

pp. 193–5. Grishkin, with her "pneumatic bust" and "Russian eye underlined
for emphasis": "Whispers of Immortality" by T. S. Eliot.

CHAPTER 7

p. 218. ". . . he strove to rrrrrrresuscitate the dead art of poetrrrrrry . . ." The
trilled *r* is Ken's imitation of Pound's reading style: "E. P. Ode Pour L'Election
de Son Sépulchre" by Ezra Pound.

p. 225. Yeats' word "rent," rhymed with excrement: "Crazy Jane Talks with
the Bishop" by W. B. Yeats.

p. 239. "Let us go then, you and I—"; "Through certain half deserted streets—
": "The Love Song of J. Alfred Prufrock" by T. S. Eliot.

p. 242–3. "Speech after long silence—"; ". . . the supreme theme—"; "Of
art and song.": "After Long Silence" by W. B. Yeats.

CHAPTER 8

p. 244. "Pound's nasty word, 'devirginated.'": "Homage to Sextus Proper-
tius" by Ezra Pound.

CHAPTER 13

p. 390. "Have you been a *good* girl?": "The Good Little Girl" from *Now We
Are Six* by A. A. Milne.

p. 403. "Beauty is momentary in the mind— / The fitful tracing of a portal; /
But in the flesh it is immortal.": "Peter Quince at the Clavier" by Wallace Stevens.
From *Collected Poems*. Copyright 1923 and renewed 1951 by Wallace Stevens.
Reprinted by permission of Alfred A. Knopf Inc.

p. 410. "In the moon barge—pale eyes as if without fire.": from "Canto
LXXX," *The Cantos of Ezra Pound*.

p. 411. "Wipe your hand across your mouth and laugh?": "Preludes" by T.
S. Eliot.

CHAPTER 14

p. 421. "That's what that Robert Graves poem was about—if you didn't have
words, you'd go crazy—": "The Cool Web" by Robert Graves.

CHAPTER 15

p. 484. "A stricken rabbit is crying out . . .": "Man and the Echo" by W. B. Yeats.

CHAPTER 16

p. 516. "The world is charged with the grandeur of God": "God's Grandeur" by Gerard Manley Hopkins.

CHAPTER 17

p. 535. "gone into what?— like all them kings you read about—": "28" from *One Times One* by e. e. cummings.

CHAPTER 18

p. 570. "—the greatness, rareness, muchness, fewness of this precious only endless world—": "Warning to Children" by Robert Graves.

CHAPTER 21

p. 652–653. "'Pull down thy vanity,' Pound told her, 'it is not *man* made courage, or made order, or made grace'": From "Canto LXXXI," *The Cantos of Ezra Pound.*

p. 657. ". . . her line was an echo of Lowell's: 'The sea was still breaking violently and night—'": "The Quaker Graveyard in Nantucket" by Robert Lowell.

The last two scenes in Chapter 6 (Gloria meeting Ken and having dinner at his apartment) were first published, in slightly different form, in *The Review* (Vancouver, B.C., Canada), Summer, 1997.